# HOLY DAYS

a novel by

Patricia Goodwin

Plum Press

Marblehead, MA

Holy Days
Copyright© 2015 by Patricia Goodwin

A portion of "A Child's Christmas in Revere," a chapter from *Holy Days* was previously published in the anthology, *Under Her Skin: How Girls Experience Race in America* (Seal Press, 2004)

Library of Congress, *Holy Days* registered © 2008 by Patricia Goodwin
Cover Design: Christina Goodwin

ISBN   978-0-692-36268-6

# HOLY DAYS

"Forgive me. I ask this of all the children who were shot, beaten, raped, murdered, burned, mutilated, stuffed in trash bags, buried alive or left for dead by the side of the road, by their fathers or mothers, stepparents, friends, strangers, priests, Nazis, I don't know which is the worst. Mine could be called a mild rape. But a mild rape was enough."

"They tried to kill me in this place of love and horror. They tried to kill me, but they couldn't because I loved too much."

- *Gloria Wisher*

To the Old Italians,

who taught me how to love


To Mr. George Doucet,

who taught me how to read literature and saved my life


and

To Joan, my angel

"Every day is a holy day."

*- Gloria Wisher*

# Book One

## Chick

East Boston

1951-1959

EAST BOSTON, 1954

I was three years old when Mama opened the door and looked into the room. She screamed.

NURSERY SCHOOL

When Grandpa took my hand we walked around the corner from the city to the country.

As we rounded the corner I saw for the first time in my life, trees!

Breathless at the sight of green softness blowing, I gasped, "Is this the country, Grandpa?"

"Yeah, this is the country," answered Grandpa, "you like the country?"

"Yes!"

I had heard of the country in books. Seeing all the swaying, lovely trees so close to our bare, ugly street, Brooks Street (but where was *the brook?*) I began to search for the something I knew was out there, now that I had reached this place called country.

Looking and looking, only three years old, toward the top of the hill, for the illusive thing, that was, like me, unformed, I looked toward the big White House, the only mansion, the only thing of beauty visible on Brooks Street. To the beautiful White House, my eyes always turned. The White House shone like the sun. On gloomy days, it glowed like the moon.

"Grandpa, what are these?"

The toe of my little red lace-up shoe nudged an iron ring hooked through the skin of the curbstone.

"Oh, that's where we used to tie up the horses."

Horses! I didn't believe him. I turned, and looked far down the grey cement of Brooks Street to our tenement and I couldn't imagine horses there! What would they eat? There was no grass!

Other children would have asked questions. Not me.

I looked up at Grandpa and saw the mischievous glint in his root beer eyes, half-lowered lids, over the constant stogie in his mouth. He was kidding me. Horses!

Nevertheless, I decided to put this idea away somewhere deep inside me and take it out someday when I could understand it better.

"Horses delivered ya coal. An' horses delivered ya ice, in a wagon, huge blocks o' ice," Grandpa explained.

"Coal?" What was coal? I asked myself, the person who did not know.

"Coal to heat the house. Every house had a coal chute, a hole in the side so the coal could go in. Our house still has a coal chute, on the side where the cellar is, a chute, like a slide. You know a slide?"

Now I knew he was making a joke of me, the way he walked, with a smile hugging that stogie. Grandpa was always joking somebody.

Only Grandma never laughed; she had a little mouth face, a little red mouth tied up in a bow, a serious little red bow.

Grandma and Grandpa were from heaven. And, Nona, too, she was from heaven, and Mama, all these were angels. This I knew.

Nona was Grandma's mother. She was forgetting English and remembering only Italian. I loved to stroke her white, white hair with one yellow blonde streak, soft as a kitten, along her cheek. As a girl in Italy, Nona had had the golden hair, a treasure in a land of black-haired beauties. I loved to stroke one finger down the yellow trail, because there I was in history. I had inherited Nona's golden hair, or was it my father's English head bobbing with curls in an old photograph, my father dressed in breeches like a lord? He looked exactly like me, if I were dressed up like a boy.

"Who do you think this picture is?" Mama asked me, holding a brown photograph.

"Me!" I was certain. Then, I wondered, why don't I remember? "I don't remember."

"That's Daddy."

"Daddy?"

"When he was little."

Daddy. I looked for Daddy in the photo, in the little boy's squinting, sunny smiling face, in his curls. He looked like Shirley Temple and so did I. But, not like Daddy. This I knew.

Everyone looked to Grandma for decisions. Her face told them what they had to know: was her mouth screwed up in a twisted red bow of disapproval or a nice red bow just straight? But, even Grandma had to do what Grandpa said. *She* looked to him.

Grandpa wore a felt fedora and a double-breasted overcoat. He was Vic. Grandma was Palma, like Palm Sunday. Nona was Nona, and Mama, Mama. All the men wore fedoras and big overcoats with big shoulders, and all the big boys too, trying to be men. But, Grandpa was the first and the biggest in his fedora and coat.

It was a lovely mystery to me why I walked to nursery school with him every morning. Why Mama handed me over to her father every morning I did not know, but I was delighted. It was a very great honor for me to walk with Grandpa. I was proud of his fedora and overcoat, and proud, too, of my dark red velvet suit with leggings, and circling the shoulders, a puff of white angora to nestle in my nose. The walk from our house to the nursery school took exactly five minutes, but the way we took it, it lasted at least ten, maybe twenty.

At the place where the sidewalk changed from cement to rosy brick, an old lady came out of the laundromat in the cellar of a house. She struggled with a heavy bag of laundry in a cart; yanking it, bump, bump, bump, up the cement stairs. Grandpa stopped to help her and I didn't want to let go of him or share him with her, but he helped her and spoke to the old lady in Italian while I studied the bricks, which were rosy and beautiful, unlike the old lady who was grey and wrinkled. She spoke Italian like a moan. Grandpa spoke Italian like a song. Grandpa told the old lady something in very firm Italian and he came back to me.

Then, we were at school and I was so glad to be there! What a pretty school it was! A little red brick house with lots and lots of green ivy hugging, up and up, round and round, making lace of the sunlight. And a flower garden and birds that came to sing! That was school!

Grandpa handed me over to the teacher and I don't remember her, she disappeared into her love for me. In those days, teachers loved their children like mothers. She must have loved me, because I was very happy to be handed over to her. She was a part of school.

Grandpa left and there was a clear division between having been with Grandpa outside, traveling in the world and now being inside, in the world of school.

School had lovely rules that kept everything neat and put away when not being played with and quiet when the teacher said so. She would speak and we would listen. We sang together and looked at pictures. Teacher read stories to us, carefully holding the book out to her side so we could see the pictures, which were puppies and ducks or girls and boys like us. We didn't have pretty books like these at home! Our hungry eyes gripped on the pages. ABC was alone for a long time and then, we were told about D and E and more and more letters unfolded right before our eyes like mysteries revealed. Knowing how to say them was like holding a key to a door that was no longer a door, but a road to a horizon.

After story, we had snack, always a little carton of milk with a straw and a graham cracker. We had graham crackers at home. Grandma piled butter on them or plain in my hand like in school, but we didn't have little cartons of milk at home, those were expensive; luxuries didn't exist at home, so the thrill of opening these cartons was never lost to me, not in all the years of school, and sticking the thin straw in and sucking up that cold, cold milk! We didn't have straws at home either. I wanted to make bubbles, to make the milk colder, but teacher wouldn't let us. She always scolded the boys, but I had to, you see, it was my only chance, so I practiced doing it quietly, ever so softly, bubble, bubble, and was never caught.

After crackers and milk, we hurried to clean up, passing our empty cartons to the teacher. Then we fetched a mat from the big stack of straw sleeping mats in the corner. Naptime was like a game, because I wasn't tired, ever. I don't think any of us thought we were tired and I would have sworn that none of us ever slept, but, of course, we fell asleep quite suddenly and unaware.

We knew what we were supposed to do, and there was a lovely voluptuousness in doing what we were supposed to do for someone we trusted so utterly. We put the mats down on the floor, took off our shoes and socks, lay down and closed our eyes.

One little boy (who was he?) always put his mat next to mine and this meant he liked me. I remember Mama telling me the teacher had told her about the little boy, that's how I knew it meant something bigger than just his being next to me. And, while our eyes were closed, the boy's hand would come over to my mat and blindly feel until he found my hand too, which he held with his eyes closed, and smiled.

There was only one precious time Mama came early to take me home and she came all the way into the schoolroom, not waiting out in the darkness by the door. And, I was not huddled in my coat waiting, but lying next to the little boy with our shoes and socks off and he was holding my hand and smiling.

Teacher's sweet voice called to me in my sleep, her voice sang to me, "Gloria! Gloria! Look who is here!"

And, I turned, with my sleepy eyes and there, by the window full of green leaves lapping sunlight, her soft red curls making a sunny halo, her round face lit by the love in her eyes, hazel eyes with the heavy lids and lashes I inherited, soft and round and lighted, there she was! I thought she was an angel.

"Mama!"

She and the teacher both looked down at me, smiling with love and pride.

ANGELFISH

When I was born they put me in a drawer because they were too poor to buy a crib.

One by one, all the women came. Like goddesses, they looked into the drawer and warned Mama, "She's so beautiful! Watch out for her! Take care!"

I had curly blonde hair and big blue eyes that would change to green. My forehead was broad, high and wide, and my eyelids hung thick with lashes. I mention these details because no one ever told me I was beautiful. I grew up thinking my head was enormous, grotesquely deformed and my light eyes too pale to be seen. I thought I was a bigheaded alien; in fact, I was a pearly angelfish in a dark, Italian sea.

No one petted me or caressed me with names. On television I heard neat, trim little mothers calling their children "Dear!" and "Sweetheart!"

and "Darling!" So, I went into the kitchen and asked Mama, "Do you love me?"

Mama answered, a little impatiently, "Of course, I love you! I'm your mother! What kind of question is that?"

"Because all the mothers on TV call their kids 'dear' and 'sweetheart' and you never say those things to me."

"That's the television!"

But, the world knew I was beautiful.

Mama told the famous story of the Baby Butler salesman who begged to take my photo to show off to customers. Our copy was worn and faded, folded with grease lines in Daddy's blackened wallet. In this picture, I sat suspended in the canvas seat, my huge head and bulging eyes looming over the tray in front of me. A duck, a fish, a merry-go-round, a clown are arranged exactly in the corners of the Baby Butler's tray and over my shoulder, like the Cheshire Cat, the grinning salesman, instantly and forever one of the family, in his neat suit, tall, dark and handsome and saying all the right things.


EASTER

The strong backs of men carried the long board up from the cellar.

I must have been in my mother's arms because I saw the men from above. I must have been held high; perhaps Mama went down to the cellar to supervise the carrying of the board which Grandma and all the other women who came at Easter would spread first with a cloth and then, with clouds of white flour into which they would plunge headlong up to their elbows.

In the house, the young men were slaves to the women: they fetched and carried, they moved twice their bulk upon their backs, huge bureaus or refrigerators, up stairs and down, negotiating treacherous corners or thresholds with the maneuvers of generals moving armies through mountainous passes, with the ceremony of a thousand natives supporting tributes to their gods, they climbed ladders and stepstools to reach up into the stratosphere and bring down a bowl or a cup, they knelt behind toilets, crawled blithely into other dark, damp holes where it would be unthinkable to send Grandma or Mama and like disembodied voices from these dim caves, they would call the mysterious finale at which everyone would sigh in relief, "That's got it, Ma!"

Only Grandpa never fetched or carried: he sat with his stogie, no matter what. He was the King and Grandma was the Queen. Nona was the Queen Mother.

Easter was Nona's birthday. The whole family came.

The men carried the board, which was really a heavy old door, up the cellar stairs. The muscles in their shoulders bulged through their T-shirts. Their waists were slim in the blousy trousers of the day. One light bulb dangled halfway down the wooden landing. The cellar's limey stonewalls were rough and white, and the men's' shouts made a rhythm like a slave's song, "Watch out!" "Yup!" as they struggled and sweated under their cumbersome load, shifting from side to side. The scrapes of their weighted shoes on the gritty wood, the smell of dank, wet brick, grimy wood, the same smell as the warm skin of men, as if filtered through their skin, equal somehow to the promise of rum cake and chocolate: it was the start of Easter and I knew it.

Now, in the fierce, white light of the kitchen, the women instructed the men how to place the board. Every year, they placed the board on the same table spread with towels, evenly, as though leveled by some celestial, inborn leveler the women carried in their heads. They placed towels to protect the valued Formica surface of the kitchen table, poor people's marble, the lovely cherished swirls of gold and brown, from being scratched by the harsh old board, smoothing and smoothing the towels, all the while singing their commands, "Here, here, like this, like this," the men suffering being told, year after year, chanting back, "I know, Ma," "Yeah, Ma," "Don't worry, Ma," suffering their awkward, meaty hands being thrust aside.

The women, magicians and priestesses, with white turbans wrapped around their heads (a popular style after Carmen Miranda) and red, red lipstick like ceremonial paint, would take ordinary objects, such as a discarded door, bags of immaculate white flour (bags of clouds!), eggs (pure white shells enclosing God only knew what magic!), water, pinches of mysterious savories, broken parts of broom handles worn smooth to roll and roll over the doughy mixtures, mix, press, roll, cut, all the while chanting in a language only they understood, half Italian, half American, old voices mixed with young voices, I listened rapturously to their song without understanding a single word, not a single clear idea, except one - until they had transformed the clouds of white flour, the water, the eggs, the pinches of potions, into that idea - Easter - what *we* thought of as Easter - the ravioli, manicotti, covatelli, rich dough wrapped around meats and cheeses, simmered long and deep in the tomato sauce that was our communal blood; the sugared bows, eggshell thin bow ties luscious with powdered sugar; the honeyed balls, little balls of fried dough swimming in honey pools; the chewy almond cookies, pink, green, white; the rows of white rice pizziolas, low, round cakes of rice and egg as sweet and airy as the holy host itself.

Grandpa was in charge of the wine, which came from his brother-in-law's vines. Uncle Albertino made the wine himself. It was unthinkable to buy wine in the store. Grandpa poured this wine with as much pride as if he had given birth to it himself, instead of its being tithe from one of his loyal subjects. And Grandpa was in charge of the fruit and nuts. The fruit he sliced upward in his hands with a huge, sharp knife that only he and Grandma dared to handle, and he passed the slice, thick and juicing, to you on the blade of this knife, held secure by the tip of his thumb.

"Mmm, thank you, Grandpa."

And the nuts fell into your little inadequate palms from his great one. He cracked them for you, and the shells and skins fell upon the tablecloth and the floor and our laps, along with spots of red and flaking crusts of bread.

Nona sat in state; children gathered round her knees. Her old, white head like newborn fluff nodded to one side. She grinned, loose and noddy, with gap teeth, some gone black. On her little ears, soft as dough, the diamond chips in blackened filigree she'd worn since infancy, the ones I begged for, but, no, Nona had to be buried in them, sparkled now like the joke in her old eyes. She always had a joke glimmering deep in her eyes.

The cake was for Nona. From the bakery. No one dared bake it themselves. Enormous, enough to fill everyone there and still a big hunk left over, lighted by close to a hundred candles. "How many, Mama, how many?" "I don't know! A hundred!" "Can Nona blow them all out?" "No! She's too old!" "Then, how will she get her wish?" Thick with Italian whipped cream, sculpted whipped cream, rosettes, leaves, letters, vines, buds of whipped cream, an architectural wonder to rival any castle. Under the cream, layers of chocolate and vanilla rum puddings, yellow cake meat soaked with rum. It was a cake even Grandma wouldn't attempt; she liked to make only the sturdy, practical dishes that nourished every day life, the pastas and breads, the meats and fishes. Of course, Nona couldn't eat this cake even though it was for her birthday, it was too wet and rich for someone so old, she would've died and gone to heaven. The rest of us stuffed ourselves with it. I loved to squeeze gently the soggy flesh of cake in my hand before oozing it over my tongue. I began to eat this cake long before Easter. I began to eat it somewhere in the shivering, grey January - this luscious sweet hope of cake.

And there were other boxes from the bakery. One of the women would lift the brown cardboard cover and fold it back with an expert snap, revealing a treasure chest of cannoli, filled with whipped, sugary cheese or thick yellow cream and chocolate; cream puffs, little mouths gaping, overflowing with whipped cream; the marzipan cookies, baby colors, pink, green, and yellow; bismarcks with their surprise of raspberry jam; éclairs, Napoleons - these I didn't recognize except by exclamation of one or another aunt - "Oh! The éclair!" "Madon', the Napoleoné!" - semi-familiar aunt mouths full and groaning with ecstasy.

And, Mama sat with an open box of chocolates on her lap, Fanny Farmer (What a name! She must, I thought, be a farmer with a big, fat fanny from eating too much candy!) The kind of candy each in its own paper basket that rustled when you put your hand in. "Which one is the caramel?" Mama had a way of picking them out. She didn't even have to answer me, she could keep on talking with Aunt Louisa or Aunt Teresa and her fleshy, round finger would touch one. Mmm, how did she know? At home, the candy was locked up and doled out by these same round fingers, piece by piece, and it was hard candy, suckers, never chocolate. But, today was Nona's birthday and Easter; the thrill was infectious and every day rules did not apply.

Crack!

Over fifty heads turned to see what broke. Grandpa was sitting on the linoleum floor, on top of the remains of my little pegboard, its teeny seat he'd tried to fit in squashed somewhere under him, the table-top grid of holes and colored pegs flopping like a dead, tropical fish on his stomach. Stogie clamped tightly in his teeth, Grandpa studied what he'd done.

"Ha! Ha!" he laughed in the stunned silence. All the men roared with laughter.

Grandma yelled at him, "And, what you do? What are you thinking?" All the women groaned and yelled at their husbands for laughing.

My mouth bulged with sweet caramel and chocolate. My blonde curls flew back and forth from Grandma to Grandpa in bewilderment. My pegboard! And Grandpa! What a crazy combination! What did Mama think? She was looking away from the disaster, but her mouth was drawn tight like a purse with the strings yanked hard. The blonde curls flew. Grandma's mouth, a taut red bow. They flew. Every other woman's mouth, the strings pulled tight.

"What about my pegboard?" I cried to Mama. Mama pressed her fat finger hard against her pursed up lips; she twisted the finger and pushed it against her mouth, urgently, hard, hard, warning me. I pressed my lips tight, too, wondering about this gorgeous taste of sweetness, that it was now combined with tragedy, and I shrugged away my pegboard, gave it over to the adults, to Grandpa, whom I loved beyond question.

The men roared again and again as Grandpa struggled to get up.

LITTLE NAZI

Daddy brought home soft, yellow chicks, handfuls of them, overflowing and running, cheep, cheep, out of his hands, running round the bathtub, trying to run up the sides, sliding down, tumbling on one another, running, bumping headlong into the porcelain tub.

"Can I hold one? Can I hold one?"

It scurried in my hand, clawing at my baby plump skin. Suffering the sharp end to claim the soft, I patted its fluffy head. My baby finger went right through its fluff like air and touched bone! A boney head that shifted nervously, cheep, cheep. I was delighted!

Daddy brought home a rabbit! And put it in the tub with the chicks. Alas, this inferior rabbit was brown and I wanted it to be white. The chicks ran from side to side, bumping into the rabbit that didn't seem to mind, he just chewed and chewed. Lettuce and carrots were in the tub, too, until Mama told Daddy to make a hutch for all the animals. "And get them out of my tub!"

"We're gonna eat them," Daddy said.

How can we eat them? They're running back and forth with feathers! They got feet! I can hear them scratching, trying to get out of the tub, trying to claw their way up the sides of the tub.

The chicks weren't yellow and fluffy anymore. Was it the hutch that had done that? In the tub, they were the first thing I ran to in the morning and the last thing at night. But now, I'm losing interest. They're not yellow. They've changed to a scruffy grey brown and I don't really want to touch them anymore. They're not round babies. They've stretched to long-necked, gawky adolescents, still scampering back and forth, pecking at the screen in front of the hutch Daddy built, snapping at my fingers poking in at them.

"Oooh! He bit me!"

"That's what you get for sticking your fingers where they don't belong!" Mama scolded.

"We're gonna eat them," Daddy said again.

"How are we gonna eat them?"

"We're gonna kill 'em, then we're gonna cook 'em and eat 'em."

Now, I was intrigued. I abandoned any loyalty I ever had to them when they were soft and golden. Why? Had they been disloyal to me by losing their pretty color and pleasing shape? Would I have defended them to the death, screaming in tantrums, kicking Daddy and biting Mama, perhaps setting preteen chicks free in the night, had they remained beautiful? I was a curly, yellow chick, though I didn't know it and beauty was affecting me even then. A little Nazi, I was ready to hand over my imperfect pets in order to see what slaughter was.

I wasn't supposed to see. Mama didn't know I was down there. And the men, what did they know, or think about a little girl, almost too small to be seen, walking around the dirty cellar. Maybe they didn't think of sending me away because I was invisible, because I wasn't wearing a dress. I wore my play clothes: pants and a shirt, dusty lace-up shoes like a boy.

Daddy paced nervously. He smoked a cigarette with his fingers cupped over it, the way men smoked and never women, squinting into the smoke, concentrating. He paced, back and forth, like the chicks, back and forth, only deliberately, not frantically the way the chicks had scurried in the tub. Grandpa sat on a box. He clapped his hands against his knees.

"Might as well start, Bill," Grandpa urged.

"Yeah. Just let me finish this cigarette."

Men make such a ceremony of killing, when Grandma told me she'd had to flush plenty of kittens down the toilet, whole litters of them, because you can't keep them and nobody could afford to get the cats fixed. I didn't want to picture her doing it, but I believed her to be a very matter-of-fact, efficient killer and if I admitted what lurked under my blind horror at her murdering soft and mewing cuddliness: I was proud of her.

Daddy threw down his cigarette butt; ground it on the gritty stone floor with his black work shoe.

"Which window for the coal, Grandpa?" I asked suddenly, out of the coal black grimness. I chose the grimiest one in my mind and waited for his reply.

"What? Ah, that one for the coal." He pointed vaguely over his shoulder, his eyes tending Daddy. I still don't know which window it was. "Hey! What are you doing down here, girlie? Go uppastairs!"

But, Daddy already was taking a trembling, adolescent chick out of the hutch. He cradled it gently in his hands. I decided to disobey Grandpa. I lingered, my huge chick eyes gaping, bulging round out of my bulging round forehead.

Peep, peep. Its eye rolled over.

"I got it," said Grandpa, taking it from Daddy, who went to get the ax. Grandpa cupped his hands tenderly over the wings. He placed the chick's head down, stretching its long, gawky neck on a stump of wood. The stogie smoked between his gripping teeth.

I could hear his breath, hiss, hiss, through the saliva gathered round the stogie, sharp stinking, burning my fragile nostrils.

Peep! Peep! The chick's eye rolled trying to see who had him in his grip.

Daddy lifted the ax. Down it went! Chomp!

The chick's eye stared. Blood squirted up like a fountain from its neck. Grandpa took the wriggling body by the feet and tried to tie it up to a wooden beam, but the body wriggled away from him, to the floor, where it ran and ran, smacking into boxes, smacking into Grandpa's shoes, spurting its red blood over his pants.

I felt my face go cold. I didn't scream. I sucked in deep breaths that sounded like whimpers. I began to heave in whimpers watching the headless chicken run its life out till it fell over and its feet kept scratching, trying to find the ground.

"Ah!" I said.

"Get upstairs! Go!" Grandpa shouted, remembering me. He was leaning, reaching his empty hands for the chicken. Daddy was going for the next one.

"Rosa!" Grandpa hollered upward through the cellar's beamed ceiling, hollering through the kitchen floor to where Mama was, "Get ya daughter out of here!"

He shoved me up the landing with a bloody hand.

Later that night, Mama carried me down the cellar. Cradling me in her arms, she pried my tiny fingers from my eyes to show me death.

"See, there's the chickens. The ones that ran in the bathtub."

All in a quiet row hanging from their shocked feet.

We ate the rabbit, too. Chunks of it, buried deep in the spicy tomato sauce, scooped up, ladled into our waiting mouths with hunks of crusty, Italian bread. I don't know how it was murdered or by whom. I was cowardly enough to eat it without having witnessed its slaughter.

A COOKING HOUSE

Grandma's house was a cooking house. Her house cooked, upstairs and down, from the roof to the cellar, with food, yes, with the rich aromas of wonderful food, so that you could almost be nourished by the aromas alone: of coffee percolating on the stove; of homemade sweet butter thick on slabs of bread; of fish frying in olive oil, grated cheese and aromatic spices; onions crackling; tomato sauce brewing on an eternal flame; meats stuffed and rolled and sewn with string; pastas curled with a quick twist of the floury thumb or churned out of a pasta machine like old fashioned laundry. The oven steamed perpetually with vanilla, cinnamon, almond, apple, currant and blueberry.

Nona cooked on the roof. Mama cooked on the second floor where we lived. Before we lived there, Angie and Uncle Vic (sometimes called Vickie not to be confused with Grandpa) lived there, but they didn't cook. They ate downstairs. Grandma cooked on the ground floor. On to that dead concrete street she sent out the smell of people living as did every other house on the block, which was otherwise dead except for people.

Yes, the house cooked with food, but it cooked with people too. The doors slammed open and slammed shut. All day long, up the stairs and down the stairs, the people came and went; the boys and the young men galloped down the stairs like young stallions. They took the stairs two, three at a time, up and down, and I tried so hard to imitate them with my short legs, stretching, straining them to the alternate step and hauling myself up by the railing or by the wall.

And, in the night, the sleeping house whispered with people, softly shuffling on slippered feet or giggling, clicking high heels, scraping leather soles, "Vickie, is that you?" (sleepy moan) "Yeah, Ma." (drunken smile, girlish giggle) "Is Angie with you?" (sleepy moan) "Go back to bed, Ma, we're all right." (giggles, clicking heels, laughy moans, shuffling grown up clothes, silky, scraping up against each other going up the stairs)

Grandma had four sons. Mama was her only girl and the oldest, so Mama was like a Mama too. She held the babies for Grandma, babies almost as big as she was; she fed them, changed them, put them to sleep, took them for walks in the carriage. She played with real babies instead of dolls.

Uncle Vickie was the oldest boy; he was always in trouble, followed closely at the heels by Uncle Freddie, who had red, red hair and liked trouble just as much. All the pictures of Uncle Vickie, with his chubby Grandpa face and wavy, black hair show him with his gang of smirking young boys in miniature, double-breasted overcoats and miniature fedora hats tipped down over their narrow eyes, smirking boys always handing money to Uncle Vickie. Lots of pictures of Uncle Vickie: curly, black hair tumbling over his luminous dark eyes, holding out his hand, getting dollars counted into his extended palm. "Hey, Vickie!" He turned his naughty cherub face and squinted forever into the sun, click, holding on to dollars.

"Vickie! Been shootin' craps again, Vickie?"

"Nah! I don' shoot no craps, Pa, you know dat."

"How much ya get down tha' onna corner?"

"Nothin'!"

"How much ya get?"

"Aw, a couple a bucks, dats all."

"Chicken shit."

Uncle Freddie tried to be like Uncle Vickie, but he wasn't as sharp. He couldn't be as sharp, so he would be mean. He did mean little things just to seem tough. He ate to be mean; he'd eat anything, everything. He'd take the last piece or the best and biggest piece, anything, just to be noticed, to have people cry out, "Freddie!" He got fatter and fatter till you were sure he'd bust his skin if he ate another bite. And, he laughed, with your piece of cake all chewed up in his mouth.

Uncle Salvi was a saint. He was good in everything. Quiet and tall, he carried Grandpa's huge liquid eyes, but he filled them with, not mischief, serenity. Broad-shouldered, handsome, he smiled tenderly on all the crazy commotion of the house. When I tell you he was a saint, he did a lot of the same things his brothers did, but he did them in such a way, a soft, sweet way that made them seem okay. After Grandpa died and Grandma was the boss, she wouldn't let anyone smoke. Daddy had to go outside, Uncle Vickie wouldn't visit as much, but gentle Uncle Salvi was allowed to light up right at the table. Uncle Salvi laughed at my clothes; if they had a hole, he chased me, poked his finger in and ripped them so Mama would have to buy me new ones. Uncle Salvi's saintliness was an illusion perpetrated by Grandma in which we all believed. He taunted, "You stink!" to which I countered, "I 'tink pretty! I smella powwa!" I meant "powder" which Mama spread over my tummy every morning. Everyone laughed at my charming error, "I smella powwa!" Their enjoyment mixed with the sweet confusion of the hurt he caused me in that tiny chest covered with baby powder when he tore and left my shirt in shreds mingled with the intense love I felt for him and the knowledge I had that he could do no wrong.

If you think Uncle Salvi was Grandma's favorite, think again. Uncle Sonny was her baby; he was a baby doll. Only seven years older than me! There's a picture of him, grinning with only four teeth, sleepy dark eyes, naked, four years old, giggling because he was caught naked by the camera, his bulging, naked tummy, smooth and sleek as a little black seal laughing with appealing black seal eyes.

Daddy was a shadow. I see him standing in the kitchen upstairs, smack in the middle of the linoleum and tile kitchen, deep in thought, fingering the wooden red apple that hung from the ceiling light, a florescent double circle. The apple hung on a long red ribbon, frayed at the end, tied to a dirty string that was, in turn, tied to the light's rusty chain. Mama loved this apple: it held her marriage and her family, her future that she was building. Mama stood while she was on the phone and played with this red apple, rubbing it absent-mindedly. I wondered at this phenomenon that was a simple red apple, it was higher than my eyes, I had to tilt my head to look at it, bat it with my outstretched fingertips if I jumped high enough. I needed to touch it because everyone else did. The apple was filled with energy from all of us. Whether we fingered it with contentment or frustration, the apple absorbed our feelings. If you said, "the apple," everyone in the house knew what you meant.

Daddy was a shadow. Grandpa was the Big Father of the house and beside him all the other men were boys: Vickie, Freddie, Salvi, Sonny, even when they were full grown men; Daddy and his friends, which included his two brothers, Jake and Harry, from the foster home around the corner. The house overflowed with men who ran through it like wild animals at play.

Even though it was the 1950s, they all still looked and talked like they had during the war. The war was who they were. They talked about the Nazis every day. "The Nazis fixed everything, they fixed," Mama said. "Everything, they fixed." Men and women still dressed like a war was on. Mama still wore bobby socks, which, of course, could be washed and worn over and over, making them perfect for poor people. But Mama liked to pretend things were like they used to be; she told me there were no silk stockings or nylons because of the war.

"Why not?"

"We gave them to the boys to make parachutes."

What was silk? What were parachutes? Who were the boys? The mystery was lovelier than the truth, so I turned the words round my mind and savored them instead of asking.

Another rosy mystery was "Rosie the Riveter," which Mama liked to say.

"What's a 'Rosie the Riveter'?" I finally asked one day.

"Oh, that's what we used to call the girls who worked in the factories making the airplanes."

Mama also used it to refer to any independently minded woman, like Aunt Bettina, one of Grandma's sisters, who sounded like a man on the telephone.

Or, one of the men would grab a woman and swing her like a jitterbug around the kitchen. Or, Mama would start to sing, "I'm Dancing With a Dolly With a Hole in Her Stocking," which always made me scream with laughter, because they sometimes called me Dolly like they sometimes called a girl, though I never had a hole in my stocking, because any hole was sewed up quick.

Mostly, the men would get exasperated, and holler at somebody, "Aw, take a long walk off a short pier!" or "Ya Mutha wears combat boots!" which made Grandma yell in Italian.

And how many times did Mama sing, "Can you tell me boy, is this the Chatanoo-ga Choo Choo?" I never did find out the answer to what a

Chatanoo-go Choo-Choo was; she'd just give me her mysterious smile, like the one on the Madonna of the Grapes in Grandma's bedroom, and say, "It's a song!" The question drove me crazy, but perverse as I was, I loved being driven crazy, and I loved the question infinitely more than the answer.

The men still tried to get into uniform. Joining the service was still a very proud thing. Uncle Vickie joined the Navy. His black ringlets tumbled out of his regulation white sailor cap like mischief. He looked like he was ready for trouble, making his bellbottoms and sailor blouse look like a special uniform for trouble. But, Uncle Salvi looked like an Air Force saint in his uniform, like he was going to fly into any country and just take care of things. Daddy joined the Merchant Marines. He couldn't get in anywhere else. He was too skinny even for that. He had to eat bowls and bowls of bananas and cream for weeks until he weighed barely enough. I didn't know the Merchant Marines was no good, that Daddy was no good. For years, I told people proudly, "My Daddy was in the Merchant Marines!" until some smart aleck enlightened me that the Merchant Marines were all hoodlums, like jail on the ocean. And I remembered that Daddy was an orphan passed from foster home to foster home and, once, he'd said, choking back the tears, the first time I ever saw him cry, that Grandpa never wanted him to marry Mama or even talk to her, because Grandpa thought he was no good.

BROOKS STREET

At the highest point of Brooks Street stood the White House, a great queen in a beautiful white gown, a three-tiered white wedding cake, a white embossed invitation beckoning me.

Looking toward this house, upon their backs, the tenements held up the hill like workers wearing the same plain uniform, every one dressed alike in old, slatted wood and faded brick. Sometimes, the backs of these workers sagged under their heavy loads; the roofs and porches slumped in the middle, exhausted, not giving up exactly, just hanging on.

On every corner was an awning. Nature had abandoned this part of the street; the oasis stood a top the hill leaving a concrete desert. With no trees for shade or softness, men made their own places of refreshment. On every corner was a corner store and men, women and children were physically yanked out of the plainness of their houses toward the brightly colored awnings and advertisements luring them to have a Coke or a Lucky, to take an Ex-Lax, anything to get out of the house. Groups of people clustered at the corners under the welcome shade of the awnings, smiled at by the angelic Breck girls, comforted by Aunt Jemima.

These stores were named after men. We called the stores Luigi's, Giuseppe's, Martinello's or Joe's. Even though they might have a sign that said, officially, Brook's Market, these dark caves, fans blowing sawdust, reeking of stogie, sweets, pickles and perfume, were named and called after men.

Once, or even twice, a week, if I were lucky, one of my uncles would take me the enormous distance of three houses to Brooks Market, past the long, windowless men's club, and across the street on a quest for penny candy. I might find a penny on the sidewalk, and Mama would give me a penny, and I was suddenly wealthy beyond words. I'd start to think about maybe saving a penny for another day, but, no, I might lose it or maybe no one would take me for a while, too long to wait, too chancy. Besides, you could get three candies for a penny, so the possibilities seemed endless.

Who was holding my hand? So many people did then, it could've been anyone, but it was probably Uncle Sonny. Because he was only seven years older than me, I sometimes forgot to call him uncle and he would remind me proudly, "*Uncle* Sonny!"

My big eyes bulging with anticipation, we crossed the hot summer street baking with cars and sun.

The bell on the screen door jingled.

"Sonny! Who's dat wich you? Cinda-rella?"

"Good morning, Mr. Martinello. This is my niece, Gloria, my sister's little girl."

Uncle Sonny felt like a man saying "my niece, my sister's little girl" as though all girls were together and he was aside, a man. And Mr. Martinello, sucking a stogie, almost like Grandpa, but not nearly as elegantly, was pleased, pleased that, rightly, little Sonny had a niece because his older sister had rightly married and rightly had a child.

"She's bootiful, Sonny, bootiful! An' where did she get all de yellow curls from, huh? Da fairy godmutha?"

A lot of this conversation, and many others, went on about three feet above the yellow head, but, this remark, I could tell, was directed downwards where I was trying unsuccessfully to glue my bulging eyes to the glass case full of sparkling, colored candies.

I turned to look at Mr. Martinello who was leering down at me. I didn't have to say anything; one look of the chick face was enough. Mr. Martinello laughed happily and asked Uncle Sonny, "So, what're ya gonna have, a tonic?"

"Yeah, I'll have a Coca-Cola."

A Coca-Cola was an unheard of luxury to me! It always amazed me, too, where did my uncles get money, when, according to Mama and Grandma, none of us had any?

I'd never had a Coke, never had put my hand into the dark depths of Mr. Martinello's ice chest like Uncle Sonny did now, taking out the glistening, dripping bottle, asking me as he squished his Coke open on the teeth of the metal bottle opener on the side of the sweating ice chest, right by the scroll "Coca-Cola," "Do you want a tonic, Gloria?" How I longed to do something so sophisticated and wonderful, as I watched the gas rise from his open bottle, but Mama didn't want me to have Coke because something about Coke wasn't good for me.

"Can I have a orangeade?"

"Sure!"

I watched his hand disappear again into the chest and come out dripping a bright orange bottle this time, squish, and it was mine, icy and wet.

"How is your mutha, Sonny?"

Their conversation faded over my head as I grasped my orangeade and pressed myself against the glass case of delectable shapes and textures, sparkling colors you could eat with your eyes. The red licorice coins were best, not especially for the flavor, but for the flavor that lasted. Embossed with a crest like a checkers piece, you got three for a penny and you could hold one in your mouth and suck on it for an hour if you concentrated and didn't forget and bite it by mistake. Nonpareils had an awkward, suspicious name and I wasn't crazy about those teeny white pebbly things that stuck in my teeth. Daddy ate malt balls: those didn't interest me. Hard candy I could get at home, though I studied all the colors there in the case, faithfully, anyway, to see if there were any I hadn't tried yet. I bought the licorice coins as an investment and decided to splurge the other penny on caramels; you only got two, but I adored the creamy, mysterious bull's eye in the center and the thick, familiar flesh of caramel.

Outside, my cheeks bulging, my lips oozing gritty, sugary cream, cold orangeade clutched in my hand, we passed the boys playing stickball across the street from sidewalk to sidewalk, using the street as though they owned it. They played with a piece of broomstick or a mop-stick and a white pimple ball sliced in half. Halfball or stickball. I strained to watch them play, savoring that I was walking with Uncle Sonny, savoring my cheeks overfull of flavor. When a car passed, the boys paused quietly, tapping the stick against the curb, causing an echo, a resonant echo, sharp, yet deep, the sound of hard wood against stone, echoing against streets and houses, finding its way into the blue sky and the tiny ears of a girl: the sound of boys.

And, if a car had the nerve to honk and get in their way while the game was hot, watch out! Down came that stick on the shiny fin of somebody's car, smack! And the boys would holler swear words and the driver's arm would come out the car window in a fist; or, the car would screech to a stop, the boys ran fast, and the raging driver would get out and find himself alone in the middle of the street, and other drivers honking at him.

Some boy would have to make a crack to Uncle Sonny because he was with me. I couldn't understand what was being said, much of it, especially on the street, out of the mouths of boys, was still a foreign language because I was small and in a foreign country - my home. I'd look up to see if I could maybe read what had been said from Uncle Sonny's expression, but his eyes were as soft and loving as ever, unlike as they could be from the dangerous, narrowed eyes of the other boys. He was the true meaning of turning the other cheek. This he did, opening the front door, nudging me gently into the house.

He liked to take me places.

EAST BOSTON, 1954

I was three years old when Mama opened the door and looked into the room. She screamed.

Her life was changed forever.

SEXUAL LAW

When a young woman stepped out of the house, her sex went up like a shot and young men, standing around all day in the company of other men - like soldiers or sailors who'd been deprived of softness and a sweet smell - stood alert suddenly, even though they seemed not to have altered their slouches against the tenement wall or the store window. They squinted over their cigarettes and a hush, as though decided communally, instinctively, fell over them and inwardly, their feelings swelled as she walked by. Maybe one or two didn't look at her: they watched her without looking. The others gave her the eye, up and down, through the haze of smoke. In the hush, the tension gathered, to be let out as soon as she passed, when they could still smell her, when she could still hear them, they'd let it all out, swoosh, as remarks she could just barely - or not - hear, but could feel, in a rush of heat through her veins.

I've seen pictures of my father taken with many other women, some pretty, with regular, pleasing features and others, downright ugly, big nose, teeny eyes, but, ever present, the red, red lips of the time, and, in every photo, laughter. The laughing eyes and mouths, on the street corner, at the beach, at a train station just after the war, a modest Japanese couple walking by peacefully in the distance.

I was glad to see my father had had other girl friends. I held in my small hands evidence that he was fun. Plainly, you could see how much fun he was, that he had joy.

Almost all the photos were taken on the street. Mama always took a shy photo. How Daddy must have loved her hooded, hazel eyes, her red curls and painted lips! He loved her body, too. Full, it was from Grandma's relentless cooking. Daddy always said, "Look at her! She's not fat! Look at that!" He'd grab a handful of her ass through her soft housedress.

But, before they were married, Mama was sweet on Daddy's brother, Jake. Jake had hooded, disreputable eyes, even I could see that; even as a baby, I did not trust Jake. I cried when he held me; I squirmed. All the brothers were blonde: Jake, Harry and Bill. Jake and Daddy wore the love curl, like Alan Ladd, all the women said, "Your Daddy looks just like Alan Ladd." But Jake looked more troublesome than Alan Ladd. Daddy wore his Lucky Strikes folded up in the sleeve of his white T-shirt. The brothers lived in a foster home around the corner on Trenton Street, a whole world away. There must have been a mighty tug on Mama to put on her lipstick and go down to the store for something so she could pass by the good-looking brothers hanging on the corner of Trenton Street.

Grandpa tried his best to put a stop to Mama's going out like that. Grandpa knew that sex was out there, everywhere, in every move she made - and Mama could be frighteningly pretty just by lifting her hand, and so could Grandma, and my sister and I have inherited those graceful movements that can send shivers through a man. So, Grandpa set the law down. He wouldn't let Mama roller skate. He wouldn't let her ride a bike. Grandpa knew how provocative these motions could be: her limbs rising and falling, her behind, a smooth, stiff outline, her red curls beckoning in the breeze. Mama on a bike! Mama on roller skates! I can feel Grandpa's shudder going through me!

But, Grandpa's law couldn't stop sexual law and restraint made Mama even more innocent and desirable. Especially to the bad boys. Boys like Jake and Daddy. Mama was really good. She prayed and went to mass and confession. She received Holy Communion every Sunday. She obeyed her father and her mother. She had that good look: round and soft and unaware of her power, a labyrinth of red curls, chubby legs in ankle socks and thick high heels stepping up into the corner store. The bad ones, without jobs, without homes, dropped out of school, squinting through the haze of cigarettes, were pulled right to her, without knowing what on earth had happened to them.


GARDENS

The tenements were close, less than two feet of alley separated them. Sometimes one wall held two houses together. Clotheslines crisscrossed, colored flags flapped from them; women's voluptuous arms tugged the ropes and pulleys. Windows slid open and women's arms tossed buckets of water out the windows. The women sang out to each other all day, their voices calling Italian like a song. We lived window to window, door to door, radio to radio, telephone to telephone - how many times did Daddy answer another man's phone, picking up our receiver, saying "Hello?" into the dial tone? How many times did he look across to see another man's wife naked in the dark?

The alleys were dirt, flanked by high, slatted fences. Bad business could be done there. I heard a boy's voice, "Come here, come into the alley." I don't know who he was, but he called to me. Behind the fences, weed trees sprouted every Spring, unfolding like evil palms, pushing right up through the iron fire escapes, ugly, straggly, even though they were green; they had a papery look, almost fake, crummy, taking from the beauty of Spring rather than adding to it. These evil palms burned bright red in autumn like maybe they had come from the Devil after all.

The dirt alleys, the tall, wooden fences, the weed trees led the way like the walls of a maze from the barren streets to a land of gardens. Maybe because the streets were lifeless except for the sexual power of the men and women upon them, behind the houses, burst a Garden of Eden, cut in neat squares by the individual yards of the tenements, a garden filled the center of a city block formed by the houses with their backs turned, lush, breaking with open blue sky, sea gulls and the scent of ocean, maples, oaks, elms, peach trees, grape vines, flowers, bent and swayed in the wind, tall corn, tomatoes, lettuce, carrots, squashes, pumpkins, marigolds reflecting the bright sun off their orange faces, incredible, incredible, I never would have believed such a world was back there, hidden and brave, till I was old enough to stand up and recognize it with my own eyes. The streets were night, the gardens, day.

The Italians never left Italy, but crossed the sea toward a rebirth of Italy, toward a promise they made to themselves, with seeds sown into the linings of their clothes, with memories closed up in lockets, waiting, like babies wait to be conceived, to be planted in the New World.

In the back of the tenement, when you stepped out on to the weathered wood, the sun-whitened wood that made up all three porches out back, cascading down two landings per story, with charming picket gates and white railings, nothing but air under your shoes though they made the sound of leather on wood, and the wooden screen door snapped shut behind you and your eyes went up and out and out and out, for as far as you could see was open and blue and white and green, shining, swaying, growing, splashed with sunlight, laundry lapping up sunlight, like a dream, like Italy.

Seagulls called; they cut through the blue sky and white clouds like freedom. Little I was, but out I flew with them; seagulls lifted my heart. Two, or three feet tall I was, but I could feel the wind over their feathers, their wings that could cut the blue sky like white knives and soar without flapping. Their cry! They were superior! They only flew out back, never in the front. They were wise.

The old man who lived next to us walked out every day in his old straw hat. He walked slowly, bowed, pushing a large, wooden wheelbarrow; he was already old when I was young. His garden was the largest. Old and bowed, he cared for his vegetables every day. Grandma knew him. They spoke over the fence in Italian. He had every vegetable. Grandma respected him. I could tell from her tone when she spoke of him. If she said, "He goes out every day, every day," I knew she respected his diligence. If I asked, "Does the old man have peas?" and she said, "Of coursa he has peas! He has peas!" then I knew she respected that he had all the right vegetables. If I asked, "Does the old man have the biggest garden?" It was as far as I could see, the biggest! Grandma would say, "Oh, yeah! Who else? Around here?"

Then I knew she respected him more than any other gardener, maybe even herself.

But, Grandma also knew how to grow things, and Nona, who had taught her, also knew. The right seeds and the right soil were not enough. Soil, seeds, sun, water, the sudden, clean air of the back, none of these were enough; another, sixth sense was needed to breathe life into the scraps of earth hidden behind the barren streets. I could feel this sixth sense rising out of the skin of Grandma's and Nona's fingers as they touched the very thing they knew and loved, the tender plant, the soft dirt, the seed, the root; knowledge came off their fingers, devotion was transmuted from flesh to flesh. Nona had this sense and Grandma, and the old man, the dirt clinging lovingly under their fingernails and working its way into the miles of fine lines that told on their wrinkled skin. I could not have this knowledge, I thought. I thought I was no more than a blob of dirt, a pebble, an underdeveloped curled leaf of indistinguishable new growth, all the while capable of both giving and receiving, all the while, having knowledge without knowing. Like babies, the old people were also innocent of themselves and capable of much.

The old man had plum tomatoes, rows and rows of them, taller than he, stooped over as he was. He had a fat peach tree. Good peaches, Mama told me, like in Italy, juicy and sweet.

"The Irish lady on the other side, she has one for the flowers, for the flowers, she has one," Mama declared, wrinkling up her nose. "Those Irish peaches are green and hard, even the birds won't eat them. That tree is wasted on her, wasted."

Peaches had soft fuzz on them. Plushness, wet from Mama's washing, from Mama's dripping pink hand to mine, wet fuzz tickling my nostrils. Held up, a peach was a sun, radiating light. A new world with miraculous, inner flesh that could be discovered, tasted, digested and was still miraculous and not in the least understood, even though it had become a part of me.

Lettuce grew low, crisp and tender. The old man had every kind: butter lettuce that melted in your mouth; crunchy Romaine; chicory, tickly; bitter spinach, all catching the rain, the clear, washing water, in cups green-furled. Before the long zucchinis arrived the old man handed over the fence, the yellow blossoms of zucchinis never-to-be, pilfered from the harvest. Grandma sautéed the yellow flowers with eggs. Me, Mama, Grandma and Nona (who mashed hers with no teeth) sat together at the noon table scooping eggs, spinach and blossoms into crusty bread; silent, except for an occasional moan of delight, soft and personal.

Our garden was a tiny square of earth cut out of the concrete yard crammed next to the shed for the trash cans. A telephone pole was stuck in it. Round about was a wire fence.

It was Nona's garden, really, though Grandma and Mama also worked in it. Nona carried the water in buckets down all the flights of wooden stairs, back up again to refill the buckets, then down again and again until the garden was fed. She was eighty. Agonizingly slowly for a little girl behind her who wanted to skip down the steps as though flying through air, way high up, from the third floor down. But, I waited and mused, sending my mind and heart out instead, as I, no bigger than the bucket, waited behind Nona's blue velvet scuffy slippers with the toes cut out for her veiny, swollen flesh, her beloved blue velvet slippers, her beloved veiny flesh.

She never poured the bucket of water directly on the plants. No. She held the heavy, sloshy bucket with one hand, wobbling with one hand, or set it down, if she could, and with the other, formed a gentle scoop, so that she splashed the plants at the base and patted the soil with drink.

This care was the sixth sense, this mysterious, deep knowledge that not everyone had, none of the young bodies strutting out on the streets, all of them had forgotten their legacy of the gardens. What was this mysterious sixth sense but love, that made things grow, that brought recognition of need and understanding without self-consciousness, without theory, that brought life to the garden?

Nona grew the love plum tomatoes, too, as did everyone Italian; they were a staple of the Italian diet and garden, straight up they grew, tied up to tall wooden sticks. Because he liked us, because we never complained like the other neighbors about growth that would steal out of his slatted wood fence into our yard, the old man let us keep anything that spread from his garden to ours: the blossoms of squashes or pumpkins, the morning glories that twined and wound about, the marigolds that poked their heads and spied on us, the greens gone wild and erratic. Nona grew the hot, red finger peppers that Grandma hung in bunches to dry, that she and all the other grown-ups sprinkled lavishly over the steaming red gravy drenching the macaroni. Mama's eyes filled up with hot pepper tears and her nose blossomed red and ran with mucus, and Mama sniffed and blinked her eyes and whispered huskily, "Oh, that's good!" and took another bite.

Nona grew tender lettuce, but, most tender of all was in a whole separate section, the whole other side of the little red brick walk that ran down the center of the garden, devoted to - the arugula. No more than three inches tall, with leaves the size of pennies, bitter and marvelous, like nothing else and only for adults: arugula burned my mouth. Nevertheless, I knew from the rapt faces of the arugula eaters, the bitter little plants were worshipped. Mama's eyes closed, her moving mouth moaned. Grandma nodded and chewed. Grandpa jutted his chin in an expression of divine justice. Nona, like me, was not allowed to eat them. Arugula. Pluck them - I was allowed to do this, tenderly, a pinch of little finger nails - and they continued to grow, ready for the next time.

"How long before the arugulas grow up again, Nona?"

"Eh?" She shrugged and laughed, toothless, black filigree in her mouth like her diamond earrings, "Who knows!"

A telephone pole poked itself into the arugula garden. And at the foot of the telephone pole, a small Madonna, dressed in blue robes and white, her palms held upward, her eyes closed, she smiled serenely, blessing the garden. I liked to wash her face when it got dirty from the dark soil. I dipped my fingers in the watering bucket and washed her face.

"Why is the pole here, Nona?"

Nona shrugged and threw out her hand, as if to say, "Whaddaya gonna do?"

I was insulted by this horrid wooden pole that had numbers on it and a metal tag. It looked like business, which had nothing to do with the garden. But year after year as I followed Nona down to the garden, I believe the pole grew roots like everything else Nona fed, because after a while it seemed to change to an organic thing.


FEELING THE WORLD

What a riot, what an orgy of living my little life was for me! I wondered at the peculiar mixture I was of Mama and Daddy, Nona, Grandma and Grandpa and all the things I saw and felt and ate and breathed. A part of me was perverted as though the good in Mama and all her generations had met the bad in Daddy and all his generations, had somehow twisted like a curious string of DNA creating this perversion, putting me beyond them both and everything.

All babies are crazy to play with water and I was no exception, except that my sexual response never separated to my genitals, not entirely, from the rest of my body.

Mama gave me bowls of water to play with, to plunge in my hot baby hands, out on the sunny white piazza. She gave me water dancing with sunlight, sparkling, thrown up in the sunlit air, tickling down my fat arms, I turned to Mama and laughed my toothless grin.

By the time my little sister came -

I was six. Mama put out the little wading pool. Marie and I filled up the pool with as many toys and cups and saucepans we could find, and then, sit in it. Why? To feel these objects against our skin, pushing against our bodies, ooh, it felt good! It was my idea to fill our panties (which was all we wore) with them, as much as we could fit in, till we were fat with objects in our panties. Feeling, feeling, wanting more feeling! The cool water seeped in, nudging the lips of our little vaginas in a strange new way, the objects pushed against us when we moved, we laughed!

Mama came outside and cried, "What are you doing?"

We looked down at our bulging panties full of cups and pans and bath toys, and looked back up at her. We didn't know what we were doing. Mama just shook her head. Kids are crazy. Living with a kid is like living with a crazy person. Kids walk backwards, sit in a chair upside down, yell high-pitched cries just to hear how the sounds. I was a kid *and* I was perverted. What was I doing? Feeling the world! And it felt good.


LOVE PARTIES

The house banged and stomped and ran with people; it called out and answered in happy shouts. They didn't talk to each other in normal voices, they bellowed from deep in their bellies, with joy, with rage, with a deep relish of their joy and rage; from room to room, up the stairs or down, from the refrigerator to the stove, from adjoining beds, they loved the sound of themselves.

It was music. English rolled off their tongues with the texture of sauce and pasta, mixed with Italian like a song of tinkling bells. They kept my ears ready and my eyes opened. My curly head spun from one of them to the other. Grandma gibbered breathlessly in Italian to Nona who grunted in agreement till it was Nona's turn to jibber and Grandma's to grunt. I didn't understand a word, but I loved to hear them talk. I was a contradiction of adoration: I loved that I couldn't understand the Italian words they spoke and I wished the words would unfold for me magically.

Uncle Vickie hammered the house when he came in from outside, his friends still warm from him, calling to him from the street. He shrugged them off his shoulders. Grandma caught his gesture.

"An, whadda they wan', Vickie, eh? An whadda they wan'?"

Uncle Vickie blushed, "I dunno, Ma. Wha'do I know?"

He winked at me. My upturned face lit up! What an honor that he should take this uncomprehending blob into his confidence! What a thrill that some something was going on out on the street that Uncle Vickie was savvy about!

Then, Uncle Vickie was no longer a boy in an overcoat and a fedora, but a man in a sailor's uniform with his naughty black curls peeking out from his crisp, white cap. Uncle Salvi tossed his Air Force hat and it landed on my head. My baby hand went up to the shiny rim like I was saluting, my fat legs curled under my frilly dress like a pin-up girl. Someone snapped a picture.

Mama and Daddy had friends in, men and women shoved into the kitchen, a cramped, smoky little room with a linoleum floor in line with dozens of other cramped, smoky little rooms in a row down the city block of tenements. Cards, and glasses of booze, cigarettes and matches, ashtrays, were flung down on Grandma's pristine tabletop. Frank Sinatra or Bing Crosby swooned them into each other's arms.

They loved to touch each other; they would in a minute for any reason, an arm, a thigh, a knee, for emphasis in a conversation. The men slapped the women's asses, screams and squeals! Slapped the men back, the broad backs of men. Laughter, all laughter. A man's loud voice, Daddy's, calling out a joke on another man, he answers back a joke on Daddy and the whole room aches with laughter. Mama's laughing, turbaned head peaks out from the teeny bedroom she and Daddy shared with my crib, a pantry, really, not big enough for a cot and a crib; you had to walk in sideways. Tucked in behind Grandma's washing machine, like a big pressure cooker, big as a man; she'd clamp the lid down and it rumbled the clothes clean, secretly, locked inside. A man, I can hear his laugh distinctly, though I don't know his name, he leaned on it, laughing. It was something to lean on at parties, too round on the top to rest a drink on. No one paid attention to it, they were so happy to be celebrating themselves and each other. But, I was crazed with intellect, and to see him leaning on it and laughing, I knew its ominous presence meant Grandma had to work hard soon, after the party was over. I wondered at its workaday presence, waiting for the celebrants like a policeman, but what did they care? The haunting presence of work was nothing to them! It was a reason for a joke, a slap, a kiss, a drink, a laugh! They played like children, but crazily, intensely, hungrily, really, they had a hunger for each other and for their brief, drunken times together.

They loved to make Grandma laugh. It was a supreme challenge to make her laugh. Grandma was not a little old lady. Nona was hunched and old, her slippers scraped. But, Grandma was a slim lady in a thin-waisted dress with padded shoulders after the war. She wore nylons, seams always straight, and thick, high-heeled shoes. Her light brown hair was rolled back smoothly at the temples and crown, after the style of the war years. Her forehead was high and clear, intelligent; Grandma had a knowing face, her chin was set and strong. During parties, she frowned or pursed her lips in a fine, red bow. Maybe she knew she shouldn't let all the parties go on, where was Grandpa? I don't see him there. Maybe he was gone already. He died when I was four, suddenly, from his own heart; it killed him. If he was gone, then the fine, red bow would loosen and someone would make Palma laugh. Then, all the men and women would light up with delight at their

power and the rightness of their celebration, because, there, at the edge of
the red bow, the red ribbon had fallen loose, had slackened into the hint of a
smile, and as everyone partied up to her, the red corners of her mouth lifted
and joined them, and, dumbfounded, they sat her down, gave her a root beer
and she allowed herself a few more laughs.

"And where did you come from with your blonde curls?" But, they
weren't really interested in me.

The women, with red lipstick smudged on their cigarettes and painted,
red fingernails, said, as they took a puff, "Your Daddy looks just like Alan
Ladd."

My big eyes would follow their red fingernails as they floated on
smoke in the air, drifting down a cloud of smoke to settle round a highball,
clinking and shining with ice and cheap bracelets, "just like him, just like
him."

When they said so, Mama dipped her head and privately smiled, a smile
like the Mona Lisa, and Daddy dipped his head, with the love curl nodding a
jaunty, slick wave over his eye, like the curling tip of an ocean wave, and he
smiled too, that same secret smile. Daddy was tall. And, he turned and told
me, with some pride, "You know, they had to stand his leading lady in a
ditch so he could kiss her."

I didn't know what he meant. But, I loved to listen to the sound of
them.

"You dames'r all alike!"

"Watch out or I'll slip ya a mickey."

"Aw, he's all hepped up on goofballs!"

"Hey, who's got the church key?"

Mama wore a frilly, white nylon blouse with a slip under to cover her
and a black velvet bow tied primly at her throat. She got awful silly on a
highball and once, she, probably also under the influence of her long-lasting
infatuation with Daddy's brother, Jake, Mama yanked her blouse out of her
skirt, lifted it up and hollered, "Hey, Jake, wanna havva naval battle?"

Everyone's mouth gaped. Even Daddy blushed.

"Rosa, was that *you?* "

Mama turned bright scarlet red, red as her lipstick. She'd do that, get to
feeling good and let one out like that and never live it down.

Sometimes, I was there, silent, small, forgotten, in the chaos of their
being alive and drunk on each other, unnoticed, invisible and watchful, as
ever I wished to be. Sometimes, I was asleep listening to the black rhythms
of their voices, listening with one ear, and the sudden, violent bursts of
laughter woke me open. Even in half sleep, I opened myself and took them
in, their hunger and thirst for themselves, for each other, for their time
together, their freedom to drink and sing and dance and laugh, the high,

pungent odor of liquor and perfume sweating out of them, filling my nostrils till I could taste it. They couldn't get enough of each other and I couldn't get enough of them.

ANGIE

Angie was a minx. To look at her, her eyes clenched the spirit of an elf, a minx, a nasty nymph. Not round Italian eyes, Angie was not Italian; narrow, untrustworthy eyes, the way they had of pinching in the corners when she laughed, or silently smiled, what was she up to?

Uncle Vickie brought her into the house. She was his first wife. They lived on the second floor when we lived in the tiny pantry of Grandma's kitchen and Nona lived on the top.

Uncle Vickie made his eyes like Angie's when he was with her. He couldn't keep his hands or arms or lips or legs off of her when he sat next to her; his body pushed so close to hers, as though trying to get closer then he physically could.

She had nipples. That's what I loved about her, as well as her eyes. She wore a tight sweater and her nipples stood up. I positioned myself right in front of her and matched my eyes to her nipples and I couldn't take my eyes off them, so perfectly did they stand right up in the centers of her round breasts.

Angie didn't mind. She smiled her minx smile at me. I was too young to be ashamed. Standing in front of her, I thoroughly enjoyed the exactness of her nipples, which other women didn't seem to have. Mama and Grandma and Nona, and all the other women, seemed to have corrected their nipples into bras. Did Angie know some secret? Angie winked at me. Her whole body was a wink.

Every Saturday morning, she and Uncle Vickie would come for me - no, just Angie would come. Uncle Vickie waited in bed. Up the stairs in her nightgown, Angie hopped in bare feet, her breasts swinging, she called out, "I've come for the baby!"

And, Mama? What did she know? Proudly, Mama handed me to her, and Angie took me and carried me upstairs where she and Uncle Vickie played with me in the bed.

"There are worse things," Mama told me years later, when I confided in her some horror that had happened to me. "There are worse things." What? What?

"All I'll say is, when you were three years old, something happened that was so bad, I almost killed myself and you too. That's all I'll say."

What? What? I asked myself, not Mama. But, every time I questioned her about Angie, her face went pale, her chin, haggard, "What do you want to know for?" she scolded me. She warned me, aged and exhausted, with the warning eyes of a soldier who doesn't want to talk about the war.

What did she see? What happened in that bed? Where was my baby mouth? Where were Uncle Vickie's hands? Where were Angie's beautiful breasts? What did Mama see that was the first thing to make her go pale and want to cut life dead? The first thing to begin gnawing at her, the worm that ate a line across her smooth, clear forehead and dragged the corners of her red mouth till they turned down forever.

"There are worse things."

What is the worst thing, Mama? Do you mean when the enemy does not come marching down the street behind roaring tanks, when the enemy does not carry another flag or wear another uniform? When the enemy is your brother or your brother's wife? When you must learn to live with the enemy? When you must learn to love the enemy?

Mama taught me that day that I am not so important, that bad things may happen to me and Mama was not so important, that bad things may happen to her. That a family learns to live with the enemy, not to forgive him exactly, but know him, because families love, not in spite of faults, but also faults. The faults were named Vickie. The faults were named Angie. We learned that Uncle Vickie was a gangster and Angie was a gangster's wife. We learned to love the gangster as well as the uncle, brother and son.

But, what if nothing had happened in that bed but warmth and flesh? Maybe, Angie wanted to cuddle a baby. She was having one soon herself. With one inside, maybe she couldn't resist snuggling with me and her husband under the sleepy morning sheets.

Maybe, the enemy was someone else. Who? I think he must have been in the house already.

Was it Jake, Mama, who I never trusted, who used to hold me while I squirmed, with his hand up under my dress? Jake who delighted you because he could hop into a convertible car without opening the door? Was it Daddy? Mama? Was it DADDY? The one who protected us? Was that what turned your angel face so dark?

Once, when I was asleep in my crib, Daddy was the only one home. He was in the bathtub when he smelled gasoline and smoke. He leaped out of the tub, threw on his robe and ran downstairs without covering himself. An arsonist was setting fire to the hallway. Daddy thrashed him to within an inch of his life, sobbing all the while at the thought of me asleep upstairs; his eyes blurred with tears and bath water as the man fled. From that day, each time the front door opened, a sharp buzzer went off which Daddy had invented to keep us safe.

When I thought of me sleeping safely, I wondered who was already in the house. Who? My mind searches for him, while the child sleeps.

Mama wouldn't tell me what happened, but I could read the lines and shadows on her face and they read - sex. What else would make her want to die? The answer lay under her skin like a dried up riverbed, the lines twisted into a grainy pattern I could decipher only so far.

A man spills blood; a woman cleans it up. They blamed Angie because she said Uncle Vickie kicked her in the stomach and that's why she lost the baby. And, she said, he had girlfriends, something about black girls "on the floor" at the club. "That's what she said," Mama told Grandma, "I don't know how she could say such a thing."

"That's why Angie and Vickie got a divorce," Mama shrugged, as if to say, how could anyone divorce, that was so ignoble, when there was endurance and there was suicide.


PIGEONS

Grandma brought up her children during the Depression. For her, the Depression was the war; it was the fight; it was the struggle. The Depression had taught Grandma and Mama how to live, and, even though most people, history tells us, were doing well in the fifties, we still lived by the rules Grandma and Mama had learned during the Great Depression.

"People used to scrape the insides of the garbage cans with a spoon," Mama said, "that was their food! They licked the trash can covers!"

I looked skeptical.

"You think I'm kidding you? You think I'm lying?"

She showed me pictures in a big book called Life of bombed out cities and I, the little pervert, was fascinated by the naked asses of bodies sprawled in the streets.

"Where's their clothes?"

"Blown off! By the bombs! That's war!"

Perverse, perverse, war turned me on. I'd take out the book when she wasn't looking and stare and stare at the naked asses.

Nevertheless, these lessons Mama had learned. Her values learned by the great lesson teachers: the war, the Depression. Food was the most important thing. After food, cleanliness. Cleanliness was like not being bombed. And food, like Grandma's and Mama's, was like the greatest, most luxurious tastes and textures in the world, better than the best restaurants of Paris or Rome: all the food they couldn't get during the war and the Depression.

Yet, no matter how fancy the food got, a simple hunk of bread with a crust to bite and soft buttery flesh melting round our tongues was heaven. In our house, fresh Italian bread with butter was worshipped as the basis of all food and glory, as holy as the Heavenly Host. I may not have known how to express it, but I learned early that food was an orgasm, an indescribable, overwhelming flood of sensations beginning at the mouth and nostrils, overflowing the banks of every nerve as it traveled round the body, to be renewed on the tongue over and over.

We had nothing in our hands but food.

For entertainment, we looked out the window.

Grandma had a small blanket folded on the windowsill for her elbows to rest. Up and down the street, you could see the immigrant women leaning on their elbows, gazing with downcast eyes at the concrete rivers that passed below. Occasionally, a woman would come out of the house with a bag on her arm.

"Ah, Angelina's goin' shoppin'," Grandma mumbled. My head followed the old lady down the street as if she were on the most important diplomatic mission. But why did an old lady hunched in black have a pretty name like Angelina?

A piece of newspaper flew by, lifted by the city wind between the buildings. I watched till it was out of view. Straining, my face pressed to the glass, I tried to see a corner of the White House.

"Get away from the window, you make a mark on the glass! Look! Look, how the pigeons eat!"

Our bread was fresh every day. Grandma always fed the pigeons day old bread. She dried it for the birds and broke it up. Sometimes, she soaked it for them, but I never could figure out why she did one and not the other.

"Pigeons are beautiful," I said admiring their shimmering, peacock necks, their soft grey feathers, their fat bottoms trailing the ground. They pecked and pecked, following the crusts of bread to the gutters, following the crumbs out into the road, pecking bravely between the rushing cars.

"Ah, they're dirty! Dirty!" Grandma shook her head and made a face.

Right before my eyes, their grey feathers got dirty. The sleek green and purple of their necks, was that dirty, too?

"They're so pretty!" I said. They cooed like doves and wobbled like jollies. Were they dirty? Were they?

"Filthy, filthy birds! They have bugs! They shit!" Grandma said with force.

You could see their shit all over, the sidewalk, the gutter, the street. The birds, it was true, ate right in their own mess. Filthy, that was it.

Disappointed, a sad lowering of the eye; like the other immigrants leaning out the window, you could witness me from the street. A small thing, but I couldn't like pigeons if they were dirty. Dirty was the first thing I knew that was bad.

When my Daddy's sister came from out of nowhere to live in our crowded house, huge with an illegitimate child, I toddled over to the women, Grandma, Mama and Aunt Doris, working together at the steaming stove.

"Doiten!" I handed the offensive dust ball over to Mama, thinking I had done a wonderful thing by finding it under the bed and getting it to her.

"But, where did you find it?" Mama cried out.

"Unda the bed!"

And, as if I hadn't answered them they cried in unison, "But where did you find it?" They sang together, like a Greek chorus, their denial of anything dirty in their lives.

EAST BOSTON, 1954

I was three years old when Mama opened the door and looked into the room. She screamed.

Her life was changed forever.

Daddy and I looked up.

DRUMBEAT

I could see their skin next to my eyes as though it were my own skin. I could breathe them all, as through cloth and skin. Grandpa, of wool and tobacco and old, tough skin thick with years and years of wine and meat. Grandma, through flannel and vanilla, her pale arms dusted with flour and spattered with sauce, and, under her fingernails, the fierce scent of oregano and amanda. Mama was cotton; I breathed her through flowery cotton and heavy breasts like pillows puffed with baby powder and Ivory Snow. Nona was almost evaporated; she was harder to breathe, half blind and forgetting words, first English, then Italian. All that remained of her were her black and gold diamond earrings that stretched the pierced holes in her ears like dough, her ephemeral, silent giggle, and her fine, white hair, soft as air, with its streak of bright yellow to remind you she was once solid; once, she was made of more than giggles and air.

Aunt Sophia, who was Mama's aunt and, therefore, my Great Aunt Sophia, had a blue twinkle in her eye. She leaned over me on the bed, leaning on rolled fists, her arms on either side of me. I looked up, kicking my fat baby legs, this twinkle, blue as heaven, this skin, smelling of holiday cooking and holiday perfume, my fat legs rejoiced in them, kicking, and my fat arms, kicking too! I laughed, I laughed, my eyes lighted with her twinkle, which she never lost as though Aunt Sophia was a baby too.

On either side of her were her sons, nine and ten, John and Joseph, Johnny and Joey, and she showing me to them. "See her, isn't she beautiful?" and I was, really beautiful, like an alien child: tufts of Nona's white blonde hair, enormous globes of deep blue eyes, a nose that came from Daddy, the intelligent, English nose in a fat, baby face. Those two boys, embarrassed and fumbling, looked down out of obedience to their mischievous mother, and saw a baby and grimaced, but, something had clicked, and, their reluctant eyes kept returning to me, rapt and kicking on the bed. Their flesh was darker than my own pink and white flesh. They were my family, but they had their father's Italian eyes, like Arab eyes, eyes that had crossed the Mediterranean out of Africa, eyes that held the drumbeat. I was white, but, underneath, I had this black blood, lying on that bed under their liquid eyes, under their mother who smelled of holiday cooking and holiday perfume, under their sleepy grins, their reluctant black eyes that kept returning to me.

Five years later, they extracted their revenge when they gleefully stuck pins in my doll, which lay, pink and white, on the bed, kicking her fat legs and arms. They stuck pins in her, because they wanted to stick pins in me; they wanted me, and their mother had set them up to want me, deep in their memory they both loved and hated my power over their wantings, their mother's sorcery, the power of her skin and my skin. "See her, isn't she beautiful?" My five-year-old fluffs of hair would make them crazy with wanting, so they killed my baby doll instead of me.

And I would cry. The splits in my dolly's head, they were horrible. They made her head look like a deformed baby. The boys had made her mongoloid, ugly! I cried and cried. And, they laughed. Johnny and Joey, Johnny and Joey. Aunt Sophia comforted me.

She sat me down in the kitchen, smiling a secret, satisfied smile at her sons' power and at her own mischief, and she gave me cookies and milk. My parents were there, smiling. Aunt Sophia's calico cat, which Mama used to call a money cat, leaped on to the table and meowed. Her name was Cookie. This calmed me as I ate my cookies that the kitty's name was Cookie too: this satisfied me.

Johnny and Joey eyed me from the doorway.

"We wanna kill that doll!" they called.

I hugged her, closer, deformed as she was; my eyes bulged further with horror and admiration. I loved them. I brought that doll with me every time we went to Aunt Sophia's. I had to bring her. I looked forward to these visits more than any other place we went. I adored Johnny and Joey, and, as I grew older, I wanted more and more their dark eyes over me and their mother's approving smile.


MORE HOLY THAN CHURCH

When my sister was born, Mama stopped going to church. But, she wanted me to go. One Sunday morning, she got me all dressed up and told me I could walk down the hill by myself.

Overcome with a sudden panic, I couldn't believe what I was hearing! She wouldn't even let me play on the street because it was too dangerous; maybe she thought church would protect me.

Tears blinded me as Mama pushed me out the buzzing door.

"Go on, just walk straight down the hill," she encouraged me.

I didn't know about independence. I only knew about terror.

I looked down that long concrete hill and I could not see the church, The Church of the Sacred Heart, which was no more than a pile of bricks with a cross on top and an iron fence around like a prison. You may as well have told me to walk down to hell.

Already, I knew I had to go to church. I knew it was a sin not to. Already, I was studying my catechism to prepare me to receive my First Holy Communion. Soon, I would be a seven-year-old bride in white veil and dress, white gloves, shoes and stockings, squinting into the sun in front of that holy brick pile.

People were walking by, dressed for worship. Ladies in high heels and white gloves; some had corsages pinned to their shoulders, like girls going to a dance. Men in suits and hats. They turned to stare at me, also dressed for worship in a frilly dress and socks. But, I was screaming with tears.

"Look! Everybody's going to church! Walk with them!" Mama told me, getting angry and embarrassed.

Maybe she thought I would somehow attach myself to the flow of these people going down the street, like a little barnacle on a whale or a motherless heifer stumbling off with a strange herd. But, I would not. For love, I had great courage, but, for the outside world, I had none.

"Here! Go with these people! Will you take her to church?" Mama suddenly asked a lady.

The lady hesitated and stopped. Even at seven years old, even through my eyes swimming in tears, I could see her distaste. She didn't want to stop. She didn't want to concern herself with us. She was on her way to church, after all, which was pleasant, why should she interrupt her peace with the problems of heathens? Coldness, correctness, went out from her toward my mother standing in the doorway in supplication. My mother, who had her hands so full with a new baby, she shouldn't have been standing at the frantically buzzing door for minutes! Minutes! Grappling with me.

"Yes," said the Lady of Disdain, "I'll take her."

Who was she? Just a lady who didn't like us.

"Thank you. Can she walk back with you, too?"

"Of course."

She leaned over to take my hand. Mama was saying in my ear, "Now, you be a good girl." Mama kissed my cheek.

The lady leaned over to take my hand, but I would not give my hand. I screamed at her instead, loud, giving her at once all the terror I could muster in this emergency. I became the devil. Here, lady, meet the holy devil on a Sunday on your way to God Almighty mass!

Her stiff, benevolent face turned ashen; she folded her hands inward and hurried past.

Mama was furious. She yanked me back into the sanctuary of our house. The buzzer stopped. The dim hallway enveloped me softly as Mama yelled at me. Not only had she gotten me all dressed up for nothing and stood downstairs while the infant, Marie had screamed for her upstairs, but, now I had a mortal sin on my soul because it was Sunday and, for the first time, I had not gone to mass. I would have to confess this sin to God!

I was more terrified of Mama than God. Still choking on my tears, I trembled at the prospect of going down to the brick pile another time for confession, but I could feel, as the church fell away and the house took me in, my inner peace building. Grandma's sweet cooking aromas of meat bubbling in the Sunday tomato sauce enveloped me like a warm bath. Home, I was sure, was more holy than church.

## NONA BELLA

I was sitting on the kitchen table in Grandma's. The tabletop was gold Formica, a word I heard since before I could speak English. The tabletop was cool under my pants.

Mama had taught me to sew, but, since I had nothing to sew, I sewed buttons out of a jar on to the legs of my corduroy pants.

Mama and Grandma could sew anything, in a minute. By hand stitch, or by pushing the cloth under the metal teeth of the sewing machine, brrrrr-clamp, brrrrr-clamp. Grandma's machine was a Singer made of black iron lace with a pedal she worked with her black, lace-up shoes. All sewing machines were Singers. Mama's Singer was blue. It plugged in to the wall and didn't have a nice lacey pedal like Grandma's which she let me rest my little hand on while her foot made it go up and down.

Grandma made potholders out of scraps of towels or dishcloths. Mama made housedresses. Both made the bedspreads and curtains out of pieces of worn out bedspreads and curtains they spliced together with the nonsense of immigrants who didn't know what matched and what didn't. Brown plaid bedspreads with orange cowboy ruffles for boys' beds, navy blue striped curtains to match. Old chenille bathrobes sewn together for a girl. Even the sheets had seams going every which way. And, these scarred sheets were destined to be pillowcases. But, the pillowcases did not become handkerchiefs. Handkerchiefs were sacred: Grandpa carried them. They were real, made of fine linen from Italy, religiously washed, pressed and folded by Grandma as fine altar cloths by nuns.

"Where did you learn to sew like that?" I asked Mama. I asked her constantly, every time she sewed, and she loved to answer me.

"I was an operator before I was married."

"What's an 'operator?'"

"Oh, that's a factory girl who operates the machines."

Before I was born, when I was, like Daddy said, "a twinkle in my Mama's eye," Mama wore dresses and coats and white ankle socks with thick high heels. She rolled her hair and wore red lipstick. She sewed all day in a row of Singers, a long, black shiny row, whirring and banging, in a row of permed heads, red lips and painted fingernails, women singing and shouting as they worked above the roar of the workplace. Mama loved them. She said their names, Marina, Maria, Edie, Cora, Franny, like a song that only she knew.

"Do you know them now?" I asked.

"No!" Mama snapped, as though I was being ridiculous, "I'm married now! They're gone."

"Gone, where?"

"Oh, they're probably all gone and married, too."

Marina, Maria, Edie, Cora, Franny, Rosa, Mama was proud of them, proud of having been an operator, a girl in a row.

"On Kneeland Street, we worked, on Kneeland Street," Mama sang like a song.

Grandma was soaking clothes. In one half of the sink, she had the whites in bleach n' water, bleach n' water, bleach n' water, like one word, one sound. In the other half of the sink, Grandpa's shirts soaked in liquid starch.

Nona and I were sitting at the table. I was on the table, sewing button after button to my pant leg. Nona and I couldn't speak much English, or any other language, maybe just a few words, but, even then, we weren't too sure of the meaning. She liked me a lot, though. I could tell. Her old eyes lighted up when our eyes met. I had her hair. Maybe she remembered that. I was beautiful: she knew it, but I didn't. She and I had a game we loved. Nona called me, "Brutta!"

"What is it she called me, Grandma?"

"Huh? Oh, 'brutta' means ugly." Grandma said in her overworked, exhausted voice. I didn't know it then, but she was taking care of everyone from her daughter's daughter to her dying mother and she was tired.

"Nona, brutta!" I countered with delight.

Ha, ha, ha, Nona's toothless mouth opened wide with joy, she laughed silently; she hadn't enough breath for sound.

"You, brutta!" Nona returned, shaking a little with laughter in her thin faded dress and sweater.

"Nona, brutta!"

We could go on like that for a long time, while I peacefully sewed buttons to my pants, until some adult made us stop, probably to get me off the table so we could eat.

I loved Nona to distraction. We lived in a serene and secret world together: in the house, in the garden out back, or on our journeys to the Square while she was still able. The Square was a large, open-air market blocks and blocks of barren concrete roads away that suddenly opened out to a square full of colorful fruit and vegetable stalls tumbling out of the tiny, overfull grocery stores. I held on to her metal cart, an old lady's cart that folded out for carrying the shopping, while Nona pushed it along, a little old widow in black and a little yellow chick in a pale summer dress. She sat me down on a curbstone and - only a lady as old as Nona could do this (Mama never would) - she plunged her old hand into a box full of pea pods at the grocery stall like she owned it and thrust a handful of pea pods into my pea pod hands. She stuck a green pod in my face, and split it expertly with her thumb, all the fat peas rolled out delightfully into my palm! I sat on the curb and slowly broke the pods open with the intense concentration of those bulging eyes and looming forehead, placing the round peas on my tongue, curiously, crunching into their sweetness with the knowledge that, over my head, Nona knew what I was tasting for the first time, trying the pods, spitting out the bitter skin, thinking of her laughing at me, silently.

Nona was the only one who could make the concrete streets seem like the country. Under green awnings, the dark Italian men would come out to greet her, to try to sell her something. Nona always said no and went inside, into the dark cave for the better produce he was hiding. The baskets and boxes of rich and glowing colors glinted in the desert sun, the desert of the street.

She filled her cart and gave me a juicy peach, much bigger than my hands, to eat on the way home. She left me at ninety-eight. She really became hard to take care of in the end. All of Grandma's sisters took turns, but Grandma had the hardest and longest turn, none of the sisters took Nona for as long, and Grandma had the most to do and the least money to do it and she made it seem so much harder because she moaned and groaned every inch of the way, but who are we to say, especially me, when I did nothing to help at all but play with Nona and love her?

Nona. Nona, bella. That was the other half of the game. I never could tell which half of the game she thought was funnier. She threw back her old head and laughed joyously whether she was called ugly or beautiful.


## E.B. HIGH

Grandma and I looked out the window; she, with her elbows on her folded pad and me, dashing from one sill to the other. One of Grandma's cats wove in and out of our arms, brushing soft, purring fur against our lips. We looked and looked, like immigrants did, looking, it seemed, for that promise we were supposed to find here. We watched the pigeons eating, the old men carrying rolled up newspapers, the many, many widows in black dresses and kerchiefs who came out of their houses daily to do their shopping, the boys playing stick ball. We watched whoever and whatever wandered into our vision.

We had a date once a week to watch the trash men. Even Mama came to watch them. They were wondrous! Dirty men, caked with grime, they were blackened, performing a blackening job. Strong men, stronger than Daddy or my uncles! They were our heroes because they could lift a metal trash can with one hand and crash it down on the lip of the huge green monster truck, tip its end and empty it into the monster mouth with one swooping gesture amidst their growling shouts and the truck's monstrous groans and aching creaks.

"Look at that," Mama admired.

"Mm," agreed Grandma distracted, "Marina's going to the store, mm," her eyes grieving after her friend, another widow.

Then, the trash men tossed the barrel back on the sidewalk careless of the deafening metal clatter, careless that the barrel rolled afterward into the road. They whistled sharply and leapt gracefully back on to the filthy truck that choked us with the smell of rot. We watched in awe as the great jawed truck swallowed up our mess and took it away forever.

"Look, look, the kids are coming home from school. Look, Gloria, look!"

Grandma and I liked to watch them, the high school kids; she said they were all dressed up. The boys wore skin-tight pants, black leather jackets and white T-shirts that set off their jet-black hair with shiny comb lines standing right up. The girls wore tight black leather skirts stretched over their behinds and soft sweater sets. Their hair, too, went straight up like black nests on their heads. You could see the black, charcoal eyes of the girls painted almost to their ears, ears from which hung bright plastic earrings. They had a way of leaning back so their breasts, packed into pointy bras, pointed aggressively up. They leaned back, the girls, leaning their books on their slender waists. The boys didn't carry books.

They all smoked, but not like adults, who smoked slowly, thoughtfully, inhaling serious thoughts, and exhaling wisdom, flicking the ashes into the ashtray with authority, because they knew something. The kids smoked with their bodies. They lit up in a concentrated huddle, shoulders hunched, eyes squinting, staking a physical claim on the cigarette. The boys shrugged their leather jackets. The girls shifted their weight from one high heel to the other, causing their tight skirts to dip and rise. They licked the tobacco bits stuck on their lips or picked them off with their fingertips like, conscious, sexual signals to one another.

They weren't quiet. They poured down the hill from the High School like screaming lava. E.B. High, another huge, brick box, like several Sacred Heart Churches lined up forever, stretching over a city block. Some distance from the White House on Eutaw Street, it spread itself over the top of a huge dead mound of tar surrounded by a dead chain link fence.

When we drove by, on our way to visit somebody, I'd sneak a glance at its ominous bulk, its forbidding, dead eyes, some of them knocked out, snarling words scrawled across its cheek with dripping paint, and every time, I asked, "Mama? What's that place?"

"East Boston High School."

"Do we live in East Boston?"

"Us? Yeah!"

Horror scorched my tummy. "Will I have to go there?" Mentally, I began calculating my remaining years on my fingers.

"No!" said Mama, "We'll be out of here by then."

I made her tell me that every time we went by.

I was sure East Boston High was a prison. I thought the kids, dressed so tough and hard in black leather, must be incredibly brave to go there everyday, live and function inside and actually come out alive to stream so powerfully down the hill and past our waiting window.

*"FUCK YOU!"*

I heard it for the first time, there, at that window, coming out of the fierce bodies of the high school kids packed tightly into leather, the word that was all sharp edges, echoing sharply down the street, beginning with the hiss of an F, and the savage way the kids screwed up their eyes and twisted their mouths to get the FUCK out.

"Tsk," said Grandma. "They should be ashamed! Ashamed!"

Simultaneously, Mama gasped and my head flew from one to the other.

*"FUCKIN' ASSHOLE! I'LL KILL YA!"*

"That's it!" Grandma said, getting up, "That's enough window!"

She yanked the window down over the rumble going on in the street. I pressed myself against the glass to see the bodies seething past, a few boys and girls scuffling off into the road, being blasted by car horns, arguing visibly with the drivers.

"Come on, come away from there! Go draw a picture, go!"

I didn't have a clue what the word meant, but I knew it had made us stop looking out the window. What incredible force was in these kids, I wondered, as I stole a few more moments to gobble them up with my eyes. What made them pour down the street out of every opening in the red brick prison, roaring and screaming all the way down the hill? What made them seem to burst out of their clothing? What was the word they shouted with an effort of their entire bodies, from the roots of their hair to their extended fingertips, from their crouching knees to their rigid toes? What was the word so alive with their hate and pent up feelings that they had to scream it at the top of their lungs to get it out? What did it mean? No one at home ever said a bad word. Since I knew it was bad, the idea of saying it, trying it out on my little tongue didn't even occur to me, but - I kept it, hidden and struggling inside of me, alive as it was with their hate and, yes, even their love and their passion in that place that was alive only with people, they cursed sometimes with love and complete abandon.

THE FRONT

"Why can't I go out, Mama?"

"Where? Out the back?"

Had I heard relenting in her voice?

"No, the front," I said, hopefully.

"No front! No front!"

I stood with longing at the front window. Mama wouldn't let me play in the street. I could see other children my age playing out there. Carol was out there; she was mad at me right now for decorating mud pies with dog shit.

"If you put that stuff on there," she'd said, "I'm going home!"

There it was, sparkling caramel brown in the sun, a neat, little pile from Grandma's terrier and there was my mud pie, black and dismal. I couldn't resist placing an inedible caramel topping on an otherwise inedible mud pie. Carol went home disgusted. After I'd done it, the deed held absolutely none of the satisfaction I'd thought it would. I was disgusted, too.

Anita was with her, hopping over hopscotch while bossy Carol tapped her foot, impatient for her turn.

"The other kids are out there," I whined.

"I don't care what the other kids are doing! You can't play in the street!"

"Can't" was another of Mama's favorite words. Mama specialized in "You can't!"

"Why not?"

"It's dangerous!"

The cars, probably, I decided. There, in the gutter, was half a pigeon. Maybe, she was afraid a car would suddenly go crazy and speed up over the curb and slice me in half, sitting on the front steps. Sometimes, we heard a yelp and then, loud, frantic yelping would continue down the street. Mama would tsk, "They hit a dog."

They, I sensed them, those dangerous people out there who, like the Nazis, had more control over her life than she did.

I had other reasons for not wanting to go out back, besides my self-conscious embarrassment that I had played with dog shit. Nine months of the year, the back was not a garden, but a concrete slab. Our little garden turned to ugly black mud and bare stalks, its gate shut. The rest of the concrete yard was where the dog "did its duty," where the grey metal trash barrels were piled up along the alleyway. The alley bordered against a tall, wooden fence whose blank face was all I could see unless I climbed on to one of the porches and looked down. Nothing was there. Iron balconies, someone's dirty cat prowling around, rags stuck between the railings and flapping in the wind, and brown leaves - all the leaves turned a coarse brown - dried up and rustling down the alley.

But, what was dangerous about the front?

I thought of the buzzer. Most of the time, I laughed at it, thinking it was funny to have a buzzer on a door. But, the adults didn't laugh. When the buzzer went off, their backs froze, their heads turned toward the front and they waited. There was an entry way and if our doorbell rang, their backs relaxed.

"It's somebody," Mama said, meaning it was a friend, someone with a legitimate reason for visiting. One of the adults, not Grandma, if anyone else was home, went out to see.

So, maybe Mama was afraid of - fire? Yes! Fire! And Cars! And Dirt! Though Grandma washed the front stairs every week with sudsy water and a brush. Mama was afraid of Danger! And the Unknown! Sometimes, the buzzer went off, we waited, but our doorbell did not sound! Only the buzzer again, and they all just looked at each other, and, then, the ghost of the buzzer remained humming, while Mama looked at Grandma and shook her head, "I dunno know!"

"Not the front!" Mama said.

Mama was afraid, not only of cars, the slinking power of them, rusted and scraping the ground, but that they would slow down, open their doors and swallow up my blonde head from the doorstep. Men! She was afraid of men! Men stole children, but so did women! And women were better at it! Mama said there was a woman stealing children. She stole them and sold them! Mama could smell danger like an animal and like a true woman she could also know the unknown.

The backyard was home, fenced in and insulated; she could watch me there, as if playing in a pen. But, the front was the world, outside, unpredictable. We hid inside like the Jews from Hitler.

I stayed locked up, upstairs, watching through the windows, watching the boys play stick ball, watching the dirty pigeons, the graceful trash men, the cars, the rain, the dripping icicles - and if I strained my neck around the side window, I could just make out the lovely White House at the top of the hill, stately, surrounded by lush green grass or pearly white snow.

I stayed indoors pretty much, until the day I went to school.

## MY LITTLE GIRLS

A deep loneliness grew in me. It never would leave me, not as long as I lived. It grew from the concrete, fed by the cold window and the blank faces of the tenements. I asked Mama one day if I might have a little sister to play with, and she smiled one of her secret Madonna smiles, saying that I might some day. Immediately, I felt I'd done something definite, simply by speaking, and, this shadowy thought was ominous, rather than cheering. I suddenly shivered to think of another child in the house, and to think I'd sealed my own fate simply by saying the word, "sister," disturbed me, I didn't know why.

But, no sooner did the loneliness come, than my little girls appeared. I don't know who they were or where they came from, but, one day, I looked down and they were all around me. I didn't make them up, because I was just as surprised as anyone. They were really there.

Translucent, no more than five inches tall and numerous, I never could have counted them. No, I was too young to count and I was not a counter anyway. I had no interest in how many little girls there were, only that they were there, with me.

"Soocha, will you pick that up for Mara?"

"Who are you talking to?" Mama stopped her dust cloth and turned to me.

I looked up from my play, incredulous.

"My little girls!"

"Oh!" said Mama, understanding perfectly, but pressing me further nevertheless. "Who're your little girls?"

"My little girls!"

"Your dolls?"

"No! Not my dolls, my little girls - see?"

I swept my hand around me.

"Where are they?" Mama continued dusting.

"Right here."

"Oh. Do they have names?"

"Yes. Maria, she's the biggest, Mara, Moora, Sara, Soocha, Dinna, Poora."

I continued playing.

"There's more, but they don't have names."

In fact, the bodies of most of them were far too liquid and changing for names. I had named the girls in front, but even them, not too seriously. I didn't know how to pin them down; they were too fluid. The names I'd chosen, not really names, but sounds, kept changing with them.

They spoke to me and comforted me. They loved me very much, that I could tell. I could feel their affection like a warm light on my body as I sat next to them, or gathered them all under my bedcovers at night. They leaned toward me, wearing dresses of light, shaped with flared skirts and puffed sleeves. Long hair made of light rested on their hazy shoulders. Hundreds of little girls making a cushiony halo all around me.

But, the nightmares came, too.

Not monsters, but a man and a lady dancing, waltzing. They wouldn't stop waltzing! She wore a long gown with a full skirt and he wore a tuxedo. The shapes, the shapes flew around them! The couple danced close to me, quite suddenly, and scared me to death, and, then, receded so far into the distance, I was equally terrified. Between them, the shapes flew, also flying toward me and flying away. The shapes scared me more than anything! Some were thin - so incredibly thin! The feel of a single strand of hair engulfed my dreaming self with horror! Why was it thin? Thin! So thin as to be insane with thinness! And, just as suddenly, and for no reason, thick! Thick as a slab of stone, terrifyingly thick! And flying toward my face! And receding far into the distance so I could barely see its smallness! I woke up screaming and screaming!

"I can't understand it!" Mama cried to Daddy, as she clung to my trembling body, "I never let her see any bad movies, never told her any scary stories, what could have happened?"

What, what could have happened?

## CARRY

Mama said, "You can't" about everything except eating, church and - school.

One day, I was playing with my baby doll, and I decided, "It's time to name her."

I knew where to find words. I opened a book, one of Mama's paperbacks, *Love Party* maybe or *Scollay Square*. I looked and looked until I found a word that caught my eye, a pretty word. I could see the word plainly amongst a hundred other words on the grimy, yellow page. But, I couldn't read it. I held my finger on it and went to find Mama.

"Mama, what's this word?"

Mama stopped what she was doing, leaned over the book, and said, "Carry."

"Carry. That's the name of my doll."

"Oh, yeah?" she answered, preoccupied. Mama and Grandma were always preoccupied.

"Yes! Carry!"

I loved the word. I loved its shape and its presence on the page, c like arms to cradle, curvy and delicate rs to run, a y for style and flourish. Even the meaning was right, because I would carry my baby doll - yes, the same baby doll I irresistibly handed over to my black-eyed cousins so they could kill her with pins. Can you believe that I loved her and I handed her over to murderers nevertheless? I did. And I loved her killers. Yes, I wanted them to stick pins in her, because I wanted them to stick pins in me. In me! And I wanted their mother, my Great Aunt Sophia, my grandmother's sister, with the blue twinkle in her eye, to comfort me afterwards with cookies and milk and the affection of her soft cat.

I loved Carry's name. I was proud of having found it myself, even without knowing what it was. A simple word, but it was waiting for me there, on the page of that trashy book that Mama devoured in her stolen moments, her eyes all glassy with anticipation and lust. I could see it plainly: carry. Black letters on yellowed paper. Stuck in small letters in the middle of a sentence without meaning. There, I recognized myself, a startling discovery, in something new and strange, an unknown thing, vibrant and soft with feeling. Carry. A simple word that was the beginning of my lust for words. As Mama taught me the sounds of the letters, in my moments alone I began the slow process of sounding out the words, teaching myself how to read.


SCHOOL

Words, paper, pens, books. These excited me! Fresh paper, fresh notebooks, crisp and stiff, stimulated me with expectation. Words were free. I could have them in abundance! Fresh paper and pencils were provided by the school!

Pencils! Lovely things! So simple and perfect! Tilted, before sharpening, to the eye, a marvelous circle of wood making an absolute, clean sphere of flesh colored wood around a black core. And, the sacrament of sharpening! The long, slow moving line of patient, reverent children scuffling one by one to the window sill where the pencil sharpener sat upon its pedestal. Some children had handfuls, but I took only one at a time and sharpened it carefully, religiously, used it to the nub, and then, kept the nubs, secretly. How I loved the smell of sawdust and shavings that flew from the overflowing basket on the sharpener into the sunlight like fairy dust. And, the slow, laborious motion of the handle, the grating and grinding until you got your rhythm and you knew it, the handle spun gloriously and the pencil emerged trim, pointed, ready to go to work. Work became a wonderful word. We had work to do in school.

School. I learned to spell the word as soon as I could manage; it wasn't an easy word, but it was one I wanted badly. I had special clothes: school clothes. White ankle socks in warm weather; thick, black stockings in cold. Red plaid dresses with white collars. Sweaters that buttoned up the front. Shiny black shoes with a buckle and a strap instead of laces. When I came home, I had to change immediately out of every item of school clothes and hang them or fold them to keep them nice. The black shoes stood shining in the dark closet waiting for the next day. I changed back into my home self: brown corduroys and red lace-up shoes. School waited.

I was good in school. Grandma said so, "Gloria is good in school," she said, with authority. Mama said so, telling Daddy, "Gloria is good in school." "Oh, yeah?" Said Daddy, as though to say, "Of course she is." It was an important announcement, I could tell, one they had been waiting to say.

School was just around the corner; you turned left on Eutaw Street instead of right, which was the way to the nursery school. It was a thick, grey building filled with grey marble staircases and glowing brass railings. Miss Towers was our principal. She was as towering as her name, high and great in a blue silk dress, the same silk dress all teachers wore, but Miss Towers commanded the dress. In the hallways of grey marble, down the staircases of up and down lines of children gazing up at her in wonder; we could barely see her face, but identified her by her great shelf of breasts in blue silk and the top of her grey hair sitting on that shelf like a bowl. Children feared God in those days and we trusted Him; in the same way, we feared and trusted Miss Towers. We also loved God with complete adoration and we were able to transfer that love with utter abandon to Miss Towers, to all authority, in fact, to the building and the institution itself - school. The shining marble steps and brass rails were trophies of hope. Children of immigrants, we clung to the railings and glowed with pride to climb the marble staircases, and, if Miss Towers appeared in front of us and descended the stairs, the sea of children parted for her, and if she would touch one or the other of us, or fold her hands in satisfaction across her broad stomach, and nod, "Good morning, children," as she passed, we were blessed.

The kindergarten teacher ushered Mama into the schoolroom, where, really, the world of Mama and home did not belong, but, she had to show her, she had to show her, "Mrs. Wisher, you must see Gloria's drawings!"

Since no one had ever said anything before, I looked at them, as though for the first time, with Mama and the teacher.

"They are the best in the class!"

Where? I studied my awkward figures with their long, gawky necks and wondered, "What does she see?"

I looked to Mama.

Mama beamed like an angel as she had that day in nursery school, against the golden, sunny leaves.

"She has real promise, Mrs. Wisher! Real talent! I've never seen anything like it!"

Their two heads nodded in agreement and wonder at my drawings. In Mama's mind, if the teacher said so, it must be so.

All the way home, Mama told me how proud she was, that she'd always known I could draw. It was true, I'd always drawn pictures to amuse myself, but never had such a fuss been made. But authority had spoken, and now, I was officially the artist in the family.

At home she told Grandma and Nona, who frowned and asked Mama, "Que va?" Mama was too shy to speak Italian, she understood it, but she didn't like to hear herself making the beautiful sounds. She hesitated, so Grandma yelled impatiently in Italian at Nona, "Gloria! Gloria! She can draw pictures!"

Nona grinned big, her toothless grin.

"Brutta!" she said.

We had a silent laugh together over Mama and Grandma's heads.


I was in the first reading group. By now, I had decided, I had to be in the first group. Words and drawing had become vital to me: they were me. I had to be first and best in them because they were all I had; if I wasn't first or best, then someone else would have them. To achieve this status, I needed only to bend my head and concentrate on the page. I had to try, it wasn't completely easy, but I loved the trying as much as the succeeding. This was freedom. School. Words. Pictures. Music, too. I loved to sing. The little girl in front of me turned around one day and said, "You have a pretty voice." I was stunned and happy, I sang out! I was coming out! I was discovering myself and the new world and it was like discovering America. I was beginning. I had work to do and talent.

The teacher asked me to read. We sat in tiny wooden chairs gathered round her feet, Group 1, while the other reading groups wrote in work books at their desks.

In those days, we stood to read or speak, pushing aside our chairs quietly, decorously; it was a point of honor to be able to do this well. I did, not to please the teacher only, but to please myself. I loved the discipline and the challenge of it as well as the quiet scraping of the wood against wood. At home, we had linoleum on the floor and chrome with rubber tips on the chairs. Those made a screeching sound or no sound at all. But, wood against wood was an intelligent sound, a school sound.

I stood and read from "Dick, Jane and Sally." I thought they were enormously stupid because they repeated everything over and over, but, as a good student, I repeated their words dutifully, thinking the sentences were actually quite clear and pretty the way they were arranged in fine rows on the page. "See Spot run! See him run!" Quite orderly and nice. And the repetition began to sound nice, sing-songy and sweet, clear and simple. I finished reading, feeling good. I'd done a good job.

"Would you look behind you now, Gloria?" the teacher said.

This was a bizarre request from the teacher. Nevertheless, I obeyed, turning my body and looking round.

There stood Mama! Can I tell you the joy of seeing her there, once again, glowing with pride, surrounded by sunlight filled with dust, the dusty sunlight of school?

I was in love with school. What could be better than having work to do that I loved every minute of doing and being good and seeing the beaming faces of teachers and Mama's gentle face alight with how good I was? With each new thing I learned, I grew larger and larger. The approval of Mama and my teachers was delicious; it was a sweet ice cream they served up to me every day after the nourishing bread and meat of work well done.


THE CALAMARI

You see, Mama had said she was going to make the calamari. She had them, there, on the sink defrosting all day while she washed windows. That was it, I guess, she had gotten wrapped up in washing windows, dirty and tired, and the calamari were still sitting there showing her they needed to be done. After long hours of scrubbing and getting up and down on the step stool, the calamari had started to look like too much work and Mama had decided she would do them tomorrow. She'd sighed, "Ah, I don't feel like doing the calamari today, I'll do them tomorrow, maybe." And, she put them away in the refrigerator.

But, Daddy had kissed her good-bye that morning and she had said she was going to make the calamari. And Daddy had had the taste of calamari in his mouth all day.

When Daddy came home and saw the hunk of cheese on the table, the bread and the knife, he said to Mama, "Where's the calamari?"

Mama said, "I didn't feel like making it; I was too tired. I washed windows all day."

Daddy had had a very hard day. The one thing he'd looked forward to all day was Mama's calamari.

I don't remember the rest. I just remember the screaming and Daddy's back as he flung the hunk of cheese through the window. The sound of crashing glass made me turn my head and there he was, forever, in my memory. The screaming, the breaking glass, crashing dishes, "Jesus, Jesus, Jesus! Christ Almighty Christ!" The glass screamed out to hell with bosses, to hell! Christ Jesus! If Jesus only came every time He was called. The window! The window, Daddy! The ice-cold winter came rushing in for us! He was sorry, he was sorry, don't cry, don't cry, all of us crying.

## MACHINES THAT MADE OTHER MACHINES

Only the women at home did work that was their own. The men went out to do other men's work, to work for other men.

Daddy worked in a factory full of machines that made other machines. He came home growling, hating, spitting his dinner from clenched teeth as he talked to Mama, who had already eaten. We ate early, Mama and me.
Mama sat upright in her chair at the kitchen table, her hands folded, listening quietly to long, horrible stories about how the lug nut broke or the conveyor belt was jammed and how stupid the boss was, and Christ Jesus, but not FUCK, never FUCK, why wouldn't they just listen to him, Billy Wisher, who'd fixed everything on the ship that had ever gone wrong, everyone could always depend on him and didn't they still depend on him, but they didn't know it, he knew it, by Jesus, he knew it.

I was on the kitchen floor in my pajamas with feet in them playing with coloring books, filling in spaces with perfect, seamless color, over and over, never going out of the lines, never, coloring the pictures in order lest the man come to the door, knock on the door, and arrest me for not coloring in order (there were one or two pictures further on I couldn't wait to get to), the same man who came to the door if you ripped the tag off the pillow, one of my cousins had told me. Mama tore up my favorite coloring books one day because I wouldn't eat my pastina with raw egg. The egg was supposed to cook on the hot pastina, but some of it was still gooey like snot. I gagged, but Mama was furious. She didn't understand; she thought I was being stubborn and disobedient. I cried for hours, and, later, I prayed on my knees to God to, please, have my coloring books back in my toy cabinet when I woke up in the morning. I told Mama that I had prayed and she looked sad. Immediately, I realized, we didn't have the money to replace them, so God wouldn't be able to do it by the morning. I was right: the coloring books weren't there. They were special coloring books, magic, because all you needed was water; you brushed water on the page and the color appeared like magic. I called them my magic coloring books, but they were gone forever.

This night, I colored with regular crayons, glancing at Mama now and then, watching her pretty mind wander from Daddy's stories, watching her hazel eyes turn inward while her back sat straight, her hands folded. She listened like that for years.

"Ah, he's a college man, they always give it to a college man. They get all the promotions. By Jesus, I never finished the sixth grade; I had to go to work. I know the machines better than anyone, but they give the foremanship to a young guy just out of college." Daddy wiped the gravy up with bread. He dropped the bread. He held his head with his large, thick hands, coated with gravy at the fingertips, black with machine grease in the deep lines of his skin.

Mama sighed deeply, the Queen of Sighs.

"Gloria should go to college, Rosa, she's smart. Maybe we can send her."

Mama brightened.

"You think so?"

"Sure," Daddy picked up the bread, more hopeful now, "She's smart enough! Smarter than some of these college guys. She should go to college."

"She'll be the first one in the family."

"Yeah, mine too."

Daddy drank some beer.

"Ah, my ship's comin' in. Any day now! You watch, my ship's comin' in."

The work of women is so real. Mama had to wait, sit and wait till Daddy was finished eating and talking before she was released and could finish her work. But, I didn't know: her work was listening. Listening, touching, wiping, washing, feeding, healing.

I was afraid to say, "My ship's comin' in, my ship's comin' in," the words, they have a way, a magical way, of causing fate. Daddy chanted this chant all his life, all his life, all his life.


SOPHISTICATED CLOTH

I sat on Grandma's kitchen floor and with the grave seriousness of a little judge, I pondered the serious job I was doing - sewing scraps of what I thought was the most sophisticated cloth, grey wool, into a business suit for my Barbie doll. My stitches showed, huge, black and awkward, but I didn't know that. To me, Barbie was ready for work in her no nonsense grey skirt and box-like hat. I even sewed a bit of "fur" from an old bathrobe around her neck and cuffs.

"What kind of dress is that for a doll?" some tall person leaned down to ask me. "Look at that!" said this idiot, "Everything matches!"

"It's an outfit!" I told her. "Barbie has a career! She's going to work!"

Where did I get that? Did I copy Rosalind Russell or Katherine Hepburn sitting casually atop desks on black and white television?

"Are you going to have a career? Aren't you gonna get married?"

"I'm not getting married! I'm going to college!"

"Oh! College! Is she going to college?" the tall person asked Mama.

Mama shrugged, "She's smart enough! She'll be the first one in our whole family to go to college!"

I had no idea what I was saying. Except, I knew, somewhere in my simple mind that Grandma's mouth was pulled tight like a purse and Mama's was getting turned down at the corners and screwed up in a funny new way, twisted, like someone had taken a key and stuck it in and just twisted her lips, when I knew she was mad, really mad and carrying that madness around. And the ladies on TV got to wear suits and really high heels, something elegant that I'd never seen on Grandma or Mama, and, amazingly, their faces were bright and clear and ready for action! And college men were always getting the "promotion" and that was something good that Daddy wanted and never got because he hadn't gone to college.

"So, what are you gonna be when you grow up, Gloria?"

What an idiot, I thought to myself, I had just finished telling her!

"I'm going to college!" I repeated to this unfortunate stupido.

I never thought beyond college. That was my ultimate goal. What could be better? I wanted nothing more.


WHAT ARE YOU GONNA BE?

Of course, it was part of my wisdom and confusion to believe Mama's work was the only true work and still plan to work outside the house myself. I was able to see everything all at once, to contradict myself and still believe passionately in what I was saying: I was insane, I suppose, that would be the sane answer. Knowing that, consider this: I did choose a career once.

Finally, I was allowed to play out front - only on the doorstep and the immediate sidewalk.

Carol, Anita and I, were playing hopscotch. Who needed chalk? We scratched the hopscotch frame on the sidewalk with a broken piece of concrete, snapped apart by a car or a boy, and, then used the bits of concrete as game pieces.

Or, we played marbles in the city water covers. BOSTON WATER carved in three dimensions. Marbles were like penny candy, colorful and plentiful, for a price. Subtle and deep, the only works of art in the neighborhood, you could search for colors in marbles forever and never find them all, but they were in there: soft greens shot with purple you could almost taste, breathtaking blues swirling ocean, cloud and sky, barely distinguishable shades of grey, and the big, inky blacks, which, if you believed the boys, only they could have.

We were a bunch of dirty little girls. Our hair was caught up in tangles. Mama couldn't get me to stop screaming while she tried to yank a comb, ignorant hairdresser that she was, mercilessly straight down my head from top to bottom. Usually, I ran under the bed, tears streaking my face, until she got tired, "I don't know what I'm going to do with you!"

"Can I go out?"

"Go! Go out looking like a gypsy, Esmeralda! Go!"

Something else would claim her attention. Our mothers tried hard and exhausted themselves trying, but we had reached the age of going outside and we were dirty now during that glorious time between school and bed called play. Snot dried on our lips and was shoved along our cheeks by fingers black with street dirt, the worst dirt in the world according to Mama. But, finally, I was allowed to play on the doorstep or "Right in front of the house, don't you dare move!"

Anita was my best friend. I loved her name because of its neat little sound, and when I learned to spell it, its neat little arrangement with a's on both ends and a "neat" in the middle. She was my age and size and she liked to draw, too, which made her sublime. Sometimes, Mama would take me "over Anita's" and she would sit inside in the kitchen having coffee with Anita's mother and Anita and I were allowed to sit outside the kitchen door, on the landing steps between the closed front door and the closed kitchen door; a wooden staircase, lighted and empty, except for two serious artists, their papers and their active pencils.

I loved Anita even more because she knew what I was saying. She completely understood this new method of drawing I came up with and was able to produce drawing after drawing along with me. You see, we would take our pencils and shade the area *around the shape* creating a silhouette in negative. We were able to draw anything like this: people, cars, dogs, horses, houses, you name it. Perverse little rebels, we had found a way to rebel even against ourselves!

There, on Anita's steps, we also devised a way to make our own dot-to-dot drawings, arranging the main dots first by eye, numbering them, then filling in the dots. Or, we traded and did each other's dot-to-dot! I loved Anita!

Carol was older and something of a pain. She had to be older and taller all the time. Carol was beautiful, that's why I liked her. She looked like Natalie Wood, while Anita looked like a little mouse with her brown hair and her long nose in her little face. It made Carol crazy that I liked the little mouse better, probably because she knew the mouse had talent, which, she, Carol, could not bully from either of us. You know I'm a sucker for beauty, until it turns ugly, sometimes by turning inside out. Carol turned inside out a lot and after a while, she didn't seem so beautiful. Nevertheless, we kept her for her ugliness too.

Carol, this day, was rather violently hopping scotch over our bent heads as we sat waiting our turn on Grandma's front steps.

"What're you gonna be when you grow up?" was Carol's question to us, which we were supposed to be pondering. "Teacher or a nurse?"

Teacher, nurse, mother, nun; those were the choices. I probably would be a mother anyway. I didn't want to be a nun.

"What're *you* gonna be?" we stalled.

"*I* asked you first!"

"Yeah," I said, "but we wanna know what you're gonna be. Do you *know* what you're gonna be?"

"Of course *I* know!"

"What?" asked Anita.

"A nurse," she replied in her "of course" tone, towering above us on one hopping foot. "Now, you tell me what you're gonna be."

Yuck. I'd had enough relatives in and out of the hospital to know that nurses had to change bedpans and wipe people's bums and give them baths and enemas. I couldn't imagine Carol doing any of that, but it made me laugh to think of her finding out too late.

"What are *you* gonna be?" I turned and asked Anita.

"I don't know," she shrugged. "How about you?"

"I'm thinking."

"Maybe, a teacher," Anita decided.

That must have satisfied Carol, she had no comment, only a smug smile and more hopping.

"Gloria Wisher?" She called me by my school name.

"Yeah, what?"

"Come on! What're you gonna be?"

I was thinking. Boys always wanted to be firemen. That was no good, riding on screaming trucks and actually *going* to fires! Too dangerous. Or cowboys. That wasn't so bad. You got to ride a horse. But, I was a girl. Girls weren't cowboys, except for Annie Oakley, but, I'd seen her in a musical on TV and she was stupid looking. I definitely didn't want to be her.

A teacher or a nurse, neither of these was good enough for me. What was the very best thing anyone could be?

Well, my eyes wandered, as ever, toward the White House, serene, graced by the only green grass on Brooks Street.

The White House and I, we had a communion between us, as though, just by turning my face in its direction, the whole street of grey cement, pigeon shit, broken bottles, newspapers, garbage, cars scraping the ground and spitting smoke into our mouths, there, on the doorstep, boys swearing, men's club on the corner boarded up for privacy, all disappeared instantly, just by turning my head; it was just me and the White House and dreamy, summer green.

If you think I wanted to live in it, you're wrong. I wanted to live with Mama and Daddy in Grandma's house where the smell of cooking mingled with the smell of people's skin and laundry, clean and dirty, the smell of dust or disinfectant, the smell of Mama's slippers, like roasted nuts, I loved them, no one's slippers smelled like Mama's. Because I was so often at her feet, playing on the floor, I would embrace her slippered feet and kiss them. I did not even want the street to disappear, no, not forever, I loved it too: it was the barrenness, the dark that made the White House and me stand out. There we were, the two of us, a ragged, little girl and an elegant mansion, what did we have in common? We were one. I was the White House. The White House was me.

"I'm gonna be a princess," I said.

Carol stopped hopping.

"You can't be a princess. You have to be born a princess. You can't grow up to be one."

She tilted her "I'm older and taller" head to one side and stuck her hand on her hip like hers was the last word on the subject. She resumed hopping.

"Pick something else."

Anita's mouth was gaping open. I could tell she was delighted. Her little brown eyes lit up. Did you ever notice the wisdom of the underdog while the bully often never becomes acquainted with the truth? Anita's delight began that lesson for me.

"I *was* born a princess," I told Carol.

"You can't be a princess!" Carol hopped and yelled. "Pick something else!"

Too late, Carol. I already was a princess. Anita and I smiled at her, enraging her into a lovely tantrum with our silence.

It didn't help Carol's screaming objections that I looked exactly like the pictures of princesses in the fairy tale books. It didn't help that I had long, flowing golden hair bouncing with curls, large, green eyes, full of innocence, and, worse, knowing; Grandma's red bow mouth, pink cheeks and the broad, high forehead of a king's daughter.

It didn't help that I was surrounded at Grandma's house with a small kingdom of people and visiting dignitaries who loved me and cared for me and were amazed by me daily.

It didn't help that for the first five years of my life I was the only star, so that even after my sister was born, my selfish little star burned willfully brighter, brighter than hers ever could.

It didn't help that my November birthday was celebrated with three cakes to feed the multitudes that came. Or that my birthday marked the start of the holidays. Thanksgiving and Christmas would soon follow and everyone's face was lighted like the candles on the cakes with great anticipation and expectations.

I had already taught myself to read Grimm's Fairy Tales, Hans Christian Anderson and any other fairy tales I could get my hands on, so I was already familiar with all the things a princess could do and a princess could perform the most arduous tasks. She could carry water in a sieve, spin straw into gold, kiss the blindness from a man's eyes and kiss a frog into a prince.

I was not intimidated by these abilities; they rang true to me, I identified with them. Somehow, I, too, had wandered for years in search of a lover; the older I got, the stronger this feeling grew. I knew what it was like to race against time and evil, sewing shirts to free your brothers from a wicked spell, tossing the shirts over their heads just in the nick of time, all complete but for one sleeve, shuddering with happiness as their swan bodies changed to men's, with the exception of one feathery, white wing.

Somehow, I knew what it meant to love a beast. I could not have told you who or what the beast was, only that I knew how to love him.

I knew magic. Magic was beauty. Magic was talent. At will, and I had such a strong will, I could make beauty out of nothing. Name a thing and I could draw it. A horse, a house, big or small, real or fanciful, a dog? A cat? Angry or nice? Like magic! And I could rhyme words and spell them and read better than anyone! I could sew and I could look out the window and I could eat Mama's and Grandma's fantastical cooking, which, clearly was the greatest magic of all because it could send you magically heavenward!

"I'm already a princess."

"You can't be a princess!"

"I am a princess."

PROPHESY

Uncle Sonny took my hand. He was fourteen, maybe fifteen when he first took me. I was seven or eight. The two of us, hand in hand, poor kids, dressed up to go to town in our best clothes, still looking like immigrants in pants too short, eyes too big; we had to walk through the Combat Zone.

"But they'll have to go through Scollay Square!" Mama protested.

"It's not 'Scollay Square' no more, Rosa," said Uncle Vickie. "It's gonna be Government Center now."

"What? No more Scollay Square?"

"Naw! They cleaned all dat up years ago!" Uncle Vickie waved his hand as if clearing all of Scollay Square off the table.

"Come and see Uncle Vickie's watch!" Mama called to us. "Look! It has no numbers, only diamonds!"

Mama had forgotten about Scollay Square. She trusted Uncle Vickie that it was gone. She held his wide wrist now in her own small hand and smiled proudly down at the watch.

We all looked. The watch had a black face and four diamond chips where the 12, 3, 6 and 9 should be.

"How do you tell time, Uncle Vickie?" I asked in awe. He must be awfully smart, I thought, to tell time without numbers.

"Aw, I just know."

"Where'd you get a watch like that?" I asked, thinking, a watch like that must come from someplace far away, someplace exotic, like Nice, where my favorite doll that Uncle Salvi brought me came from, the one I called "the Mama doll" that looked like Mama and had "Nice" embroidered on her black lace apron. Or, maybe, this amazing watch had come from Italy itself.

"Aw, some colored girl give it to me," Uncle Vickie laughed.

Grandma stopped dead in her tracks, her hands dripping with soapy water.

"Listen to that!" she tsked. "Now, what'd he say a thing like that for?" she turned to ask Mama, as though asking Uncle Vickie was hopeless.

"I dunno," Mama shrugged, laughing.

Mama whacked Uncle Vickie off the back of the head and Uncle Vickie laughed heartily.

Laughing there with Uncle Vickie, Mama forgot about the dangers of Boston. Besides, I could tell, whatever waited for me there, on the other side of danger, where Uncle Sonny would take me, was worth the risk - no, whatever it was, it was essential, something Mama felt I *had* to experience.

"I used to work around the corner from there, on Kneeland Street," Mama said as she curled my pliant hair around her fingers. She had a way of twirling a finger full of hair and then pulling her finger out so that when she was done, I looked like Shirley Temple. This delighted Mama, and me too, of course.

"I remember," I told her, knowing even then, how important these memories were to Mama and how important they should be my memories too.

"It's all Chinamen now, and Jews, but, once, it was the garment district."

Chinamen, now and Jews, garment district, Mama said them with such fondness, like a song singing in my ears, Chinamen, now and Jews, Kneeland Street, the garment district, mixed all up with the love of anticipation of doing something new.

"Take care of her!" Mama warned Uncle Sonny.

"She'll be fine. Ready?"

"Yes!"

I went off eagerly.

"I love the bus!" I said.

"Oh, yeah?" Uncle Sonny was counting change, not that it needed to be counted; the money had been counted into exact amounts by Grandma and put into separate pockets by categories. Bus money, called the magic words, "car fare" by Mama and Grandma, was ready in his right front pocket, special money in his back pocket and return "car fare" in his left front pocket.

The bus, old and rickety, picked us up at Bennington Street. We sat on dark green plastic seats, ripped, yellow stuffing popping out. I had to hold on tightly to the rail, even though I was sitting, the motion of the bus spun me violently from side to side, till we pulled up at Maverick Station to change to the subway train.

"I love the train!" I said.

"It used to be white down here!" Uncle Sonny said.

"No suh!"

"Yup."

I looked around. The walls and floors were black, dripping heavily with black water into puddles where people had thrown papers and garbage.

"White walls? Or floors?"

"White everything! I saw a pickcha!" Uncle Sonny explained.

"Hey," he continued as we stepped on to the train, "maybe we can see rats if we look hard enough, running along the tracks."

"Ok," I answered, getting ready to look real hard. "I love rats!"

Hand in hand, we walked down Tremont Street, Uncle Sonny had those oily black eyes, I had large and green, a gypsy and a princess, we walked past the Old Granary Graveyard, "Oh, look-it! Benjamin Franklin's buried there!" I nodded, not knowing who that was. King's Church, the Old South Church, the Parker House where people lunched close up to the windows.

"Are they drinking champagne?"

"What? Ha! Yeah, I guess so, who cares, they're rich!"

Past the ladies, a bunch of them, wearing high heels, higher than I've ever seen in my life, even in the movies, wearing black stockings with runs and holes showing pink flesh through! Grandma and Mama *sewed* the holes in their stockings; they'd never leave the house looking like that!

Past the garish five and dime stores, all of a sudden, hundreds of 'em, blasting music in sudden bursts out on to the street, and a man's voice yelling about some really great deal on some incredibly strange stuff. Lots of glossy white statues of a fat, bald man, naked, sitting cross-legged and grinning red-painted grins, almost scary. I couldn't decide if they were scary or just creepy, each with a round clock in his belly. Every little fat grinning man, was exactly the same, milky white and shiny. But all the clocks were different: some had silver numbers, some gold, some fancy with the letter kind of numbers, some ordinary.

"Who's those fat men?" I asked.

Uncle Sonny said, "Those are Budd-has." He pronounced the word to rhyme with bud, like a rose bud.

"Budd-has?"

"Yeah, come on, sailors buy 'em."

There were a lot of sailors, walking two by two across the narrow sidewalk in white caps and snapping white bell-bottomed trousers and navy blue ties that caught the breeze like flags. They walked, so straight and full of themselves in their uniforms. Like Uncle Vickie, whose black curls had snuck out of his cap like mischief.

"Is this where Uncle Vickie got his watch?"

"Naw, that fell off a truck."

"How come it didn't break?" I asked, pondering this.

He laughed, "That's how come it don't have numbers."

The numbers, I could see them, bouncing off the face of the watch as it hit the road, bouncing all over the pavement. Lucky Uncle Vickie was there to pick it up before it got run over.

"We're here."

I looked up, my head went straight back. We were standing in front of the Paramount Theatre. PARAMOUNT in huge golden letters was written across a large sign like an arm reaching out from the theater. The doors in front of me were glass reflecting our dwarfed bodies standing outside, both our heads tilted back, both our mouths gaping open. Scrolls of golden ivy grew round and round the entrance.

Uncle Sonny grabbed hold of a golden handle, carved with leaves and wooded vines, and swung the door open for me.

I entered between red ropes on golden poles. Gold tassels hung from the ropes. The ropes were shining like hair in the sunlight. I touched them - they were as soft as flower petals. We stepped on a red carpet, our feet sunk into the softness. The walls were red with designs cut out. I could feel the texture with my eyes, plush red designs sticking out, surrounded by more golden leaves and vines and many, many lights like candles sparkling off the gold, illuminating everywhere we stepped.

Uncle Sonny walked up to a golden box with a man in it like a confessional, except everything was lighted and beautiful. The man was wearing a toy soldier's uniform. Uncle Sonny asked for two and the man gave him two tickets. We walked along the carpeted room to another man in the same toy soldier's uniform, blue with dark blue ribbons down the sides of his pant legs, gold buttons and gold tassels on his shoulders, who took the two tickets and ripped them in half! Then, he smiled and handed Uncle Sonny the ticket halves and said, "Enjoy the show!"

Uncle Sonny put the ticket halves in his pocket, took my hand and we walked past a glass case with a lady behind it. The case was full up with candy in shiny packages and bright boxes and there was popcorn! I could smell it! The lady smiled at me, but we walked past her.

No other people were there. We had the whole place to ourselves.

We were suddenly facing a red and gold staircase that was very narrow at the top, but opened like welcoming arms at the bottom where we stood. The stairs were carpeted in red and the railings ran toward us in shimmering gold and above our heads, a crystal chandelier, bigger than any light I'd ever seen, big as a fountain, it pulsed light down on us.

"Is this Church?" I whispered, dumbstruck.

"Ha!" laughed Uncle Sonny, "It's the show!"

He showed the half tickets to another man in a toy soldier's uniform, who took a flashlight down an aisle of seats and pointed with the light to two. Along the floor, pins of light came out like stars and made us seem to float in darkness.

"Enjoy the show!" he smiled, too.

The seat was velvety soft and slid down when you sat on it. Uncle Sonny took my hat and coat off, carefully wrapping my hat and gloves into one of my coat sleeves. He then placed the coat on the seat next to him, along with his own.

Now, we faced a stage covered with an enormous red, velvet curtain. The lights were dimming, the little candles on the wall twinkled out.

The music flared, the trumpets! And shall I tell you what I saw when the curtains parted? Do you know I was transported to heaven?

I sat in the darkness and light came from the tremendous screen and struck through my tiny body, heart and soul, till I shone like a lighted girl. And I believed in what I saw and heard and felt there, as much or more than I believed in God, there I found my faith, virtues I would believe in, causes I would champion for the rest of my life, I would be a missionary of what I learned there, no matter how many set backs or rude awakenings I'd suffer, like a growing plant run over by a truck, I would snap back. I believed simply by believing I could make my creed be so. The more you told me I was dreaming, the more determined a dreamer I became. Thus, even by failing, I would succeed.

What did I see? What did I hear?

A royal blue field, velvety as the theater, a choir of beautiful voices sang to only me, "I know you, I walked with you/ once upon a dream/ I know you, the gleam in your eye is so familiar a gleam/ yet, I know it's true that visions are seldom what they seem/ You'll love me at once/ the way you did once/ upon a dream." More music, dancing music, and then -

A golden candle, a golden book titled, "Sleeping Beauty," encrusted with jewels, the book of a king, opened and a man's voice like no voice I'd ever heard before, read:

"In a far away land, long ago, lived a king and his fair queen. Many years they had longed for a child and finally, their wish was granted. A daughter was born to them and they called her Aurora. Yes, they named her after the dawn, for she filled their lives with sunshine. Then, a great holiday was proclaimed throughout the kingdom, so that all of high or low estate might pay homage to the infant Princess."

The people came from miles around and they sang! "Hail to the Princess Aurora/ All of her subjects adore her / Hail to the King! / Hail to the Queen! / Hail to the Princess Aurora! /

"Health to the Princess/ Wealth to the Princess/ Long live the Princess Aurora/ Hail Aurora! / Hail to the King! / Hail to the Queen! / Hail to the Princess Aurora!"

I believed completely in the Three Fairy Godmothers, Flora, Fauna and Merryweather. I believed in their gifts: Beauty, "One gift, Beauty rare/ Gold of sunshine in her hair/ Lips that shame the red, red rose, / She'll walk with Springtime wherever she goes." Song, "One gift, the gift of song/ Melody her whole life long/The nightingale's her troubadour/Bringing his sweet serenade to her door."

Somehow, it seemed familiar that Merryweather was interrupted by storm and evil in the shape of the villainess, Maleficent: "The Princess shall indeed grow in grace and beauty, beloved by all who know her. But, before the sun sets on her sixteenth birthday, she shall prick her finger on the spindle of a spinning wheel - and *die!"*

When Merryweather gave her gift: "Not in death, but just in sleep, the fateful prophesy you'll keep till true love's kiss the spell shall break." The choir sang, "True love conquers all!" I was sure that was right.

The cottage grown from the trunk of a tree, the berry picking, these became sacred. But, of all, it was the song. The voice of Aurora, Briar Rose, her peasant name, and being a peasant who was really a princess, oh, that was important! I knew in my heart there was more to being a princess than just birth. Her voice went out from her straight to the heart of a prince, the voice, that was the most important thing of all, I was convinced.

This was my first time, but there would be many times after it, and Uncle Sonny would take me, faithfully, to those glorious churches of dreams, whether the Paramount, the Music Hall or the Tremont, all of them decorated like palaces.

I learned and learned, eating voraciously and transforming what I learned into me. Here, is what I discovered:

I believed that when man entered the forest, evil came with him as surely as night follows day. I believed that children could fly, and, if they chose, go to a place where they would never grow up. I believed, absolutely, that growing up was a very wrong thing to do. I decided never to grow up, no matter what the cost. I believed a prince could awaken a princess with a kiss, and, no matter how much Mama and Daddy fought and yelled at each other, I knew I could do better. I believed in the wishes of the fairy godmothers. Beauty and Song. What were they but talent? I believed that if a girl was true of heart and strong and never gave up, she could make her dream come true. But, most of all, I believed in the fact of what I had seen and heard and felt: the lulling, stabbing, delicate, bright and brilliant colors lighted from within; the graceful, dashing and subtle movement; the sweet, sublime and fearful music, and the voices! Oh, the voices! Big, big voices, vibrating me till I disappeared into tingling voice! Dear, loving, treacherous or cunning! The words spoken unlike any words I'd ever heard, rolling or clipped, sneering or horrified, words sung and spoken with love on the tongue, lips and teeth coming together in pronunciations that left me quivering. The undeniable fact of it all that would pierce me over and over, I believed and believing was wonderful!

That was really how I knew I was a princess. When I walked out of those theaters, I was overflowing with princess.

THE BUDDHA IN THE ALLEY

We walked two miles to the beach. Poor Mama carried a cold, sweating thermos of Kool-Aid, bags of blankets and towels, beach toys and the potty whacking against her legs making her look like a one-man band. The city sun was brutal and merciless, not a cool green leaf to shade us. You had to be strong to walk to the beach or you had to rest many times along the way - like me - collapsing on a stone doorstep. Mama got impatient with me, "Oh, not there! What's she doing now? Come on, Gloria! I just wanna get there!" The stones were gritty and burned against the tender young skin of my buttocks, unprotected by the nylon bathing suit I was wearing.

I liked to keep my head down, studying the gutters for anything interesting, anything shining a little too much, hoping for anything as valuable as a dime, maybe. I picked up colorful papers or bits of smooth green or brown glass and ask Mama, "What is it?"

"PUT THAT DOWN! THAT"S GOT GERMS! OH, MY GOD, WHAT AM I GONNA DO WITH HER?"

Sometimes we walked to Wood Island Park by the airport and the train station, where the kids played and splashed in a sea-blue fountain, knee-deep in dazzling blue water and mothers waited under the almost cold, green damp of the cluster of trees that was an oasis around the plaster fountain. On weekdays Wood Island was a park for women and children. On weekends fathers sat in rolled shirtsleeves with the mothers under the trees, but most of the time Wood Island was only for women and children.

Though airplanes roared over our little heads, we were conscious only of the frosty blue water and the warring politics of splashing and being splashed. If you happened to look up, it seemed you could touch the fat, silver bellies of planes. You got used to the closeness of huge monsters: the strong odor of gasoline that you didn't even smell any more following the scream in your ears that you didn't even hear any more.

While we splashed Mama waited under the trees flickering with sunlight and shade; she had sandwiches and cold, sweet drinks. Mama had a long, sharp knife only she could touch that she wielded upon a long, crusty bread, slicing it quickly and sharply into sandwich sized pieces that she expertly slit open into mouths gaping for the fillings. She then took hunks of meat, homemade cutlets of veal or chicken, breaded and already fried, or fat Italian sausages, and shoved the meat into the open bread. These feasts she handed out to us, one by one, leaning toward us with her long line of cleavage standing out of her rubber bathing suit and her fat arms reaching eagerly, her face glowing with sun and sweat, and pride at the plenty she was able to provide so far away from the comforts of home.

We gobbled up every crumb of sandwich and drop of sweet drink, so starved and parched we were, so appreciative and frightened of leaving the oasis for the long dry trek homeward. We acted as though we'd starve without Mama, and, in fact, we would have.

Sometimes, we walked the extra three blocks to the beach itself: Orient Heights, blue and yellow, on fire with light. It was a name I repeated over and over, Orient Heights, Orient Heights, but where was the Orient and where were the Heights? I asked Mama as many times as I sang the name to myself, what did it mean? I searched the flat skyline for heights and the sands for Chinamen. There were hills, down the road and behind another train station, and a top one of the hills, a fifty foot high Madonna that was supposed to stand upon a building, her bare feet clutching a top the roof on the highest part of the hill, to greet the sailors, the men coming home from the sea, but she was too tall for the planes, too tall for the planes and they made her stand down lower, at the base of the building, where you can go and kneel and pray. She turned black over the years. Now, she was the Black Madonna, still holding her hands palm upward for peace.

But, I was content to not know the meaning, to know only the asking, and the hot, baking run down the sands to the crashing blue sea, where I stopped out of fear and squealed at the waves crashing and chasing me as I ran away from them! Back up to the hot sand, no, no, I kept going back, until I could get my feet and legs, and finally, my seat wet by sitting in a tidal pool and splashing water over my stomach.

I was terrified of the ocean, though I loved it instantly and forever.

"If you drown, I'll kill ya!" Mama yelled from the blanket where she was setting up house.

She was only repeating what Grandma had told her, making her too scared ever to learn how to swim.

I liked to sit at the shore line and feel the treacherous waves try to pull me out to sea with them, try to toss me like a dead fish on to the wet sand, sucking the sand out from under me, causing the ground to race like the road under the car, making me dizzy. If the ocean drowned me, Mama would kill me again, it made no sense, but I was paralyzed with fear.

I wouldn't pee in the ocean. Poor Mama, she had to carry the potty every time we went to the beach. I was horrified at the idea of peeing in the mighty ocean, horrified!

The same white birds, seagulls, I saw flying over Nona's garden, dipped and soared overhead. I was visiting them in their home the way they visited me at mine. I felt good visiting them, comforted and flattered by their closeness, thrilled, too, when a big fat one, with silly curved beak waddled close to me. How big they were! Even with wings folded! As big as me! Or, as small as me, their rounded chests as wide around as my own small chest heaving with great excitement to be waddling on the ground with these gorgeous white flyers. Solid bodies, unlike other, hollow birds. What are seagulls? I wondered. Are they birds or people with wings? They seemed so much smarter than birds. Inching closer to my small body, I felt threatened and strangely, welcomed their threat. I screamed and hid behind Mama, causing the gulls to blink warily and turn away from our blanket.

"They're looking for food," Mama explained.

Then, I knew: I'm more powerful than the gulls! Gulls are afraid of me, though I am no bigger than they with their enormous wings closed up, walking in foreign people territory. But, let them take off! The white wings unfolded and gulls claimed the sky! They soared with the emotions of people, with pride and exultation, power and determination! The gulls couldn't fool me! They were human and I knew it!

"Ah!" cried Mama, "I love it when they do that!"

A white gull, filling his wings with ocean breeze, hovered effortlessly above the rolling water.

On summer Sundays, what a joy to bury Daddy up to his neck in the sand! Me, in my bouncing blonde curls and ruffled bathing suit and sneakers, because the sand was so hot, screaming with glee in my power as I threw each little plastic shovelful over his laid-out body, till, finally, absolutely seriously and business-like, patting it down around him making him look like he was already in his grave. Except for his head, grinning on a cigarette, cracking jokes, "Hey! Somebody feed me a beer, will ya?" His jaunty curl like Alan Ladd's, like an ocean wave, bobbing up and down, saying, "Yes! Yes!"

The men wore tight bathing suits like wide rubber bands snapped over their private parts, which bulged suddenly, curiously, in front. The women wore much larger versions of this shiny, rubber band pulled across their mountainous breasts and bellies, groaning across their planetary backsides and hips, large and round as the earth itself.

I was fascinated by all these sudden bulges and curves, especially in the men, which did not seem to be a part of their bodies, but seemed stuck on in the front of their suits, just for the summer, maybe.

"What's that?" I asked, over and over, usually ignored.

"What's what?" Mama replied at last, not taking her eyes off the damp magazine, "True Confessions" she devoured with rabid eyes. Every book or magazine she read was "not for kids," what Mama called, "raw."

"The big thing in Daddy's bathing suit."

All the adults turned their heads and screamed with laughter. Mama smiled secretly and turned even redder than her lipstick and her sunburned skin. All her hair was twisted into tight, little red pin curls, getting set for

Saturday night, looking like a bathing cap of coiled snails and bobby pins, but she wore her red lipstick anyway to the beach.

"Hey, Billy! What the hell's that big thing in your pants?" his brother, Jake hollered. "Better do something about that, Rosie!"

Daddy grinned, real proud.

Aunt Sophia was there, sometimes, and Johnny and Joey, who were very busy swimming and never bothered with me at the beach. But, their father had the black eyes of an Arab, Uncle Joseph, who was greatly tall and big as a king, with a great, booming voice to match his size, a friendly, joking voice, a jovial king who wore a metallic gold bathing suit that shone like gold, and his bulge was much bigger than that of any of the other men. And, Aunt Sophia had that blue twinkle in her eyes. Grandma said, "Oh, I wish I had the blue eyes like my sister. But, I got brown! Old brown!"

No one had answered my question, but now I knew the bulge was important, something "not for kids," something "raw."

We were staggering home from Orient Heights and Daddy wasn't with us so we were walking. The sun was blazing hot. We scraped up to Grandma's doorstep, dragging the bags against the pavement, making a scratching noise on the rough canvas.

"Pick that up! You're getting it dirty on the ground!" Mama groaned, exhausted.

I picked up the bag, trying to catch it on my shoulder by the soft rope that ran through the top, when I looked up and saw, well, I knew it wasn't what I said it was, but since I didn't know what to call it, I called to Mama, "Hey, look-it! There's a Budd-ha in the alley!"

A Budd-ha, like the ones Uncle Sonny and I had seen in the sailors' store in town, fat and gleaming white, as though someone had brushed milk over his skin the way Grandma does on the pasty white dough when she's making pies. He was sitting straight up against the wooden fence behind the men's club, as naked as a Budd-ha, facing toward Grandma's house. No clock rounded his belly that I could see. The only interruption of his stark white color was a neat red circle next to his eye and a drip of red paint from that circle, down his neck.

"Don't 'hey' me! What tha hell's a 'Budd-ha'?" grumbled Mama, coming up behind us.

"Oh, my God!" I turned to see Mama change from sunburn to as pale as the Budd-ha. "Get in the house! Get in the house!" she screamed at us, shoving us so hard that the plastic thermos hit Marie who stumbled against the cement stair, scraping her leg. She started to wail.

"What's the matter, Mama? What is it?" I begged, my own lips trembling.

The buzzer went off as we entered the door. Mama turned and shoved the door closed behind us as though the Budd-ha would get up and follow us into the house. Then, she jammed the heel of her hand on the bell to Grandma's house as hard as she could, over and over.

My heart thumped in my chest as Grandma opened the inner door and shuffled up to us, crying, "What's the matter, Rosa?"

"Call the cops!" gasped Mama, flinging us into the house. Marie still wailed, her mouth open like a tunnel, her face streaked with dirty tears.

"What, Rosa?"

"Thank God I didn't see nothing," Mama said.

"Mama?" I begged. "What is it?"

"Nothing!" she told me. "Never mind."

The cops came, cars and cars of them, wailing sirens, spinning blue light and red into the sunny day. Mama went outside in her housedress thrown over her bathing suit, but she came right back in.

"Shot in the head," through the open window, I heard the men's voices.

"Dumped him in the alley. Buck ni'ked!" he chuckled hoarsely, "It's a message, awright."

Mama shoved us into Grandma's bedroom, "Stay here and be quiet! I have to talk to the policemen out in the kitchen."

In the dim light of Grandma's bedroom, the Virgin held her hands out from Grandma's bureau and Jesus, on the wall, wrapped in cellophane, also held up his hand in the sign of the Holy Trinity, pierced at the palm, and on his chest, the flaming Sacred Heart.

I tried to figure out what was happening from their faces. Both Jesus and his mother looked sorrowful and kind. Why were they sorrowful and kind?

Marie cried in my lap, mostly from being pushed and shoved by Mama. Finally, curiosity got the better of her, and we both got up and stood at the paned glass door where we peeked through the lace that smelled of Chanel #5, like Grandma during the holidays. We stared through the patterns of lace and perfume at the huge policemen in their dark uniforms and big shoes filling up Grandma's kitchen.

"Those are cops," I explained. She nodded, not understanding.

"Kin we watch tellabision?" she asked.

"No!" I whispered, "It's in the other room."

She started to cry again.

"Shut up!" I whispered harshly, "do you see a television in here?"

She didn't know what I meant. And I was too stupid to know she was little. I thought she was the one who was stupid. She cried, so I started telling her a story about rabbits.

Still sticky with suntan lotion, gritty with sand and drowsy from the beach, we sat on Grandma's chenille bedspread; I told stories till I couldn't think anymore about rabbits, no stories would come, because our drooping lids had finally slammed shut. We collapsed together in a deep summer sleep, hungry and floating, our nostrils tickled by chenille. I dreamed of people sitting around a lighted table, far off in the night, they were singing songs with one voice. I opened my eyes and thought I saw them, lighted, a few houses away, having a party while we were having an emergency. I closed my eyes again and drifted. Then, Mama's face was next to ours, her breath smelling of cigarettes. Strangely, she was telling us to get up, that it was time for supper. Light was streaming in behind her. Over Mama's shoulder, Grandma passed by the doorway carrying a bowl, a cloth draped over her arm.

The policemen were gone as if I had dreamed it all and Grandma's kitchen was back to normal.


I had renamed my oldest and biggest girl Maria Rose, after Briar Rose in "Sleeping Beauty." The next day, Maria Rose told me not to worry about the Budd-ha. She said the Budd-ha had gone back to where he'd come from. I assumed, logically, that meant the sailor store, a much larger sailor store than the one I'd seen, judging from his size.


THE NABBYS

We started going to Revere Beach, which Mama said was famous, known worldwide. We got there in what Daddy called the "skush-a-bunk," which Daddy drove so badly it made Mama scream and whack him, which made us kids and Daddy laugh.

"There!" She pointed to a long finger of broken down pier sticking out into the ocean. "That's where it happened! Out there, right on the water, there was a big Dance Hall! It burned down and everybody was killed!"

Happily! Proudly! She informed me. Why was she so happy about it? It had happened so long ago, perhaps, it was impossible to feel the pain, only the romance of hundreds of men and women glittering in gowns and tuxedos, drowning, burning! Beautiful people who had gone out that night to have fun, I understood that much even then, I was seven, but I thought of their screams, their struggles, trying to hang on, trying to swim, why did they die? Why? Couldn't they swim? I thought all adults except Mama and Grandma could swim.

"Why didn't they swim?" I asked Mama.

"Oh," she said, slogging through the hot sand, "they wore a lot of clothes then, in the old days."

"The clothes got wet and dragged them down," Daddy explained.

None of this made sense. I was confused. But, every time I went to Revere Beach, the ghosts of the partiers drifted upon the empty water, forever dancing in the festive lights of the turn of the century Dance Hall. Every time, every time, dark night or sparkling day, I saw or heard some shadow of them, some memory, in a reflected light upon the lapping waves, in the long trail of the rising moon, in the waves lapping the rickety old pier, in a colored kite or streamer, a man's joyous shout, a woman's lilting laugh, the clink of a glass, and music, music, elegant violins, harp, cello, jovial banjo, horn, drum, flames upon the water.

Just as the alley now, always held a Buddha.


The men drank a lot of beer. They always drank, and drank too much. What had always seemed right, the credo of "eat, drink and be merry" after the war, was becoming less and less interesting and attractive. Was I getting older? Were they getting drunker?

It had something to do with the skinny people. All of a sudden, Mama began introducing me to skinny people, and for the first time in my life, with the exception of Daddy's brother, Jake, and he was family, I was meeting people I didn't trust.

Who were these bony knees? Mama introduced me with such excitement. "This is Cousin, this is Paul, her husband, Bubba, his mother, this is Ooda and her brother, Little Paul."

She had to be kidding! They were so skinny! And what kind of a name was Ooda? She was a tall, floppy kid with pointy glasses and a limp, blonde ponytail. Little Paul was anything but little. He was much taller than Ooda. He had his father's thick lips, jumpy Adam's apple and pocky complexion. And, sure enough, though I doubted it at first, Paul did keep referring to his wife as Cousin! Did he think she was his cousin? Was she? And was Bubba really his *mother?* I couldn't imagine calling my mother Bubba! I wondered, where did Mama find these people, the Nabbys, with their Nabby knees sticking out and their pointy eyeglasses that could stab you to death? They all wore these pointy eyeglasses, except Paul and Little Paul. I had a vague idea they must be hillbillies like in cartoons. That was the only explanation I could come up with.

And, why was Mama so crazy about them? Her hazel eyes lit up with rapture when she spoke of them. There was a feeling of discovery. The Nabbys lived right by Revere Beach in a place called Beachmont, a hill overlooking the beach. When we visited, I could plainly see that Beachmont was one of those places on earth that should have been as desirable as Hawaii or Italy because it was just as breathtakingly beautiful, with panoramic views of the ocean, little white houses cascading down the side of a hill to the blue sea. But, the Nabbys lived in a shack that was sagging in the front and sinking into the ground in back, which Mama thought was great because it had "a rumpus room" in a "finished" basement. A "finished" basement was like the Tenth Wonder of the World to Mama. She started talking about fixing up a house in Revere.

These suddenly, weird, skinny people! The only other person in my life who'd been skinny was my godmother, Margaret Flannagan, who was sacred. Mama said she was thin because she was Irish and not Italian. The Irish, Mama told me, didn't know how to cook, so they starved, traditionally. In Ireland, they had nothing to eat but potatoes. These Nabbys weren't Irish. These Nabbys were something else. White people. People who ate out of cans. Canned things. And frozen things. And chips out of bags. That's why you could see their Nabby bones, Nabby nubs moving under their skin! Most of the people I'd known up till then had been round and soft and generous. I didn't trust these new people. I knew there was nothing of *me* in their hard bones! There'd be no comfort for a child in their fleshless embrace!

We went with these Nabbys to Baboosic Lake in New Hampshire, which wasn't even a real lake, but a manmade lake made by someone called a "developer" who'd hit water while digging the foundations for ranch homes, Daddy said, so he built cabins instead around the fake lake. Ooda took care of me and her brother, who was "more my age" as Mama liked to say, though you'd never guess, since he was three times taller than me. Ooda took us down to the "beach," which was sand put down. No waves, but a gentle lapping and a roped off area in the water for kids. Ooda was very nice to me. She helped me put a dead fish on a string one time and say I caught it. That was my first real lie because it had been so planned. But, on the way back to the cabin, I grabbed hold of some tall grass and it sliced my hand, so God got me good for lying, even before confession, even before the actual lie. Sometimes, Ooda lost patience with me, though. I never blamed her for that, only for being skinny, after all, it wasn't her fault she was stuck taking care of a perverted kid.

I can't tell you when my personal fascination with Nazis actually started, probably when I first started to hear about them. Mama and Grandma talked about the Nazis all the time. We were all fascinated by them. We became a nation of Nazis. In order to keep it from happening to us again, we became them. The Nazis taught us that we had to be physically perfect. They taught us how to be horrible, how to kill, how to torture. Mama was fascinated. "The Nazis fixed everything, they fixed, everything!"

she used to say. She meant the Nazis had taught us things. They taught us what was possible. No matter how bad we were, we could never be as bad as the Nazis, right? It was a perverse comfort. It allowed much. The war had ended only a few years before and had still not been settled in people's minds. Daddy never said much about it, but he watched movies with a religious conviction, war movies; he watched John Wayne kill people, and I watched too. I loved movies about the French Underground, their jokes, their laughter, their steady hands and cool expressions of absolute control; I loved their sense of justice and bravery - no compromise, no regrets. I learned a lot from the Underground, but what I learned, I already knew. The Underground simply reinforced my ideas, which were, at this point, unformed emotions, about fighting back, struggling, feeling, "Yes! That must be right!"

Yet, the Nazis, the villains, they were the most fascinating. I had already noticed that people loved villains. Their eyes lit up with a maniacal glow whenever they talked about bad characters. Secretly, they preferred the villain to the hero. People admired the villain's strength and intelligence. They admired his ability to conquer. If the villain was handsome (and Nazis were mostly blonde and tall and handsome), then he was truly better than the hero in the eyes of people. People experienced a sense of loss when the hero finally overcame evil in stories. Something was lost.

I always "played" before I went to sleep, and being captured by Nazis was my favorite play. I was especially fascinated by their medical experiments, which I had seen glimpses of in movies on television. Of course, my play was based on foolish ignorance. I had no idea what I was fooling with. Still, having read horrific deeds in fairy tales, such as people being eaten alive by giants or burned at the stake by the king, nothing the Nazis had done seemed worse than what I had read about in fairy tales. I was young enough to not know the difference between fairy tales and stories about Nazis. Fairy tales seemed absolutely real to me; I was not entirely sure they had been made-up. And, I had no real life reason to fear the Nazis. I'd already drilled Mama's limited store of knowledge about them.

"Would the Nazis kill me?" I asked.

"You? Ha! They would have loved you! You're exactly what they wanted! Blonde hair and green eyes! The Italians! Now, the Italians, we would have been next after the Jews! The Italians changed sides, they changed sides."

"But, Grandma's Italian and I'm half Italian!" I worried.

"Ah, next they would've started on people with freckles," Daddy grumbled.

"Do I have freckles?"

"A few," Mama said.

So, I would be next, after all, my expression told her.

"Don't worry, the Germans lost the war!" Mama laughed.

I was just as worried about *The Three Little Pigs*, or, actually, the Wolf. I continually asked Mama if our house was made of brick.

"No," she said, in Revere, "It's made of wood."

"Is that the same as sticks?" I trembled.

"I guess so, why?"

"'Cause in *The Three Little Pigs*, the Wolf could blow it down."

She laughed, "Nobody can blow this house down."

Of course, the house in East Boston, Grandma's house, was made of brick.

At Baboosic Lake, Ooda and I shared a cabin bedroom, she in one bunk, and me in the other. Cozy in bed, I began my play.

You see how idiotic I was. I was tempting the Devil in tampering with Nazis, in conjuring them up, so to speak, to kidnap me, or torture me. When I played, I was stretched out on an operating table, helpless. The glaring white operating light was turned on me. I was wearing a thin, white shift. They hadn't killed me, because I was exactly what they wanted. Blonde and green-eyed. The Nazi doctor, dressed in a doctor's white coat, stood over me.

"Will it hurt?" I whispered in the dark, looking right into the light. All I could see was the doctor's white coat. His face was a blur of light.

He answered. No, it would not hurt.

"Are you sure?"

This line I could not get quite right. Like an actor rehearsing, I repeated, "Are you sure?" with a different inflection. No, still not right. I concentrated harder. "Are you sure?" I whispered carefully, delicately, I thought, but still, I could...

"Be quiet, Gloria!"

A sharp voice cracked the fantasy. It was Ooda, in the next bed.

"What?" I asked sleepily, as though she'd been the noisy one, waking me, instead.

"You keep saying, 'Are you sure!" Cut it out and go to sleep!"

"I am not! I was asleep!"

My indecent fantasy was suddenly public. I lay in the dark, my stomach icy with the fear of being caught, and I wondered, what was it like to just lie down like Ooda, like one of those, normal, skinny, bony white people, thinking of everyday *stuff* and finally, just drift off to sleep?

The dark seemed so empty. I had nothing to do, lying on my back, my hands decorously folded across my tummy. I tried to be normal, to go to sleep like a normal person and I felt so - disappointed. So very disappointed.

Disappointment being worse than annoying Ooda or getting caught, I began my nasty play again, even more quietly this time - totally in my imagination. My tiny vagina responded to every insinuation in the Nazi doctor's voice, feeling warm and full, like I had to pee, only more pleasant. As the doctor played with my body, it throbbed, but only slightly. Maybe I did have to pee.

I got out of bed and pulled the potty out from under the bunk, scraping the sandy floorboards.

"Now, what are you doing?" Ooda grumbled, half asleep.

"I gotta pee!" My water sprayed against the empty bowl.

"Geez, are you ever going to sleep?"

I shoved the potty back under, scra-a-a-a-pe, and pulled up my shorty pajamas wishing I could wipe myself, cursing cabins and Ooda, as she was cursing me.

"Go to sleep!"

"All right!"

Ooda's mother had a moustache. I decided the Nazis wouldn't keep her for anything. Ooda was pretty, but she wore glasses, and, unless I was mistaken, she was also beginning to work on a moustache of her own. You had to be perfect, that much I knew. The Nazis had taught us well.

Lying there, I didn't feel like playing any more. I hated not being alone and free to do what I wanted. I couldn't help feeling my thoughts were not only strange and disturbing, but loud, loud! And Ooda, normal and unaffected, was trying not to hear to them in the dark.

We went to a lot of barbeques in Beachmont. Mama couldn't get enough barbeques. She loved everything about them: the hot dogs, the hamburgers, the beers in tubs of ice, the highballs out of tumblers, the bright plastic swizzle sticks she collected in her fist. The way she talked about how she had to make the potato salad or bring the tonic, you'd think the Pope himself had called her up and asked her to bring him potato salad. But, I loved barbeques, too. It was a chance to eat potato chips out of a huge bag and stick them in the mysterious and deliciously gooey stuff adults called "dip."

The women wore sandals and peddle pushers, cropped pants that ended just below the knee and the men wore T-shirts and baggy trousers. Daddy started wearing Jesus sandals right about now. He wore them with white socks.

The adults drank. Bubba, Paul's mother was trying to show me a book, but I could hear them giggling. The adults were wrestling down on a blanket. It was dusk and the Chinese lanterns, fluttering in the trees, were turned on, glowing red, orange, blue, yellow. I could hear Mama screaming with giggles and Cousin's low, guttural chuckle. I looked and there was

Paul on top of Mama and where was Daddy - on top of Cousin! I scowled at them. That wasn't right! It wasn't the right mother and father!

I went along on these barbeques because I had to: there was fear and confusion, but also some joy and mystery in them. Beachmont was beautiful, sunny and blue as well as unbearably ugly, broken and sad. The beauty and ugliness of Revere lived side by side: the bent petals of flowers growing out of a pile of abandoned tires turning brown in the sun; a shopping cart when there wasn't a store in sight; a wet mattress by the curb. I stuck my face into food to forget what was happening. I craved the taste of the strange and fierce food, strong relishes and mustards I wasn't used to, the hot dog bun that disappeared in your mouth like it had never been real, the red ketchup they said they used in movies instead of blood. But, now I felt a new sensation I would feel again and again and again and would come to associate with Revere, this feeling that my stomach was twisting like a dishrag runny with dirty water and wet food, twisting.

Not long after, Mama announced, "We're moving to Revere!" She was quivering with expectation.

HALLOWEEN

It was Halloween night, the first Halloween I was to be allowed to go out with my friends. I had plans.

"My costume is all ready!" I protested.

"I know. I'm sorry. Your father and I have to go out."

She wasn't smiling. I knew she meant it.

They were all dressed up. Mama was sparkling with rhinestones and red lipstick. Daddy wore a suit and tie that sat on him crookedly. He looked uncomfortable, like a little kid who'd dressed himself.

"It's a party at Daddy's work. We have to go."

I knew there was no hope. I was already in my pajamas and tucked in bed, but my spirit was not there. My spirit was climbing Brooks Street for the very last time, in my Halloween costume, a princess.

I was determined this time, now that I was older and it was definitely my last Halloween in East Boston. I climbed the hill, though I dutifully kissed Mama's perfumed face as she dipped it to me, and Daddy's shaved, but still bristly cheek, as he offered it, burning my lips with aftershave.

"I'm sorry," Mama whispered.

"I know."

I climbed the hill. I was determined. This time, I would do it.

Mama and Daddy left. I could hear Mama's high heels going down the steps.

I was almost there, climbing my own steps, gracefully lifting the long skirt of my costume. Now, I would reach up. Now, finally, I was not afraid. I knocked on the door of the White House.

THE BEST ANGEL

We didn't move to Revere till after Christmas. There was going to be a play at school.

We were so happy! We were running. A few of us, younger girls, had been set free downstairs in that great stone school, running ecstatically through rooms we didn't know.

We were going to be angels in a play about the birth of Jesus called "The Nativity." The older girls were making our costumes. We were supposed to be waiting for them to bring us our costumes, but our excitement couldn't be contained in one room. We burst in upon them, there, in the sewing room, like angels themselves, older girls, mysterious and magical to us! Sunlight filtered through the tall windows upon yards and yards of white cotton, upon rows of black lace sewing machines, ironing boards lined up. The girls held up our angel dresses with long bell sleeves; like beautiful ladies in waiting, they tossed them billowing over our laughing heads.

Miss Towers was going to be at the play and Oh! I wanted to be the best angel I possibly could be. We were brought up on the stage and told to kneel and pray with our heads bowed and our hands in supplication. We were told to close our eyes. I knew an angel would obey absolutely and I didn't want to disappoint Miss Towers.

When the curtain parted, I was so tempted! The stage lights glowed red under my trembling lids, but I never opened my eyes. No. Purely an angel, a devout spirit in attendance, I never saw the audience or any of the other actors. I never saw the play.

# Book Two

## The Mighty Blossom

Revere

1959-1964

NOT A REAL HOUSE

I liked to ride behind Daddy in the car on Sundays when we went visiting. I stood up. My sister and I were free to bounce around the back seat as much as we wanted. We wished we had a station wagon, so we could roll around even more. We dreamed about having one to take us to the drive-in, where, most of the time, we were not allowed to look at the screen. We were already in our pajamas and had to lie down with our heads at either end of the back seat. Cramped and hot, our feet worked furiously at kicking each other until Mama finally screamed at us or Daddy's hand came flying over the back seat. That hand brought quiet.

I liked to stand up and ride behind Daddy because his coat was the same cloth as mine. A dark navy spattered with colorful nubs, white, pink and baby blue. These clothes were not homemade or bought together and it was a real wonder to us that they were the same. I admired his shoulder, then my own, his, my own.

We didn't have a station wagon. We had what Daddy called a "skush-a-bunk" and Mama called a "shitbox." That meant an old broken down car, any kind, as long as you couldn't tell any more what kind it had been; it made a "skusha-skusha-bunk" sound when we drove. The muffler had a hole in it and was tied on with a twisted coat hanger. One or two of the doors in our car were always broken. Mama had to remind me, "Don't touch that door! It doesn't open! You have to get in your father's side!" and she'd purse up those lips in disgust. The broken door was usually tied with a rope woven in and out of its exposed guts where the upholstery had ripped open.

Mama wouldn't get in the car to go visiting on a Sunday until Daddy laid out a fresh white sheet over the front seat for her. We got one too, in the back, if we were dressed up. She had special "short sheets" she saved for making pillow cases: these were sheets that'd worn so thin from washing that, in bed, your foot went clean through them. "It's still good! It's still good!" she liked to say about junk most people would throw away. Slips of paper - "Use the back!" Elastics - boxes of them saved from bunches of carrots or broccoli or the newspaper, blackened with ink. Mama saved thumbtacks, corks, dried ballpoint pens, empty aspirin bottles, broken pencils, stray screws or nails, you name it. Anyway, she just cut the hole right out of the old sheet, (kind of Alice in Wonderland, if you think about it) and kept the rest for sewing or patching or for the car.

"I'm not getting in that shitbox until you put a sheet down on that greasy seat! That goddamn grease is everywhere! He's got that goddamn grease everywhere, he's got." Then, she grunted.

"Did he put a sheet?" she asked us. "Did you put a sheet?" she hollered out the front to Daddy.

"Yeah, yeah, yeah, goddamn pain in the ass!"

"I'll pain in the ass you! I'll pain in the ass you!"

She started repeating herself. Well, she always had, a little, but now, she repeated a lot and violently, in a losing, flailing way as though her speech were limbs fallen asleep, numb, desperately, uselessly, striking out. And, her lips were often, almost all day every day, a purse pulled tight, so tight they curled in on themselves and disappeared, swallowed up inside the purse. When? When had this happened? Maybe when Mama found out the house in Revere was never going to be fixed up like she wanted. Like she'd dreamed.

Sometimes, men are like salesmen. I learned early, I was eight. Daddy had these skills: carpenter, electrician, plumber, roofer, plasterer, painter, all self-taught, none of them official and he had sold Mama on this hundred year old house in Revere instead of a newer house like she wanted. He'd sold her by promising dreams, promising to shape the old walls and floors according to her very own dreams with his very own hands. He'd sold her on romance and love, on air, on her own heart and the wishes, the desires in his heart of hearts that seemed possible at the time he spoke them, but became less and less so as he too flailed away with hammer and saw at the old rooms, at Mama's dreams, until the money and the energy and the dreams ran out. Mama would kick at the mess of a half torn down wall, purse her lips and grumble, "Look at this, look at this! This is supposed to be my new bar, my new bar it's supposed to be!" "Promiser! Promiser!" We kids would call each other if a promise were broken, the moral equivalent of an Indian Giver, a deep and shameful sin.

The house in Revere was a hundred years old, bought from a woman who was herself a hundred years old. I must have come along once when they went to fix the house. I wandered by a long dark blue sink, speckled with white and a dark blue stove with a chimney. I was mesmerized. "What are these things?" I asked Mama. "A sink and a stove," she said. I didn't believe her. "That's what they used to have in the old days, enamel." Mama explained. But, soon, these dark things were headed out the door, tumbling into some junkman's truck. Mama bought gold appliances. She had a thing for yellow. She painted every room yellow and green. She thought that was so pretty.

In front of what Mama lovingly called "my *bay* window," stood a large and very ancient bush of heart shaped leaves. Mama said, "It's blocking my view," a view of another old house across the street. The men tore it out. After she got to know the neighbors, who were, of course, watching all this tearing out and tossing away, she learned the bush had been a lilac. Mama felt the horror of someone who'd accidentally killed someone. She ran around with her hands flying over her head, "I didn't know! I didn't know!" It wouldn't be ten years later when we realized all the blue enamel she'd thrown out would be worth, well, almost as much as the down payment they'd put on the house.

During the time Mama and Daddy went crazy "fixing up" the new/old house, Marie and I stayed with Grandma. Our old apartment stood empty between Grandma's and Nona's, which was also empty and ghostly. I slept on a cot in the secret hush of Grandma's bedroom. The silence of her widowhood was enormous. The French doors to the kitchen were covered with intricate patterns of Italian lace; these were my meditations in the half-light. I don't even remember where Marie slept. I only recall, lying there alone, wrapped in Grandma's dark bedroom, deeply content. I could have remained there forever.

Uncle Sonny and Uncle Salvi were at home too. They were funny. They never fought. This was the time Uncle Salvi was making whipped cream and he whipped it too far - or was that when Marie was born and Mama was in the hospital? Grandma said, "Oh, boy, I'll have to make pancakes now!" In the morning, we had pancakes like only Grandma could make them, white white, with white flour and egg whites, so light they were like crispy clouds, with the homemade butter that was a mistake with sugar in it and vanilla.

Life was homemade sweet butter and night viewed through lace until the night Uncle Salvi finally took me to the new/old house to stay.

The wooden steps rang hollow in the dark. In the trees, the silvery undersides of leaves fluttered in the street light, illuminated, agitated against the night sky, as though my troubled soul followed me inside.

"Are these the steps to the new house?" I trembled, the corners of my mouth turned way down, about to cry.

The porch was wooden and black where it fell away from the lighted doorway.

"Is this the porch?"

I could hear voices, laughter at a joke I didn't share, hammering, Daddy was putting up something Mama was nuts over called "cabinets."

Uncle Salvi knocked at the big wooden door. Windows rattled.

"Come on in! The door's open!" Daddy called proudly.

Mama turned and cast me a big grin, her chin nestled on her red hair curled round her shoulder, so proud of herself for having a new house to show me, her first child, who'd arrived like an uncertain guest.

A card table held cold cuts piled on wax paper, a loaf of bread, and plastic cups. Was that supposed to be the kitchen table? The room floated in sawdust. Somehow, Marie was already there.

Mama was washing dishes. The sink worked, I told myself. My eyes followed down her legs and saw - pipes! Pipes sticking out under the sink!

"This isn't a real house!" I screamed.

I turned and ran, thinking of nothing but getting back to Grandma's house in East Boston.

Uncle Salvi caught me. To this day, because I trusted Uncle Salvi so implicitly, because he was a saint, I can't help but wonder if his carrying me over the threshold into Revere meant God, in His infinite wisdom, wanted me to live there.

The adults laughed and laughed while I cried without hope, "This isn't a real house!"


THE HEATHEN

Daddy went over the bumps in the road too fast, so that the car seemed to fly off the road for a second and your stomach flipped up to your throat and sent a delighted little gasp of air out your mouth.

"Oh, Daddy! Do it again!"

"No!" Mama snapped from the passenger side.

We ignored her.

"Do it again, Daddy! Do it again!"

He liked to let go of the steering wheel. He put his hands up high, like he was under arrest. We leaped off the seats and stood up.

Mama cried, "Sit down in the car!"

We ignored her.

"Daddy! How can you drive without hands?"

"Oh, the car knows where to go."

"Billy! Put your hands on the wheel! Goddamn it, I'm gonna get out and walk!"

The more Mama screamed, the higher Daddy put his hands and the more we squealed with delight, making Mama more and more unhappy, pulling the purse strings tighter and tighter on her red bow mouth.

"Billy!"

"E-e-e-e!" We squealed as Daddy flew the car over a bump with no hands.


"There's one, Daddy! There's one! Right here! Right here! - You went past it!"

I was pointing out the Dairy Queens, and lesser ice cream stands to Daddy as though I were doing him a great service. He ignored me till about the fifteenth time I hollered in his ear.

"Siddown!"

No ice cream.

We were coming back from Arlington or Somerville or Dorchester where we'd been visiting relatives on Sunday afternoon. Mama and Daddy had a party with relatives while we kids were thrown outside in summer or into a room in winter and told to play.

Arlington was good.

Arlington was Daddy's sister, Doris and the large house on Ariel Street, which was a forest and a dead end that went straight up like an ariel antenna and really had an ariel antenna at the top! The house was built into the rocks like the cottage in "Sleeping Beauty" had been built into the trunk of a tree. The grounds sloped down and down in the back making it great for running which I did as soon as I was let out of the car which was parked pointing to the sky.

I ran and ran, breathlessly running. Mama yelled after me, "Stop at the trees! That's someone else's property!"

Round about at the trees and a fast run back. All the kids ran with me, Marie toddled behind, and Aunt Doris's two kids, Ruthie and Ronny, who were younger than me. We ran till we couldn't breathe, then sat down and just looked at all we'd run, heaving for breath, surveying the long, long yard, the secret places hidden behind sheds and arbors we hadn't looked in yet.

"What's there?" I asked.

"I don't know. That's not our yard."

I was off and running again.


Neal was Aunt Doris's husband; I skirted him. He had the wrong kind of smile. Aunt Doris disapproved every time he smiled; she was embarrassed by it. She covered his mouth with her hand.

Eventually, he had to be divorced. I babysat for Ruthie and Ronny, before and after the divorce. Neal would say how much I'd grown every time he saw me, and Aunt Doris would cover his mouth.


Somerville was one of those places you can't believe people actually live. I always considered it a negative space around Boston, like East Boston, Revere and all the other suburbs. Somerville was exactly like East Boston, only richer and bigger. The tenements were further apart and finished in aluminum siding slapped over peeling wood. Clumps of gas station petunias and, sometimes, roses, gassed and covered with road dirt, grew out of narrow strips of earth choked up against chain link fences spray painted silver. Silly house ornaments, whirly-gigs, Madonnas in bathtubs set on end to resemble the grotto of Lourdes, American flags, plastic bunnies or ducks looked about as cheerful as holiday ornaments in hospitals. Not everybody had that kind of money, though. Most people suffered in sagging tenements on endless grey streets. Mailboxes were torn up by kids who'd never written a letter, and never would. The streetlights hung broken. Sneakers dangled in pairs over the wires. Sometimes I saw the same lush gardens as East Boston's cared for by the old Italians, dug out of inches of space, trellises of grapes hanging heavily and the same gargantuan harvests of fruits and vegetables.

My smart cousin Bernadette lived there. She was fatter and smarter than I was. She wore pointy glasses and a ponytail. I could never tell whether her hair was brown or shitty blonde.

The second we got there, the adults would shut us up in her room and close the door. First thing she said was, not hello, but "What did you get in Religion?"

"I don't take Religion," I said.

Bernadette looked smug, but she was careful to also look a little sorry for me, that I was a heathen from public school, which I knew I was. The heathen was wondering if her Aunt Louisa, Bernadette's mother, had made cake. Probably not. This house was not a cooking house.

"What did you get in Grammar?"

Sister school had some very strange subjects.

"Do you mean English?"

"Is *that* what you call it?"

By now, I was actually thinking about finding Marie.

She made me compare grades. If we hadn't gotten report cards, she'd ask about test scores. Her marks were always higher, you know, A+'s instead of A's. *And*, she liked to remind me, sister school was *harder*.

There were times, though, when I'd call her Bernie, which I think made her tingle, times when she was the only intelligent kid I could talk to. We could talk about books, even if we hadn't read the same ones, she was still able to understand, and, of course, so was I. She wasn't smug all the time.

I stayed over a few times when we were really close. I remember Aunt Louisa coming home from a function - they, my family - actually called special events like weddings, funerals, parties, *functions*; it sounded like a bowel movement and it drove me crazy. Bernie and I were hushed in the dark because we were still awake and Aunt Louisa and Uncle Stanley were home! I heard Aunt Louisa call, "Uh-oh!" at some noise we made, some giggle or bump in the night. Her husband, Stanley mumbled ineffectually, something about "No more sleeping together."

I've always loved that "Uh-oh!" I've kept it, close to my heart, it was a moment I shared with Bernadette, a moment of unintentional rebellion when we drifted bodiless in the dark, in time, poised, absolutely together. The only two intelligent beings I knew.

One hot summer night, they let us, Bernie and I, walk down to the corner store to get Italian slush. The street was sticky with a summer's worth of slush and tonic, candy and gum melted to the sidewalk. We weren't aware of danger, but had a heightened awareness of the night, a new treasure. The hot darkness was intense with nightlife. Around us in the glaring street light moved older kids eating melting slushes, sweaty men smoking cigars, women smoking cigarettes or hurrying, carrying a frosty half gallon of milk back to open cars filled with dirty half naked kids. I walked in awe, my feet almost nabbed by the gum and grape juice tacky on the sidewalk trying to suck in my sandals.

Suddenly, at the very door of the store, open to the clammy night, a girl nearly bumped into us, coming quickly out. She was about our age and she was naked to the waist.

I gasped.

She had rich, dark skin and lovely new breasts with thick, brown nipples upturned to the steamy summer night. She clutched a dripping popsicle in her fist.

She said, "Some people take their shirt off when it's hot, you know."

I wondered if her mother had told her to say that if she had any trouble.

Bernadette clicked her tongue and said it was a sin. I agreed, as we walked into the store, it was a sin to show your breasts. Yes, Bernadette was right, the girl was too old to go without her blouse. Tsk, tsk, a sin.

But, another voice told me differently, more a swelling in my own chest than a voice. Bernadette sounded like Aunt Louisa; it was an old cranky sound that rattled out of her mouth. And, that girl, who was she? A rich-skinned island girl who had as much right as a man to take her shirt off in the heat, a beauty, the heathen thought, she was a beauty, lovely enough to justify her nakedness. She walks, forever in my mind, dark and shining with heat, right through everyone else.


## THE SAINT AND HIS BROTHER, THE DEVIL

The worst place was Dorchester.

Pealing houses, weak and thin, stood on small lots, waist high in lot weeds. On the porches, old couches and living room chairs regurgitated their stuffing. The same wet mattresses, tires, shopping carts, ripped out mailboxes, and stripped cars I was used to seeing occasionally in other places, decorated every block in Dorchester. Every Friday and Saturday night, you'd hear on the news that someone was shot and killed in Dorchester.

Dorchester had black people. In the early '70s, some black kids in Dorchester doused a white, female social worker with gasoline and set her on fire. I understood: they didn't want her there. Everyone said, "That's Dorchester." That's what Dorchester meant.

And this:

Dorchester was Peter and Jakey, Uncle Jake's sons. They had a stepmother, Rena. Their real mother, Anna, had died of tuberculosis. In her photos, Anna had the vacant stare of someone who had sunk far down and could not be rescued and knew it. Her gentle face bore the complacency of the weak; it floated, ethereal, somewhere above her wheelchair; already her body had lightened to the weight of a bird's skeleton, already she was half ghost.

I loved her deeply and at once from her photos: she smiled a weak, loving smile, wrapped under bundles of blankets in her wheelchair outside the Veterans' Hospital in Bethesda, Maryland where Jake had taken her over and over in a failed attempt to cure her. Peter and Jakey stood by her side, holding on to the wheelchair for their own lives. The Washington Monument, the Lincoln Memorial, the Capitol building, figured here and there behind their futile little group. Nothing could save her, not America, not the Best Hospitals in the Country, not her sons' desperate longing or Jake's. Nothing.

Jake drank like a fish after that; like a man made of alcohol, also breathing it, waking up in it, swimming in it. He went limp and useless. Rena supported him by waitressing. I don't know how he met her or why she liked him, but, in a way, it made sense to me as a kid. Rena drank too. Once, very quietly and uncharacteristically, Jakey confided that Rena locked him in the closet when he was bad. He said she made him and Peter get the ashtray for her, even if she was closer to it. Peter did the housework, he said. Then, Peter caught him telling me and told him, "Stop telling!" So, that was all I ever learned about their situation, which I immediately figured must be worse than Peter wanted us to know.

Peter was the good one. He had a real coonskin cap and a Davey Crockett record that he played over and over for us on his little record player. Peter was older; he'd inherited his mother's spirit. I didn't know why he didn't get his father's name, but I was glad. Peter welcomed Marie and me into their room, which Jakey hated. He wanted all Peter's attention and I don't blame him. Peter sat us down and asked if we were comfortable (which made Jakey fume) and handed us each a toy. Jakey ripped the toys out of our hands and hit us over the head with them just to see us cry.

"Jakey, they're little girls," Peter explained with the patience of a saint.

"I don't care!" Jakey screamed in his face.

Their Dad hollered from the kitchen where the adults were drinking and smoking, "Jakey! Knock it off!"

Rena: "What's he doing now?"

Peter: "Nothing, Ma! He's fine."

Mama: "Who's crying?"

Daddy: "Shuddup an' play!"

Peter put a finger to his lips and miraculously, Marie and I stopped crying.

"Do you wanna play Monopoly?"

We nodded eagerly, though we had no idea what Monopoly was.

"They don't know how to play Monopoly!" Jakey groaned.

Gently, Peter opened the game board, which intrigued us with all its weird symbols.

"We'll teach them."

"That'll take forever," sneered Jakey.

Peter handed each of us a playing piece.

"You be the iron, Gloria. Marie can be the hat."

He placed them tenderly in our outstretched palms. We stared at the strange, pewter objects in our hands.

"Do you want to play, Jakey?" Peter asked.

"Not with them!" he sulked in a corner, making loud fart noises the whole time.

Occasionally, I'd look over to see him glaring at us as Peter explained the game to our blank faces. He wanted to kick the board over and maybe kick us a few times too.

It was a sad day, but it shouldn't have been a surprise, when Jake and Rena were declared incompetent to take care of Peter and Jakey, who were sent to foster homes.

Daddy cried at the kitchen table and Mama's face turned white, her lips disappeared in a pale, taut line.

"I went from foster home to foster home. Nobody wanted me. He's my brother's son," Daddy sniffed.

I didn't know exactly what a foster home was, but I knew it wasn't a real home with your real parents. When Daddy cried, an emergency went off in my stomach, and when Mama's face went white and her lips were gone, I was terrified. I stood dumbstruck watching them for clues to my own future.

Daddy wanted to adopt Jakey. Because, in my parents' incredibly simple minds, he was more our age, mine and Marie's and WE COULD PLAY TOGETHER! Peter was going to the Nabby's, where he, being older, was supposed to have a lot in common with Ooda and Little Paul. That way, too, you see, the brothers could still see each other, we could all see each other all the time and all play together!

Everyone wants to go back and change something. Everyone has at least one thing they wish never happened. I wish we had never adopted Jakey.

"I wish we'd never adopted you!" I screamed the worst, most unkind words I could think of after Jakey had picked up the black telephone, heavy and solid in those days, and lifting it over his head, whomped me with it against all the foster homes, against every stupid kid like me who ever called him brother when he wasn't their brother, every strange room he'd had to sleep in, with other people's crummy furniture and other people's sickening smells, and most of all against my father's charity and tears.

"Yeah?" Jakey growled and bared his teeth like a dog. "You should'a kept me with my brotha'!"

Mama had left me "in charge," but that was a joke. What had happened? Probably, I'd pressed my authority a little too far. Maybe I'd insisted he sweep the floor like he was supposed to, maybe I wouldn't let him go out.

Sniveling on the floor, I was lucky, I'd moved just right and the telephone, instead of killing me, had clipped me on the forehead. Marie was shivering in the corner, as far from the commotion as she could get. A lump was growing, and a cut oozed red blood into my eye. "Red blood," Marie would tell me later, "red blood." But, can you believe, at Jakey's words, tears came to my eyes for his suffering? Really, it's a good thing I never went to war. I may have felt sorry for the enemy, sorry enough to help him kill me.

Of course, I thought, my head pounding and swelling, we took him away from Peter, no wonder he hates us. I cried for him, and for me, too, at what we had done. Given a choice, Peter would never have abandoned his little brother. Given a choice, I would never have taken Jakey without Peter.

Sprawled there on the floor, the bloody telephone making wild noises, I felt the loss of Peter enormously, like a great holiday suddenly cancelled, Peter, where was he now? Wasted on the Nabbys when we desperately needed the gentle peacemaker.


THE LITTLE AIRPORT

"Feast your eyes!" Daddy told us, "You'll never see this again!"

We were coming in from Saugus down the mountain to Revere. Below us, we could see a long, low building made of sweet wood and white paint gone grey from time and too much sun; on its roof, slanting off to the horizon were the faded, blue letters R - E - V - E - R - E.

"What does that say on its roof, Daddy?"

"Revere. That's the name of the airport. That building is a house for planes."

A house for planes. Amazing.

"Why is its name on the roof?"

"That's for the planes to see when they're flying in. That's Revere Airport."

We pulled in. Two sleek white planes sat like gulls waiting expectantly for flight. Magically, their wheels rested on lovely green grass.

"Look at that!" Daddy purred appreciatively.

"Can we fly in one of those planes, Daddy?"

Daddy laughed.

"Those're private planes. Only rich people fly in those. Pretty soon, they'll have to go down to Logan with the big planes. This place is going to be a shopping center." Daddy said as he whipped the steering wheel round with one finger.

We were leaving! I'd never see this neat little airport again! I jumped to the rear window and greedily watched as the crisp white planes on the grassy runway got smaller and smaller. Already they had been a memory when I first laid eyes on them, little ghosts of planes, graceful little ghosts, elegant and rich little airport, receding further and further, disappearing forever.

I was worried about these little planes at the big airport being bumped or crushed by the huge jets I'd seen scraping the roof tops in East Boston.

"Won't the big planes hurt the little ones down at the big airport?"

"Nah, don' worry."

Something else nagged at me.

"What's a shopping center?"

Again, Daddy laughed.

What was this thing that was more important than pretty planes and soft, green grass?

"They're building it so people can go there to shop," Mama said. "Stores."

Stores? Like in the Square in East Boston? With sidewalks and streets and windows and lights? Out here? In the country?

Down below us were green squares cut into the ground stretching on and on to other roads and houses, pink and yellow, like a picture. One of the houses was long and white, like the airport, but it had also a glass house filled with green plants.

"What's down there?" I strained my neck to see as we went past.

"Farms," said Mama. "Those'll be gone soon, too."

"Why?"

Mama shrugged, "All the farms are gone. This used to be all farms."


Years later, Daddy found a raccoon in the parking lot of one of the new stores, Zayres, where we went for cheap sneakers and school clothes.

"Ah," said Daddy, "he probably wandered up from that little valley down there between the highways."

Daddy knew just how to hold him, under his little armpits.

Then, the raccoon did something that made us, all of us - me and Mama and Marie, and even Jakey - gasp with delight. He brought up his long claws, shaped like slender human hands, and covered his eyes.


## WORSHIPPING

I woke in the morning to the large, pear tree in full bloom outside my window, which was open for one of the holy, first warm days of Spring, the glass clean, curtains freshly washed, bed sheets crisp and smelling of holy Ivory Snow, of babies, of Mama and comfort. I opened my eyes to the swaying pear blossoms, softly white and green, drifting a soft green perfume into the room.

Mama taught me that Nature was holy. How did she? She never said so. When we went for a ride, along the highway she searched, hoping for -

"A birch tree! How beautiful they are! I love birch trees!" she brightened at the birch trees flashing by, lighting up the forest with their speckled white bark.

"I love birch trees, too!"

Mama and I, our heads together at the car window: hers red and curly, mine, yellow and fluffy; our eager faces reflected back at us, getting clearer and clearer as darkness covered the sky.

At home, the last light of day ignited the dust at the foot of the huge maple tree that Mama said was holding up the whole embankment behind our house. We would watch the sparrows, there, in the dust shining with sunlight splashing powdery golden light over and over themselves and twittering ecstatically.

"They're taking a sand bath - look!"

Gold dust flew in puffs of tremendous energy from the tiny wings. Insignificant, ordinary city birds were flashing golden before our eyes.

"How happy they are!" Mama whispered to me.

A secret. You gave me a secret then, Mama, and I took it into my heart.

Revere was the country, and only immigrants with empty pockets could think so: we snatched what country we could from its embankments, from Sundays with a view whisking by us in cars. An inch of country was still country. And, if the sparrows could find ecstasy in a small pile of dust, so could I, so used to finding happiness in nothing: what if I had only dust turned golden by a moment of sun to throw over my wings instead of water, refreshing and cool?

I was wrong to be content, even joyous, with nothing. It was dangerous to be so content.

I learned how to climb a small tree on the embankment with an apple and a book and nestle in its branches, perfect for holding me, spread out as they were, like an open hand. This tree had purple berries; I dared to taste them, they were horribly sour as if they hadn't ripened. Their seeds were huge, taking up most of the berry's flesh. I named it, The Huckleberry Tree, after a boys' book. Sometimes, I sat on one of the tufts of long grass like steps going up the small hill to the highway and studied the grass life, minutely, as though I could be the size of an insect and walk in the grass as in a forest.

I carved an Indian Camp for myself: a neat clearing round a few trees where I brought a table (a board) and chairs (large stones) and a few old dishes from the house. I dug a small circle in the dirt, surrounded it with smooth stones and called it my campfire. I loved to gather firewood, bring it back to camp and stack it neatly next to the campfire. I never lighted this fire, I only pretended. Wearing the white mantilla for mass, I performed a ceremony to declare the Indian Camp sacred ground. I brought a bowl of water from the Mama's kitchen, made the Sign of the Cross over it, because it was only from the faucet and not holy in the usual sense, and, solemnly, splashed it with my fingertips on to the earthen floor of the Camp, chanting, "Holy, holy, holy! This ground is henceforth sacred to all men!" In those days, I considered "men" to mean me too.

I lived in the Indian Camp daily. I worshipped by curling up into the trees like a rabbit or a deer asleep in the thicket; I worshipped by breathing the wet smell of earth, by getting myself black with earth, my skin and clothes, my belly as I lay flat down on the dark soil, until I, too, smelled of earth. I worshipped by looking up, deep into the layers of swaying branches, searching for pieces of sky, by gazing far into the grooves of bark or the bulging veins of leaves, looking that had no end.

I prayed that I could be good enough, holy enough to be canonized as The Saint of Trees. When I heard of the huntress, Athena, who wanted to be wild and virginal and live free in the woods, I understood. And when I learned of the nymph, Daphne, chased down by the god, Apollo, who, rather than give in to his desire, prayed to the gods and was changed into the laurel tree, I thought she was the luckiest girl! My heart and mind were boundless. My adoration was a long taproot sent deep into the earth.

THE WAY TO THE LIBERTY

At first, I didn't know what our new home, Hichborn Street, was. It took months, even years, for me to gather that knowledge. At first, I knew only the house, the yard, the way to school, the way to church, and, of course, the school and church themselves.

Loneliness bore down on me whenever I had to leave home. I did not recognize myself in anything beyond my backyard; therefore, I began to reach out for whatever small thing gave me any pleasure at all, or any pain.

The road to the Liberty School was filled with things to keep me company. Hichborn Street curled over the crest of a hill. Along that crest, ran Franklin Avenue to the Liberty School, where it disappeared into Centennial, the steepest street in the world, which, in turn, took you down to the beach.

Because the lovely walk on Franklin followed the shore so closely, dazzling white seagulls like the ones that had flown over the gardens of East Boston flew with me every day, calling over my shoulder, singing out in front of me, swooping down in the blue or grey sky to show me how graceful and lovely something could be. No, sometimes, that wasn't true, sometimes, I felt so lonely, even the gulls seemed far, far away, happy or troubled in a world of their own, a world I couldn't share; they were circling souls, specks as high as the day moon, which frightened me with wonder when it was pale in the day sky.

Mrs. Padder had brilliant orange hair that stuck out from under her police lady's cap and brilliant orange cheeks and lips to match. She crossed us at the four-lane highway that crashed over our house all day and night. Up went her uniformed arms, like Moses parting the Red Sea, so we could walk, a row of ducklings, through the stopped surge of cars, growling to get going, inching forward, growling, inching, till our feet touched the curbstone on the other side, she stepped out of the way, and the drivers sped out as though devils bit on their necks from the backseats.

"Do I have too much makeup on, kids?" she asked us every morning, rubbing at the persistent orange spot on her cheek.

"No!" we answered dutifully, every morning, knowing she did, but not knowing how to tell her. Instead, we told each other, as soon as she couldn't hear us.

"What a Paddypuss!" laughed Jakey, doing his best to make fun of her name, all the while rubbing his cheek with his grimy fist. "Do *I* have too much makeup on?"

"Sssh! She'll hear you!" I said.

"Who cares? She looks like a stupid clown." Jakey checked over his shoulder, anyway.

"Yeah," said Rick Likus, one of the bigger boys who didn't need Mrs. Padder to cross him. "She might let the cars go on ya, watch out."

Even Jakey wondered about that, the bared teeth of the cars were always eager to chew up the road and our little bodies along with it.

Past the yucky yellow mud in front of the truck stop, Santoro's. We couldn't step in it and survive. Only truckers could because of their big yellow boots. We called it The Quicksand after all the quicksand we'd seen in the Tarzan movies and the many horses that had been sucked down screaming in the westerns Daddy watched on Sundays.

Past the Shinbuck house, leaning precariously atop its own impenetrably wild hill.

"It's got a hole in the roof," I pondered out loud. Gulls could fly through.

"Yeah, but people live there! It's a foster house."

"No, sah!"

"Yes, sah! I seen them!"

"What's a foster house?" I asked timidly. So, that's a foster house, I said to myself.

Jakey didn't answer, but the older kid, Rick Likus, did.

"They take orphans in fa money."

"They do? They got orphans in there?" I asked, gazing up at the tall shack.

"Yeah! They're crazy. They got their own family and a bunch of kids with no parents."

"How many kids?"

"I dunno, about a hundred," said Rick. "Why? You wanna go up there?"

Rick Likus had been hit by a truck when he was little and the accident had left a scar over his left temple, stringing his eyebrow and eye together, and making Rick Likus crazy. The first thing anybody said to us about Rick Likus was that he had been hit by a truck when he was little and that now he was not right. No one fooled with him.

You didn't seem to go past the Shinbuck house. It was never out of sight; it hulked behind you, tall on its weedy hill full of wild trees and trash - years of bottles and wrappers that normal people threw at it as they walked by. A long line of dark concrete steps led the way up the steep hill to broken wooden front stairs that lurched drunkenly against the Shinbuck porch. The house stood, three stories tall, grey slats of wood leaning into each other for support. None of us wanted to go there, ever. But, some of us thought about it more than others. You could see the Shinbuck house's threatening bulk from our kitchen window.

The wild rhubarb was next. It grew in a wild spot across the street; I could see the horseshoe shaped leaves flopping over the sidewalk, the shiny red stems. I don't know how I knew what it was. I'd never seen rhubarb before.

"Must be rhubarb," I thought, tempted to try it.

I crossed the street, hoping no one was looking at me. After the highway all the kids were usually far ahead of me, so if no one was looking, I snapped off a red stalk, bit into the stringy flesh and chewed slowly, sucking my mouthful, sucking the red juice, pretending I was Tarzan. I liked to think I was Tarzan; I liked to think I could live without houses and streets, without school or church, like Tarzan.

Next, a low brick wall like a ramp that ran up and down a little hillock of a green front yard. This I ran up and ran down quickly and happily!

Next, The Tulip Tree spread its branches over a neat square inch of front yard at Judith Salter's house, a huge frothy cake on a silver chain link tray. I wondered how such a pale, limp girl could live beneath such a magnificent pink tree and still be pale and limp.

"Magnificent, magnificent," I repeated the word to myself, in Spring, on those few glorious days in Spring when The Tulip Tree was in full radiance, as I planted myself underneath and looked up.

Ah! The sharp fleshy smell of green stem, the winey smell of browning petals white and pink as skin, but brown lines forming on some and sending up a high, pungent urgency! Clouds of them, clouds, layer on layer, white and white rippling with pink and creeping brown.

The last soft thing, the last pretty thing before the black tar of school, the penmanship on green lines that encircled the room, the dead Presidents, the alphabet, all had a faded, temporary look. All this is temporary, they said, bear with this a while and you can go home to where the real work is: your own true books, the Indian Camp, the Embankment, the Huckleberry Tree.

The last soft thing: the last bright sea gull stubbornly circled the squat, red brick school I was entering, calling out to me, reluctant to leave me alone.

CORRECTION

"What are you DOING, dear?" Miss Dunkee squawked.

She yanked the paper out from under my freshly sharpened No.2 pencil almost snapping off the point.

The paper covered her face.

"Oh, no, dear! We don't use cursive in the first grade. You'll have to print. I'll get you another piece of paper."

Her tone hurt me. She made a smug, simpy smile with her chicken lips: she enjoyed finding fault with me. I had never experienced a teacher being happy that a child was mistaken.

I studied her in her stiff woolen suit, grey wool and padded shoulders. I had seen such suits in the movies about World War II, was she a Nazi? Not really a Nazi, but like a Nazi, she enjoyed torture.

"Did they teach you cursive where you came from, dear?"

Another piece of paper was snapped in front of me.

"Yes."

Fresh and white, innocent, it had nothing to do with the Dunkee, still, I wouldn't enjoy this piece of paper as much.

"Well, they taught you wrong."

She beamed a nasty smile my way.

"When you get to the third grade, you'll learn cursive."

I already knew cursive.

"We make our letters differently here. You'll learn."

The other kids were enjoying the scene too. Every face was twisted in a smirk. Seeing me suffer made them feel better. That was a law in Revere.

Law #1:  Make someone feel bad, you'll feel better.

I loved cursive. I mean, I was in love with cursive. The graceful letters spun and wove; they had long, trailing scarves; they danced on toes. They lifted my heart that I could form them exactly right. In East Boston, we had been taught that our cursive would get better and better. Cursive was mine. If this dried up prune thought she could take it from me, she was sadly mistaken. Now I was learning the skill of duplicity; it would be the first time, but not the last, I would pretend to be dumber than I was. Ever so neatly, I printed my name Gloria Wisher in the nicest letters possible, I printed along the line and in perfect harmony with the margins.

"That's right." Miss Dunkee smiled like Cinderella's stepmother. In fact, the entire class wore the same Nazi, stepmother smile.

Now Miss Dunkee had taught me that some teachers like to teach in the negative; they teach what not to do, and there she was, absolutely satisfied with my progress in the negative.

Law #2:  Go backwards, just for spite.

I had arrived with a head full of Shirley Temple curls. The first day of school in Revere, Mama twirled my hair round her fat finger and yanked it through to make curls like a bowlful of macaroni. How proud she was! I believed her and I was proud too.

But, when I got to school, Miss Dunkee stuck me up in front of the class and announced who I was, "This is Gloria Wisher, class. She is our new student. Please say hello."

"Hello!" said the class, their eyes like scissors snipping off my curls.

I smiled, happily, thinking they would all welcome me as they had been asked to by their kind and wonderful teacher, Miss Dunkee, as I thought all teachers must be as kind and good as Miss Towers. But, I was wrong. I was told later by Vicki Carlo that they'd all hated me because I was blonde and pretty and that, mentally, they had shaved my head bald. It was the first time I'd heard the word "pretty" referring to me and I heard it first as a bad thing.

I was in the cloakroom, alone for a moment with a little boy. A dark tunnel of a walk-through closet where we hung our coats and hats on the shadows of hooks we felt for with our hands feeling along the wall.

Somewhere, I had heard or read that you should be friendly to other people, new people, maybe Mama had told me to "make new friends." I turned to this little boy and I said, "Hi!" cheerfully and my curls bounced.

"Yick!" He turned in horror and ran.

"Mama!" I cried when I got home. "I'm never wearing my hair in Shirley Temple curls again! The boy said, 'Yick!' to me!"

"Oh, that's all right, what do you care about what the boys say?"

"No more curls!" I sobbed, miserable at having offended an uncouth boy.

So, I let Mama be disappointed and her precious curls were flattened forever and held down by two barrettes over my ears. From the front, I looked plain enough, but nothing could stop the curls from breaking loose behind and cascading down my back in a shiny golden tumble.


BEATRICE

In the basement entryway, dark and damp, we sat in a row on a narrow, wooden bench putting on our boots out of a jumble of rubbers and damp wool, stepped on scarves, hats, crushed mittens smeared with mud.

He pulled my small boots out of an indoor puddle. He knelt in front of the loneliest, lightest girl.

"Beatrice," he said. "How are you today, Beatrice?" he asked me, pulling my boots up snug.

Why did he call me 'Beatrice'?

The old janitor, tall and tall, he went up and up when I looked at him, thin and caved in, his chest and cheeks, sunk in. He shuffled when he walked in old janitor shoes. He shuffled by the line of us, filing along the dark corridor in the basement. He carried a white rag and stuffed it into his uniform pocket.

"Beatrice," he called me with an old voice, shaking, lisping a little on broken teeth, and my head, lit up by the bare light bulbs hanging between the pipes, turned.

His faded blue eyes caught me.

"How are you today, Beatrice?"

I knew he meant me. His weak eyes were so happy when I looked back. He meant me, but why did he call me 'Beatrice'?

I was home and the doctor was coming. Mama couldn't get me well, she was somewhere, but the shapes were always around, in and out, sweating, my hair stuck to the back of my neck, my pajamas stuck to my chest where Mama had rubbed Vick's Vapo-Rub to help me breathe. My throat was swollen and the doctor was coming to give me a shot. Mama moved me down to the living room. I had to put on fresh pajamas because the doctor was coming. Mama tugged them, scratchy from the laundry soap, over my aching head. When the doctor came, I would be well. As soon as he stuck that needle in my bare bottom, I'd feel better right away. I could smell the cough syrup. It smelled like whiskey. I lay buried under the damp sheet at my throat and wished the doctor would come.

Dr. Nathan looked like the naked Budd-ha in the alley. His skin was milk white, brushed with milk like Grandma's pie dough. He smiled down at me like an old, pale-eyed Nazi, anticipating what he was going to do.

"How are you today, Gloria? Not so good today?" he sighed those last words as he sat down beside me on the couch where I lay. "Not so good," he sighed as he sat and the couch sighed too, "not so good."

"Well, we'll see what we can do." He opened his stiff leather bag that was on the coffee table. "Bah!" the bag opened. Dr. Nathan rummaged his instruments, metal against metal, like spoons and knives, I thought, spoons and knives, and needles.

He took out a needle and did some mysterious things with the needle and a small, clear bottle he stuck with the needle and turned upside down and sucked up all the clear liquid that was going to get me well.

"We'll just give you a shot of penicillin," declared Dr. Nathan.

Mama turned me over and pulled down my pants to show my bare bottom and Dr. Nathan pinched a hunk of feverish pink flesh and stuck the needle in me. This process was repeated every month or so because I was sick a lot. I was glad to see Dr. Nathan. When I saw him that meant I would soon be well.

After the shot, I was better and, under mounds of used tissues, empty tea cups and plates of crumbs, I sat up on the couch and read magazines sent over by the lady across the street, Connie, who, Mama said, "never throws nothin' away." (She should talk. Mama had every bit of paper, every elastic, cork, dried-up pen, pencil stub and blackened eraser she ever owned sticking out of the kitchen drawer that couldn't close.) I ate those glossy magazines with my eyes, devouring those little squares of words around and under the pictures, they were so neatly and beautifully expressed, they lilted with rhythm, but I still couldn't tell what they meant. "Lime, cool and sassy, lemon, sweet and sunny, dress UP for Spring, dump those dreary blacks and browns, let's SWING into Spring! Think fuchsia!" "A serene island getaway awaits you, caressing winds, warm blue waters, your own private lagoon, soft beaches that never end."

"Look," Mama said, smiling secretly, "something came for you."

She read the long, white envelope. It was addressed, simply, "Beatrice." One of the kids had brought it home with my homework.

"Who's that?"

Still a little sick and unsure, I didn't recognize myself. I had forgotten.

Mama opened the envelope and took out one of those long, funny cards that were just invented. On the outside, there was a garish cartoon character that wasn't on any of the real cartoons saying something weird about being sick. On the inside, Mama read, "Thinking of you, Beatrice, Gabriel Landis."

"Gabriel Landis. Well, you have a fan. Who's that?"

What did she mean, a fan? One of those folded things ladies fanned themselves with in the old days? Mr. Landis was the janitor. As soon as Mama said the name, it had a school sound and I knew what it meant.

"Mr. Landis is the janitor," I told her.

"Oh! He likes you!" she beamed.

"He calls me 'Beatrice'," I said.

"Oh!"

"Why does he do that?" I looked down at the crazy card, trying to make heads or tails out of it.

"I don't know," Mama said. "Maybe he likes that name."

I looked at his signature. His handwriting was like a boy's, not very good, the letters cramped and wobbly, as though his hand shook. But, imagine this - he had a first name, Gabriel. The name of an angel! I liked him better after that and I looked for him for the first time when I finally returned to school.

He wasn't there.

He wasn't by the boots, not under the black iron stairwell, not by the noisy boiler, or by his wide janitor broom or his mop and pail of black water. No one knew who he was when I asked about him. I never saw him again.


LOVE CHILD

The specter of the Shinbuck house hung over our kitchen table. We saw it constantly while we ate, looking down at us with the blank eyes of its smashed windows.

"Ma, what's a foster house?"

When did I start calling Mama, "Ma"? Sometime in Revere.

"Where'd you hear that?"

We were eating vinegar peppers and eggs, shaking hand-grated Romano cheese that melted gracefully over the hot, fluffy eggs and peppery pieces, shoveling the meal on to hunks of fresh Italian bread. We often ate together, because Ma said I was the only one who appreciated what she made. Marie, Daddy and especially Jakey, had developed quite a taste for canned stuff, packages and American inventions like peas frozen in a bag or miniature marshmallows, things Ma twisted her face up and called "Junk! Junk!"

"The Shinbuck house!" I pointed to it with my fork. "All the kids say it's a foster house."

"Oh," she said, ominously confirming everything the big boy, Rick had said, "It's called a foster home. That's like where Daddy had to go, where kids go whose parents don't want them."

"What?"

A real fear shook me. I'd never heard of parents not wanting their kids. Daddy had had no parents after his mother, like Jakey's, had died of tuberculosis, his father couldn't take care of him. Suddenly, I was overcome with a big fear, not exactly for myself, but bigger, for the world.

"Some parents don't want their kids?"

"Nope," she cleaned something out of her teeth with her tongue. "They give them away. Oh, sometimes, they're in trouble and they can't take care of them," she added. "Like your Uncle Jake and Rena; they drank." She made a disgusted face.

When she said "in trouble," I pictured the ragged ladies in silent movies struggling to walk against the wind and rain or the snow. What that had to do with drinking, I didn't know.

"Did you want *me?*"

"You! You were my love child! I was madly in love when I had you!"

"You don't love Daddy now?"

"I love him!" she shouted into her dish. "He's a jerk!"


Ma could point to any kid in my class picture and say, "He's Jewish, he's Italian, she's Irish, she's Jewish."

"How can you tell?"

I was amazed! I stared and stared at the familiar faces, but I couldn't see a difference. I only knew who was absent on Jewish holidays and who would appear at Sunday School or mass.

"She's Jewish."

"How do you know?"

Ma shrugged. "He's Italian."

"Yes! How can you tell?"

She wasn't looking at their names, but if she had been, I still wouldn't have known how she knew.

"He's not Italian. What is he?"

I didn't know.

"What's his name?"

"Michael Setlow."

I wrinkled my nose.

"He has Setlow germs."

"Oh. He's Jewish."

"God! How do you do that?"

She laughed heartily at her trick.

"Does he like you?"

"God! No! He smells like garbage! You know, like a burp! And he wears a ton of pencils and pens on a plastic thing in his pocket and behind his ears, and he puts a plastic book rack on his desk to hold his book open."

"Oh, yeah. What's his father do?"

"I don't know," I shrugged.

"If you married him, you could be rich."

I was horrified. Marry Michael Setlow, just to be rich? And how could she tell I'd be rich if I married him?

She pointed to a face.

"What's his father do?"

I shrugged again.

However, by fourth grade, I could answer these questions as fast as Ma could ask them. Jewish, Jewish, Jewish, Italian, Jewish, Italian, Irish, Jewish, Doctor, Doctor, Dentist, Sells cars, Sells jewelry, Sells meat, Sells Insurance, Lawyer, Dentist.

## THE LOVE NOTE

Anthony Salomoni sent me a note. That was new. I'd never had a note before. It was clammy, folded many, many times; each fold was stained black; the lettering that said my name was smeared with pencilly fingerprints. It landed on my desk.

Shelley Werner had passed it. I looked up to see her glaring at me like she could kill me.

Anthony Salomoni was thin and dark; I thought he was one of the cutest boys in school. His black hair was slicked back. His black shoes were pointy. We called that look a Haircut, I don't know why. Haircut meant he was bad. He wore a black leather jacket, but I liked him. His points, his blackness gave me the shivers.

I opened the note.

> *Doll,*
>     *I like you. Do you like me? Write back.*
>         *Tony*

I didn't know anything about notes, but getting one was very exciting. I looked inside my desk for a stray piece of paper. In those days, lifting the lid of your desk was extremely risky and paper was never stray. Every piece was accounted for. I used an old scrap of practice math paper, thin and grey. I tried to make my note just like his, with smeary pencil and fingerprints, but it turned out neat. What did I write? I don't really remember. I must have said, "I like you, too." Then, I folded it a million times, smudging it carefully. I tried to pass it to Shelley Werner, but it fell on the floor.

"Gloria Wisher!" Miss Dunkee cried out. "Was that a note?"

She got up from her chair, scraping it ominously along the wood floor. I watched, fascinated with horror, as she bent over, a long-snouted skeleton in a grey wool suit, and picked up my note. I was suddenly frightened for the little piece of math paper, now emblazoned with a declaration of love, because it was in dangerous, enemy territory, Miss Dunkee's hand.

I looked to Shelley Werner for some show of support, after all, she had passed Anthony's note for him. Her mouth was twisted into a horrid little smile. A chill went through me! Why, she'd dropped the note on purpose! This meanness frightened me more than Miss Dunkee: it was a Nazi thing to do.

Miss Dunkee read the note. As though she had bitten straight into a lemon, she winced. I heard satisfaction and contempt in her voice, as though she had expected such behavior from me, when she said, "Anthony Salomoni and Gloria Wisher, stay after school."

Now our names were joined in public. The class, thrilling with malicious joy, had been informed that our names were now joined. Dunkee had married us in our misbehavior.

I don't know how Anthony Salomoni spent his time. Dunkee wouldn't let us do our homework. We had to just sit. He tried to look at me twice, but Dunkee smashed her ruler down on her desk both times, causing him to turn back. I was determined that she was not going to punish me. Already, she had invaded my privacy, I knew that instinctively. Wasn't it against the law to touch someone else's mail? We'd be taught the U.S. Mail was sacredly private.

If only she could have seen my mind! She would not have been smirking as she leaned like a leafless tree into her huge yellow ledger - what did she write down in that thing? If she'd had, for an instant, the eye of a mother, or a poet or even, a real teacher, she would have seen my rapt expression, round cheeks flushed pink with happiness, eyes too eager to be imprisoned, sunlit hair stirring in the breeze from the open window; she would have known immediately, she would have jumped from her chair and pointed - THAT CHILD IS NOT BEING PUNISHED!

Oh, no! The day was too eager itself - too blue and white, too yellow and wet green. The trees were whispering and the dirty window was open letting in small ocean waves of scent mixed with mud and green stems. Where else would I be? Did I know the secret of flight so I could sit chained to a pen-stabbed, mutilated hulk of desk and an iron seat? If she could have really seen, she would have seen an abandoned desk, an overturned chair. She'd have had to run to the window and look up into the sky. There! There I am! I am holding hands with Peter Pan! What did I want with a real boy? Not earth bound Anthony Salomoni! Oh, if she could have seen! What a disturbing picture we'd have made for her empty bones and her cobweb eyes! Strands of cloud caught in our hair, green vines and the last flowers of summer dripping with dew hanging from our mouths and clinging to our chests. Seagulls accompanied us like angels. Was she blind? Didn't she see my dreamy, orgasmic grin?

Why, she'd given me a gift! She'd invited me to sit and do nothing! She may as well have tried to do something kind! Old Dunkee, when you looked up with your self-satisfied stepmother smile, when you mumbled through your veil of cobwebs, "You may go," didn't you see? Did you have enough energy to be amazed? Didn't you see my quick sink to disappointment? My flight was over too soon! Didn't you notice my sudden, vertical landing; didn't you see the vines and flowers tumbling down over me?

Anthony Salomoni snuck a furtive glance at me as he sulked out of the room. He also hadn't seen me tumble down to earth.


## MISS PLUM NO LONGER

What had happened to my adoration of authority? When authority returned, so did my affection.

Beautiful authority returned in the fifth grade in the form of Miss Plum. Sweet and friendly as the surprising insides of a ripe, soft plum, she had black hair, white skin and heavy, red lips. What was she but a welcome, wet fruit? She had a young bosom! A waist! A round behind to rival Ma's soft melon! And, when she stood in front of us one day, like a movie star shyly, nervously, accepting an award, and spoke in a careful tone, "Class, the next time we meet, I shall no longer be Miss Plum. I shall be Mrs. Love." Well! My heart jumped up to applaud! My eleven-year-old body sat back in the stiff wooden chair and thrilled. Mrs. Love, I repeated to myself, Mrs. Love.

I pictured Mr. Love's tall, dark shape, loving her.


## CAMELOT

A time of Camelot came in the sixth grade with the reign of Mr. Mario Lanza. He was a great, broad man who wore suits and smelled sweetly of aftershave. He was a great king. He was kind and gently stern. His presence in the room commanded everyone's eye and ear, with pleasure. With enormous pleasure, we loved him. He was a great block of a man with rounded edges where corners should be. He had the deep, brown eyes of my Grandpa. He looked like Perry Mason, but when I told Ma his name, she clapped her hands together and gasped, "Oh! Mario Lanza! He played Enrico Caruso in the movie!" She asked if he sang to us. No, Mr. Lanza did not sing to us. If he had been musical, I wouldn't have gotten my first B. But, that is another story.

When Mr. Lanza taught at the Liberty School, we entered a Golden Age during which education flourished and great prosperity was enjoyed throughout the land. By the time Mr. Lanza became the principal, which seemed inevitable, President Kennedy was in The White House and the entire country entered the Golden Age along with us; it was called Camelot, after the President's favorite musical. During this era, the bankers and jewelers, the dentists and doctors, the cleansers and the used car dealers prospered, so that the fashion and hair-dos, the jewelry and cosmetic surgery of their children multiplied also in accordance with their vast fortunes.

Some of us, however, missed this prosperity, though it occurred all around us like a sea that would drown us. Daddy worked three jobs, Ma said, "to keep our heads above water." I pictured myself unable to stay afloat, gulping huge mouthfuls of ocean, trying to calm myself, talk myself into being calm and just float. Of course, as Daddy got more and more jobs, there were more and more jobs he could be fired from, more bosses he could argue with, more promotions he could miss. Daddy was proud. He said he "wouldn't take no shit from nobody, especially no Christ Almighty college piece of shit in a suit with his head up his ass."

My class reflected the marketplace: Isod Lacoste, in the subtle form of a tiny, happy alligator waving its tail was emblazoned on the rainbows of the boys' adolescent chests; the girls were buried up to their sculpted noses and chins in pink and white clouds of mohair, their snug, little bottoms wrapped in pastel wool with knee socks to match; Bass Wejuns, as solid as mahogany, held their perfect feet, and, on gym days, Jack Purcells, dazzlingly white.

I wanted all these. I wanted shiny, new things. At night, I studied my long nose in the bathroom mirror. Daddy's nose, big and bulbous on the tip. What was I doing with his nose on my face? I wanted a "nose job." All the Jewish girls, and one Italian, whose family owned a whole square of Italian marble at St. Anthony's Church with their name carved in it, had nose jobs. They'd gotten nubbin' little noses, Irish noses, Mademoiselle model noses, sculpted like the noses of angels out of the huge blocks of ethnic nose they used to own. I wanted a Breck girl nose. And, a narrow, Natalie Wood forehead: one that just peaked out of lush, dark hair; one that just topped a delicate, ski-jump nose. And dark eyelashes, not the white blonde lashes I had that disappeared and made me look eyeless. To make matters worse, I had the huge, bald forehead of George Washington and the long, noble nose of an aged Roman senator, frightening on the face of a little girl.

Once or twice a year, I got a couple of paper bags from Ma's cousins, Grandma's nieces, Marion and Diane; they were about twenty and they "worked," which, in Ma's language, meant they spent a lot of money on clothes. You wouldn't know it from what was in the bags.

First, I was in the sixth grade, but I dressed like a twenty-year-old woman; second, none of the clothes fit me. I had to roll the skirts at the waist and pin them. These pins were always bursting and sticking into me at school. All the girls at school wore gorgeous pastels and creamy colors. Marion and Diane favored browns. I remember finally getting a mohair sweater, when no one else was wearing them anymore. It was striped with horrid colors, green, orange and, of course, brown, and since most of the fluff had worn off, it reminded me of an old tiger cat that had been in a fight. I hated it. I dreaded getting the bags and looking into them. I hated all the clothes, hated having them on me, on my back, being judged by them, heavy and brown. I knew they were wrong. They had nothing to do with me. But, in time, they did have something to do with me. The oppression of these hand-me-downs, the darkness, the heaviness, that's who I was; that became my character in school, shy, nervous, silent; that's who people saw when they looked at me. I was wrapped in silence.

I wanted braces. All the Jewish girls had them. They spoke with little lisps because their mouths were huge with silver, mouths shining with rows of silver machinery gripping their white teeth, working, even as they sat recumbent in class, working to make them straight, fine, more and more in sync with the Nazi image, the perfect magazine model, the beautiful actress on TV.

I had a crooked tooth. How had I gotten it? Chasing a word, of course!

It happened during a visit to East Boston. How strange the place was! Plywood boards covered the corner store; also the blank face of the men's club, bandaged with plywood; also some of the tenements, boarded and struck across the face by slashes of graffiti, words I'd heard before and whispered to myself, secretly, in my room, just to hear the sound of them.

The White House stood unmolested on the top of the hill.

When we drove up, Uncle Sonny, who was in high school now, had planted a tree in front of the house, but "they" had pulled it up and he stood in front of the house holding half the slender tree in his hand, the little plastic fence he'd put around it dangling from its broken branches.

"They pulled it up," he told us.

Ma and he clicked their tongues at it for a few seconds. Daddy smoked a cigarette, because Grandma didn't allow cigarettes inside.

"Eh, whaddaya gonna do?" Uncle Sonny shrugged, placing the tree gently back into the hole in dirt, patting it down with his foot till the little tree stood again, slightly lopped to one side. Uncle Sonny fixed the white plastic fencing, slightly bent now, to go round the tree again.

We went in. Uncle Vickie was visiting too, with a new boxer dog for Grandma.

Uncle Vickie took one look at me and laughed, with the cigar hanging on his mouth; he didn't care what Grandma allowed, and he said, "Let's call the dog, GiGi, after Gloria!"

I hated having the boxer face, all slobbery and sneezy, named after me, but it was Uncle Vickie, so there was nothing I could do about it. GiGi slobbered her kisses all over my face. She seemed nice, but she wiggled so much I couldn't hug her. While we were there, Uncle Sonny and Uncle Salvi were wrestling on the twin beds and GiGi's head went through the wall. Grandma went crazy and the two boys, two men in a room too small for them, in a house too cramped, busted with laughter at her, tried to hold in their giggles, but their cheeks burst with spit and laughter. I didn't know whether to be horrified or amused. I looked at the gaping hole in the wall, a black hole in the faded, flowered wallpaper. I couldn't imagine this event happening when Grandpa was alive. I didn't remember the boys *EVER* laughing at Grandma when Grandpa was alive! When no one was looking, I went over and put my head in to see what was inside a wall. It was dark and splintery around the edges. I wondered if the darkness went through to the next room.

Later, Uncle Salvi told me I couldn't spell his last name, Grandma's last name, and Grandpa Vic's last name, Buonocorso.

"I can too!" Ha! What a joke! I knew exactly where to find the answer!

"Nah, you don't know how! You're too stupid!"

"I'll betcha!"

"Okay! I'll betcha!"

I ran out front to where the doorbell was with its little nametag underneath.

"B-u-o-n-o-c-o-r-s-o" I memorized as I hopped from one stair to the next, hop-hop, I tried the door, but it was locked! I'd locked myself out! So, I rang the doorbell and hop-hopped, while I waited.

"B-hop-u-hop-o-hop-n-hop" - then my foot slipped and wham! I landed with my bottom front tooth jammed backwards against the edge of the step.

I leaned on the doorbell and screamed.

Grandma opened the door saying, "Who is it?" to a screaming, bloody mouth.

"But, how did you get out here? What happened to you?"

How much ice has been applied to my head? How many times has the world come smack up against my hard head? The time I walked round the corner of Eutaw Street where Mama had told me not to go alone and pow! I walked right into the path of a plug on the end of a wire being swung swack, swack, swack by a boy. The boy was horrified. My eye swelled up so hard, I couldn't see. Two very old girls, maybe fifteen, helped me home. The time I was bouncing outside the house in Revere, bouncing on an old mattress spring taken out of somebody's trash, giving a smug wave to Annette, Rick's sister, see me, see how much fun I'm having, when my foot caught in a spring and I went flying backwards, one of the jutting rocks on the unpaved street pierced my head. Or, bouncing on my cousin's bed in Connecticut, I landed on the floor and my barrette stabbed me in the head. Lots of ice, wailing louder than a siren rushing to the hospital. Only, we didn't rush to the hospital. We piled into somebody's skush-a-bunk, Ma yelling at me all the way for being so stupid, and drove to the Relief Station in East Boston, where moaning, bleeding poor people were treated for free.

This time, we didn't go anywhere. Grandma applied ice to my tooth and chin, and yelled at Uncle Salvi.

"You know better than to send her out there! What are you thinking sending her out there?"

"I didn't send her out there!"

I struggled with the face cloth blocking my speech. Through blood and bent tooth, I won my bet. "B-u-o-n-o-c-o-r-s-o", I grinned triumphantly. Of course, I didn't get anything but satisfaction.

But, now I had a crooked tooth and a legitimate reason for braces. Every time I saw those sparkling cages in the Jewish girls' mouths, I wanted one in mine. I didn't remember any of *them* having crooked teeth.

I asked Ma for braces.

"What do you want those for?"

"I got a crooked tooth," I grimaced, showing it off.

"We can't afford braces! Do you know how much braces cost?"

"No. How much?"

This was interesting. How much did those kids' parents spend on them?

"Thousands of dollars! As much as a house! As much as Daddy and I spent on this house!"

She always said, "as much as a house." I always believed her.

"Whaddya think money grows on trees?"

What a good idea! Money should grow on trees, I thought. But, then, of course, people would strip the trees naked. I hated money because I loved money. I wanted to cover myself with everything money could buy and parade myself in finery in front of everyone who had money and paraded themselves in front of me.

"You can't even see that crooked tooth of yours." Ma said.

"I know," I admitted in a slump.


## WELCOME

We'd hung an awkward sign, WELCOME, over the front door, a tentative banner made out of crayons by two little girls. Jakey had glared at it like he could kill the ones who'd made it and hung it there, like he could slit the throats of all those who welcomed him.

Ma said she loved us all equally. But, Jakey didn't love us, so it was hard for Ma to love him. I know she tried. I could see her trying, for Daddy's sake, it meant so much to him to save Jakey, to have a son and "keep the Wisher name going."

She asked Jakey if he wanted more potatoes - she had made them the way white people make them, mashed, just for him - but he said no, he wouldn't. She washed boys' clothes, strange and bulky, along with girls' socks and panties, plaid pajamas along with flowered, she folded them just as nicely and set them aside for him to put away, which he never did.

She gave us chores. Jakey was terrible at sweeping the floor. He liked to sweep the dirt over my feet and I had a horror of the dirt going over me, soiling my white socks, sifting under them, getting grit between my toes because Jakey had done it to me. He just laughed. He laughed like Rick, whom he spent a lot of time with, though Rick was older. Jakey was Rick's shadow, always watching, always learning. They laughed like Nazis: a secretive, nasty chuckle, like they had plans to do something nasty or were remembering something deliciously terrible they had done. Ma told him to stay away from Rick, even though she was best friends with Rick's mother, Annie, she told Jakey Rick was too old for him; he'd get him into trouble. She couldn't have given Rick a better recommendation.

For a long time, we went every weekend to the Nabby's, so Jakey could visit Peter, but it didn't help. Jakey was lost to Peter now. He wouldn't listen to him. When Peter asked, "How's school? How they treatin' ya?" Jakey shrugged and went off to a corner as soon as he could. It was obvious that Ooda adored Peter and Little Paul worshipped him. They laughed and joked about things we didn't understand. I took the opportunity to eat plenty of white people's food we didn't get at home: greasy, salty potato chips; gooey dip; powdery cheese curls; sweet tonic. But, it wasn't fun.

As soon as we got home, Jakey ran out into the dark light of evening to find Rick. He belonged to Rick.

After we'd all gone to bed, Marie snuck over to my bed and Jakey slipped into the room, in his strange, plaid bathrobe, leather slippers and boys' pajamas, with a brown pattern of cowboys and Indians. He sat on the edge of my bed. He was a strange creature, propped up on an elbow, a boney wrist protruding and weird, thick, boney ankles sticking out the other end of him.

There, in the dark, I told them stories, whatever I knew or could imagine. Peter Rabbit, how he was caught in Mr. MacGregor's garden; "The Bright Red Color," how Ninita and David used the color red to destroy the witch who tried to capture them; "A Dog For My Sister," how Patrick brought his sister's dog back to her; "A Pirate Friend," Jakey's favorite, how Hank followed a trail of gold only to be led to pirates.

Words floated in the dark. Words caught their breath and held it. Words caused their disembodied laughs to echo back to me.

Ma yelled from downstairs.

"What's going on?"

Jakey thought that meant him, that he should go. Immediately, he started to get up.

"Stay!" I grabbed his boney wrist.

He fell back, resting again, ready to listen. And, suddenly, I had power over Ma, over all power, it seemed, because I was telling stories.

My bedroom was deepening like a soul. The more I read there; the more I wrote or studied; the more I cried, face upward on the bed waiting for Daddy to come home so he could smack me with his belt because I'd done something wrong, the more I meditated, lying there, on the cracked plaster shapes in the ceiling: a wrinkled old man, the Lamb of God, The Sacred Heart, The Holy Spirit, an apple, an island, (Sometimes, he was too tired to hit me, sometimes, he didn't think what I'd done was important enough.) the deeper the darkness grew until I could slide into its presence like a black hole in space and time and pull the chamber closed behind me.

I liked letting Marie and Jakey into my bedroom, though I shared the room with Marie, my side was by the window where the pear tree spread its leaves and softened the silhouette of the city of Boston and the oil tanks against the red sky at dusk and the black lace of the Mystic River Bridge, and Marie was by the door, as though she were always about to get out of bed and leave.

Someone suggested I should write the stories down and I did, in a little blue book, an examination book that had been left blank by Uncle Sonny. I printed them, hoping the little examination book would appear more like a real book. I wanted desperately to show my stories to Mr. Lanza.

Mr. Mario Lanza honored me by asking me to stand beside him at his desk in front of the room and read my stories to the class. When I had finished, he asked to see the book. His great brow furrowed and he said, "Gloria, I thought you liked to write cursive. Why have you printed?" I explained and he congratulated me. He reached across his wide desk and finding what he wanted, he fixed a large gold star, larger than any I'd ever seen, to the cover of that blue book.


HICHBORN

Now I was learning about this new world around me. The street began to settle and take shape:

Hichborn Street was broken in half by a four-lane highway that ran along the top of the hill. The two halves of Hichborn fell down each side of the hill, crowned dubiously by the splintered shell of the Shinbuck house. Our side was the short side. It was the only side I knew.

We were a small village, shaking in the arms of highways that raced past us on three sides. On the fourth side, the B&M Railroad trotted along in a parallel line with our street. In fact, all the houses had been built one hundred years before for railroad workers. Ours was the biggest. It had been built for the foreman.

The Wisher house stood in an elite position, big and alone on the odd side of the street, looking down the hill at all the other, smaller houses. A bay window and a wide, open porch with a wide railing - upon which I sat many mornings and afternoons – hung from its dirty white facade, causing the old house to seem much more grand, much more refined, than the others. We were alone under the highway, our backs up against the embankment, rich and dark with growth, a lush backdrop of greenery: wild, rough open land, plus our own yard with two large maples back and front, and a sprawling elm, at the end of our long, sloping lawn, the pear tree gracefully placed in the center. The street was alive with fruit trees and roses, wild lilies and lilac, thorns and milkweed. Our yard ran down the hill beside a thick clump of growth that we called The Bushes. These were a frightening mystery where the bad boys played; I wasn't supposed to go in there. The Bushes rustled with boys and the dangerous games they were up to, hidden in the dark jungle. I tried, but couldn't see into its depths. On either side of our house was more wild land, which everyone on the street assumed belonged to Daddy, but it didn't. Nevertheless, everyone on the street, it was a cliché, "everyone on the street," couldn't shake the image of all that land, The Land, Ma called it, being attached to our big, important house. It remained ours in spirit the whole time we lived there, which was forever, though the highway always threatened. From the day Ma and Daddy bought the house, the state said they would widen the highway and take Hichborn Street with it. They never did.

We shook from the heavy trucks that barreled over our heads and rumbled the house, rattling dishes and vibrating under the soles of our feet. Ma assured me a thousand, thousand times, "No, the trucks won't come crashing into the house."

The crash of the barrel was terrifying. When the truck hit the road, it blasted our ears like a bomb: the explosion hit, rolled, hit, rolled, hit, rolled, and slammed hard over the second bridge, the overpass at the foot of the hill. And the next truck came. Cars whizzed by, screaming little whistles.

I watched them with big eyes.

"Are you sure they won't come flying over that little white fence and come straight in my bedroom window?"

"I'm sure," Ma tried to comfort me.

At night, I shuddered under the covers as each truck hit and rolled. I was sure one would come crashing through the wall behind my headboard.

We were a mile from Logan Airport and the planes came too. They came low, so that their wheels seemed to scrape our roof, their bellies hung huge over our heads and their deafening screech screamed on and on in a rhythm that finally ended in a high-pitched sigh of release from the engine.

The train, which ran behind all the other houses on the even side of the street, was romantically slow. Once in a while, it burst through at a break-neck speed, rattling the house, sweetly blowing its horn with a long, lonesome wail. But most of the time, it rumbled along the tracks, its cars bumping into each other like herded, lowing cattle.

The bad boys played on The Tracks. They ran along them and hopped on the trains for rides. "Tsk," Ma said, "tsk, they're gonna get killed. Killed, they're gonna get! Killed!" Rick and his friends ran in a gang of bad boys, wild boys running along the tracks. They liked to put things on the rails just to see what would happen to them: a penny, a rock, a pipe and - a jackrabbit.

Jakey said to me, "There's jackrabbits down on The Tracks."

"No suh!"

"Yessuh! Come on, I'll show ya!"

He took me down to the end of the street and around the corner, the way to mass, and we stood on the bridge overlooking The Tracks. I expected to see bunnies hopping about.

"Look down there! There he is!"

He was splayed out over the tracks, on his back, his arms and legs lay open. He had armpits and thighs like a human, and big jackrabbit feet that looked like they could wear shoes. His long ears fell backward like hair. He looked like a human boy, lying dead on the tracks.

"They shot him with a BB gun," Jakey told me.

"Who shot him?"

Jakey just grinned.

"Who shot him?"

He shrugged.

"I'm not telling *you!*"

"Why did they shoot him? He looks like a boy!"

"A boy! Get out of here! You're nuts, a boy! Whaddaya gonna cry? I shoulda known you'd cry."

I did have tears in my eyes, but I fought them back, so Jakey would still tell me things. I wished he would tell me everything he did and saw and everything the boys said whenever I wasn't around. They never did or said the same things when I was around like they did when they were off together somewhere like The Tracks or The Bushes or Death Valley. I wished I could be invisible and follow Jakey and Rick and see and hear everything they did.

People threw their trash down on the tracks. Big trash like refrigerators and stoves, mattresses, couches, tires and great chunks of dead fences. Small trash, like crushed beer cans tossed from the highway, gaping old shoes, bottles and bottles and bottles, stinking of stale alcohol, like Daddy's breath when he kissed me.

I could stand on outstretched toes and just see this splayed out body of a jackrabbit, the carcass of this big, wild creature that belonged on the prairie. It belonged to the land of cowboys and Indians, what was it doing here, shot, laid out amongst rusted beer cans and broken bottles, with the dumbfounded face of a bucktoothed boy? Why had it come here to eke out a living, like us, along the short pieces of land caught between highways?

Death Valley was the largest embankment. A deep V cut into the land between highways. It was overgrown with long grey grass tangled with thorns and wild roses, pink as raw meat. Wisteria climbed over the tops of the coarse berry trees; I could see the purple flares of color as we sped by on the highway and strange berries where they hung in poisonous, red bunches. I strained my neck to see into Death Valley where the bad boys disappeared all day. Purple irises beckoned a girl in to the depths; orange day lilies spotted the green jungle like tigers. However, it was clear, the place was surrounded by poison ivy that spiraled round and round the white guardrail, vividly crimson in autumn, shiny green in summer. The mystery was how the boys got past the poison ivy every time, how they kept from getting stung by the swarms of bees and wasps that feasted there.

I wondered, "Why, Jakey? Why is it called 'Death Valley'?"

"I dunno." He wasn't even interested.

Maybe someone, a boy, had died there. I wanted to be kissed there by some romantic boyfriend, someone I imagined to be like the good pirate, Errol Flynn: he would wear one of those billowing white blouses. I could feel him take me in his arms. Of course, the grass was soft in my daydream, not sharp; there was no poison ivy to threaten with its fiery beauty; no Jakey, no Rick.

The boys crossed and re-crossed the tracks; they entered the jungles and emerged from them. They wrote their names under bridges; where the ugly trolls of stories lived, the boys lived too. The bad places, the tracks, the valleys, the corners, the cellars, the crawl spaces under porches - these were owned by boys, simply by virtue of their presence there, by virtue of the acts they performed there, by the many times they carved their names or cravings or rages with knives, by the mud they carried back clinging to the soles of their half-rotted shoes. They allied themselves with the worst places where they staked their claims, where they marked their scents like dogs.

## MUSIC

The benevolent reign of Mr. Lanza was marred only by the treachery of a member of his cabinet, Miss Gutty, the music teacher. Once a week, for our music lesson, we were forced to file across the hall to face the crumbling stone wall, Miss Gutty, who would teach us to sing. Surely, there were stone walls more musical.

She stood erect as a weed frozen in winter. Puckering her dry lips to a round pipe, lips that sometimes stuck because they were frozen, she blew a high-pitched beep, which we were supposed to imitate, ensemble.

We sang out of books.

"Way-o, the sun is setting an' I wanna go home!"

A song about working on a banana boat.

Somehow, this Gutty managed to teach us how to read music, which I loved. The mysterious symbols on the page suddenly became clear and beautiful. You could hear them! You could sing them! Sometimes, Miss Gutty let us choose a song. For months, I'd raised my hand, hoping she would choose me, and one day, she did!

"Beautiful Dreamer," I requested.

She turned up her spotted nose. "That's too difficult."

A flood of hands went up. She chose someone else.

She loved the boys. Her favorite thing was to let Michael Setlow play the piano. She tortured us with this at least twice a month. He only knew one song, the "Boogie-Woogie."

I asked the girl next to me, "What kind of a song is named after snot?"

She giggled. Miss Gutty snapped her stiff back around. Giggling, of course, was not allowed. Fortunately, Gutty couldn't locate it.

Michael Setlow took his seat at the piano bench with his lower lip hanging open and drooling with delight. Then, he began playing the bangy notes for about the thousandth millionth time, drooling happily, looking up occasionally, grunting with happiness. Miss Gutty nodded her approval.

I don't know what came over me, because I truly loved being good. Being good was a voluptuous luxury around truly good people. I never got in trouble with Mr. Lanza. But, suddenly, my usually obedient self began tilting her head from side to side, opening her mouth wide to the music, so that each note seemed to burst out of her little mouth.

Everyone around me broke into laughter, releasing all that Gutty tension they'd held in for so long. Michael Setlow loved it; he didn't care if you made fun of him, he always laughed; he was so lonely, any attention was welcome.

But, Gutty didn't like it. I was scolded in front of the class. I was told my "class participation" grade would be coming down, that it hadn't been real good to begin with, which was funny because I loved to sing, even with the Gutty. And, what was even funnier was, that was probably the only time I actually did participate fully in what was happening in class. On that day, a secret admiration was born in me for the class clown. I began to think they were wonderful to be able to make the whole class laugh, even the teacher sometimes; I began to think they had tremendous courage to go against what they were told to do and do what they wanted instead. I realized the funny kids knew something about life we serious kids would never know, and it wasn't just about laughing. They were simply better at life than we were.

So Gutty gave me my first 'B.' In Music.

Ma said, "A 'B' is good. But, how come? Is Music hard?"

I explained to her what had happened. Ma nodded wisely.

"Yeah, sometimes that's what those old ladies do, they like the boys." Then, she repeated, "A 'B' is good."

Not Mr. Mario Lanza; he frowned in a kingly manner.

"A 'B,' Gloria? I don't understand. I thought you loved music."

"I *do* love music, Mr. Lanza."

His frown deepened, but he said nothing.

The frown of a king told me all I needed to know. That Ma had frowned in exactly the same way, confirmed what I knew. In fact, no matter what mark Miss Gutty had given me, in Mr. Lanza's eyes and in Ma's, I deserved an 'A,' therefore, in my mind, an 'A' is what I had received. I had crossed a Gutty line by being a girl, and again, I had crossed her by being pretty (at least prettier than she was!), and again, by being smart, and again, by being fresh. That was fine, because I loved adversity almost as much as comfort. I was beginning to love rebellion, beginning to feel my little soul rise up in my chest. These women who were not graceful and motherly, soft and generous, they shocked me and I would forever be crossing them. A 'B' is a small scar, but the body was small. My king and my mother had frowned at this wrong. What could be better? Little rebel, little red badge of courage, a little hero wounded, however slightly, in a battle, however small.

## MAGGOTS

I was sitting cross-legged, wrapped in blankets, studying my History book in the Indian Camp. I loved to study outdoors, especially History, which tended to put me to sleep. I loved to flip the pages ahead and gaze at the paintings and artists of each period located at the ends of dark chapters about wars and finance, offering me hope and a little understanding of what people were really thinking. I also liked to go to the library to find the music mentioned at the end of the chapters, listen to it and try to understand the times. There wasn't much available at the Revere Public Library. I found Beethoven's Ninth. Ma was tired of hearing it.

The cold kept me awake. I held in one hand, a steaming cup of coffee, thick with milk, but no sugar, quickly losing its heat to the dry winter air; Ma had to let me drink coffee early because I'd begged her and begged her until she gave me spoonfuls of coffee out of her cup in my milk, the many spoonfuls increasing until I had a true cup of coffee. I was ten.

"There she is," a voice said.

I looked up. How I hated to hear, "There she is." It meant someone was coming, someone who would intrude on my solitary world.

It was Jakey's voice. He had two kids with him. Rick and Annette. My heart started pounding. What were they doing in our yard?

Most kids waited at your gate and asked to come into your yard. Yards were sacred. Kids didn't just walk in. Unless their mother was in your house, that was different. Annie Likus, Rick and Annette's mother was probably in mine. Annie Likus, also known as "Rick's mutha," and called that more frequently than her own name, was a fat woman with a coarse Irish beauty that sat, almost buried, dead center of her fat face. She never dressed. She wore housedresses in summer, vague pants and sweatshirts in winter, hardly different from pajamas. She never brushed her hair or wore make-up. Her shoes were slippers. In summer, I was frightened by her crusty feet; I experienced a real fear whenever I chanced to look at them, that these feet were coming to get me, waiting for me when I got to be Annie Likus' age. Her fat legs were carved with bulging blue veins, she limped and she said I would limp with veins one day. She'd heave herself into a chair and sigh greatly, "Oh, Rosa, my legs today." Annie was fond of telling me things: "Face it, Gloria, (if I wore yellow) yellow's not your color." Her favorite: "You're not gonna be blonde forever, you know, Gloria. One day, your hair'll turn *brown*." Brown. That's what had happened to her red Irish curls and she was furious about it. Or, she'd take one look at me and cry, "Where the hell'd *you* come from? *You* don' look like nobody! You come from the paperboy!" Then, she'd look at Jakey and say, "Oh, now I see who she looks like!" I guess she couldn't see past the blonde hair I and Jakey had; she couldn't see my resemblance to Ma, my large, heavily lidded eyes, Daddy's long nose sitting in the middle of my face. No, she had to say I looked like Jakey, which gave me the creeps. He had blonde hair and blue eyes like Uncle Jake, that's all. I had green eyes! Green, you stupid cow! Over and over, just about every time she saw me, she told me I looked like Jakey and I came from the paperboy.

Annie and Ma were best friends. They spent hours locked up in Annie's car, parked in front of our house or across the street in front of Annie's, smoking cigarettes and talking, dressed in their shapeless housedresses, coats thrown over, clasped tightly against the cold. In summer, they sat in a car oven, glad to be alone. The car would fill up with smoke making our mothers invisible to us. We kids banged on the windows and asked them for stuff. We got into a lot of fights just to get their attention. They ignored us, occasionally rolling down the window to scream, "Whaddya wan'? Jesus Christ can't I get a minute? I can't fart, I can't fart!" Sometimes, I'd just look in at them, at their eyes locked far off, concentrating hard on somebody's tumor or nervous breakdown or adulterous affair I was unaware of and wouldn't think was important, because it came from the boring world of adults.

I couldn't believe Annette and Rick were walking into my yard. Rick and Jakey went right over to the garbage pail. Annette, to my horror, was coming straight toward me, straight toward my Indian Camp! No other kid had ever been in my Indian Camp before! I didn't know anyone I wanted to invite, certainly not Annette.

I got up, dropping the blankets and the History book, but she kept coming.

She was in the Indian Camp!

"Whaddya doin'? What's this?" she asked, looking around at the dishes, the mock campfire and rock seats. She sat on one.

"It's my Indian Camp," I said.

She laughed, "You're kidding, right?"

"No. I live here."

"Yeah, right. What are you, some kind of squaw?"

My back went up! Squaw!

"I'm not a squaw," I told her. "I'm a brave!"

She laughed again. Annette, if you'll pardon the expression, was "my age" which always struck me as ridiculous. She was way below me in school, at least two grades, because she'd stayed back twice. Ma thought we should "play" together since we were "the same age." I hated Annette for her stupidity and her lank red hair, dull and brownish, which seemed another expression of her stupidity, and her coarse face, a smaller version of her mother's, scratched here and there with childish scabs, making her look like she had been gnawed by rats. Annette's favorite game was telling me she could "take" me, and that her sister, Linda, who was Marie's age, could "take" Marie. "Yeah, but can you spell it?" I always thought to myself. Of course, I was too terrified of her to say it out loud. Annette and Linda had that hard skinniness; they had solid, thin bodies that wrapped around your neck or chest like snakes with a power that astonishes as it pulls you down. On the way home from school, I was careful not pass Annette and Linda. I carefully stayed behind and walked slowly. But, they would stop. And wait for me. If Annette saw me carrying a paper, she'd ask, "Whaddya get, Gloria?"

I dreaded that question, but I answered anyway. I was proud of my grade.

"A+."

Fists came down hard on my face. Once she pushed my face into the snowy bushes. I wouldn't fight back. She screamed at me to hit her, and I said, "Jesus wouldn't hit someone like her." I closed my eyes. As my head went down under the pressure of her hand, as my face fell into the soft snow on my forehead and cheeks, icy sticks scratching my lips and nose, my closed eyes traveled neatly into the spaces between the knife-like twigs. I was lucky I wasn't blinded that day. I thanked God every time I thought of it. I had come so close.

"You can't be a brave, you're a girl. Girls are squaws." She looked around, her lip curled like a dog's when it growls.

"I'm not a squaw."

"You ever eat dirt?"

"No. Why would I do that?"

I was shocked. Indians never ate dirt.

"It's good."

She was already scoping the ground for some choice dirt to eat. Having zeroed in on some, she scratched out a handful, brought it up to chest level - was it really going into her mouth? - and began sifting through it, taking out the white pebbles.

Well, weren't those like nuts? Why take them out? Maybe she was one of those fussy eaters who don't like nuts in things.

"Aren't you afraid you'll eat a bug?" I asked, cautiously.

The handful was lifted and shoved into her mouth. She answered, "No," by the side-to-side motion of her head, savoring her black mouthful of dirt that crept out the corners of her mouth like black chocolate. Her teeth were white stones.

"What about worms? Did you ever eat a worm?"

She shrugged and swallowed. She swallowed! Annette had eaten dirt right in front of me! I'd seen it with my own eyes, but I still did not believe it! And, even though she knew I saw her, she still treated me like she was superior. I watched while she looked around for another mouthful.

"Hey, Gloria! Come here!" Jakey called me.

I put down my coffee cup. It was a chance to get Annette out of the Indian Camp. Annette got up too and went over to the garbage pail. I followed, keeping her between me and Rick, who was grinning that Nazi way I didn't like.

"Look in here!" Jakey said, proudly.

The two boys had the iron lid pulled back, exposing the insides of the garbage pail below ground. I'd never looked in there before. Ma always took out the garbage and the garbage man came and took the closed can away.

Annette peered into the hole.

"Ugh! Gross!" Then, she grabbed her brother by the neck, shoved his head into the pail and took off running.

Rick came up laughing and screaming, "I'm gonna kill ya, where the fuck is she?" He scooped up something from the pail and took off after her.

I could hear Annette screaming across the street, "Ugh! Ma! He put maggots down my back!"

"What's maggots?" I asked Jakey.

He was laughing.

"Look in the pail."

I edged closer to the pail and looked in. The stink swept over me. White worms, fat and wet, swarmed over the garbage, over and over each other's slimy little bodies. I felt my legs go all watery and my face grow cold. The worms seemed all mixed up with the stench and the cold creeping over my skin.

"Wha-What are they?" I whispered.

"Maggots," laughed Jakey. He knew something, something else. I could hear it in his voice. What was it?

"How did they get there?" I spoke, almost breathless.

"Ya mutha put 'em in there!"

It was Rick's voice! Behind me! That's what Jakey had known.

Too late, he grabbed me, and my legs gave way from just the thought of what was in his fist held high over my head.

He fell on top of me, grinning, his blue eyes, his scar directly over my own eyes, his damaged eye half-closed. I thought, "He was hit by a truck. His eye fell out and they had to sew it back in. He wasn't right after that. He wasn't right."

He didn't put them down my shirt. It must have been too easy for him.

"Here they are, see?"

He showed me what was in his fist, maggots soiled from his dirty hand. They squirmed free, landing on the grass by my hair.

Were they in my hair? I squirmed too, as if for my life, but Rick wouldn't let me up. Then, he did a strange thing. He pushed himself hard up against me, the zipper part of his dungarees, which felt hard, twice he pushed, hard up against me, and he fell forward so that his face brushed mine. I felt his wet lips on my cheek, which was cold from the frosted air; his lips were warm. He smelled, like all boys, of icy air and earth, of the dirty, wet fur of dogs.

"Gloria!" Ma yelled from the house. "Get up!"

Rick tore off me and ran out of the yard.

Ma was hollering at me.

"What's going on? Whaddaya think you're doin'? That's not nice! Don't ever let him get on top of you like that again!"

I jumped up so fast my head was reeling. Then, I remembered to check my hair for maggots. There were none. I didn't know what Ma was talking about. I hadn't *let* him get on top of me. I was confused.

She was still looking at me, angrily, questioningly, while I stumbled into the Indian Camp and picked up the blankets, the History book, the coffee cup and went into the house. She held the back door open for me. It creaked on its rusty hinges.

"What are you doing studying outside?" she asked more softly.

I wanted to say, "I have to be outside," but I couldn't speak. I didn't know what had happened or what to say. My whole body throbbed with the impact of Rick's upon it.

Jakey had watched the whole thing, pleased as hell.


## THE IMMACULATE CONCEPTION

Marie and I exchanged the long, kerchiefs of lace we wore to church, the mantillas; we made a game of it all the way. The white mantilla was my favorite, but it was small, the black one was bigger. The white made you look like a bride, the black turned you into a widow or you could pretend you were a Spanish lady, that was better. The mantilla you held by the time you got to church, that was the one you wore.

Marie was a beautiful bride. She had big, root beer eyes, a cute, turned-up nose I was jealous of, and full lips, unlike my narrow chicken lips. Her dark skin made her teeth flash white when she laughed. She was a pretty, monkey bride and she liked to laugh.

How many times did I call her, "Stupid!" till she believed me? How many times did I tell her to shut up before she did? I could've brought her up better, if I'd known better - I wish I had.

We walked along a white avenue that ran from the foot of Hichborn Street straight to the Immaculate Conception Church; Winthrop Ave was named for the man who first came there, John Winthrop, but, for a long time, I thought it was named for the white beach, Winthrop Beach. Winthrop Ave was like a beach: sparkling, white concrete, in a white neighborhood, lined with straight white houses, extremely cared-for houses, neat as houses drawn on Hallmark cards. They had window boxes filled with startling red and yellow flowers; they had neat picket fences and neat walkways straight to the front door. They had real American flags on real flagpoles. And green grass cut in perfect squares, exactly like God's handkerchiefs in the poem.

Ma said the Irish lived there: Catholics, who were rich enough to send their kids to the sister school where I only attended Sunday School and rich enough to fix anything in the house that needed fixing and not have to use it broken.

You could see the tall, white church from far down the straight avenue. The Immaculate Conception Church. I had no idea what Immaculate Conception meant. Nevertheless, we walked toward it every week without knowing what its name meant, it was some adult big-word mystery, a conglomerate of concepts, like the President, the Government, the FBI, Wall Street, Cold War, Communism, Russia, Mortal Sin, Excommunication, it meant unknown things, it hovered like dark confusing clouds and determined our path. The church loomed ahead of us, getting bigger and bigger as we got closer and closer.

Week after week, we approached, sometimes trembling with guilt and fear and filled with sin as we walked to confession on late Saturday afternoons. We opened the monumental carved doors, which creaked with sanctity, crossed ourselves with holy water, thick, from the oils of many hands, (I thought it was thickened from having been blessed.) crept down the rich, rich caramel staircase, the wood permeated with incense and fear, to the confessionals. We slid on to the pew, worn smooth by the worry of so many sinners, their bodies polishing, polishing, punishing the wood, sliding toward the rich curtain with a yawning priest behind it, sliding closer as each sinner dropped to his fate.

Sometimes, you could hear them confess! "Bless me, Father, for I have sinned. It's been one week since my last confession. I had base thoughts," we heard spoken in a stranger's voice, an adult! Woman or man? A titter passed nervously down the pew; to cover the sound of the rest of the confession, we laughed. Our hands flew to cover our mouths, to cover our own sins.

On the stained glass windows, Adam and Eve stood naked except for vines, the Tree of Knowledge between them entwined with the snake, all forming an arch pointing to heaven. The sufferings and the ecstasies of Jesus, told in The Stations of the Cross, where we knelt during the Novena. The vibrant colors! The deep blue of our Lady, the calming blue of peace, the scarlet robe of Mary Magdalene, the whore. I was sure, such a loving man as Jesus must have fallen in love with Mary Magdalene, the woman who washed his feet, and dried them with her hair.

You could hear the boys shout from outside; you couldn't see them, you couldn't see out but you wished you were out there shouting with them. You wished you were a boy outside shouting wildly, blindly, while the meek confessed. While the people inside slid along the pew and dropped off and you got closer, you wanted to run out and howl in the cold, fresh air and the warm, sweet sun and the smell, you wished you could smell, too, of dirty dog fur and laugh from your gut like a boy at the idea of sin.

At mass, Marie and I saved a place on the pew for Jakey. He showed up just before the blessing, puffing with fresh air, he slid in beside us, grinning secretly, as if to say, "You don't know what you're missing."

The mass was beautiful then. The choir sang, "Sanctus, Sanctus, Sanctus, Dominus Deus Sabaoth. Pleni sunt coeli et terra gloria tua. Osanna in excelsis." The altar boy chimed the bell and ministered to the priest, golden plates and golden cups. The priests folded the lace. We knelt and prayed to the disembodied voices of the choir. No one dared turn his head to look! If one of the Sisters, lined up in the back rows, saw someone turn around in mass, it was mentioned later in Sunday School. The choir's voices carried us, carried me, through my prayers. How I loved the singing! But, I didn't dare turn my head to see whose voice it was. They sang in the dead language, Latin. It was dead, nobody spoke it but priests in mass and prep school boys in exclusive schools; doctors, who said the names of diseases and drugs and the unknown, unseen parts of the body and experts in the unpronounceable names of flowers, insects and animals.

We fell to our knees, on the wine velvet stools, and beat our chests, "Mea culpa, mea culpa, through my most grievous fault." We rose to our feet and flew on the wings of soprano voices, "Gloria in excelsis Deo!" Shivers engulfed my back, tingling up my neck, traveling through my hair, "Gloria! Gloria!" It must mean something, I thought, shivering that my name was sung by angels!

When the collection basket came around, Marie shyly handed me her sweaty dime to put in with the dime Ma had given me. Jakey pretended to put in his dime, but instead, he pulled a dollar out of the basket and shoved it so quickly into his pocket, no one saw what he'd done but me. I think I turned completely white. Jakey grinned.

How had he stolen from God? Did he think he'd get away with that? I remember asking Ma, "Who gives a dollar to the collection?"

"Ha! Rich people!"

They must be rich, I thought, to give a dollar away like that. And, now, Jakey had stolen from God. I knew I would never tell anyone.

The Gospel was my favorite part, next to what I thought were the gorgeous voices of the choir, because the priest told a true story about Jesus and then, explained what it meant to us in our lives. Before that, he gave a list of notices, which I thought were incredibly boring and totally irrelevant. After that came the beautiful Communion: the bells, the incense, the sweet, airy taste of the wafer which was the body and blood of Jesus; the serene holiness of going to the altar in frightened anticipation of receiving the Son of God in your mouth, and then, returning on shaking legs with Christ melting on your tongue, burning in your nostrils.

After mass, Jakey took us over to Tony Roma's, the store on the corner across from the church. Revere High School stood across the street on a hillock of black tar. The building was worrisome, a big brick square; it waited for me.

Father Corro came out of the rectory without his coat and stood on the corner smoking a cigar with the big boys, as big as men, who hadn't graduated high school, but stood there, in front of Tony Roma's every day, smoking, hollering at their friends, stopping cars going by, leaning on the open window, talking to the guys inside, or, just standing all day gazing over at the High School as though wishing to get back in.

Tony Roma fed the High School: subs, Cokes, chocolate chip cookies, potato chips. Kids could buy cigarettes there, and candy. On Sunday mornings after mass, you couldn't get another body inside, but Jakey was going to try to squeeze in three. My heart was already banging around in my chest at the idea of going inside. The noise was crazy, even outside the door. I hated seeing Father Corro out there with those older boys. I was terrified to see him there. We should have been going home to dinner, that's where we should have been going. The warm scent of Ma's sauce struck me full in the face in my imagination and I yearned for its loving presence on my tongue.

"I can't believe you've never been in here!" he bellowed over his shoulder at us.

Jakey pushed through the crowd falling out the open front door, smoking on the steps. I held Marie by the hand with two of my own. Her eyes were very large, her palms poured sweat into mine; I knew how scared she was. It was a problem she had, more severe than most people. She was very ashamed of it and that made her sweat more.

Nobody let us by. Jakey was ahead, so I pushed a little and the bodies parted some, but closed behind me, so that Marie and I were nearly smothered by the coats of people shoved up against our faces and pressed there. The smoke was blinding, I could only see the backside of coats and if I looked down, the slushy shoes and muddy floor. The heat was intense, like the blast from the oven when Ma opens the door to peak in.

We inched our way forward, keeping Jakey's dark blonde crew cut in my view. He was calling to his friends. He waved; a lighted cigarette was in his hand! Women, young women, high school girls, sat cross-legged on the barstools, smoking, turned outward, away from the counter, their coats were open and their breasts stuck out of tight sweaters tucked into tight skirts, sashed with thick leather belts. Their hair didn't look real. One of them laughed, a deep guttural laugh, dangerous, I was afraid of her because of the way she laughed: she was tough.

The scream of noise was steady; it was a roar. But, every now and then, we heard a single, distinctive voice, maybe Tony Roma's, screaming, "What the hell'dya wan'?" or a huge laugh from someone or a high pitched squeal.

I sweated into my coat and hat. Marie's hand slipped from mine, but I managed to clasp it again. Jakey was at the penny candy counter. I squirmed my way up there in desperation to get by his side. Strange, I struggled to get to him, this boy I loved only with doubt and fear. Someone stepped on Marie's foot and she let out a wail. Her mouth opened wide. She had a black heel print across her little white boot.

People started and turned round looking and looking for the source of this new noise. When they saw her, they laughed. A woman looked down, "Aw! What's the matter? Aw! She's so cute!" Then, she turned back to her friends.

Marie wailed and wailed, till my eyes stung and I wanted to cry too, I didn't think I could take any more of it, then she sniffed a couple of times and stopped.

Plenty of kids my size were already pressed against the grimy glass of the case, their Sunday clothes all askew. The reds and greens of the candies looked dirty through the dirty glass.

"Whaddaya wan'?" yelled Tony Roma.

All the kids hollered at once, it seemed, yet somehow, he understood them, and handed them candies, snatching the money from them, dropping it behind him, in a can, I thought, I could hear the clink, clink, and yelling back at them, "Whaddaya wan'?" Then, Tony Roma, with his fierce black eyebrows look right at me and screamed, "Whaddaya wan'?"

Jakey turned to me, "Tell him."

"I don't have any money," I said, "I gave it in the collection."

"Suck-er!" Jakey laughed.

He pulled out several dollars. My eyes bulged out of my head. There was a miracle! How had he changed one dollar into so many?

"So, whaddaya wan', come on," Jakey slurped his words, I suddenly realized, like his father used to do.

The idea of picking out candy without warning confused me. I was being pushed and bullied by elbows and knees and feet and Marie looked like she was about to cry again.

"Aw, come on!"

Jakey turned around in disgust and ordered a bunch of stuff that he liked. Then, he shoved his way out so fast I could hardly keep up with him. The cold air blew right through my soggy clothes. It felt good at first, but almost immediately, I felt like I was dressed in ice.

"So," Jakey said, handing us globs of red licorice, tossing nonpareils into our hands like showering coins, "What did you think of Tony Roma's?"

My heart still pounding, I said, "I hated it."

Jakey threw back his hand and laughed thoroughly, sucking on a licorice whip, cramming the whole long thing into his mouth at once.

Marie's face was already smeared with chocolate and little white grains of sugar. We started walking home, together, which was kind of nice, until Jakey saw Rick Likus and ran off and that scared me, it always did.

I took a bite of licorice. It was damp from Jakey's fist. Faintly, it tasted of smoke and dirty hands and some kind of metal, I thought. But, it wasn't metal. It was the flat, chrome taste of my fear.


RULES

"How come you don't go to church, Daddy?"

I asked his slicked down head as it hovered over an open paperback, *Love and Mutiny*. He was busy, unconsciously filling an ashtray with the little bent corpses of a hundred cigarettes.

"Wha'?"

His attention was taken by fictional captains and the heaving breasts of sluts at sea.

"Why don't you ever go to church?"

"Aw, it's been too long."

Back to his book.

I thought a moment. I was a devout student of my catechism as well as my grammar. I spent many an afternoon pacing my bedroom, absorbing the rules of religion and grammar. Neither made any sense. These were not the kind of rules you could learn by knowing the reason why or how it worked;

these were arbitrary rules, it was so because the book said so, that's all. You had to learn them cold, by rote. I walked back and forth, back and forth, in my room, repeating to myself, "Thou shalt not kill," "Thou shalt not commit adultery," "Thou shalt not covet they neighbor's wife," "Thou shalt honor thy father and mother," "The subject of a sentence can be a noun or a pronoun", "An adverb modifies an adjective, verb or another adverb," "An adjective modifies a noun," "A pronoun takes the place of a noun." Of course, I knew what "Thou shalt not kill" meant, but the chances of my being tempted to kill someone were so remote, learning the commandment seemed far removed from my world. I learned it anyway, and devotedly. It was a matter of pride to me that I could recite these rules impeccably, not only to Sister, but also to Mr. Lanza. But, what the heck "coveting thy neighbor's wife" was, nobody I asked seemed to know, not even Ma, and asking Sister was ABSOLUTELY OUT OF THE QUESTION, which meant, on some level, I must have suspected its meaning had something to do with sex. I had about as much understanding of the rules of grammar, which was a shadowy, intuitive, half-faithful, half-apathetic understanding of rules I must follow whether I understood them or not.

One of the elements of Catholicism we learned in Sunday School is that you can always return to the Catholic Church. Theoretically, all you have to do is confess, or even, have contrition in your heart, and God would rejoice to take you back. Of course, this was before I had anything more to confess than being mean to my sister and I had no idea what sins Daddy might be guilty of, or why he might not want to go back to the loving arms of Christ, if ever he had been there, and I assumed he had, at least once, when his beatific mother had held him in her caress at birth and had looked down upon him with hope and adoration and named him, "William."

So, I said to Daddy, "Why don't you just go to Confession! God will forgive you! You can always go back to Church!"

It took him a while to realize I was still talking to him. He looked up slowly from his paperback, which had half the cover ripped off, the lady's head was gone, just her breasts remained.

"Wha'?" His teeth were rotting, I noticed, in the front, they were yellowing, like Uncle Jake's had always been.

He jerked his stubbly chin toward the highway, which was slamming by behind my head, "Go play in front of a nice, shiny Cadillac."

He went back to his book.

Daddy worked three jobs sometimes; he wasn't home a lot. Ma kept his dinner warm and he hardly ate any of it, the mounds of food were cold in the middle and crusted around the edges when he got it, though, when we'd had the meal, it had been fresh and steaming, buttery and divine. Often, he put his head down and fell asleep long before the last bite of food had passed his lips. The television would still be blaring some game show and he'd be snoring right along with it.

Sometimes, just for fun, Jakey or I would jostle one another and say, "Watch this!"

While he was still awake, one of us would ask, "Hey, Daddy! How old am I?"

"I dunno, what? Ten?"

"Ha, ha, ha! I'm nine! How old is Marie?"

(Jakey and I were nine months apart. This boggled everybody's mind. Better than that, for three months of the year, we were the same age.)

"Get the hell outta here!"

"What's my middle name?"

"Get outta here! Go play in traffic!"

He was hoping, he told us, that we'd get hit by a pretty nice car so he could sue the owner. It was supposed to be a joke.

Daddy never went to church. Ma never went to church, not since Marie was born. On Hichborn Street, on a Sunday morning, all the adults met outside. If the weather was summery and warm, they gathered up lawn chairs and set them side by side on the pavement, or, in the street, as hardly any cars went by. On cold days, Daddy visited each house, house by house, till Ma said he "couldn't see straight." Once, when Daddy was trying to teach me how to ride a bike, it was Sunday and they were all out there. I fell and Annie Likus let out such a laugh, I got up and vowed never to get back on that bike again. Never.

But, I did get back on, days later, when the street was silent and almost dark. I started at the bottom of the hill and inched my way up, cautiously, it took me weeks, till I could fly straight down from the top.

That was why I wouldn't ride, not because bikes were too fast. I just - I didn't want to ride with the other kids, or have anyone see me. I didn't trust them. I always waited till the street was empty. I just wanted to ride alone.

There were times, when no one was around and the street was mine, it was eerily beautiful, especially in autumn, when the air was wet and cold: the sky went dark, the leaves crumbled and the wild things hung crazily from the trees, weeds cracked in the wind, the berries turned black and hard, the Chinese lanterns glowed orange by the crumbling corner of the foundation of our house, the silver dollars swished their silvery skins against the broken stone. Then, it seemed, the street was mine: it whispered my name in the hush of swirling leaves; it drew my portrait with flowers, twisted and stripped naked.

I rode my bike when no one was around. Or, I sat in the Indian Camp and simply looked and loved.

Sometimes the street broke my heart with its ugly beauty.

## THE BLACK ITALIAN

The nuns of the Immaculate Conception Church lived in the pee yellow brick convent across the street from the pretty white church and the elegant white mansion, which housed the priests. It puzzled me that the nuns had the ugly building; it seemed to me, the nuns should've had the prettiest place to live and the priests should've taken the ugly, blank faced yellow brick. It was as if the women were shut up, shut away from the world and as if the priests were meant to be open and take part. The "rectory," Ma called their beautiful, white house. "Rectory" sounded a lot like rectum. That confused me too. What did rectory have to do with rectum? I looked both words up in the dictionary – *Latin, rectus, meaning straight; ruler, governor, director, guide.* The *rector* was supposed to guide us in a straight direction.

What did the nuns *do* in that pee yellow building with the teensy tiny windows up high over their heads so you couldn't see in, not a lamp or a table or a lady's face at the window? Did the sisters ever take off their long, black veils and crisp, white hoods?

Were they bald underneath?

"No! They're not bald!" Ma laughed into her oily dishwater. "They used to be! But not any more. They don't shave their heads any more."

"Is their hair long, then?" I inquired. This long hair was vital to me, to my sense of identity and womanhood.

"No! They cut their hair short!"

"How short? Like a man's?"

Did they all look like men underneath? Some looked like men from the front! Some had moustaches and a hairy mole, like Sister Benedictus! Some were stunningly beautiful, and I couldn't decide, was a beautiful nun more frightening or more holy than an ugly nun?

Ma lost patience with my questions, most of which I didn't even ask her.

"I don't know!" she yelled, finally, her hands dripping with dishwater.

Who cut their hair? Men? Did the priests cut their hair? Did they cut their own hair? Did Mother Superior cut their hair? Was she superior to all mothers? Did she do it? Don't tell me they went to the hairdresser! No, don't tell me that.

A hairdresser was too thin, too electric, too linoleum, too plastic, when I could envision a cruel Mother Superior visiting each cell in turn, by candle light down a thick, caramel corridor of carved, sacred wood, hushed with the whispers of frightened, young nuns, whimpering voluptuously over the loss of their hair.

Sister Benedictus pointed her finger from out her long, black, bell sleeve of doom, a black sleeve like Death's, knowing full well she spoke to the terrorized children of immigrants who feared God and but were too poor to go to sister school, who knew, one day, they'd be going to the horrid place she pointed to, the red brick box across the street, Revere High School.

"There!" she warned, "There, is where the Devil goes to school!"

She was ugly as a man, which meant she was justly, a nun. If a nun was beautiful, and, perhaps, you would see one in your lifetime whose features cast a light of their own from beneath the starched white hood and black veil, we would say, in unison, "What a waste!" But, Sister Benedictus was ugly and we were comfortable with her coarse nose and hairy lip because she was so mean and it was no waste that she was a nun.

We believed her, of course, about the High School. Rick Likus went there. Blankly, the old brick building looked back at us with the face of a decrepit old man. Its broken old windows stared ahead, the crumbling window shades hung by a thread like tired old eyelids, the Devil's own handwriting slashed across his weathered cheeks. Was Rick Likus the Devil? I could still feel the weight of his body on mine. I shivered, not unpleasantly, and an evil ounce of me began to look forward to the High School.

After all, Johnny Strummer went to the High School. He drove his own car and brought home a new girl every afternoon. Johnny was slender, graceful and tall, he played basketball and hockey and ran track, whatever that meant, but I did know it meant he was fast and strong and very beautiful, with blonde hair always falling in his blue eyes. He called me, "Bleachie!" teasing me that I'd bleached my hair blonde. But he said it in a way that meant he knew that I was naturally blonde. He winked and smiled down at me. He crouched down, sitting on his heels, or sat on the porch steps with us, if he had a minute. We all came running down the hill the second his Volkswagen bug puttered round the corner, all of us about an inch high, surrounding him, a giant.

Even Johnny's old dog, Sam got up from the middle of the street and ever so slowly strolled over to Johnny. Nothing and no one could ever coax Sam to move. Sam spent the entire day sleeping in the middle of the street, the cars made painfully slow arches around him. Sometimes, a bunch of us would holler at him to try to get him away from danger, but he wouldn't budge. Sam made his way painfully over to Johnny, just as happy as we were to see him. He nuzzled his gooey, sandy snout in Johnny's outstretched hand, "Sam, good boy."

I remember sitting next to Johnny on his porch and he told me I was a hairy ape when he saw the blonde fuzz on my legs and I went right home and cried and shaved my legs for the first time till Ma caught me and made me stop. But, I knew he wasn't trying to be mean. He had a kind way of saying things. He was just older, that's all. The older girls loved him. I dreamed about marrying Johnny Strummer, but I always knew it was just a dream. Sometimes, when I played about Robin Hood capturing me, I made Johnny Strummer one of the band of outlaws, but it really didn't feel good, because I knew he'd just laugh.

Johnny had an Uncle John who came and went from the house frequently, but didn't live there. Uncle John came to visit Johnny's pretty mother, Celia, who worked nights as a nurse. Uncle John never shaved, but he must have shaved sometime, because he always had stubbles and not a beard. Ma told me to stay away from there because the Uncle sat on the porch steps and drank, and when he did, Sam always sat next to him, not in the street. Sometimes, I thought Sam was waiting for Uncle John when he sprawled like that in the middle of the street. I asked Johnny, once, if Uncle John was his father. He said, "No, silly, he's my uncle, except he's not really my uncle. I just call him that." "Where's your father?" I asked. "I don' have a father," he shrugged, then he ruffled my hair and called me, "Bleachie." I loved him. Johnny Strummer had a great apple tree and I could never stay away from that; I had to climb it before the apples were ripe and steal as many as I could while they were still green. There was a perverse kind of challenge in it, I wasn't supposed to, the apples weren't ready to eat but I ate them, and it made sweet tempered Johnny Strummer furious with me. I suppose I got back at him that way for being so marvelous and inaccessible.

Tim Duffy went to the High School also. His house was the best on the street, the only one that was "kept up" as Mama explained it. The Duffys had money she said, they could buy a plant to hang by the front door if they wanted to, and a porch swing and keep a light on over the gate all night. His parents were teachers, possibly the most intelligent people on the street. In fact we wondered what a family like that was doing on the street at all. Tim Duffy made me a bow and arrow for my Indian Camp. He made it just the way I would have; in fact, I copied it and made another just for the fun of making one. He used a bendable branch and a tight string tied round and round and caught on notches on the tips. He made real arrows, too, out of smooth sticks. He put a smooth notch on one end and a point on the other. He didn't put feathers on them, but I didn't care. I was overjoyed, but too shy to hug and kiss him like I wanted to. That was during the brief time he and Jakey spent together as friends. Too bad, Tim might have been a good influence on Jakey; he did his homework and got all A's. But, more than likely, Jakey would've wound up getting Tim killed somehow. Tim was weak and blonde, like me; he wore glasses and I still have a fondness for boys with glasses because of him.

Yet, the goodness of Johnny Strummer and Tim Duffy could not outweigh the fear Sister had put in us, our fear of what could happen, what might happen in that red brick box. She told us we should learn our catechism to save ourselves from evil, from temptation and from the degradation that would surely stalk us there.

I paced the cracked linoleum floor of my room like a true Christian soldier carrying my weapon on my shoulder, the word of God, which, with each step, I committed to memory as armor against evil. If Rick Likus tried to hurt me, I would know my catechism. If the Communists came marching down the street, I was ready.

In Sunday School, I recited flawlessly. A curly blonde angel, a white faced dove, I stood by my desk - actually, I stood by the desk of someone who really went to school there - and bravely repeated the word of God, believing in my heart that if I did well, Sister Benedictus would *have* to approve of me and if she did, I would be saved.

There was a prize, for attendance, not for reciting and I watched while someone else won it, a lovely statue of the Madonna, small enough to hold in your hand, like the one in Nona's garden, just like the tall one outside of the church, with her hands outstretched in supplication of peace, her robes, blue and white. You had to have perfect attendance and I was always sick. How I wished the prize had been for perfect recitation, then I might have had a chance.

Phillip Nerone watched me as the prize went to another girl. When he caught my eye, he smiled at me so sweetly, I felt the warm rush of his affection, the warm, beatific softness of his gaze that put to shame all the beatitudes of the saints themselves looking down from pictures and statues, I felt it flowing over me, my face, my shoulders, down my back. His deep black face and short wavy hair. His black, dewy eyes. He smiled at me for years, every Sunday, and his smiles blessed me.

When I told Ma about him, she wrinkled up her nose.

"Nerone!" she said. "He's Sicilian! That's a black Italian!"

What did that mean to me? What did his darkness matter to me? After all, he didn't mind my light. I drank in his holy, gentle smile every Sunday; I looked for it with real need, to erase the fear planted by Sister Benedictus, and always, he gave it. Phillip Nerone was a deep comfort to me. Not even the Christ child could have smiled so lovingly.

## A FATHER WHO CALLED, "HONEY, I'M HOME!"

One morning, Mr. Lanza sent Rita LaRosa out of the room on an errand. As soon as the door closed behind her small, thin body, her short, black hair that hugged her narrow skull, her nose and black-framed eyeglasses which were the largest parts of her, Mr. Lanza folded his big, square hands in front of him and sighed.

"Boys and girls, the reason I sent Rita out of the room for a moment is because her dog died last night. Rita loved her dog very much. She is very sad, so we must all try to be especially kind to Rita today."

I was stunned by this speech. Since I had no intention of being anything but kind to Rita, I thought instead about Mr. Lanza.

I wondered if he had any children. I thought he must be a wonderful father to them, as he was to us. I couldn't imagine my Daddy making a speech like that. I marveled at the idea of having a father who wore a clean white shirt, a suit and a tie every day and actually looked like he belonged in a suit, unlike Daddy who looked terribly uncomfortable and messy whenever somebody died or got married and he pulled out his only suit and grouched until he could get it off. I tried to imagine a house with real furniture and real pictures on the wall, and a father who called, "Honey, I'm home!" Daddy always said, "Here I am, you lucky, lucky people!" And, this father would put his briefcase down and a mother would skip out to greet him wearing a dress and pearls. Imagine, I thought, a father who smelled of aftershave, not machine oil. A father who was smooth-shaven, not rough. A father whose fingernails were clean and white tipped, not black and cracked and caked with grease. A father who spoke in sentences, not grunts, who never told a dirty joke about females stinking between their legs. A father who never scratched his crotch in front of you. Imagine, a father who folded his clothes and put them away, who didn't drop them, reeking of range oil on the kitchen floor for Mama to run and pick up, whose shoes were polished, not dull and filled with jungle rot. A father who never spit green and left globs of it in the sink! But, most of all, imagine a father who knew your age and name and reached over to kiss you on the cheek or pat your head out of love and affection?

One day, Mr. Mario Lanza's usually calm face was grey with pain. He gathered us around him again, simply by asking for our attention. Thirty-five eager pairs of eyes looked to him.

He began.

"Last night, when Mr. Lanza was driving his car, the road was dark and Mr. Lanza didn't see" - he took a deep breath - "Mr. Lanza could not stop in time."

He began again.

"Last night, Mr. Lanza killed an old woman with his car. I couldn't be more sad or sorry. I wish I had seen the old lady, I wish - I could have - stopped.

"Mr. Lanza may lose his license because of this sad accident, I don't know yet. The court will decide. I wanted you to know about this, class."

Can I tell you how much I loved him at that moment? That my eleven-year-old body filled with tears? An old lady was dead and I cared only for his sorrow. He was never the same after that day. The next year, he became principal with the sad calm and grey face that never left him. I would have given my right leg and hobbled, gratefully, for the rest of my life to have been his child, to have been different, to have been born with nice blood in my veins, and not my own.


MONEY

"Gloria," Ma said, "I'm going back to work."

A stone fell on my universe.

I was sitting at the kitchen table doing my homework, when something as big as one of the planes that screamed over our heads, dropped, fell through the roof, fell through without breaking or smashing anything, but my entire world of school, church, books, Indian Camp and street shifted on its axis. Was Mama the axis?

"Why?" I asked, about to cry.

"We need the money," she spoke flatly, her mouth gripped tightly in disgust.

"Why? What do we need money for?"

"Ha!"

I couldn't understand this concept of not having any money and living just fine and still needing money to live.

"Will you be here when I get home from school?"

"Nope."

"Will you be here in the morning?"

"Oh, yeah. I'll be here in the morning, but I'll leave before you. I'll take the bus."

What was *that* going to be like - coming home to an empty house, a house without Mama?

"I got a job."

"Already?"

It seemed like she'd gotten a job while we were talking.

"Yup," still, the disgusted, tight line of her mouth. "It's in a sportswear shop in East Boston. I'll be a stitcher. You know, what they used to call 'operators'?"

Of course, all the Italians turned to East Boston, like turning to the nearest Italy, in any time of need. If Mama needed curtains, she went to East Boston for them. We lived in Revere because it was the closest country to Grandma and East Boston.

"Sometimes, my boss will pick me up at the top of the hill, but, the rest of the time, I'll have to take the bus."

Her voice gripped hard on determination and disgust.

Another day, I came downstairs to find her staring out the living room window, which looked down the street, at the black arm of the Mystic River Bridge reaching over a city of oil tanks, the ghostly skyline of Boston in the distance.

Her back was to me and I hopped around the front of her about to shout, "What're you looking at?" when I saw she was crying.

She looked old. My heart fell. Tears dripped down her cheeks. At her chin, they shivered a moment, then dropped off. Her thin lips trembled. They were white.

I was frightened that she could suddenly get so old! Dry lines collected around her beautiful eyes, bags of flesh thickened under her once laughing eyes. How could she have gotten so old so quickly? How could she? I felt she was a traitor to herself and to me! I would never do such a thing! I would never get so old! I was so frightened that she was crying.

"What's the matter? What are you crying about?" I gasped.

She continued to stare out the window.

"Money."

Money! I hated money. I wished I had some, I'd give it all to her! Even then, I knew she wasn't crying about money, not really. She was crying about Daddy. I can hear her yelling, "He spends it all in the barroom! The barroom!"

No matter what she was crying about, Mama was crying. There, at the same window where I would watch her over and over, a thousand days since, her grim, disgusted form walking short-legged down the street, on rainy days, the pleated, plastic rain hat on her head, a fat vinyl pocketbook on one arm, another bag, too, for her lunch, always a chunky Italian sandwich, her work sweater and, in winter, her shoes, to replace her boots.

My heart broke as the bus stopped and opened its doors for her. I watched her disappear into its bulk, I saw the silhouette of the bus driver - he didn't care about her! My heart cried out as the folding doors flattened behind her. She was caught inside! The great bulk lurched forward and took her away.

"Mama! Come back!" I cried. "Come back! Don't leave me alone!"

## OODA AND LOLA

Ooda came for a while to babysit every day until Ma came home at 4:00, but then, she stopped coming. Then, I was in charge, which was a joke as far as Jakey was concerned.

When Ooda came, it was fun. We watched her coming up the street, from the same window I watched Ma go. You couldn't see her for a while because of the trees clumped together at the corner, but then, she'd come into view and we'd shout, "There she is!" and rush out to greet her.

She had grown to be so pretty and slim. By now, we knew it was good to be skinny, now we knew that *we* were wrong because we were fat. Ooda had beautiful blonde hair that stood in a perfect flip at the ends, like Shelley Fabares on "The Donna Reed Show," or like Sandra Dee in the movies. Sometimes she brought her girlfriend, Lola, who was dark as an island girl with long, black hair that fell to her waist. Together, they were night and day, civilization and paradise. We ran out to meet them, falling all over each other to be first; we knew they were all the things we wanted to be.

The girls wore matching sweater sets: A-line skirts that skimmed their tiny behinds, soft sweaters covering the pointed bumps of their neat breasts, another soft, matching sweater with pearly buttons open over their slim shoulders. Their boney ankles slid around inside their nylons, their boney knees pointed as they walked. They carried transistor radios tuned to the same station, tucked neatly a top their wallets, held in their slender hands like a small package.

Johnny Strummer went a little crazy when Ooda and Lola came up the street. It was a sight to behold: Johnny Strummer dashing out of *his* house. We watched from the porch as they stood together and talked in a little group, under the basketball net nailed to the tree in front of Johnny's house. This casual meeting of demi-gods fascinated Marie and me. When the girls finally arrived at our house, we shouted, "What did he say? What did he say?" "Oh," Ooda replied, "We just talked." Just talked! How I would've loved to be a teenager and "just talk" to Johnny if he came running out of the house to see *me!*

Ooda and Lola could sing any song on the radio by The Supremes, The Shirelles, The Temptations, Frankie Valli and The Four Seasons, any group! They knew all the words. They taught me and Marie how to sing "The Name Game." "Banana-fanna-ro-ramma-fi-fi-fo-ramma-the-name-game!" It took a long time to learn, as hard as catechism, but I finally got it. Ma wouldn't let me sing it; she hated it. But *she* sang, "I-yi-yi-yi-yi-yi- I love you! I-yi-yi-yi-yi- I think you're swell!" all around the house, dancing like Carmen Miranda. Daddy thought he was Bing Crosby; he'd sing half a line and then croon, hitting a few notes perfectly so that it actually sounded great, but then his voice broke with a crack and he hummed because he forgot the words.

One day, we watched Ooda and Lola come around the corner, up the hill, but something was wrong. As soon as I could see what it was, my eyes kept trying to alter reality, no, it can't be, but it was - Lola had cut off her hair. She looked like Brenda Lee, or like one of Ma's friends. Marie and I were horrified: Lola looked ordinary.

Johnny Strummer didn't seem to mind. He ran out of the house and held them there for a while, as usual. But, afterwards, Lola seemed to drag herself up the hill.

Ooda made signs to us over Lola's bent head: she put a slim finger to her lips. We fell back from them without speaking as they passed into the kitchen where they put down their wallets and transistors grimly, silently, and got some tonic out of the refrigerator, without speaking, seeming to pay a quiet tribute to the lost romance of Lola's hair.

## THE CELLAR

*I was down in the cellar, but this never happened, it's only in my mind. I'm stalling; I'm trying not to tell you.*

*The cellar was beautiful to me because, like a castle, it had stone walls and brick walls and a stone floor. I felt at home there in the dark dampness. I must have lived in a castle once, a long time ago.*

*It was cold and the window above Daddy's workbench was closed tightly, but the wind whistled through anyway, fluffing my hair over my forehead.*

*It was hot and the door to the yard stood open; Daddy was cutting the grass and I could hear him, faintly, the click-clack of the rickety old mower - and I could smell him, giving off a trail of the sweet, miraculous scent of cut grass.*

*I was opening and closing the many drawers of his tall, wooden tool chest. I slid them open and peered in to see filthy old nails and screws and drill bits and nuts and bolts and dies. I slid each one closed and opened another, peered in, and closed it.*

*I was looking for something of myself in a man's tool chest, but I didn't find it.*

*I lied. This did happen. More than once.*

RAINBOW

*The pear tree had tried to tell me in the morning. I woke to find glaring blossoms illuminated like frothy lights against a threatening, black sky. It was about to storm.*

*But, it never did. In typical, New England fashion, the sun came out, and at the same time, a soft, spring rain fell, making a full, pastel rainbow over Hichborn Street. We all ran out to the middle of the street, fresh with rain. We looked up, amazed.*

*Forgive me.*

AUGUST 5, 1962
HOLY DAY

Daddy walked on to the porch where his brother, Jake, and some other men were working. Daddy dipped his love curl to light a cigarette - he was already my husband by then - rolling the remains of a pack of Luckies and matches up into his T-shirt sleeve.

"Jake. Did ya hear about the great loss to womanhood?" Daddy asked, speaking into his hands as he lighted his cigarette.

The porch wrapped around one side of the house and cupped its hand around the front where I'd sat on its broad rail at the age of ten and wrote my first story, "The Bright Red Color," now immortalized in the little book with the star on it given by Mr. Mario Lanza. I loved to sit barefoot on the wooden porch rail with a book or a paper and pencil, feeling paper in my hands, holding the pencil, feeling wood warm on my bare soles. I loved to nest there as much as in a tree, its branches open like a hand to hold me.

The afternoon sun lighted the sawdust round the workmen so they seemed the haloed angels of workmen. I stood at the front screen door, where Daddy had just passed through, watching their hard, white T-shirts aglow with the setting sun. Their cigarette tips burned fiery red; pencils were stuck behind their ears; their belts looped with tools, hammers, T-squares, wrenches. Ma was making them re-do the porch; under Ma's command, the men were screening in the porch, killing the broad wooden rail with a screen right down the middle, right between my legs where they'd go on the flat railing, my summer home, no more.

Uncle Jake, Paul, Daddy. Also, Uncles Salvi and Sonny, who were good carpenters and good men: out of their league here like priests helping to reform criminals, they lent a hand.

I loved to watch them, softened by the lighted sawdust. In the world of men, I was invisible at the screen door, though I could be seen clearly enough. I was a fat, blonde child bursting her shorts, sticky with sweat, sticky with the black drips of watermelon and popsicle on her unshaved legs, her lumpy, mosquito scabbed legs.

Uncle Jake, reaching for a board, turned his licking mouth grin to Daddy, who sucked on his cigarette, mysteriously holding in his secret a moment longer.

"So, what's this great loss to womanhood?"

"Marilyn Monroe committed suicide."

"Ya shittin' me!"

"Get outta here!"

"I just heard it on the radio."

Jake wiped his face with his handkerchief.

"Jesus Christ."

"Jesus - ya sure?"

"It wuz just on the radio."

"Well, wa' happened?"

"She took a bottle a' pills."

"Jeez'!"

"Why the hell'd she do a thing like that?"

Silence.

The men looked down at their feet; they poked the sawdust with their work boots. Jake scratched the board he was holding with his black thumbnail. Uncle Salvi frowned his disapproval of suicide; Uncle Sonny looked impressed. Daddy smoked thoughtfully, mingling grey smoke with clouds of golden sawdust. Perhaps, he considered the magnificence of his message.

"She wuz naked when they found her. Sprawled naked on the bed."

"Naked?"

"Naked?"

"Yeah."

"Who found her?"

"The maid."

"Christ."

They were silent. Deep lines instantly creased on their foreheads and held there, till Jake broke the silence with his three-toothed grin.

"Wish I wuz on that reconnaissance," he joked.

The others agreed with a low murmur and a shuffling back to work, which continued in a silent tribute to her made by the concentration of the hammer slowly banging against the nail, the patient saw, the meditative sandpapering of board. I watched their tribute, their hard muscles flexing under their straining shirts, the square asses of men, broad across, leaning into a job, Daddy's love curl bouncing vigorously as he worked thinking about - her.

They knew her in a way I didn't. To me, she was flat as a television screen, painted like a doll, sparkling with color and diamonds, which she said, "were a girl's best friend."

They were thinking about her white skin, about the heat caught under her heavy white breasts, about the dewy moisture that grew there - and in the other place, like under arms, inside her thighs, wet, warm pockets to slide their hands in and that hard, dry thing always seeking - always - the warm, wet putting place. How they knew her.

But, they did not know her painted red lips; those were less real than the rest. Less real: her white blonde hair. Her bottomless eyes, far less real than her very bottom, their fingertips, their penis tip, quivered every time she turned around.

If I were Daddy, I would have carved her name, MARILYN, into one of the boards and, turning the board inward, secreted her name into the porch forever. But, I wasn't him and he was not so much like me - reverent. Maybe he wasn't even thinking about her anymore. Maybe he was thinking about the hot sun burning on his back, about the dry sawdust in his throat, maybe he was thinking about his next ice cold, throat-burning beer.

But, I was thinking about her. Thinking there was more to find out about her, more I didn't know, but would, soon.

I would think men made her do things. "Put your leg up, Miss Monroe, there, that's it." "Smile, Marilyn!" "Yeah!" But, maybe, she didn't need to be told. Maybe she knew what to do and the men just thought they were in control. She knew how to lift her leg, how to roll in the surf, and bend, pleadingly, from the waist, how to stand over a blasting hot grate so that her skirt filled famously with the wind of trains, so that trains blasted through the crotches of every man who saw her, always smiling.

I would learn she wished she was a housewife, but she wasn't a housewife. She wished to lean, sleepy-eyed and barefaced out the sunny morning window. She wanted to be on the cover of Good Housekeeping where she said she never would be. She told a serious actress, "Oh, no! Don't wish you were like me! People respect *you*!"

As I watched the work of men, I saw much to admire. Their dirty, used tools, black with oil, powdered with wood dust and curly chips, tools that worked so often, they were never cleaned by the kind of men who quit at quitting time. I saw their muscles work and grow big and wet so that their T-shirts melted to the skin of their backs making wide, sacramental rings under their arms and ceremonial wet spots dead center of their hard breasts and between the wings of their shoulder blades. My father's neck was written with black rings. Black hair came from his nostrils and his red brow dripped black lines down his pockmarked cheek. Jake grinned every grin lasciviously, whether he meant or felt lascivious or not, with only the three, blackened yellow spikes that remained. Paul was there, foolishly lapping up the atmosphere like a little brother tagging along. When Daddy or Jake lit a cigarette (Paul couldn't light a cigarette worth a damn, he wasn't bad enough.), and hushed their hands over their mouths in deep communion with the wrapped tobacco bitterly burning their lips, burning a wet hole right through the cool, white paper, I smelled the quick, startled pungency as the cigarette caught fire and Daddy's head went back pulling smoke like lava into his lungs, letting it pour round his lungs, breathing it out his nose and mouth like a dragon breathing fire and smoke, then, no one had ever lit a cigarette before, no, not James Dean or Robert Mitchum or Marlon Brando - no one.

Sawdust and the slanting, orange sun and smoke filled the porch, now getting smaller and tighter with screen, losing more and more the sweet, green air of trees.

I looked down at my nubs of breasts that were the tiniest tips of icebergs, the very topmost points of pyramids buried in a thousand years of sands, and my fat stomach, as though I had swallowed a balloon that would carry me aloft to wondrous lands, which I saw, at that moment, as my inadequacy and my gluttony and my cushion against the onslaught of the world, and I thought, I couldn't help thinking, "What a poor substitute I am for Marilyn Monroe in my Daddy's life."


IT WAS A SATURDAY

Now, I will tell you. The pear tree had tried to warn me that morning. I woke to find glaring blossoms illuminated like frothy lights against a threatening, black sky. It was about to storm.

But, it didn't. In typical, New England fashion, the sun came out and, at the same time, a light, spring shower fell, making a full, pastel rainbow over Hichborn Street. We all ran out to the middle of the street, fresh with rain. We looked up, amazed.


I was standing by my closet door.

How many times have I repeated that phrase to myself? That image I have of my still innocent self, standing by my closet door.

What had I done moments before that had been so sexually provocative? I'd been downstairs, probably, in my play clothes, watching TV. Had I leaned over, stretched my shirt against my budding breasts? Had my shirt come out of my pants in the back? Maybe, the corduroy had pressed an outline of my rear end that he couldn't resist.

I was smiling. I remember I was smiling. I loved Saturdays. Ma went food shopping in the morning, so we had Danish for breakfast. Ma liked to turn them over and slather the frosted squares with a thick layer of butter on the bottom and stick them, upside down into her waiting mouth, so that the frosting hit the tongue first, then the butter, and a sip of hot coffee, melting together deliciously. We were allowed to eat two, lemon and raspberry.

I did chores in the morning. I was responsible for the whole upstairs. I dusted and polished the furniture. I vacuumed. I washed the bathroom sink, tub and toilet. I loved to see everything come clean: it was a beautiful sight. I especially loved to polish my mother's big, mahogany bed with the pineapple tops and the spool and spindle posts, in and out, round and round the beautiful carvings, deepening the richness of the dark brown wood. I loved to handle her heavy, silver brush set. The mirror was too dull to see in. After I looked in it, I'd look up at my reflection in the bureau mirror to check if I was still okay and not all blurry. The brush bristles were too soft for my thick hair; they slid over the surface like an infant's brush. People in the old days, I thought, must have had soft, delicate hair. I used a tough, pink plastic brush bought at the 5 & 10. I replaced everything on Ma's bureau so exactly that she asked me, "Did you remember to dust my bureau?" "Yeah, why?" "Mmm. Nothing's moved." I was very proud of the job I did upstairs.

Saturdays had a holiday atmosphere. Ma made hot pastrami for lunch and we ate onion buns from the store. She boiled the meat in mustard and water in a huge pot, like for lobsters in summer or at Christmas, when Daddy said, "Here, lemme show you!" and he took the nutcracker from my small, struggling hand and snapped the lobster shell open for me with his strong grip and handed me the soft, sweet meat; and the same boiling pot for steamers, "The little ones are the sweetest," on hot summer Saturdays served first with fresh salt water to wash them in, then melted butter and corn on the cob. Also on Saturday mornings, Ma sent me to the meat market to get an order. The counter was very high and behind it were some of the cutest boys I'd ever seen in my life; they had black hair and blue eyes, big boys, football players from the high school. I refused to speak the order. Ma had to give me a note, which I handed, mutely, to one of the boys. They were always incredible kind and never made fun of me for not speaking. That was in the rich part of town by the church, where I imagined the boys were well brought up. I was handed a fat package of meat, fat and heavy and solid. That was the Italian cold cuts for the week, for lunches, mortadella, salami, prosciutto, mozzarella cheese, provolone and Swiss cheese, and, of course, the fresh pastrami. There was a fierce smell of meat in the store, a smell sharp with cheese, yet clean and white, like a well-kept kitchen, like Grandma's kitchen.


I went to confession later, after the Tarzan movies. I came into the kitchen to show Ma: I mouthed the words while Tarzan's voice from the other room spoke, "White men go! Go!" or "Jane lead, Tarzan follow! Always!"

Ma cried out, "Look at that! Look at that! You know the words! You watch too much television!"

I had been to confession, to the hush and sweetness of incense and solitude, of bowing my head and confessing: "I hit my sister. I yelled at my sister. I said a swear word. I lied."

I said my penance, five Hail Marys and five Our Fathers. Careful to genuflect first because of the presence of God, then kneeling at the lavish white and gold altar of the Immaculate Conception Church, my hands clasped perfectly together, finger to finger, thumbs crossed dutifully in reverence of His Death on the Cross, hoping God would know I meant it, that I was sorry for my sins, that I would try harder next time to be patient and kind. I truly wished to be better.

My hands, clasped by my nose, smelled of dirt from the Indian Camp, mixed with the warm spring air, penetrated the cloth of my hooded sweatshirt; my profile peeked out as I prayed.

A nun crept behind me. She floated behind me and reached a spiritual hand, which, like a thought, settled on my shoulder.

"My son, you must remove your hood in church," she whispered, in a voice like a breath, like you wished all nuns spoke.

"Sister, I'm a girl," I whispered back.

"Ah!" She was pleased.


I was standing by my closet door. I was smiling.

Daddy came into my room!

"What're ya doin'?" he asked, quietly.

"Daddy, what are you doing in my room?"

"Oh, I just wanted to see you. What're ya doin'?"

"Oh, I'm just picking out my clothes for mass."

I actually thought, maybe he'd like to see what I'm going to wear tomorrow.

"Oh, yeah?"

"Yeah! You wanna see what I'm gonna wear?" I started to get my dress out of the closet to show him.

"No. Come 'ere. I want to see how you've grown."

"Oh, okay," I thought.


After confession, as a reward, every Saturday afternoon, I crossed the street and went to the library. The Revere Public Library looked like a small temple, with a central dome of concrete astride two red brick wings. A high stone wall surrounded the courtyard. Inside the courtyard was a pretty garden of plants, shrubs and small trees. I walked along a circular path to the front steps, which opened gracefully as a theater staircase.

Once closed behind me, the double glass doors cut off the sounds of the street, the screams, the swears, the car horns, the engines, the roaring, the bodies of cars scraping and clattering, the oaths, "I'm gonna kill ya!" "Fuck you!" blocked, as if the Great Cupped Hands came down from heaven and muffled the street's screaming mouth, or, mercifully, covered my ears, for a brief respite at least.

The librarian was always glad to see me. She knew me because I was one of the few people who ever came in. She looked up over the top of her little half glasses on a cord and smiled with lips pressed together.

"Hello," she mouthed silently, still smiling.

I smiled, too, also with my lips pressed together. In perfect communion with her smile, I walked past her to the fiction, which I considered, even then, to be the holiest, most sacred books in the library; Bibles, every one, Bibles to learn from, to read the lines and between the lines to discover truths and hidden truths. These were holy because they were original works. Fiction came from a place only God knew and God gave out, sparingly, to only a few. These few were connected to heaven, and hell, in a way no one understood, not even the writers themselves. This connection made fiction great. And holy. It was only common sense, it was what I felt, instinctively, this holy rush of love for the words and the stories and the feelings they evoked, this adoration for the writers. I saw no difference between them and saints, except, I knew, writers were sometimes evil. They had to be, it was a difficult position God put them in, like Judas, who was chosen by God to betray Jesus: they could not help themselves. Somehow, this made them more holy. How could it be, while we were supposed to struggle to be good, to obey the rules, writers were meant to break them? Yes, they were thrown in, like artists. Yes, artists were the same, chosen and sacrificed at once, all this I would come to know and only felt now as I entered my beloved and sacred fiction. My heart knew that fiction was infinitely more in touch with the truth than fact could ever hope to be.

What was I reading? Only sacred things. *Robin Hood*, the language alternately staggered me with blows or rocked me in a cradle. The fairy tales of Hans Christian Anderson and The Brothers Grimm, though I suspected that women had created these stories, to keep kids from touching the spinning wheel, for instance, or from wandering off into the forest. *Black Beauty*, anything about Napoleon. I remember reading Ma's copy of *Gone With The Wind*, but the language was not as beautiful as the language of Robin Hood or the fairy tales. I read Mary Stewart until the third book, when I realized each story had the same plot – woman goes to mysterious house that might be haunted and falls in love with the dashing owner – so I had to stop even though her writing was beautiful. I wouldn't touch Nancy

Drew or any of that stuff "kids my age" were reading. I only read beautiful, sacred things.

For a blissful while, I sat in a wooden chair like the Papa Bear's chair, miles too big for me, pressed up against the long, wooden table, my book open, luxuriously, in front of me. I read until I was bothered by a bunch of kids coming in and jostling the table or until I finally had to go home for supper.

I loved to watch the librarian write the numbers from the book I'd chosen to my card, so neatly, so primly. It was a ritual that seemed sacramental in its slow indulgence.

She smiled again and whispered, "How's school?"

"Good."

She seemed to know I liked school and was a good student. Our words were like a mutual caress. We gave meaning to each other.

The library was my reward after confession, which was a sweet indulgence, when you hadn't sinned very much, as I hadn't, up till then, an indulgence and a consolation, to be gently reprimanded by the benevolent priest in the sandalwood hush of his cubicle, "You are forgiven, my child. Go, and sin no more."

"Thank you, Father."

The walk home was brimming with promise. New tulips bowed to me in the soft breeze in the trim, pretty yards of the white people. I vowed that I, too, would have a nice yard someday. I planned this future yard: greenest lush grass, soft colors of flowers, white picket fence, small white house, no, a cottage, then I remembered, the cottage of "Sleeping Beauty," built around a tree, or, maybe, a tree house, like Tarzan.

I loved to read for a while, again, once I was safely in my room. Safely in my room. Just before supper, which I could taste and smell as I read, wafting up to my room, the same meal Ma made every Saturday night especially for Daddy: baked beans, frankfurters, rich brown bread Ma cut out of a can and steamed, spread with layers of melting butter for scooping up the beans, thick with molasses and to drink, cold, cold, milk.


"I want to see how much you've grown."

Daddy's head bent down, already intent upon what he was going to do. He knelt down in front of me.

I want to go back and talk about the library. I want to say, you know, I loved the library. Supper was over, but I thought of the library, of its solace and its sanctuary. But, it could not save me!

I looked down as Daddy unbuttoned my pants. I could see the top of his head. I was used to Mama pulling down my pants, but I was always informed of what she was about, checking to see if I'd peed myself, checking if I was hurt, helping me to go the bathroom, but Daddy pulling down my pants was something I couldn't understand.

"Daddy, no!" I whispered desperately, wasn't it wrong for a boy to pull down your pants?

"It's mine," he coaxed, "I made it."

What did *that* mean? Wasn't it mine? And, didn't Mama make it, when I was inside her?

"Oh, yeah, you've really grown!"

"I have?"

I looked down. It didn't look any bigger to me. I was about to tell him so, when my smile, my home smile, my Saturday smile, left my face forever.

Daddy's tongue darted into the pink folds of my vulva.

An alarm went off in my head, in fact, over every inch of me. What was he doing? What did it mean?

His tongue floated me up on a tingling, warm wave of my blood. I thought my feet would leave the floor.

He made little eating noises. He moaned.

"Does that feel good?" he stopped for a moment to say.

"Yeah," I responded, weakly. And confused, what was he doing? I couldn't believe he had his mouth where the pee came out.

I wasn't thinking about the library or about church, but I could see them both plainly; they were shadows, shapes, behind my shoulders watching, like guardian angels that could not help me.

"Oh, oh," I moaned. "Daddy," I whispered. Instinctively, I knew to be quiet.

"Mmmm," was his answer, his face buried in the soft, pink skin, a few soft, brown hairs entered his nostrils.

"Daddy," I groaned, "Don't, it feels funny."

My knees became fluid; I stumbled.

"Hold on to the wall," Daddy said.

Obediently, my hand went out and I was balanced. Then, something happened.

Daddy's tongue hit the right spot; over and over he licked it, opening the gates of a flood. His hands moved behind me, cupping a chubby buttock in each of his big hands. I began to pulsate and fall backwards. Daddy held me harder, so that the pulsing became fiercer, pointy, not round, my blood insisted what I could not deny, I could not, no, I could not.

"Whaddya think o' that?" Daddy laughed with red, swollen lips, sitting back on his heels.

"I don't know."

He laughed, eyes shining.


After Daddy left, I lay flat on my bed, looking up at the ceiling. This position was also where I'd find myself when Ma yelled, "Get up there an' wait till your father gets home!" I would watch the ceiling like a clock, as darkness ensued, keeping watch over the changing shapes of the cracked plaster: the Lamb of God, The Holy Spirit, the decrepit old man, the apple, the island. I knew every mark and imperfection, every split and gaping hole looked at me like an old friend. They kept me company. I'd watch the light and shadows alter the shapes, and I'd wonder, how much is it going to hurt this time? Maybe, he'd just groan because he was too tired. Those seemed, suddenly, to be innocent, simpler times. When Daddy would be inspired to discipline me, beating me with his belt, in one of his bursts of fathering.

"Don't do it again," he'd grunt and go away.

What had I done? I doubt if he knew.

For a while, I'd wail and weep until the red, hot flame on my buttocks finally began to lighten and subside.

This Saturday night, darkness seeped into my bedroom and I didn't turn on the little light, the one by the bed. I thought, how strange everything looked, all my things seemed slightly altered by coming darkness and cold fear inside me, growing with the shadows, covering the familiar shapes: the bedside light, a pink girl in a dusty – I'd forgotten to dust her - illuminated pink ball gown; the bedspread, pink chenille from a bathrobe, edged with roses from old curtains; the fake wood linoleum floor, with its black holes Daddy called "pussies"; the yellowed blinds hanging crooked because Daddy had left a piece out when he put them up. Their sameness scared me. They were the same, but changed - everything, even the street outside, where the darkness came from - all exactly the same, but painted over with my astonishment, altered by the shadows creeping, by the icy fear crawling over me that something had happened and I didn't know what.

What had he meant by "It's mine. I made it?"

"Glor-i-a!" Ma called suddenly from downstairs.

My heart leaped out of my chest.

"Yeah?" I said, uneasily.

"What's the matter?"

She could tell from my voice.

"Nothing."

"Come down. We're having ice cream. Come and watch Jackie Gleason. What are you doing up there?"

"Nothing."

I could hear her footsteps coming up the stairs. I could hear Daddy, already laughing with gusto, like the commercial said you should. I could hear the theme music, usually so promising, promising a really good laugh on a Saturday night.

She had ice cream ready for me. A huge, white glacier in a yellow plastic bowl.

"How come the light wasn't on?" Ma asked me. "An' you're not in your pajamas yet?"

"I don't know."

How'd she know the light wasn't on? The ice cream tasted cold and sweet, thin with ice, water flavor, not vanilla like it should be. It would be the last thing I ate until after I received Holy Communion in the morning. I froze, hot and cold at once. Could I receive communion now? I ate more slowly. Everyone chuckled at the show. I hadn't heard a thing. Daddy didn't look at me. I didn't dare look at him. I just looked down into the softening cream. I heard his jungle rotty feet scraping together, *kwish, kwish, kwish, kwish,* as he scratched them, each against the other, under the table.

To receive Holy Communion with a sin on your soul meant a mortal sin and to receive with a mortal sin meant Excommunication. Had I sinned? What if it were a mortal sin?

"Gloria?" Ma asked, impatiently, "What's the matter?"

"Nothing," I insisted.

"You sick?"

"No!"

I thought I'd better at least pretend to watch the show. Art Carney was acting drunk at the bar where Jackie Gleason pretended to be the bartender. I never could understand this part. I could never tell what Art Carney was saying; he slurred his words and fell off the stool while Jackie Gleason patiently wiped the bar with a cloth. Daddy roared with laughter. Marie and Ma laughed whenever Daddy laughed. Jakey laughed at everything.

I fed ice cream to my guilty face. Then, Daddy started to laugh on the snide as Jackie Gleason, in a tuxedo, was being circled by a young, beautiful girl wearing nothing but a bathing suit and high heels. Why was she wearing high heels with a bathing suit? I never understood that either.

Suddenly, a new feeling started to creep over me, not guilt, not fear, not remorse, not confusion - anger! A grey, sickening shiver of complete revulsion crept as if in my blood, over the skin of my shoulders, up over my skull, down my arms, tingling in my fingers as though I could kill someone! A hot rage burned in my chest. How dare he! He was fat and old! She was so beautiful! What was she doing there? Why was everyone laughing? It wasn't funny! It wasn't!

This new feeling would grow. A terrible seed was planted that night, the seed of my rebellion and my revulsion from the home and the family I still loved and needed so much, the beginning sprout of my lust, my shame, my hatred, my love and my great yearning for more.

## HOLY COMMUNION

Little girls wore girdles then. I was sitting in church, feeling like stuffing in a fat girdle attached to a pair of nylons, nervously listening to the priest inch closer to the moment of Communion.

He raised the host out of the wine goblet.

"Take this all of you and eat it: this is my body which will be given up for you."

The choir responded, "Lamb of God, who takes away the sins of the world/ Have mercy."

He turned in his starched, pristine robe. There was an exchange of goblets with the altar boys.

Jakey slid into the pew, laughing silently.

"What's a' matta'?" he asked me.

"Nothing," I said.

"Take this all of you and drink from it: this is the cup of my blood, the blood of the new and everlasting covenant, which will be shed for you and for all men so that sins may be forgiven. Do this is in remembrance of me."

People began to rise and file up to the altar to receive Communion. That's what it meant, I suddenly realized, we were supposed to eat and drink the very same food and wine together like a family.

"Lamb of God who takes away the sins of the world/Grant us peace."

Tears came to my eyes. I felt so alone. There was no one to ask. What if I received and I had sinned and I was excommunicated, not officially, of course, because the Pope didn't know about me, but in God's eyes?

"Lamb of God who takes away the sins of the world/Happy are those who are called to His supper."

"Aren't ya goin'?" Jakey smirked, with his Big Jake-like grin, even though he had all his teeth.

I didn't move.

"Lord, I am not worthy to receive you, but say the word and I shall be healed."

"Whaddya do since ya went to confession? Whaddya rob a bank?"

Cold terror flooded my body. I swear I could feel every inch of my clothing, from my stupid straw hat with the paper flowers to my white gloves and white patent leather shoes, each floated over prickly flesh. Deep sobs rose from my empty belly - I hadn't dared do anything deliberate to sabotage my Communion, like eat breakfast - from far down in my belly, where I knew, I knew, I'd done something, if not wrong, I'D DONE SOMETHING. God knew, even if I didn't, exactly what that something was. And, the nuns, lined up behind us, at the rear of the church, they knew, even if I was too ashamed to ask them. The fact that I shivered deep inside my body and was afraid to ask, the fact that I instinctively hid, this fact should have alerted me, but I had nothing to compare it to - what had happened? Whatever it was, Daddy had been there, so how could it have been wrong?

Jakey leaned over and whispered sharply, his breath smoky and bitter with - stale beer? - "I'm tellin' Ma ya not receivin'!"

I was up like a shot. My lips were pulled tight and determined as Grandma's and Ma's ever had been. I climbed over Jakey's legs.

"You're not going?" I don't know why I asked this; he never had before.

"Are you kiddin'? I don' wanna go to heaven."

At that moment, I would have risked hell rather than have Ma know I hadn't received Holy Communion. She would know, you couldn't fool her; she would know I'd done something - wrong.

Ooda had told me, and I was getting old enough to understand it, my breasts were budding, my pubis was softening with hair, I was beginning to understand and yearn for things in life according to the movies and the popular songs, Ooda had told me and I could feel it was true that the worst thing a girl could do was steal another girl's boy friend.

Daddy was Mama's husband, had I stolen him? This fear would grow. For the moment, my fear of Ma was stronger than my fear of God or the Pope or the Devil, and I doubt seriously if, at that moment, I knew the difference between any of them.

I half expected the host to sizzle when it touched my tongue. I noted, interestedly, that it did not. The priest did not flinch as he reached his hand into my mouth - the Devil was not sitting on my tongue.

Holding the dear host preciously light on my tongue, I walked back to the pew, my hands together, fingers pointing to heaven, thumbs crossed. I was afraid Jakey might have something nasty to say, but he was already bored, turning his head to the back of the church to see if any of his friends were around.

I closed my eyes and knelt, letting the paper thin wafer dissolve into spirituality, adoring the taste, believing undoubtedly it was the flesh and blood of Christ, (and, at the same time, that it had been baked in the rectory kitchen by nuns or trucked in from a factory in New Jersey), delicious taste of paper, sweet and clear.

Comforted by the presence of God in my mouth, I began to think perhaps nothing had happened, after all.

MA

The little animals who made their insecure homes in the surrounding green troughs between highways, sometimes got confused and burrowing through the ground one day, would suddenly find themselves surrealistically scurrying across a linoleum floor or swimming frantically in a dark, flooded cellar.

A mouse scratched across our kitchen floor. It hid as best it could, pressing its trembling body against the woodwork, eyes bulging, sniffer going wild.

"Oh, it's only a field mouse. They come in to get warm."

She called Daddy who beat it to death with his steel-toed work boot. Would it have been so bad, I thought, to have a little mouse in the house? Like Cinderella?

I must have asked Ma because she laughed at me.

"You can't! One mouse means there's a hundred!"

One day, Ma had to kill a rat.

She'd just come home from work. Ooda was still there, talking to her. They talked together like grown up ladies about grown up people they both knew who were married or having kids or sick with something disgusting.

Ooda talked from the kitchen while Ma went straight for the bedroom as soon as she came in the door. There, she unhitched her garters and stripped off her girdle, grasping the rubber with weak, but, determined fingers, grunting breathlessly with each tug, squeezing her ample buttocks, wriggling her chubby thighs, stopping for a rest, inching out slowly and painfully. The second she could breathe, she let out a sigh like the earth must release after an earthquake, after holding in its breath for a million years.

Then, she rolled her nylons down to her ankles, which Daddy hated and for which I was paying, dearly. (But, I never blamed her. No. I always thought tenderly of these nylons round her ankles.) She put on old slippers, cut out at the little toes for comfort, like Nona used to wear. Then, she went straight to the stove to start cooking supper. Sometimes, Ma put her purse down and started supper with her coat on.

We still ate like kings - peasant kings, but kings, nevertheless. On this day, she already had the pizzaiola, the rough corn bread bubbling in the iron skillet. Already, I had washed and soaked the sandy, curly escarole leaves when I came home from school; Ma took the dripping greens, she chopped them while the garlic sang in the pan. Later, she'd add the sliced pepperoni and we'd eat with red wine, crusty bread, and bitter wedges of Romano cheese.

Ooda said she would never eat that stuff. She cracked her gum with an amused smile.

"You eat junky food," Ma teased her.

The afternoon was prematurely dark and damp, but, this being the only time she had, Ma was going out back to hang clothes.

She put on an old coat she kept "for the yard." The ground outside was grey and muddy. I called it "Poland, 1941," after a picture in a book.

Ma never used a basket. She had a system of piling the wet clothes on her arms and shoulders, socks on top, larger items on the bottom. The clothespins were in a bag on the line; she took four at a time in her mouth.

I watched her at the screen door. I had a deep, romantic need for her. Something had happened to me and the loneliness and guilt, the fear, that she wouldn't love me anymore, was breaking my heart. I needed desperately to watch the pattern of her work. I needed her to be exactly as she was: round and generous, soft and kind.

First, she took the socks, one on either side of the line, by the toes, with one clothespin. Pants by the waist. Shirts wide open by the tails. I had the artist's adoration for the housewife, images that I devoured hungrily at the end of every history chapter, a woman holding a child, working in the fields, baking bread, washing clothes, but no work of art made me happier than watching the real thing. Her shape was beautiful, homely, bulky and round in her old coat, the piles of clothes dwindling, altering her silhouette. Her brilliant hair was still red, but getting dull with age. Her bare legs were still fat and solid, like a fat child's. I watched her reach on her tippy toes, her fat calves, her effort to reach, seemed to show her love for me...

"Oh, my God! A rat!" Ma screamed, dumping the wet clothes in a heap on the mud.

"Ooda! Come here!"

Ooda pushed past me. I watched through the door as Ma grabbed a long pole that was in the yard for God only knows what purpose, just a part of the junk pile. Ma pinioned the escaping rat. One end of the pole stuck on the rat's wriggling back, Ma clung to the other end, literally ten feet away, as though for her dear life.

Ooda hopped nervously from foot to foot, biting her lip, clenching her fists.

"What do you want me to do?" Her voice was strangely high pitched.

"Throw stones! Throw stones!" Ma's eyes were curiously bright with energy; they shone weirdly. Then, she laughed with the excitement of the kill.

The rat was by the autumn remains of the Chinese lanterns and silver dollars I loved so much; their shriveled red and grey corpses shook in the struggle, rustling against the stone foundation.

"Oh, my God, it's so close to the house!" Ma yelled.

Ooda began to laugh too, nervously, at first. Then she picked up a few stones and pitched them, delicately, at the rat's head. They came close, but missed.

The rat's eyes rolled, searching for a way out.

Ooda laughed and clawed at the mud with her manicured nails, giggling with little hisses through clenched teeth. She hit him! And his head flipped horribly from side to side. His claws dug into the mud. His thin grey tail beat the ground.

Ma strengthened her grip on the pole.

"Gloria! Get out here and help us!"

Never! It wasn't the killing that suddenly turned my stomach - no, it was the ugliness! I would never help kill a rat! I didn't want Ma to do it either!

The rat's pointed snout darted over his shoulder. His eyes glared with human emotion - hate! At Ma! He wanted to kill her, too!

"Gloria!" Ma screamed, leaning hard on the pole, trying to pick up rocks, blindly, with her other hand, thinking better of it, and grabbing back on with both hands.

Marie appeared at my side.

"What's goin' on?" she asked, in her slow, drowsy way.

"They're killing a rat," I shuddered.

"Oh, yeah?" she said, with interest.

She went outside too. Some other kids came too, from other yards, having heard the shouting from the street.

"Throw stones! Kill it!" Ma yelled urgently.

Soon, all the kids were throwing stones. The rat squirmed and wriggled; he tried to back away from the pole, he tried to run forward. The kids shouted with happiness. They ran around to the front of the rat and dropped the biggest rocks they could find on his head till they killed him.

His snout lay broken, upturned, teeth bared as if still fighting.

Ma picked up his limp grey carcass between two sticks like salad tongs and, laughing, grimacing, carried him over to The Land, where she dumped him.

Over the trees, he sailed, his claws limp as sleeping hands, his eyes still fierce with anger. The tree limbs bowed, the leaves ripped as he passed through them, and then, the branches bounced back up, neatly concealing him from us forever.

Ma turned with a satisfied air, which quickly changed.

"Oh! Look at the clothes!" she cried, holding her head with her hands.

Busy, killing feet had trampled them in the mud.

DADDY

Forgive me. I ask this of all the children who were shot or beaten, raped, murdered, burned, mutilated, stuffed in trash bags, buried or left for dead by the side of the road, by their fathers or mothers, stepparents, friends, strangers, priests, Nazis, I don't know which of them is the worst.

Forgive me. For the rest of my life, I'll know *it was nothing, nothing* compared to what other children suffered. Still, it changed me forever. No, not changed, added to, I became that, I had been colored over like a black and white picture smeared red with paint, polluted like a clear stream running with waste.

But that's not all that worked on me; worked and worked, trying to kill me, to smother me with its heavy chest, to choke me with its adult penis. The street worked on me and the city, the men and the women and their children, worked. There was a lot of work to be done.

They tried to kill me in this place of love and horror. They tried to kill me, but they couldn't because I loved too much. I could not be killed, though they didn't know that yet. I loved them all in their beauty and in their ugliness. I even began to love the pain they inflicted upon me, as my companion, as myself. I began to love the noise and the screams, the barreling of trucks and the whine of sirens, the smell of horseshit in the air, sweet as grass and the sweet, sweet blossoms of the pear tree. They couldn't kill me with these things, though they tried.

I came downstairs one night to find Daddy sitting at the kitchen table, his back to me, his legs crossed at the ankles. I also sat that way at the table. It was a habit of mine too. He was working on another kid's Science project, something to do with electricity, there, at our kitchen table, late at night, after everyone else had gone to bed.

Daddy was a pillar of the community. The whole adult population of the street looked to him for help in time of need. On blowing, frigid mornings, Daddy could start anyone's car. If the telephone rang in the middle of the night, he'd leave his bed, no question, to fix a neighbor's flat tire out on the empty highway. One by one, as each toilet broke down or sink backed up, he'd snake the pipes or re-work the plumbing in each and every house on the street till the map of pipes and joints of each and every house was imprinted on his brain. He was proud to do it.

But, Daddy couldn't get our TV to focus, no matter how much he banged the set with the heel of his hand, wrestled with the rabbit ears or swore, "Jesus! You son-of-a-bitchin', friggin', Christ All Mighty!" Once, Daddy beat up the TV repair guy because he asked Daddy for a new thing called a $12 service fee just for coming to the house and he hadn't even fixed the TV. Daddy had so much electricity shooting through his body from accidents at work that he couldn't walk by the television without an alarm of static going off. We'd all yell, "Daddy! Get away from the TV!" As soon as he passed by, the picture returned.

Ma couldn't get him to finish a job around our house.

"Your father! Your father!" she'd yell, like it was a swear.

She only asked him to do tasks she absolutely couldn't do herself. Then, she got mad because she knew she'd have to wait forever for a door hinge to be re-attached or a drawer to open.

Meanwhile, kids dropped off their limping bikes. Daddy pressed the sagging tire into a pail of water and we'd all watch for the bubbles to appear. "There's the leak!" We'd watch, raptly, as Daddy got out the bicycle repair kit, found a rubber patch, glue, and glued the patch over the gaping split in the tire. Our house had other people's toasters, hair dryers, and radios waiting to be fixed. Daddy knew the intricate workings of every electrical matrix on the street. He knew which car would break down next and what part it would need. He could fix a screen door, a window or a washing machine. I've seen him birth puppies and break up a fight. One time, when he was driving drunk, the cops stopped him and he said, "I just live ovva there," and the cops escorted him home.

But, he had trouble remembering our middle names and never could get our ages straight. Once, when he was helping me with my math, which I never could get right, he finally got aggravated with me: he smacked me so hard, my body tried to go through the table. One of my breasts was bruised, crushed against the edge. I cried a long time with the pain and Ma yelled at him, "Whaddaya think ya doin'? She's a girl!" I never asked him for help with my homework again.

No matter. Really. I was so proud of him already, for being busy and sought after and capable. For being good at everything he did and for being able to do everything he tried. I thought the other adults must be stupid. After all, even *I* would get phone calls from grown men asking me, "Gloria, how do you spell - ?" Besides, it was quickly and insidiously becoming true that I did not want Daddy to know our ages or our middle names. Soon, I would not want to see him or smell him; I'd move, not to touch him or anything he had touched.

Still, I was proud of him. Proud of his talent, proud of his looks, his love curl, his shoulders, the way he rolled his pack of cigarettes up in his T-shirt sleeve, the way he smoked, the way other men looked at him.

Just proud. Made no sense.

I stood on the stairs for a time watching him working at the kitchen table with the only light coming from Ma's corny daisy chandelier, making a ring of daisies above his head. Then, I snuck back upstairs without getting the drink of milk I'd gone down for. I didn't dare cross in front of him, alone, in my pajamas, after everyone had gone to bed. I had to be more careful now.

Instead, I used the bathroom sink, scooping handfuls of cold water, sucking it up gratefully, as though it were the last water on earth. Quietly, I returned to bed, knowing I could never be quiet enough for Ma not to hear me, but happy to be alone and sleepy and doing nothing I didn't want her to hear.

## THE NAZI

The Nazi officer came into the room. He looked at me where I was, on the bed. There was nothing in the room but a bed, lamp and table. No curtains on the window, which looked out on a bleak, winter field.

The Nazi was handsome. He was always handsome. I wasn't afraid of him. I loved him because he kept me safe in this room and he was never cruel to me; he was always kind.

Never was there any question of my family or my friends, never any betrayal, or any politics, only this handsome man slowly removing his uniform, coming over to me where I was on the bed.

I was naked, under the covers. Warm and naked. I was giving him something he could not get outside this room.

He lay on top of me, but, suddenly, he was wearing his full uniform again! He pushed himself hard against me, and again, hard.

Then, he was naked again, and he held me. His warm, wet lips brushed against my cheek, which was cold, exposed as it was to the chill in the room.

## THE LOVE RING

"Come in here, I want to show you something," Ma called from her bedroom.

She was making the big bed, hers and Daddy's, with the white chenille cover. Ma could make a bed with one hand tied behind her back. It was a marvel how she could whack the cloth with a karate chop and send it perfectly tucked under the pillows.

"Watch," she said as I appeared in the doorway.

Ma sent the sheet high in the air, high and full as a sail, while her little toy terrier (Ma always had a new toy terrier), Teeny, leaped on to the naked bed and whipped around and around in circles, her sharp, racing claws scratching the mattress. As the sheet settled on Teeny and she disappeared from view, she stopped suddenly and sneezed under the cover. Her little head sniffed quickly, side to side. Then, Ma lifted the sail again. The dog took off, "Yap! Yap!" she cried ecstatically, "Yap! Yap!" until the sheet settled once more and she stopped.

Ma jerked the sheet away.

"Get off there, you! You don't belong there!" Ma pretended to be mad.

Teeny licked her chops, nervously.

For a joke, Ma made the bed around Teeny who seemed to chase her tail underneath the tucked-in covers, searching for a way out.

Then, Ma pulled out a corner, put her head under, where she was licked up. "Come here, stupid." Teeny wiggled out into her arms, slurping her face all over.

"You didn't laugh," Ma said.

"Yes, I did."

"I didn't hear you."

"I laughed inside."

She made a face.

"Here, I got something for you," Ma said.

I followed Ma to her jewelry box, that mysterious, carved wood casket painted on the lid with a garden of roses in full bloom.

Ma opened the box, revealing an overflow of dazzling rhinestones and colored glass. She dug into this jumble and pulled out two small rings.

"These should fit you now."

One was emerald and gold.

"That belonged to your father's mother, Alice. She died of tuberculosis before you were born."

An emerald!

"You mean, it's real?"

"Yup!"

Silently, she handed me the other one.

It was a slender white gold band in which was buried a diamond chip flanked by rubies under heart-shaped cutouts.

"Where did you get this?" I gasped. It looked like a love ring. Did Daddy give it to you?"

I noticed she'd been smiling. A secret, love smile.

It didn't seem like a ring Daddy would give: it was too delicate and sensitive a ring.

"It's a 'sweetheart ring.'" Ma explained.

But, *who* had given such a beautiful ring to Mama?

"Did another boy give it to you?"

She nodded, with a dreamy, far away look in her eyes.

"Who? Uncle Jake?"

"NO!" she shook her head scornfully. "Another boy," again, she went all dreamy.

"Who?"

"Someone."

"Someone," I thought, as Mama slipped the pretty ring on my finger. Someone else, other than Daddy, had loved Mama. Good. I was glad.

This someone else, I knew, had grown up to be a good man. He was handsome and honest, brave and true. This someone gave me hope because he had chosen this ring.

Teeny snuggled and licked Mama's chubby forearm as I admired the twinkling diamond, soft rubies and shining white band on my finger.

The prettiest ring I would ever see.


## DADDY WAS TAKING A BATH

The bathroom door was ajar.

I hurried in because I had to go so bad; I had my pants down before I realized, Daddy was taking a bath in the tub!

In a half-squat over the toilet, I gasped and yanked my pants back up.

"Daddy! I didn't know you were in here!" I said as I dashed out.

He grabbed my wrist as I passed.

He hadn't looked a bit surprised to see *me*!

"Daddy," I whispered, "Let me go."

He laughed. He was pulling my hand down, into the water.

"Daddy! No!"

I tried not to look in the tub. He was laughing at me. He put my hand on his penis. It was floating, hard, in the water. It was hard, but the skin on it was soft. Daddy started to move my hand up and down on the soft skin.

I didn't dare look.

"Oh," he moaned, "the water makes it so good."

Suddenly, my hand was free! I ran out, dripping bathwater over my legs. I could hear him laughing at me.


A moment later, I snuck back. I had an idea I should close the door so Marie wouldn't do the same thing I'd done.

I crept toward the open door. Through the hinged side of the door, I could see his head, there, against the back of the tub! What if he saw me? I made a dash for the doorknob, which I grasped and tugged shut with a whack!

"Who the hell's that?" he yelled, angrily.

Then, he laughed.

## THE KRAUSSES

I made a friend. Dorothy Krauss. She was very pretty and very fat. She had wavy brown hair and brown eyes which her mother, Hazel thought were beautiful. Maybe they were. I didn't think so. They were too small. I never could get excited about small eyes, but small, brown ones, forget it. Actually, I thought her little beagle, Tuffy, had the only beautiful brown eyes in the family, large and dewy, sweet and expressive, but, of course, I never pointed that out.

Hazel Krauss. Jakey and I called her Witch Hazel. We couldn't help it! It was so obvious! Her black hair grew in wiry tufts half-plucked from her bare scalp. Her chin competed with her nose, long and pointy. I never saw a better example of beady eyes than Hazel Krauss's, so I will call them beady, black and beady. Not only were they round and hard, they spun in their whites. And, she had a way of walking, that was suffering, really, she groaned as she walked. She would turn, suddenly, like a large crow, flicking her neck and the beady eyes spun and I felt - no matter what she was saying - that she was lying, whether she knew it or not.

Hazel was always sick, she shuffled painfully from the kitchen to the den where she sunk, with excruciating slowness and pain you could almost feel, into her old green armchair, whose lumps and bulges had been bullied to fit Hazel's own lumps and bulges till she was about as comfortable as she ever could be. There she lit a Marlboro and told me how terrific Dorothy was, in every way, somehow excluding me from each and every quality Dorothy supposedly possessed. Dorothy bore most of Hazel's suffering for her; Hazel never stopped complaining to her, but to me, she praised Dorothy. It was an efficient system really: this way, she made us both feel bad.

The most amazing thing about Hazel Krauss was that she had a boy friend. The Krauses called him Cousin Harvey.

Mr. Krauss knew about him, of course. Cousin Harvey drove right up to the front door in a huge Cadillac with fins, a glistening white convertible with flashy red seats. Hazel would make her way, trembling with sickness and pain, down the stairs; she was all made-up, like a hag with lipstick on, her tufts of hair curled. She waved goodbye to us with a jingling costume jeweled hand, leaving behind a good whiff of Avon hair spray, stressed deodorant and Jean Naté Pour Le Bain. Then, the three of us turned and went into the house. Mr. Krauss took care of us while Hazel went out with Harvey.

Hazel and Cousin Harvey always went to the dog track. I suppose Mr. Krauss, Will, felt the track was a good place for them to go, since he went there too, often. We were blessed with two tracks, one on either end of

Hichborn, a dog track called Wonderland and a horse track called Suffolk Downs.

A stream of grey men poured out of Revere Beach train station twice a day. These men walked with their heads down, their shoulders collapsed. They walked with the last effort they possessed, across the highway, while a police officer wearing an orange bib held up his hands like the priest in mass to stop the cars for them. We would watch from our waiting car. The men wore the oldest clothes I'd ever seen, dark clothes, thin, faded plaids, blurred tweeds, dusty shoes, they looked like they smelled old and stale as attics; they smoked cigarettes as if to keep warm by the tiny well of embers cupped in their hands. Racing forms, worried, smudged and blackened from worrying, rolled up, protruded from their pants pockets as they walked.

"Who are those men, Ma?" I asked.

"I don't know. They're going to the track."

"They don't look rich."

Ma and Daddy laughed. "They lose! They lose!"

"I wonder if they drop any money in the parking lot." It seemed a long way from home, for me to try to go there and look. I figured the boys probably went all the time.

"You're dreaming! They don't have cars. They don't have any money to drop."

Sometimes, we would see the losers walking back to the train station, the discarded racing forms fluttering at their feet. Another weary stream of losers poured toward them from the train station.

But, Cousin Harvey didn't look like a loser. He wasn't. Harvey *shone*, like his Cadillac. He even dressed like his Cadillac. He wore glistening white patent leather shoes and a glistening white patent leather belt to match, pressed red slacks and a short-sleeved white nylon shirt that billowed in the summer wind. However, his fat belly bulged over his belt tucked far below it for comfort; his shiny slacks stretched tightly around his big buttocks and thighs; the toes of his fancy shoes turned upward in the strain of trying to hold on to his fat foot.

As I watched Hazel and Harvey drive away, I knew they were going somewhere Ma had warned me about. "Don't go near there!" she warned about the track. "Walk on the other side of the street!" even though Uncle Vic owned a lounge down on the beach, about a block away from the track, called The Tom Tom Room. I wasn't supposed to go anywhere near there either.

Hazel and Cousin Harvey amazed me, because they were ugly and, at that time, I didn't know ugly people could fall in love. I had learned from the Nazis. It made common sense to me that only beautiful people met and fell in love. I thought ugly people got married because either they had been better looking when they fell in love or they just got married from a practical view because no one else would marry them. I thought ugly people made love only to have their ugly children. I couldn't imagine, Hazel and Harvey actually kissing, or, heaven forbid, getting hot and petting.

Will Krauss was the opposite of Harvey. Will Krauss was a milkman. He drove a milk truck for Hood. He was slender and trim in his red and blue uniform and a jaunty cap to match. He carried a metal basket clinking with glass milk bottles with little red caps. I loved to see him step down from his little white truck in his smart blue uniform and cap with the dark blue visor. He was tinkling and fresh. He looked exactly like the actor, Fred MacMurray. I thought Dorothy was so lucky to have such a fine, real father! I thought any father who wasn't having sex with you was a real father. You could probably even sit on Mr. Krauss' lap! I loved to say, "Hi, Mr. Krauss!" as he stepped down from his truck and he'd call, "Hi ya, Glor-i-a!" and he'd make a salute against his cap. He was great!

But, Hazel didn't think so.

The Krausses lived on Winthrop Place, a side street of about five houses that curved off Hichborn like a quiet, circular driveway.

This day, I walked down to the Krauss', hopefully, to use their bathroom. At the foot of our yard, the street suddenly changed to sand, yellow sand (just like the yellow quicksand mud of the truck stop just above it on the highway), that was the arch of Winthrop Place, scrunch, scrunch, I pretended it was a country road. On one side, a huge field, impenetrable with tough weeds that rose to a continuation of the embankment in our yard. On the other side, a small lot, more or less flat, that stood dry and parched in summer, but flooded every winter. There, we'd skate over frozen clumps of weeds that tripped us mercilessly until we trained ourselves to skate around them. Winthrop Place, once discovered by the great John Winthrop, once lush with new vegetation, once singing with new birds.

Hazel opened the storm door for me.

"Dorothy got her period today," she informed me, sucking her cigarette. "She's a woman now."

I walked in, my eyes shocked by the sudden darkness. I never could get used to the sudden, yet ever constant, darkness of other houses.

"I was wondering if I could use your bathroom, Mrs. Krauss? Daddy's in ours."

She laughed, gesturing toward it, "You know the way. Couldn't hold it, huh?"

"No."

Dorothy met me at the top of the stairs.

"Hi! I got my period!"

"Yeah, great, I guess. I gotta go."

I shut myself in. I hated other people's bathrooms. I had to use them all the time. Other people smelled different. That must be the scent dogs picked up, all the different family smells we have. The Likus', which was another dark house, smelled of cabbage and the inside of shoes. It also smelled of darkness, if that's possible; if you think, yes, sunlight smells fresh and clean, then, it follows, that darkness smells damp and dirty. The Krauss' house reeked of stale cigarettes and - dried blood - their bathroom especially. I supposed that was because Dorothy had gotten her period. In magazines, bathrooms looked clean, absolutely clean. It was just a part of the Nazi thing, this perfection of magazines and television. In reality, and reality was scary, bathrooms looked used: the towels sank in soggy folds; the rugs were suspiciously stained; the shower curtain or doors were crusted with black mold; the floors caked in black and powdered with dust at the corners. These horrors pursued me. The spiders and cobwebs on the ceilings were nothing compared to the fungi that fell off of human bodies. I was terrified of having to pull down my pants around these unpredictable terrors, terrified of *actually seeing* them - mold, pubic hairs (which Anne Frank had gotten in trouble for leaving behind in the sink after she used it), globs of food from teeth, grey water - from my own family unnerved me enough, but someone else's! I had to teach myself to not breathe, to suck myself in so as not to see, not to feel the terror. I tried to ignore it, but it never went away. I held my breath until *I* went away.

"What's it like to have your period?" I asked Dorothy. I hadn't really been able to relieve myself; some of it still felt heavy and stuck up inside me.

She shrugged, "I have to wear a pad and a belt."

"Yeah, I know. They gave us a booklet in school."

"Really? Sister Benedictus never said anything."

"I wonder if nuns still get their period."

"I don't know."

"Sister Benedictus acts like she has it all the time."

We laughed.

"You mean 'cause she's so grouchy?"

"Yeah."

"Too bad you can't just duck an' cover when it comes."

Again, we had a good laugh.

"It works for the bomb," I said, "but not for your period. Too bad."

"Wanna play?"

"Ok."

"Who you gonna be?"

"Ah, Maria Montez."

"Oh! Did you see that movie?"

"Yeah!"

"That was great! I should've said her, can I be her?"

"Come on, I said it first."

"Ok," she said, disappointed, but I wouldn't give in. Maria Montez had that *authentic* island look. "I'll be Dorothy Lamour."

I was still shaking after what had happened in the bathroom at home with Daddy. But, I was beginning to develop a method of silence, a way of continuing with what I needed to do - in order to live on - what I - *what I* - in *my world* - was supposed to be doing.

Dorothy was part of my world. She was precious. I would never tell her what had happened to me. I needed her to be free of it.

Our play always involved a romantic scene about a handsome, evil pirate capturing us and an even better looking good pirate rescuing us. We kissed Dorothy's pillow if we played in her room; we kissed the swings poles or trees if we played outside. The swings poles were great because they formed an A and you could sit propped up in them and pretend you were in the pirate's arms and kiss him at the same time.

Ma called me home at twilight. Her voice sang out over the street, it filled the street as the sun set orange behind the black lace bridge and the black oil tanks and the trees became silhouettes against the midnight blue sky, "Glor-i-a! Glor-i-a!" We played another minute or two; we hadn't been kissed enough, we weren't finished with our play, we hovered halfway between distress and rescue. "Glor-i-a!" Ma's voice filled the street at twilight, like the choir at church, "Glor-i-a!" I always listened for a moment before I gave in to it, then I walked home along the sandy road.

Dorothy was also my book friend. She was one of the smartest people I knew, including teachers. She went to sister school; of course, Hazel wouldn't have had it any other way. This made Dorothy smarter and closer to God than I was. She wore a uniform that signified this sanctity: a blue blazer, plaid skirt, white blouse, and blue tie. If the uniforms were meant to make all the girls look alike, they failed. As Ma said, "Some girls look better in their uniforms than others." Dorothy did not look good in hers. Dorothy's fat and the school uniform fought hard, but the battle was lost at certain stress points: under her sweaty arms where the crisp, white shirt melted into yellowed, knife-sharp creases; across her middle, where the waist band folded over an avalanche of "midriff bulge," which television told us was undesirable, unwanted in the struggle for the Nazi ideal, and at her backside, where her skirt, pleated and balloony, perpetually caught in her protruding butt causing her slip to show, frothy and indecent. My slip always showed too. My hems kept ripping; they hung in thready messes. I also had midriff bulge, as did Marie and Ma. Dorothy's fat was as much a companion to me as she was. Her weight was repellent but it was familiar.

Ma always said, "The nuns crack the whip." Sister school was hard, but it was fascinating for me, because, in a way, I got to go to sister school too. Having Dorothy was like having a spy there.

"Listen to this," Dorothy said, reading to me from the poems and stories *they* read, each one of them, careful Christian doctrine. *"The wealthiest farmer of Grand-Pre', / Dwelt on his goodly acres; and with him, directing his household, / Gentle Evangeline lived, his child, and the pride of the village. / Stalwarth and stately of form was the man of seventy winters;/ Hearty and hale was he, an oak that is covered with snowflakes;/ White as the snow were his locks, and his cheeks as brown as the oak-leaves. / Fair was she to behold, that maiden of seventeen summers. / Black were her eyes as the berry that grows on the thorn by the wayside, / Black; yet how softly they gleamed beneath the brown shade of her tresses! / Sweet was her breath as the breath of the kine that feed in the meadows. / When in the harvest heat she bore to the reapers at noontide/ Flagons of home-brewed ale, ah! fair in sooth was the maiden/ ... When she passed, it seemed like the ceasing of exquisite music."*

"That's beautiful." Goosebumps tingled over my skin; this was why I loved Dorothy. "What are 'kine'?"

"Sister Dominick told us they're cows," Dorothy explained.

"Why do all the nuns have men's names? And Sister Dominick is so beautiful! She should be called Sister Mary Angel, or something like that. It seems right, though, that she teaches literature."

"Yeah, I know."

"You had to read the whole thing?"

"We had to memorize it and recite it."

"The whole thing! What's it called?"

"Evangeline."

"Evangeline." Lovely.

I wished we did things like that, and then, instantly, I was glad we didn't. I was in the seventh grade, now. Evangeline had no place where I went to school. I couldn't even imagine it. Mr. Dolan and Mr. Scanlon were dueling Science and English teachers, respectively. Mr. Scanlon never touched literature. He stuck to grammar where the rules were set. Mr. Dolan liked to poke his head into Mr. Scanlon's room and say, just to be funny, "Dick, Jane and Sally. See them run! See Spot run!" The whole class roared with laughter. Mr. Dolan did scientific experiments. Mr. Scanlon peeked in the door with his military crew cut and cranked this siren he'd bought, "Did Mr. Dolan set the school on fire yet?" he asked. We laughed a lot. Seventh grade wasn't too serious.

Another time, Dorothy showed me her book, *Ramona*, about a young Mexican woman in early California. Ramona was kissed in a mustard field.

"What does mustard look like?" I asked Dorothy.

"Sister said it's tall, taller than Ramona, and yellow and fluffy."

It sounded beautiful. I got *Ramona* out of the library. I was thrilled to find it. Ramona was like a new girl friend. She taught me a trick: if you are careful, while peeling potatoes, you could make a wish - a love wish - and if you peeled the potato in one unbroken, spiraling piece, your wish came true. I practiced this often with the potatoes Ma left for me to wash and peel after school. I made the long spiral several times and held it up to admire. I wished I could give it to Ramona, whose knife always slipped. I imagined her working barefoot on the hot terrace, her dark foot on the sun-warmed terracotta bricks. I wished I were next to her; I wished I were her sister, or her friend. I would have long, light hair, she, long and dark. She would let me comb her hair; comb the sun into her hair. We would talk and laugh together. I talked to Ramona often. But, I was lonely for her. The more I talked to her, the more real she seemed, and, at the same time, the further she slipped from me. All my life I would be lonely for people who did not exist, except in literature. I was deeply lonely for fictional people and sometimes for their creators, the writers themselves. When I read books, I knew these people, I understood them, I longed for them. I spoke to them. Though they spoke to me in their own language, they could not really answer me in mine. The best I could do was talk about them to Dorothy.

One day, Dorothy informed me, "Sister told us, if you're raped, you have to resist to the DEATH! Only a dead virgin can go to heaven."

"What?"

"God knows," Dorothy nodded. "Sister says you can't fool God. He knows if you don't resist all the way. If you have *one teensy speck* of desire in your heart, then it wasn't rape and you go to hell. Sister said."

My heart was pounding. Had I been raped? What exactly was rape? Can you be raped if you don't know what rape is?

"What's rape?" I whispered.

"Ha!" she laughed, thoroughly. "You don't know what rape is! Ma!" Dorothy called downstairs, "Gloria doesn't know what rape is!"

"Ha! She will!" You could hear the cigarette in her mouth.

"It's when a man forces you to have sexual intercourse with him."

I didn't dare ask what sexual intercourse was. But, I went home as soon as I could to look it up in the dictionary. I was big on the dictionary. The dictionary was pretty often as close as I could get to real answers.

On the way, I passed the boys playing street hockey. I could feel the scrape of the stick against the cement as though it scraped against my back. The scrape of their shoes as they slid themselves along the sandy street, the scrape, scrape of the sticks, the brutal POCK! sound the puck made as it slammed hard against the broken crate that was the goal. The boys had carried the crates up from the tracks where they'd been thrown as trash to tumble down the hillside, the wooden slatted crates they used for goals, they'd carried them over their heads to Hichborn Street, making silhouettes against the blazing orange sunset like men carrying a safari. Afterwards, they dragged them off the road when they were done playing hockey after the sun had set with another scraping sound that echoed along the drowsy street; every night you could hear the boys dragging the crates and the *slam, slam* sound as they piled them in Rick's driveway.

As I passed him, Rick Likus shouted, "Two points! Two points!" slamming the puck into the broken crate as he spoke, leveling that scarred blue eye at me. "Two points!" The other boys tittered with laughter, because the score was one point and the two points were the points of my two full breasts as I walked by. My breasts had suddenly grown full, and the boys never stopped looking at them.

At home, I picked up the heavy dictionary and balanced it carefully on my lap.

The dictionary is where I had found all the words to describe the parts of my body that Daddy kissed. On this day, I found *sex u al*, adj. *of or affecting sex, the sexes, the sex organs, etc.* (The word itself seemed to stir my sex organs.) Then, *in ter course, 1. communication or dealings between people, countries, etc.* (That was boring. Sounded like The United Nations. That wasn't it.) *2. the sexual joining of two individuals; copulation: usually sexual intercourse.* (Copulation, wasn't that in the Bible as being very bad? That word was exciting. It scared me.)

Still, I had no answers to my questions. But, the emotions which accompanied the questions - these were my answers, trembling and fear, and desire - yes, desire, even now, my panties were wet and sticking to me, there, underneath where Daddy touched me. Whenever he wanted to. While we watched television, when Ma worked at night! He slid his hand up the leg of my pajama (while Marie and Jakey were right there in the room too watching television!), all the way up until he found what he was feeling for, and the warm, gushing waves began to vibrate over me. I was afraid, I would go to hell for my desire, yet, privately, in my room, in my bed, when Daddy wasn't there, I desired that he, or the Nazi, would do this or that to me, yet, I was afraid, of myself, of my feelings, of the pictures that ran through my head. I touched myself! I was the Nazi! I was afraid of the Nazi and I desired him. He was always ready. He slid under my covers in the dark like a snake, silently, then his tongue licked my legs, he was there! And, God was watching me! He was in my head, listening, watching what I was thinking, watching my hands! I didn't dare confess! There was no question: I could not confess! But, Daddy wanted me to do these things!

Daddy said to, how could it be wrong? Should I, was I supposed to tell the priest *that?*

I'd been turning pages, frightened, thinking, frightened of thinking, frightened now of the definitions of words that used to be so comforting, glancing with one, cautious eye I saw - far down on the page  - **incest** - it jumped out at me. I'd heard that word before. Had Dorothy said it? I could hear "rape or incest," that was when you could get an abortion, no, you couldn't get an abortion, you had to suffer. What did it mean? Did I dare look? *sexual intercourse between persons too closely related to marry legally. Latin < in, not + castus, chaste, not chaste.* Castus, I interpreted, cast out. Not chaste.

I shut the book.

# Book Three

## The Saint of Trees

Revere

1964-1965

LOOKING FOR CLUES

I crept downstairs after everyone was asleep. In the darkness, I turned on the blue light of the television. I crept up to the screen, close, where I could hear their voices, whispering to me, telling me, convincing me. There, alone in the womb of darkness, I watched movies.

But, I didn't just watch movies. I studied them. I was looking for clues. Clues on how to live: how to walk, how to talk, how to move my hands, how to act in every imaginable situation. How else was I supposed to learn? I wanted to be like *them*: glamorous people like Myrna Loy and William Powell; they became my new parents. I listened to them. I imitated them like a curious infant, how they spoke, walked, carried themselves, how they sat in a chair, smoked a cigarette, talked on the telephone, lifted a book from the shelf, sipped from a cup or a glass, even how they spoke to the dog, which was still much better than any speech I'd ever heard, even in school. Even Tarzan and Jane spoke better than anyone I knew. I practiced Maureen O'Sullivan's lovely accent. Over and over, I repeated her lines. "Your jungle has become my jungle, darling." "Oh! Wouldn't it be wonderful, if, one day, I, too, should be brave!" (The idea that Jane wasn't brave! I watched in awe as her father and all of civilization walked away and left her alone in the jungle with a strange creature, half man, half beast!) After a while, I could roll the r beautifully. My eighth grade teacher would tell me that my French accent was amazing. Why not? I'd learned from the charming Annabella. I learned how to set my chin high from Katherine Hepburn, not to mention how to look a man straight in the eye and say - Ha! But, that would come later.

For years, I snuck downstairs after everyone had gone to sleep. Maybe, Ma heard me; I can't imagine her not knowing everything that went on in the house. No, I mean that fully, I can't imagine her not knowing *everything* that went on in the house. Funny, how it creeps into every subject, but it does and always will. Because *that* is what I am.

I watched whatever I could, I ate them all up greedily. I swallowed them and was transmuted. I saw every single James Cagney film ever made. He really knew how to die. I saw "Man With A Golden Arm." I saw "Mickey One." I saw "The Pawnbroker." I saw "The Story of Temple Drake." "Of Human Bondage." "This Property is Condemned." "Splendor in the Grass." "The Sound and the Fury." "American Tragedy." "King Creole." I'm not sure of the years, or the titles, I did this so often and for so long. I'm not sure at what point I took in the movies and the heroes and the bad guys, the scenery, whether New York slum or Southern mansion or English countryside, and the women! The beautiful, the old, the demonic and the angelic! Their clothing! Soft blouses, billowing sleeves, tight satin gowns, fluffy feathers, the gentlemen in starched tuxedos, heavy overcoats, fedora hats, so much, I couldn't tell where they ended and I began. Surely, I chose them, but, also, I saw myself in them first, before I chose.

I saw a lot that I wasn't supposed to see. Once, I must have dozed off, because I woke to find myself watching a British pornographic film. They all had Cockney accents. I must have been older, because I knew this: they were dirty English. There was only one girl; she had bleached blonde hair and too much black eye make-up. She was very pretty, but her hair and makeup were messed up like they'd all been fucking for hours. When I opened my eyes, the boys were coaxing a dog, a German Shepard, over to her. They had her bent over, on all fours.

I held my breath! What was this? The blood began to pound in my ears! My heart beat hard, hard in my chest! This was wrong! Yet, I couldn't take my eyes away!

They had to coax the girl too. One of them held her by the shoulders, "You'll be fine, don't worry," he told her. They spoke more kindly to the dog. "It's all right," another boy said to the dog as he gently shoved him forward, "That's it, that's it." "There's a good boy!" The dog, off camera, whined louder and louder. The other boys groaned appreciatively. The camera was on the boy's eager face as he held her; you could see her hair moving.

I was astonished and thrilled to my fingertips, throbbing with absolute lust and shame and fear all at once!

Afterwards, the girl was smoking a cigarette on a bunk bed, talking to one of the boys. I don't remember a word they said, I was so amazed that they were now, nonchalantly, lounging and chatting.

Scared and shocked, I still began to wonder what it would be like to have a dog do that to me.

Too bad, there was always the Nazi. The devil had found me, there, in my cinema.


DREAMING

I was asleep in my bed, dreaming of catching the ball next time instead of ducking and covering my head; dreaming of riding my bike straight and swift instead of wobbly and unsure; dreaming of collecting the loops off the backs of boys' shirts like the pretty, popular girls, knowing, even in my dreams, I never would. When, suddenly, in my sleep, I felt pressure, pressing against me in my bed, nudging me aside and my eyes opened slightly to sense a dark shape in the smudge of light given by the nightlight in the hall, a dark shape pressing itself on me and I was frozen with terror.

"Sssh!" Daddy whispered, he pressed up against me, holding me in his arms. His rough stubble burned across my cheek.

"Daddy! What are you doing?" I whispered urgently, sleepily.

"Sssh! Don' worry. I just want some hugs and kisses."

"Where's Ma?"

"She's asleep! Sssh!"

"Shove ovva," he said, and I slid over to give him room.

His hands started to move over me. "Mmm," he stroked my breasts, over my fat stomach, slid into my pajama pants.

"Daddy!"

"Sssh!"

"Marie'll wake up!"

"Not if you're quiet, ssh! She's asleep." He turned, as if to check, to reassure me.

I still doubt to this day that Marie could have been asleep every time he did this. We must have woken her up sometime. We must have.

He circled his finger round and round in my vulva until I didn't care what he did.

"Daddy, something's tickling me, your hand."

I reached down, expecting his hand, touching my leg. But, it was soft and hard at the same time.

"Oh," I said.

Daddy laughed, affectionately.

Then, he slid down under the covers till I wondered how he could breathe! His huge bulk made a hump like an elephant. He pulled my pajamas down and completely off.

Ma would kill me!

"Daddy!"

"Sssh!"

He opened my legs wide – this made me crazy with desire! Then, he buried his head deep in my vulva. Sometimes, I think, his tongue went inside me, I was too overcome to know anything for sure.


THE RAPE ARTIST

Ma and I were sitting at the kitchen table eating at a pile of Saltines, a stick of butter and a bottle of dark Karo syrup.

"I love to eat with you," Ma said as she opened wide her little mouth for a Saltine thick with butter and dripping with Karo. "You really enjoy your food. You make it look so delicious."

This was a fact. Marie was not fun to eat with. She was no longer a baby. She was seven years old and knew better; nevertheless, she smeared her food all over the table with a real concentrated effort, as if she were trying to rub the vegetables into the Formica to get rid of them. Mashed potatoes were squeezed slowly through her fist till they oozed out her fingers in sickening, grey worms. Believe it or not, Marie cremated her food long after she was seven. It made Ma really furious and got her attention. You could see that self-satisfied smile on Marie's face, like she'd gotten exactly the reaction she wanted. I yelled at her too, for trying to aggravate Ma; once, I yelled so much that the vein in my neck almost burst, but it wasn't my attention she wanted.

Jakey had a more direct method. He filled his mouth up with food, asked to be excused to go to the bathroom, then spit the food into the toilet and flushed. Daddy started calling him, "Shithead" because he went to the bathroom so much. Ma was more refined. She called him "Toiletpaperhead." They actually thought he was going to the bathroom.

I thought Jakey and Marie were crazy. The food was orgasmic. When Jakey was upstairs, flushing, I ate from his plate. Ma scolded me.

"Stop that! He needs his food!"

"Why? He's not going to eat it!"

I knew he'd eaten already, probably a sub or pizza at the poolroom or down the beach.

I ate religiously. I not only ate from other people's plates, I sucked on the strips of fat that edged a steak or chop; I gnawed the bones until I'd gotten every bit of marrow out of them. I chewed and chewed, rolling the textures and sweetnesses round and round my mouth to see where they tasted best, tip of tongue, back of tongue, center, roof of mouth, lips. I licked my lips, buttery, creamy, bitterly green, sweet, succulent corn and squashes, crusty skin of bread and soft white flesh, dripping in gravies and butters, crunchy lettuce soaked in Ma's oil and vinegar dressing. And when I was done, I picked up the gooey plate and applied my face to it; I licked it clean like an animal. I sucked on each finger, one by one, even digging my teeth under my fingernails to unearth any marrow or meat or flesh of vegetable that remained. All the time, I moaned and grunted unconsciously, as though I ate in a trance, as though I entered my own body on a physically spiritual plane, the sweets and bitters, the oils and meats transported me as though they were drugs or wines or spiritual states of being in themselves, my eyes turned inward, the lids fell and I saw only the vague shapes of my rapture.

This was true of Christmas dinner or Saltines and butter. On this day, I replied to Ma's "You make everything look so good" with a smiling slurp of buttery Karo and "Oh, yeah?" I was very flattered that Ma loved to eat with me.

Our house was the kind of house people ran in and out of all the time, so it wasn't surprising when Marie dashed into the kitchen breathlessly, with Rick Likus' younger sister Linda right behind her.

"Ma! Gloria!" she cried, "The Fantasis are having a fight!"

We jumped out of our seats and ran outside. The Fantasi fights were something you didn't want to miss for a second. It was like watching a plane crash right before your eyes. Horrible, but you couldn't look away.

Sure enough, there they were, a ragged assembly outside their rickety brown tenement, the worst house on the street.

The Likuses were already down there, facing a large crowd of Fantasis. Both families yelled and rushed forward, shook fists at each other and fell back.

"He put a dead rat on our porch!" Junior's father screamed.

That must have been Rick Likus, I reasoned, not for a moment did I think the Fantasis were lying.

"You're crazy! Your whole family belongs in Danvers!" Annie Likus shouted back. By Danvers, she meant the mental institution. She'd defend Rick to the death, I thought, because, something weird happens to women who have boys, especially Irish women who have boys. Annie smoked and flung her cigarette in the Fantasi's direction. "You're crazy!"

"We go to mass every Sunday!" Junior's mother crossed herself. "My God, I say the rosary every day!"

"You're filthy! And you're crazy!"

"My God! Madon'! I wash clothes every day! Twice a day!"

It was true, every day dingy clothes hung from the Fantasi's clothesline out behind their tenement, but, grimy and slipping from their clothespins, they looked like they'd been hanging there for years.

Every one of the Fantasis was fat beyond comprehension. The Fantasis were fat in a terrible way - the way of strange families. I knew some of their names; the others seemed to morph into fat objects. They were: Junior Fantasi, about "my age," shorter and fatter than his father; Junior's mother and her mother; and Fatima Fantasi, Junior's sister, older than me, Rick Likus' age. In spite of her name, Fatima was the only Fantasi who wasn't fat. Rick called her "Fat is Ma" so everyone else did too, but she was tall and slender, quiet and, I think, the most intelligent Fantasi. However, she was not very clean and, though you couldn't understand why, she was not very pretty. She had pleasant enough features, but since she didn't have anyone to show her what to do, she did everything wrong, her hair, her clothes, her shoes. She dressed like a poor farmer's wife in dumpy brown dresses and thick shoes. She wore pointy glasses that made her look like Zelda Gilroy on "Dobie Gillis." We all thought Fatima was a sad waste. She seemed the only Fantasi who could actually be worth something. She was lost in that family.

The Fantasis were scary. Pale bags of fat swung from the women's arms as they shook their fists. Their housedresses were dingy; I wondered if they could afford soap. The bra straps fell from their shoulders and dangled, grey or yellowed with age, and this frightened me. I made solemn oaths that my bras would never get dirty and that they would never show. Their armpits were not shaved. I vowed always to be shaven there. Under their arms, the bras were stained in rings of perspiration that smelled pungent as an unwashed garbage can. I was terrified of them. The men held barrels under their shirts, tucked into their wide pants. They bellowed at the Likuses, yet they were not as loud as the women, who wailed like sirens, not the seductive kind from Greek mythology, but the screaming kind on fire trucks.

"What's it about?" I asked Marie.

"They're fighting with the Likuses."

I looked at Linda.

"What's it about?"

She was only seven. She shrugged. I looked at Ma. The lines on her face sagged.

"What is it, Ma?"

Whatever it was, it was adult, it was beyond me, and it was serious: all this I read in the sagging lines of my mother's face.

The Likuses were gathering a crowd of supporters. Families I didn't know and the Krausses who came out of their house and stood in front of their gate just a few feet from Richard Likus' broad back. Richard, Rick's father was usually a jolly man with a round belly like Santa Claus' that shook when he laughed. This day he frowned and shook his fist instead. Annie was there in all her slovenly glory. Richard's mother, Coreen, also very fat, who wheezed when she talked, wheezed and hollered like a banshee. Annette Likus kept getting sent home by her mother; she backed up the hill a bit, but snuck down toward the fight when her mother wasn't looking. Annie and her mother-in-law smoked cigarettes furiously as they screamed at the Fantasis.

"Take it to Chelsea court!"

That was something Annie said a lot, if Ma complained to her about anything at all. "Take it to Chelsea court!" Only this time, she wasn't fooling.

The Fantasis responded in a burst of Italian.

"What'd they say?" I asked Ma. She shrugged.

Then, Marie and Linda ran off to stand with Annette and, a second later, out of the blue, Ma spoke. "They're saying he raped Fatima Fantasi."

"Who?" My breath caught in my throat. I didn't doubt for a moment, it had to be Rick.

"Who else? Rick."

I could still feel the weight of him on top of me, still feel the thrust of his hard dungarees. I felt - chosen. I scared myself. I was insane, I had to be; even then in my total ignorance, I suspected it was my own romantic interpretation of being forced.

Ma took out her cigarettes and lit one. She took a long drag.

"They say he's a rape artist."

I laughed, in spite of the fear looming icily in my chest.

"Ma, there's no such thing as a rape artist."

"Oh, yeah? Then, what is it?"

"A rapist. A rapist."

"Well, they say he's a rapist."

"The Fantasis?"

She nodded silently.

"Oh, my God!" I cried.

The Fantasis were marching up the street in a solemn procession. Junior's father was in front next to another man, they carried a huge statue of the Virgin Mary on their shoulders; she was dressed in blue and white; she held her merciful arms open, palms upward, toward us. Junior's mother followed and her mother, their hands clasped in prayer. Junior came behind the women, his breasts swayed, larger than the breasts of any of the women. He carried a banner.

"What does it say?" I asked Ma.

It was a blue silk banner that shimmied in the breeze, like Junior's fat. As they marched slowly by us, there on the screened in porch, I could see the Holy Ghost on the banner, a white dove with golden light streaming from it.

"It looks like a priest's robe," I said.

Ma just shook her head and smoked. She knew it was true. Rick had raped Fatima. She didn't want it to be true because Annie was her best friend, but she knew. Annie was crazy about Rick. She bragged that he had stolen her a whole dinette set out of the railroad cars down by the tracks. Her affection for him was as demented as a mother's love for a son.

As the small parade passed the Likus house, Annette and Linda doubled over with laughter. Their hard, unforgiving bodies. I remembered how hard Annette's arms had felt around my neck that cold, winter day as she stabbed my face into the snowy bushes because I wouldn't fight. Another time, she'd tried to rip apart my sewing bag because she'd hated sewing class, but my stitches had held. She tore at a spool of thread instead, clawing at it with her fingernails until all the thread was broken. She'd handed it to me in triumph. The thread, suddenly a pile of shredded petals in my hand, had been a soft rose, the color of the dress I was making. It was very hard to find thread that exactly matched what you were making and Ma had to steal thread from work, which made thread even more precious. I couldn't believe Annette had torn something so dear to bits. Then she said she wanted to kill me, she spat in my face because she said I thought I was better, I thought I was so great.

I watched her now, and her sister, both of them doomed to be as fat and stupid as their mother.

"You think you own the Holy Ghost? You think the Virgin is on your side?" Annie yelled at the Fantasis.

But, the Fantasis no longer responded. They marched slowly as if to a solemn dirge only they could hear, humming in their strange heads. The police came and broke it up. The officers called everyone by name. They told Annie and Richard, they didn't even need an address any more; they just came straight here when they heard the name Fantasi.

The word rape was never mentioned.

The families went back into their houses. The street was empty. Then, Rick snapped open the Likus' aluminum storm door; he flipped his head like the dying rat, checking up and down the street. I was sure he looked directly at me though I was behind the darkness of the porch screens. Then he smirked complacently like you see criminals smirking in court sometimes on the news. His twisted eye landed on me with an almost physical jolt to my stomach. He smirked with great satisfaction. Then, he let the metal door slam; its echo reverberated over the street. And, I realized, as though it were at once a hard punch in the stomach and merely a subtle fact of life: only Rick and Fatima had been absent during the whole incident.

NOVEMBER 22, 1963
THE MOMENT

What difference does it make to history or anything else where any of us were at the precise moment we heard?

The difference is this: that was the moment we all, collectively, stopped believing.

We stopped believing in goodness.

Mama used to click her tongue, whenever she thought about it, in her vague, muddled way: "The Nazis fixed everything, they fixed everything, they fixed!" She was right. The Nazis made it so we could get used to anything. Someone, a man who had survived the death camps, talked once about being forced to shovel graves for the Nazis. He talked about how enormous the hole was and how cold he and the other shovellers were, how very cold. He talked about seeing a weed blowing in the cold wind and thinking how happy he was to be alive, just to see that weed, to know the weed was alive under the freezing snow and how grateful he was to feel the terrible cold because he was alive - and he knew, then, that human beings could get used to anything.

For a long time, the Nazis were very far away. First, they were in Europe, then, they were in the past. The Nazis were not us, but we became them. We invited them in.

From the moment the shot rang out, the Nazis, like the devil himself, rose up from hell and rushed to our side. From that moment on, we learned to turn our heads and check our backs; we learned suspicion and fear. At first we were horrified at ourselves and then, we got used to our fear. And then, we got used to our horror. And, then, we became proud of our horror and began to wear it ahead of us, not as a shield, as a medal.

We were so frightened by the Nazis, that we became the Nazis in order to keep it from happening to us again. We had the comfort of knowing, no matter what we did, no matter how evil, we *could never* be as bad as the Nazis.

In Revere, bad had become a virtue. Bad was *it*. I heard of kids who wouldn't come to Revere. That struck me as funny, because there were other cities, like Dorchester and Roxbury, where I was afraid to go, even in the car with my parents. Sometimes, bad is all there is. It starts to look good after a while. Bad makes you tough. It makes you ready.

I was walking out of school at lunchtime. I was looking down. I always did, looking introspectively at the black tar of the schoolyard that plunged downhill, watching the bits of broken glass twinkling in the sunshine.

Someone spoke in a normal voice: "The President's been shot."

I watched as the black tar ran out from under my feet, ran backwards, ocean waves of tar sparkling with glass, running out like the ocean, pulling the earth out from under my feet, the black tar ran on and on, spinning endlessly, and I went cold with fear.

I looked up to see everyone running, kids were running home. As though an air raid had been sounded, as though we were being bombed, kids ran for shelter.

The President can't be shot, he can't be! He's the President! That alone should protect him! He was so beautiful, so perfect! So good and fine. Didn't *those qualities* protect him? How could anyone *dare?* How could anyone *not love him? What more could anyone want?*

I thought of him sailing as I, too, ran home and the seagulls flew after me, cawing hoarsely after me, "Dead! Dead!" He was sailing, his hair filled with spray, and also in the boat, his fine wife and children, sun-colored, flying on the wind! What more could anyone want?

When I got to the highway, Mrs. Padder was crying, the tears making a trail of black eye makeup in her orange rouge. When I got home, Ma's nose was red and swollen; her beautiful eyes were swollen with sorrow. The television was on and everyone on TV, women and *men*, cried openly. Men choked when they tried to speak. Daddy came home early from work. He put his head down on the kitchen table beside his beer. When he lifted his head, he rubbed his eyes over and over.

The whole world was crying. The television was on for days. There was no school, but Ma made me watch the funeral.

"You sit there and watch this, this is history!"

"I can't stand it! I wanna go to the library!"

"The library's not open! Everything's closed! Look! It's history!" She was right. The streets were deserted.

But, I couldn't bear it any longer. Black, black, black, the slow march of black.

"Why don't they wear white? Isn't he in heaven? Why isn't everyone happy?"

I couldn't imagine him anywhere else. I was sure he was an angel now.

"Doesn't the priest wear white for a funeral mass?" I asked.

"Shut up and be quiet!" Ma sniffed.

I was tired of mourning already. I'd watched the television enough! John John was saluting. They made him do that. The riderless horse frightened me. It was ghostly. I wondered if the President had ever ridden a horse. I couldn't remember him on one, but I thought he'd look perfect. Then, I confused the lone horse with the headless horseman, and I remembered it was Jackie who'd ridden.

I was confused for days, as the TV droned on and on, the funeral procession marched for days. John John saluted all day long, the black horse rode alone, Jackie's suit was covered with blood, and we had a new President, President Johnson, who was a joke on the Vaughn Meader album. We'd all sat around the kitchen table, it seemed like years ago, in our pajamas. We had my little record player on the table and we laughed and laughed, as the little boy rang the doorbell at the White House and asked for Caroline. President Kennedy himself answered the door (really Vaughn Meader doing an imitation, who, afterward, refused to do another album) and told the little boy that Caroline was in Hyannisport with her mother and the little boy said, "Well, then, what's Lyndon doing?" I'd needed it explained to me, but, after that, it was hilarious.

And before, during the election debates, hadn't Ma knelt down and smooched Jack Kennedy's handsome young face on TV and didn't she turn and press her round ass to the set, and cry "Kiss my ass!" whenever Nixon's ugly mug had come on?

And, simultaneously, while the funeral marched endlessly and the eternal flame burned in the dark rain, young girls were being strangled to death, one by one, because they'd trusted too much in their mutual sorrow and let the Boston Strangler in the door.

It was evil; evil had wormed its way into Camelot.


## EXILE

Fat girls are delicious to sleep with, or, pretend to sleep with, if you are playing a sleeping scene.

Dorothy and I were on her bed, lying so closely, our eyelashes flitted like butterflies' wings across each other's cheeks. Through our cottony undershirts, our breasts touched nipples, almost painfully. Down in my panties, a sudden awareness of our closeness broke open in a gush of stickiness.

Dorothy seemed to know about this. She smiled. A sudden look of knowledge took hold of her features; it frightened me, her brown eyes looking down, where did she suddenly get her knowledge?

"This feels good," she said, softly, so no one could hear.

Not that Hazel would have. When we'd passed her in the living room a few minutes before, she'd been completely entranced by a game of solitaire. Cards were spread over the vinyl hassock between her veiny legs, a cigarette stuck to her shriveled lip, a game show screamed at her from the TV.

Dorothy's hand wormed its way under the tight elastic of my underpants, came back out, and unzipped my pants. My big stomach fleshed forward, Dorothy smiled.

"What are you going to do?" I whispered. "Is this all right?"

"Of course it is. We're both girls. You can't get pregnant from a girl," the little expert informed me.

I ignored the questions which melted as I melted and fused more and more into Dorothy and her bed, into the fat girl smells, of pungent folds and creases between our legs and rolls of midriff, sweet with excesses of chocolate and vanilla, strands of our hair caught with peanut butter, fingers marked by ballpoint pens, now slippery with ooze.

Once or twice, I broke the surface and thought about Daddy and wondered if this was like that, but Ma had warned me about boys, not about girls, not - about – Daddy.

Walking home between the thick overgrowth of the embankment, the highway screaming with cars and the street itself, silent and abandoned at five o'clock, I pondered, inching my way along the yellow stones of Winthrop Place, I wondered, once again, what had happened to me.

I could hear voices in my memory, clear, official voices from television and from government films shown at school: "Ask your pharmacist." "Talk it over with your guidance counselor." "Don't be afraid to go to your parents." All of these choices were equally ridiculous. If I went to any of these people, I would be severely punished. I would be instantly "from the wrong side of the tracks" like Connie Stevens in "Parish," like Natalie Wood in "This Property is Condemned." And, how could I go to Ma? How could I go to Daddy, when *he* was the problem? How could I tell Ma about Daddy? She would die! I felt this rather than knew it: her pain would be enormous! It would be a nightmare, a *real* nightmare! I couldn't bear causing Ma that much pain.

There was only one person to ask.

Sister said the priest is God's representative on earth. The catechism told us we could ask our priest anything we would ask God. But I didn't want to ask the priest. I wanted to go straight to God. I had to find Him.

Instinctively, I turned toward Church. But, it was late afternoon, a weekday, if I went to Church, I'd be late for supper and Ma would know something was wrong.

Was the Church open? I asked myself and just as quickly, answered, the Church is always open.

The pull of that little white church was enormous. It wanted to lift me from the empty road of sand.

That was another thing. If I were to suddenly change direction, someone might see me. It would be Gloria, as seen through one of the windows in the Likus house, *"She's walking home, watching her feet as usual. She always walks with her head down." "So, what happened?" "I don't know, she just suddenly turned and went down the street. Maybe I should call Rosie."*

I checked. The Likus house had closed eyes. So, also, did the Strummer's, the Duffy's, the Fantasis, even the Krauss' - dark, unseeing windows.

My body decided for me, it turned and walked straight and very fast toward Church.

Sure enough, Dorothy's amused voice called to me from her bedroom window. "Gloria? Where are you going?"

I looked up, but all I saw was a blank screen. I wondered how many of the other windows held a hidden face, also watching me, but I said nothing and hurried on.

Around the corner, there used to be a little grocery store, when we first moved there, and Mama sent us, sometimes, to buy a few things, "I went to the store/ to buy a loaf of bread/ to buy a stick of butter" was a song I used to sing as I walked, alone or with Marie, and the track people lived there, above the little store and next to it, in tiny apartments, in apartments so tiny, they left the doors open and they hung in the open doorways.

"Stay away from them! Don't talk to them!" Ma cautioned as she combed our hair, or stuck the little slips of paper listing bread and milk and butter and the money into our hands.

"But, what if they talk to us?"

"Don't talk to them! Just keep walking!"

They came to work the tracks, the dogs and the horses, and, sometimes, they came to work the stalls down on the beach, where Jakey liked to go, where people went at night to play their chances at winning against what Daddy called a "rigged" game, to throw balls at a target, to knock down pins or catch a cheap toy on a swinging magnet. People seemed to like the odds that way: challenged by the sneers of the carnies, they spent dollar after dollar as sweat poured down their backs. There was a certain justice in being a victim, a justice they seemed to herd toward.

The track people always watched me, and now, as I passed, a man stood in his doorway. He was too thin. His bones poked out of his face; as he looked my way, he smoked a cigarette and squinted into the smoke. He heard the others calling to me from their cars.

"Hey, baby," he spoke quietly. Nevertheless, a woman, deep in the shadows, turned at the sound of his voice.

"Who's that?" she asked, suspiciously.

I passed by quickly. I heard him giggle. I could feel his eyes following me, his eyes piercing the back of my head, yellow and soft, staring with hungry eyes, eating eyes, eating me; if he ate me, he wouldn't have to look at me anymore.

I turned in time to see her too, standing and watching me, her arms folded over her chest, but she was serious, not amused like her man.

As I walked along the highway, an evil chorus went up of horns honking and men shouting to me from their trucks and cars. As soon as the blonde hair came around the corner and hit the wind like a flag to the bulls, a blonde flag signaling the urge to cry out from deep in the genitals, the men leaned out their windows and cried to me, from deep within, they cried and flailed their arms at me, a twelve-year-old blonde girl, walking. Often, they stopped their cars and opened the passenger door and said, "Hey girlie, wanna ride?" I could have been killed over a hundred times if I had been a more adventurous girl, one who would take a ride. But, I was a quiet girl who preferred to walk and be alone.

On Sundays, they left me alone. The highway was soft with the occasional soft rush of a car and I could step out alone or with Marie and was instantly protected by the day itself, and my hair was covered with the mantilla -

I didn't have the mantilla.

My heart fell. I wouldn't be able to go into the Church. I stopped in the middle of the highway, rigid as a spooked squirrel, cars swerved around me, honking angrily, men yelled at me, and I ran, like squirrel, to the other side, avoiding their wheels and their shouts.

But, the mantilla. I continued on, worried, but determined. Perhaps, I would find a Kleenex on the ground. Some of the women pinned Kleenexes to their heads if they'd forgotten their kerchiefs or hats. But, now, I was in the white neighborhood, and in this neighborhood, there was nothing on the ground, just a few cigarette butts pushed to the edge of the gutters and a smattering of glass sparkling against the curb.

I could smell and hear people's dinners cooking. White people's. I could smell the boiling white flesh of potatoes. The meat smelled thin and clean, washed too much and apologetically boiling in water. Not inviting. Not rich and deep, oily and thick with juices, spices, aromatic vegetables, not a strong aroma like Mama's cooking, strong enough to lift you like a cartoon character and carry you to its source - Mama. The liquid smell of Mama's cooking made me wish for a piece of bread with which to gather the aroma to my mouth.

The white people clinked metal spoons against their metal pans. I could hear the echoes as I passed by their perfect little pink and white houses, "clink, clank," an unnerving, foreign sound, alien as a conqueror's language. Ma said they were rich here. They frightened me with their metal spoons and aluminum pans. Ma used enamel pots and iron, her wooden spoons made a soft sound, "donk, donk," a loving sound. The white people ate from factories, canned things, industrialized foods like cubed carrots and miniature marshmallows that didn't look or smell like food, food that had all the dirt scrubbed off it, food that was chemically colored beyond recognition. Ma said. Ma said. The sounds of them preparing food like that, the antiseptic odors of empty, neutered food frightened me, the conquerors with their wealth and their church and their plastic food. There was something immoral about them because they had never bent to pick dandelions like Ma and they would laugh at her, I remember, once, she wouldn't pick them because a white person was watching, they put chemicals on their lawns to kill the dandelions, she said, and that's when I found out dandelions were weeds.

I was at Church. I opened the caramel door and expected Him to be sitting in one of the pews. There, He was! Resplendent and white, all light, filling the church with glorious rays of light!

But, He twinked out immediately, He was not there, I had imagined Him.

I realized God was not in Church. He was only there the way He was everywhere.

I went in anyway. I genuflected deeply. I remained on my knees, there, in the red-carpeted aisle, alone in the silence and the dark beauty of an empty church. I could feel He was not there.

"God, please show me where You are."

I didn't want to see Him. Right away, I was afraid He would show Himself to me and I would have to give Him my life. I was a coward.

Suddenly, I was yanked upward from my collar and pulled to my feet.

"Hey, girlie! Whaddaya doin' down there in the middle of the aisle?"

Father Corro had me in one hand, his bulldog jowls not six inches from my face.

"I was praying, Father."

"You're supposed to pray in the pews, that's what they're for!" he whispered harshly, dragging me toward the front door. "An' why ain't you at home eating supper? There's no confession now. And whaddaya doin' in Church without a kerchief? Huh?"

"I was praying, Father."

"Go home and eat your supper."

"Yes, Father," I crossed myself, genuflected and ran out.

I really didn't know what I'd done wrong, though I shook so much, I could hardly walk. I had to sit down on the curbstone and wait for the tremors in my legs to stop. Kids sat on the curbs a lot, so it felt a lot like home, only the view wasn't right, it wasn't the Likus' house or the Duffy's, it was the rectory and the church and the convent to my back, the library and Tony Roma's, so I knew something was wrong, seeing all that from the low angle of the curbstone. Eventually, I got "my sea legs" as Daddy always called it, and started for home. I didn't blame myself so much as I blamed Father Corro. I couldn't believe a priest had thrown me out of Church. Tears came to my eyes because a priest had thrown me out of Church and I was afraid. I was terrified, what did it mean, that he could smoke cigars and throw kids out of Church? We always said, if you want a light penance go to either Father Corro or Father Dougherty: Father Dougherty cared too much to give a mean penance and Father Corro couldn't care less.

But, sunset was warming the sky all around me. I had to walk very fast to beat it home.

The kids were back out on the street, playing, after supper. Johnny Strummer, easy and cool, was shooting baskets outside his house. He stopped to look at me as I passed.

He frowned. "Hey, Bleachie, you okay?"

He had a brother's eye for me. I loved him for that.

"Yeah," I said and kept on walking, my head down, as usual.

Jakey was whacking a can with Rick Likus' hockey stick, he called to me, "Where were you? You missed supper. Ma's looking for ya."

"Is she mad?"

"She's over Annie's," he shrugged, slamming the can against the curb; it ricocheted, bouncing painfully off my ankle.

"Hey! Watch it!" Johnny yelled at him.

Jakey had to do what Johnny said, because Johnny was considered a higher species, but he laughed anyway. "Oh, yeah? Whaddaya wanna kiss her?"

All the other kids laughed, except Johnny. I heard the basketball bounce and slap the street, but I didn't hear his voice. A rush of love went out from my heart to his eloquent silence, better than a kiss and a kiss would have been a dream.

If Ma was over Annie's, that gave me time. I had another idea.

A felt something switch inside me. This hour was mine, this hour of sunset, when the sky cries out in a blaze of glory before losing the battle to midnight blue, the final color before darkness. I was born in this hour, in autumn, in the sunset of the year, in the last scream of color, the color of life, before life curls up into hard, black buds and goes to sleep, a time between breaths, private, secret, deep, hidden, when, at last, shadows lead you into their depths and shades of darkness become your colors.

I followed the half-light into the backyard, along the path by the pear tree. The grass was hard and the mud between had dried to cakes that crumbled beneath my shoes as I walked.

I could hear the dishes tap, and I felt a sudden twinge of guilt that Marie must be doing the dishes by herself. A yellow light streamed from the kitchen onto the darkening grass, making the path glow artificially. I held my breath and tiptoed foolishly - a bluejay cawed, scaring me, I froze, then a sparrow sang, little and gentle, and I sighed with relief.

"I don't know where she is!" Marie cried out, annoyed as hell, as I crept past the kitchen window and made my way toward the Indian Camp.

How strange such a familiar place looked in the dimness! I hadn't been there for so long! Look! Look at the dirt pressed down by a stranger's hands! I could see shadows, indentations of the fingerprints, the open palms, there! In the black dirt packed down to make the floors of the Indian Camp! So innocently! So diligently! So industriously!

Who had done this, I wondered, standing at the edge, afraid to go in. Whose fingerprints were they? Whose palms?

God had done this! Look at the mud pies He'd made! All dry and cracked! I should eat them for my salvation! And the firewood so neatly stacked! And a leafy curtain He had hung over an imaginary window! The leaves all curled and crumbled!

I didn't dare go in, though I knew God was in there. I didn't dare.

I went away. I climbed the hill where the alfalfa grass made clumps like steps to sit on. There I sat, looking deeply into the dried grass for comfort. The pale stalks rose out of the earth like the trunks of a million, miniature trees, an infinite forest where I could walk and walk, at least in my mind. But, my vision became blurred and I realized, I was crying, there, in exile, while the cars barreled and careened not five feet from my head; rumbling, screeching through my chest, and, I wondered, what in the world was real and which way was I supposed to go, towards home or Church, Indian Camp or highway?

I sat there a long time. The damp earth seeped through my pants and I was cold. By the time Ma came home, I was shivering uncontrollably, my teeth banged together. I could hear her voice cry out from the kitchen, her most frightened and annoyed voice, "But where the hell *IS* she?" and I knew, I would have to go in. I heard Marie shout, "I don't know!" I didn't hear his voice, but plain as day, in my ears, his crusty feet scraped together.

His penis was like the trunk of an old tree, big-veined, ending in bushy stuff, the only penis I'd ever seen. It was always erect. But, I didn't know that then.

He'd said, "Kiss it."

Quickly, I gave it a sweet kiss, right on top.

He laughed at my innocence.

"No, no! *Kiss* it!"

He thrust it closer to my mouth, but I still didn't understand.

He could have shown me, he could have made me, but he didn't, he let me go. I didn't know that then.

"God, please, help me!" I cried. I prayed, inside, as quietly as I could, but God doesn't answer you so soon, not in your waiting heart.

As soon as I could, as soon as I stopped crying, I went into the house.

Ma screamed at me, "Where the hell have you been?" so that I felt her pain, and it hurt.

I could hear him already snoring somewhere, probably the couch. "Thank you, God," I thought.

"I was up on the hill," I told her, which was a lot less suspicious place to say than church.

THE NAZI

The door to the bare room opened and a dog burst in, jangling on a leash, and the Nazi behind him, holding the leash. The dog saw me in the bed; he locked his eyes on me. He began to growl and bark in sharp snaps.

The Nazi spoke firmly to the dog in German. The dog sat down, but he continued to glare at me. The dog licked his lips, whimpered and turned his head toward the Nazi several times, anxiously, anticipating another command.

The Nazi spoke soothingly to the dog. Reluctantly, the dog attempted to relax, sitting back on its haunches.

Now, the Nazi turned to me.

I had not taken my eyes from the dog. I did not know what kind of look I should have on my face to please the Nazi. I had heard of the dogs tearing women apart after the Nazis had tired of them.

I had a look of terror on my face.

The Nazi smiled to himself. He was pleased.

The dog made an attempt to stand; he barked again, anxious not to have the proper command.

The Nazi ignored him. He began to undress. He came toward me. He touched my trembling face and spoke kindly to me in German. His hand travelled to my neck, down my throat and entered my vulva where the Nazi turned his fingers until I moaned, causing the dog to bark louder, causing liquid to gush from me. The Nazi grinned and spoke again kindly, he whispered in my ear, he thrust his hard penis into me and crushed my breasts with his hands. The dog whimpered and barked, louder and louder, as the Nazi thrust himself into me over and over, harder and harder, causing tremors to shudder up and down my legs.

MUSHY GUSHY

I tried to stay away from Dorothy, but I couldn't. I missed her; she was the most interesting and intelligent kid I knew. Plenty of times, we'd fight over who we were going to look like in our play, or some vital point, such as, whether Douglas Fairbanks was too old to be a pirate by now, and I'd leave in a huff and go home and Ma would say, from seeing the look on my face, "What happened?" singing it, like it was a joke to her, "Dorothy and I had a fight." I'd reply, missing my friend already.

She was the only person I knew who read books for fun. The kids at school were separating now into nerds and beauties. The beauties were golden limbed and shining in new clothes, gold and jewels. Beside them, the nerds were deformed fetuses, all brains and stunted torsos, with gnarled hands and clubbed feet. I was a nerd, but I was terrified of nerds; horrified to touch or be touched, however inadvertently, by them. I knew they had "hobbies" like astrology or chemistry, but none of that interested me; that was science, and, science was cold and unloving. Besides, if I spoke to one of them, I'd actually have to breath the same air, like being in a nerd gas chamber! I could die, or, worse, become like them, smelling of vegetable soup in a can, frayed and grimy at the edges, wearing white socks, black eyeglasses and pants that ripped open at the buttocks. I wanted to be golden, but I was poor and fat. Dorothy was my secret and my consolation; no one at school knew about her. She was smarter than anyone, even adults, even the smartest nerd at school, that would be Michael Weinstein, who got A's in everything, but everyday wore smelly black suits covered with dandruff, like a sleazy grown man you wouldn't want to sit next to on a bus. Then, there were others, like Annette and Linda, Rick Likus' sisters. Dorothy could speak in whole sentences, even paragraphs, while these others could only grunt. She could think, while they picked their noses and ate it, for a change, from eating dirt. But best of all, Dorothy could invent and discover, where the others couldn't even follow.

She showed me things. But, I wasn't always able to take what she showed me. In Revere, you're supposed to be able to take things. I wonder, even now, how much should we be able to take?

Nevertheless, I've always been amazed - and seriously confused - by the way we seem to participate in our own torture.

When the Nazis herded their prisoners into the gas chambers, they told them, "Breathe deeply. Tell your children to breathe deeply, the gas is good for them." And the people looked down into the faces of the little ones who trusted them completely and they told their children, "Breathe deeply, the gas is good for you."

Why should innocent people ever imagine evil? What confusion when the gas actually *hurt*, and more and more confusion building to terror as the gas hurt more and more, and the children choked and the people cried out, choking, as conscious life slipped away and the realization, for one stunned millisecond, that, *this was real! Real! And God had let the children be there!*

How was it, and what did it mean, that I sucked in my fat tummy and pushed out my inadequate breasts, once, when I passed by him, knowing he would respond! He jumped up from the kitchen table and followed me! And I led him down the dark hallway, pretending to myself that I was alone, hearing his footsteps coming closer all the time till he caught me on the stairs, at the shadowy curve in the stairs, he lifted my jersey, he grabbed it and yanked it out of my pants, he stuffed his face into my still-forming breast and sucked, and I fell backward into his hands.

I was ashamed. And, excited.

So, one day, when Dorothy called and said, "Meet me at my house, hurry up! You gotta see this!" I didn't want to go. I hesitated.

"See what?"

"I can't tell you over the phone, you gotta come down. There's some people in the house behind me - you know, the red one - they're crazy! You gotta see it! Hurry up!"

"I don't want to see crazy people."

"Yes, you do! Get down here or I'll never speak to you again!" Dorothy whispered, harshly.

I knew I had to go down. I was drawn to Dorothy; I couldn't give her up.

She was waiting for me on the porch. She was pacing with the grin of a little demon on her sweet, fat face. Her bright, brown eyes looked me up and down, from my questioning face to my shoes and back again, making it suddenly clear to me, with a nasty twist of her cherub mouth, I was going to do something bad again: I wondered what it was.

"Come on!" She grabbed my arm and pulled me around to the driveway. "My mother told me not to go here anymore."

The red house hid itself way down at the end of a long, blind driveway, a far away and an almost invisible, undiscovered land, next door to the Krauss' little green house. I'd always pretended, in my childish, pastoral imagination, that the squat, red building was the Krauss' barn.

As we crunched down the gravel driveway, the red face of the house seemed to jump closer at us, instead of us coming closer to it. It changed shape. It grew and altered from the storybook face of the Krauss' barn to the menacing face of a stranger; its red door stretched in length, its white-framed windows widened in interest at the two approaching girls. It looked suddenly strange, unfamiliar and - ordinary, which scared me most of all - as we came close upon the dull grey aluminum door.

I could hear what sounded like hundreds of kids running and screaming inside the house – no, squealing with crazed delight and taking their squeals from one room to the other, like a whiplash through the house. I didn't like that sound, I shrank back, but Dorothy pulled me forward and the aluminum door opened and a dark-haired lady in something misty red and silky shouted to us, "Hurry! Hurry!"

As we scooted in past her, I could hear the urgent scrunch, scrunch of a man's urgent footsteps rushing up behind us: the storm door slammed at our backs and the woman pressed down the teeny lock with her thumb; water from the garden hose smashed hard against the glass and a thousand kids screamed with emergency. I turned to see her standing nose to nose through the glass with an ugly man; his features smeared through dripping water, his dark hair melting into his burning face, his lips open and screaming, his words drowning, his mushy fist inches from her happy, happy mouth.

Then, I thought I heard him yell, "Hazel! Let me in! I'll kill ya! I'll kill ya!" all gurgley with water, as he walked away. "It's my house, damn it!"

"Who's that?" I asked Dorothy.

"That's Barry."

"Who's Barry?"

"Hazel's husband."

Another Hazel. Now, slamming the inner, wooden door and locking it. She walked toward us, younger than the other Hazel, beautiful as an exotic dancer, languid as an Arab princess, her black curls lapped around her neck and shoulders like garlands, her long, red peignoir, open and flowing as a ceremonial robe, a cigarette worked steadily from her painted nails to her overfull, over-painted lips. Thin breasts fell limply into a red bra as she leaned down. And horror! Clumps of black hairs hanging like little animals out of her red nylon panties, hanging like upside down animals between her legs!

"Hi, kids," Hazel said, dully.

"Hi!" said Dorothy, obviously impressed. "This is Gloria."

"Hi, Gloria. Make yourself at home, honey," Hazel replied, without looking at me.

She sat down at the kitchen table and took up painting her toenails, which were very long and had been painted so many times that the layers of paint were thick and high. She took puffs on her cigarette and reached over to paint a kid's fingernails from time to time. Her legs were wide open. I couldn't take my eyes off her.

I'd never seen black hair like that on a woman. Was it because the hair on her head was black? Ma's pubic hair was light and dainty. But, this! Bushy and fierce! And strange, a stranger, another Hazel! Another!

"Why won't she let her husband into the house?" I asked Dorothy, aside.

Dorothy laughed. "She never does!"

Daddy was always saying, "A man's home is his castle." I thought everybody wanted a castle. *I* wanted a castle. How could she get away with not letting him in? She must let him in sometime! Did she let him in at night?

"Where does he sleep?" I asked Dorothy.

She laughed again and shrugged.

"Come on," she said, tugging at me, "Hazel lets us wear her clothes."

For the first time, I noticed, all the kids around me were wearing lacy peignoirs, high heels, ruffled dresses and heaps of costume jewelry over their corduroys and jerseys and their faces were finger-painted with lipstick and mascara. I wondered if any of the crazed maniacs were Hazel's kids.

I tugged off my laced shoes for a pair of sparkling, strappy high heels. Dorothy slid a blue nightgown over my head and the kids screamed through a world of bright blue nylon.

As my head popped through the sweetheart neckline of the nightgown, the scratchy blue lace against my cheek, I saw Hazel dashing from window to window, slamming them shut, still gripping the cigarette between her fingers, her breathy laughter, guttural, from her throat, followed by hoards of screaming kids, because Barry had picked up the hose again and was blasting the windows with jets of water like some sort of desperate fireman.

"Haze-el! Haze-el!" he screamed, forlorn as a howling dog, at the shut windows.

She just kind of hugged herself in that peignoir, serene and silent, she smoked and watched him run around all crazy.

I never really saw Barry up close. I saw him from the street sometimes, far away down the driveway, watering the few flowers and thin shrubs that grew around his little house and I saw him through the windows from the inside of his house, where he wasn't allowed. I didn't understand any of it. It was wild, like entering a nightmare house where the ceiling was the floor; a new adult world, another kind of reality thrown at me, a frilly dress thrown over my head and my face painted to be another face. Their name was Church! Barry and Hazel Church! What did *that* mean?

I knew I was supposed to go there and run around like a maniac, because I was a kid and I was supposed to actually like running around screaming in a strange lady's nightgown and high heels, and, one time, Hazel let all the kids take down every box and bottle of food on the shelves and mix it all together into Mushy Gushy. Rows of kids around the kitchen table, each with his own bowl of grey goop, stirring in oatmeal, cat food, cocoa, beans, milk, coffee, noodles, tuna fish, eggs, peanut butter, anything they could find, screaming kids wearing earrings and nightgowns over their clothes, makeup accenting their wide open mouths and crazed eyes, daring each other to eat it, and laughing, laughing like they were all insane.

Hazel laughed with them, while Barry tried to open a window with a screwdriver. We could hear the window rattling furiously with his rage.

I was supposed to like Mushy Gushy, but I was scared of it; scared, too, of the little red house and the windows that grew as I approached, scared of Hazel's black clumps of hair coming out of her panties, scared of the man who couldn't get in - what if he *did* get in someday? Would he kill everyone? Did he hit Hazel, was that why she locked him out? I was scared of the kids wearing Hazel's silky things over their play clothes, scared of the weird paint on their demonic little faces, scared at the way they treated food, Ma and Grandma had always treated food so reverently, what would they say if they saw mushy gushy, grey and lumpy, reeking of throw up, and Hazel in her panties, laughing?

I didn't want to go back, so I told Ma about the Churches. Dorothy would have murdered me, if she knew. I told her everything: mushy gushy, the clothes, the makeup, Barry trying to get in. I told her about the black hairs sticking out of Hazel's panties.

Ma's face sagged grimly; her no lipped mouth, a pink line. Slowly, she shook her head from side to side.

"I don't want you to EVER go there again!"

But, she wasn't looking at me; she was looking sadly into herself.

Oh, thank you, Ma! Thank you! I felt released!

"All right," I said, quietly, all the while, wondering at her deep, inward expression.

For a while, Dorothy and I got into our Roman phase, inspired by "Spartacus," "Jason and The Argonauts" and other sexy, slave pictures, during which we ran around her fixed-up basement naked, wearing only flimsy red scarves flung upon our bodies. Our Roman phase lasted until Dorothy started doing slave experiments on me, laying me down on cushions, rubbing my legs and buttocks soothingly, saying she'd like to put something in me, maybe a pencil, but she wouldn't push it in hard, like some people, she said.

"Who?" I asked, half dreamy, half alarmed.

She mentioned a girl from the sister school. I got really scared. Dorothy was my friend, but I had a place to go to get away from her. Not the safest haven in the world, but in a crazy way, more stable than the craziness of other people's houses.


A CHILD'S CHRISTMAS IN REVERE

Margaret Flannagan was my Godmother. Every Christmas, she sent me a sacred card, all my own, with the Virgin and Child on it. I waited for this holiest of cards, this slip of colored cardboard, every year and when it arrived, I asked Ma to open the envelope because only she could do it neatly, with her long, red fingernails like a knife, without losing the name and address in the corner. Carefully, I took the card out. I kept the envelope, tenderly setting it aside. Then, I sat down and looked at the card, the beautiful Madonna and Child. I stared and stared at the picture, thinking about Margaret holding me in just such a pose. I was thinking also about the Holy Virgin: what had it felt like to be chosen and then to give birth to the

Son of God? What did it feel like to love Him as your child? What was this incredible mystery of motherhood? And what did it mean to be a godmother?

"Ma? What's a godmother?"

"Oh, a godmother takes care of you if anything happens to your father and mother. She makes sure you're brought up a Catholic."

"What's gonna happen to you and Daddy?"

"Nothing!" she laughed. "Just in case something happened."

"Like what?"

"Oh," she sighed, "we could die in a car crash or a car accident." She shrugged, "But, that's not gonna happen."

"Do I have a godfather?"

"Your Uncle Vickie!"

This made sense, because Uncle Vickie was connected, but what I couldn't understand was, why wasn't he married to my godmother?

But, Ma was tired of my questions. She cut one hand through the air like she did when she was fed up, "Don't worry about it! Jeez! You think too much, you know that? You think too much!"

I saved all the Christmas cards Margaret Flannagan sent me. I didn't have a ribbon, so I chose the color of the rubber band I would put around them carefully. I chose a wide blue one, from Andy Boy broccoli, the most like a ribbon I could find. I kept the envelopes too with Margaret's handwriting on them addressed to me, which I imagined were written with love.

And the cards! The colors of stained glass windows above the altar in Church! Renaissance vermillion, deep as a cup of wine turned to blood; the fathomless blue of the Virgin, her eternal blue for her eternal prayer for peace, blue as the sky of Jerusalem and blue as the sea below it; the gilded gold, dazzling as the sun on sand, and the white light of God, streaming from her brow, flashing from her fingertips.

I didn't know then, these were the colors of Margaret's guilt.

She was my godmother, but she never came to see me. Her husband wouldn't let her.

Here was a vital lesson I learned in bits and pieces.

"Where'd you meet Margaret Flannagan?" I asked Ma.

"In school. Everybody's equal in school," she replied.

I knew better, but I didn't argue though, I thought maybe everybody in Ma's school had been equal. I knew in a democracy, we were all supposed to be, but I also knew, we definitely weren't. Some kids were so much smarter, others so very pretty or so very rich. Nobody was equal.

"High school?"

"No! I didn't go to high school. I went to trade school."

"Did Margaret go to high school?"

"Yup."

I breathed a proud sigh. I knew she had gone to high school, some marvelously higher high school than I had ever seen.

"Did Daddy go to high school?"

"No! Your father never went further than the sixth grade."

"How come? Was he stupid?"

I knew kids stupider than Daddy who were in high school, Rick Likus, for instance.

"Your father had to go to WORK!"

WORK! was one of those important words Ma threw at us with a loud angry yell. KIDS! was another one. CHURCH! YOUR FATHER! POOR! TEACHER! SCHOOL! And SIN! To name a few. A sin was anything from President Kennedy getting shot to throwing away uneaten food.

Margaret Flannagan, a slim, elegant lady in a peaked hat with a half veil turned up, smiled back at me in Ma's old photographs with the delicate little features of an Irish, little eyes, little nose, little mouth. Her cheeks were bright as an apple. Her arm held Mama fondly close. But her eyes gave her away. Even with that big, apple grin, she had trouble around her eyes. It was as though she knew, standing in front of Grandma's old wooden door, or in front of The Sacred Heart's rusted chain link fence, her arms embracing Mama, she knew - she didn't belong there.

After she married Harvey, the trouble crept down from her eyes and covered her whole face.

I'd ask Ma, over and over, "*What's* his name?"

"Harvey!"

"How do you spell it?"

I couldn't help it; I had to *see* a word before I could know it.

"H-a-r-v-e-y!" Ma told me.

I thought a minute.

"Gee whiz, Ma, isn't that the name of that invisible rabbit, you know, in the movie?"

Ma laughed, "Yeah, they're both invisible."

One day just before Christmas, Margaret Flannagan called on the phone. Ma's face was all twisted, what used to be her pretty little mouth but was now a thin, colorless line all twisted in disgust.

Ma slammed the receiver down. "Your godmother's coming over," she informed me, her mouth all twisted.

My heart leaped up, but checked itself halfway to my throat because Ma had her disgusted face.

"Don't ever pick a girl friend for godmother to your kids! Remember that. Pick somebody in the family!"

Then, she picked up the broom and started sweeping the floor, real hard.

"Why?" I asked, secretly feeling a thrill building in anticipation of Margaret's visit.

"They'll disappoint you."

She was quiet, for a while, sweeping the floor, then she said, "Pick somebody in the family. Your family's always there. Always."

Ma was always complaining and I didn't know what she meant. I wasn't going to have friends who deserted me. I was going to have friends like Margaret Flannagan, elegant ladies who wore peaked hats with their half veils turned up. Despite a vague sense of sadness somewhere in my blood from Mama, I wanted to impress my fabulous godmother.

I wanted to make something Christmassy marvelous for Margaret Flannagan to see.

Besides the sad, drooping Christmas tree, Ma had some decorations up, unfolded from last year. A red-faced Santa with a fold down his left eye dangled from one piece of yellowed tape. She'd hung a gold garland, a little ragged and looped over the doorways with some chipped red and gold balls hooked on it, here and there, causing the garland to sag cheerlessly. She'd taped lights over the kitchen window that blinked on and off like a creepy barroom sign.

About a million cards came every year. Ma Scotch-taped them with a grubby thumbprint on each one, all around the archway of the door. Cards arrived in bunches; Ma and Daddy had tons of friends. I liked to take my finger and open them where they hung and read the secret message, gibberish to me, and see who they were from: I'd ask, "Who's Ida and Joe?" And Ma would tell me something like, "Oh, Ida used to work with Daddy over at Brocket Shoe."

"Was she Daddy's secretary?"

Ma grunted, "Daddy never had a secretary. Ida did the books."

Yuck. Sounded terrible, something to do with math.

"Who's Pete and Gladys?"

"Oh, they lived around the corner from Grandma in East Boston."

"Do I know them?"

"Nah, they moved to Chelsea before you were born."

I got a leap of joy if I knew who sent the card, cards that glistened with sparkles, cards with watercolor poinsettias or doorways wreathed and lighted. I could recognize Aunt Doris's handwriting, all jammed together and illegible, or Uncle Salvi's and his new wife, Dolores, who was an Irish girl, a bleached blonde like the girls Ma said were whores, but who couldn't be a whore because her brother was a priest. They always sent a manger; they already had four kids, all named after saints.

Those were Ma's decorations. She went on sweeping the floor, now and then she'd heave a sigh, deep and mournful, overfilled with giving up and carrying on at the same time, she was the Queen of Sighs.

I was looking out the window. They'll never make a Christmas card of a wintry scene in Revere. Winter turned grey in Revere; a veil came down, lowering itself over the houses, the street, the ocean, even the people, the very colors they wore, changed, as though, suddenly, everything was on black and white TV, everything fell under the city's veil of grey. The sky turned grey, dirty white clouds and clouds of leaden grey spiraled round and round, threatening and low. The once friendly trees became strangers swaying black arms, scratching the house with black fingernails; a few dead brown leaves hung on them like old dead decorations.

Beyond this stood the silhouetted city of oil tanks and the black lace bridge and the tall, silver buildings glistening along the skyline of Boston.

I wanted to make a very beautiful Christmas decoration for my godmother, Margaret Flannagan. I wanted her to see what I could make. What would be the best thing to make? A Virgin and Child, like her cards - a manger!

I told Ma. "I want to make a manger for my godmother!"

She said, "You can't!"

"How come?"

Ma always said, "You can't!" I figured it was a way to keep me in line.

"How are you gonna make a manger?" She stopped the broom.

"Well, can I have a shoe box?" I asked, timidly.

"I DON'T HAVVA SHOEBOX!"

The broom swept hard.

Undaunted, I went upstairs.

I heard Ma muttering to herself, "Now, she wants a shoebox, a shoebox she wants! I don't have enough to do! She wants a shoebox now!"

I looked at my dolls. Carry would have to be Jesus. I started to take off her clothes. Carry still had all those pinholes in her head, and she was a girl, but she would have to do. When she was naked and lying down, she had a lovely way of kicking up her fat legs and chubby little feet, a darling way of holding up her baby hands, in exultation, just like the Baby Jesus.

Ma came in, burst through my closed door like she usually did, scaring me half to death, but I was always glad to see her.

"Here!" she said, handing me a grimy Buster Brown shoebox, "Here's your shoebox!"

"Thanks!" I replied, my eyes already glazed over with concentration.

Carefully, I folded a doll's blanket Ma had made out of old towels quilted together into the shoebox. I placed Carry, naked, on top. I spread a pillowcase around the box to represent snow.

Ken would have to be Joseph, and Barbie would have to be Mary, even though they weren't married and they were so much smaller than Carry. I removed all their modern clothes and wrapped them in white Kleenexes for robes. I knew Ma would yell at me if she saw all the Kleenexes. I tried to get Barbie and Ken to kneel. They wouldn't. So, I sat Barbie down and Ken stood up. I spread Barbie's arms, but couldn't turn her palms upward. I couldn't close her painted on eyes.

I drew the farm animals, the cows and horses. I drew the shepherd and the sheep. I drew the Three Wise Men, being careful to distinguish them, their separate countries and their caskets of gold, frankincense and myrrh. I propped them up as best I could with toothpicks jammed into the folds of the snowy pillowcase.

All this I placed under my bedroom window where the stars could look down upon Him. A star! Oh, yes! It would be wonderful to have a star! The red electric candle Ma had on the windowsill every year!

I plugged it in.

Instantly, Carry's skin glowed blood red! I sat back and admired my work. I thought the whole scene was marvelous!

I called Ma in to see what I'd done. She took forever to come.

"That's nice," she said, when she got there, "you better put that pillowcase back where you found it when you're done."

"I will." I promised, gladly.

"And turn off that candle in a while, you're wasting electricity."

"Okay."

I knew that was Ma's way of saying she liked it, otherwise, she'd be screaming.

I was so happy! Eagerly, I awaited praise from my godmother as well, when she came this Christmas to see me.


A thousand Christmas mornings, grey and chill, we hustled out of our warm, cooking house for the adventure of visiting a million friends and relatives Daddy took us on a drunken path to see. Every Sunday, the many neighbors and relatives came to our house, one by one, or sometimes, in droves, for ours was a cooking house, a bustling house with both doors open, but today was Christmas Day, the day we went out to visit. Mama stayed home in a holiday ruffly apron to cook Christmas dinner. At the door she waved good-bye and mournfully instructed Daddy, "Don't drink too much! Say Merry Christmas to my mother, mmm," she moaned, releasing as she did a glorious deluge of scents into the freezing Christmas Day led by Bell's seasonings that had seeped round and through the turkey's stuffed with savories breast.

"*My* turkey has a name," Mama liked to tease the hundreds of little kids who came each year to witness Mama's frozen, naked turkey coming out of the Stop & Shop bag and going into the alternate freezer down cellar. "See!" Mama pointed a fat finger to the turkey's label, "Jenny O'Young Tom! That's its name! Jenny O'Young Tom!" Hundreds of kids nodded sagely, though none could decide, and there was much argument over, whether *it* was a "Jenny" or a "Tom."

I did not want to leave her. But, the adventure of visiting called out to me.

I left the roasting of meat, a primitive and gratifying aroma like no other, deep and juicy, stuffed and fat. Mysterious, unlike a summer barbeque which is an open, communal smell on the warm breeze, the Christmas roast is privately accomplished, secreted away in the ovens, communally secret, delightfully wafting out as jingling, shouting doors open in welcome. I left behind the simmering of richest, holiday tomato sauce, using pork and beef, peppers and onion, garlic and oregano and basil all at once; the deep dish lasagna or manicotti; hidden also, beside the bulging turkey, hidden, the potatoes in silvery wrap, roasting, the yams beside them; roasting, the squash, melting into buttery warmth; cranberry jelly cut out of a can; celery to dip in olive oil and black pepper; green and crispy salada and afterwards, vanilla cookies, spread with frosting that Mama spent a whole day making; anise wheels like stained glass windows; walnut snowballs frosted with snowy soft sugar; pies: pumpkin, apple, squash and Daddy's favorite, mince (Yuck! Too sharp!): honey balls like tiny donuts you had to fish for in golden lakes of honey; chocolate bulbs wrapped in Christmassy colored foil and a hugest bowl of nuts to crack and raisins to squish in your mouth melted with chocolate and red wine, all at once, wine and chocolate, raisin and nut meat melted and mingled in your Christmassy mouth. All these, following me out the door in a wave of sweet and spicy, warm and roasted, all these I left behind to go out into the grey Christmas Day. Grey and damp, holding Daddy's hand, studying my new, white plastic boots. Marie was skipping and wandering on his other hand, while he jerked us straight in order to cross the cold street, blackened with drizzle, pocked with black pocky snow, and yellow snow even Annette wouldn't eat, a piece of stray tinsel caught in a black pock, shivering wildly in the wind.

Jakey walked by himself.

The Likus' was the first stop. Annie opened the door for us, "Merry Christmas! Merry Christmas! Merry Christmas!" She said to each of our heads passing her as she held the storm door.

"Ho, ho, ho!" Daddy responded, "An' a Hap, Hap, Happy New Year!"

We entered the dark house, along the dark hallway; so dark I couldn't find the floor. My feet stepped down and down into nothingness, stepping and stepping as on numbed feet. I followed Daddy blindly down the dark walls in utter trust and horror, to the kitchen, only slightly less dim than the hall. I was met there by a damp kitcheny smell, warm and clammy, like watery meat. It was not a cooking house.

"Can I get you something to warm your bones, Billy?"

"Don't mind if I do!" was Daddy's reply at every house, "Don't mind if I do!"

What amazed me was how happy they all were; everywhere we went, to see Daddy! How happy they were to set his whiskey down in a simple kitchen glass in front of him!

"Over the teeth and through the gums, look out stomach, here it comes!" he sang happily.

He made me cringe. But, when I saw the beaming faces around him, Annie, in her new Christmas robe of bright red polyester quilting and Richard, in his flappy socks and workpants, beaming like Christmas stars upon him, I thought they were fools, and, instantly, I felt proud to be with him, foolishly proud to be of the same name, from the same house, the Wisher house, labeled with him, wrapped up, cooked like the turkey, smelling of him, through the wet, stifling wool of my mittens, through my skin, spices, tobacco, whiskey: I was with him.

*"You should never sit next to a man," he whispered in my ear, his scratchy stubble burning my ear, while he lay next to me in the dark, under the covers, stroking my breasts, working himself up, running his big hands up and down my body, "You shouldn't be allowed in the same room with a man."*

"Hey! Gloria! Come and see what we got!" called a far off voice from the living room, Annette's taunting voice.

"Go play," Daddy told me, over his shoulder.

Marie followed me. Jakey was gone already, upstairs with Rick. They had a way of disappearing before anyone even knew they were around.

At the threshold of the living room, I stumbled over gifts falling out of their opened boxes. Gifts filled the living room as if a gift dump truck had backed up to the house and dropped its load through the living room windows.

I couldn't see a thing beyond the sea of tissue paper. The vague shape of a Christmas tree blotted the dark window. Gradually, I could distinguish the shapes of boxes overflowing with scarves and hats and mittens that matched; sweaters with angora puffs, sweaters with turtle necks; sweaters of varied colors: gossamer pink, deep purple, dark red, green, neon yellow with pants and skirts to match; and toys and toys and toys; dolls advertised on TV (I never got any of the dolls I saw on TV, though I begged for them.); games in boxes rattling with promise, Scrabble, Monopoly, Miss Popularity; Mr. Potatohead thrust in my face; Barbie furniture, pink and smelling delightfully of brand new plastic. A doll wobbled toward me, ZZ-ZZ-ZZ, she went, till Rick, out of nowhere threw a new basketball at her and she fell over on to her back, smack into tissue and wrapping paper, still ZZ-ZZ-ZZ waving her legs.

"Aw!" cried Coreen, Richard's mother, so fat she couldn't move, out of the depths of a stuffed chair buried in the corner, nearly scaring me to death.

"What did you get?" Annette asked me.

"Boots," I said, holding up one white plastic foot.

"That all?" she laughed.

What could I say? No, that's not all. I got new soft flannel pajamas we always wear on Christmas Eve to have new ones for Santa to see. I got a new pink eraser and a box of Number 2 pencils, like in school. And paper books, some with lines for writing, some with no lines for drawing. And a thing of Scotch tape, all my own; actually, Ma never bought Scotch tape, she couldn't afford it, she bought some other kind, but she called it Scotch anyway.

"What did she get?" Annette nodded over to Marie.

"A doll."

"What kind?"

"Show her," I said. Marie lifted the nondescript doll she was holding and Annette blew spit through her teeth.

Coreen laughed from her shadowy chair.

Daddy was standing behind us.

"You kids ready? Look at all the presents! Are these for me?"

He reached down and put a girl's pink and white knit cap on his head. It sat way up on top, suddenly looking like a doll's cap.

*"Give me your tongue,"* he whispered, hot, in my ear.

*"What?" I whispered back.*

*"Put your tongue in my mouth."*

*How quickly my tongue flew into his waiting mouth! And how good it felt - down there! Between my legs! As though Daddy's tongue reached all the way down me!*

Annette and Linda, Coreen, Rick and Jakey all laughed real loud.

"What's the matter? Don't I look pretty?" More laughter.

"Well, were shovin' off!" Daddy called out. "Merry Christmas to all and to all a good night!"

As we filed out, down the dim hallway, I wondered how long before I would have to use that bright new eraser, how long before I'd have to use those perfect new pencils, how much longer could I keep them fresh and untouched?

After a couple of more neighbors' houses, we bundled into the skush-a-bunk, all fitted with Christmas sheets to keep us clean, and headed for Grandma's.

We drove past the Fantasi's grey tenement, patched with boards like Band-Aids over sores. We saw, with surprise, the Fantasi's, though poor and shabby, had a complete manger scene in the window like you'd see in a shoe store or a bank, sitting on fluffy cotton speckled with sparkling flakes, surrounded by blinking colored lights, and as we passed, the voices of a heavenly host of angels piped at us from this dreary place.

"What was that?" Jakey flicked his head around.

"The Fantasis got miracle music!" I exclaimed.

Daddy laughed.

"What the hell is miracle music?" Jakey sneered.

I had to think a minute. You had to be careful, sometimes, how you explained things to Jakey. He was touchy.

"It's the music they play in movies when a miracle happens," I said, shyly.

"Oh, yeah," Jakey nodded, like he knew that all the time.

We all listened to the choir through the steamy car windows while the car edged its way on to the highway and merged, leaving the heavenly voices fading softly behind us.

Men and women walked on Christmas Day; they walked the highway's gritty, narrow sidewalk. It was hard for me to imagine that it was Christmas Day: the people looked so dreary and forlorn. A woman dressed in black pushed a heavy baby carriage, a man walked with his head and back bowed, blasted by the oil trucks booming behind them, barreling up behind them and whooshing past, leaving a wake of dust and flying trash. We were on the highway now to East Boston. We were below the City of Tanks, a fearsome black city rising above us, fenced in chain, wrapped in warnings and flashing red lights. The tankers waited. From Liberia and Russia, from Greece and Turkey, with names painted across their massive bows in foreign alphabets, names I could not read, no matter how pained I was to decipher them; they waited for oil to be pumped into them like black milk. I could smell it: I reeled with nausea and hunger at once: the metal, the masculine, rank smell of oil. The same oil that made black fingernails and the deep, black lines in Daddy's hands and behind his ears, the creases equally hieroglyphic as a foreign alphabet, and, after you've seen the same hieroglyphic over and over a long, long time, equally clear.

The men and women walked past the City of Tanks while the grit blasted between their teeth like a sand storm in the Sahara, and the towering Virgin Mary, the Madonna Shrine, stood above them, holding her hands in the blessing; she was eight stories high, meant to stand a top the highest hill to greet the ships sailing into the harbor, to be the welcoming first sight of sailors, but she was too tall, too tall, too tall for the planes coming into the airport so low and searing, you swore they would scrape your head. They put her down; she stood at the foot of the building, the Black Madonna, now black with age.

The men and women walked on Christmas Day pushing their babies on narrow sidewalks, past the City of Tanks, past the Black Madonna, their heads bowed, their shoulders shuddered with each barreling oil truck, breathing the burning exhaust from diesel trucks, and above them, high on the hill, the Crucifix, a hundred feet tall, lighted at night, taller than the billboards bright with tropical visions, bubbling with liquid refreshment, the Crucifix stood next to the projects, where the poorest people lived, where you could see a smattering of colored lights, two windows that were celebrating Christmas out of rows and rows of dark warehouse type buildings like concentration camps for the poor. The cross was a landmark for illicit meetings: there, at Christ's broken feet, people made love in the dark, they wrote their names on the steel, they smoked and drank and smashed their beer bottles against the cross like drunken Roman soldiers throwing dice.

We drove under the black lace bridge.

In East Boston, we inched our way along crowded streets, pausing for Cadillacs double and triple parked, as long lines of cars waited patiently to go around the bulky bodies.

"Ah, all the mobsters are visiting their mothers," Daddy growled.

Daddy wasn't so jolly here, because it was so hard to drive and at Grandma's, he wasn't getting any whiskey or beer, only coffee and he couldn't smoke or swear.

Jakey and I counted the sneakers hanging on the telephone wires.

"Eight pairs!" I said, wondering what the kids told their mothers when they got home about where their sneakers had gone.

"You're nuts! I got fifteen! Didn't you look up the side streets?"

"How did the sneakers get up there?" I asked.

"Ha! You're stupid! One kid says, 'Gimme your sneakers, asshole!'"

"Hey! Watch yer language!" Daddy hollered.

"None of these stop lights are working," Daddy complained. "They just break them so they won't have to stop."

Grandma met us at the buzzing door with the same greeting she gave us every year, "Mmm," she moaned, "Where's my Rosa? Didn't Rosa come? Hello, children, Merry Christmas," she kissed us one by one, while the boxer dog, GiGi, did a wiggle dance on our feet.

"No, Ma, Rosie's home cooking Christmas dinner," Daddy explained annually, kissing her soft, soft cheek, as we all did, our puckered lips sinking deeply into her old flesh. She was now a slightly stout old lady, now in an old dress she had made out of pieces from old bathrobes to be warm, with a towel tied round for an apron and white old lady shoes, like nurses wear in old movies, like nuns wear, only white, with the little toes cut out for comfort.

Past the glossy photo of President Kennedy covered with Saran Wrap, past the ancient colored picture of Jesus and His Sacred Heart burning in His chest, also covered with Saran Wrap. Completing the little shrine by the door, a small wooden table made by Uncle Sonny in school shop, a yellow plastic doily and a vase of plastic roses and daisies, every week the table lovingly polished and the flowers lovingly washed in a tub of frothy soap and water.

Sneaking up to our faces, the sweet scents of vanilla, ginger, nutmeg, cinnamon, apple, squash, pumpkin, mince. Jumping at us from behind these, the richness of meat, spices and turkey roasting, sneaking up, the rich stuffing, potatoes, yams, the bubbling tomato sauce, the layers of lasagna, the bowl of extra meatballs, hunks of pork and beef. All with Grandma's certain scented touch, deeper than Mama's, older. Piles of nuts piled round green and yellow pears, purple grapes, figs, dates, oranges, bananas, red apples and pomegranates greeted us as we entered the hot white kitchen, burning white, almost too white from the searing cleanliness of her widowhood.

She gave us each something to eat, "Just a little, Billy, just something to hold them over."

I went over to the side counter, under the cabinets, where Grandma kept the small pieces of donut and cake she couldn't finish, the little halves she'd saved wrapped in the tiniest pieces of plastic. I loved to ask for them and she let me eat them, she only let me, have the other wonderful half of her secret treats.

"Who's coming today, Ma?" Daddy asked, stirring sugar in his coffee. If Grandpa had been there, Daddy would have had anisette in his coffee. "Here, Billy, let me sweeten that for you," Grandpa would have said, pouring the thick licorcey liquid into the cup. But Grandpa wasn't there anymore.

"Oh, Salvi will come and Dolores, and the kids. Maybe Vickie, if he can get up, if he can get up!"

Daddy laughed.

"How many kids Salvi got now?"

"FOUR! Already! And she's pregnant again!" Grandma sliced the air with her hand, "Can you believe it! I told him, 'Whaddya think you're doing?'" She shook her head.

Daddy laughed again. He knew how many kids; he just wanted to see her get mad.

"He's a good Catholic," Daddy smiled.

Grandma looked at him, disgusted, "You gotta be kidding me! He don't go to church! *I* go to church!"

"Well, nobody goes to church more than you, Ma." Daddy replied.

"Dolores, God bless her, she takes the kids to mass. God bless her."

"She's a good girl," Daddy said.

"Yeah, yeah," Grandma nodded. "You want another piece of pie?"

"No, no!" Daddy said, and my heart went cold and the little piece of donut stuck in my dry mouth because I knew we were leaving. I never wanted to leave her, never. Once I was with Grandma, my heart rested and was at peace. I never wanted to leave her.

Grandma stood on the outside step with the door held open, the buzzer screaming wildly, GiGi shivering at her feet, watching us, making sure we got into the car okay.

"Watch your hand!" she called, gently to Marie.

"Ma, go in!" Daddy told her.

She ignored him; she nodded, then waved him away with her old hand. We waited till she went inside.

"Why do you call her, 'Ma'?" I asked Daddy, as we were driving away.

Every time I heard him say 'Ma,' it hurt me. He had no right to call her Ma, she wasn't his, she was mine, and Mama's and Marie's, and even Jakey's more than his. He didn't even like her. He made fun of her all the time and called her, in a mocking tone, his "mother-in-law," whatever *that* meant - what kind of law, I wondered, made Grandma *his* mother?

Daddy didn't answer me. In those days, parents didn't feel they had to answer kids.

As we turned on to Eutaw Street, I saw the White House, as big and grand as ever.

I never wanted to leave her.


After East Boston, we went to Chelsea. Don't ever go to Chelsea on Christmas Day. Chelsea was a negative city, a minus world, decorated with the kind of Christmas decorations that took away from Christmas, instead of adding to it. Chelsea was the poorest city I knew. Every year, they dragged out the same red and white plastic candles, now scratched and yellowed with age, and stuck them on the light poles. Every year the same tarnished tinsel draped drearily across the vacant avenue. Leering Santas cast glances at us from the corner drugstore, from the laundromat, from the gas station. Faded decorations hung everywhere thin and colorless, their color drained by so many hopeless eyes.

No cars snaked along the empty streets, no cars, only us. No Cadillacs were double parked so that Mafioso could visit their mothers. No people walked. On Christmas morning, the streets were empty.

Uncle Gus and Aunt Lennie lived in this ghostly place. Their apartment was a minus house: no wallpaper, no curtains, no furniture. Tea cups, a few plates and odd cans of food were placed on bare wooden shelves inside the exposed wall. To this barren house on Christmas Day, Daddy brought the bottle, tall-necked and fat, wearing a happy Christmas bow.

"You're a good boy, Billy," Uncle Gus scraped up the words from somewhere deep in the crater of his throat.

"That's aw'right, Uncle Gus," Daddy said, handing his Uncle the bright new bottle.

Uncle Gus wrapped his boney grip round the neck and gave it a sharp turn, crack, the seal broke.

"Heh, heh," laughed Uncle Gus.

"Here you go," smiled Aunt Lennie, handing cloudy old glasses out to the men.

"You kids want a drink of water?" Aunt Lennie offered.

We all shook our heads, "No!"

They were skeleton people. They moved about the kitchen like people already dead. Their skin stretched taut on their boney frames caved in under their thin clothes. Their clothes were much too thin for winter!

Gus's grey stubbly chin and pointy Adam's apple stuck out of the neck of his grey, woolen long johns. He resembled an old Humphrey Bogart, the criminal Humphrey Bogart; he rasped like Bogart, his voice was scratchy as his chin.

"Ah," he drank heartily, "you're a good boy, Billy!"

"Aw, I'm just a young lad starting out in life, Uncle Gus!"

At this, they busted out laughing, raspy and rotty-toothed skeletons, laughing with Daddy.

How they scared me! The track people were terrifyingly thin; they were a mean thin, hard and solid. But, Uncle Gus and Aunt Lennie scared me. They were wispy thin, caved in, ghostly. They seemed perfect to be relatives of Daddy's.

Just before we left, we each got a skeletal embrace from them, all warm and squishy from the whiskey.

"Oooh, so goood to see you, kids!" cried Aunt Lennie, stinking warmly of whiskey.

"You be good, now!" hugged Uncle Gus, scratching our cold cheeks.

As soon as I got home, every Christmas morning, I ran to Ma for an explanation.

"Ma! How come Uncle Gus and Aunt Lennie are so skinny?"

"THEY'RE POOR!" she shouted.

"And their teeth! How come, they have no teeth except black, old, rotten ones?"

"THAT'S WHAT HAPPENS TO YOU WHEN YOU'RE POOR, YOUR TEETH FALL OUT! YOU THINK YOU CAN JUST GO TO THE DENTIST ANY TIME YOU WANT WHEN YOU'RE POOR?"

I didn't want to think of them, despite the frightening, familial link I could not deny.


Margaret Flannagan was the last visit. She lived high a top a hill called Beachmont where the white houses overlooked the blue summer sea and the dark road spiraled round and round the hill on its way to Margaret's house.

The sun split the sky for one second as we climbed the hill and the clouds shone gold and the sea splashed cold and blue. I wondered if the ocean did that because it was Christmas; did the ocean and the sky know it was Christmas and that I was going to Margaret Flannagan's house? Just as suddenly, the sun disappeared and the clouds and the sea returned to being grey and sullen.

Up the bleached wooden front stairs my young legs lifted themselves, icy pink under their Christmas stockings. Daddy rang the doorbell. I tried to peer into the windows: was she rushing to greet me, all flush with smiles and breathless hellos? Their unlighted Christmas tree blocked the front bay window like a curtain of dark green and I vowed, one day, I would keep my Christmas lights on all day and night.

Was she coming? We waited, shifting from one frozen foot to the other, the seeping cold making its way through our bodies. I clutched her clumsily wrapped bottle of cologne from Woolworth's.

Faintly, I heard music. Where was it coming from?

There she was! My Christmas curls fell to one side as I dipped my head in adoration - there! My Margaret! All pink cheeked and cheery Irish! Surrounded by a sudden rush of music when she opened the door - someone was playing the piano!

"Bill! Come in! And the children!"

"Mer-ry Christmas! Mer-ry Christmas! Ho, ho, ho!" Daddy bellowed like Santa Claus.

"Gloria! Oh, thank you! And I have something for you too, dear!" chirped my beloved. Except for teachers, she was the only one who called me dear.

"Oh, Marie! And Jakey! How big you've grown! You're so tall! I'm just amazed at how much he and Gloria look alike!" (I could forgive only her for making this observation.)

"That's my brother's boy!" Daddy beamed, proudly.

Harvey slinked by us, standing in the foyer in a group. Out of the corner of my adoring eye, I saw his stern expression. His sweater was a lovely soft blue.

"Come in!" Margaret hugged me, "Patrick was just charming us with some Christmas carols."

"I wouldn't call my playing *charming*, Mom," Patrick remarked from his place at the piano.

Margaret simply tossed her lovely little hand his way.

Patrick was her only child, twenty-eight, tall, blonde and good-looking, wearing a thickly cabled sweater of jeweled colors. Ma always said, Patrick "had a good job." He was about to be married. His fiancée, plump and palest blonde, wearing pearls and winter white, stood with her hand on his shoulder. They looked like a greeting card, a card rich people would send to each other.

In fact, the whole room was a rich, luxurious Christmas card. Garlands of real greenery were twisted round and round a white banister. Real holly and real mistletoe hung cheerily from the mantle and the archways. Candles glowed in brass holders. The long, wooden floors were spread with thick colorful rugs of intricate, twisting designs edged in fringe; here and there, between the rugs, the wood flickered warmly with the reflection of the real fire in the real fireplace. Real poinsettias burned like red ribbons.

In all of this finery, the Christmas turkey, vegetables, sauces, sweets and spices, though slightly more bland than Ma's or Grandma's, scented the splendor with their own riches.

"Please, continue," Harvey told Patrick, in a commanding tone.

He did. And the room was filled with beautiful, swelling notes unlike any I'd ever heard. Involuntarily, my eyes filled with tears and little shivers ran down my spine. I recognized the song, but only vaguely. I would come to know it as "Greensleeves."

Margaret leaned toward me her cheek brushed mine, "Would you like some eggnog, dear?" she whispered.

"Yes, please!" I whispered back, delighted I was finally getting to use that phrase.

"What's wrong?" she whispered urgently.

"Nothing!"

"Are you sure?"

I nodded.

"Well, maybe, it's just coming in from the cold. Would you like some eggnog, Marie? Jake?"

She went into the kitchen.

The song ended.

Daddy rubbed his stubbly chin.

"I never heard *that* Christmas carol before! You know 'White Christmas'?"

"Sure, Bill! Want to sing along?"

"Don't mind if I do!"

Daddy launched into his imitation of Bing Crosby, his chin sunk deep into his chest, his cheeks puffed up with air. Jakey and Marie laughed and Harvey looked solemn with anger. I thought he could seriously kill Daddy.

Margaret returned with three cut glass cups of eggnog, floating with nutmeg.

"I'll have something a little stronger, if you don't mind, Margie!" Daddy said, brightly.

Harvey looked grim.

"I knew you would, Billy!" Margaret called from the kitchen.

She returned with a drink for Daddy, golden liquid in a chunky cut glass. The colors of the room danced in the glass as she carried it past me. I vowed to have glasses like that one day. I vowed to have music and wood and candles, rugs and a piano and a son in a jeweled sweater to play it, and his fiancée in pearls. When my eye fell on Harvey, I decided, I would not have him.

*I'll let you see a glimpse of me: The sun has filled our seaside home, streaming in through tall windows. Barefoot and in a white cotton dress, I run down the white hallway filled with light to the source of the music, light, airy, sweet as the keening of doves. I run on toes barely touching the long, tile floors, to the source: my daughter playing her flute.*

Margaret reached under the Christmas tree and pulled out a long, flat box.

"How come your Christmas tree isn't lighted, Margaret?" I asked, timidly, not wanting to offend.

"Oh, isn't it?" Margaret rummaged under the tree for the switch. "Oh, well, maybe Harvey or Patrick can figure that out. Patrick is an engineer, you know."

"There it is!" I said, suddenly spying a contraption on the wires. "Can I do it?"

Margaret looked worried, "Go ahead."

Fearfully, I pushed the button and burst Margaret's Christmas tree into sudden glory.

"Well! Will you look at that? Harvey, look at the tree now! Gloria discovered the lights weren't on! Aren't we lucky you came by today?" she cooed. Harvey sent spears my way.

"Aren't you going to open your gift?" she asked, "Let's open them together."

We ripped our packages open.

My heart sank. I couldn't believe it. She'd given me one of those gift boxes of handkerchiefs you buy in the drugstore. The handkerchiefs were folded perfectly. You could never get them folded like that again, if you disturbed them. In each corner, was nestled a little, red embroidered rose. Immediately, I wondered if Harvey had made her get such a gift for me. It was the kind of gift you would get someone you didn't like very much but had to get a gift for, it was so - sad - and cold.

"Oooh! Cologne! Evening in Paris! I love it!" Margaret fairly sang.

I brushed my disappointment aside. Why, I would *love* using them because *she* had given them to me. I'd keep one in my pocket every day. Ma would never let me blow my nose on them.

I told her I loved the handkerchiefs. Evening in Paris, I explained, was my favorite scent in the whole drugstore.

"Well, it's my favorite too!" she said. "Would you like to see what the doctor gave me for Christmas?"

This, of course, was the doctor for whom she worked. She was receptionist for my pediatrician.

She opened a small, velvet box.

"See," she said, "it's jade."

I was looking at a necklace, a gold chain and a deep green pear dangling from it.

The words, "jade" and "doctor" turned in my mind. "Doctor" had something to do with "jade." Behind me, Harvey circled and cast glances my way, wondering what I was doing there, wondering when I'd leave, considering to himself what kind of people didn't have doctors giving them jade.

Suddenly, I made an important decision, though it was not a decision. It was much more a physical longing, a yearning back to a horrible place, a craving for those skeletal arms about my neck. For instantly I knew I was better than bones and bad teeth, just as I knew I was worse, far worse than jade. Suddenly, from out of this foreign place of pearls and pianos, out of tension and false manners, grew a fierce love for them, skin and bones, as familiar as war and Depression, as comforting as deprivation. Their yellowed skin, their blackened teeth frightened me, but they had welcomed me with arms already dead; failures, failures, waiting on the sunken docks of Chelsea for ghost ships that would never come in, I knew them, I was related to them. "Pick someone from the family!" I understood them. I trusted them far better than I ever would all this terrible wealth and splendor.

Just as we were leaving, Harvey unwrapped a joke gift Patrick had given him. A walking Santa in a red velvet suit, ringing a silver Christmas bell. Who had money for such an expensive joke? They burst out in bells of laughter, and chinking glasses as we left, the little walking Santa ringing, ringing its tiny bell, working hard to please them.

Margaret never stopped to see my manger that year. Harvey beeped the horn and Margaret ran breathlessly to our front door where she handed Ma the last gift she would ever give me. I don't remember what it was.

I could hear their whispery, urgent voices, "can't...can't!" I pressed my head awkwardly to the frosted window. I twisted it so I could see the dark street blinking with the reflected red lights of the car. The car door was still open for her; in the driver's seat Harvey's rigid silhouette looked straight ahead.

Then, her permed head came into view. She skipped down the front steps; she was so thin and graceful!

Then, I saw her lovely, slender leg pause for a moment in its high heel as she climbed back into the car. That was my lesson. That perfect, extended leg. "Better than you," it said, "No time for the likes of you." Then, it disappeared into the car.

My only consolation was my homemade manger. Carry, as Jesus, kicked her chubby feet happily, lifted her rounded arms; Barbie, white in her Kleenex gown; Ken, for once, a young god in his white robe, all, a flame in the red light of a cheap, but holy Christmas candle.

Ma stood at the kitchen window, smoking one Tareyton after another, peering out the night window that blinked with Christmas lights like a pinball machine. Whimpering and clawing at her legs was another of her little terriers, Tareyton, named after her cigarette, and the commercial for the cigarette where all the Tareyton smokers had a black eye, just like the terrier.

"Jesus!" Ma growled through her teeth, clamped down on the cigarette as she bent down to pick up the wiggly little rat, "She's killing me! My legs!"

Ma resumed her gaze out the window, sending bullets of radar into the car lights rushing toward her.

"Christ All Mighty, where the hell is he?"

I didn't pay too much attention to her. I was running into the kitchen to get my fiftieth snack of the evening, an apple, maybe, or a piece of cheese, sliced clandestinely from the large chunk in the refrigerator, getting smaller, a hungry mouse nibbling it away.

I was running back to my all-consuming life in the living room, which, of course, I have forgotten, though not completely. I also have not forgotten how seriously I took these fantasies and fables to heart. Maybe it was "The Addams Family," after all, Ma called me Morticia, because of my long hair; maybe "Robin Hood," to whom I played Maid Marion in my mind; maybe "The Wonderful World of Color," by Walt Disney, which we got in wonderful black and white. Jakey and I used to argue about what the colors might be. If you knew one color, like Santa Claus's suit, maybe, you could almost tell what the others might be. Always, I was sure I was right; it's a lost skill, or, maybe, I was always wrong.

How deeply we lost ourselves in the darkness and the flickering blue light. It erased the floor, the ceiling the walls, and everyone around you. Only TV Land existed. Unless, of course, your father was crawling his fingers up your pajama leg, though, once, a boy friend sucked my breasts while I watched the little dolphin, Flipper.

I was intent on getting back to whatever drama was playing itself out on the screen, but as I rushed past her, Ma's torment pulled at my careless mind and body. I didn't have any idea how much she needed Daddy to set up the Christmas presents under the tree, that Christmas might not happen without him. I was old enough to question the existence of Santa Claus, and young enough to forget I questioned it.

Besides, she was always waiting for him, always standing right there at that window, smoking, begging the horizon to produce his car lovingly zooming toward her over its edge. I'll never wait for a man! I vowed as I ran by her, convinced she was an idiot; yet, half my heart remained with her, standing at that window, hugging her squirmy, maggoty dog.

Deep in TV Land, once more floating in the virtual world, I heard the front door open with its peculiar, ssquee-runch! It stuck in damp and swollen weather.

"There he is!" Ma's heart sighed audibly, while her dog burst into the frenzied howling of a terrier.

Daddy's cheerful, proud of himself face came in, beaming full, catching the streetlight from outside. But what was that with him? Against the black night behind Daddy's shoulders was a black shape following him, then eyes, shiny bits of white, staring eyes. Eyes, flipping from side to side. Tall eyes at first, then short eyes, flipping even faster, two little pairs of them.

Colored people!

What were colored people doing in our house?

Terrified little children, a boy and a girl, about four and five years old, backing up close to their mother, tall, pretty, eyes cautious, staring. Next to her, a colored man, taller than Daddy, angry, chin set hard, eyes furious as a man in chains.

The children inched backward into their mother, her eyes round and determined. She held her kids by their shoulders as they shivered with fear, then gently, pushed them forward; patient, she was. Slowly, the children came into the living room, where three white kids sat gape-mouthed and cross-legged on the floor. The man, angry as hell, and Daddy, a beacon of hospitality, stood in the doorway. Daddy introduced his kids.

He got our names right, but not our ages, not that anyone cared. I didn't know then how drunk he was, or if he was drunk, only that he was Daddy bringing colored people in.

Ma ran in from the kitchen, stubbing out her cigarette, tossing her howling, clawing dog into the spare room and quickly shutting the door, getting her brain in order: my husband has brought colored people home with him, there are colored people in my house - what to do?

Rush to the door and welcome them.

"Their car broke down on the Parkway," Daddy explained to Ma. "I said, 'It's Christmas Eve! Come home with me, don't stand out here in the cold, come home with me! The little lady will make us some coffee, get warm! Eh, we'll go back for the car later!' Make us some coffee, Rosie, will you?"

The two trembling kids were deposited with us in the dark living room, while the adults went into the kitchen. Kids were always just dumped with kids; adults went with adults.

It was Jakey who spoke to them. He was used to colored people, though I don't know how - maybe from the carnies on the beach or it might have been from the track people, though neither of these groups seemed especially colored to me. The one other time I saw a colored person, I was about two. She was a little girl and she was standing on the other side of a chain link fence in Connecticut where we were visiting Marie's godmother, who was a lot nicer than mine and pretended to be my godmother also, only she wasn't pretending - she meant it. The second I saw the little colored girl dressed in a frilly, pink dress I busted out screaming. I thought she was a monster in a pretty little dress. The adults came running out of the house and laughed at me. "Oh, Gloria! Don't be silly! It's just a little girl, see!" But, I was terrified. The little girl just stared at me; she nibbled on her finger. Maybe she was wondering what the heck I was, maybe some kind of screaming alien, with a big mouth, an enormously high forehead, feathery yellow tufts and bulging green eyes.

"You ever watch this show?" Jakey asked the little boy.

He nodded vigorously. All five of us kids returned to TV Land and floated together. We didn't say another word to each other.

Which was why we could hear every word from the kitchen.

Daddy's voice boomed, large and generous.

"We're all equal! All equal! I've always said, 'We're all equal!' In the eyes of the law and the eyes of God!

"You want another beer?"

A quiet answer, angry.

"Go on! There's more where that came from. Some of my best friends in the Merchant Marines! There was Joseph, we called him, Black Ben because he wore those little half glasses like Ben Franklin, ya know; and Cookie, what was his name, what a guy! Give you the shirt off his back, that guy! By God, you're all equal out on the sea! You can't fool Mother Nature, you know! She'll drown a white man quick as a colored any day, she doesn't know the difference!"

"She doesn't know the difference," his eyes going blank over a long sip of beer. His upper lip curled a funny way over the lip of the glass because he didn't have all his teeth anymore. His lip curled and I felt it curl, in my tummy, the horrid sensation of his lip.

"Ah!" he swallowed a whiskey chaser. "Don't worry about the car, now! It's too cold to worry. Don't worry!

"We're all equal," Daddy's eyes, bloodshot and liquid. He wiped a tear.

I was there, in the kitchen. I must have ventured out to the adult world.

The women drank coffee.

"That Martin Luther King, an' Jack Kennedy - they had the right idea, by God! Damn shame, it's all our shame, by God."

On the edge of their seats, the women quietly drank coffee. They exchanged a few, soft words.

I remember the fierce jaw of the man. Maybe he didn't like a little blonde girl staring at him. Maybe he didn't like Daddy.

I wondered if he wanted to be helped. It was his family's Christmas Eve, too. Maybe he didn't want us in his Christmas.

As if in conspiracy with the colored man, Daddy took out his oily wallet and from its secret black folds, he pulled an old piece of folded newspaper. He moved carefully, as though the yellowed, soiled paper were an archeological treasure, the black oil of a hundred machines caught in its dry creases, his thick, blackened fingers, suddenly graceful, as they must have been handling the infinitesimal body parts of the gargantuan machines he fixed everyday. How much blood had Daddy poured from his veins into the machines? How much of his flesh had been chewed by the oily black teeth of gears? How many volts of electricity vibrated through his tendons and bones? Careful, as though unfolding a great secret, he spread the newspaper, which turned out to be a photo of a machine as big as a room. In front of this machine stood Daddy, in his work uniform, the young Daddy who looked so very much like Alan Ladd with the love curl curling, and another man, in a dark suit. The man in the suit had his arm tightly around Daddy. Both men were grinning like devils.

Daddy pointed his smallest fingernail at his own tiny head in the picture.

"That's me," he said. "Don't tell me I don' know what it's like to be colored."

The man's jaw twitched ever so slightly. Daddy handed him the photo. In his big, black hands, carved brown and pale as coffee with cream on the palms, in his hands, the photo looked small. It looked almost white.

"I invented that machine," Daddy explained. "Ever hear of the shrink-wrap machine?"

The man's head rose quickly. He knew.

"I had to find a way to heat the wrap - that was the problem, you know - I had to find a way to heat the wrap without cooking the food underneath." Daddy grinned like the Devil. "How do you think I did that?

I did it! I solved it!"

And Daddy told the man how he'd finally perfected the shrink-wrap machine. But, I didn't understand a word, because I didn't care anything about shrink-wrap at that time. I cared more for the television I was missing, or the food I decided to get. If I had known how close I once had come to waking up a princess!

"'An who do you think got the credit? Whose name is on that machine now? Who got the patent? Who got rich?"

I turned just in time to see that huge, black finger point to the employer's sinister, smiling face.

"He did." The only words I heard him speak, with a strange, thick drawl.

"You're right! Goddamn it! You're right! The man who paid for it! That's who! Tell me I don't know what's it's like to be colored!"

The man left with Daddy to go out into the freezing winter night to the highway where Daddy would fix his abandoned car with a flashlight and his toolbox. The women remained in the kitchen, nearly silent, drinking coffee.

We kids watched a lot of TV that night, until Daddy and the man returned and the parents ushered their children out. As they passed in front of the TV, TV Land shifted from a vital, three dimensional reality to flat shapes with talking mouths. As the man passed, his jaw was just as hard set and cold as it had been when he entered, as hard and cold as the frozen road under Daddy's back as he'd lain under the car like Michelangelo under the ceiling of the Sistine Chapel. I wanted to shout from the place I was, in the blue dark of TV Land, shout to the man, "He means it! You don't know him! Just 'cause he's drunk doesn't mean he doesn't mean it!" But it wouldn't have been enough. Being drunk and sincere wasn't enough.

Daddy missed Christmas that year. He slept through it.

Somewhere, in the diluted grey morning, Ma, who'd tried for hours to wake him and couldn't, phoned her saintly brothers, Uncle Salvi and Uncle Sonny, to come and set up Christmas for us. They put my new bike together and brought the games and other boxes over from Grandma's, where they'd been hidden. The bike was from Uncle Vickie, who got it "off a truck," and the games were from Uncle Salvi. Uncle Vickie also gave me two plastic dresses like they wear on *Hullabaloo*, only with the price tags still on them.

Daddy woke up the day after and held his sick head in his hands and sipped a Bloody Mary in that funny way with his upper lip suspended over the rim of the glass.

"A hair of the dog that bit me," he usually said, but not this time.

Daddy vowed never to abuse drink again, because then he'd have to give it up, and, "God forbid, God forbid."

JAKEY

I was on the floor in my room, drawing a picture of a horse, when Jakey came in.

Jakey was not a welcome visitor. If I'd been a cat, my fur would be standing straight up. I'd be getting ready to hiss.

"I know what's wrong with it!" he offered.

He always said that when he looked at my drawings. Jakey could draw, too, but he never did. He just liked to criticize my attempts.

"I don't want to know what's wrong with it! So what if it's not perfect, horses are hard," I countered.

Daddy always said, whenever he saw me trying to draw a horse, "Ah, horses have more curves than women."

I just kept trying. I could see the horses, so plainly, as I remembered having seen them through the crack in the fence at Suffolk Downs when we walked by with Ma on our way to the beach. The horses, so graceful, so lovely, tied to ropes like a clothesline, circling like a carousel, circling to get exercise, circling, they tossed their manes. If we were lucky, they whinnied.

I loved to draw, especially when I was alone. From the first line – and writing was like this too – the drawing began to look back at me. If I was doing it right, there was a recognition of the very line that had magically come out of my pencil, magically guided by my very hand, there was a sense of power to draw well, a sense of companionship and enveloping love with the subject I was drawing and with the larger world around me. If I were alone.

"Hey!" Jakey said, sitting on my bed, "How come you always have that piece of nightgown sticking out of your drawer?"

I looked at the fold of nightgown I kept just out of the drawer where I could grab it if I needed it. It was one of Ma's old, ripped nylon nightgowns, the only feminine piece of nightwear I possessed. It was the closest thing I had to what Wendy had been wearing in "Peter Pan," and it was there in case he came for me. I knew he wouldn't have enough patience to wait for me to change into a nightgown, so I planned to just grab it and change later in Neverland. It had been so long – years! I was beginning to run out of hope for him. Yet, somehow, I couldn't tuck that nightgown away.

"None of your business!" was all I told Jakey.

He got up on his knees on my bed.

"Hey, look Gloria! This is how a guy fucks a girl!"

I looked up to see him pumping his buttocks like a dog.

"That's not how!" I yelled at him, really upset. "Dogs do that!"

"Yes, it is! You just don't know anything!" he laughed at me.

I wanted to yell again, "Aurora and Prince Phillip didn't do that! I know what they did! And Robin Hood and Maid Marion, *after* they were married! And Cinderella and her Prince, likewise! Snow White and Prince Charming! And every heroine and hero I knew lay together in their snowy white conjugal bed, surrounded by roses and singing cherubs, their lips joined, his penis inside her, they didn't move, they didn't move!"

But, I couldn't tell Jakey that. I couldn't tell him to leave either, though I wanted to scream, "Get out of my room! Get out!" Ma wasn't home to yell at him, so he'd just stay even longer.

I went back to my drawing, a lot less happy than before. Pretty soon, he got bored and left.

After I'd finished drawing, I walked over to my bed to straighten the covers after Jakey had been on it. I glanced towards my bureau to the top of the lovely decoupage jewelry box that Ma had just given me, where I kept my rings, tucked neatly into the curves of its scalloped edge, to see with cold shock - my rings were gone! The emerald that had been Daddy's mother's which had been in *my* safekeeping - gone! The little love ring I loved so much that had been given to Mama when she was loved by another boy. Gone!

I ran to look for him – his room was empty, I ran downstairs - he wasn't in the house.

The second Ma came home, the second I heard her exhausted shove on the door I ran to see her. My feet thundered down the stairs.

"Ma, Jakey took my rings!" I gasped breathlessly. Somehow, I thought she was going to fix the situation.

She shook her head and her lips disappeared into a bloodless white line.

"He's stealing from us," she said, as she put her bags down.

"Who?" I asked.

I had to hear her say it.

"Jakey," she said. "Who else?"

Then, she added, "I think, his friends do too. That Rick when he stands in the hall waiting for him. I think he takes the change out of my coat hanging in the hall closet."

"Your coat pockets!"

I couldn't believe it. Her coat pockets? Her sacred coat pockets that even *I* had to ask permission to go into?

"They both take money out of my coat pockets," she said, "and out of my drawer where I keep it."

Her drawer! That was like robbing a bank, no, a church! That money was to pay bills! We couldn't live if that money was stolen! Even Daddy didn't touch it!

"What are you going to do?" I asked, marveling that this could happen, wondering if they would call the police now and send Jakey to jail. I felt glad, at first, then, terror for him. We had to protect him! Would we?

"What can we do? Nothing! I asked him. He said he wasn't stealing, that we just didn't like him. Your father cried. I don't know what to do with him. I treated him the same as you girls. I gave him the same food, the same clothes and the same toys. I'll just keep my money in the bank from now on, that's all!"

She had her coat off, but not the plastic rain hat. With one hand she took out a pan, and, with the other, and her foot, she opened the back door for Tareyton.

"What shall I do?"

"You! You're lucky, you got nothing left to steal!"

I cried a good deal over those rings. I began to hate. Hate was so simple, really. I knew the rings were on someone's fingers, someone I didn't know but hated: a cheap, disgusting girl, the "kind of girl" men liked, whose fingers I could have torn off! Had he sold my rings to her? Or, worse casually *given* them to her? How could anyone steal such beloved things? Who would *want* someone else's rings?

But, it was more than that. The little rings seemed to hold every event and emotion, every vision and plan I'd ever held dear within their delicate frames of gold; if you put them on your fingers, you would feel all my terror, my affection, my rage, every sensation from every experience, as well as all the hopes and dreams and sorrows from the lives of Mama and Daddy's mother, multiplied a thousand, thousand times concentrated within the small rings. You would be overwhelmed by memories and dreams, unstoppable, fantastic and terrifyingly ordinary: the calm face of the benevolent doctor as he told my father's mother and father that there was no hope, the creaking bed and the small heads of her children gathered round for whom she hadn't the strength or means to care; Mama's shy mouth being kissed by another boy, not Daddy, who loved her; the gentle smile of a kind, innocent dark-skinned boy at Sunday School who loved and didn't know the sister hated his darkness; the noses of planes searing toward my window; the penis of my father in my face; Nona's pink ears nestling the diamond studs in Florentine filigree; the sweet, bitter taste of arugula; the Holy Host like water on my tongue; too large, too close, too powerful for her small heart and mind to hold. It was a wonder she, whoever she was, didn't die the second the explosive metal touched her flesh.

Sometimes, I thought, with a smile, maybe I'd hear about it on the news.

I began to wear a chain around my neck from which hung a very small key.

People smiled and teased me, "Is that the key to your heart?"

I shook my head, no. I wouldn't tell anyone. I hid the key under my blouse. It was the key to my shame.

At home, it opened a small, teak casket, a miniature hope chest Ma had given me to lock up anything I didn't want Jakey to steal. She'd gotten this caramelly colored box as a free gift when she'd purchased her life-sized hope chest almost twenty years before.

I was ashamed to use Ma's little hope chest this way. I was ashamed to have to hide my possessions under lock and key from my own brother. I really had nothing of value left to put in the little box, which I knew could be smashed and emptied by a thief anyway.

I think I was in the eighth grade, maybe the ninth, when I finally tucked the nightgown into the drawer forever. I know I was stubborn. I held up much longer than my beliefs. Whether Peter Pan "forgot, as boys often do" or whether he didn't exist at all, it didn't seem to make any difference after a while.

## USHERS

Every Saturday afternoon, Dorothy and I made a B-line to the Revere Theater no matter what was playing, but if an Elvis Presley, Haley Mills or a Beach Party movie was up, it seemed we couldn't get there fast enough. Seeing movies was a pilgrimage of absolute necessity; we treated each movie as a quest we must make, a measure of our worth, a holy mission. Had we seen the latest, Beach Blanket Bingo? It was vital that we should. Annette's bathing suit, the long line of her cleavage, Frankie's crooning voice, his gorgeous smile, the bright beach colors, even the flipping of the party girl's pink fringes: these were essential. We were projected to the Revere Theater on Saturday afternoons by cosmic energies disguised as our will but infinitely stronger, and by heavenly and earthly forces moving our feet more immediately and more urgently than the moon and tides.

Our destination, The Revere Theater, was a bombed out shell of a theater. Except for the blazing light and romance upon the screen, it was not a desirable place to be. Take the grandeur and glory of the Paramount and the Tremont Theaters downtown with their scarlet carpets and golden braid, sweet cherubs and ornate woodwork, with the fantastic chandeliers lighting your way up the grand staircase and pin-lights guiding you along the aisles - then fight a long, agonizing war inside over a period of twenty years, battle, plunder, hold prisoners, hide refugees, house soldiers, let them piss and shit in the corners, throw sticky food at the screen, grind sticky food underfoot, knock out the flame-like bulbs of the wall sconces, scratch their names and their despair, claw the red velvet wallpaper off the walls - all to make their surroundings look more like the pain they felt - that would be The Revere Theater in the 1960's.

Dorothy and I paid our quarters to get in, then nervously followed the crowd of screaming, shoving kids toward the black cavities that would lead us to the movies themselves, cautiously traversing, like a mine field, the black floor tacky with years of gum and candy, the huge perimeter of sopping carpet around the water fountain already engorged with chewing gum and garbage, around the riot of kids waiting to drink.

It wasn't enough for us to see the movies; we went also to flirt shamelessly with the ushers. Even with the giggling groups of strange boys who gathered in the dark to throw popcorn and jujubes in our hair, we were distracted by the mature, red jackets of the ushers, by the official flashes of their lights in our faces. I suppose it started by our having to complain about the boys, but once we realized we could get the ushers' attention, we couldn't stop.

These gawky older boys became our purpose. We dressed for them, trying on crazy outfits of hand-me-downs, and, in Dorothy's case, whatever Hazel could find her in the chubby, or maternity section. We tried desperately to get them to kiss us in the dark. We followed them like little streetwalkers down secret passageways around the screen, up hidden stairways, knocking timidly upon closed, forbidden doors.

I never knew their names. Boys who spent their Saturdays in the sticky darkness. Boys too thin or too fat for their uniforms. Boys who swung a disinterested flashlight over the heads of rowdy kids they'd rather trade places with than discipline. Boys who didn't mind flirting with soft, fat girls in the mysterious, shadowy caverns of the old theater. We were never successful. Never kissed by them.

We were strange girls, contradicting ourselves over and over. For instance, I'd sworn off Dorothy, but I didn't mind going places with her. I couldn't be alone with her in her room, that's all. I was so used to this maneuvering, this flirtation I kept with sexual danger. The chance that sex might happen meant it was always happening: always sex was there, lurking behind Dorothy's twinkling little eyes, in her charming voice and the girlish movements of her hands. I loved her and I was wary of her. There was no one else. She was the only one who could communicate instantly with that other side of life I loved so well, like my cousin Bernadette had that night when our disembodied voices had curled round each other in the dark. Sex had not been absent that night. Bernadette was crazy to have someone love her. We all were. The caresses I gave myself in my own bed were always from an imaginary lover, one I was controlling, one I could trust. I craved to be touched by a trusted lover. There was no one. Only myself. Dorothy could reach my mind and heart and respond to me, at will. Besides, she was my movie friend. Did you ever have a movie friend? They are uniquely sympathetic souls.

Once, the movie scared us. We found ourselves caught like frightened birds while fierce, naked African natives pounded the theater with their drums and bare feet, while they chanted and howled in rhythmic joy and pain, and tossed their naked body parts in our terrified faces.

Dorothy and I ran out, the natives yowling and pounding at our scurrying backs. Outside, we burst into guilty tears.

"That was a dirty movie!" I cried, trembling with shame.

"We didn't know!" Dorothy was quick to rationalize. "You couldn't tell from the title, 'The Sky Above, The Mud Below'! What's that? It sounded like a nature film!"

Of course, it *was* a nature film, but the Catholic Church had so successfully frightened us away from nature. The terrorism of religion was the real reason sex was frightening and dangerous. Our guilt bore down on us like the Sorrows of Gethsemane. We had seen naked women - and men!

"Are you gonna tell the priest in Confession?" I asked, my pubis still pounding with the drums.

Dorothy looked at me, horrified at the suggestion.

"No! Of course not, he'd nevva undastand! We left didn't we?"

I sniffled in agreement. Usually, we trickled into Confession after the movies on Saturday. On this day, we had lots of time to kill during which we worried and wandered the streets like two soldiers lost from their regiment.

The day was as hot and blistering as the desert. The theater had been air-conditioned. We had no money. We wandered down to expensive Broadway where white people shopped and pressed our faces against the lusciously cake-filled window of the Liberty Bakery. We ate with our eyes huge pastry boats bearing mounds of whipped cream; with our eyes we tasted the crusty breads and sugared tortes. We named the confections to each other as though we knew them and described their essential flavors which we remembered from past celebrations: the luscious Italian cream of the yellow cannoli as well as the frothy cream cheese filling and the egg-like shell of the white variety; the roasted walnuts drowning in the moist, deep chocolate of the brownies frosted with thick clogging black chocolate, the sinful lushness of the knee-deep frosting on the wedding and birthday cakes.

"Did you ever get anything here at the Liberty Bakery?" I asked.

"No," Dorothy said, sadly. "It's too expensive."

Neither had I. Ma was loyal to another bakery, Rizzo's, where Daddy bought the Italian bread every Sunday morning, besides, Italian pastries had been reserved only for special occasions at Grandma's and there hadn't been any of those since Nona went to heaven.

We traveled in the dazzling sun, past the Horatio Alger House, back toward the white Immaculate Conception Church. Dorothy balanced on a white picket fence and sang in her clear, high voice, the voice of a child really, simple and clear, she sang what she called the lonesome song. She balanced along a narrow wooden ledge behind the jarring pickets, scaring me to death.

I can't remember all the words.

*Did you ev-er hear the whippoorwill/ sing out his lonesome song/ it seems he's lost the wi-ll to live/ and I'm so lonesome I could cry/ I-I-I could cry/ I could cry-y-y/ I-I could cry/ I could cry.*

I listened as to an Arabian flute that lifts a snake and defies God's laws. It was as though the sweet, high notes held Dorothy aloft. I also envisioned a train whistle crying away into the night and I remember the song as the lonesome train song, the day Dorothy sang the lonesome train song.

Another time, we went to the movies on a very momentous day specifically to witness Hayley Mills' first screen kiss in "In Search of the Castaways," or was it "The Moon-Spinners?" Unfortunately, the kids were especially rowdy that day, or maybe we had passed some kind of milestone, but we couldn't hear a thing the actors were saying, their mouths opened and kids' yelling and laughing came out, so we complained, of course, to the ushers, whom we thought were our friends, but they didn't listen to us. They were too busy. We decided to take matters into our own hands and sneak up to the balcony, which was closed, but, also, we reasoned, cool, quiet and a sanctuary. It was, for about five marvelous seconds, until the manager himself, a weasily little fat man with a too short tie, a too small jacket and a too thin mustache, caught us and threw us out.

We spent the rest of Hayley Mills' magical first kiss outside on the rickety iron fire escape. Enraged at being mistaken for bad kids, we smashed our feet for almost two hours, the length of a movie, against the metal door we hoped led to the manager's seedy office.

The Revere Theater was torched some years later, leaving a gaping sore of crumbling concrete from which wires twisted and writhed like veins from a severed limb. Finally, the Revere Theater looked like it had been bombed on the outside too.

BOY SCOUTS

It was all right to have sex with Daddy, but not all right to have sex with boys.

Daddy had a Boy Scout Troop. Can you believe they let Daddy have a Boy Scout Troop? He didn't desire boys, as far as I knew, which wasn't very far. All those camping trips, the tents, the sleeping bags, the Masters drinking and carousing after the boys had gone to sleep, and that joke Daddy used to tell about the sailor I never understood.

*"This sailor goes ta sea, it was his first time out, see, so it's Saturday night 'n the guys have this barrel an' they're all havin' a good time, drinkin', an' one by one, they're puttin' their dicks in the hole in the barrel an' when it's this sailor's turn ta fuck the barrel, he says to himself, he says, "This ain't so bad." A few Saturday nights go by and one night, they're drinkin' an' havin' a good time and the guys slap 'im on the back 'n say, they say, "Hey, fella, it's your turn in the barrel!"*

Daddy was always telling jokes I didn't understand.

Every three weeks, the troop met at our house in the den, that is, the front room with the bay window, where the lilac would have been if Ma hadn't made the men tear it out. It was hard, sometimes, for me to figure out which room was which; they were always changing. Ma was never satisfied; she always had a new plan. She and Daddy sat at the kitchen table and drew with stubs of pencils on scraps of paper they turned round and round between them. Soon, the plan was implemented. Men came: Daddy and two or three of his friends. Their screeching saws excavated the house into dunes of sawdust and stacks of boards. For months, nails rolled beneath our shoes, cabinets stood on the floor, and the backside of the refrigerator was exposed.

Our house was never finished. But, for a while, the front room was the den, really an extra room where odd furniture was thrown in, and it was also where the Boy Scouts met.

I wasn't allowed in the room during meetings. Nevertheless, I got dressed up as best I could. I washed and set my hair in rollers, or beer cans for a looser curl. I teased and sprayed it, trying to get the ends to curl up in a flip, but the flip always flopped. I dabbed the pasty medicated make-up on my fat, pulsating pimples. I rolled my red corduroy pants as evenly as I could around my rolly stomach and put the safety pin in to hold it secure. I sucked my breath in, but not too much so the safety pin wouldn't bust open which it often did at school, it's nose stretching achingly on the sharp point of the needle, till, finally, bursting and stabbing into me in class. I stole Ma's Evening in Paris, which made me think of Pepe LeMoco and Gabby, I don't know why, because Paris was the one place he dreamed of but could not go, since he was an outlaw and couldn't leave the Kasbah. "Par-is," I repeated with his accent, as I spotted the liquid from the blue bottle on my temples and throat. I also reached into Ma's drawer and took out the Plexiglas earrings with the red rose caught in them that screwed on your ears like a vise.

The Boy Scouts arrived one by one in a doorbell ringing, feet shuffling, voices murmuring ceremony. I waited a while, then crept downstairs and stood outside the doorway in the hall. I peeked in.

The Boy Scout den was thick with smoke from the hundreds of cigarettes the Scoutmasters smoked. In the thick haze stood Daddy at the blackboard he borrowed for the occasion from the VFW Post. Daddy stood like a Strategic Command General briefing his troops, gesturing his cigarette over the heads of all the boys, who sat on metal folding chairs (also brought from the VFW) like good soldiers. His gesturing arm made ceremonial, all-inclusive, benevolent sweeps of the smoky room.

Daddy wore a man size Boy Scout uniform. So did Paul Nabby, who stood next to him. And fat, bald Chuck McDermott, who rolled around the room like a big fat ball, making sure all the boys behaved themselves. Paul smiled, approving of Daddy's battle plan. Chuck nodded his approval. It was a Boy Scout joke, Daddy in the Boy Scout uniform, and Paul and Chuck McDermott were even funnier. All three of their sons were in the troop, Jakey and his brother, Peter, Little Paul, Chuckie, all in brown uniforms with red kerchiefs slung over their necks like little youths for Hitler.

I hung in the doorway like a whore.

I positioned my body so it looked good, which wasn't easy and had taken a lot of practice upstairs in my room. My legs stretched to the opposite doorframe. I sat against the other side, sucked in my tummy and pointed my breasts. I didn't know I looked like a whore. I thought I looked good.

Chuckie McDermott was coming!

"Hi!" he said in a sly, little whisper. "Your Dad wants another beer."

Chuckie was not at all like his father. Chuckie was tall, lanky limbed, dark haired. He stood above the other Boy Scouts; he moved like a slow cowboy.

"Hi," I smiled.

"Gloria!" Daddy yelled. "Get upstairs!"

I giggled and ran up the stairs. I stopped on the landing where Chuckie could still see me. I hung in the shadows thrown by the lamp on the hall desk that no one ever used except to store old papers. Chuckie turned and I let him look. Just at the right moment, I leaned into the light, letting the light flash off my hair, it reflected fully, off the wave on my shoulder.

"Blondes are indecent." Daddy once told me. "There outta' be a law against them."

"You're so fuckable," Frank would explain. "He couldn't help himself."

"You shouldn't sit next to a man." Daddy said. "You shouldn't be allowed in the same room."

I believed them, all of them. It was Christian doctrine to me. From their teachings, I was learning how to act.


TRASH HEAP

The cute little grocery store on the bottom corner of Hichborn Street was gone. Once tucked behind the Fantasis, it couldn't stand being next door to the track people, it left. In it's place, they made more apartments for more track people.

But, this was not the track season. It was chilly and damp, a Saturday. An icy drizzle licked our faces. Chuckie and I had no place to go.

"Let's go for a walk," he whispered in my ear.

I'd just read Stephen Crane's *Maggie: Girl of the Streets*. I felt Chuckie's breath on my cheek: *he was Pete whispering to Maggie. Maggie's mother was on the floor in a drunken stupor. Pete whispered in Maggie's ear, "Ah, what deh hell, Mag? Come ahn and we'll have a hell of a time."*

"Come on," Chuckie whispered.

*"'Ah, what deh hell, Mag, see,' whispered he softly into her ear."*

I wasn't supposed to read Maggie. I'd found it in the Revere Public Library in Fiction. I thought it would be like Ma's thin novel, *Scollay Square*. It looked like *Scollay Square*, thin and small, with a faded, lurid cover. My heart beat fast. I wasn't supposed to read a book like that, but Maggie's voice spoke to me in my heart; she told me to go ahead and read the book and trust her.

We walked down the street and around the corner. The track people were gone. It was cold and wet, not track season, which was hot and arid as the desert. Track season blew gusts of sand high as yellow clouds around the highway. But, now it was grey and brown, stumps of brown weeds stuck up, frozen and stiff around the mattress behind the track apartments. We sat down, and, immediately, the wet seeped through, cold as pee, into our clothes.

"We'll be wet!" I jumped up.

Chivalrously, Chuckie turned a slab of plywood over for us. He wasn't wearing his Boy Scout uniform, which was a shock: his black hair was slicked back. He wore tight black pants and pointy black shoes.

"Maybe, we should go to Death Valley." I said. I thought Death Valley would be prettier.

"What the heck's Death Valley?" he asked, breathing in my ear.

"It's over there!" I pointed.

"I think we should stay here," Chuckie said.

He put his arm around me, he kind of gripped my shoulder with his grubby fingertips and pulled me toward him and kissed me.

It was my first kiss from a boy! And, it had happened, I realized, on a trash pile behind where the track people lived!

I'd always imagined a meadow. I couldn't help it. When I had planned my first kiss, I saw a prince leaning down from his white steed; I saw him, perhaps, dismount and walk boldly, irresistibly, toward me. I would be wearing a dress as soft as air and when our lips met, birds would sing, flowers would fall from the trees.

Some version of this scene is what I'd hoped for myself, what Robin Hood and Maid Marian had enjoyed:

*And so they were married, the lovely bride decked out with many beautiful jewels that were gifts from each one of the band. On this day, the great oak, as well as the whole glade, was festooned and garlanded with sweet flowers - jessamine, eglantine, honeysuckle and wild roses, forget-me-nots from the brookside, pied daisies and cowslips. The sward was a thick carpet of sweet-smelling posies, and the merry birds, when they saw the glade turned into a garden, came to the twigs and branches and sang a glorious melody together, while the happy bride and the brave groom walked slowly, hand in hand, to their new and beautiful bower, where they lived together in great content for many a long day after.*

As Chuckie kissed me again (the second kiss!) and I tried to imagine the railroad tracks and the trash heap as a green meadow, or, at least, a field, but the tracks and the used tampons and the brown beer bottles wouldn't go away. It was my only chance, my first kiss, and there wasn't going to be softness or beauty for me, when I realized once again, like a flower crushed underfoot that springs back up with the rain: it was the words, the words had been the meadow, the music, the flowers and the birds, the words were calling out to me, the words were all I had.

But, I liked Chuckie. I liked his face close to mine, liked his boyish arms tugging at me to hold me tighter. His kisses getting harder now, his hands starting to move, in circles around my back, inching closer to that area under my arms where my breasts swelled.

I remembered Ma's "True Confession" magazines, in which the boys worked so hard to get the girl's bra off. Chuckie was running his hands over and over the back strap of my bra, as if it would pop open by itself.

I liked being kissed and touched. I liked his breath as he moaned for me. His boyish breath, smelling of candy and cigarettes, entered my mouth. I touched his face, too, and he moaned a little and he said my name, as though I'd hurt him.

His hand slid down my neck and stopped, in a gentle curl at my throat. *And Pete whispered, again, "Ah, what deh hell, Mag?" And, I remembered Maggie, crying afterwards, begging Pete, over and over, to tell her that he loved her, and the old woman neighbor who'd overheard them, laughing at his response, "Oh, hell, yes," she laughed, gnarled and toothless, "Oh, hell, yes!"*

And, I couldn't. I couldn't let him. You see it was all right to have sex with Daddy, with the Nazi, or anyone else I could imagine, but not with boys. Boys were forbidden. Boys could get you pregnant. They could talk and laugh about you afterwards. You had to go to confession. You wouldn't be able to go to college. College. That's where the beauty was, that's where the words were, waiting for me.

My hand covered his.

"I'm going to college," I told myself.
"No," I told Chuckie.

## MARIE

I worried about Marie. I tried to listen with her ears in the dark when Daddy was in my bed and she was asleep in the next bed and some of the things I heard through Marie's ears terrified me.

She was such a dirty little kid. I thought of her blackened skin in the clean, clean sheets Ma gave us, her dark monkey skin, blackened further from play. Ma couldn't keep her clean. But, Marie was so lucky, I thought, there, in the dark. Sometimes God blessed me and I could hear her sleep. I could hear her gentle breathing. She was so lucky to be asleep.

At times, Daddy wasn't there and I touched myself. Robin of Locksley would be bad; he captured me, because he couldn't help it. He would lie on top of me, but, because he was out of character, he would instantly change into Daddy, and do the things Daddy did, but with my hands. And, I would wish Daddy was there, and next time, I promised myself, I would beg him to put it in me, then as I built and built to the rush I tried to postpone and prolong as long as possible, I promised myself, I'll ask him to, I'll ask him to. But, I never did. Think of it! I would have been terrified of the huge, dark animal on me, the huge hairy animal, reeking of stale beer, the monster that would smother me, crush me, fill me too much, hurt me beyond belief. I would have gone insane.

Could I keep Marie from going insane? How much do innocent people need to know? Already, her eyes and ears had seen and heard more than enough. The fights Ma and Daddy had were crazy with noise: terrible crashing of pans against dishes, Daddy's fist through the wall; the vicious swearing with teeth clenched; the see-through opening in his underwear, the blood and curly-q hairs in the bathroom. It happened slowly, like pollution, a slow release of poisons into the system, into the pure, clear water. A little seemed to make no difference, it was diluted so much that the poison disappeared. Maybe it wouldn't make you sick, but the water was no longer clean...more was released. Perhaps Mama bent over too far and Daddy came up behind her, or someone left the door open a crack, "Oh! That'll be aw'right!" But, it wasn't.

At school or on the corner, other girls had dulled, narrow eyes and the snapping tongues of snakes, while Marie and I were able to keep our innocent faces, our round, bright eyes and our eagerness for life - and I wondered, *what had those girls seen?*

## THE MOUNTAINS OF BETHER

In the eighth grade, we walked to school, past the Liberty, past the little park, really an island with two benches and a tree, where Hazel Krauss had pulled down her pants and shat one evening behind one of the benches (while Dorothy stood guard) because she couldn't hold it till she got home, down a dirt path that entered a wood, down a old wooden stairway overgrown with scrub, down three tiers of hillside, the third tier of which deposited us on the black tar playground of the Coffin School.

The voices of other kids, the footsteps and shouts followed closely and also far behind me. I walked quickly, but the beauty of the way was not lost on me. The mantel of green softness around my shoulders, the rays of sunlight alternately striking and shaded, the feel of leaves and earth under my shoes, the company of songbirds. I couldn't believe such a place existed in Revere. I didn't think it was safe there, but I dearly treasured the minutes I was allowed to be in that "leafy bower." I wished I had a sword and could wield it like Maid Marian who knew how to defend herself.

*"Troubled in mind, she bethought her of her childhood friend, who, she heard, had become the famous outlaw, Robin Hood of Sherwood Forest...Well aware of the danger of traveling alone dressed as a woman, she decided to array herself like a youthful page and range through Sherwood Forest till she found her dear Robin Hood. So, clad in youth's attire, with quiver and bow, sword and buckler, she started on her way..."*

*"What is thy business, young stranger, and where dost thou go in this wood?"*

*Thinking Robin was some rough thief, the youthful stranger boldly replied: "What is that to thee? I go where I list. Mind thine own affairs and leave me to mine."*

*"That will I not," quoth Robin. "Not one step shalt thou stir without my leave." Then, drawing his sword, he stepped forward threateningly.*

*But the youth drew out a thin, bright, glistening blade, and fell to with such quick blows that Robin had all he could do to guard himself...*

*At last the stranger, whose sword was lighter and more easily handled, gave a sudden thrust which cut a deep flesh wound across Robin's cheek, so that the blood ran fast down his face.*

*"Oh, hold thy hand, young sir," said Robin..."Hold thy hand, and thou shalt be one of my merry men to range the forest with bold Robin Hood."*

*Then Marian remembered the voice of her [childhood] lover, and said: "Ay, Robin, 'tis thine own self. At last I have found thee."*

She and Robin walked with me and it would have been a surprise to anyone who bothered me, to find such strong bodyguards with me. If only reality had been as strong as my imagination and will.

The way was medieval, so it as quite a shock to emerge from the woods into the twentieth century of paved sidewalks, cars backed up, honking, parking and pulling out; boys sitting on top of mailboxes, pounding them mercilessly with their heels, booming deep metal echoes over the street, trying to outdo each other's frightening noise; shouting kids, whistling or screeching like airplanes, cars screeching on their brakes to let the flood of kids pass.

The little grocery store on the school corner, half buried with kids stuffed into its open mouth, kids squirmed their way in and out like maggots. Kids sucking on bottles of Coke, thrusting handfuls of potato chips over their faces, stuffing pink cakes into their mouths, cramming candy bars in their pockets; girls who wanted to be thin, eating chewing gum like it was food.

Every now and then, the owner would come racing out after a kid who'd shoplifted, "Hey! Hey! Come back here!" and another kid slipped in behind his back to shoplift.

The whole street laughed at him.

"Someday I'm going to get him!"

"Ah, what are you open for? You just want our money!" some girl, smoking a cigarette, hollered back.

The owner went back inside where his wife was overwhelmed with kids who couldn't buy and steal fast enough.

Stepping out of the woods, leaving my protectors behind, I was afraid. Afraid of the noise, the anger, the pushing, the screwed up faces, the bared teeth. I had to stand with them, by the doors, or I'd be late. Afraid of their rage, so close to my ear, tearing off threats at each other; afraid of their dirty hands on my back, shoving me into the bricks; afraid of their laughter like Nazis, so glad of someone else's pain; afraid to stand with them, up against them. They smelled like dirt and sugar and smoke. Pushing, pushing, waiting for the teachers to come and open the doors for us, freezing and sweating, freezing on the outside and inside my coat, sweat pouring from under my breasts, my feet stomped like cigarette butts into the cement, pushing. I couldn't get away from them, looking into their runny nostrils, directly into their blackened pores. "Stop your shoving'!" the teacher finally yelled, releasing the pressure on us by unlocking the doors.

The Coffin School, where we stopped having a Valentine Box.

"Don't you think you're a little old for that?" Benny Mann told me when I asked about it.

Benny Mann was one of the most popular, collegiate boys. He was dark and fat and outrageously funny in class. His shirt could never stay tucked. He sucked in his breath when he talked. His father owned a meat company and drove a meat company truck with the family name, MANN MEATS, on the side. How Ma would have loved me to marry into that! "Meat men are rich!" She told me with that glazed look in her eye, probably imagining piles of money! Benny was going to prep school next year, along with all the best boys - the most popular, collegiate boys.

He sat next to me, in alphabetical order.

"How do ya feel?" Benny asked me one day.

"What?" I asked, timidly.

"How do ya feel?" he repeated.

"Fine."

"You sure do!" His hands flew over my breasts so fast I wasn't even sure it was happening.

I turned away as he bent over his desk snickering at me. My face burned with shame and horror while he giggled.

It was because my breasts were big now, as big as Fatima's had been when Rick Likus had raped her. We never saw her any more. She never came out. That was why Benny had done this, I told myself, because my breasts were as big as Fatima's.

And, my blouse was as poor as hers. If I'd had a tennis sweater like Benny's, like the popular girls wore, he never would have done that to me. If I'd had the proper armor: a tennis sweater, Bass Wejuns and an ice cream plaid skirt. Would he?


Exiting their classrooms and walking toward each other, Mrs. French was tucking in her blouse and Mr. Warren was adjusting his pants and everyone said they were getting ready to go to bed together.

Mrs. French taught us French and she cupped her long, maroon-taloned hand under my chin, squeezed my lips till they puckered and recited, "Bon, bon, bon!" I repeated through lips shrunk to rosebuds, "Bon, bon, bon!"

"What a wonderful accent!" Mrs. French cried.

After years of listening to Grandma and Nona, after a decade or more of macaroni, wine and bread, my tongue knew how to tuck itself behind my front teeth, to twist and turn itself into the thick nasal vowels and consonants, heavy and full of the romance languages.

She was hard on me, though. She pinned me, in class. From her desk, far away, "Gloria!"

"Yes?" Meek and frightened, always.

Her severe eyes pinned me, over the tops of her glasses on a chain; the brown curls of her hair tumbling down, her enormous breasts pressing against her wine-colored silk blouse suggested a looser attitude underneath. "Gloria! Did you ever hear of an eraser?"

"Yes." She'd caught me crossing out with dark smudges of pencil, trying to be like the other kids, but I was being held to higher standards.

"Do you have an eraser?"

"Yes."

"Oh?" More scrutiny over the glasses. "I'm glad to hear it. I was afraid you didn't have one."

Mrs. French taught us English, too. She made us read *Lorna Doone*. The print was so tiny and the pages so thin! The kids groaned and said it looked like the Bible and they couldn't read it. She told them them they'd survive.

I read long passages aloud in my room. When they spoke to each other, John Ridd to Lorna Doone, my heart beat alternately in his strong chest, in her fragile frame, though he would prove fragile where she was strong.

*She flung her little soft arms up, in the passion of her tears, and looked at me so piteously, that what did I do but kiss her. It seemed a very odd thing, when I came to think of it, because I hated kissing so, as all honest boys must do. But she touched my heart with a sudden delight, like a cowslip-blossom (although there were none to be seen yet) and the sweetest flowers of spring.*

*She gave me no encouragement, as my mother in her place would have done; nay, she even wiped her lips...as if I had used a freedom."*

No one could finish the *Lorna Doone* test. When Mrs. French called time, everyone groaned at once and kept writing furiously. She called out, "Anyone caught writing will FAIL immediately!" A sudden rustle of papers being thrust at her. Kids clustered round each other for comfort. The room buzzed with, "How did you do?" "How did you answer the third one?" "I think I really screwed up."

They looked at me. Lea Diamond, her sweet blonde flip swished my nose as she turned.

"What about you?" she asked.

Me. They wanted to know about me.

"I finished early. I had to copy it over though, it was a mess."

They stared at me like I was an alien spaceship coming in for a landing. Preston Pierce frowned and stared.

"How do you think you did?" Lea demanded, wrinkling up her nose.

"I loved the book," I said, confused.

I didn't dare add, "I'm gonna miss it."

Lea turned her little nose away from me. They didn't really want to know about me.


"I shall be telling this with a sigh/ Somewhere ages and ages hence:"

Skinny and pale, Donna Pagano was shivering and stumbling through her recitation. Two nerds in the front row spit giggles at her.

"Louis and Martin!" Mrs. French reprimanded them from her perch, one of the empty desks in the back of the room, an uneasy place to balance her voluptuous bulk. "You're like a bad vaudeville act!"

They flung their heads down on their desks and tried to suffocate their derision of poetry, but you could still hear them, like two tires going flat.

Donna Pagano continued.

"Two roads diverged in a wood, and I -

I took the one less traveled by,

And that has made all the difference."

Louis and Martin farted through their mouths into their hands. Mrs. French wrote silently in her book.

"Frances Dudley," she said.

Fran, who dressed in dark colors and chain smoked whenever school stopped for a second, got up quickly, strode to the front of the room, turned to face the class and recited:

"Reflections on Ice-Breaking' by Ogden Nash

Candy

Is dandy

But liquor

Is quicker."


Half the class laughed outright. The other half turned to look at Mrs. French.

Mrs. French gazed coolly over her glasses. She then wrote in her book.

"I'm going to fine you for contempt, Miss Dudley."

"What's that mean?" Fran's mouth hung open. We could all see a blob of purple bubble gum.

"D for Dudley," Laura Borman said. She was a small, pink beauty who never wore the same outfit twice.

"No, F for Frances," piped in Harry Gordon. Handsome Harry, dark, with big features, they called him Ha for reasons they wouldn't tell me. "Oh, it's complicated," Laura had droned, following the curve of her auburn pageboy with polished pink fingernails, bored at my question, when I finally got up the nerve to ask her.

The beauties snickered together, a shining web of influence, a golden filigree of absolute security permeating the room.

"That's enough," Mrs. French told them. "Get rid of the gum, Miss Dudley."

Fran shrugged and sat down real fast, still snapping her gum.

"Laura Gorman," Mrs. French said.

"Oh! Ha, ha!" the beauties laughed heartily.

Laura looked smug and very happy. She pulled a sheet of pink notebook paper written in pink ink out of her binder, bowed slightly to her friends and sashayed to the front of the room.

"Miss Gorman, the assignment was to *memorize* and recite a poem," Mrs. French told her, pointing her pen at the pink notebook paper. "Have you memorized this piece?"

Laura twisted her lips as though she'd been caught. Her friends moaned, "Uh-oh! Now you're in trouble!"

"No! I know it!" Laura laughed, hitting Preston Pierce's blonde head with the pink paper. Preston, who was leaving for Newman Prep next year, who was going to be a doctor, sat in the front row, his long legs stretched far out in front of the desk.

He smiled at her, like they'd known each other forever, and silently took the paper from her.

"I know it," Laura said into Preston's blue eyes.

"Then, let's hear it," replied Mrs. French.

Laura cleared her throat. Laughter sprinkled the room. She was pink and delicate and she could do anything, maybe breathe, and entertain everyone.

"O Romeo, Romeo! Wherefore art thou Romeo?" Laura said in a normal voice. The class roared with laughter. Laura grinned.

Mrs. French looked black.

"QUIET! Is this a joke, Miss Gorman?"

"No! It's poetry," Laura laughed. Again, the beauties laughed, coolly.

"Please, continue," Mrs. French said in a warning voice.

"Ah. Let's see," Laura hesitated. "Ah, I know it!"

"Oh, yeah! Let's see - ah, 'Deny thy father and refuse thy name: - ah, (she laughed) - ah, (she thought she had it!) And I'll no longer be a Capulet!"

The beauties burst into thunderous applause. Laura bowed and curtsied and sat down.

"That's it?" asked Mrs. French.

Laura turned around.

"There's more," she explained, as if to someone fabulously stupid, "but I didn't know I had to memorize the whole thing."

Mrs. French sighed and wrote in her book.

"Gloria Wisher," she said, suddenly.

A bear trap snapped shut on my ankle, shattering the bones to pieces, sending cold blood racing out of my face and body. And I'd tried so hard, for days and days, a week and four days of recitations, to hide behind Elaine Sherman, to make myself as small as I could, but she'd found me.

"Gloria," she repeated, calmly, as if she'd known all along that I'd been hiding.

That was all she had to say. I got up and walked to the front of the room, dragging, in my imagination, my wounded foot and the trap behind me. But, I'd studied and practiced in my room, trying different tones and voices, until I'd found the perfect combination of Joan Fontaine in "Jane Eyre" and Jean Simmons in "The Robe." As I got closer to the front of the room, I began to feel my faith growing in the words themselves. I knew they were beautiful.

I didn't even know what the piece was, not really. Only that it was called "Song of Songs." I'd found it in The Book of the Month Club Poetry Selection I was dusting one day in Ma's bookshelves.

Now that another nerd was in front of them, Louis and Martin went back into action. They began a low snicker.

The bear trap tightened, it seemed, this time around my throat.

Seeing I couldn't begin, they snickered again, louder.

Preston shushed them.

Everyone turned to look at him. Especially me. I couldn't believe it. I opened my mouth and began to speak. I looked away from him, but I could feel him with me nonetheless.

"I am the Rose of Sharon, and the lily of the valleys."

Mrs. French's head shot up. She too was listening carefully.

"As the lily among thorns, so is my love among the daughters.

As the apple tree among the trees of the wood, so is my beloved among the sons. I sat down under his shadow with great delight, and his fruit was sweet to my taste."

"Wooo-oo!" Louis wailed. Martin echoed beside him, "Wooo-oo!"

Preston shot them an angry look. They covered their mouths with their hands, stifling their giggles unsuccessfully.

"Louis, Martin, once more and you'll both get an F on this assignment!" Mrs. French gave an ultimatum. "I've had enough. Please continue, Gloria."

"He brought me to the banquet house, and his banner over me was love.

Stay me with flagons, comfort me with apples: for I am sick of love."

I realized it was my own voice I spoke in as Preston kept his eyes on me.

"His left hand is under my head, and his right hand doth embrace me."

I recited, until "he cometh leaping upon the mountains," Louis and Martin lost control again, and once more with, "the voice of the turtle is heard in our land," and "the tender grape give a good smell" but, by then, I didn't mind so much, I was able to smile at them and Preston smiled, encouragingly.

"O my dove, that art in the clefts of the rock, in the secret places of the stairs...

"Take us the foxes, the little foxes, that spoil the vines: for our vines have tender grapes."

Now, everyone was listening.

"My beloved is mine, and I am his: he feedeth among the lilies.

"Until the day break, and the shadows flee away, turn, my beloved, and be thou like a roe or a young hart upon the mountains of Bether."

I finished. A murmur spun along the golden web. Preston frowned deeply, looking at me, as I had seen him frown and look many times before: as though he were trying to figure out who I was or how to travel that infinite black hole between us, that gulf separating the haves and have nots, what he had and I didn't, what I had and he would vomit, if he ever tasted it.

I went back to my desk.

"Incredible," Mrs. French whispered as she wrote in her book.


She was the hardest teacher I'd ever had, the first teacher I'd loved for her hardness.

When Mrs. French was leaving and everyone, everyone, was glad, I made Ma, absolutely made her, bake a cake. It was large enough to feed an army; it had to be wheeled in on a cart; it shone with sixty-five candles to represent every kid in the eighth grade class.

With tears dropping down her cheeks, Mrs. French placed that long-taloned hand on my shoulder and said, "You're a good writer, Gloria. Don't ever give up your writing."

A writer! I was stunned with a new hope.

"I won't," I promised, looking into her yellowy, blood-mapped eyes.

Mrs. French nodded, "Good."


G*L*O*R*I*A

In the ninth grade, every ninth grader in Revere went to the Adolf Hitler School for Young Adults, a long red prison that stood on a half mile of sand flat, like the pillar of Ozymandias, whipped by a wasteland of blowing sand.

I'd come out of school and they'd be standing there, across the street in a gang and a younger boy, fat Earl Rizzo, who'd just moved on to our street, would call out, "Hey! G-l-o-r-i-a! Hey! Glo-ri-a!" like the song, the song that followed me, "G-L-O-R-I-A!"

I kept walking. After a minute, I turned and he was telling them something and they all laughed real loud so the street echoed with their giggles like hyenas laughing at their prey, thin, evil, high-pitched, a promise in the night of a feeding frenzy, hee, hee, hee, teeth sinking in, saliva and blood running down your skin.

It was because my breasts were big and heavy, suddenly, big and heavy, and it was because of Rick, what he'd told them about me when the darkness streamed out of Nat's Pool Room, and the sidewalk was darkened by it's negative light: the whispers about my breasts, about the nipples, hard against Rick's palm as he told the other boys he'd cradled them, heavy and swelling in his dirty hands, about my pubic hairs, soft and blonde tangled with his own black wires, about my big fat ass, what it felt like squishing against his balls. He told them anything and they imagined from there, whatever they wanted. They called out to me, "Gloria! Gloria!" as though I would stop right there and pull down my pants for them.

"Gloria!"

A whisper, hoarse as a rat's claws on the backs of boards. Earl Rizzo huddled in the gloom of his brother's car.

"Hey! Gloria!"

It was night and I was walking home from somewhere, maybe someone's house, or the sub shop on the highway where Ma made us go for rolls or cigarettes. The beams of cars like long searchlights that swung onto your shape and cars honked.

I had developed the instinct of not turning when my name was called, when "girlie!" was shouted on the highway; instinctively, I knew, don't turn!

"Gloria! Wanna see my brutha's car?"

The scurrying feet of rats ran up my back. I shook them off. As though seeing his brother's car was an ambition of mine!

How close the boys were, how very close I came! There were so many gangs. Earl led a gang of young boys, younger than Rick's gang: they roamed down Hichborn or Franklin, roamed the beach or Shirley Ave., the tenements on Thornton. They hung for hours outside Nat's Pool Room where they were too young to get in but where they learned everything they needed to know. There were gangs on the other side of Revere, the Irish side, a block past the Immaculate Conception Church, by Broadway and Gateway, by the Dublin Bar, gangs who fought, it seemed to me, over wearing white shoes or black, over being Irish or Italian. Over who was dirtier, who was meaner, who was poorer, richer, better.

Earl was dirty. He was poor and mean. His brother worked and had bought a car. He parked it down by my house and Earl sat in it and waited for me.

"Gloria!"

The fat silhouette of Earl Rizzo, vague and shifting with the passing headlights of cars, but the two eyes, glared at me, sealed with intent, human like the eyes of a wolf.

"Gloria! Come on, I want to show you!"

Maybe it was that blonde hair flying up like a flag or a gunshot at the hunt, that blonde hair had kinetic power to move men. At times, it was a power I didn't want.

Maybe, like little dogs, the bad boys, Rick and his pals, reacted to the change in me as though a stiff smell had gone up from between my legs after Daddy had been with me. Maybe they sniffed the air, their masculine chemistry quickly altered and they went after me as surely as their little penises pointed the way.

Maybe I wanted someone - a boy, softly, to whisper my name, to stroke my cheek, my hair, while the moonlight shifted in the depths of trees. Maybe I wanted someone, a prince, a faun, a young god, to kidnap me because he couldn't help himself, overcome by love, and keep me for a while, under the trees, loving me softly, then sadly, letting me go. Someone. Not Earl Rizzo. Not Daddy.

I read books and books protected me. This brain was all I had to shield me, this huge head, this round, bulging forehead, "all brain," Jakey called me.

In the shade of my room, in the arms of the Huckleberry Tree, I was loved by words, soothed and loved. I gave my faith to heroes who did not exist. Robin Hood, Tarzan, Peter Pan. John Ridd.

*"Here was I, a yeoman's boy, a yeoman every inch of me, even where I was naked; and there was she, a lady born, and thoroughly aware of it, and dressed by people of rank and taste, who took pride in her beauty, and set it to advantage. For though her hair had fallen down, by reason of her wildness, and some of her frock was touched with wet, where she had tended me so, behold her dress was pretty enough for the queen of all the angels! ... All from her waist to her neck was white, plaited in close like a curtain, and the dark soft weeping of her hair, and the shadowy light of her eyes (like a wood rayed through with sunset), made it seem yet whiter...Hereupon it went hard with me, not to catch her up and kiss her...only it smote me suddenly, that this would be low advantage of her trust and helplessness."*

I was supposed to take the school bus, but I was terrified of it. I'd seen the bus for the Adolf Hitler School pull up at Hichborn Street, long before I was old enough to go to the Adolf, the school bus had terrified me. I could hear it from the middle of the street where I was playing or riding my bike. The doors would slide open and a roar of screams and swears would rush up the hill toward me, and I'd turn to see silhouetted against the black windows arms and legs flailing about and feet kicking up over the seats and I thought, that's the Adolf Hitler bus; I'm not getting on that bus.

So, I walked a long way, don't ask me how far, two miles, maybe, I didn't care. I was determined to be alone and free of them all.

There were so many of us, we had to go to school in shifts. Like the streams of workers who filed into the General Electric plant in Lynn, we went to school day and night. The first shift was in early morning, from 7:15-1:15, the second shift from 1:15-5:15. I always walked in the dark.

It wasn't unpleasant. The sun made long red stripes behind the oil tanks, which floated forward from out of the dark sky. A few stars still winked in the lush, lightening midnight blue; a single white sea gull, ever faithful, still followed me, calling.

I walked along the highway, busy already, swishing with cars and trucks and lighted city buses. Occasionally, a weak burst of horn, tentative as the crossing of night into day, and a plaintive cry out the truck window to a young girl, "Sweetheart!" Look at me, the cry said, look at me. I didn't look.

Under the overpass, walking on a thick carpet of pigeon shit, trying to step in clear spots - there's a place clear - there's another - no more here - none - there! My whole body lifted, levitated, over the pigeon mess. The birds seemed barely awake; I could hear them, quietly cooing under their sleeping breath. I could see their nests, creepy and drippy, hanging from the steel rafters, caked with the black soot of a million years, vibrating above me. Men stopped their cars, leaned toward me and opened the passenger door with a reaching arm. "Hey, honey, wanna ride?" "No, thank you." I scurried faster.

Back out, it took a minute for my eyes to adjust, even into the cool, blue light of a receding moon sparring with sudden flashes of sun.

After the overpass, I walked along the base of a tall embankment, like Tarzan's escarpment, it hung over me, the site of Dorothy's club, which she had named, Ecstasy.

"What's 'Ecstasy'?" I had asked.

"It means the highest form of excitement," Dorothy had informed.

And Dorothy knew, because the nuns had told her. The nuns were experts in passion and abandon, which they interpreted as religious. *Ecstasy: a sublime state of arousal during which the participant might levitate, see visions or revelations, perhaps, see or speak to God, or suffer Christ's wounds.* Transportation out of the physical burden, yet, actually brought about by, and experienced through, the physical. But, not to nuns - to them, it was spiritual alone, yet induced by slow torment of the senses: flagellation, torture, anguish, deprivation, fasting, meditation to exaltation. The body was responsible, the body, for the denial of itself, for the extreme lengths of passion and pain the spirit could encounter and feel, the nuns did not know, but the body was responsible for the ecstasy they taught in school.

In Ecstasy, we read literature. *"I broke my heart with weeping to come back to earth; and the angels were so angry that they flung me out, into the middle of the heath on the top of Wuthering Heights, where I woke sobbing for joy."* We read aloud to each other. That was nice. Reading was all the ecstasy I needed from Dorothy. That, and the beautiful flowers we found there.

Strange flat-faced, open roses grew thickly, pink and fierce smelling with petals like pink sugar and stems and thorns so thick you couldn't reach into their depths to pluck the flowers out. Purple irises stood very tall, poking their heads out of the high grass. These too were unyielding; their stalks were tough as a reptile's hide. Though I grappled with them, they were unrelenting, till I came up with the roots, swinging dirt over my bare legs, which were cut and bleeding from the razor sharp blades of the wild grass. Somehow, we invaded this tangled chaos and made a space for ourselves.

Sometimes, she surprised me and brought another kind of book, *"His sinful stare took her breath away. Her full bosom heaved tumultuously as he ripped open her bodice and thrust his face into the hot flesh between her breasts where he kissed her soft orbs till she trembled with ecstasy...he fit perfectly inside her, she knew he would! How wonderful he felt! His throbbing staff seemed to suck away her breath with every thrust, and yet, she craved more and more, till she could barely breathe..."*

Till my heart beat wildly with fear and my panties stuck to me with the warm juices of my own passion.

"Did you hear that? Ecstasy! That's the name of the club!" Dorothy said proudly.

"My mother doesn't want me to come here," I said.

"Why not?"

"She says it isn't safe."

"Why did you tell her?"

Why? So she'd tell me not to go. I led Ma to tell me. Because if I went, I knew Dorothy would try to have sex with me again, only I didn't think to myself "have sex with me," I thought, "Dorothy would do that thing to me."

"I thought this club was supposed to be a secret," Dorothy grumbled.

These were my thoughts as I walked alone to the Adolf Hitler School for Young Adults on the sand flats down by Revere Beach. I decorated the walk with my thoughts, as I always had, thinking, too, of the too tall boys who went to school there, tall and big as men, who towered above the other kids because they'd stayed back so many times. They *were* men; they skipped school, waiting till they were old enough to quit. And, after they quit, they stood outside in the sand half the day, staring up at the red brick building like prisoners let out for exercise, like they'd made a big mistake and longed to get back in.

I thought of the reason I called it the Adolf Hitler School: because the English teacher there, English, which was my only freedom, knew how to ruin a subject, but not how to teach it. She taught only grammar, which I already knew. She was not acquainted with literature. Her idea of poetry was to measure the meter. I couldn't believe I was back where Deenie Loomus and Francie Nolan had been, standing before a teacher in a too crowded classroom trying to talk about the meaning of the words and being told to sit down, they only had time to count the syllables. Why Deenie and Francie had lived in the Depression and Francie, in the slums! Hadn't we learned anything since -

Into these thoughts and thoughts like them, not so often that I could prepare for it, Rick Likus would spring out of the bushes and jump on me. He didn't have to be in school for an hour yet and he spent the time stalking me.

He got a good grip and yanked me off my feet into the bushes where I lay flat on my back, my stack of text books, the only thing between our bodies, protecting me like a shield. A shield Rick ignored. The books dug into my ribs as he pushed his body hard into mine, as his mouth searched my neck where he actually bit me, and my blood and his saliva ran down my throat. He laughed.

He lifted up his chest, to look at me.

"Hi, Gloria!" he said.

"Get off me, Rick!" I hissed, angrily, surprising myself.

He laughed.

"You're a goddamn vampire!" I struggled in my fury to get up. He decided to let me.

I shoved my way through the bushes, scratching my hands and tearing my jacket.

"I want to SUCK YOU!" Rick laughed from the bushes.

Leaves hung from skirt as I ran down the highway.

Men honked their horns at me because I was running, agitated.

Ma would've been mad about the jacket, but I didn't tell her. I fixed it myself; I was very good at sewing. I didn't tell her about Rick. That might seem stupid to you and I suppose it was, but Rick's mother was Ma's best friend. I didn't think much of Annie Likus, as you know, but Ma thought the world of her. Annie made Ma laugh - a lot. It may seem stupid to someone who was brought up better, who had more going for them, to think I would sacrifice myself so my mother could have a friend, but it didn't seem stupid to me.

I didn't want my family and Rick's in the middle of the street fighting like the Likuses and the Fantasis; I didn't want a parade of the Virgin for me.

Besides, there was a feeling of privacy. My privacy, my desire, my experimentation. Rick could be mine for a while. Maybe it was my own depravity, my own terrible perversity that I was flattered, that I wanted him to chase me. I wonder what goes through the mouse's mind as he runs in front of the cat. Was I crazy or brave? Was I so lonely or so untaught? I marvel sometimes at what really goes on in the mind of a person, how attracted we are, even at an early age, to the bad things, even if we are afraid, how we push and prod them to find out what they are, or maybe it was my own self, that I was really half devil, from Daddy, and half angel, from Mama.

## THE SAINT OF TREES

"There's something so feminine about you," a man once told me.

I know what he meant. I'm small. Men imagine they'll feel their size against me. I'm light and delicate. My big eyes seem naive. I am naive. It takes tremendous bravery to be naive. He meant that I was like a victim: someone who could be acted upon. I was small, round, and soft. I was romantic, devotional.

I wanted to be the Saint of Trees. I thought about becoming a nun.

I had another friend, Colleen Callahan, who was a couple of years older than me. She was a big tall Irish girl with a snub-nosed, chinless face, freckled as a giraffe, good-natured and kind; she was going to be a nurse, the next thing to being a nun. Colleen was a calm relief after Dorothy. Her family had recently moved into the big yellow house next to Ma's friend, Connie; they were a big family of big Irish boys and a mother who looked just like her, who was also big boned, chinless and a nurse.

"Do you think I could become a nun?" I asked Colleen.

"You?" she laughed. Her blue eyes twinkled down at me; at the same time, her grim mouth turned down at the corners. Poor people have a sad way of laughing sometimes.

"Don't be a nun," she said, "They'll cut off all your beautiful hair."

She was so much taller than me and so much broader, as well as being older, that I consulted her quite seriously on many subjects. In return, she did not disappoint me. She spoke with all the authority of her size and advanced age. Colleen was fifteen to my thirteen.

"I have to be a nun," I explained, "because I want to become a saint. The Saint of Trees."

We were at the Quicksand, the seeping yellow mud that encircled the truck stop. We were getting ready to cross the highway. We kids spent a lot of time crossing the highway. It was second nature to us; we were good at it.

We talked about sainthood without ever taking our eyes off the traffic hurtling by us; we began by standing still and studying the rhythm of the traffic. We advanced slowly, learning the oncoming rush with our bodies' sensors, sending out waves of mental and sensual radar, allowing the waves to bounce back and vibrate over us. We timed our crossing precisely by intuition and rhythm, breathing against the skin of the cars, timing the return of our breath with extended nostrils, crossing without benefit of stoplight or cop, weaving in and out of the rushing cars by wisdom, faith, guts and sheer luck.

"Now!" we shouted together.

We dashed out and began the weaving, our bodies instantaneously judging fragments of time and space. If a driver panicked and the car slowed down, it was a deadly interruption of rhythm, we had to alter in mid-flight. Sometimes we came so close, we could tap our fingers on the steel back flying past. We leaned into the blast of cars as much as a construction worker leans into a stiff wind at forty stories, balancing his life on a fickle breeze and six inches of steel beam.

Slowing down to a walk on the other side, Colleen resumed our conversation as though it had never been interrupted.

"You can be a saint without being a nun," she informed me. "People will pray to you. Do you want people to pray to you?"

"No!" I said, horrified. "Pray to me? No, I don't! Why would they?"

"Because," Colleen laughed, "that's what saints are for."

"I thought you were going to be a writer," she added, as we sat down on her front steps.

"Saints can write," I told her.

"Ha!" She laughed out loud. "You're pretty funny. Saints don't have time to write. They're too busy praying."

But, I was a saint. Though I was barred from the sacred ground of the Indian Camp, I could nestle into the rough arms of the Huckleberry Tree. In rain, its wet, trembling leaves protected me. In cold, my toes separated numbly from my body; in sun, I was blessed with cool shade. Close, below me, my sister called to me but could not see me. Close, above me, the cars and trucks and planes zoomed weightless over the fragile eggshell of my head. There, in the tree, I achieved sainthood, within the book I held in my hands I climbed peaks of snowy mountains encircled by clouds; I saw the vistas, blue and gold, misty or bright. The peace, the purity of heaven was visited upon me, there, within the eggshell, swirling, an embryonic galaxy; the power that is life itself being formed inside me, I felt it, absolutely pure and undeniable. I mistook it for sainthood, which is servitude, which, at that time, I thought was an ultimate power on earth next to God's, which I did not realize, I possessed already.

Already, I was holy.

## THE LAST TIME I SAW THE NAZI

The last time I saw the Nazi, he came to me in that barren room, in the dead of winter, the wind screaming low and mean outside. He carried a large white box. He placed the box on the little wooden table.

"This is for you, you must wear it for me. Now!" he told me.

I was in the bed; I was naked. He opened the box, rustling with white tissue paper. He motioned with his hard chin, for me to come to him. I did.

He lifted out of the box, a film of gold, a golden skin he gave to me.

"Put it on," he said. And, he sat back in the only chair to watch.

The silk seemed to melt in my shivering hands, it was cold as it slid over my body like the skin of a snake and fell heavily to the floor in a golden puddle around my bare feet.

He reached into the tissue and pulled out a pair of golden shoes. He knelt and placed them, one by one, on my icy feet. He remained there, kneeling, his head fell back and he looked at me. Slowly, almost imperceptibly, his rigid lips began to tremble. He resented their shudder; he tried desperately to control them, but his lips betrayed him. His eyes, also, wept. He let his head fall back in abandon and he cried like a child.

I felt a remarkably cold affection for him; I waited while he cried. Long minutes passed while he hugged my knees and poured tears down the golden folds of the dress. I didn't dare move. What could I do? If I fell down with him, perhaps, he would kill me for recognizing his pain? If I tried to lift him, perhaps he would beat me until I was lower than him. He wept, then, the weeping stopped and he hung his head silently about my legs. I waited. Darkness climbed over the wailing fields outside.

At last, he stood and took me in his arms. He spoke something, brief and tender, in German. I understood.

He was mine, the Nazi. I belonged to him.

# Book Four
## Rebel

Revere

1965-1967

GODS AND GODDESSES

When the boys and girls came down the street on summer evenings, after sunning all day at the Beach, the boys' pastel shirts stood out against the buttery tan of their necks, the girls' athletic knees strode surely and strong, their hair a shade lighter than when they'd awakened in the morning, tinted with sun and surf; they laughed cruelly and gaily at each other. My heart leapt to see them, luminous and gilded; my heart sank to be excluded from them. I watched them from afar, from the confines of my porch and my fatness, my ignorance of smart manners, my terrible shyness and fear of anything graceful, anything glowing as they were, a rank of young gods and goddesses straight from their mother's dinner tables on their way to a Little League baseball game.

Preston and Ha were already at the ballpark. Calling him Ha out loud in front of people was forbidden to me, but I called him that secretly when I was alone. Ha and Preston were in prep school now. They strode past wearing real baseball uniforms that shone beautifully in the setting sun, grey and sparkling white, with blue and white socks that shaped their firm legs like colonial pantaloons and stockings. I snuck down after they'd passed my house: the crack of their bats, their shouts, the way the girls sucked on straws stuck in real Cokes. There at the baseball park I studied them: the murmurs of players and the scraping of their cleats in the dugout, and if I stood on top of the dugout, I could feel through the soles of my sneakers, the vibrations of real people doing real things.

I meant to write about Rick Likus and his friends, the group of boys and girls Rick went with, but my own classmates strolled down Hichborn Street instead. Rick's group was very much like them, except for age, of course, and religion. The popular kids in my class were Jewish. Rick's friends had no religion; they were wild.

If the boys and girls I knew were gods and goddesses, Rick and his gang were satyrs, centaurs and nymphs. They ran around the streets and islands, in and out of the houses and cars, their little goat hooves and bare nymph feet flying as fast as the pandemonium they left behind.

Frankie Carter, tall and blonde, quiet, always watching. Jerry Finley, skinny, with long, curly red hair that shined copper in the sun; he delivered our Revere Journal. On the days he collected, I answered the door if I didn't have a pimple. "He's here to collect," Ma said, like a song, "He's here to collect." I was in love with Jerry Finley for years because he was so skinny and his red hair shone like golden metal when he slapped on our steps that rolled up Journal Ma devoured. She clicked her tongue over the stories and obituaries, repeating Revere names, "Leach, tsk, tsk," "Roposo, tsk, tsk."

She made me sick every week. The sound of everyday Revere names made me sick, though the sound of magical Revere names, Frankie Carter, Jerry Finley, Rick Likus, Ha and Preston, resonated over Ma's and Daddy's, Jakey's and my tongues, ringing bells of familiarity, inspiring adoration sometimes strangely mixed with contempt or fear.

Other boys whom I didn't know were in Rick's gang, their faces and bodies merged with the group as vague dirty brown jackets and dungarees, dirty brown hair and faces. The girls were tough as tree bark; they had harsh voices like crows cawing that cut across the street, laughter like sin. They wore ruffles on their bathing suits even though they didn't need ruffles to flesh out their figures. Their long, bronzed legs shone out of cut off dungarees; they had stiff, sun-bleached hair that whipped their faces like dirty mops.

I didn't dare look at the girls too closely. I didn't know their names. I was afraid to look at them except sideways. If they'd caught me, they would've beaten me. I could hear them calling Annie Likus, "Hi, Rick's mother!" Everything was Rick's. They didn't call Annette or Linda by name, the girls sang out across the street, "Hi, Rick's sister!" from where they dangled their wondrous legs over the side of Rick's little Triumph.

Rick's gang played hockey for the High School. They were a fierce team, eager to fight, proudly limping, sneering with scarred eyes and broken teeth and lips torn up and pasted back together a little lop-sided.

Even amongst demi-gods, one god stood out. He didn't need to be the strongest or the handsomest. He didn't need to be the King.

I saw him on a summer morning when the pear tree shone green in the bright sun bearing heavily its load of tough, fat pears, while Daddy was mowing the lawn, sending the sweet smell of green into the air, while I sat on our porch steps reading a book, I looked up and he was walking down the street, as it turned out, to Rick's house.

Our eyes met across the street. He didn't know who I was, or wasn't, so he reacted normally, kindly, as he would every time he saw me as long as we were alone with the street between us. A soft boy, gentle, he had light brown hair and brown eyes, a round face, a kind smile. He hung on the outer fringes of Rick's little gang; he was the soft one, the sweet one, softer and sweeter than any of the girls. They called him Tweetie.

I looked up from my book, across the street into those gentle eyes.

"Hi," he said, softly.

"Hi," I returned, unsure that he could be so kind.

I was in love.

I couldn't believe what I was seeing when he opened Rick's door and went in.

Who was he? I ran in and asked Jakey.

"What do *you* want to know for?"

"Who is he? How come he went into Rick's house?"

And Jakey told me all he knew. The boy's name was Richie Silva. I couldn't believe his first name was the same as Rick's. He lived - I'll tell you where he lived, where I snuck down in the middle of the night to stand in front of his house. It was a dear little forgotten road, half-paved as though the city had run out of tar right there, so the wild roses and lilacs, the morning glories and lilies, the skunks and stray dogs and cats took over. The scrub trees and bushes, black green where I stood under the street light, smelling the fierce odor of skunk, praying I wouldn't be sprayed; Ma would kill me. I sniffed, trying to filter out of the smell of skunk and diesel fuel, always present on the air, to find the perfume of roses and the salty scent of the sea flying straight up the hill to my nose. This little street would be so dear to me, just kitty corner from the park where Helen Krauss had squatted and shat on the way home because she couldn't hold it any more.

One night Richie came home with his friends; he stood on the curb, he laughed, "Ya, right!" into the car. He laughed, "Ya, right!" into the car. I could repeat that forever, strong as it is with memory, love and terror. "Ya, right!" He laughed with his friends. He didn't see me. I wish I'd run up to him. I wish I'd run up and kissed him. At least once.

I saw another movie late at night. The night is filled with things. If I went down and turned on the television, in the middle of the night, I would see a thing I knew I wasn't supposed to see: a true thing, a secret thing, hidden under the black screen of TV Land. Just turn it on, that's all, just turn it on. There. A girl. She was on a bed in the dark. I could see nothing but her face, her hair, her shoulders. I knew she was on a bed because under her head were the black and white stripes of an old bare mattress. But, something was going on. The door of the room kept opening, throwing a weird light over her; she'd squint into the light at the boy coming in. Sometimes, she laughed. Her dark hair was spread out on the black and white stripes, flung out about her laughing face. But, then, if she didn't like the boy whose turn it was, she made a grimace at him and his head blocked out her face for a moment; she reappeared over his shoulder and she looked angry. Several boys went into the room for her, but it was the last one she loved. Her face lit up with joy when he entered and came toward her. She held out her arms to him and in her mind, she whispered, her silent face rapturous over his thrusting shoulder, "You're the only one, my love. You're the only one."

When I thought of Richie Silva and I thought of him every day and night, I thought of him that way. I knew I was the girl on the bed and the boys were all coming to me, one by one, Rick, Jerry, Frankie, the Nazi, Daddy, but when Richie Silva entered the room, he was the only one.

It was strange, eerie. A few years later, when I met the beautiful Junie, out of the blue, she said, "I'm gonna call you Tweetie!"

## SAILORS

When the sea sparkles in the blue eyes of a sailor, don't mistake it for love.

When the handsome sailor, sparkling in his white uniform, leaned over the rail of The Constitution, his white arms reflecting the sun like a mirror, I saw the glint of something in his eye and I wondered if love could show like that.

What was a smart girl like me doing hanging around sailors? Why did Colleen Callahan and I get ourselves all dolled up, go into Boston and throw ourselves in front of the sailors down at the elegant Constitution, white sailed and shining with brass and caramel wood like a floating church? Or any common, dull grey battleship we could get near? Sometimes we chose the metal battleships with cornball Mid-Western names, like Michigan or Wisconsin, stark and naked as giant maggots. But usually, we gravitated toward the beautiful Constitution. It was as familiar as Paul Revere's House, where we'd been taken as children, over and over, for field trips, The Constitution, The Bunker Hill Monument, Paul Revere's House.

One of her four or five brothers was a sailor on a ship in town. I never was sure how many she had or even which one actually drove us into town with him to his ship. We got out of the car pretending to walk downtown to do something else, but we'd go back and flirt with sailors. Sometimes, we'd tell them where we lived and they'd come all the way to Revere for us and take us out for a date. I told Ma Colleen's older brother had introduced us.

A sailor dressed in street clothes is a sorry sight. The first time I saw a sailor out of uniform, standing at my door in his weak polyester shirt and pants, I got scared. This was not the person I'd invited to see me. From his regulation hair, causing his ears to stick out without his lovely white cap to tuck them under, to his uniform shoes, large as clubfeet poking their swollen noses out from under cheap 5 & 10 men's trousers, he unnerved me. The thin little Hitler moustache, simpering on his upper lip, the only extra hair they were allowed, scared me the most.

The handsome ones were too smart to go out with us. We attracted the skinny, ugly sailors, the stupid ones and we experimented with them like the little Nazis we were.

It began with my cousin Peter, Jakey's brother. Peter became a sailor. He brought lots of sailors to our house. I loved my cousin so much because he was the best person I knew. And, as if by magic of Peter's wonderful virtue, all the sailors he brought to our house were as good and kind as he was.

Peter took a sailor named Ship to see us. That was his real name, Shipman, called him Ship. Ship sat silently behind thick glasses; his brown eyes magnified like fishes caught in bowls. His nose, mustache and lips threatened to come off with the glasses. Peter kept assuring us that Ship was a lot louder on the ship. He never talked except to respond to Daddy's friendly man-to-man growl, "How's it goin', Ship?" "Fine." I'd turn my head in surprise! Ship had spoken!

Peter and his sailors came to our house to eat. Ma cooked huge pots of what Peter called "pasta poosta" because he couldn't pronounce pasta fasciola, that is, pasta noodles cooked in a rich stew of beans and tomatoes, basil, garlic and oregano, dunked with hefty slices of crusty Italian bread. They drank gallons of orangeade or ginger ale, only occasionally downing a few of Daddy's Miller High Life's, but never ever getting drunk. Not that you could see. They were always gentlemen, all of Peter's sailors, and I loved to watch them eat and drink and say silly things about each other. Peter would tell them, proudly, about me, how I was smart and going to college.

Once, he brought someone handsome. He had dark hair, cut trim and neat round his fine head and blue eyes like the sailor whose eyes had sparkled with the sea, not love. I don't remember his name, but he was smart. In my mind I call him, Starsailor, because after we ate he and I talked for hours about the stars and navigation by the stars, then constellations, then myth, then the universe, and time and the nature of time and space. He told me about wormholes and black holes, star births and star deaths. He said the birth of a star looked a lot like a human embryo, only millions of miles big. He was older and smarter and I loved that. I don't know where he came from or where he went to, but for an evening I had him there and we talked feverishly.

Halfway into our conversation, Ma shook her head, "I don't know *what* you're talking about! I haven't understood a thing for an hour and half!"

But, I could tell she was proud that I could talk about something she didn't understand at all.

"Do *you* know what they're saying?" Ma asked Peter.

Peter smiled proudly.

"Nope!"

One day, many years later, Peter brought some lace his fiancée's sister had made. He showed me pictures of the girls who were from another country; they were ugly as horses in dresses. Peter's girl was the least ugly of the sisters. I wondered why he was marrying her. But, I wasn't interested in her. I was enamored of the lace and said I wanted to learn how to make it, so mysteriously intricate and perfect, so delicate to look at, yet as strong as a fisherman's net.

"No," said Peter, "lacemaking isn't for you. That's only for girls who can't do anything else."

Why couldn't they do anything else? Because they were so ugly? I was excluded from lacemaking, which seemed, somehow, a privilege of plainness, a cloistered duty transformed by the secrets of sisterhood, the whispers and giggles of girls visited clandestinely in ancient castles under stained glass windows and stone walls by sailors.

It was Peter's influence that sent me searching for sailors of my own. But, my sailors were not as nice as his.

The worst sailor, the final sailor, was Dinghy. That's not his real name.

Dinghy came off one of the battleships near Colleen's brother's ship. We could walk the sun-bleached docks and in five seconds have attracted twenty sailors from out of the dry wood. Or, maybe we met him and his friend down by the swan boats where the sailors were as hungry for girls as the ducks for bread.

Dinghy came from one of those places that still existed in the United States where people get married at twelve or thirteen, sometimes to their cousins, and live in a shack on a mountain. I imagined, horribly, that the women wore faded housedresses, raised chickens and children while the men fished, hunted squirrels, and made moonshine, or some other illegal trade, sometimes racing from the authorities in the dead of night over bumpy moonlit back roads. He had an accent when he spoke, which wasn't often, an accent that seemed to come from the other side of a jail cell, and his voice was too quiet to be calm.

What was I doing with a guy like that? What had possessed me to bring Dinghy home? He was ugly. Dinghy's Adam's apple, which was nearly as big as his head, jumped out every two seconds as he swallowed his nervousness down. His hands were clammy as he held mine. He was small and thin as a bone; every so often, his narrow frame twitched like a bug after it's been smashed. I can't believe I kissed him, turning my sweet pink and white face to avoid his lizard-like nose. I must have been punishing myself for - you know.

Dinghy was rabid with sex drive. He was all over me the moment we were even remotely alone, in a movie theater, in the den, or watching television on the old couch. Dinghy's mouth would be ravenous on mine. His hands thrust themselves downward from my throat so forcefully I thought he'd strangle me if I didn't let him grope me further. After many struggles, one day his eyes glazed over as he leaned toward me with his open mouth and told me to marry him.

I froze solid; my life snapped in front of me. I saw myself fat and pregnant, trapped in a trailer, my stringy hair reeking of fried food and spit-up, babies screaming all around me, diapers hanging on a make-shift clothesline over my head because we were too poor to have a washing machine and dryer, and in my daydream, Dinghy, his quiet suddenly turned evil, got up from watching a blurry TV set and smacked me across the mouth. Worst of all, I couldn't say I wouldn't have deserved it just for being around a guy like him in the first place.

I jumped right out of Dinghy's scrawny arms and went to find Daddy.

"He wants to marry me, Daddy," I said. "Help me."

Daddy sighed, heavily.

"Wait in the kitchen," he said.

I could hear them shaking hands as Daddy entered the den. My heart beat hard. Guilty sweat beaded up in my palms. I heard their masculine voices murmuring, soft guttural negotiations, the deep rumblings of their mutual grievances against women and frightening silences during which I imagined Dinghy would scream and come rushing out at me.

However, twenty minutes later, Daddy escorted a subdued and defeated Dinghy to the door.

I felt my stomach empty of him and all sailors forever, my bloodstream ran clear. It was better than confession. I felt light, fresh, a bit older, and jittery with hunger.

Daddy came to the doorway of the living room. He stood and looked at me.

"Thanks, Daddy," I said uncomfortably wondering what might come next.

He didn't reply. Except with the expression on his face, which was disgusted, resigned and a little proud.

I had to agree.


AUGUST 18, 1966
THE BEATLES COME TO REVERE

We were forbidden to go, but a historical event was about to take place only a mile away from my house and no matter what I thought of them, whether I admired them or not, (at this time, I actually preferred Elvis) it was a matter of honor, there was no question in my mind, the Beatles were coming to Revere, therefore I was going to see them.

It didn't take much persuasion to get Colleen to go with me.

"Want to go see the Beatles?"

"No, what do you think?"

Neither of us had any money, which meant we also didn't have any tickets. Still, we knew we were going to get in. How? We didn't know that yet, but the excitement of finding out was almost unbearable.

Since early afternoon, we could hear the kids screaming from our house as they lined up a mile away to get into Suffolk Downs Race Track. Occasionally, the roar of a man's voice bellowed on the loud speaker, like the roar of the ocean heard from far away or the roar of a truck approaching. The voice of the man commanded, like the voice of God, but his words were unintelligible. "What did he say?" we asked each other all day long. "I dunno," was the answer. The high pitched squeal of the kids grew and grew all afternoon till by twilight, the still air heavy with diesel oil and a day's worth of growing heat, while Colleen and I walked along the darkening highway, the tar sticky from hot exhaust, amongst streams of dirty kids in dingy, sweaty, summer clothes, getting closer and closer, their voices became one huge voice, louder than the highway, bigger than the sky, and suddenly the squeal swelled incomprehensibly louder, becoming deafening, an emergency howl and a long scream of agonizing yearning, hurting our ears and drowning out all other sound.

"The Beatles are here!" I cried out, but no sound came out of my mouth. Nevertheless, Colleen nodded in absolute ecstasy.

We were at the gate, which was being crushed by throngs of kids' bodies, hot and desperate, pushing themselves in one mass toward the guards who flung their own fat bodies upon them and pushed back.

The decorum of taking tickets had long since passed, yet there didn't seem to be any hope of getting past the police. Uniformed men were everywhere. Orange construction horses blocked the way. The police spoke silently into walkie-talkies. They pressed the kids bodies with sticks held across like bars and the kids fell back.

The hill behind Suffolk Downs was covered with people as though some god had poured them down over the hillside. The crucifix stood thirty feet high among them and kids dangled their feet from its cross.

Colleen and I stood off to the side of the gate entrance, against a chain link fence and waited for a space to appear in the crowd flooding the gate.

Then, two kids made a break for it very close to us and the security guards by us dashed for them, throttled them and walked off with their struggling bodies. Without conscious thought, as the guards' backs were turned to us, we pivoted our bodies through a small opening where two chain link fences didn't quite meet and we were in.

We ran into the stands, merging easily with the swirling bodies of kids.

But, where were the Beatles? I could only see the backs of people. Many adults were there, pressed together, milling, churning. I thought I heard for a second the far off tinkling of music.

Could *that* be them?

I had to find a way to get above the people. All the seats, really folding chairs, were taken, but some of the kids had begun standing on the backs of the chairs. Again, without thought, I knew this was my only chance to see the Beatles, so I climbed on to the narrow, top rim of the back of a man's chair.

He looked round and smiled at me. I smiled, too, and peered beyond him as he turned back to the show. I barely touched his shoulders with my knees in order to keep balance and stay on. My feet wobbled slightly in low sneakers that had long ago lost their laces.

There they were!

Way down on the field on a little white box of a stage, they appeared to be black ants trying to stand and play tiny guitars and drums!

They looked up in abject terror at the massive crowd of thousands screaming with mouths open and hands and fists shaking at them.

I couldn't hear them. I never got to hear them. I couldn't hear anything, not even the screams. Only a whoosh and a painful, aching vacuum in the air, like silence, as though the crowds' ensemble scream had passed through the sound barrier into a kind of negative silence that swelled against our eardrums and hurt.

I could tell they were singing different songs, because they seemed to pause in their playing, confer together, like little ants meeting in the center of the stage, and then, go off and begin playing again. But, I couldn't hear the songs.

Then, just as suddenly as they had come, the Beatles were scurrying from the field! Each clutching his guitar and Ringo, his drumsticks, they fled to two black limousines waiting on the grass with doors open! The doors snapped shut and the limos sped away!

Everyone kept screaming and waving in the direction the cars had gone.

It was over. The Beatles were gone.

Suddenly, I realized, I was standing on the back of a folding chair.

I got down, thanked the man, who grinned idiotically and said it had been his pleasure.

Colleen and I walked home again. I hadn't been conscious of her presence, but she'd been right beside me the whole time, standing on the seat of a chair, as she was a much bigger girl.

Kids, frustrated and dazed, streamed down the highway yelling, whooping, some crying. Bottles were thrown, some fights broke out. Kids wandered across the highway, out amongst the cars, feeling invincible, feeling the need to stop traffic. The terrified drivers honked and continued their course, weaving nervously around the lines of aimless kids.

When we got home, the adults had set up their lawn chairs in the center of the street where they'd sat in the dark listening to the screams.

"You think you're smart!" Ma yelled at me as I approached her and Daddy, Annie and Richard and the Krausses. But, I could tell she was a little proud of me, too, and Daddy and the rest of them wanted to hear all about it.

You could still hear the kids, screaming here and there; they didn't want it to be over, but the Beatles had fled Revere. At that very moment, they were making a mad dash for the airport; running for their lives to a private jet; shakingly lighting cigarettes in the back of the limousine, terrified that their music had been silenced by ravenous kids, wishing they never had to do that again.

## BETTINA AND SUSIE

"In the home," Daddy was saying, his voice cracked with sobs, "they never let us..."

"Take it easy, Billy," consoled my mother's Aunt Bettina, with her deep voice, "that's all over now. You got a nice family now and a nice home. You made it out of there. Right?"

With her own strong grip, she held his trembling hand across the kitchen table. He didn't often do that, break down about the home in which he had spent much of his childhood, but, occasionally, if the conversation hit a nerve, he crumbled.

They'd been talking about my reading at the dinner table, how I always had a book and whether or not it was a good thing. Daddy broke down because the priests wouldn't let them read books. If they were caught doing nothing, as the priests called it, they'd be given work to do, like scrubbing the toilets or the long staircase in the rectory.

Aunt Bettina had a voice as deep and gruff as a man's could be. She fooled me every time she called on the phone.

"Rosie, there?" she asked in the playful tone of a man, who was strange to me, but who seemed to know Ma secretly and very well.

My back went up like a little porcupine. Who *was* this guy who thought he could talk to my mother like he was her boyfriend? Annoyed, I handed Ma the receiver.

"It's a man," I said, disapprovingly.

She looked quizzical. Her insurance broker? A salesman?

I could hear the male voice laughing, deep and loving, echoing along the little space between Ma's ear and mine.

"It's a man, Rosie! It's a man!" Aunt Bettina teased.

Ma laughed, looking my way and shaking her head.

"It's your Aunt Betty, you stupid," she said, affectionately.

We were supposed to call her Auntie Betty, but I couldn't resist calling her Aunt Bettina, which was a much prettier name. She was a small woman who wore her thick brown hair short and combed straight back from her noble forehead. She smoked more cigarettes than Daddy. When she visited Ma, she drank Lipton tea, but I always envisioned a heavy set glass of whiskey rather than Ma's crockery mug with the tea bag's delicate string and label dangling out that seemed so fragile in front of her square body. Aunt Bettina was Grandma's sister, but our family was the only one who would receive her.

She came, always, with her girlfriend, Susie, who called her Tina, in a secret pet way, which was lovely to hear. Susie had pressed gold hair that she wore in the style of the glamorous movie stars of the Thirties, like Carroll Lombard or Betty Davis, in permanent waves cascading close to her skull. She held her neat, golden head very erect upon her tall, thin frame, like a ballet dancer.

Bettina and Susie had to have a purpose for coming, usually to do something for Ma. Maybe, that was their way of rationalizing this risk to Ma's standing in the family. Ma just smiled her Mona Lisa smile and said she didn't care. I had no idea why Aunt Bettina wasn't welcome at Grandma's house, Grandma, who was the most generous person I knew, but the only thing different about Aunt Bettina was her voice and her hair, so, I assumed, whatever these were clues of, that was the reason. This "reason" floated above Bettina and Susie like - curiously enough - halos, since it seemed to single them out for a perverse kind of sainthood.

In fact, there was something uncannily sweet and fine about Bettina and Susie. Bettina and Susie. Why do some names ring out like the bells of heaven? And others like the tolls of hell? Bettina and Susie, two saints, two angels kicked out of the church, but, I was sure, not out of heaven.

On this night, Susie stood and retouched Ma's hair with Blondex while everyone talked. I was reading Dickens, "real reading," not for school. I always read every book the author had written, not just what I had to read for school. "Real reading," sometimes called "sacred reading," was a theme song of mine.

Ma sat without her glasses, her beautiful eyes puffy from the shampoo, a towel spread over her shoulders, the squirmy terrier in her lap. Susie called Tareyton, "La Pishashta," in bastardized Italian, the little pisser. Ma handed Susie bobby-pins as Susie sectioned the wet, dark red hair, spun the ribbons of hair on her finger and pinned them in little circles against Ma's head, till Ma's hair disappeared and she was wearing a bathing cap of tight red spirals. Daddy sat with us, which was a phenomenon, a tribute to Aunt Bettina, really. He kept trying to give her "a little shot" with her tea.

They were asking me about the fine print and the thin pages in my book.

"Look at the pages! So thin! Like the Bible! How the hell kin you see those words, Gloria? You're going to ruin your eyes! Billy, you should get her a magnifying glass, no shit."

Daddy laughed, kind of proud of me, "Ah, she loves that stuff! The smaller the print, the thinner the paper, the better! What's that? Shakespeare?"

"Dickens."

I called all the books by their authors now, no matter what the title, they were Dickens or Collins or James.

"Oh!" he said, like he knew.

"She should be a teacher," Aunt Bettina advised.

Susie agreed. She nodded, bobby pins jammed in her mouth.

"I'm going to be a writer," I said.

"Mmm!" Susie murmured, impressed.

"A what? What, like for a newspaper?" Aunt Bettina growled.

"No, like for books."

"That's no good! Be a teacher! You get your summers off."

Everyone agreed, I could travel, they said. I'd get paid for my summers and have them off too.

"She's always reading," Ma told them.

"Oh, yeah? You should be a teacher, then."

"She even brings a book to the table. I have to tell her every night, no reading at the table," Ma said, proudly, handing Susie another bobby pin for her mouth.

"Oh, that's no good. You shouldn't read at the table," Aunt Bettina told me.

"I can't stop," I said.

That's when we noticed Daddy's eyes had gone all red and the tears started to drop, one by one, on the table. He sniffed and Aunt Bettina asked him what was wrong.

He told us about the orphanage. Things leaked out from time to time about his past, things leaked, just like his tears, one by one, and fell before us. I still didn't know everything I should about my father's life, all the mysteries, all the reasons. But, I couldn't stand to see him cry. My stomach hurt, as though someone powerful had grabbed it full in his fist and twisted it mercilessly. Tears gathered in my own eyes, Susie looked pained and Ma looked down at the pins held tightly in her red-tipped fingers.

"I keep having this dream," I said, quietly.

They all looked at me.

"What? Like Martin Luther King?" Aunt Bettina joked uncomfortably, trying to break the tension.

I smiled. "Kind of. The Communists come marching down the street. Right down Hichborn, with tanks and soldiers doing that step - what is it?"

"The goosestep," Daddy sniffs.

"Yeah, the goosestep. I can see them and hear their feet coming right down our street where we used to play and I'm terrified. Next thing I know, they're storming up the steps to my room; they make so much noise it scares me to death. They have guns with bayonets and big boots and helmets, like the Nazis. I keep getting them mixed up with the Nazis. They start tearing the books off my shelves and they're going to arrest me and take the books away and burn them. One of the books they take is *The Diary of Anne Frank.* And in my dream, I walk right up to the leader, the sergeant, or whatever he is, and I say, "You can't take them from me. I've already read them."

They were silent a minute, then Aunt Bettina said, "You should come down and talk more often, Gloria."

It was true. I never came down from my room. I'd created another world up there with my books and my heroes. But, I'd made a special effort this night because Bettina and Susie had brought me clothes. Beautiful clothes. Aunt Bettina's old cashmere sweaters that had a faint odor and coating of dry cleaning which clung to my hands like a film of oldness after touching the soft cushy fabric, but I didn't mind; the colors were deep blues and greens, the colors of the sea and the forest, and no one had ever given me anything so fine. There was also a fuchsia wool jacket of impeccable tailoring, not that I would have known what such a thing as impeccable tailoring was, I just knew it when I saw it. The jacket had short sleeves and I marveled that a woman could be cool enough to need a jacket, but warm enough to not need sleeves.

It was then that Jakey walked in the back door with Rick right behind him.

"Where *you* comin' from?" Daddy asked Jakey.

Jakey shrugged, "Nowheres."

Aunt Bettina studied them both. Susie went on with Ma's hair as though she had no need to study them, she already knew what she'd find.

"Clean your feet!" Ma hollered, but they were already on their way upstairs.

As he passed me, Rick mumbled, "Body by Fisher" and Daddy's head jerked round in my direction.

"What did he say?"

"I don't know," I lied. It was from a car commercial, something about the sleek body lines of the car. Earl Rizzo had started calling me that.

"He's a little scumbag, huh?" Aunt Bettina asked Daddy.

Daddy polished off the dregs of his beer.

"You said it!" he agreed.

"What the hell happened to his face?" she asked.

There was an awkward silence for a minute while we waited for each other to answer her.

"He was hit by a truck when he was little," I said.

"Jesus!"

"Want some more tea, Betty?" Ma asked her.

"Sure, Rosie."

"Kin I interest ya in a wee drop o' the creacha', Betty?" Daddy teased with a mock Irish brogue.

It was amazing how quickly and how often my loyalties shifted. How war wasn't as simple as it should be - it was more like the stories people tell afterwards, as when a prisoner actually has to live with his enemy and the enemy takes care of him, nurses him back to health, and, finally, hides him from his own side and helps him to escape. There was never a time when I could forget, never a time when I could believe that Daddy was my father. At times, he was the enemy and I was his prisoner, and at other times, I was caring for him and hiding him, sorry we were enemies. Never did I plan his escape. No, in fact, I was sure I should kill him. If I were honorable and brave, I would have killed him by now. No hero would have eaten his food or drunk with him at his table. I should have run him through with my sword a long time ago. That much was clear.

What was not clear was why his tears cut through me like a sword. Why it made me proud sometimes to think of him. Why it repulsed me right now to watch him getting another drink, and absentmindedly scratching one foot with the rough, peeling skin of the other. Why I let Rick talk to me like that. Why I was proud to have him think I had a Body by Fisher. Why I was proud that he'd been hit by a truck and was so tough he was still walking around. I should kill them both. I should kill them. Why didn't I? Why?

EAST BOSTON, 1954

I was three years old when Mama opened the door and looked into the room. She screamed.

Her life was changed forever.

Daddy and I looked up.

Daddy laughed.

## MY LOVE PARTIES

The year of the ninth grade, this curious nether time involving my thirteenth year, when all the ninth graders were thrown together into the Adolf Hitler School for Young Adults. It was a sinking time, like the Dark Ages of Europe, a sinking into a murky place, a time I can't remember clearly, during which I sank deeper and deeper into the mud, acting out the only predetermined path I knew. If an angel hadn't reached down her hand for me when I was just about to sink below my nostrils... if she hadn't seen my light flickering there, in the dark muck, I would have gone under.

There's a catch phrase in Revere to excuse bad behavior. When little kids are bad, their mothers tsk in a mournful tone, "Ah, he doesn't know any better!" In Revere, it's a phrase for a whole city. It's true of politicians and police, it's true of nuns and priests: they haven't seen better. The only place we saw good behavior was on those corny, half-hour TV shows like "Lassie," "Leave It to Beaver" or "The Andy Griffith Show," and we were told that wasn't real. The very things we were trying to escape, we were told were the facts of life. And, curiously, "the facts of life" was a catch phrase for sex. Sex, as well as reality, the way things were whether you liked it or not.

When Ma was at work, I had boys in the house. Girls were there, too. Don't ask me who they were, I don't remember. Jakey asked some boys to come over. Jakey wasn't always with Rick. He was younger and he maneuvered quite dexterously from one gang to the other.

The stakes were serious now. One Saturday morning while Marie and I were watching cartoons, I sneezed and got my period. I opened more than I ever had and the gush that came out was unfamiliarly thick and urgent. I just knew it was my period. Ma checked on me and she said, "Good. Your blood is a good color, nice and red." Now - I could get pregnant. It was a matter of intense pride to me that no one should be able to say, "You know Gloria Wisher? She got pregnant and had to quit school." Never! I was going to college! Still, I never knew when the quicksand would overcome me, some moment when I wasn't capable of lifting a limb to save myself, some millisecond when I paused to take a breath only to swallow the mud that would fill my airways forever.

Once, some boys came from East Boston in a dark blue van where they played cards with the van doors open to the street like the doors of the old-time paddy wagon that used to come to get the criminals off the street. They wore black leather jackets, jeans and high-heeled, pointy-toed boots; the cards tossed with dirty scrunched up bills littered the van and me, begging one of them, "Will I see you again?"

Little Paul came over. Tall as two of me, with pale skin stretched too far, pocked red with the scars of acne. His nose and eyes and lips were too big. I gazed at the beautiful boys; they walked past me on the street. One had looked at me dreamily with the brown, languid eyes of a doe, not at all out of place in his gentle face. "Hi," he had said, but the beauties were not for me. I was too afraid of them; I hung back and punished myself with boys like Little Paul, where I felt more comfortable, more at home. He was a giant and I was his goose.

Maybe I was trying to recreate the love parties in Ma's romance magazines. Imagine the grainy black and white photos, a living room of lumpy furniture, girls flopping across the laps of boys, boys' sweaty hands twisting the bra straps, getting the bras soggy and grimy along the thousands of white cotton stitches in a spiral round the cup.

Yes, at that time, I was going through the Boy Scouts. Little Paul was just one of them.

We were alone on the couch in the Boy Scout den. Couples were strewn all over the house. I'd taken something from him, something small and silly, maybe the cap from his beer, maybe a quarter he needed to get home.

"Give me that," he warned.

"No!" I felt powerful (why?) with this little thing in my hand.

We were kissing; he put his huge tongue deep in my mouth. He began to open my fingers. So easily! He'd get it!

Quickly, I tucked it into my bra.

"Now, you can't get it!"

"Yes, I can."

But, no boy had ever touched my breasts before and I didn't think it was possible. I didn't think he'd dare.

He kissed me again, circling my mouth with the tip of his tongue. He mashed my lips, churning his mouth round and round them in a circular motion while I melted into a puddle of mush made by our lips and the sudden surge of liquid in my panties.

His hand knew what his lips had done to me because it suddenly was on top of my breast, stroking the soft green cashmere of Aunt Bettina's sweater. The lips of my vagina opened against my will and the liquid flowed faster.

His hand left my covered breast and slid up the cool skin of my back. Now, he'd gone under! He wouldn't! He'd never done that before.

His strong hand, big as a man's, covered my breast, dug it out of the cotton cup with probing fingertips. Softly, even, efficiently, he laid the breast over the top of the cotton bra where he could stroke it, running his finger with surprising expertise over the stiff nipple, all the while his mouth pressed round and round my own. My lips pulsated as he pulled his own away and whispered, "I got it."

Gotten what, I wondered? I remembered when I looked down at the small object in his palm and couldn't believe my foolishness. It seemed ridiculous to have traded the privilege of touching my breasts for such a piece of junk.

Little Paul was too big for me, a giant with the brain of a split pea. In those days, we were taught to save ourselves for a hero. Little Paul had nothing to inspire me. He sucked my breast while I watched Flipper, the brave little dolphin who was more interesting. It wasn't long before he wanted to go down into my pants. He used his enormous size to become insistent. I couldn't control him. When he called he whispered into the phone, his breath causing a blast of wind like someone blowing into a bottle, "Wear a skirt!" My traitorous vagina gushed with juices, causing me to react stubbornly, I refused and appeared in tight, black pants. In the hallway, when we kissed hello that night, he grabbed me by the crotch and lifted me up to him, "I TOLD you to wear a skirt!

Jakey, who was hiding in the hallway, witnessed this peep show. Later, he said, leering conspiratorially, "I know why you broke up with Paul," and he grabbed his own crotch and gave it a squeeze. Fleetingly, as the headlight beam of an oncoming car, the thought that Jakey might be sexually dangerous to me rushed my brain. Of Little Paul, I became scared, really scared. He was so big, so persistent, it seemed his size and strength alone would get me pregnant in no time. I broke off with him and sent him home that very night, where I hoped he'd stay.

I remember his mother, Cousin, proudly telling Ma how he'd allowed her to look at a gigantic boil on his groin.

"He's a man, now!" she beamed insanely, with the demented pride of a woman who has had a son.

What the hell is a boil, I wondered? It sounded horrendous. I could only imagine what infectious growth had lay in wait for me in Little Paul's pants, what microscopic monster had burrowed under his red-blotched flesh causing it to bubble up in a pus-pounding sore that could impress only a mother gone mad from having given birth to a son.

Fred Shat. His name alone must have been absolute torture to him. But, to make matters worse, he was shorter and fatter than me. His hair stuck to his head in a greasy mass and he wore the colors brown and tan a lot, cheap, ill-fitting clothing that seemed to slip and bunch-up on his lumpy body. I suppose he resembled a turd. He thought he was going to be a famous disc jockey. He had to explain to me what that was. He practiced at Fleetwood Recording Studio in Revere, where he had pals who let him in. I think he was the one who brought the boys from East Boston in the van. Too bad for me, Fred Shat had a brain I could love. He gave me a penny sculpted into the shape of a heart. I took to wearing it slung alongside the "key to my heart" on the chain around my neck. Thank God, he never dared to kiss me.

We smoked cigarettes and made drinks out of tonic and whatever we could sneak. Things were heating up. We broke a lamp, but that didn't alert Ma, though she punished me for it. Neither did the time I got so mad at the kids, Marie and Jakey, for not listening to me that I slammed the front storm door and, to my horror, watched as a long crack raced behind me from one corner of the glass to the other as though stabbing me in the back. She punished me for that. Nor the time Jakey slammed the phone receiver on my head causing a huge lump and blood to appear on my skull, though I didn't get punished for that. No, it was this: in a moment of insanity, to impress and entertain everyone, I wrote on a scrap of paper a bastardized version of a hit song and then burned lacey cigarette holes to decorate the page. Here is what I wrote:

*You don't need anybody to fuck you*
*Here I lay with my legs open wide*
*You don't need anybody to fuck you*
*I'll keep you satisfied.*

Ma found it on the end table where I'd appropriately left it, a classic case of wanting to get caught. Maybe I was trying to use her as a contraceptive. Maybe things were getting too close to disaster.

Ma was devastated.

"Is *this* what you do when I'm at work? I thought I could *TRUST YOU!*"

"You can!"

"I never used such words in my life! Where did you *hear* such words? Not in *this* house!"

I was too stunned to think. The picture of Ma sitting on the couch where God knows what had occurred, holding this evil paper in her dear little hands was too much to bear. I was too amazed to feel anything but just that: ice-cold amazement at my stupidity. As I looked at the paper shaking in her hand, it seemed to have been written a long time ago by another person all together, didn't she know that?

The paper, the words, put an end to my love parties. I was back peeling potatoes with Ramona again, and, in a way, glad of it.

EVER SO GENTLY

The rough stubble of his beard brushed my vagina like a stiff wire.

"Oh, Daddy, it hurts!" I whispered, turning my face under the covers where he was.

"Does it hurt good or hurt bad?" he chuckled, a voice in the cavernous blankets.

Just at that moment, I was rushed by an intense wave of sensation.

"Hurts good," I shuddered.

He giggled with his breath alone, blowing over my wet, secret hairs tickling his nostrils.

After he left me alone with Marie's innocent form snoring delicately in the bed beside me (briefly, I thanked God for her innocence) I imagined Richie Silva approaching me from the lighted doorway as Daddy had done.

He knelt by my bed. He held my hand in his and ever so gently (how I loved that phrase, "ever so gently!") lifted my hand to his lips and kissed it with such affection, tears came to my eyes and I cried.

"Don't cry!" he whispered. (Another favorite phrase!)

"No one's ever kissed me like that before," I answered.

Visibly touched, his features softened even more, if that were possible. He leaned toward me where I lay on the pillow and let his lips touch mine with so much love I burst into very real tears. I sobbed with a lonely heart and hid my face, to muffle the sound, in my pillow, which I didn't have the strength to pretend was Richie's boyish chest, as I had so many times before.

I can't tell you how much I loved him. I loved him walking down the street. I loved him getting into Rick's car. I loved his voice calling out to one of his friends when they all played hockey on the street. I loved his laugh like a little kid's and the way the others would laugh at him when he laughed and he looked sheepish and good-natured, I loved him. I loved hearing about him, how he had a girl friend and I was glad when I saw who she was that she was not pretty, but she had big breasts for his pleasure and his prestige, I loved him.

I loved the way he'd sneak a glance at me, across the street, and smile so gently, ever so gently, and sometimes, silently mouth, "Hi."

I was so in love the pain was love; it was delicious. The pain kept me company.

## DIRTY SOAP

When he came home from work, his big work boots scraped dirt on to the linoleum floor. He dropped his greasy coat and asked, "What's for supper?" like he didn't care and Ma told him, "Pork chops." He took off the greasy uniform shirt, heavy and thick with black oil from the shop and dropped it on the floor and Ma picked it up, almost before it hit. Then, he went over to the sink, stuck his blackened hands under the running water and grabbed the bar of pure white Ivory soap and turned it over and over till it turned black from his hands and he scrubbed till his hands were rubbed red and raw, but not clean. The smell of the soap and dirt together filled the kitchen so that I gagged sitting there, right behind his greasy black buttocks, eating my pork chops and apple sauce, sucking on the juicy fat and gnawing the luscious marrow from the bones, and, after finishing off my own, reaching for everyone else's. I gagged and Ma said, "What's the matter?" her little mouth full of crispy, hot pork.

"Nothing," I said, "the dirty soap."

He'd splashed thick, grey soap all over the counter and sink and faucet and it smelled so bad, so evil.

"Eat, don't make trouble," Ma told me.

"The money's clean," Daddy said, wiping the rest of the grey soap off on one of Ma's clean dishtowels, like he was the lord of the manor. I wanted to kill him, just for his smell.

The money smelled like dirty soap.

I might have loved the smell, you know, if things had been different. I can smell it right now; I can conjure it up anytime; it haunts me like his Jesus sandals in the hall, like the furry knotholes in the fake wood linoleum he called pussies.


## BILLY WISHER

I want to tell you now about Daddy. I want to tell it the way I saw and heard it, as if I were reading a story about Daddy. I want to call him by his name, Billy Wisher. This was the answer I received when I asked myself how it might have come about:


Billy Wisher was dog ass tired that night when he pulled up to the windowless exterior of the Chelsea Men's Club. His Chevy rattled and kept running after he shut it off. He swore choicely as he cranked the driver's door open, lifted it on it's damaged hinge and slammed it shut, just so, you had to do it just so, or it wouldn't shut at all. His throat burned like hell from the three packs of Luckies and he needed a beer so bad, he'd swear he'd been drinking salt water all day.

He lit another cigarette as he entered the blank door of the club. For a minute, all he could see was blue smoke till his eyes adjusted to the sudden darkness. Then, a red light appeared over the bar; then it melted into the script, Schlitz. Several other lights appeared, yellow dots, white, the shadowy heads of the fellows bent over their beers, hugging their beer bottles with one hand, extended fingers holding on to a smoke. The television was on really low: Walter Cronkite whispering the news. He couldn't hear it till he got close and sat down.

"President Johnson's War on Poverty..."

"War on Poverty, my ass," Billy interrupted as he nestled on to the barstool next to Ray.

Cronkite's voice got muffled in the ensuing debate.

"Hey, Bill, how's it going?"

"My dog's got dogs, how about you?"

Ray chuckled, took a swig of beer, "They're getting all the breaks, huh, Bill?" He nodded toward the screen.

"Hey, what are you going to do? It'll get worse before it gets better."

"That's for sure! Ah, maybe we can keep them out of Chelsea."

"Keep them out of here!" grumbled the barkeep, Phil as he slid a cold bottle of Miller High Life to Bill.

"Ah, we got a couple of nice fellas down at the plant," Billy said.

The fellows looked at him, on down the line of barstools, Ray, Phil, Sully, Manny. They looked for a minute; they liked Bill and didn't want to disagree with him. They nodded together over their beers.

"You're right, when you're right, you're right," said Manny.

A disgruntled Last Supper, each man took his own thoughts on the matter into himself, glad the issue was outside the club, especially on this night when each man was so wrecked.

"Hey, Bill, got a minute?" Ray asked.

"Yeah! What?"

Ray looked blank, lost, in fact. His pudgy face twitched just a little in the dim light, almost a foot below Bill's tall frame.

"Want to go over to a table, Ray?" Billy offered.

He took his beer and whiskey over to one of the tables next to a couple of fellows playing cards.

"Over here, Bill, huh?" Ray motioned to a table in the darkest corner of the shadowy room.

"Right-o!" Billy answered.

The two men sat down in the shadows.

Ray twisted his lip with his fingers, blackened like Bill's from decades on the machines.

"I did it, Bill, I did it!" he confessed.

"Did what? What, did ya rob a bank?" Billy chuckled.

"No."

To his surprise, Ray's face had suddenly collapsed and gone grey.

"What did you do?" Billy asked, softly, thinking maybe Ray had killed someone.

"I fucked her."

Billy licked his lips. Whoa, this was different, he thought.

"Who'd you fuck?" he asked, quietly, you might say, respectfully.

Ray leaned in and whispered, "My kid." But, he choked on the word "kid."

"Jesus Fucking Christ!"

Ray inspected the room to see if anyone had heard; if anyone had changed his expression by a hair. No one had.

Ray took a deep breath.

"Bill," he shook his head side-to-side, "I got to tell you, I got to tell somebody, it was like nothing else!"

Billy got an immediate hard on, but, at the same time, he didn't want to hear about it.

"Yeah?" he said, politely.

"Yeah! I'm telling you! The young ones are so sweet, oh, they cry and moan like you wouldn't believe. Ya got to comfort them and tell them it's all right." Ray blew air out his mouth several times as he spoke, "Jeez,' I'm coming in my pants just talking about it, man."

"They whimper like puppies, 'Daddy, please,' and you think you're going to explode, I'm telling you."

Ray checked around the room one more time.

"Jesus, Ray, are you telling me your dick *fit* in there?"

Ray looked shocked. "No! I didn't *fuck* her! Just with my tongue! Jeez, I didn't want to scare her!"

He thought for a second.

"You think, Bill, huh? You think you can fuck them that small?"

Billy considered, "I don't know. Man, you wouldn't want to *hurt* them!"

"Nah! I wouldn't want to hurt her! Jeez!"

The two men reflected silently. They talked about the Bruins for a few minutes, and about the new clock at work being ten minutes slow. A few minutes of silence and Billy said he had to go. Ray grabbed his arm.

"This is just between you and me, right Billy? You and me, right?" he pleaded.

"Yeah! Sure! Don't worry about it!" Billy assured him.

"Hey! Listen, I almost forgot. Her little purse broke."

Ray pulled out a small pink purse. Billy recognized a cartoon character on it, a duck. It was sticky with candy or something when Billy took it.

"The strap broke. You can fix it, huh? I told her you can fix it for her. You can fix anything, Bill. Bring it to me anytime, Bill."

He stuffed the little purse into his coat pocket; the pink strap dangled out.

His cock was aching as he walked back to the car. He wished he could stick it into something hot and juicy right now. He shuddered at what he'd heard, but his cock throbbed right back as if in reply to his conscience.


MISSING GET SMART

One night, I was alone with Marie, watching something incredibly engrossing on TV, I'm pretty sure it was "Get Smart," that comedy of errors about secret agents. The doorbell rang and in a television fog, I went to answer it, carrying a TV around my head, pondering deeply the question of how Agent 99 could stay so undisheveled while crime fighting: how her knee socks stayed up, how her slacks stayed pristinely white, how her hair settled so shiningly perfect around her sincere and eager little face. We always opened the door in those days. We just answered the door. No one ever asked, "Who is it?" I swung the door open, never expecting an enemy on the other side.

Rick Likus was in my house before I knew it and I was shoved into the den and down on the old couch. He caught me as I tried to get up and run.

"No! I came to see you! I need you!" he whispered, so Marie couldn't hear.

He couldn't have chosen better words. Instantly, I forgot Marie and "Get Smart." An aura was created, accurately targeted to the heart of a Catholic girl, one who passionately wanted to be held and, at the same time, absolved of all responsibility in the matter. It was, as if a movie was about to begin in which Rick Likus needed to hold me: a movie about a girl who wished to be needed as well as wanted. *The idea that Rick could need me!* Only the devil could have tricked me so perfectly.

I sat down next to the devil.

He put his arm around my shoulders, like he would have on a real date.

We sat like that for two seconds. Then, his face turned to mine and he leaned toward me (and I thought, is Rick Likus going to kiss me?) and he kissed me, really kissed me, like a boy friend.

His kisses were full and concentrated; his hands were patient, touching my skin lightly as though exploring this person, Gloria. They were Rick Likus' hands, I reminded myself, as if he were a movie star, and he was, in a way, a star in my small world, recklessly, handsomely scarred, desirably wicked.

He kissed me a long time. My God, I loved being kissed by him! What am I, God? What am I? I wondered somewhat desperately as Rick Likus held me in his arms.

Then, he remembered why he'd come and his hands moved to the areas he'd come for: he opened the cotton shift I was wearing, an old housedress of Ma's that wrapped around. All he had to do was untie a bow at my waist and the limp, old fabric fell open. His hand slid in, up my belly, rigid with fear, and cupped, around the soggy old bra, my large breast in his small hand. I heard the sharp intake of his breath at the size and heaviness, the sudden energy of his grasp.

"Rick!"

"Sh!" God, he commanded like the Nazi! I was dreaming, no, I reminded myself, this was happening!

"Rick, stop!" Meanwhile wishing he would absolve me, somehow.

He took his mouth from mine and leaned me backwards. He began to pull at my huge white panties. My underwear seemed to glow in the dark, grotesque and phosphorescent, saying, "Now he'll know how fat you are! He'll take advantage of you now and laugh at you later! You're fat! Fat!"

"No!" I gasped, grabbing the elastic out of his hands.

"Gloria! You're going to love it!"

His open mouth breathed steam on my face as he pressed himself against me, again and again. He pounded me with the hardness of his crotch with motion as fluid as a worm, just like Jakey had shown me, just like dogs do!

Once I had decided, no, I could suddenly hear the television; suddenly I could hear his kisses slurping. His kisses missed my mouth, wiping my cheek with his saliva, my neck, my lips by accident, as I twisted and turned in his arms, he continued to tell me I was going to love it. I could smell him, he smelled dirty, like a wet dog. He smelled of leaves half rotten, earth and his own skin, sour and musky.

Marie came in, sleepy and dopey. She said, "Who was at the door? Where are you?" Stupidly, she scraped the wall for the light switch.

I rolled off the couch, hitting the floor on my hands and knees as Rick ran out the front door, knocking a groggy Marie against the wall.

"Who was that?" she asked, as if in her sleep.

"Nobody," I said.

I tied my dress, quickly, and by the time we walked back into the light, she seemed to have forgotten. An Alka Seltzer commercial was on television, "Plop, plop, fizz, fizz/ Oh, what a relief it is!"

"You missed 'Get Smart,'" Marie said.

For weeks I carried a strange sad sense of loss, as though I had missed a chance to be raped by Rick Likus, a chance, to be held, to be seduced. A sense of loss, however perverted, mingled weirdly with terror that he would come again. I began to imagine scenes, the scenarios of my seduction.

"Gloria!" His hands were blackened by earth. As he touched my face, I smelled them in the dark, black and earthy.

"I can't stop myself, Gloria," he kissed me.

"I know."

"What are you doing to me? I'm fucking out of my mind because of you. You're killing me." His words were muffled, spoken with his lips against my skin, spoken through my skin.

He kissed me down to the grass, to the couch, to the floor.

He kissed me - did I dare imagine, even in front of myself - down to the bed, the most depraved place of all, where Daddy had done things to me?

"I can't get enough of you, Gloria."

Tears crept from his eyes. I kissed his tears; I licked them from my lips.

"I have to, I can't help it, I have to," he confessed. "There's something about you I have to fuck."

"I know," I answered.

"I can't help it," he wept.

"I know. I want you to do it."

"Oh, God!"

I dreamed of Rick waiting for me in the bushes. I dreamed of his friends, like the movie I saw late at night on TV, taking turns on me, or not taking turns. Sometimes, I dreamed of heroes or princes. Sometimes, I dreamed of devils. Often, Richie Silva held my hand while I slept or he whispered, "Don't worry" or "Don't be afraid" in my ear, after they had all gone and I was alone. I conjured up sweetness, gentility, or evil, as I willed. I imagined I was precious to Rick: I imagined that he would never tell anyone because he wanted me all to himself. I imagined Richie sneaked in to make love to me when Rick wasn't around and he was happy with that because he knew Rick was one thing and he was another. I dreamed evil could be kind. And that kindness could be evil.

Of course, it was all coming from me. I was the one who provided Rick with tenderness. I was the one who taught Richie what he could do to me. Me, my touch, tenderly on my face or breasts or vulva; my kiss, desperately into the cold pillow or the burning crook of my arm. I created from my love love that did not exist outside of it. It was my romance, my craving, my strength. No one could love me in the ways I created. It was all coming from me. All of it.

But, twisted in that special way only a place like Revere can teach.

If you asked me why didn't I tell you a nicer story, why didn't I make up a nice story about nice people, I would wonder myself, why didn't I? Why couldn't I? All I can answer is this: This is the story God gave me. This is the man silhouetted in my doorway. This is the creature that crawls in with me in the dark.


UNDER THE PORCH

I went outside - when I hear that phrase, I can just about taste that peculiar odor of our house, simmering with the depth of cooking meal after meal after meal, permeating our clothing, our skin, our hair, as though we were the bread and meat and vegetables, the macaroni and the sauce, soaking in the pots and sweating it out again, into our socks and shoes and slippers, our underarms, our breath, our bed clothes, the walls themselves, their seams seeping with spices, as I opened the door and walked out of the simmering pot into the open air that rushed my nostrils with the mellow, sweet brown of overgrown grass, the stirred up earth of dogs, and, in season, the fragrance of lilacs, roses, lilies, pear blossoms, the clotted mass of rotting berries, the herbal sting of wild highway flowers, the diesel fuel scorching out of trucks, the roasted, sweet aroma of hay and horseshit from the racetrack, the clean wash of salt from the sea. My ears were blasted with the tortured screams of airplanes scraping the roofs of our houses, the slow groan of the B&M railroad rumbling the ground I stood on, the agonizing cry of trucks barreling the road, the nagging bark of dogs, the maniacal shouts of kids, the innocent chirps of sparrows hiding in the trees.

I went outside to nestle in among the pumpkins I was growing along the back of the house, quite successfully, though Ma often had stolen the early, yellow trumpeting flowers that would have been pumpkins to squander them in what she called "mmm, a delicacy," scrambling them up with peppers and eggs. I cradled a new book under my arm and I was smiling a little with the anticipation of leaning my elbows on the firm shoulders of pumpkins and reading a story.

He was standing there, by the little door under the porch where Daddy kept the lawnmower and tools.

I bumped into him because I walked with my head down and I couldn't see what was coming. He held me for a moment by my shoulders as surprised as I was and I thought for that moment that he really loved me by the expression in his twisted eye of shock and regret.

"Gloria!" he whispered.

I backed away. His surprised grip let go of me and instantly reached for me again.

"What are you doing here?" I asked.

But, I knew. It was Jakey's B&E period, when he was working with Rick to rob houses. During this time, Jakey attracted weird characters to himself, guys with lumpy faces whom he called by weird names, Chickie and Eddy D. And Rick who walked right into the house one Saturday morning while we were doing chores and saw Jakey kneeling under the kitchen table rubbing the white, chalky Bon Ami against the chrome legs up and down, up and down, and Rick said, "Practicing?"

Loudly, Ma had tsked and told Rick to "get out of the house and wait for him outside." And, she had muttered to herself, "Like flies to shit, like flies to shit, the two of them."

"Gloria!" He was opening the latch on the little door that led to the space under the porch.

"Come on!" he whispered harshly.

The sun was nearly down. It crossed my mind; I wouldn't have had much time to read anyway. The last lights made the grass turn grey, caked with mud and crushed brown leaves. The autumn coolness kissed my cheek like a dark angel.

He was already under there, under the porch. I couldn't see him, except the whites of his eyes moving and his teeth against his dark skin.

"Gloria!"

I could smell the rank earth floor of the room under the porch.

"Gloria!"

He pulled out a crushed pack of Marlboros with only two or three cigarettes left in it. He stepped out a little into the yard. He held out the smudged, crumpled cigarettes to tempt me, like I was a dog.

"Gloria!"

I could get a flattened pack of cigarettes anywhere. Ma had her matches neatly tucked under the cellophane. Daddy left his lying around just as dirty and crushed as Rick's: he forgot them and opened a new pack. But, I was tempted by these filthy, mashed cigarettes, when I could get them anywhere - except from the front dungaree pocket of Rick Likus, a tight space, warm from his body. The cigarettes would be warm from his body.

I was a dog. I wanted them.

"Come on, Gloria!" He held them out to me. "You'll like it!"

Yes, "it!" That snapped me to. That's what he meant, he wanted to throw me down in the dirt and do "it" and tell everybody about "it" and come back and do "it" again and again and brag about "it." And I would be that and only that and I absolutely couldn't be that.

I turned and ran into the house, back into the warm smells and the relatively safe walls, leaving Rick Likus under the porch, in the shadows, where he remained in my heart for weeks, for years, forever, lurking.

## AN OUNCE OF PRIDE

Romantic and idiotic as I was, what gave me that ounce of pride to keep myself safe? So many kids before and after me went under, looking for love in an alley, oblivion in a bottle or bliss in a joint or a needle or a pill, hit by a Mack truck, rolled and left under an overpass, buried under layers of pigeon shit. So many kids ran away from home. I knew I was supposed to run away, but I was afraid.

I thought street kids must be very brave. I admired them that they were filthy and slept in doorways and drain pipes, that they ate out of trash barrels like refugees of war, a trash can lid for their plate, maybe scraping it with a spoon. I admired them that they coughed and bled and washed in the gutter, that they went crazy with disease and malnutrition and the street. They were brave! Brave!

I, on the other hand, ate and drank at my father's table. I sat right next to him and sincerely laughed at his jokes. I snuggled under the cool, crisp sheets my mother washed for me and, on them I had sex of varying sneaky, cowardly sorts with her husband, her boyfriend, my own father. Under the illusion of a contract of innocence and obedience, I let my parents keep me safe - yes, safe - from murder and robbery, beatings and what I came to think of as violent rape.

But, there are so many subtle violences. And I was tormented by guilt. For having done bad things, for having enjoyed them much of the time, for having become these things out of doing, memory and time, and for not having the guts to run away. I was guilty. I didn't want to leave my mother's lap, soft and flowery in her cotton housedress. I used to sit at her feet and kiss them in their old slippers. I loved their smell, like warm, roasted nuts just out of the oven. I couldn't leave her refrigerator that I could open anytime for fresh bread and butter, a half wheel of Romano cheese, pounds of sweet ham and hot salami, cakes, pies, ice cream, puddings, apples, peaches, grapes, strawberries, milk and cream. The warm, steaming windows dripping with cooking and tables warmly full of people as the winter howled or sizzling barbeques outside in summer. I was weak and as I tasted these things and wrapped myself in warmth, I nearly vomited with shame. And, among these things, I wouldn't leave my books and my drawings. And, on Sunday nights, as though I deserved it, I wanted to watch "The Wonderful World of Color," in black and white and imagined the colors. I reminded myself of the Jews who stayed in Berlin because they couldn't bear to leave the piano and of the Jew who admired a weed blowing in the icy wind because he knew it was as alive as he was, while the bodies he buried were not alive.

Why didn't I go under? What gave me the pride that swelled in me like the dirty grey storm waves at Revere Beach, the pride it took to not get pregnant and the gall instead to tease Boy Scouts and sailors? What gave me the madness to bat Rick Likus about with my paw? It was Mr. Lanza giving me a large gold star for my stories. It was Mrs. French and her long-taloned hand on my shoulder telling me I could write. It was Ma and Daddy - yes, Daddy - bragging that I might be a teacher, that I was going to college and that I would be the first in the family, telling their friends and neighbors with pride about the books I read, about my grades, asking me for information like I was an expert or an encyclopedia. Grown men and women, neighbors, calling on the phone to ask me how to spell a word. They let me know I was worth something: but, they didn't know how to help me. The very people who confused me, hurt me and neglected me also exalted me. They gave me life, but it was a long struggle out the birth canal.

And, my angel was out there, looking for me. I had one more very important step to take before I could meet her.


GETTING SMART

I lost weight. I decided, if I was smart enough to get all A's in school, I could figure out how to lose weight. I made up a diet for myself, based on all I'd read in the piles of glossy magazines that had kept me company through my many illnesses and fevers, telling me all about the glamorous life, the smart life. I allowed myself only 1,000 calories a day. Then, I devised a program of exercise meant to burn all the 1,000 calories while strategically slimming me as close to the ideal as I could get - thin legs; flat tummy; narrow waist (according to Scarlet O'Hara, 17 inches was the desired measurement); perky buttocks; large breasts; slender, graceful arms.

I learned this ideal on television. The real lessons of life were on television. There, I discovered that a woman must be - at the very least - perfectly beautiful. Perfection was the minimum daily requirement. After that, she could be any of these she wanted: a housewife, a nurse, a teacher, a secretary, a dancer, a waitress, even a movie star. A perfectly beautiful woman might sometimes be allowed to be intelligent; she might be allowed to be talented. But, if she wasn't at least perfectly beautiful, she didn't exist. The greatest sin was being ugly. If a woman got a man's dick hard, he hated her; if she didn't, he hated her even more.

I blamed the Nazis for this ideal. "The Nazis fixed everything!" Mama said, "The Nazis fixed everything!" Women were the only ones who had not escaped the concept of the master race, even after the war was over. I watched the perfect beauties, each in their own way perfectly lovely, waltzing around and around with Lawrence Welk, old and shriveled in his tuxedo. Their sweet dewy cheeks rested close to his wrinkled, sunken skin.

I asked Ma, "Does he ever try to kiss them?"

"How do I know?" she yelled at me for my stupid remark.

But, it wasn't stupid, because then, she laughed to herself, just a little, and I knew, it was true. I imagined back stage at The Lawrence Welk Show: a wrestling match between crumbled, old men and perfect, beautiful women. The men won each match, pinning the woman down until she did what he wanted. Maybe he gave her presents, maybe flowers or jewelry. But, always she was beautiful and he was ugly and old.

I watched "Combat." The beautiful French girl said she had been "liberated" by the French, "liberated" by the Russians, "liberated" by the Americans. She said she was tired of being "liberated."

Women were still occupied.

I watched any show, even the news. All the important women were beautiful. They had impossibly big breasts and impossibly long legs. Their hair was never wind blown. Their nails were never broken. Their stockings, never ripped, never sagged at the knees and ankles. Their flips never flopped like mine; the ends of their hair turned up in perfect, architectural points. Their breasts were full, their cleavage, deep. Their slips never slipped.

It was an impossible ideal to reach, yet there I was, on my bedroom floor, night after night, walking on my fat buttocks till I could feel the bones hitting each time I grunted and groaned my way across the floor. "Hate, hate, hate!" I chanted comically, like an angry child. Hate directed at Daddy and at Rick Likus especially, and for what? For using me, and making me hate myself and because I was fat! I saw with revulsion, as I pushed my bulk along the floor, my gargantuan white panties glowing in the dark as Rick's eager and dirty hands had pawed them. Hate, hate, hate propelled me across the room and back again, over and over, day after day, until I was so thin Daddy exclaimed every time he saw me, "She's lost enough weight! Look at her! She has to spin around twice to cast a shadow!" or "If she turns sideways, she disappears!" or "If she wears red, people'll think she's a thermometer!" I ignored him. Maybe he wanted me, his victim, to be fat. I lost more weight out of spite. Only my huge, Italian breasts stayed pretty much the same, thinning slightly on the sides and top.

Getting thin was a fine revenge. As the fat, rippling flesh fell away I seemed to grow inside with strength and independence. Fine, new bones poked themselves through, lifting the new, tight skin in strong new shapes, at my knees and elbows, along the edge of my jaw, defining my new long neck and a funny, lovely slender bone along the outside of my knee that curled and straightened as my leg bent and opened.

I sewed new clothes for myself. The Mill Store was down on the tracks, on the East Boston side by the City of Oil Tanks, where Rick Likus had stolen that whole brand new dinette set still wrapped in plastic and his crazy mother had been so proud of him. Though it was dangerous to go down there, I walked by myself through dead tracks and past dead train cars, I risked my life to get a scrap of cloth. I never saw a soul. The Mill Store was a factory outlet standing on a sand pit by the abandoned tracks where you could get precious scraps, odd pieces left on the ends of a bolt, for about fifty cents. Since I was so small now, I only needed a yard or two to make a skirt or a dress. I made mini skirts and baby doll dresses out of flowered cotton, with ruffled, lacey cuffs and empire waists. I wore my hair long and wavy. I washed it every day and brushed it now, rather than combing, until it was shiny and soft as silk. From the magazines, I learned how to give myself a manicure; I chose light pink polish or clear and wore my fingernails only moderately long. I bought a cute pair of blue granny glasses for $1.50 at Woolworth's and wore them demurely on the tip of my nose. I bought a pair of suede sling backs down Shirley Ave. for $3.00 and to Ma's horror, I stole her old fashioned cake and brush mascara and applied it carefully to my lashes, discovering in the process, that they were longer than I'd ever imagined lashes could be.

Like Natalie Wood in "Gypsy," I realized with a shock: I was truly pretty. Strangely enough, becoming pretty felt less rapturous than I'd thought, it was more like a business arrangement. Good, that's done, now I can go on to other things.

Now that I was pretty, I attracted the pretty girls to me.

I got a new friend in school, Bonnie Freeman. She was cute as a button, if buttons can be cute, little and dark, rich and adorable. Her large brown eyes glistened with a liquid playfulness. She had a nub nose and a face as round as a plate. We cheated off each other's tests. Cheating in school was something I learned after being pretty. Cheating was a lot of fun. It was a challenge, a comaradie. I didn't need to cheat, so I felt it was okay. I don't know what was going on in the History teacher's head. He'd tell us to exchange papers after a test; then he'd turn his back and write the answers down on the blackboard. We'd switch our papers back and correct our own tests ourselves. I ask you. Even though I hardly ever changed an answer, it was great fun and fodder for friendship. My gleeful eyes met the gleeful eyes of other pretty girls; we giggled together, silently and conspiratorially.

But, things didn't happen as quickly as I wanted. There were nights when I listened to Elvis up in my room and his voice would sing inside me, filling my chest with pain I knew wasn't his, but mine. I had one album, which I took out of the library again and again. I played "Blue Moon" on my little record player where I'd played my one Disney record, "Hi Ho, Hi Ho" on one side and "Someday, My Prince Will Come" on the other. The album stuck out over the edges of the turntable, but it worked. "Blue Moon, you saw me standing alone, /without a dream in my heart, /without a love of my own." His perfect voice vibrated inside me. And, one night, after my exercises, after the curlers were in my hair, after I'd done my homework, I stood up and played that record and hummed along looking at the black shapes of the tanks and the bridge and the city against the midnight blue sky on the horizon till I cried and banged my fist on the wall. I sobbed, "I have so much to give! I have so much to give!"

What I meant was: I wanted to be held and kissed, loved and treasured, and to give all I am in return. It seems foolish now, wanting to give, because that's how women get themselves in trouble.


THE BEAUTIFUL JUNE

Bonnie Freeman had a sprawling ranch house on the other side of Hichborn Street, which was like another world I never knew existed. A beautiful blue pool filled the backyard, a walkway of brick coiled around the pool, followed closely by professionally landscaped bushes and trees.

Bonnie, her friend Junie White and I stood at the sliding glass doors, steamed up from our breath and admired the pool's slumbering form under its dusty black cover.

"It must be beautiful," I imagined the dazzling sun sparkling on the water. I imagined the beautiful Junie diving straight as an athlete into its serene blue depths.

"It is," Junie said and both her head and Bonnie's nodded dreamily as though Bonnie's was attached to hers, for Junie's was the stronger.

Bonnie had insisted Junie and I should meet. Junie had lived two doors from her in a white house all their lives. I repeated to myself, "Junie White in a white house." Junie was slim and white blonde. She had a sculptured turned up nose, like you're supposed to, and high cheekbones and full lips. Her eyes were bright blue. Junie, when I first saw her standing in Bonnie's mother's mushroom grey carpeted living room, shone like her own sun, but she shone white, not yellow.

We played records. Bonnie had all The Beatles albums, even ones that repeated songs. She had a Polaroid camera and took flash pictures of us, which we were able to look at right away. Still, Junie was impatient and got her thumbprint stuck over Bonnie's and my face more than once.

Junie asked me if I liked The Beatles.

"Yeah, I like them," I admitted, reluctantly.

"Did you see them on TV?" Junie wanted to know.

"Yeah. I saw them at Suffolk Downs too."

Junie was visibly impressed. Her slender chin rose almost imperceptibly, that I had done this and she hadn't. Her parents wouldn't let her to go.

"What did you think?"

"I didn't know what I was looking at. They looked like ants."

She and Bonnie laughed.

"Which one is your favorite?" Bonnie asked me.

Which Beatle was your favorite was a test in those days of just who you were. It was a good gauge.

"George," I answered.

Junie's eyes narrowed and her beautiful head nodded in approval.

"How come?" she asked anyway.

"He's the smart one," I said.

"How do you know?" she tested.

I shrugged. "Well, he's quiet and I like that and I read in a magazine that he was smart." I blushed. I know I blushed. I would blush in school if the teacher so much as called my name. Even if I raised my hand by my own choice, I blushed.

Junie nodded.

"Who do you like?" I asked her. I already knew Bonnie liked Ringo.

"Paul."

Junie was right. She'd have more than a chance with Paul.

"Bonnie tells me you like Elvis," Junie said.

This was the real test. I liked Elvis because nobody else did. I liked him because he was beautiful and he was mine. But, what would Junie think of my liking somebody so out of style?

I thought I might have to choose between Junie and Elvis. I chose.

"I like him because he's beautiful and I can have him all to myself."

Junie twisted her lovely lips in a knowing smile. I'd passed. Later, Junie would tell me it was my liking Elvis that had convinced her to come and meet me. She'd been intrigued. Besides, she told me, she'd known for a long time she was losing Bonnie to Bonnie's new boyfriend, Larry. Larry Kilman, a much older guy who made a lot of money though he didn't seem to have a job and took Bonnie out on weeknights to the drive-in at Suffolk Downs.

"In the future," Bonnie said, "there won't be any more songs, just beeps and honks and kids will dance like this -"

She showed us, twisting her cute figure in all sorts of unnatural angles and spasms. Junie and I laughed and joined in, dancing like our bodies were broken.

THE BEACH

I met Junie a few months before we went to Revere High School. Junie had gone to St. Mary's in Lynn and she was about to change over to public school. One day I saw her standing with a group of girls down at Bell Circle that noisy, filthy intersection where the highways and the tracks meet. I didn't want her standing in such a crummy place amidst the shards of glass, sticky candy blobs and leaky beer cans thrown out of cars. She'd just gotten off the bus and was saying goodbye to her friends. She was wearing her plaid uniform skirt, rolled up at the waist to make it shorter. It tumbled down her slim legs, which were stuck into the biggest shoes I'd ever seen, "dink shoes," Junie called them. Really, saddle shoes the nuns made them wear. Junie was crushed that I had seen her in her uniform. I was so touched to hear her say that, warmed by how much she liked me. "You couldn't look ugly in anything," I told her, "even if you had to wear a burlap bag."

I'll probably know what year it was from now on, because as I've said before, to Frank, whom you'll meet later, when he asked me how long I'd known Junie, I hesitated for a minute and answered, "I've known her all my life. I didn't start to live until I met Junie."

On the day before school started at Revere High School, the last day of summer, Junie, Bonnie and I went to the beach.

Two girls were having a vicious fistfight as we approached the sand. Screaming curses at each other, they pulled at each other's stiff, teased hair; they tore at each other's leopard-print bikinis; maybe that's what it was about, they had on the same bathing suits; they grunted and groaned like lovers as their bodies sent out waves of sharp sand and sailed together this way and that in a strange, passionate grip. We had to maneuver carefully around their locked forms flying dangerously close to us at times. An eager crowd of on-lookers had gathered to cheer them on.

We had to be careful, too, of our facial expressions. If someone caught one of us turning up her nose, they could decide to fight us too, and, as I'd warned Junie many times, her nose was *always* turned up.

"They're fighting over some guy," a boy laughed as we continued on.

Sitting on lawn chairs like Roman spectators were thick set, bronzed older boys and between their sprawling, hairy legs, like long, silken scarves, the slender, greased bodies of their girlfriends had eased themselves. The faces of the girls and boys, one a top the other like two-headed, sexual monsters, looked out on the scene with supreme boredom from behind dark glasses. They observed the fight with only sunstruck interest and flicked the flying sand from their oiled skin. I recognized Richie Silva among them. His doe eyes were blanked out by sunglasses. His girlfriend, Gina was between his open legs. She wore a purple bikini. Her stomach was nonexistent; her swelling breasts formed a line of cleavage nearly eight inches long.

It was not a time to say hi to Richie, nor for him to say hi to me, not even silently. Whether he saw me or not, I don't know. I wanted him to see me; I was wearing my first bikini. It was pink. Junie had one too. Hers was navy blue; the color sent her blue eyes sparkling. We'd bought them together, trying them on in a giggling tussle in the fitting rooms of Jordan Marsh where the salesgirl had kept calling in to us, "May I help you, ladies?" I knew I looked beautiful; I was tanned as a golden brown bun; my hair was sun-bleached and whipped blissfully by the ocean wind. But, Richie would not acknowledge me today.

"Larry!" Bonnie hollered, running awkwardly toward him through the sand. Before we knew what had happened, she'd disappeared from our side, as she had every day that summer, to sit with Larry and his older friends on their blanket.

"We didn't even get a chance to say, 'See you later,'" I said.

"They creep me out," Junie confided, "the way they wear clothes at the beach. It's weird."

It was true. Larry and his pals were sitting on the blanket in black socks and shoes, black pants. They'd taken off their white business shirts to show off scrawny white chests with thin patches of black hairs. They pulled up to the beach every day in a wide black car that an older businessman might drive.

"How come her mother lets her go out with him?"

"He's Jewish," Junie said. "He's got money and he's somebody's son."

"Oh." That'd just about do it, I thought.

"They never tan even though they've been here every day," she mused.

"They're spiders, that's why they don't tan," I said.

Junie liked that. She laughed, but it was a painful laugh. She missed Bonnie.

Junie and I stayed at the beach all day. We agreed on everything. Suntan oil: baby oil and Mercurochrome, a dark red antiseptic meant for wounds, which we applied liberally for its deep, rich color. Reading: large and paperback, always classic. Writing: letters. Radio: none, and hated sitting next to anyone with a radio. Money: none. God knows we'd spent it all on our bikinis. Lunch: nothing. We took a walk instead, tucking our clothes under our shoes, worrying appropriately over our belongings, enough to keep them from being stolen. Our movements on the blanket and off were comfortably and naturally choreographed to slip around each other with ease.

"I'm gonna call you Tweetie!" Junie said, suddenly. "You're a lot like her, little and tweet."

She was being affectionate; the pain to be so joined with Richie was a secret delight.

"Tweetie always wins," I told her.

She nodded as if in sudden realization of this fact.

We were walking in the water, which, at Revere Beach, was always a sickening greygreenbrown. It appeared blue from far away, but when you got up close, it slapped the grey shore with layers of brown seaweed, tampons and applicators, sopping sandwich remains, ropes of plastic bags, cigarette butts. Occasionally, if we were desperately hot and dry, we plunged our baked bodies into the greyish soup only to run out screaming and laughing, "Ugh! Ugh! I can't believe I did that!" Once, Junie had a man's bikini trunks wrapped around her ankle. You'd think it was a jellyfish, the way she trembled, "Get it off!" I didn't want to touch it either, but, for her, I knelt down and wrestled with it till it came off. We looked at each other, not knowing whether to laugh or cry.

I told her about the dancers from the old dance hall, how I always saw them and felt their sparkling, tragic presence waltzing over the waves then sliding under. Junie listened silently, looking out over the water where she saw them too.

It was the end of a summer, and this was the day we walked all the way down to The Point of Pines where the sand ended in a concrete wall dotted on top with colorful lawn chairs, then back, by the Bandstand where a decorous, overdressed crowd of old Jews, bringing their own folding chairs, gathered every Sunday afternoon for an old fashioned concert. This day, the Bandstand was empty of old people and crawling with tanned, young bodies. The Bandstand was where the older kids hung out.

Johnny Strummer was there as we passed, he called, "Hey, Bleachie!" And, there he was, shining with sun, wearing only cut offs and sitting on the sidewalk, his back up against the sparkling sea wall.

Come here, he motioned with his handsome chin; his sun-bleached hair floated about his face.

Junie and I walked toward him. I was glad to bring Junie over to someone so beautiful; it was a sweet blessing drawing myself and Junie to him. What would he say?

Up close, his blue eyes were lighted with sunlight peeking out from under the waves of shining hair passing over them, he said, almost sadly, "Bleachie, I'm getting married." He pointed to her.

There she was, the girl Johnny Strummer had chosen, the girl the whole street had waited years to see. She was smoking a cigarette. Her teased dull brown hair stood high above her little forehead. Her small underdeveloped features squinted into the face of the girl she was talking to. She was tiny and skinny and inconsequential in a black one piece.

"She's not pretty enough for you," I heard myself say.

Johnny laughed, all full of sun, all blue and golden brown. "Oh, yeah," he said, his own hand reaching up to take my hair out of my eyes.

"Who's this?" he asked of Junie.

"This is my friend, Junie White." My friend, Junie White.

"Hello," said Junie.

I squatted beside him, this Junie giving me new courage, this chance maybe being my last to speak to him. "How come you picked *her*?"

He turned so close to my face, he said, "I have to get married."

This shock, this tremendous waste hit me hard, that it had happened to the Great Johnny Strummer! But, it was none of my business. My face must have shown what I didn't want to say, as my face always betrays me.

He smiled, gently. "Did you think *you* would marry me?"

I smiled, too. "I thought you would wait for me."

"I couldn't wait for you," he said.

Junie and I said goodbye to him then and I tried not to think life was over at marriage. Nevertheless, Junie hunched her shoulders as I told her who Johnny was, how long I'd admired him, watching him play ball, turning my radio up high on the sunny windowsill, hoping he would hear the music and turn his head my way. He was my myth, my Johnny, like a thousand Johnnies, who are handsome and fine, who are your dreaming, but who cannot make your dreams come true.

Bonnie came over to our blanket later and informed us she was not going home with us, she was going home with Larry.

"As if we didn't know," Junie remarked to her pretty back skipping away from us.

She and I took Centennial home, to get the hill over with right away. By the time we got to the top of that vertical antenna, you'd think we'd crossed the Sahara we were so parched.

The next day was the first day of high school.

"Are you scared?" Junie asked me.

"Yeah. You?"

She nodded that delicate, white blonde head.

There, at the crest of Hichborn, watching the cars whip by us, waiting to time my crossing just right, Junie said something momentous.

"We might as well be friends. Bonnie's never coming back."

There's a photo of us, me and Junie, snapped by her tall, good-looking father, Ted, who just happened to come down to the beach that afternoon to pick up Junie's brother, Joey, who was around somewhere. Junie and I, huddled on our blanket, faced her Dad's teasing "Smile!" with weak grins, our arms crossed and knees up to cover the bikinis we were suddenly embarrassed about in front of him, giving, instead, the impression that we were naked and shielding our private parts from view.


THE HIGH SCHOOL

The most important thing about High School was knowing your way around. While I had a terrible sense of direction, Junie's was excellent. It took me three years to learn where the exits were; the south door was more of a mystery to me than the South Pole. I knew where the South Pole was.

They put Junie in the College Course and me in Accelerated. I liked being apart from the other kids, except that it meant I didn't see Junie most of the day. We met at strategic points and times.

"The double doors," Junie commanded.

"What double doors?" I panicked.

"Tweet," she heaved a big sigh, "you know where your English class is?"

"I think so."

"Just go out the door and down the stairs."

"Which door?"

"Just stand at the teacher's desk and turn left."

Out of the swarm of kids I saw Junie's body bob out of the crowded doorway, our hands joined, notes, folded and refolded and tucked neatly into themselves in the official Junie White manner, were exchanged, palmed expertly; she shouted, "Lunch, lockers!" I shouted, "- K!" as our bodies were pushed along the tide.

The tight clique of bleached blonde cheerleaders spread over the whole width of the corridor as they passed, loud and nasty. They were following skinny, pale little Donna Pagano, walking up real close to her all the way upstairs, pushing her, pushing her until they had her up against the wall. Right outside the classroom door, Donna hugged her huge pile of books, her eyes glazed over. The fat comfort novel, "Hurry Sundown," sacred reading not for school, slid around on top of the pile, jabbing her in the deep cave of her collarbone.

One by one, the girls spit in her face. Each had the exact same color hair, done in slightly different, perfectly smooth pageboy styles or flips; each had perfect white teeth like dew drops in the folds of the frosted pink petals of their lips; they laughed with the teeth of angels. Their spittle dripped down Donna's stony face.

"What are you looking at?" one of them said to me. "Huh? What's this?"

She flung my scarf in my face. It had been sewn with the same pastel plaid wool as my skirt, but it wouldn't fling up like she wanted it to, because I'd pinned it down with a little silver cat pin with green rhinestone eyes.

"Get out of here!" she screamed when she failed to take my scarf.

She kicked me instead, kicked me into the classroom, with one hefty Bass Weejun to my calf. The pain throbbed, but I was glad to get away.


They say you can smell a rotting body right away when you walk into the room; they say the smell literally knocks you over when you open the door. The girl's bathroom at Revere High School was like that, you'd swear there was a rotting body in there, and in a way, there was.

As Junie and I walked into the girl's rotten bathroom, we overheard a gleeful voice, "He pissed in her mouth!" When I saw the short, heavy set girl who had spoken, she had bristly red hair, brown-blood red at the roots, orange at the frizzy tips, I pictured her down on her knees, him letting loose in her mouth, but it wasn't her, she was telling the story, but I saw her like that, spitting out his piss and crying.

They changed the subject when we came in.

"You goin' to the fight tonight, Rhoda?"

"Who's fightin'?"

"The Dublin's fightin' Chelsea."

"Where?"

"Unda the bridge in Chelsea, you goin'?"

"I dunno."

"Eddie's gonna be there!"

"Yeah?"

There were no doors on the stalls, so Junie stood in front of me while I used the toilet.

She faced me. "Don't sit on it!" she hissed.

"I won't, don't worry."

"What? You gonna watch her?" The red-haired girl yelled at Junie. She took a drag on her cigarette, waiting for Junie to answer.

Junie ignored her.

"Hey! I'm talkin' to you, Blondie!"

Squatting in midair, I looked up at Junie to see her reaction and it was like we were the only two people in there. Her expression was calm and open, as usual. Lighted, even in this dark hole, by its own inner lamp of rosy health and generations of fine, Swedish bones.

"Mona, for Chrissake, you gotta fight everybody? They're goin' ta tha baf'room, for Chrissake!"

"Yeah," Mona agreed. She snickered, checking her thick eye makeup. "Luxury accommodations."

It was Junie, you know, she had a way of rising above it all. So aloof, so soft, it was like the girls couldn't see her, or a soft mist of forgetfulness enveloped them and they could think only good thoughts. I remember her brother saying she had carried a whole pizza into the movie theater once and no one had stopped her.

Just as the girls stubbed their cigarettes out in the rusty sink, a teacher came in, one of those typing or business teachers, a square cow in a dress.

Junie gazed implacably over her shoulder.

"Put out the cigarettes, girls," she ordered weakly, a few seconds too late to challenge anyone. Her eyes ran a quick check over us.

"What cigarettes, Mrs. Borren?" Mona asked, innocently.

"Aren't you two supposed to be in detention?"

"That's where we're going if you move your fat ass outta the door," Mona said in a singsong mutter. The other girl giggled.

"What?"

But, the three of them were out the door, which slammed with a monstrous metal on metal boom down the hall.

"Are you finished yet?" Junie asked, suddenly impatient with me.

The whole equilibrium had shifted. We were alone now and I was taking too long.

"I was afraid to come out," I said.

Junie laughed. "Flush with your foot," she ordered.

"How come you came to public school, Junie? How come you didn't stay with the nuns?"

"I don't think it's safe to use those sinks," Junie told me as I started to wash my hands. She ripped off a piece of cardboard paper towel. "Here, spit on this."

"So, how come?"

We walked out. Junie held the door open with the paper towel.

"My mother didn't want me coming home on the bus through Lynn anymore. It's too dangerous."

"Yeah, Lynn is so much worse then Revere. 'Lynn, Lynn, city of sin/ stab you in the back and do you in.'"

Down the hall, we could hear shouts. Several of the bigger boys who were football players were assembled at the foot of the stairs, blocking the way. They were angry, shouting, shaking their fists toward one of the classrooms.

"We don't want you here, you pussy!"

The word "pussy" spit out of a distorted, angry mouth. The boys' chunky football bodies strained in tight chinos or white slacks, stuffed into pink or yellow polo shirts about to burst with muscles bulging with anger.

"We're tired of seeing you pussy footing around here!"

Junie and I slid past their meaty fists, our eyes large with listening.

"It's Mr. Cameron," Junie whispered, and I turned to see his trim little body in its light blue suit and his pale, agitated face as he tried to ignore the taunts and carefully pack up his briefcase with the day's papers.

"What do you think you're going to teach us, how to walk in high heels?"

"Do you have him, Junie?" I asked her.

"For French," she answered.

"Get the fuck out of here, you swishy, little bastard!"

You'd think I'd know what homosexuality was, but I didn't. Vaguely, I was aware the Mr. Cameron was smaller, softer than other men I knew, but that was all.

"I wonder how long he'll last," Junie said. "They do that to him almost every day. They can't be in the same room with him."

"Do you have a lot of homework?" I asked her as we came outside.

"No."

"You want to go down the Ave so I can get those shoes?"

"Call me when you get home."

That meant she had to ask first.

We offended Mrs. Potter's sense of neatness, dawdling there at the highway while she was trying to herd the children across. She kept trying to mosey us along with the others, but we shook our heads and kept talking, our bodies doing a little swaying dance, hugging our books and swaying forward and back as we talked.

Then, Junie said she would go and to call her the second I got in the house, and she chose her time perfectly when Mrs. Potter wasn't looking and dashed out and wove around and through the hard, colored missiles and it was a joy to see her. When she got to the other side, she reached her hand up so very high; she jumped for joy, goodbye, waving high! She backed up toward her street, facing me and jumping and waving so that with each jump and wave she cheated the horizon one more time, laughing and jumping and waving, and me too, laughing from deep in my belly and jumping and waving till she was only a small hand over the top of the hill and she was gone.

I carried a tender smile down the hill to my house.

The phone rang the second I got in.

THE AVE

"You just left her!" Ma yelled while the phone was still ringing.

I swear, I could tell it was Junie by the sweet trill of the ring.

"Hi!"

"Hi! I thought I was supposed to call you?"

"I decided to call. I can go. How soon can you get here?"

"Half an hour?"

"What? What do you have to do?" she demanded.

"Nothing."

"Then, what's going to take you a half an hour?"

"I have to go to the bathroom."

"You just went!"

"I gotta go again!"

"Well, hurry up!"

We talked for another half hour anyway.

Whenever I could, as we sat next to each other or walked, when we did our homework, or at mass, or on our way to school, I feasted my eyes on Junie, especially on her profile. I had, from what I could see, when I twisted myself around in front of the mirror, the profile of a chicken: a high forehead, a hooked beak, thin lips. However, Junie had the right profile, the kind you were supposed to have: narrow, delicately sloping forehead, turned up nose, full lips. I looked at Junie the same way I would have looked at the Pieta, if I'd had the opportunity to see it. Her finely chiseled lines were just as amazing to me, and, like the Pieta, whose polished marble reflected the light of God and the artist's devotion from every curve and crevice, her skin glowed: from out the edge of her profile, the sun burst in glaring, Northern rays.

I feasted my eyes now as we walked toward Shirley Ave. Past Mrs. Ratby's house at the foot of Hichborn where some dirty little kids were trespassing on Mrs. Ratby's perfect green grass, throwing trash on her perfect lawn, the only clean yard at the bottom of the street, and yelling for her to come out which she did, smacking a broom against the sky and swearing choicely at them. They screamed with delight and ran over the lawn like crazed insects.

As we walked, we planned our lives in detail.

"Are you going to get married?"

"Never! You?"

"Yeah - I might ever!"

Past the short ghetto of tenements that clustered at the bottom of Junie's side of Hichborn like trash barrels at the back of a house. The people wore dark, shapeless clothes and hung out their doorways or on their steps staring at us as we walked by, just staring like the track people, only these people were there all year round.

"What about kids? You want kids?"

"No kids! No, I'm going to write books and paint and live absolutely alone except for my work and friends and lovers, other artists who'll come to visit me and talk about art."

Past the chicken coop, a cement garage clucking with filthy chickens, its doors open in summer, spewing feathers and chicken shit outside sticking to the sidewalk.

"Does your mother get her eggs from there?" Junie asked.

"From there? No way! Rosa might ever! Our Egg Man comes from a farm!"

Past Nat's Pool Room where the boys eyed us minutely up and down, so you felt their eyes on your ankles, your knees, your thighs, up under your skirt, over the back of your ass as you passed by, "Ni - ice!" "Ni - ice ass!" They called from across the street. We never walked on the same side, never ever. The song from out the door of the pool room, the song that dogged me, "G-L-O-R-I-A /Gonna shout it every day!"

"There's that Aaron Goldman," I said, he was leaning at the doorway watching her pass with those blue eyes, deep and meaningful under his dark curls.

"He looks at you."

"I know," said Junie.

She closed her eyes. She walked past Nat's with her eyes closed.

Past Shirley Beauty Parlor, stinking of perms and gluey hair spray. Past Myer's Bakery where Junie went in to buy a moon pie, where all the pastries looked too plain and anemic to me, an Italian who liked them thickly stuffed with real cream and rum and rich with flavors of chocolate and vanilla, almond and anise, not thin with plain white sugar for white people.

"I'd like to have one kid, maybe, just to see what it's like, I mean, you gotta have at least one. Right?" I volunteered.

"I don't even know any kids I like."

"Yeah, I've never seen any. Except for Connie's kids. They're kind of cute. When I baby-sit, they like it when I toss my hair over my head and chase them around like Cousin It."

"That's cute."

"Yeah, and they never fight. I let them stay up and they're real good. Once, Nancy, that's the little one, she got up and tried to go to the bathroom in an open drawer."

"No!"

"Yeah! I caught her just in time."

"Oh, that's so cute."

"Yeah, it was pretty cute."

"Do you think it's possible to have a nice kid, Junie?"

By now, we were fingering the crepe blouses for sale at Ideal Cleansers. I put my hand under the ruffle of one, to feel it against my wrist, landing softly, in a romantic curl around my hand.

"Wow, I don't know, do you?"

"I'd love to have a little boy or girl with beautiful blonde hair and big eyes, blue or green eyes, very pretty, nice and sweet, a little artist. That's what I'd like."

"That sounds beautiful. You'll probably have one just like that, Ria." Junie called me Tweet or Ri or Ria, but never my full name, unless, like a mother, she was angry with me. I sometimes called her Pie, after Junie Pie, but that's all.

"That would be great," I mused, "but, no husband!"

"No!" she shook her head.

To Shirley Shoe, where the shoes cost from $2-3.00 up to $12-18 for velvet evening pumps. Sy was there, and his wife, Pearl, who gushed at you the second you came in the door; they looked you over, checked the cost of the shoes you were wearing, checked how expensive your purse was.

I tried on a pair of princess heels for mass and Pearl watched to see if I had peds. I did, nice clean ones Ma kept tucked in the corner of her drawer for wearing with her sandals.

"Oh, those are stunning on you! Just stunning! Sy, aren't these stunning on her!"

"Stunning!" Sy replied from somewhere in the dark, back room.

"I wish I could wear such a delicate shoe!" Pearl continued. Her own feet were swollen and stuffed into short, apricot pumps. "You taking those, sweetie? Three fifty, hunny."

While Pearl stuck the shoes in a used bag from Stop & Shop, I pointed to pairs of shoes and called them by the names of girls we knew. Some of the shoes were so shopworn, they looked like they had been worn for years, but Sy and Pearl would sell them to you for $4.00 and tell you they looked stunning on you. I pointed to a brown pair, with turned up toes and flaking creases, "Cheryl Hotstetter." I said, and Junie laughed out loud. I loved to make her laugh. I studied her sense of humor since the first days we were together, when we'd walked up Centennial after the beach. I studied what made her laugh and then I did that and watched. She was lovely to watch. She loved to make fun of people for their special qualities. Sometimes it was affectionate, sometimes derisive. I pointed to another pair, purple leather with missing rhinestones along the toes, "Judy Delaney!" Junie shook her head and giggled.

"When I have my baby," I said, as we walked out, "I want a cradle made of real wood, maybe handed down in my husband's family. You know, a real cradle, handmade, not one of those stupid things from the furniture store."

"Yeah," dreamed Junie.

"With real lace curtains hanging from the canopy."

"Yeah."

EAST BOSTON, 1954

I was three years old when Mama opened the door and looked into the room. She screamed.

Her life was changed forever.

Daddy and I looked up.

Daddy laughed.

"Cut it out, Rosie! She's okay. It doesn't hurt her!"

WHITES

I learned to sit up very straight, so that when we stood after mass, for instance, people were surprised to see how much taller than me Junie was. But, on the subway, I had to sit forward on the seat, or else my short legs dangled six inches from the floor. One day, we were on the train going into town and my feet were dangling off the floor and Junie was horrified.

"Gloria! It must be awful to be so short! Look at your feet! They're disgusting!" Her lovely face twisted into a knot.

I looked down and she was right. I was always surprised to see how small I was. I never felt small. I felt big until someone tall stood next to me, or until, Junie let loose on me.

She couldn't help it. She would laugh at me sometimes, that Nazi laugh, and it was really a shock to hear it come out of Junie's angelic face directed toward me. To understand Junie's need to be cruel to me, who could take it so well and love her still, you had to know Agnes. Her mother.

I'd climb the wooden back stairs of Junie's house, stairs that resounded with a wooden echo along the paved driveway and out along the highway that whooshed with cars every other second, to the kitchen where I knocked formally on the half-opened Dutch door.

"Oh! Gloria! Come in!"

"Hi, Mrs. White. How are you?"

I'd never called a friend's mother by her last name before. No one on our side of Hichborn ever wanted to be called Mrs. anything. It was too formal and affectatious for life on the other side of Hichborn. But, not too formal and affectatious for Agnes.

Agnes was standing at the counter dressed just like Mary Tyler Moore on "The Dick Van Dyke Show," slim as a tulip in cigarette pants and ballet flats. Her hair was done in a short, neat style straight from the hairdresser: light brown wisps stylishly frosted in spikes of whitish gold.

"Just fine," she hummed, just like a little hummingbird going from one flower to another, she flitted from one task to another, "and how are you this beautiful day?"

"Fine, thank you."

This was white people's talk. I was learning how to talk to white people, how to walk, talk and dress like white people. I learned from TV, but I also learned at the White's. White people at the White's.

I sat down in one of the captain's chairs, resting my arm on the pretty plastic tablecloth, decorated with a busy federal pattern of eagles and American flags. Each seat was marked with a federal blue placemat.

Spread out on the counter in front of Mrs. White were a matching set of six or seven little blue bowls. Inside these delicate blue curves, as though cupped and ready in blue hands, was every item she needed: eggs with yolks; egg whites, flour, sugar, brown spices of varying hues, vanilla, milk.

"What's all that for?" I asked, peering now, over her slender shoulder.

"I'm baking a cake!" she announced cheerfully. "Haven't you seen anyone bake a cake before?"

"Not like that."

"Well, I measure everything first and set it out. I like to have everything ready. Doesn't your mother do that?"

"My mother doesn't measure."

"She doesn't measure! Well, of course she does! Everybody measures! They have to! When you bake, you have to measure!"

She was right, in a way. Even though Ma seemed to toss the flour and sugar around like fairy dust, powdering herself as much as the cakes and cookies, the pressed pizzaiolas, the domed walnut balls, the mushy coconut macaroons, flicking pinches of nutmeg and cinnamon like the secret ingredients of a witch's brew, she was measuring all along by intuition, memory and blind faith, not along the absolutely level flat of an aluminum teaspoon on a leash of level teaspoons like Agnes.

Agnes hummed a tune to herself as she danced lightly at her work. "Are you goin' to San Francisco? / Be sure to wear some flowers in your hair/ if you're goin' to San Francisco/ you're gonna meet some gentle people there."

Watching Mrs. White was a revelation to me. I wasn't used to the ways of white people, and I wasn't sure what to think. Which was the better way? Ma's or Mrs. White's? For instance, when Agnes sewed, and she could sew anything, she employed every single sewing gadget ever made. I'd seen a lot of these gadgets in the store and couldn't figure out what they were for until I saw Agnes use them. She began by washing, drying and pressing her fabric. She outlined her patterns with waxed chalk. She pinned using a ruler to check the distance of each pin from the seam line, a pincushion nestled on her slender wrist in one of those pucker, soft elastics. She cut slowly along a flat surface using pinking shears. She measured and basted three quarters of an inch from the selvedge using a contrasting thread with the cloth flat on the table. She ran the seam evenly and smoothly and slowly through the presser foot of the whirring Singer. She ironed each seam open. Agnes's movements were so meticulously slow they were both painful and wondrous to watch.

When Ma sewed, she slapped the cloth down, cut an estimated shape and stuffed it under the presser foot anyhow. She never washed, dried, pressed or pinned. The shape that emerged from the machine was puckered and warped, caught up where it should hang straight, hanging loose where it should be caught up. When I pointed this out to Ma, she shrugged, "That's all right! Nobody cares!" But, I did.

The shape that emerged from Mrs. White's machine was pristinely perfect. Better than store bought. The seams were flattened by a steam iron, at the exact setting for the fabric whether cotton, silk or nylon. Ma never used the settings, just one, steam. Once, Mrs. White made an orange windowpane hopsack jacket for Junie. Simply the idea of having a jacket made of orange windowpane hopsack meant you were rich to me, because I'd have to have the kind of jacket you could wear with anything, that is, white or black or navy blue. Mrs. White put something I'd never even seen before under the lapel - a funny white paper she called "stiffening" to make the collar sit properly against the neckline. It was illuminating.

Also, Mrs. White made her own buttonholes! In any shape! Ma said, "I can make buttonholes! What do you think I do all day at work?"

Ma didn't think the Whites were so great.

"I don't know why you think that Junie is SO BEAUTIFUL! She's all skin and bones, she is! All skin and bones! She must be STARVING!"

I think I spent the first few times at the White's with my mouth wide open.

Junie had three brothers: John, Paul and Joseph, called Jack, Paul and Joey. Named after saints, of course. The names of boys, the names of saints, the names of ball players, other names - the Kennedys, Pope John Paul and Cardinal Cushing - were bandied about the White's house like sweet music, like prayers directly connected to celestial favor, like magic words tossed back and forth to each other like baseballs, and magically, the word was God Absolute, no question.

It's true what happens to a woman who has sons, and Mrs. White was no exception. I was not immune to being in the same room with the White boys. The first time I saw them, they tumbled into the kitchen wearing real baseball uniforms, smelling of fresh air and the green of smudged grass. In the huge bulk of their bodies alone, broad backs, long legs, wide feet that threatened a room, their male power was unmistakable. They smiled at me with the same fine bones as Junie: the same narrow cheeks, flashing white teeth and shining blue eyes. Jack was big, he filled the room, and his hair was dark, setting off the blue sparkle of laughter in his eye. Paul was tall, quiet and blonde. Joey, who stuttered just a little, was a small promise of Jack. Even June's father was handsome. Fathers, except the ones on television, weren't supposed to be handsome. They were supposed to be lumpy and bulgy with too much nose and stomach. Ted White didn't have a stomach. His pants rested against a flat terrain and fell in graceful folds I would come to fear because they signified a man in control.

The house was as finished as a house in a magazine. All the woodwork was finished white clean and met neatly at the corners. Our woodwork toiled along chipped and flaked and slimy with black and yellow grease; it hid itself somewhere behind the couch and never came out again. Mrs. White had the first garbage disposal I'd ever seen. The first time she hit the switch, I thought a car had crashed into the wall and stuck there with its engine grinding.

In the White's house, all the colors matched. The Presidential blue kitchen curtains picked up the blue of the American flag under the eagle's claws repeated over and over on the wallpaper. The amber sofa in the living room echoed the sunset in the painting above it. In Junie's room, I stopped at the door, confronted by something I'd admired and run my grubby finger over in the Sear's catalog: Princess curtains: those white nylon wonders of ruffles drifted like clouds over the window, where they were kept from floating off by brass flowers. Every piece of furniture in her bedroom - bureau, desk, nightstand, vanity - were all members of a matching set, caramel colored like the soft cornered wood in church, with little matching brass handles and curled feet.

The enormous cellar was also finished. Down there, Mrs. White had a real laundry room with a sink. The boys and Mr. White had a real pool table. There was also a woodshop where Paul had made his mother a real white picket fence, as painstakingly slowly and patiently as Agnes cooked and sewed.

When I came home and told Ma about these things, I said, "Why did you tell me this stuff only existed on television?"

"They must be rich," she said, "What does HE do?"

I assumed she meant Mr. White.

"He's an electrician."

"Oh! That's gooood! They make a lot of money! That's what your Uncle Sonny wanted to be."

"Why can't he?"

"Ha! He's has to learn how to read first! AND go back to school!"

"Uncle Sonny can't READ?"

"HE DIDN'T PAY ATTENTION IN SCHOOL, HE DIDN'T PAY! What do you think? You have to pay attention!"

"Can I teach him to read?"

"He won' let you teach him! You're a girl! You're too young! He's a man!"

But there was a dark side to the White's perfection: exactness as hidden and as keenly interlocked as the precise movements of gears inside a clock. The constant standard of excellence that Mr. White pursued and expected others to pursue, that drove him to poke his long finger over and over into the thin pillow of flesh on Junie's shoulder, "Look at the clock! Look at the clock!"

We had to run a lot. We had to have Junie home exactly on time; even two minutes late meant she'd have to stand still and listen to him.

He wouldn't let her read before she went to sleep. He said it was a bad habit; she shouldn't rely on reading to get to sleep. But, we were in a frenzy to read all of Thomas Hardy – because of the delectable beauty of the natural way of life we found there - and Junie couldn't resist stealing Ted's flashlight into her bedroom at night and reading under the covers what seemed like forbidden stories of lust and tragedy until Ted saw her light on one night and took the flashlight away and took all the fun out of it by yelling for forty-five minutes about obedience and respect until reading wasn't worth having to listen to him.

But Mr. White was an amateur next to Agnes. It was Agnes who had the special gift that would send Junie climbing out through the Princess curtains, running blinded by tears across the lonely highway in the nether hours to throw stones at my window. Shivering together on the damp grass, her thin arms as insubstantial as the cool pear blossoms that broke loose with the night air and showered on us, hands as fragile as a child's clutching at my pajamas, "Ria, am I stupid?" she begged me, "Am I ugly?"

"No! No!" I protested, where had she gotten such ideas? "You're the most beautiful thing I've ever seen!"

I hadn't witnessed Agnes at work yet. Hadn't heard her comments, so subtle and cunning at first, comments that fell into your psyche until you stepped on them like unexploded bombs moments, days, even years later.

Mrs. White was cooking. It was around 4:00 in the afternoon, just about the time Ma came home from work. I was there, in the White's kitchen, waiting for Junie, and it was as though Mrs. White had forgotten I was behind her, sitting quietly at the kitchen table. She was at the sink, looking out the window, which faced the highway.

"Oh, look at that!" Mrs. White cried out in a singsong making fun voice, "It's little Rosie coming home from work with all her bags and that big old cigarette going. And those little legs! Look at them go!"

I jumped up from the table, and, I could tell, the motion startled her: the captain's chair scraped back and she turned with an expression of horror.

Quickly, she recovered her poise. Quickly, she smiled smugly at me and began to hum. She left the room.

I looked out the window.

There was my mother walking up the hill on the narrow sidewalk that stretched along the highway between where the East Boston bus left her off down at the crazy tangle of Bell's Circle and the long walk up the hill to home. She walked slowly, dragging a little because she was tired. Every few steps, she put the cigarette to her mouth and when her hand fell down again to her side (I knew, so the blood would go back into it); it fell with such weight, I could see how exhausted she was. It was summer and she was wearing her good peds, ugly little half-socks with her sandals. Her legs were unshaven, pale red and fuzzy. The sidewalk was a desert of sand and garbage and glass shards. A newspaper flapped against her legs, she shook it off.

It was my mother and it broke my heart. What did Mrs. White know about taking the bus to work every day? About lugging bags of groceries for miles when she had to shop? Mrs. White had her own car. She didn't have to work.

But, it was my mother's legs that hurt me so much. A struggle of opposites went on inside me and I nearly choked on my horror and adoration of her. Her short legs, they were my own legs, too stubby to carry anything but the smallest person, deformed, ethnic, the very legs that Junie had made fun of dangling, as she described, "disgustingly" over the subway seat.

"But, I'm much bigger on the inside," I'd reassured her.

She brightened once again, after being all disgusted and grim.

"That's what I love about you," she'd said. "You say things."

You see, she couldn't help it. Agnes drove her to make fun of me. I would try to drive Agnes out of her.

Take the incident of the green grapes, for instance.

We were in Ma's kitchen this time. There was Ma in her flowered housedress, nylons rolled to her ankles, torn slippers, washing in the strainer the huge mound of green grapes she'd just brought home from the Italian market in East Boston that was on her way to the bus stop from work.

When she'd finished running the silvery water over them, she plopped the strainer down in front of us, dripping and sparkling, lusciously wet and cold.

I couldn't wait to reach for them, which I did, popping a fat one in my mouth, snapping it between my teeth.

"Mmm," I advised Junie, "have one!"

Only then did I notice the tense anger on her face. Why, it was Agnes White sitting across from me!

"No plate, Gloria? No napkin?" she sneered. Just like her mother would have. Calling me *Gloria*, which she never did.

I laughed.

"You should see yourself! You look exactly like your mother right now! Have one! They're fantastic!"

Nothing could have been worse then telling Junie she looked exactly like Agnes because Agnes had aged a hundred years too fast. Agne's once pretty face had become gauged like a dried up river bed with the deep lines of her disapproval. Junie was already terrified of winding up like that.

Junie and I used to say it was because Agnes had given up her dancing career to marry Ted. The dance troupe was just about to go on tour when her father had made her quit. Her family had been fierce Irish Catholics and the idea of going on tour with a group of dancers, staying in cheap hotels unchaperoned, undisciplined, unprotected - it was immoral. So, she got married. The babies came quickly. Ted left her home a lot to go to the French Club during the first years of their marriage. Not a day went by when Agnes didn't mutter something about "the French Club, the French Club."

One day, Agnes showed me her high school photo.

"Who do you think this is?" she asked me.

It was the same trick Ma had played on me with the old photograph of Daddy in his curls and short pants. I knew that trick, but I was fooled anyway.

"It's Junie."

Agnes laughed.

"Look again."

But, it was Junie. The same sun was caught inside the same exquisitely sculpted form, but Agnes had lost her sun. It was Junie's now.

"Have one!" I tempted her. I knew she wanted a fat, wet grape. "Which one is looking at you?"

"That one."

"Take it."

I could see the meanness gather in her half closed eyes. She took a fist full of grapes and threw them across the room.

I was furious.

"Listen, Agnes, we don't throw food here!"

A long moment of silence followed. We just looked at each other. I didn't know how she'd react. I thought our friendship might be over.

Instead, she plucked a glistening grape and put it in her mouth.

"I should be grateful they're washed," she said, smiling apologetically at me.

I picked one up from the floor and wiped it on my shirt. I knew I should make her pick up all the grapes she'd thrown, but I also knew that would never happen.

"They taste good with dirt on them," I said.

"You're so natural," she grimaced, taking another.

I ran out of Junie's house that day, calling across the highway, "Ma! Ma!" I ran to her and in my heart, I fell to her fat, tiny feet, I hugged her pokey legs. "Ma!" I called, careless of the cars that screeched and blasted their horns at me.

"What the hell are you doing? What's a matter?" She sucked heavily on her cigarette with alarm.

"Nothing," I shrugged. "I saw you from Junie's and decided to walk with you."

"You scared the shit out of me! Where's your sister?"

"At Linda's."

"Oh."

Junie ran up to us and we walked Ma to the house together. I told her what had happened. I told her everything. Except one thing. That was really the thing that made my legs feel so short.


JIMMY PRIESTLEY

Agnes was really dangerous by the kitchen window.

"Look at that! Look at that!" We heard her yell. We came running out of Junie's bedroom to find her at the kitchen sink pulling off her big yellow rubber gloves with comical, urgent pucky sounds. Ma never wore rubber gloves.

"Look!" She pointed out her kitchen window. "That's marijuana! Look! I know what it looks like because I looked it up in The Encyclopedia Britannica!

Gleefully, as gleeful as Ma when she hears the news or reads the paper, she pointed next door to the field of tall grass and scrub bushes, chicory and milkweed that was her view every day and used to be the yard of her dead sister's house.

"That Jimmy Priestley is growing marijuana! Look at that!"

Junie and I were not as acquainted with marijuana as Agnes, but we did know who Jimmy Priestley was. He passed us often out on the street, caved in, starving, frail as a prisoner of Auschwitz. In fact, I had seen him many times myself before I knew his story, out on the Revere streets, walking as though he walked the earth. He passed us daily gnawing on a cigarette as if for food, and Junie and I would watch, respectful of what he was: a heroin addict, a spirit already dead, passing by in another dimension.

"No wonder his eyes are always red! I'm gonna call the cops!"

"Mom," Junie tread carefully, for this was not only Jimmy's life she was handling, "if you call the cops, they'll arrest Jimmy."

"That's right! I'm going out there to get some so I can prove it!"

She ran outside. We watched her wading up to her waist through what looked like wildflowers and weeds to us. Gleefully, she ripped a bunch and ran back.

Before we knew it, she was in the kitchen, breathing excitedly and spreading the narrow fan-like leaves over the flags and eagles on the kitchen tablecloth.

Junie and I weren't sure if that was marijuana, but I know it crossed our minds to sneak out to the field and get some later.

"Mom," Junie tried again, "if Jimmy goes to jail, who'll take care of Billy? What'll he do? Are *you* gonna take care of him?"

Billy was Jimmy's little brother. They lived together in their dead parents' house. Jimmy sold drugs to support them both, as well as Jimmy's habit, which was, most likely, a demanding roommate. Everyone knew this but Agnes.

Agnes just stared at the leaves stuck to the plastic tablecloth. She grinned to herself. She shook her head from side to side.

Junie must have gotten through to her, because she didn't call the cops. Agnes had a lot of energy left over, you know. She had to do *something*, because she had never been a dancer.


WOMEN

We were on the floor in Junie's bedroom. She was doing math. I was flipping through the pages of my history book, the way I always did, skipping to the back of each chapter where the culture of the time was depicted. Through the ages I noticed paintings of women doing the simplest things: formal, straight-faced portraits; goddesses or saints in landscapes; the Madonna and child; women in their bath; women washing clothes; women cuddling babies; women reclining, women reaching, dancing, reading, sewing, playing the piano, arranging flowers. I began to wonder: which was more important, the painting or the woman. I decided it had to be the woman.

"You know, what women do is the most important thing."

Junie looked up.

"What do you mean?"

"Well, all the most important artists painted women."

"They're beautiful," she declared, returning to her work.

"Yeah, but what women do is beautiful too. Anything they do. Even working in the fields or doing housework. Women make it all beautiful. Hemingway talked about the woman who cared for him, saying that she worked, that she rose early to care for her own family before coming to his house in the morning to care for him, then she went home in the evening to care again for her family. He equated what women do with writing, he called both 'work,' saying that she 'worked,' and it was the greatest compliment. He made work beautiful. He told us the work was full of love.

By the way he described everything he did, how reverently he described everything, by lingering on every detail of eating, drinking, fishing, working, loving" - here I paused – "he told us it was holy."

Junie smiled at me and her eyes shone with love.

"I wrote a new story," I said.

"What's it about?" Junie asked, turning away from her math book. She loved a new story.

"You. It's another 'Georgia' story." Georgia was always cruel.

Junie liked nothing better than a story about herself.

"That's good. When can I read it?"

I pulled it out of my notebook. Her eyes lit up and she took it from me eagerly.

These moments when Junie read my stories were like those first moments of a story beginning for me too, like the opening of a movie when you're in the dark and the music and images start to fill you, whether sweet or harsh, reverential or assaulting, it feels wonderful coming into you from somewhere outside of yourself. Sometimes, I thought it was so lonely to be only one person at a time. When Junie read my stories, I was so many.

"Wow! Ria, am I like that?"

"Yeah."

"I hurt you like that? I'm that mean?"

"Sometimes."

She looked away.

"I'm sorry. You know?"

"I know."

I hadn't given her the story to confront her. I'd given it to her in spite of confronting her, because she was Junie.

"I really think," she hesitated, thinking, "that your writing, and your art, when you paint or draw, I could never do any of that in a million years. I think it's incredible."

"You could draw, if you wanted to."

I really believed that. I couldn't believe someone like Junie couldn't draw.

"I can't though. It's a great story."

"It's gonna be in the school newspaper."

Once a month a mimeographed wad of papers was sent around the school called "The Lantern," named after the famous lanterns of Paul Revere's ride, of course. The faculty advisor said she liked my writing, but she never failed to criticize it. The "Georgia" stories she found, "too weird and emotional."

"I love it when your stuff is in print! I feel so proud, like I've done it too. Someday, I'm going to say I knew you."

"No, someday you're going to say, "She's my best friend!""

"Right."

I flourished around her. She gave me love just by thinking of me, just by being in my thoughts.


## RUSTIC DREAMS

"What kind of house are you gonna have?" I asked Junie.

We sat on the guardrail high over the embankment behind my house. In those days, the guardrail was made out of chipped white wood, friendly and inviting for sitting on in the afternoon. Soon, the rail was changed to steel, curved with a sharp edge to keep kids from sitting on it.

We swung our legs over the highway side. The cars whisking past made a hot wind causing tall weeds to blow against our calves. We checked now and then to see if any poison ivy was hitting us, because it was there, growing as low as rats right under our feet, turning dangerously red along the edges of its glossy leaves. Every so often, a horn would blast and a man would scream for us.

"It's our hair," we both agreed.

"How many is that?"

"18."

"No, 25! 18 was a long time ago!"

"Oh."

"So, what kind of house are you going to have?"

We were fifteen and dead serious, because I'd been told over and over in English class that the worst thing you could do in life was leave your dreams behind. None of the great writers or artists had ever done that and I was determined not to do it either, not even the smallest dream.

"I don't know. What kind are you going to have?"

"I know it's crazy, but I've always loved that cottage in "Sleeping Beauty" that was built around the trunk of a tree."

She gave me one of her brilliant, excited looks.

"Oh, yeah! And the drawers opened out of the trunk! That doesn't seem real, but it was a great house! I want a cottage too, but right on the beach."

"You could roll out of bed and go for a swim every morning."

"Yup."

We were silent, our inner eyes filled with visions of blue oceans and white sands, while the cars sped by in a blur.

"I might want to live in Paris for a while, you know, like Hemingway. Or Italy, I want to see Italy. But, eventually, I want a cottage somewhere with an English garden, you know, almost wild, just crammed full of wildflowers," I mused, "and lace curtains on every window and a white cat with blue eyes."

"I want hollyhocks by the front door," Junie said.

I waited to speak while a plane screamed over our heads.

"What are hollyhocks?"

She shrugged.

"Nana Adelle had them in the backyard in Chelsea. They were the first flower I ever saw. They were on a tall stalk with flowers one above the other and the smell was incredible! I remember standing in front of them; they were way taller than me and there were tons of bumble bees. It was like being in a different world. I've seen them in books too. I saw them pictured in *The Secret Garden*."

I still couldn't believe Junie had been born in that forgotten city, Chelsea. Or that wonderful flowers called hollyhocks had grown in Chelsea. Or that Nana Adelle, a delicate, graceful old lady, no bigger than a fawn, had come from there and the beautiful Ted White had been born there, in the old tenement, in Nana Adelle's old bed. Once, Junie and I had visited her in the dark, musty apartment. She gave me a little green leather manicure case, full of miniature instruments as delicate as she was, because she'd been cleaning out her things the way old ladies do sometimes, anticipating their death, wanting to be sure their things were with good people. With her smooth little hands, the hands of an adolescent girl, she put the case into my hands. "This is for you," she'd said, and I knew she approved of me as a good friend for Junie and that I had been blessed by Junie's Nana Adelle.

"Were you named after Nana Adelle? A middle name of hers, maybe?"

"Are you kidding? Agnes would never name me after the Whites, 'the French,' as she says."

"Yeah - so?"

"So what?"

"June - what? Allyson?" I asked, kidding.

She turned red as beets.

"No!"

"I hate you!" she said.

"No! June Allyson? Jeez. 'Meet Me in Saint Louis.'"

"Was she in that?"

"Yes."

"My mother thought it sounded sophisticated."

"I suppose."

A car beeped. I turned my head in time to see a light blue pick up truck fly by and standing in the back, leaning on the rim I saw -

"Elvis!" I screamed and jumped down as if to follow him. All the while knowing better, I let myself get excited, "It was Elvis! Junie! He was so gorgeous!"

"I saw him!" she said, raptly.

Her face was all lit up, gazing down the highway after the small blue truck which was long gone and the tall, sweet-faced boy with abundant black hair who had been standing in the back. She knew better, but still, she understood.

"Ria," she said, "Elvis doesn't look like that anymore."

"Yeah, you're right." I agreed, sitting back down on the guardrail. "Elvis isn't Elvis anymore. But - he was for a minute!"

She laughed. In a moment, she said, "Paris isn't Paris."

"England isn't England," I grinned.

"Milk isn't milk."

"Chickens aren't chickens. Eggs aren't eggs."

"Tomatoes aren't tomatoes."

Our grins were broad as the list went on and we celebrated the modern degeneration of everything good. Many horns honked. We also planned our wardrobes for high school, dates, college and a double wedding. These included lush velvets, tanned leathers, gold braids, ruffles of real lace at the cuffs and throat, lace stockings, pearled slippers, real flowers and pearls woven through our hair, good dungarees and sturdy boots. We filled our houses with handmade antiques we called real furniture, real wood floors, real stucco walls like a peasant's cottage, the elegant, rustic simplicity of which, we agreed, was the only real way to go.


AT MY GATE

Bonnie was with us. Junie had brought Bonnie over to my house. Her eyes gleamed with nervous possession and excitement standing next to Bonnie because she knew it couldn't last. Bonnie was with her this one day because Larry was out of town. Bonnie was sleeping over with her, she told me, nervously, and even Agnes and Ted and the boys were excited. She and Bonnie were going to cuddle together in that narrow white bed. I didn't like sleeping with Junie in her small bed. I didn't enjoy sleeping so closely with another person; it surprised me that I wanted space more than flesh when I slept, but I was jealous anyway. When I slept with Junie, she woke with skin as fresh and rosy as a newly opened flower. I woke like unwashed clothes. She and Bonnie stood together like they were the friends and I was alone. It was unbearable.

The evening was warm, a close and muggy early spring twilight, when the trees were still barren and the grass was still matted and brown. Ma was working nights. Do you know what that sentence means to me? When I hear that phrase, I panic as one who remembers they will die one day. The same panic I felt when Ma said, "Oh, don't worry about the bomb! When it comes down on those oil tanks, you won't feel a thing!"

Daddy was reading at the kitchen table, his dinner dish of cold fatted leftovers pushed away from him, a dirty yellow Q-tip and a handkerchief wadded up with green spit-up next to his scrubbed red elbow.

The three of us were up in my room. Bonnie had brought over some records and we were playing them on my little turntable. Bonnie laughed about that, that I didn't have a hi-fi. She had everything imaginable. She said there were speakers now, separate from the turntable and a dark glass lid that came down over the record to keep it safe. She said Larry had given her a hi-fi and it was in a mahogany cabinet. I didn't know what mahogany was, except that Ma's bed was made of it. I said so, and they both laughed at me.

Someone was calling my name.

"Glo-ria!"

But, it sounded weak. Was it outside?

Bonnie was brushing Junie's glorious hair, while telling me I needed a new brush.

"Sh!" I said.

"Glo-ria!"

Was the voice crying?

"What?" Junie giggled.

"Glor-i-a!" the voice moaned, a boy's voice. It was coming from the front.

I ran to the front window in Ma's bedroom. The girls tripped after me, giggling, "Who is it?"

They crowded around me as I looked through Ma's curtains.

It was Richie Silva swinging on the front gate, moaning, "Gloria!" His body was swaying with the gate.

My heart leaped in my chest. I felt my throat go icy and my head reel, every time he fell forward and swayed on the gate, every time he groaned, "Gloria!" I felt his voice inside me, groaning.

The two girls got crazy. They fell on each other pretending to be drunk. Was he drunk? They swayed to and fro, almost tumbling down the stairs. They were going outside to make fun of him!

I ran after them.

"No! Don't!" I called to them, but they were already outside, falling against each other in the middle of the walkway where they'd stopped. Right in front of him, they started singing a drunken song, "Oh, show me the way to go home/ I'm tired an' I wanna go to bed! / I had a couple a' drinks about an hour ago/ an' they went right to my head!" They hiccupped and fell down.

Richie looked at them miserably.

"Gloria!" he said, quietly, as if to himself, when he saw me.

He saw me, and his face seemed to clear with hope. Hope! Did the sight of me give him hope? I was awestruck with love.

"Gloria!" He tried to lift himself.

I held out my arms to him and he stood off the gate. I wanted to run to him, hold him, kiss him, whisper to him that it was going to be all right: I was there. He would hold me in his arms the way he had in my dreams, tenderly, reverently.

But Junie and Bonnie bumped me like drunks and I fell forward on the cement. I landed hard on my knees and skinned my palms like a little kid. Daddy came out to see what the commotion was and he started hollering for Jakey.

Jakey came outside and I didn't want to hold Richie in front of them all. He was down on the gate again, just hanging there. The girls were still singing and falling down.

"Take your friend home, Jakey, and put him to bed," Daddy advised.

I watched helplessly as Jakey picked Richie's limp body off the gate and started dragging him up the hill. Richie moaned something struggling to look back over Jakey's shoulder and Jakey laughed, "Yeah!"

Junie and Bonnie followed them up the hill, falling on each other and hiccupping, singing and laughing. There was nothing I could do but go inside.

I was sickened and disappointed. In the house, the cooked meat smell of dinner, the sour potatoes, the black soap around the sink where Daddy had washed up, his work shoes, sweaty and greasy in a heap under the table, the handkerchief wad and the yellowed Q-tip - I wanted to puke.

I thought of Richie, soft and loving, and how I could possibly break out of the house to see him. Ma came home around nine-thirty and Daddy was already snoring on the couch. Marie was watching television and I pretended to watch too. Then we went to bed and I lay there thinking of Richie, watching the shadows creep over the ceiling, smelling the outside through the open window like a little dog, wanting to whine for the outside, wanting to scratch at the door and whine.

Did Richie long for me at that very moment?

The thought was too much. I jumped out of bed and threw on some dungarees. Dungarees and pajama top: that was my emergency outfit. I crept out of the house, knowing Ma might hear me.

"Gloria?" I heard her moan from her bed.

I didn't answer and kept going.

In the beautiful grainy darkness, I made my way to Richie's dear little street, across from my beloved Liberty School, kitty corner from the small park where Hazel Kraus had crouched and shat. There, the lilacs fought hard with the stench of diesel fuel from the highway and the airplanes. A skunk tiptoed disgustingly sideways, leaving behind its fierce scent. I was terrified of getting sprayed; Ma would kill me. I'd be better off getting hit by a car.

Richie's house was dark: every window was a closed eye and the screen door in front was clamped shut like a mouth.

I wondered which window was his and if he was there, behind it. I wished he would appear in one as if by magic. Carefully, I walked around the house. Though I crept around carefully, I still cracked twigs underfoot; I rustled through shrubbery, causing branches to smack the walls. I waited for all hell to break loose, but there wasn't a sound.

Was that window his, nestled in that gable? Or was it the one on the first floor? In a crazy impulse, I felt at my feet for a stone and heaved it as hard as I could at the upstairs window. The light came on and I backed away from the house to stand under the streetlight where he could see me.

"Richie!" I heard myself call, hoarsely.

"Get the hell out of here, you little whore! Richie ain't home!" a woman's coarse voice snapped from behind a black screen.

His mother! I ran away as the downstairs light came on, running up the hill to the school playground where I stopped, unwilling to let his street out of my sight.

I leaned on the rusty chains of a swing; I sat on the wooden seat and let myself swing back and forth as Richie had on my gate. I cried for him the way a baby cries. I cried for his gentle touch, which I had imagined alone in my bed to be as gentle as his brown eyes that had looked at me from across the street and his soft voice that had said, "Hi" only to me. I tortured myself voluptuously with thoughts of him and I wondered if it was all coming from me - no! No, Richie had come to *me!* And I knew there was no way for me to see him until he decided to come to me again.

Frustrated and lonely for a boy who was only as far from me as a house and a mother and a world, I swung on the swing for a few minutes till a cruiser whooped by, flashing its blue light and I got scared Richie's mother had called the cops and I went home.

## BONNIE

We were always running to school because we were always late. We ran till we couldn't breathe and then we'd run gasping. Junie hated to be late. It was always my fault, because I spent so much time getting ready. Junie was ready in a flash. She was beautiful before she started.

Bonnie couldn't run. She was way, way far behind us.

"Junie," I gasped. "Wait for Bonnie!"

"No, she can't run!" Junie called. "Don't worry, come on!"

I could see her way back there. She was so tiny. And I could see by the way her head kept falling over her books that she was sobbing.

"She's crying!" I hollered, trying to catch up to Junie.

"She's pregnant!" Junie yelled back to me.

That was the last day Bonnie went to school. I never saw her again.

## JOHNNY STRUMMER

One night, I was on Ma's bed studying Shakespeare for a series of classroom plays we were doing in school. I had already played Casca. Wrapped in bed sheets, wearing a paper wreath of laurel leaves on my head, I'd happily been the first to stab Caesar (played by David Santoro) to death in front of the class. I'd been Juliet's nurse and was about to play Polonius. I liked to study in Ma's room sometimes. That way, if Junie called, I'd be right there, cozy and snuggled on the chenille bedspread, to answer the pink Princess phone.

The phone rang. I snuck in one line of dialog before I picked it up.

"Hello?"

"You wanna go for a ride?"

It was Johnny Strummer!

"Johnny?"

This couldn't be real.

"Yeah. You wanna go for a ride?"

He sounded drugged or hypnotized, as though he could only repeat that one phrase.

"I can't. I'm studying."

I didn't understand, Johnny knew me. He knew I didn't go for rides.

"Come on, let's go for a ride, me and you."

"Johnny, aren't you married?"

"Yeah. Come on, come out for a while."

"I can't."

"Why not?" He strung out the words in slow motion. I wondered if that's what strung out means.

"Because it means too much."

"To who? It means a lot to *me*." This sounded so fake, I almost laughed.

"It means a lot to your wife. And to me. I gotta go, Johnny."

I hung up, gently replacing the receiver, feeling a pang of regret for the Johnny I thought I knew, feeling betrayed by him, the one who would never have called me like that, the one with the sun-bleached curls blowing around his handsome, teasing face. He knew how important he was to me. What did he feel for me? I decided it was too expensive to find out.

I knew I couldn't go, but I wished I could. In my heart, he'd made love to me many, many times - every time he waved to me, or turned and winked at me, or drove by and his long hair flew out the little window of his Volkswagen. I loved him and I had thought he loved me.

I really did love too much.


FANTASY

This was the horrifying little fantasy I used when I was alone in my bed:

*I'm fifteen, sometimes thirteen or twelve, or eleven. I'm washing dishes at the kitchen sink. It's summer. The window over the sink is open. The warm breeze washes my face, washes through my hair, over my neck, through the cloth of my dress. I can feel it like a breath on the soft flesh of my breasts and between my legs. I'm looking out the window at the hill where I played when I was small.*

*He comes in, my father. Sometimes he's got a beer belly and he's old. Sometimes he's my young Daddy, handsome as Alan Ladd. He comes up behind me.*

*With one hand, he lifts my dress. I'm not wearing any underclothes. With the other, he unzips his work pants, takes out his big, hard penis and lifting my buttocks, he slowly, little by little, begins pushing himself into me.*

*I continue to wash dishes.*

I could always rely on having a great, gushy orgasm with that fantasy. But, afterwards, sticky and itchy with guilt, I'd lie in bed wondering if I was going to hell, or if I was already in it.

## THE CLEANSING OF THE SOULS

The White's oldest boy, John White had been named after St. John, but, when Jack Kennedy became President and was further canonized by being assassinated, John White became Jack. In the White's house, the Kennedys were sainted. In fact, a framed photo of Jack Kennedy hung next to a framed photo of Cardinal Cushing in the White's kitchen. When Mr. or Mrs. White wanted to swear, they would very decorously pronounce, "Je-sus, Mary and Joseph!" as if it were a prayer. In our house, when Daddy couldn't get the TV to work, or if one of us made him mad, then poor Jesus was picked up and flung about with a whole set of scary words, "Jesus Almighty Jesus Friggin' Asshole Almighty Christ Jesus Frig it ta hell, Christ Jesus!" We held our breath and waited for the lightning bolt to blast him.

Every so often, there was a religious crackdown in the White house. Mr. and Mrs. White would sit the family down after dinner, after Junie and her mother had finished washing, drying and putting away the dinner dishes, and in the dimmed light of the kitchen chandelier, a garish, faux Tiffany lamp hanging from the ceiling on a brass chain, Mr. and Mrs. White quietly and seriously expressed an *urgent need* for the kids to get themselves to confession, to dig down deep and make a clean breast of it. This was called "cleansing the soul."

At the table, Jack's blue eyes danced happily and healthily while his mother, her own eyes solemnly downcast, told them that the entire family was going to have a "cleansing of the souls." This very Saturday at confession they would have to tell the priest everything they'd done, without exception.

Junie, catching Jack's merry, carefree eye, chuckled a little, uncomfortably. Paul and Joey looked worried and miserable. They were still young enough to be terrified of telling the priest they'd stolen the ball during a game or chewed gum in class.

Junie told me about this family ritual that had taken place deep in the secret sanctity of her mother's household and about why she thought this particular cleansing had been called: Jack had started having sex with girls.

We knew right away, the morning after it had happened. Jack told Junie that morning: he'd poked his adorable, sleepy head into her bedroom and announced, "Guess what I did last night!" By lunchtime, Junie and I stared at him while he sat at the kitchen table blithely consuming a bacon, lettuce and tomato sandwich complete with pickle and chips, napkin, placemat and cutlery as well as a tall glass of frothy milk finishing the picture as perfectly as a wholesome milk ad in a magazine. He ate with vigor, the way Jack Kennedy had recommended enjoying all aspects of life, meanwhile chatting merrily to his mother about something; Junie and I were too absorbed to hear what.

"Doesn't it seem like he shouldn't be able to talk at all?" I whispered to her. She nodded.

We decided to call him Happy Jack, after the song. You know, "Happy Jack was a man..."

Junie figured Agnes had sensed this sexual activity of Jack's through osmosis, but since Jack had the advantage of being the eldest Irish son and handsome beyond belief, he had a power none of the others possessed that gave him instant innocence. In the perverse way of the Irish mothers of stunningly beautiful Irish sons, we were all guilty, since Jack could never be guilty. Jack laughed gaily while we cringed. As a member of her spiritual family, Junie insisted I needed to cleanse my soul too. We went to confession.

Junie had no idea what was going on in my soul. Unlike the lily in her breast, maybe a little yellowed along its pure white petals, my soul was the black dirt at the lily's root. I burned and froze at the same time whenever I considered what I would have to tell in order to cleanse it. Nevertheless, I went to confession with Junie. I told the priest, and we picked a benign one, every evil thought, word and deed I could think of, except one.

"Ah!" Junie breathed deeply as we came out into the Saturday afternoon, "don't you feel clean?"

"Yeah!" I lied, oops, that was another sin. No matter, I was sorry, and I'd say another Hail Mary, no, an Our Father, since I liked that prayer less.

I gulped down the Host the next day and begged God's forgiveness, hoping I wasn't committing a mortal sin that would result in excommunication. I half-expected God to sear His image on my tongue.

"Oh, Gloria! I feel so good!" Junie gushed.

I felt dirty. And small. And fat, though I no longer was.

And guilty.

I couldn't sleep. I fell asleep because I was tired, but woke up terrified and terrified of being terrified. My heart pounded at the thought of being guilty. My hands started to sweat. All day long, my palms sweat. Things slid out of my grip on the Biblical flood in my palms. I panicked every moment of the day and night.

The sight of Daddy getting up in his old plaid pajamas terrified me, the crumpled faded fabric of his pajamas! The way it was limp and frayed with wear! The flannel hung thinly, the navy blue piping worn through to its white underside! He yawned, showing his gold teeth, toothless pink gums. His grey stubble that I'd felt in the folds of my vagina, there! His tongue stretched and yawned! Oh, God! If only I could throw up! Then all the sins would pour out of me! The shuffle of his bare feet, hard and dry with dead skin: brush, brush on the floor. He shuffled over to the refrigerator and got the milk out and poured it with one hand. It spilled over the glass, on to the counter. Toothless, he drank milk. Spreading his upper lip over the rim, protruding his lower lip to grip the glass, he drank.

I wanted to die! Why couldn't I just die?

Days of this horror went by, everything familiar, Marie's musical giggle, the way Ma snapped the newspaper or lifted her cigarette to her mouth, Jakey's evil sneer as though the devil himself had caught me, made my heart pound with terror, filled me with guilt, till, I reasoned, what could be worse than this? I decided to tell the priest.

## FORGIVE ME, FATHER, DON'T HELP ME

I was sure I'd chosen the right priest. Portly, kindly Father Dominic. He was soothing. He was gentle. He would be gentle and soothing to me. Shaking and tortured, I slid along the pew, suffering the murmurs of other people's sins until it was my turn. I found myself in the dark confessional, under the wine velvet curtain, closed silently as angels' wings behind me. I faced the dark grid.

"Forgive me, Father, for I have sinned. It has been one week since my last confession.

I yelled at my sister. I told three lies." Here, I braced myself with the euphemism I'd rehearsed. "I did dirty things."

"With whom, dear, did you do these things?"

Earth disappeared from under me and I was sucked into outer space, gasping for air.

"With my father," I replied, weakly, with no strength left to lie. Lying in confession would get you excommunicated in the eyes of God. I couldn't struggle any more.

There was a silence. Then,

"Do you want me to help you, child?"

"Yes, Father."

What else could I say? God, no, Father! Don't help me! I don't want you to help me! What about Ma? He'd tell Ma! She'd kill herself! She'd hate me forever! What would I do without Ma's love? And they'd take me away and put me in a home like the one Daddy cried about, like the Shinbuck house with no roof! I screamed silently on the inside while fat, kindly Father Dominic gave me a gentle penance and a kindly absolution.

How could he help me? He couldn't! The damage was done and now he was going to do more!

Nevertheless, I fell down on my knees before God on His altar and said my meager penance. Then, I went outside and stood by the door to wait for the priest.

Every Catholic I knew and some I didn't know paraded in and out of the church door. Boys and girls from school. Denise Pettillo came by; she would never be in my situation. She wore the tiniest white mantilla pinned atop her perfect bouffant flip; she could sew as straight a seam as Mrs. White, so serenely, so painstakingly slowly did her cloth travel through her presser foot. Statuesque as statue of the Virgin Mary, Denise resembled Uncle Salvi's bleached blonde, sainted wife Dolores, who also would not be in this situation since her brother was a priest.

"Are you waiting for someone?" she asked me on her way in. "Are you *still* waiting?" she asked me, sweetly, on her way out.

"Yeah," I nodded, waiting for someone, that's what I'm doing.

That's what normal people would be doing waiting by the church door. Beautiful, precious, normal, white people.

I waited through all the looks and chuckles that I was still there. All the questions, actually the same question, over and over, "You still here?" "Yeah," I said, ha, ha. I became acquainted with every cigarette butt, coffee stain, glass shard, pebble, candy wrapper and wad of gum on the sidewalk.

The priest never came. I opened the door and ventured into the hush of incense and caramel wood, my mouth dry, my heart pounding the tears back. The empty pews sat straight backed as the ghosts of worshippers. No one was there. I breathed a quivering, anxious sigh of relief. I was safe. Uneasily, I realized, I had done it. I'd cleansed myself.


THE FIRST SHOT

My best friend didn't know me. That's all I could think of. I'd escaped the priest, but the thought that Junie didn't really know me, and if she did, she'd hate me, this thought wouldn't go away. If Junie were the kind of person to cleanse her soul, what would she want with a friend like me? I no longer cared about the priest. I only cared about Junie.

Junie had given real meaning to the words, "best friend." Her brilliant light was enough to make me worship her. The white sun blazed from her head, the clear blue sky was caught in her eyes. The fact that this angel needed me broke my heart, that she needed my physical presence by her side in order to stand up at all - that hurt. I would have been her monkey.

I paced back and forth in my room, already dressed for bed, Noxema on my face. I thought about what I'd be giving up. All our walks down the Ave came to mind, our talks on the guardrail and in her room. Sleeping beside her, me, sweaty and grubby, she fresh and rosy. And the time she slept over my house and we were brushing our teeth at the bathroom sink when tiny white spiders started to descend over our bent heads.

"What was that?"

"What?"

"I thought I felt something!"

"Oh, my God! Spiders! They're so little! You can barely see them!"

"They're white! I didn't know there were white spiders!"

"Look!" Our heads bent back, our frothy mouths open foolishly, "There's more!"

Millions of white spiders were parachuting down. I expected the big Mama to come down after them, fat and furious, ready to kill.

"Do something!"

"What? We can't smash them all!"

"This calls for technology!"

"What?"

"The vacuum cleaner!"

It worked magnificently.

"Wow!" admired Junie.

Of course, the vacuum cleaner also brought Rosa.

"What the hell are you doing? It's one o'clock in the morning!" she yelled.

Junie standing there in her baby dolls, frail and white. Me, vacuuming the bathroom ceiling.

When I thought of these things in bright flashes of memory, the blood rushed through my veins, warm and full of love. She was everything good in my life, everything light and clean. When I looked at her, I was so full of gratitude and warmth and wonder, I could burst, truly as though a sun were inside me.

I thought of losing that feeling forever, and all of a sudden, it didn't matter what I had to suffer. I had to tell her. That was a real friendship. She had to know. It was late, but it had to be right then.

Hurriedly, I washed the Noxema from my face and shaking violently, threw on the emergency outfit of dungarees and pajama top. Once again, I rushed out into the darkness, determined to tell Junie who I was, even if I lost everything good in my life.


She looked so fragile and childlike, rubbing her eyes with her knuckles, when she came to the window.

"Ria, what is it?"

Tears covered my face. The lights on the highway had streaked and danced before my eyes as I had run toward the nightmare I was about to create.

My voice sobbed, "June," though I hardly ever called her that, but that's all that would come out.

She looked quickly behind her. For Agnes, no doubt.

"I'll be right out."

I stepped back and waited for her. "God, God, God," I thought. "God."

The Princess curtains swished. She was climbing through, a jacket over her pajamas, unlaced sneakers on her feet.

"What is it?"

Her eyes were squinty, she yawned, big and innocent. She threw her arms around me, like this was going to be an ordinary crisis.

I backed away.

"You may not want to touch me after I tell you," I said.

"Why?" she yawned. "Did you kill somebody?"

I just stared at her.

She laughed a little.

"Who'd you kill?"

"No one. But, I think I should."

"Who?"

My face went icy.

"My f-father."

She just stared a minute. Probably, she understood how someone could want to do that. She was thinking about herself then, I knew it.

"How come? What'd he do?" she asked, absolutely serious.

I loved her so much. I think I was trying to direct all the love I had for her, into her, in that moment before I spoke.

"He's been, Junie," I broke down, sobbing, "you'll hate me," I sobbed, losing courage.

"No, I won't," she declared, holding me with one arm, leading me up the hill. "Let's sit down, let's go up the hill and sit down."

She walked me up the hill to the Brothers' house where twin brothers lived together. They were sweet as circus clowns, always giving Junie and her brothers too-colorful sweaters from the sweater factory they owned. The Brothers' house was friendly territory.

"Sit here," she put me gently beside her on the ice-cold curb, reeking of rotting tree berries and gasoline. "Tell me," she said. "What did he do?"

Looking into her sleepy, troubled eyes, I loved her so much, I handed her my life and let her decide.

"He's been having sex with me," I told her.

On her sweet face, her bottom lip quivered and her eyes instantly submerged in tears.

"Ri, has he -?"

"No, I don't know what's going on, he does all kinds of things to me, but he h-hasn't done th-that yet. I g-guess I'm lucky."

Heaving with sobs, I buried my face in my knees, which trembled and knocked numbly against my forehead.

"Ria," her thin arm tightened around me and I thanked God. I prayed gratefully in my soul, the way I did everyday when I turned and saw her walking next to me, carrying the sun inside her.

"It's okay," she told me. "It's okay."

Her own face was stiff with fury.

"How long has he done this to you?"

"I-I've counted so m-many times, since my mother went to work, I can't b-believe it every time I count."

"How old were you?"

"Eleven!"

Eleven sounded much too young, much too soon, much too horrifying.

I know what Junie was thinking, what she had been doing at eleven.

We sat in a shivering silence, the cold stone eating through my pajamas.

"Do you hate me?" I asked, at last.

Incredulously, she whipped her head around, "No! Never!"

"I actually liked your father. He's so funny."

"Everyone thinks he's funny."

"I love the way he says that thing to your mother when he wants money. 'Shoot the money to me, honey.'"

"Hang the paper on me, draper.'"

"I suppose, I should hate him," she said.

"I hate him!" I cried without thinking. "If I were brave, I'd kill him, or at least run away. But, I'm not brave."

Then, Junie gave me the greatest gift anyone ever could. She gave me a view from a mountaintop. She gave me solace.

Very softly, she said, "I think you're brave. I think you're very brave."

I couldn't be happy with solace; however, I had to try to tear myself down in front of her. I told her how I sometimes enjoyed the things Daddy did to me, how I wanted him to when he wasn't there, how it was different than I'd imagined when he was.

Again, she said something incredible.

She said, "We're supposed to like it. God wants us to like it."

"How do you know? Did the nuns tell you?"

She laughed, "No, I just know. He wouldn't have made sex so nice if we weren't supposed to like it."

I told her about Dorothy and Rick Likus and about Richie Silva, how much he meant to me.

I watched her face flashing white with each passing headlight then burning red as taillights went by. I watched for signs of revulsion, but all I saw was - serenity. The more I unloaded my burden on her, the lighter hers became.

"Bonnie and I," she said, plainly and simply, "used to suck on each other's breasts." she smiled, "We used to say it was so relaxing."

I was the one who was shocked.

"Does everybody do that?" I asked.

"I don't know."

All this time, her arm held me. She never let go.

"Once, I was standing next to my Uncle Bob," she began in a strangled voice, "I don't know why, but we were standing in the kitchen looking out the back door at the highway. He took my hand and put it down the front of his pants. I was about six. I don't know why he did that."

White people, too! Beautiful, rich white people, too! My beautiful, rich white hope cracked in my chest. There was nowhere safe to go.

"My brother, Jack says - and don't tell anyone I told you this - some of the priests at his school have sex with the boys."

"What! Priests! They have a vow of chastity!"

My hope was fast drying up. Strangely, a feeling almost of relief crept in: if there wasn't hope, then I wasn't so bad off.

"It's true. Jack knows someone who did it."

"Why would a priest do that? And - what is it? How do two males have sex together?"

She shrugged.

"I don't know. Jack says 'up their ass,' but I don't believe it."

We were silent. This information was the kind that had to be put away for the future.

"When we were cleaning our souls," I told her, "I told the priest in confession."

She was aghast.

"You're kidding! What did he say?"

"He told me to wait outside for him, that he'd help me. I was terrified they'd send Daddy to jail and me to someplace like the Shinbuck house."

The Shinbuck's stood right in front of us at that very moment, spectral and rotted, wooden shards and tree tops reached for children in the cloudy night sky that could be seen through the hole in the roof.

"No! Man, what did you do?"

"I waited, but he didn't come."

"Which door?"

"The one by Tony Roma's."

"How come you didn't go to the one by the rectory?"

"No way I was going to that one! That's the parking lot! Anybody could've seen me! The Krausses or the Likuses for cryin' out loud!"

She nodded.

"Jeez, Ri, you were so lucky he didn't show up. Your mother! My God!"

"I know, I know!" I started crying again. "That's all I think about is my mother! I wish I'd thought about her right away, but I didn't know what was happening. I didn't even know what sex was! I kept thinking that's where you go pee-pee!"

"Jeez."

"Maybe we should take some kind of class in 'What Can Happen,' you know, some kind of basic training."

"And," I continued, "I think a girl should get five shots, five legal shots at birth. She should get five pink bullets and a pink gun, numbered like a social security number, handed to her on her tenth, or maybe her eighth, birthday. If anyone bothers her, she has the legal right to shoot, but she has to decide, whether to use the bullets up or not. After her fifth shot, it would be murder. But, you see, the beauty of it would be, no one would know how many legal shots she had left! Men would have to be on their best behavior. And" - I added, considering that girls might need to be protected before their eighth birthday – "any woman who has a daughter, right in the hospital, she should be given a special mother's gun with an undetermined number of shots, no one knows how many, not even her, to protect her daughter."

Junie laughed, "You're dreamin'!"

"I know, but think how careful men - and boys - would have to be! How - respectful! It would be hilarious to watch them cower!"

We were silent for a minute or two, then I heard myself say, "Johnny Strummer called me up the other night and asked me to go for a ride with him."

"No! What did you say?"

"I told him he was married. But - I wouldn't have gone anyway. He means too much to me."

"How much do you mean to *him*?"

"I can't think about that. I need - the idea of him. He's my Johnny Strummer. Everyone needs a Johnny Strummer."

"Yeah. Jack's always been mine."

Junie and I talked about Richie Silva and me, about the myth of us, the story that would probably never unfold, the longing with a street between.

"I'm sorry," she said, "about that night. About acting so stupid, singing that stupid drunken song. I was just so happy to have Bonnie there again."

"I wanted his arms around me," I said.

We talked like that for hours. Finally, we were quiet and sleep began to creep over us again, like children who find themselves forgotten at an adult party, our heads fell on each other's shoulders. The sad Revere sun washed the night into a familiar grey city sky. Instead of the strong arms of men or boys, Junie held her thin, birdlike arms around me. So thin, as Ma had said, like a starving child, but so able to hold all my pain.

For me, the first shot of the sexual revolution was fired that night. But, it was a shot in the dark. It began when kids, like us, embracing on curbstones and in cars and alleys all over the country and the world, decided they were not going to feel guilt or shame over sex, or over something bad done *to them!* It began with telling out loud. It began with Junie's calm, unflinching love: the ability to look our nightmares in the face without fear, the skill of turning our demons into life itself. Soon, it would not be possible for bad people to do bad things in secret. This was the sacred trust of the revolution and it would be the good side of no longer being horrified by evil.

It was the first shot. I had a long war to go.

EAST BOSTON, 1954

When Mama opened the door and looked into the room, she screamed.
    Her life was changed forever.
    Daddy and I looked up.
    Daddy laughed.
    "Cut it out, Rosie! She's okay. It doesn't hurt her!"
    Mama cried and ran to pick me up.

## HEART OF DARKNESS

I wasn't finished with guilt or priests.

My hands wouldn't stop sweating. My heart beat loud and sore in my chest. I woke up fine and normal in the morning and, remembering, my heart tore into a frantic rhythm, the sweat burst from my palms like blood from stigmata.

As we walked to school, Junie held my hand, as though she could keep it from sweating. Her dry palm seemed to absorb some of the moisture; her brave touch calmed me.

The kids whistled at us and made kissy noises.

"Get a love seat!" they called.

"What's a love seat?" I asked Junie.

"I don't know. Don't pay any attention to them."

I slid my hand out of hers, so she wouldn't have to suffer, but she snatched it back.

The whistlers went wild.

I couldn't sleep. For long hours, I lay in bed wide-awake, my heart racing in a panic. My body, which seemed separate from me, begged me for rest, while my mind raced. Every night, I went to bed exhausted, looking forward to the clean softness of my cool bed sheets, the floating absolution of sleep, only to fall into a shallow doze and wake as if I'd fallen from an airplane, sweating with emergency, getting up with wet feet on to the cracked and cold linoleum, creaking like a ghost across my own floor, worrying like a spirit lost.

Aunt Lennie and Uncle Gus were living with us because their house had burned down. Ma and Daddy took the opportunity of live-in baby-sitters to go to Florida to visit Aunt Doris where she and her new husband had started a miniature golf course. We kids were left alone with the two skeletal old people sleeping in our parents' bed.

I paced outside their bedroom, terrified of being awake; terrified of saying anything to them, too scared to sleep, scared of not sleeping. The house crept around me with strange familiarity of shapes in the darkness and familiar smells, fierce and terrifying.

I found myself shaking her, "Aunt Lennie! Oh, Aunt Lennie wake up! Wake up! I can't sleep!"

She lay, old and crumpled, on the pillow, grey and still as death.

I shook her and shook her. I whispered as loudly as I dared, "Please, wake up! Please! I can't sleep, Aunt Lennie! I can't sleep!"

Finally, from a far away place, she rolled toward me and groaned, like a corpse in a horror movie.

"Oh, that's too bad, Gloria!"

The everyday objects in my room, the lady whose glowing pink ballgown was a lamp, the chipped bureau stuffed with old clothes, the curtain bedspread, the bedspread curtains, the grimy, crooked blinds, were traitors in their repulsive coziness. Why weren't they agitated, disturbed, vibrating and leaping from their places? I covered my eyes with my hands, I didn't want to see them, but my hands were clammy and I realized, these hands had touched his penis! And I yanked them from my eyes.

But, my hands were a part of me.

I told Junie, "That's what I am, I'm him. I've got him in me!"

"You're not him."

"Yes, I'm part him."

"You've made him better. You've made him good!"

After Ma and Dad got back from Florida, it got worse.

I began to have a re-occurring nightmare in which a monster Daddy was eating me alive from my vagina. He slurped and slurped in the dream and he came up with blood dripping from his grinning mouth.

I became afraid to touch or smell or see anything that was his. The way his Jesus sandals in the hall had once terrorized me, now, anything of his became like a fiend out of a nightmare trying to get me. The work clothes in a heap on the floor, and the empty spot where he'd dropped them after Ma had picked them up. His greasy work shoes, toppled on each other, their long leather shoelaces like greasy black snakes, their toes like mean, scrunched up faces. The smell of dirty soap as he washed at the sink! I was sure the smell itself was a physical thing entering my nostrils, slithering down through my throat to my soul.

One day, for some emergency reason, Ma brought HIS TOWEL INTO MY ROOM, I knew it was his because she touched me with it and it was stiff from not being washed as often as the other towels and I screamed, I screamed and screamed and screamed.

"WHAT'S THE MATTA WITH YOU?" Ma screamed back.

"GET IT OUT OF HERE! GET IT OUT OF MY ROOM!"

I didn't care if she knew; I couldn't let it touch me! I couldn't let it in my room!

"I don't know what's the matter with her!" I heard her yell at Daddy. I heard Daddy mumble something.

It was dangerous to cry like that, but I didn't care, I didn't care.

During the day, bright and relatively safe, Ma sat at the kitchen table and chatted with Annie Likus. I slumped at her crusty feet in their old slippers. *A Separate Peace* was rotting in my hand, the acidy sweat eating through the paper, the words sticking to my skin. I was supposed to be reading it and *The Heart of Darkness*, but I was reading only words, blank words, the way you do when you're reading and you start to think of something else, but continue reading. I would find myself on a page I didn't recognize and have to go back, page after page. Finally, my head just fell on Ma's flowered lap and my eyes closed in a fuzzy, heart pounding haze that was not rest.

"What's the matter with her?" Annie Likus remarked.

Ma shrugged and stroked my hair. She smiled wistfully as though she was glad to have me at her feet again, worshipping her.

I wanted to be her little girl again. I remembered the little girl I used to be running and running in Aunt Doris's huge yard in Arlington because I thought it was the country. When I thought of that little girl running in Arlington, I wanted to jump out in front of her and grab her and run away with her to keep her safe.

Ma had the kitchen table tucked into a niche she called her breakfast nook. We had to slide along wooden picnic benches to sit at the same old Formica table with the pattern of wood. It was all the rage, the breakfast nook. Uncle Vickie took his girlfriend, Kandy Kane to see us; they sat across from me and Ma at the breakfast nook. Developed as I was, I couldn't remove my eyes from Kandy's frighteningly enormous breasts. Her fat cleavage was almost as long as my arm. Uncle Vickie puffed on his cigar with pride. When she spoke, Kandy tossed her red and white plastic earrings and bounced them off her neck. She said she always wore red and white to go with her name. "It's my real name!" Kandy repeated twice, smiling broadly. She had the kind of thick lips that left red lipstick on her front teeth.


The day was stormy, a Saturday, one of those days you can't remember which season it was, autumn or spring. Since the cleansing of the souls, sins had been cropping up like snowdrops, coming up through the muck with the carcasses of dead leaves strung over their heads like tarnished necklaces. The sin of masturbation had reared its head - if it was a sin, no one had ever mentioned it, but, of course, it must be. Once I'd begun to clean my soul, new sins appeared where I thought the ground had been raked free.

I had to confess. I had to tell Ma something. I needed to hear what she thought of at least one of my demons.

Upstairs, I lay on my bed, meditating on the broken plaster shapes on the ceiling, they were like living friends to me: the Lamb of God, "Who takes away the sins of the world, hear my prayer," the lamb's gentle head somewhat swollen now. In the flaking ceiling, I saw a bird with deformed wings and an elephant with a lumpy trunk. My heart beat everywhere in my body at once, in my weak arms and legs, in my temples, my ears, in my feet

I knew were going to carry me to torment myself further. I deeply wanted to speak to a priest.

Ma called me down for lunch. A hot bowl of pastina and eggs was steaming on the table. I slid along the bench.

The pasta was shiny and golden, glistening in its broth. Curls of egg cooked on top. I didn't deserve it. I had to tell her. I know it was suicidal, but, really, I had to get it out.

"Ma," I asked, "have you ever heard the word, masturbation?"

The atmosphere suddenly became hot and charged enough to cook eggs.

"Where did you hear that?" she spoke softly, astonished, from where she stood, her back to me, at the sink.

"I don't know. I read it somewhere. Did you ever hear of it?"

"Yeah, I heard of it," she said, disgusted.

"I've - been doing that."

"WHERE THE HELL DID YOU LEARN HOW TO DO THAT?"

I wanted to scream: "FROM DADDY! FROM DADDY!"

I'd wanted her to comfort me and cover me entirely in her soft arms. I wanted her to take all my shame away, but she gave me more.

"I never did anything like that! I don't even care for marital relations! Never mind wanting more!"

"I have to see the priest," I said, poking at my soup.

"Eat your soup before it gets cold. What do you mean you have to see the priest? You always go to confession!"

I took one guilty gulp that went up instead of down.

"No." That wasn't enough punishment. "I have to see him face to face."

"Jesus Christ! You're crazy! Thank God I'm not like you, thank God!"

No, she would never put a curler up inside herself to see what it felt like. She would never put a kitten to her breast to see if it would suck. I had done these things. The guilt was so intense; I wanted to run screaming out of my body down Hichborn Street.

Instead, I gulped down what soup I could and dressed myself in a skirt and blouse, properly to see a priest.

The walk down, as familiar as my own house, so familiar, it was hard for me to understand that I was no longer home. The walk to church, the same walk to school, to the library, or the movies, seemed an extension of home, another part of myself, though it was a long straight white path through the territory of the whitest people, sometimes enemy territory, and carried with it, on my back, emotions as different as horror and love.

I rang the doorbell to the rectory. The fear of who would answer the door was part of my private penance. I expected a priest or a nun or a prim lady in a grey maid's uniform. However, a chubby, jolly-faced Irish grandmother opened the door. She wore a blue old lady's dress and a yellow sweater pinned to her old neck with a large black crucifix. I wondered if they made her wear the crucifix to show she worked there.

When I told her why I was there - to see a priest - she looked baffled as though no one had ever come to the door with that request before. I was left to wait in the hallway where I studied the dark wooden beams crisscrossing the creamy ceiling.

Father Corro came running down the corridor, leaning forward, puffing as he ran, a fat cigar clenched in his teeth. He looked so much like Groucho Marx racing toward me dressed like a priest in black shirt and pants with that little white square at his throat, I almost laughed.

"Is there a death?" he exclaimed. "Why'd they send *you?*"

He didn't recognize me or anything personal like that. He meant that I was a girl.

"There's no death, Father," I answered. Not yet, I thought. "It's me. I need to see a priest."

He deflated fast. It wasn't to be the importance of Extreme Unction. He probably thought I was pregnant. He looked annoyed. He gestured vaguely toward his office and told me to wait.

I found it by the sound of a portable television set blasting a basketball game from behind the desk.

I waited forever, watching the men jump up and down at the net.

"What's the score?" he asked me as he hurried in.

"I don't know, Father."

He looked annoyed again. He turned the sound down, just a bit. Frowning, he asked the television what the trouble was.

I spoke to his right ear, hairy and dotted with black heads. I told his ear that I suffered from the sin of masturbation. I was very well-spoken and rehearsed. I told his ear that, spiritually, I was in a great deal of pain.

It took him a minute. His right ear translated what I'd said to his brain. He mumbled something about the play on the screen as he turned my way and said, pushing his glasses back on his nose, "You know, ah, you shouldn't do that because - ah - jeez, look at that! – it interferes with your need for your partner in marriage."

"Yes, Father."

"Is there anything else?" he asked the basketball game.

"No, Father."

I was led out by Father Corro himself during a commercial. He neatly threw me out the door with one wave of his hand and went off down the hall.

As I walked home, still shaky from actually being alone in the same room with a priest, I reasoned that if Father Corro could be so blasé, maybe it wasn't so serious after all. I thought of Happy Jack and wished I could be more like him.

The second I got home, Ma was vacuuming and she snapped at me accusingly over the whine of the machine, "So! You feel better now?"

Instantly, the guilt, which had been quieted by the nonchalance of the cigar and the basketball game, shot straight up from hell searing my legs, burning past my stomach, to my brain where it paralyzed my thoughts. The guilt, the panic, was becoming more of an entity than the sin itself. Sin was no longer a blot like they taught us in Sunday School. It was an acid eating away at the organs and the spirit.

# Book Five

## Outlaw

Revere

1967-1969

A SEPARATE PEACE

I left a lot of sweaty palm prints on the desks at school, especially the black enamel tables in biology lab, and my heart still pounded like I was running for my life. No one could help me. Not Junie, not the priest, not God. I began to think about Judas. I wondered why he had been chosen by God. Jesus had known Judas was going to betray him - he said so, but he let it happen anyway. Someone had to do it. It was an odd position to be in, that of a chosen sinner.

Oddly, the dummy class led to my salvation. How I wound up in the dummy class was a classic in Revere government thinking. As a member of the Accelerated Class, I wasn't allowed to take Art. I had to take some kind of History Class. However, they told me if I could get into an Art class, I could take it, but, they said, all the Art classes were full.

Again, I dressed myself properly and rehearsed my lines. I went up to the top floor of the High School to see the Art teacher, a plump, pretty woman of about thirty-five with thick black hair and large, expressive eyes to rival a movie star's. For a few moments, we both enjoyed perfect grammar and kindred spirits. I don't recall her name. I'll call her Miss Still Life.

"Miss Still Life, may I speak with you?"

"Surely," she replied. While we spoke, she worked straightening the chairs. There seemed to be a thousand of them crammed into the large studio room. All the dummy classes were huge.

"There aren't enough chairs," she said to my request. "Art is a very popular course. Every chair you see here is filled. They think it's going to be an easy A."

"I want to learn how to paint. I've been drawing and painting, but there's a lot I don't know. You can teach me."

"Yes," she said, looking up from her task. "But, I can't."

"What about after school?"

She was shaking her head.

"I'm not allowed to do that. You're not my student. I'm very sorry."

They put me in Current Events down in the basement with the dregs. All the teachers in the basement were ex-Marines. On this particular day, we were told to write essays anonymously on some incredibly eventful current event. Too bad for me, Shakespeare had rubbed off on me and somewhere in my essay was the phrase "the stuff that men are made of."

In order to amuse the rowdies and keep them in line, the teacher, a fairly young ex-Marine, read the essays out loud. He read in a mimicking way just to give the class a cheap laugh. Of course, he chose mine at random. Since the class was so large, he had no idea who anybody was.

I sat lost somewhere in the middle of the huge, constantly moving room, surrounded by squirmy kids who couldn't keep still any more than a pail full of maggots. They picked up their desks like angular shields and swung them along with their hard bulk whenever they laughed or reached to hit each other.

I was still sweating and trembling most of the day. I'd learned to keep my hands off the desk, somebody's fist might come down on them, or, if my knuckles happened to curl over the edge, they could be slammed between moving vehicles.

The teacher read the essays derisively while the kids laughed and whacked each other with the furniture.

"The stuff that men are made of?"

He winced as though there was a bad smell in the room.

Then, he turned around, and seeing a rusty drip splashing down from one of the exposed pipes hanging from the ceiling, he held out my essay. The water hit the paper with an audible plop. The dummies went insane. They banged the desks in celebration, they stomped each other, they screamed and karate chopped their friends. It was the best thing that could happen, learning directly from the teacher that nothing they did made any difference at all.

I stood up.

"I need to go to the nurse," I said.

The teacher looked at me. "Did you write this?" he asked.

Everyone laughed and barked and mooed.

"No." I felt like St. Peter must have after the first cock had crowed.

"Oh, I thought that's why you were sick."

To a huge crash of wood and chrome, someone actually fell over laughing, desk and all.

He wrote a permission slip for me and I made my way past the moving desks out into the hall.

I was stopped right away, because the basement halls were run like the Marine Corp.

"HALT!" echoed down the dark, empty corridor. "WHO GOES THERE?"

It was the assistant principal, Mr. Dokes. He always looked like he was running for office, slicked up slim in a suit that fit him snugly in a handsome bulldog sort of way.

"YOU HAVE A PASS?" he boomed.

"Yes."

He held out his tyrannical hand. He judged my scribbled pass and let me go.

I liked him because he was handsome and slender and good at keeping order. It wasn't hard to respect someone in that place who looked nice and was doing a good job. Most of the teachers oozed out of their bulgy clothes in large lumps. Crumbs and ashes sprinkled down their fronts, wrinkles spread across their broad butts, orange pulp hung from their yellow teeth, food stains hung on their chests like medals: all this would have been eccentric or endearing if they'd been *saying or doing something*, but they weren't.

I found the nurse in her little half-room office surrounded by those lovely wooden tongue depressors, red, white and blue Band-Aids and fluffy cotton balls.

She was a neat, trim woman dressed in a spotless white uniform balanced by the tremendous color she had applied to her face: a brilliant turquoise sky upon each lid, a dark road of black tar along her lashes and two soft fuchsia mountains upon her cheeks. Her hair was an unnatural shade of yellow, swept into a dry French twist like a sand castle. She'd eaten off her lipstick: burnt orange remnants clung to the corners of her mouth.

She seemed glad to see me.

"What seems to be the trouble?" she asked me, gently, taking the soggy note from my damp hand.

"I don't feel well."

"Sit down, dear."

Her brow knitted itself in concern as she placed me into a wooden chair made for institutions and she pulled another one up next to me. She seemed to know instinctively that I did not need my temperature taken.

She looked into my face, waiting.

"I have a very big sin," I told her.

Of course, I wasn't talking about masturbation now.

She listened, riveted.

"I've been to confession. I even spoke privately with the priest. But, my hands won't stop sweating and my heart keeps - driving me crazy."

She was another angel, you know, this thickly made-up nurse. She reached out for my hand the second I said it was sweaty and she held it; it gushed into hers.

She listened so clearly, so easily. She understood immediately. I didn't have to explain a thing.

"God forgives you right away," she answered. "But, you have to forgive yourself, dear. Forgive yourself."

Dazed as a newborn, my eyes opened to the light of birth. Of course, I was blinded and startled, but she held a hand down to me and lifted me up. She bathed my head. She washed my eyes. She gave me food. I had to relearn what light and food were. Lost, she placed a compass in my hand. Armed with food and light and compass, the care of an angel nurse and the love of another frightened girl, I began the long climb out. Slowly, in the days and weeks that followed, the sweat receded, slowly, my heart quieted. Slowly, sometimes going wild again, then falling quiet, then wild, then quiet. Slowly, I learned how to eat and sleep and breathe on my own.

I began a new relationship with God, personal and tentative, reverent and terrified. I stopped going to church. I knew God wasn't there the way everyone thought He was. I went to the ocean instead. I let the rhythm of the breaking ocean be the rhythm of my breath and of the beating of my heart. Slate grey, green or blue, I prayed to the sea, which was really God. I prayed for wisdom and courage. I had passion, so I prayed for a steady nerve. I prayed for skill to go along with my talent, and the patience to keep on. I didn't put words to these ideas, only feelings and wishes to God. I sat on the sea wall, while cars beeped and groaned and sometimes pulled in behind my back. Once, a man got out and looked at me, friendly like, but with that determination in his eye that was predatory, until he saw my face, and then he backed away, got into his car and sped off leaving rubber.

There, I asked God a lot of questions, which He did not answer except with beautiful and ugly breaking waves. I apologized for my stupidity.


CHAPEL

Mr. Luke Garante had his back to us as he leaned out the grimy window. The brittle yellow shade hung cock-eyed over his head like a guillotine; the dusty sun streamed through a hole punched in it long ago by a frustrated kid. Revere High School janitors didn't replace shades or wash windows: according to Union rules, they weren't allowed to climb ladders.

Mr. Garante was quiet, like a storm is quiet just before it breaks. He was a big man, tall and wide, with the importance of a giant, large as a hero, clean in his fine blonde crewcut and square jaw. His dream had been to be a baseball pitcher. He'd given up this dream for a good reason, he told us, but he didn't tell us the reason. I didn't know why he taught literature. But, he taught literature as truly as the truest pitch was ever thrown.

Suddenly, he whirled on us, "YELLOW!" he screamed, jolting us out of our seats.

Though we'd expected it, he'd waited till we were daydreaming to continue, his entire six foot four bulk turned on us and bellowed with the amplified voice of God, "is the color of PUTRID PUS, the color of DECAY and HORROR!"

"'A river,'" he quoted, "'amber-tinted in the shadow of its banks, purled at the army's feet...The rushing yellow of the developing day went on behind their backs...A dun-colored cloud of dust...a dead soldier dressed in an awkward suit of yellowish brown.' Which side had the yellow uniforms?"

No one answered him.

"The Civil War!" he cried, "Which side wore yellow? Mike?"

I loved it when Mr. Garante called the shy, enormously fat and uncomfortable Michael Weinstein, "Mike" as if he were a manly pal or a fleet and nimble athlete on his team.

"Um," Michael Weinstein, smiled and mumbled nervously into the collar of his shiny black suit. He wore an adult man's suit every day, worn to a thin gloss at the knees, elbows and buttocks. "Um," Michael replied, smiling, "Neither side wore yellow."

"THAT'S RIGHT! WHY WAS THE DEAD SOLDIER'S UNIFORM YELLOW?"

"Um, I don't kn-know."

"I just told you!"

"Um, it was, um, dir-ty?"

"Dirty! Yes! And decayed! And putrid!"

Michael's shy face beamed.

"WHAT is the function of the color RED in *The Red Badge of Courage*? Not the badge, name another example and tell me the use of the color red."

No one.

Mr. Garante opened his long arms broadly in supplication. I waited a long time, it seemed, while he paced moodily, the way I'd seen him pace during a basketball game he was coaching.

"Do you people READ the work?"

Cautiously, I raised my hand.

He spun around.

"YES!"

"'The red sun was pasted in the sky like a wafer.' Red is used to show violence."

"YES!" - Then, quietly - "Why is it always *you?*"

I shrugged. It was true. On my essays, Garante would write, "A+, A Pleasure to Read!" He would return the paper folded lengthwise like a submarine sandwich. It wasn't easy, I worked hard, but I was the only nerd in the Accelerated Class who understood literature without help. Michael Weinstein could answer a question about the real uniforms of the Civil War because when he wasn't doing chemistry experiments or scientifically observing the movement of the stars, he happened to be a Civil War fanatic. It was *The Red Badge of Courage* that baffled him.

"'The wounded man,'" quoted Mr. Garante, "'had a shoe full of blood... musketry mingled with red cheers.' Any other examples?"

Nothing.

"How about blue? Green? Any more examples of yellow? You seemed to have that one down. FUSCHIA?" he bellowed.

I was the only one who laughed.

"'He conceived Nature to be a woman with a deep aversion to tragedy...It seemed now that Nature had no ears.' What does the author mean by 'Nature had no ears'?"

I raised my hand.

"NOT YOU!" he yelled, exasperated. "WE KNOW THAT YOU KNOW!"

Neil Simpson raised his hand. He was the alien with the pointed head who devoured science fiction at the rate of a book a day and, who, I always believed, also always knew the answers.

"Finally!" Garante praised God.

"'Nature had no ears' refers to the noise of battle blocking out all natural sounds," Simpson said. "Do you still want examples of fuchsia? I think my mother just bought some fuchsia shoes."

Everyone, including Garante, laughed. Simpson was one of those geniuses who could make the teacher laugh.

"Blue!" Garante boomed in his more normal tone.

"'The sky overhead was of a fairy blue.' What? Peaceful? Happy?"

Nothing.

"What does a blue sky mean to *you?*"

No one responded. I wondered if I was still exiled from answering.

"All right, how about this: 'The corpse was dressed in a uniform that had once been blue, but was now faded to a melancholy shade of green.'"

Simpson grinned to himself. He often did that.

Everyone else looked down at their books or blankly up at Mr. Garante who sighed deeply. I raised my hand, tentatively.

"All right!"

"Well, some pus is green, and the uniform had suffered war, it was wounded."

"YES!" screamed Garante. "GREEN IS A PUTRID WOUND!"

Then, in a quiet, solemn voice, as though imparting a great secret, he read to us the description of the youth's discovery of the corpse.

"'At length he reached a place where the high, arching boughs made a chapel. He softly pushed the green doors aside and entered.' ("Note how the use of green changes here - but keep in mind the greater issue," Garante said, aside.) 'Pine needles were a gentle brown carpet. There was a religious half-light.

Near the threshold, he stopped, horror-stricken at the sight of a thing.

He was being looked at by a dead man who was seated with his back against a column like tree. The corpse was dressed in a uniform that once had been blue, but was now faded to a melancholy shade of green. The eyes, staring at the youth, had changed to the dull hue to be seen on the side of a dead fish. The mouth was open. Its red had changed to an appalling yellow. Over the gray skin of the face ran little ants. One was trundling some sort of bundle along the upper lip.'"

The kids gawked at Garante like he was a madman. Obviously, they hadn't read the assignment; they usually didn't. I also gaped at him.

I felt I was hearing the piece for the first time. The sound of him, his deep, resonating voice, was the dappled sunlight on green boughs, the religious half-light added to the words themselves. As he softly lifted the green doors with his tremendous voice, I looked in, shocked, to see my Indian Camp instead of the chapel in the woods of war. Aching for my Indian Camp, lonely as a soldier, following Henry Fleming running aimlessly away and aimlessly toward the field of battle, my eyes stung with tears from the emotions being born from Garante's expressive voice; I realized there was a corpse in my Indian Camp and I longed for the days it had been clean.

"Why was the corpse in the chapel?" Garante asked us.

Nothing. Not even me this time.

"Let me give you a hint," he gave in, "IS ANYTHING SACRED? Weinstein?"

"Huh? Um, no?"

Garante chuckled.

"Here's something interesting."

He read, " 'The squirrel, immediately recognizing danger, had taken to his legs without ado. He did not stand stolidly baring his furry belly to the missile, and die with an upward glance at the sympathetic heavens.' What was Nature telling Henry?"

He waited, then after a few minutes of absolute stillness, he screamed, "IT'S OBVIOUS!"

Suddenly, a white light came on in my head - *I had stood still baring my belly to the onslaught and always would! Should I run away? Should I now? Why did I believe in staying when Henry had run away?"*

"You might as well answer," Garante slapped his book against my desk.

I found my lips were trembling and tears blinded me, but Garante was pacing, he didn't see. It was as if we had this magnet and metal relationship; he paced and I spoke, pulling and building the meaning of the words.

"That he was right, that it was Nature's law to run."

"NATURE'S LAW! Thank you!" He turned to me, questioningly, as though he had noticed something on my face, then he went on: "Is it against Nature to go to war? Or is it natural? Was Henry cor-rect?"

Donna Pagano, the shyest of the shy, half raised her pale hand, "It's natural to go to war - for man."

"For man! Exactly!"

The bell rang.

"Why did Henry run and why did he return to the battle? Tomorrow!" Garante yelled over the bustle of our bodies leaving.

I had to hurry to my next class. I put away with my book, the question of running or staying to fight. For me, there was no question.


FRUIT

I read all of Crane. As always, if I liked the work we read in class, I read all of that writer's work. Now, I also read all of the literary criticisms I could find and familiarized myself with all of the associated artwork of the artist's friends. As for Oscar Wilde, Garante only showed us *The Importance of Being Ernest*, but I went beyond that. I found all the rest of Wilde. I found *The Picture of Dorian Gray*. I found *Salomé*. In *Salomé*, I found myself, and from *Salomé*, I discovered the drawings of Aubrey Beardsley.

I went to the impoverished Revere Public Library, where the ceiling now leaked over the dusty books in rivulets of rusty red. There, I found a book that should have been banned, and would have been except that it was written in a language no one knew. It had fallen through the cracks into the well of secrecy. Certain works are so pure; they communicate to so few, they can become forgotten. Occasionally, a pilgrim will unearth them.

I unearthed and opened Beardsley in my room.

There, I found my freedom. The voluptuous figures were clothed and naked at the same time. The distorted faces of old men and old women, the distorted face of beauty. Dwarfs, that should have been ugly, as well as the deformed fetuses of incest, saved from ugliness by the tender skin of the line itself.

The licentious eyes of Herod saved from hideousness by familiarity. I had seen his eyes. Herod's eyes, terrible and beautiful, had looked at me, Salomé, saved from ugliness by the heartrending sweetness of her line.

The shock of enormous sex organs exposed. The fleshy figures pranced naked and clothed at the same time. Of course the sex organs were exposed. Didn't men go about with their penises towering over their own faces?

*Lysistrata*, the heavy thighs of women were Ma's thighs as she bent in the bathroom, as she stood in the shadows of her bedroom, as she struggled out of the rubbery confines of her girdle after work on hot summer days. The schoolgirl hair of the young one, Marie, Marie, Dorothy, Marie, reaching for the dark curls of another's sex.

*Lysistrata, The Adoration of the Penis*, this was the position in which men dreamed of us kneeling; the heavy balls on her shoulders, the massive erection in her hands, her frilly schoolgirl stockings, her pigtails. The fuzzy lines under the very bottom of her rump. I could smell this drawing. It smelled of baby powder and acid, the pungency where legs meet the sex like armpits.

*Lysistrata, Cinesias Soliciting Myrrhina*, the deformed old man, his robe in disarray, in pursuit, pulling at her garments, grasping for her lithe body, familiar, familiar, the old man, I could hear him begging her with his craggy voice, "Kiss it! Kiss it!"

*Lysistrata, The Toilet of Lampito*, the imp pats a powderpuff to her big ass while he masturbates his penis bigger than himself.

*Lysistrata, Defending the Acropolis*, women farting to disperse the ugly old men. Didn't Ma fart into the face of Richard Nixon to disperse him from the election?

*The Examination of the Herald*, the power of the corruption of old men, the old man with his withered penis admiring up close the massive erection of the youthful herald: the victimization of youth, the power of the victim, the power of sweet, fruity flesh over the withered pervert.

The voluptuousness of the figures luxuriating, the surprise of bare breasts on clothed women, naked women, clothed women, naked men, the harshness of the severed head, familiar from fairy tales and the Bible, bearing the stamp of truth, the shocking truth of half men half beast, the dark secret of dark, curling hairs, the distortions done with exquisite torture, the curl of the line! Oh, the curl of the line! I could feel it curl inside me there!

*The Ecstasy of St. Rose of Lima*, the sexual intensity of spiritual ecstasy, the sexual intensity of the celibate, never reaching orgasm, holding passion like a breath forever. The celibate as artist, that he was overfull! Self-denial became indulgence, overflowing into ecstasy. The silky pleasure of humbling ourselves, bowing our heads, the supplication of saying "Father" in confession; the ravishment of kneeling at the altar, the indulgent repetition of our penance. The bending back of the head, opening the mouth to receive the Host. The strange, zombie like way the faithful marched across the road after mass, heedless of the oncoming traffic.

Beardsley's dark power overwhelmed me. I was filled with his power, weird, titillating, liberating, strange, familiar, what did I know about these things? I couldn't see them; they were *in* me! How many times did I bring myself to ecstasy holding Beardsley in my hands?

I found comfort there, as I did in all the best literature and art that was banned or shunned. There, I was understood. There, I was made beautiful.

It was Mr. Luke Garante who taught me how to read; I knew the sounds and the syllables, the meanings and the grammar, but he opened my soul to the infinite. With his booming voice, he whispered the truths only the decadent knew, those corrupted with the devil, who ate from the tree willingly because God tempted them. Because God gave them fruit.


BRANDED

I never left Marie alone. Either I was home with her, or Ma was home with her, or she was at Linda's. Jakey didn't count; he was not a protector.

One night I came home to find her crying. Even before I opened the front door, I could hear Marie's sobs, faint and muffled. My heart slammed against my chest. Where was he? Where was she?

Daddy was sitting at the kitchen table, his head bent over a paperback, as though he had nothing to do with anything that was going on: the cigarette and handkerchief, the Q-tip, ashtray, all working as usual.

Now I could tell her sobs were coming from upstairs.

Ma was holding her; they were sitting on Marie's bed.

"What happened?" I asked, my heart hammering away in my chest. Ma's lips went into a nonexistent white line.

"He wanted her to go to the sub shop. She didn't wanna go."

"Oh."

No one had to tell me why Marie didn't want to go to the sub shop. No one had to tell me who had wanted her to go.

"He threw her up against the stove. She burned her hands." Ma's voice cracked and tears dripped from her monstrous eyes magnified behind her glasses.

They showed me the burner prints like stars on Marie's fat palms.

"The men say things to me!" Marie shouted at me, her face blotched with purple blood from hours of crying, her moustache prominent on her pale lip. "They say my 'titties'!" she screamed at me as though I were the one who had taunted her. "They say what they wanna do to my ass!"

I threw my arms around both of them. We all cried, holding each other, my mouth tasting Marie's peculiar, still childish aroma of candy and Ivory Snow, Ma's tobacco and lipstick, our tears falling together.

Bad as it was, I was grateful. I was sorry that Marie had been hurt. I could feel her burns: they felt like ice water in my stomach. I'd failed to keep her completely safe. But, it could have been so much worse.

## THE BITCH GODDESS

When Garante yelled, it was a sublime vacation during which everything bad became good. The worst horrors were transformed there, in his class, by the words as well as the line, a massacre could become Picasso's *Guernica*; a rape could become Faulkner's *Sanctuary*.

"THE BITCH GODDESS!" he hollered, "Lady Brett Ashley, her hair cropped short, like a boy's, 'the long line of her neck showed in the bright light of the flares.' Is she a BITCH? Does she castrate men?"

Thirty-five of us stared at him.

"CIRCE!" he bellowed. "WHO WAS CIRCE?"

"Anyone take Greek mythology here? Last year, down the hall, Miss Delmonico? Like the potatoes?"

The class tittered. What the hell were Delmonico potatoes anyway, I wondered. Every time I saw them advertised in frozen food commercials on TV floating in a soupy white sauce, I thought of Jackie Kennedy: they sounded like something she would eat, gooey and French.

My mind was wandering. Mr. Garante had banned me again from answering. I was tired of being blamed for having the right answer. Circe was a champion of mine and I would have loved to talk about her. Circe, Lady Macbeth, Judith, even poor Tess, any time one of them struck a man, castrated him, turned him to swine, stabbed him, I cheered. Literature was a good place to accomplish the impossible.

"Circe? Miss Wisher."

My hand wasn't up. I hoped my eyes didn't glimmer too much with enjoyment while I described my favorite witch.

"Circe was a sorceress who turned Odysseus' men into swine, only they were still men underneath and knew their fate."

"THEY WERE STILL MEN UNDERNEATH AND KNEW THEIR FATE!" he repeated, pacing, slapping his leg with the book.

I thought the men had always been swine underneath, and men on the outside as a disguise. And I was disappointed in Circe because she'd fallen in love with Odysseus, the only man who could successfully resist her spell. I resented his epic journey, his long dalliances with nymphs, goddesses and princesses while his wife, Penelope waited chastely at home.

I preferred Lady Brett Ashley, a modern witch. Buxom, strong and weak at the same time, smoked and drank to match any man, short hair, clear of encumbrances, every man in love with her, "all her pallbearers were her lovers," what could be better?

"THE BITCH GODDESS!" Garante called out.

Yes, the bitch! The goddess! Three cheers! Long life!

"Why did Brett Ashley turn away from the church door? Why was she unable to enter? What is Hemingway trying to tell us?"

My back went up like a cat's. Did Hemingway think she was the devil because she wouldn't enter church? What a crock! And what was this wimpy church love of Jake's? Brett knew who she was! She didn't need the Catholic Church to tell her or justify her! Someone was answering, who? David Santoro.

"Because Eve was turned away from the Garden of Eden as a temptress."

David! Where did he get that? From catechism?

"TURNED AWAY FROM THE GARDEN AS A TEMPTRESS!" Garante repeated. "So, Lady Brett is a temptress who 'ruins' men. How did she 'ruin' the bullfighter, Romero?"

Wait a minute! Women are considered "temptresses" because the Catholic Church says sex is evil! Sex always belongs to the devil, why is that?

"Miss Wisher?"

Why'd he always call on me?

I looked at him questioningly.

"Romero?" he asked.

"He wanted to change her. To grow her hair out," I said in a daze of fury.

"Yes! He did! Why?"

"To control her."

He looked surprised.

"Not to make her more womanly?"

I was livid. "His idea of womanly. So he could control her."

He nodded, considering this.

"And how did she 'ruin' him?"

"According to Hemingway, because she distracted him from the purity of his bullfighting. He was supposed to be - like a priest."

That was bullshit, no pun intended. Priest weren't much like priests.

"Like a priest! Excellent! And - you don't think she was a temptress?" he added, concerned.

"She was beautiful. He was attracted to her. She went out of her way to encourage him," I admitted. "She didn't understand about the bullfighting.

Or she didn't care. She needed to seduce him because of the pain she felt about Jake."

"She wasn't 'aficionado'?" Garante turned to the class. "Mike?"

"I - I was h-hoping to ask y-you what th-th-that was." Michael replied.

Everyone laughed.

I didn't care if she wasn't aficionado about the bulls. Maybe she knew some things aficionados didn't know. After all, Eve was the first to eat from the Tree of the Knowledge of Good and Evil. It was the Devil who understood her, God's favorite angel, whose great sin was: "I will not serve man." Satan, the first artist, the one who questioned, the one *God made to question!* Why were artists compelled to explore and then blamed for it?

I didn't believe in the Garden of Eden. Right there, sitting in class, burning at the idea of Lady Brett Ashley's not being allowed by Hemingway to enter the church, I suddenly became aware that the Garden of Eden was just men's fear of women! Deep down, I could feel it was rooted in the terrific fear men had of the power women had over them. *We made them have an erection!* They had no control over their own erection – the most important part of their manhood! The thing of which they were most proud: their greatest achievement. Man's terror of her: fragrant, soft, round, deep, wet, warm. The lovely wet wrapping him, over and over, compelling him, dominating him: the orgasm during which he was temporarily dead. The fact that they needed us, they needed us beyond control and beyond belief! Women bore all the children! Women were the only way he could have his children. God had given women all the power! Ask me now, Garante! Ask me now!

I could see the Cardinals, 400 years after the death of Jesus, corrupting His message of love, dressed in their deep scarlet robes, sipping wine, eating savories and sweetmeats, sitting round a shiny mahogany table writing the Bible, writing the story of stories that would destroy women forever. Congratulating themselves on keeping their evil seductresses from salvation.

Ha! How little they knew about salvation!


ON THE SURFACE

When the art teacher, Miss Still Life told me there weren't enough chairs, Junie had counseled me, saying, "Don't worry, you won't stop."

She was right. Mr. Garante was head of the Drama Club as well as being basketball coach and baseball coach. Soon, I found myself working right along side Miss Still Life and the two best students in her class painting a trompe d'oleil bridge and garden for Thorton Wilder's *Our Town*. She showed me how to handle the paint properly; she gave me insights on what was happening on the movable plywood walls when I applied my brush to their surface, how the walls would be viewed from the audience and the special adjustments I needed to make in my drawings. When Mr. Garante found out I knew all the actors' parts, he made me the unofficial understudy, but no one got sick or had an accident. The play was wonderful, but only the relatives of the cast came to see it. Junie came with Marie. Ma was working and Daddy stayed home.

When I told Junie how Father Corro had just watched TV while I confessed, she'd said, "So, Ri, no sweat, right?"

About the school nurse, Junie had scolded me. "I don't see what you have to forgive yourself for." This made my heart race. I actually felt guilty about feeling guilty, but it didn't last.

About not going to church any more, we had lots of wrangles. Junie demanded that as her friend I should go with her. I said I would never go again, not even to be married. I told her I'd have to be married at the sacred ocean.

Since high school started, I've told you what was happening under the surface of our lives.

When you look at a fifteen or sixteen year old girl, don't think her life is as simple and charming as it appears, don't long for the innocence of being young again. You may see her giggling with friends, munching on chips, sucking a straw, brushing her hair, checking her makeup, but it's all just the finest veneer she puts on like a cheerful chaddur.

You know what was happening under our lives, now I'll tell you what was happening on top: the normal part everyone could see.

We weren't at the high school a month before Will Cullen appeared at Junie's locker. His dark blue eyes nuzzled hers from under thick, dark brows, incongruous over the innocence of his freckled nose. The first thing he said to her, noticing the copy of *Jude the Obscure* she carried slantwise on top of her pile of books, "Would you kill your children to save them from life?"

He smiled in a friendly way.

Junie and I, who didn't necessarily want children, but would never *kill them*, smiled back. Right away, we knew he was incredibly interesting and good-looking. Then, he said, "I've been wondering for weeks who was on the intelligent end of those gorgeous legs." He didn't mean me. He fixed his penetrating gaze on Junie's delighted expression. We both knew he was going to be entirely unacceptable to Agnes.

He was.

Agnes encouraged Junie to date boys from Our Savior Prep where Jack went to school. Good Catholic boys who came from good (rich) families.

Will's family was poor. It was that simple. To make matters worse, Will was, most of the time, caustic and intense. He would become a serious revolutionary. When we met him, his brown hair was short and neat as a prep school boy's. His cheeks were round and innocent. But, as his politics grew so did his hair; his cheeks became fierce bones. He evolved into a raving, wild-eyed preacher, complete with flowing hair, tattered clothes, bare feet. After a fight with his father over the war in Vietnam, Will lived in his old Buick Special, which he'd named, Roskolnikov, after the murderer in *Crime and Punishment*. He walked the streets of Revere, barefoot, wearing torn dungarees. When Will came to pick up Junie, who'd bathed and dressed so carefully, smelling sweet, wearing a suit her mother had sewn for her, Will wore his dungs with gaping holes and long, white frays drifting about him in a holy mist, his bare feet blackened by miles of sidewalk, his sun-bleached hair curling about his shoulders like a saint's, his eyes burning with political passion, Agnes went nearly insane with pent up, unspoken rage. Junie and I sighed with adoration.

It was ironic that Agnes wanted June to date prep school boys. Jack had introduced her to a few of his friends, and she'd gone out with one or two, but she told me, she would hardly sit in the car before they were on top of her, their thick, heavy thighs nudging open her thin little knees, their slender, well-bred fingers moving fast all over her, their panting mouths drooling into her beautiful mouth.

Meanwhile, Will burned with lust for Junie, whose flat chest had bloomed voluptuously from ice cream and candy bars, the many candy bars she ate instead of her dinner, the real ice cream sundaes we bought from Sunny's Ice Cream truck for twenty-five cents each, freezing one while we ate the other during *Star Trek*, as Captain Kirk gave his speech on the indomitable nature of mankind, we devoured real whipped cream, real ice cream, real hot fudge and a real cherry, in complete agreement with him. I didn't blame Will for aching to touch her sinking, pillowy softness; I also ached to touch her, but I didn't. I could touch her with my eyes easily enough. And Will didn't, not for a long time. Not until she said he could. Once, he even slept next to her, both of them fully clothed, the whole night, he held her chastely in his arms.

Will had an ugly sidekick, Don Don, Donald Donnelly, who looked exactly like Howdy Doody, complete with detachable wooden jaw and circular, painted-on freckles. Despite his looking like a puppet, Don Don was more real than Will, who lived on another plane entirely. Will couldn't relate to life around him, except as life related to civil rights, Vietnam, free love, the plight of the American Indians, nuclear war, the plight of the coal miners, air and water and soil pollution. Junie and I admired Will very much for his political passion, but his righteousness increasingly blocked him from real human contact.

The four of us tooled around in royal blue Roskolnikov which sounded a lot like its name as Will drove down Broadway, *Ros-kol-ni-kov, Ros-kol-ni-kov,* down the Ave, *Ros-kol-ni-kov, Ros-kol-ni-kov,* the fat, old literary motorcar idling at a red light aside a sleek and roaring black Trans Am, licked with golden flames, the rival male threatening, inching, roaring, inching. Will ignored it. A Trans Am wasn't at all revolutionary.

Don Don and I weren't boyfriend and girlfriend, we just sat in the backseat and laughed at everything Will tried to be serious about.

"Black is beautiful," Will commented about civil rights.

"Yeah, sometimes I wish I were black. Black women look so great in scarves," I agreed. "I wish I could wear a scarf like that."

"Why can't you?" Don Don asked.

"I'd look like my grandmother going to sweep her front stairs."

"I love their long earrings," Junie piped in.

"Yeah!"

"Is that all you can talk about are earrings and scarves?" Will scolded.

"Why? Is that prejudiced?" I asked.

"No, that's not prejudiced!" Junie assured me.

"Thank you, June."

"You're welcome."

Will corrected her, "That's a stereotype!"

"It is?" Junie asked.

"Why is that a stereotype?" I demanded.

"Because all black people don't wear scarves and long earrings!"

"So! I never said they did!"

"Look, they just want the same rights we have."

"Which are?"

"The right to go to school, drink out of the same water fountain as whites, sit anywhere you want on the bus, the right to walk into a store or a restaurant and be treated like a human being."

Will gritted his teeth.

Don Don and I bared our teeth to each other. It was funny, because none of us had those rights either. You could barely call Revere High a school. It was practically a do-it-yourself education, the Abe Lincoln method. We couldn't drink out of any public water fountain because garbage floated in the basins. Junie and I had to be real careful where we sat on a bus and which place we walked into. Don Don reached over and tapped Junie who caught on and also bared her teeth. It took Will a minute to notice.

"Oh, funny! Very funny! No, you guys aren't prejudiced!"

"Come on, Will, you've never been down South!" laughed Don Don. He was just happy to be out with us; we were having too much fun to be serious.

"Yeah, but I'm going."

"What?" Junie asked, alarmed.

Will's jaw became rigid with determination; Junie knew he wasn't going anywhere soon. But, he would go. He meant it.

"Will would like nothing better than to disappear into history like those civil rights workers," Don Don told us. We knew it was true. That would be an ideal fate for Will Cullen to be murdered for a cause he believed in.


## MY OUR SAVIOR BOY

June and I were riding the subway into town, two blonde girls sitting straight backed and tense in the furthest corner of the car, occupying the two seats nestled in a niche behind a pole, where no one weird could sit next to us.

At Orient Heights, several hockey players from Our Savior got on, four or five young men, in maroon team jackets, huge boys carrying huge bags that lopped from side to side. Hockey sticks poked the car. Big-footed ice skates swung from their shoulders.

They sat down across from us, their massive legs and swollen feet protruding into the train. They were ominously quiet, staring straight ahead, ignoring us for several minutes. Then, without speaking, one of them took out a pen and began stabbing the perfectly fine red leatherette seat by his side. Without humor or even a sarcastic remark, another of them took out his pen and started jabbing it into another unripped seat. They worked silently and dangerously. Our blonde heads bobbed with each stab of their meaty, red knuckled fists. There was no other communication amongst them. The four other Our Savior boys with them looked on disinterestedly. The boys stabbed with relaxed jaws and absolutely dead eyes.

We didn't dare move.

When they all got off, taking half the bulk of the train with them, yellow seat stuffing powdered the floor like dead butterflies.

Joey was my Our Savior boy.

Jack introduced me to Joey DiPietro in the summer of '67, on Junie's doorstep, around midnight. Junie and I had just returned from a Dave Clark Five concert. Joey had just driven Jack home from a double date.

The Revere night was hot and dirty. Joey and I sat on the concrete step side by side, our knees up to our chests, our thighs almost touching. I was wearing cotton hip huggers with a tiny powder blue print of bluebells, a powder blue poor boy sashed with a white plastic hip belt, which was frayed if you looked too closely. Junie and I had made our bellbottoms especially for the concert. (Agnes had done the actual sewing for Junie.) Hers were tight fitting of bold tropical flowers, which Junie could carry off perfectly. In the Mill Store, she'd sneered at me, "I knew you'd pick that print the second I saw it!" She meant my print was weak and timid. It hurt, but I also knew I would have looked fat, short and ridiculous dressed in the huge red and orange flowers that a tall, thin girl like Junie could carry off with ease.

It had been one of those bright and fierce nights of girlish independence on the dark streets of Boston. Under the black overpass by the Garden masses of sweaty kids in T-shirts and halters thronged shoulder-to-shoulder, making a field of long hair, dungarees and sandals. I'd painted flowers on Junie's bare back and down my arm. We'd combed silver sparkles from the 5&10 through our hair and I'd pasted some on my powder blue eyelids. One of the band had waved to me with his double guitar. I was flying!

Joey wore a white shirt and white chinos. He looked very Carnaby Street with his details of black belt and sleek black shoes. He said he'd seen me there, at Jack's house before, when he'd driven up in his father's long Cadillac, and he'd liked me. How a boy can "like" you from a distance is obvious. I smiled sweetly into his heavy brown eyes, not liquid enough to overpower me like my cousins' who'd stuck pins in my doll, but I was all dreamy from the heady power of an exciting night, the image still clear and empowering of the lead guitarist's double guitar in silhouette backstage as he returned my chance, solitary wave. It was my first concert and Junie and I had spent the entire day crawling over the Sheraton Hotel trying to find them. I was elected to fake an English accent and call the penthouse suite, when suddenly all five of them had burst from the lobby elevator. A sudden rush of bodies and voices, hands signing autographs, hands shoving, beautiful teeth and red lips smiling, slabs of famous dark hair framing famous faces that looked strangely unreal.

I admit Joey DiPietro resembled Davey Jones of the Monkees, with his dewy dark eyes, lovely square jaw and full lips. Joey swept back the dark wing of hair on his forehead with a languid gesture, which I would see a thousand times, strikingly cold and self-assured. He was a graduate of Our Savior, enrolled now in the two-year evening program at Wentworth Business School and during the day, a meat cutter at the new Stop & Shop. Joey would come close to having me, on top of me, on the old couch in the old spare room, both our pants pulled down, our hairs touching – *how did we get that far?* He begged me to let him, let him. I never could. I didn't trust him. He went to business school, he cut meat, and he drove his father's car. He wasn't deep enough or wild or dangerous enough for me to fall in love; his eyes didn't melt me, his eyes held no drumbeat.

Nevertheless, I would have sworn I loved him. He was fun to think about, to get ready for, to sit next to in that wide boat of a car that drifted along the road without touching the surface. He brought me to the Hilltop Steak House on Route 1, which had just opened with its corral of plastic, life-sized black and white cows grazing out front by the rows of dopey, broad-assed people waiting in line to buy meat from the restaurant's butcher shop. Inside, the lights were low for couples; the wood was dark to imitate a ranch. I'd never been to such a nice place, only to the common little Clam Basket where Daddy nearly got into a fistfight with the waiter and the manager because the portions were too small and Ma said she'd never go anywhere with him again unless somebody got married or died.

At Hilltop, I ate thick steak and a baked potato, with fat dollops of sour cream and butter melting inside. The salads came in fake wooden bowls. On them, I sampled every dressing they offered, French, Italian and Russian - they each tasted like mayonnaise mixed with a different amount of ketchup. I devoured the thin pad of butter that came in a delicate pleated paper with the basket of American rolls that changed to powder in your mouth and silently wished for more. Joey bought me Cokes, which I never had at home. Ma bought the enormous economy bottles of ginger ale or orangeade. I loved the sophisticated narrow glass and the thin, bar straw to clink the miniature square ice cubes around.

We doubled with June and Will a lot. Will and I stood in front of the wall sized modern art paintings at the new three-movie Cinema in the Saugus Shopping Center. I told Will he had to "let go and just feel them" and Junie got mad and yelled at me later. "You should've seen his stupid eyes light up!" she yelled. That was the night Will looked down at my sandals and admired my toenails polished in clear pink. Junie was furious that I'd let him see my toes, as though toes were illicit. I laughed at her. It seemed so funny that Junie could be jealous of me or that she could think that Will would ever turn his heart from her. He was lost on her. His love for June was political.

After the movies, maybe James Bond, whom Junie and I hated for bedding, then dropping women like they were dirty underwear - two virgins sitting in a dark movie theater surrounded by men and young boys whose testosterone terrified us as they stomped their feet and cheered at "Pussy Galore!" as though the name itself was a license to grab us and rape us right there in the dark - I spent a hour or more in the Cadillac struggling with Joey for my virginity.

Once, Ma came out in her old, torn nightgown, so worn, the nylon had thinned and spread apart over her swollen breasts in transparent chemical holes. Her heavy breasts swayed as she banged frantically at the steamed up windows only to find me buried somewhere under Joey. He angrily wiped his hair out of his eyes while she screamed at me to get in the house. I spent a terrible few days listening to her scream at me.

"YOU'RE OUT OF YOUR MIND!" was the lesson she taught, "WHAT DO YOU THINK YOU'RE DOING? YOU COULD GET PREGNANT!"

It wasn't the words: it was the scream itself that cut through desire. That scream became my power to remember what could be my powerless future, to remember the threat of the diapers over my head. Virginity was my power. Virginity was the life force. For young girls, virginity became the instinct of self-preservation, not sex. It was ironic, I wanted sex in everything: sexy movies, sexy music - even food was sexy with its deep, rich textures and aromas - it all seemed a part of the whole - sex, the reason we're alive. I wanted sex, but I couldn't indulge in it without wasting my life. My virginity became a sexual intensity. My virginity was my strength.

Joey couldn't give me what I wanted. There was more sex in my mother's nightgown, in the leafy trees and gnarled trunks, in the shadows and the street light dappling them, in the thick juicy steaks and the slim iced glasses of Coke and the audience's illicit cheers and the anticipation of going out amongst them than in all of Joey DiPietro.

Junie, come to find out, would have gotten rid of it right away with Will, but she was too afraid of Agnes. Agnes wedged between their hot bodies. Agnes stared over Will's shoulder. It was too much for Junie. Abstinence was infinitely easier.

To think she wanted to get rid of it! That it was a burden to her! She had someone she could trust. She had love.

Joey gave me a silver ID bracelet for my birthday. It was a pretty delicate little thing, carved with vines and flowers, on which I was supposed to get his name engraved, that was the style, that's what everyone was doing.

Unbelievably, it was Annie Likus who took one look at it and said, "Don't put his name on it, Gloria! Put your own! That's too nice to waste!" She was right. But, Joey nearly fainted when he saw how delicious it looked with *GLORIA* inscribed amongst the viney twists.


DIVISIONS

There were clear divisions at the White's house. Mrs. White spent many hours scrubbing the indentations of the faux tiles on the kitchen floor, down on her knees with a brush and a pail and the neon yellow gloves sucking on her hands like domestic octopi.

"Go around front!" She yelled at Junie when we approached the back door coming home from school, giggling, carrying our books.

"Gotta go around," Junie laughed.

Agnes, on the floor scowled at the black lines between the "terracotta" rectangles. I wondered how she could tell when the black lines were clean.

From Junie's room, we could hear the boys troop in the back door with their mud-caked cleats like a conquering army.

"Hi! Hi! Hi!" Agnes sang, brightly. "How was your day? Mmm!" We could hear her being kissed by her soldiers, one by one.

For everything the boys got away with, Junie was disciplined. If Jack stayed out late, Junie had to be home earlier. If Joey got bad grades, Junie had to study harder. If Junie asked why, she was told her brothers were boys and she was a girl and girls were held to stricter standards.

Many a Saturday or Sunday morning, Junie stood for hours cheerfully making stacks of pancakes. I didn't understand her perky laughter, her encouraging them to have more, "Jack?" "Joe?" "Paul?" and when the boys were pregnant with pancakes, she spent another hour washing up the dishes. Finally sitting down to her one cold pancake.

Agnes ate like a bird. To outdo her, Junie ate like half a bird. Junie never ate her dinner. She played with a slab of thin meat. She pushed the anemic vegetables under her plate. She wrapped cold chunks of mashed potatoes up in her napkin. She only sipped at the top of the milk and only as long as it was frothy with bubbles and ice cold. If it lingered for a minute getting warm, leaving a creamy rim along the edge, she turned up that already turned up nose.

This lack of appetite almost frightened me, who ate heartily at home and then had a second meal at the Whites – Agnes insisted - of strange American skinny sausages and frozen peas and rich cake for dessert. I was an orgy of eating compared to Junie and the flesh growing on me threatened to show it. I had to keep careful watch, carefully learning to say no politely or acquiescing and regretting and exercising like a madwoman.

But Junie ate deeply of candy bars. She ripped the bright foil from them and pressed their chocolatey flesh into her mouth, mumbling her rapturous enjoyment, "Mmm, Ri, oh, you gotta have one of these, come on, mmm, God."

"No, thanks, June, I'm getting too fat from eating dinner twice at your house."

"Mm, oh, that was good, have a Reese cup, you like those."

"No, thanks, June," I shook my head. "I don't know how you can eat those things. Anything from a factory is highly suspect. Could be a rat hair in there, or maybe the whole thing is a rat turd."

"Mmm," she licked a glob of chocolate from her lip. "I don't know how you can eat that stuff you eat, all that macaroni and dirty greens."

This coming from the girl whose hand irresistibly sneaked into my warm, aromatic bread bag on the way home from the bakery on Sunday mornings, clawing off a chunk with her nails and biting the soft doughy belly and roasty crust of bread.

I laughed, "You love my mother's food!"

"Mmm!" she nodded, her little pink mouth edged with dark brown like a wedge of fruit dipped in melted chocolate.

Late one afternoon, I came into the White's silent house, dim with twilight, a few lamps turned on, giving the rooms an abandoned, secret tone. Junie was standing in her bedroom watching something. Her expression was frozen and numb. I'd never seen her look like that, as though every ounce of blood had been drained from her rosy cheeks. Her bright blue eyes were clouded with tears.

As I came closer, I saw the bed sheets flying in midair. Closer: Agnes' hands attached to the sheets, flying, ripping off the bed and flying. Between clenched teeth, Agnes gnawed a scream, *"Tell me next time! Next time you tell me!"*

When Junie saw me, she froze even more, if that was possible, her cheeks blazed white and red. Agnes turned to the doorway, saw me, and slammed the door shut. The hall went black.

Junie would never explain. But, I knew how much pain Junie was in. And I knew why she couldn't tell me. She had to be better than me. I always understood that.

Picture the Whites eating dinner, an early meal, perhaps in summer when the sky was still light. In the captain's chair, Ted faced the window. Agnes sat in the mate's chair opposite, the children down both sides of the table.

All of a sudden, Jack's eyes bugged out in amazement.

"Look! Isn't that Will Cullen?" he laughed that Happy Jack chuckle, deeply musical and derisive and absolutely without conscience.

Everyone looked out the window.

"Where?" they cried. "Where?"

"There! He's on the telephone pole!"

Junie was mortified as Jack and her brothers and parents sat around their dinner table and laughed and laughed at Will, clinging to the fifty foot telephone pole that stood on the highway behind their yard, as though he were a hilarious comedy routine on television. Apparently, he'd climbed up high to see in the window, just to see her eating her dinner. Junie told me about it, tortured with embarrassment, but I thought what he'd done was unbelievably romantic.

I wasn't there, but I can see him, brave and insane, the ignorant Whites laughing uproariously at him. As misunderstood as a saint, on that pole, he was a flag to Junie's worth and his crazy love.

FAR FROM THE MADDING CROWD

The boys took us to the movies, but I swear, the movies meant more to us than the boys.

"Do you think they had makeup on?" I asked Junie.

"Oh, I'm sure they did, only you can't see it."

"Yeah, that was incredible. I had to watch those stupid John Wayne movies my father turned on during every Sunday dinner. Some stupid actress batting her false eyelashes at stupid John Wayne. And the hair! Always in a slick forties hairstyle! Like our ancestors had perfect 1940s hairstyles and false eyelashes and pointy breasts on the wagon trains!"

"Yeah, Julie Christie looked so natural. Well, you could tell she had makeup on, but it was done so naturally!"

"And beautifully!"

"I loved how their cuffs and the hems of the skirts would get dirty, it was so real! So liberating!"

"Which movie did you like better? *Far From the Madding Crowd* or *Romeo and Juliet*?" I asked.

"I don't know. Which one do you like better?"

"I don't know."

We were in Junie's bedroom and she was finishing getting ready for our double date with Will and Joey. We were going to see Zeffirelli's *Romeo & Juliet* for the third time. Joey didn't mind. He hoped it would make me soft.

"I love the way Romeo and Juliet were naked in bed, it was so beautiful!"

"I know! I love the song too! 'A rose will bloom/it then must fade/so does love/so does the fairest maid,'" I attempted to sing. "And the songs in *Far From the Madding Crowd*!"

"I love the way they sang their own music and played their own instruments. The way Gabriel Oak could play the flute and Bathsheba could sing."

"Yeah, I love that scene with the table by the open window."

"That's it! 'I lost my love and I care not/ I lost my love and I care not' I love those old songs. You know, when I see that beautiful English countryside, it's almost as though I recognize it as home. I get a feeling of love, like I lived there before and I loved it."

"Maybe one of your ancestor's did; you're half English."

"Yeah, maybe the memory of it is buried deep in my bones, in the memory of my cells. I feel that way when I look at pictures of Italy too. Italy is in me, too."

"Definitely, Ri! You've got Italy in you! Sing that song about the soldier."

"As I was out walking one morning in May/ I saw a young couple a making of hay/ one was a maid whose beauty shone clear/ the other a soldier, a brave grenadier.'"

"That's beautiful, not your voice, the song."

"Thanks. I love the way they talked then. The beautiful accent. I wish we talked like that."

"We can. We should use some of the words from Hardy," Junie suggested. "Why don't we?"

"Okay! Like 'afield' and 'how came you?' and 'know you'?"

"Yes!"

This was something we did for a while and then forgot, until one murderous day when it was most needed and most appropriate.

"And, they didn't show it so much in the movie, but I love the way Oak could tell the time, instinctively, by the stars."

"You can tell time by the sun. You do it every summer at the beach."

"Well, that's so obvious! The sun is like the hour hand."

"Yeah, but ten past two?"

"It's right there! I'll teach you. Listen, remember in the book how he went out from his hut in the middle of the night to carry the newborn lamb to its mother to be fed, how he stood and waited for it and looked up at the stars, just feeling the night and he thought how blessed his life was?"

"Yeah, that was beautiful."

"I want a man like Gabriel Oak. He was smart. He read books, remember? And he was an expert farmer; everyone, rich or poor, came to him for help. And how he loved her and lived for her. And Farmer Boldwood - how he killed for her."

"Would you kill for me?" Junie asked me, half-kidding.

"Of course," I said, seriously.

"Yeah, me too."

"And Will. He would."

"Yeah. He would."

This was accepted, natural.

"Joey would never."

"No, Joey wouldn't."

"You know, even when all Farmer Oak's sheep died, it was beautiful. And Fanny Robin. I like the way she was laid out in the house. I wish we did that."

"It smells bad, Ri."

"Yeah, I know. They'd probably like our funerals better, anyway. You know, everything clean and fancy. Everything done for them. But, don't you think there's a good feeling by doing something, I mean, the women must have felt a sense of rightness, cleaning and dressing the body. I wouldn't want anyone else to do it, if it were someone I loved! How could I just hand the body of my child or husband over to strangers? Those creepy funeral guys. What else would I have to do that was more important?"

"Just another thing women did beautifully. What was it, do you think?"

"I think people were more noble. Just naturally noble. A good sense of justice. Some people still have that sense of true nobility. Not royal nobility, real nobility."

"I love the way everything looked so beautiful, every little thing," Junie, continued my thoughts, "As though that sense of nobility was in everything. The lace, the candlelight, the stonewalls, hay stacks."

"Yeah, I love the wooden bowls and spoons, lanterns, cloaks. The simplest things were beautiful. Not store bought. I read in a magazine that the farms they filmed on were the last old working farms in England, farms where things were still done in the old way, that we were seeing the last breath of the last old farms. I love the old ways, even though I know it was hard. I'm willing to do the work. I wish we could make our own furniture and bowls and cups and make them beautiful and use them every day. Instead of fake plastic stuff from Zayre's. It's like the paintings, all the great ones show the simplest actions, lifting a bowl, washing clothes, planting in the fields, walking, holding a child, writing a letter, usually women, the most beautiful. That's what I want life to be."

"You make it like that, Ri. Everything you do is like that. Beautiful."

"You too."

I was helping her thread pink rose buds in her fine hair. They were stolen from Agnes's garden, which Ma admired every day on her walk home from the bus stop at Bell's Circle. Agnes would kill if she saw them, so Junie had a pink shawl she was going to throw over her head as she ran out the door.

"Don't let the stems show," Junie cautioned.

"I won't. I wonder how the island girls do it."

"I don't know. I think they tuck them behind their ears."

"Imagine, fresh orchids and wildflowers every minute!"

Junie had already braided a "pearl" necklace, really miniature mother-of-pearl beads, through mine, which was half up in a braided crown and half down my back in waves.

We looked forward to wrapping ourselves in the sconce-lighted darkness of the theater, to surrendering ourselves up to the spell that was woven there. I wonder if you can imagine what these movies meant to us, how the screen in the theater shone with, not light and color, not even landscapes and sweeping music, not costumes and dancing and laughter, candles and lace, not these, but the thing they changed into in our hearts: the screen shone with hope: suddenly, I had a way to make life beautiful that I hadn't possessed before.

When we'd finished dressing, we thought we looked grand. The boys drove up in Roskolnikov, which always put Joey in a bad mood. He preferred his father's Cadillac.

Quietly, Will came to the door in sandals, shredded dungarees, clean shirt and tie and tweed jacket. Joey, Agnes's favorite, sent a wave from the dark car to her standing in the open doorway.

"Don't be late," Agnes kissed Junie's cheek. "What's that on your head?"

"Nothing! I won't!"

As he led her to her side of the car, Will said, a little breathlessly, "You look ravishing!"

Joey took one look at me and laughed out loud.

"Who're you supposed to be? Juliet?"

EAST BOSTON, 1954

I was three years old when Mama opened the door and looked into the room. She screamed.

Her life was changed forever.

Daddy and I looked up.

Daddy laughed.

"Cut it out, Rosie! She's okay. It doesn't hurt her!"

Mama cried and ran to pick me up.

Daddy stood and zipped his pants.

I MUST BE ABOUT THE WORK OF MY MOTHER (I)

"Your Uncle Sonny wants you to teach him how to read!" Ma announced one day.

"I thought he didn't want me to teach him because I'm a girl. I thought he was embarrassed."

Ma looked disgusted. "How the hell do I know? He was supposed to learn from the night school, but he didn't like the teacher. Or something, so - "

So - I could teach him. I got real excited. I had some good ideas about how to do it so he'd like reading. I really wanted him to like it. I wondered if he looked on reading as anything more than a way to make a better living.

"He's going into the Army and he wants to learn before he goes."

She sounded angry, but I could hear the fear and the struggle to hide it in her voice.

"You mean he's going to Vietnam?"

She shrugged.

"Who knows! You go where they tell you to go."

Then, she said, "On your way, I want you to stop in the doctor's office and pick up your sister's medical records for school. And then stop in the shop for a minute, there's someone I want you to meet. Nora is working there now. I used to work with her on Kneeland St. You remember."

Her voice was slightly out of breath as she bent and reached about her cooking. I could hear all the different emotions, subtly changing as she spoke. The pride in sending me to the doctor because I was smart enough and old enough to go; the gladness that I might see my godmother, who worked as his receptionist, because she knew I would like that; the happiness of showing me off to her girlfriend; and, under it all, the tension and worry of her littlest brother, Sonny, going off to war: all this was in her voice and I read her meanings with pleasure and fear, while the cooking soothed us.

She may have been making the roast lamb with crispy potatoes laced round its edges, the mushrooms tumbling over its ribs heavy with savory sauce. She may have made chicken cacciatore or pasta fagiole or the corn bread in the skillet with the escarole soup. I used to sit in the kitchen with her during those charmed hours before supper, in the suspended animation of supper being made, in the sunset caught blazing between day and night, when she worked days, came in the door, dropped her purse and started cooking with her coat on. I did my homework at the table.

Ma turned on the Merv Griffin Show and I had the great opportunity to see Truman Capote and Tennessee Williams alive, speaking for me in musical, dulcet tones, telling me their precious Southern secrets, and that funny little lady, Totie Fields, who later lost her leg, but still came on TV, brave and funny, until she died. We watched Merv Griffin together for years, through all his diets and friendships, me with half an eye because I considered him too old to take seriously and Ma, with absolute reverence and love, "Oh, look at that! See the woman there! That's so and so, oh, she's a big star!" I'd look up and see an old lady with stiff yellow hair bigger than her head; that's all I saw, until Truman Capote died, then Tennessee Williams, and I got a glimmer of what it all meant.

I saw John Lennon and his wife, Yoko Ono. I realized Yoko was the only person in the world who could surprise and delight him because she was the only one more avant-garde than he was. I'd see them talking. Right there in front of me. Talking. Yoko said, "Anyone can be artist." John said we could have no religions, no possessions, no countries.

"What the heck is he talking about?" Ma asked me.

Looking at John Lennon, I said, by way of explanation, "I'm gonna marry a shepherd."

"You're nuts!" Ma laughed. "Where the hell are you gonna find a shepherd? Go back to Italy!"

"I'd love to!"

"Yeah, you'd like it there!"


## THE ERRAND

It was unseasonably hot, viciously hot. My perfume, which was really a Kiehl's essential oil – rose – that Junie and I had purchased on one of our trips into Boston, drew bees at the bus stop. The sun sucked my blood and the steam rising off my skin was as compelling to the bees as the strong aroma of flowers. People edged away from me. Without success, I tried to rub the overly rich oil from my wrists with a Kleenex.

Ma had made me call the doctor before I left to make sure he knew I was coming. She had made me call him at home. Is that what triggered his reaction? Was it the stimulation of my voice into the cool darkness of his elegant home? I pictured the sophisticated interior: the dark browns, deep scarlets, and the coppery gold of the carpeted staircase by the polished mahogany telephone table with its shining brass lamp. He seemed startled and confused when I told him in a cheerful voice how I was coming to pick up my sister's records for school.

I was so proud of this errand as well as this adult phone call to a doctor. I looked forward to meeting Ma's girlfriend. And teaching Uncle Sonny to read!

I'd dressed carefully. No shorts or mini skirts or dungarees. I wore an Indian print dress and delicately strapped leather sandals with a bronze Aztec sun upon the toe.

I sat straight and cool as I could in his airless waiting room, trying to keep my bare feet from the puddle fast encroaching along the filthy blue carpet, growing quickly as the exhausted air conditioner drizzled into it. Rhythmic puffs of warm air blew across my knees from the wheezing machine. Several pregnant women sprawled in the leatherette chairs, their soggy shorts and dresses hiked up between their swollen thighs. Two little ones knocked each other over as they played with the few chewed-up plastic toys and used coloring books Dr. Nathan offered.

My godmother's desk was empty. I was disappointed. Had he sent her home early? I looked at her empty desk with the cloudy fish tank behind it, the anemic little goldfish swimming nervously, visible because my godmother was not in her chair.

I read the posters that lined the perimeter of the room, over and over. I was a compulsive reader; my eyes traveled naturally to words. The posters, bearing messages of health care, were of mothers and babies, washed blue as if from a flood of blue dye that had filled the room at some point in history and, like the floods of Venice, leaving water marks on the masterpieces of Madonna and child.

Dr. Nathan himself came out of his office with a mother and a little boy who were leaving. He called me in, though the others were ahead of me. I assumed this was because my errand would be brief.

Dr. Nathan was a doughy white skinned man whose jowls hung down the sides of his sad white mouth like raw pie dough over the edge of a pie. His pale eyes ran watery with light blue water.

Oddly, I liked him, though his appearance always had shocked me, as it shocked me now. I liked him, because every time I saw him as a child, he'd taken away my pain as if he'd opened his little black bag, put my pain inside it and carried it away with him.

He stepped back to let me pass into the office. Briefly, I wondered why he hadn't just left the papers on Margaret's desk. Maybe they weren't filled out yet, I told myself.

"How's Ma-rie?" Dr. Nathan asked. He had a way of drawing out her name, like he was making fun of her.

"Fine," I said.

"I just saw Marie recently, so that's why I told your mother she needn't come in to get these. Sit down, Gloria."

I sat in the chair opposite the desk.

"I'm glad she didn't come. I'd like to talk to *you* for a while."

Dr. Nathan collected frogs. You didn't notice it so much in the waiting room. Most of the frogs were in his office. Little green faces looked out at me from everywhere. Crouched in the glass case, sprawled across the desktop, peeking out from his bookshelves were scaly plastic green bodies with bulging cartoon eyes, beady black pupils that stared at me in surprise. A few realistic plaster frogs on carved lily pads or painted blue puddles, yawned with bored, sleepy lids as though they had seen his medical exams all too often.

His statement crawled over me like little frogs. Talk to me? What could he possibly talk to me about? I was healthy, wasn't I?

"How old are you now, Gloria?" he asked with a syrupy voice.

"Sixteen."

There was a sudden intake of breath as his expression softened.

"Do you have a boyfriend?"

"Yes."

I supposed he meant Joey DiPietro.

His mouth tasted this information, mashing a simpy smile around his pasty lips.

"You could have another one."

"Another boyfriend? I don't think my boyfriend would like that."

I could see me grappling with yet another boy!

"He doesn't have to know."

His pale blue eye winked at me. For a second, I wondered if Dr. Nathan knew his eye had done this! Then, after a moment of silence like a vacuum, I realized, Dr. Nathan meant himself! That I should have sex with his pasty, white body.

"I'm a virgin, Dr. Nathan," said the little idiot in front of him, as though her virginity were a shield and a sword.

His eyes closed in ecstasy. A watery drop, not a tear, escaped down his milky cheek. His thin white lips trembled.

"That's wonderful!" he managed, hoarsely, as he got up and crossed to the front of the desk.

He stood in front of me. He reached down and clasped me by the elbows and lifted me out of the chair. He was a horrid little man. At five feet, I was exactly even with him.

"I've always loved you, Gloria!" he said, leaning his jowls toward me. He kissed my astonished mouth; he drove his pale tongue into my mouth like a strong and slimy frog.

I went rigid with shock. Shallow little breaths came fast, like no air at all, to my lungs. The information coming to my brain was sparse and incorrect. How could it be right? Until I felt the breath coming out of *his* nostrils into my own and I tried to stop breathing.

His small hand, a little clammy and cold, which had always pinched my pink and feverish buttock to get it ready for the needle of penicillin, slipped under the neckline of my dress and under my bra where it squeezed a cringing breast.

Then, he stepped back, all dreamy eyed and proud of himself.

"I can give you everything you've ever wanted, Gloria. You've seen the nice things I've given Margaret. Wouldn't you like nice things, too?"

Margaret! No! That couldn't be! Nice things! Is that how you got them? Pasty, white, raw dough, you had to eat raw dough, suck on it, green and slimy, frogs legs for the rich, frog's legs, that's what it was, green and slimy. Jade. He had given her jade, green as frog skin. And the music, the piano, the golden drink she'd carried to Daddy in the crystal glass, the colors like jewels, spinning in her son's sweater, spinning in the rug, rich rug, rich rug, rich.

"Can I have the papers for my sister, now, please?" I said, in a tiny, polite voice. Did you ever notice how polite women are when they are being molested?

His expression fell, then lifted again, as if in disbelief.

"I can give you money, Gloria! And presents! All the time! *Every* time!" he added, slyly.

The eye winked at me again.

I forgot how to be polite.

"I don't want *things*. I HATE MONEY! Do you hear me? Or do I have to scream it loud enough for everyone to hear? I HATE MONEY AND I HATE YOU! I just want my sister's papers! Now, give them to me!"

He fumbled at the loose papers on his desk, quickly handing me an envelope. Without looking at him, I took it and rushed out.

When I was safely in the waiting room, protected by the pregnant Madonnas waiting with their children, something made me turn and look back.

There he was, standing at the threshold of his office, as though he were about to usher in the next patient. He was paler than I'd ever seen him, if that were possible - erased, white-washed.


Outside, in the sun that blazed off the chrome and paint of the cars, I clutched the precious school papers against the nauseous heat, against the frogs croaking in my ears, which turned out to be the cars, scraping by on the street. I leaned against a parked car, burning my hands as on a hot stove. I was shaking; my hands, my arms, my teeth, my legs shook under me, every organ in my body, even my eyes seemed to shake in their sockets, the heat, the cars spun uncontrollably, I fell forward and vomited into the gutter.

When I was finished, I wiped my mouth on a Kleenex from my purse. I spit into the Kleenex and wiped my mouth again. I fixed my makeup in the car's side mirror. I was determined to gather myself as I walked the twelve shaky blocks to Ma's shop; I was determined I would *not* be as pale as he had been standing in his office doorway.

Dignity is a beautiful veil. Under its opaque surface, shame hides its face. I put on this veil of dignity as I walked to Ma's shop, shivering with the heat, along the glistening, deserted streets where I had been little. The landmarks built my courage as I walked. Here is where Nona and I had walked to the fruit and vegetable stand, where I had sat on the curb, where Nona had handed me a peapod to open and eat. Here is where Grandma and I, on our way to the Square, had caught Uncle Sonny in the schoolyard picking up the money some boy, who'd looked like a man to me, was throwing in the air like bridal bouquets for the other kids to catch. Uncle Sonny had run to her so proud of himself with actual dollar bills in his hand. "What are you doing?" Grandma had cried. "Get home and do your homework, nevva mind the money! What's the matter with him? Is he crazy?" "No, Ma! He's giving away money!" "He must be crazy! Crazy!" Here is where Marie fell and scraped her knee so badly on the glass Ma had to carry her screaming to the doctor's office (the doctor again, a slimy feeling slid over me) where my godmother pressed and pressed a gauze pad to her fat muffin knee until Dr. Nathan stitched a neat scar across the baby flesh. I swore I could still see her blood, a dull brown stain on the sidewalk, like all the other blood and spit and pigeon shit stains around it.

I felt my body being pressed to his again and the slime of his tongue. I went faint. But, why should I be ashamed? Why was it so repulsive that a young girl's pediatrician whom she'd trusted to touch her anywhere should want to hold her sweet young body next to his shriveled white and blue skin? Why did I sweat and shiver at the same time when it was the most natural thing in the world for him to squeeze the plump young ripeness of my breast on to his dried and dying bones as though my life force could keep him from withering? Did the victim ever feel the justice of the sacrifice?

A bus let off its burning, black exhaust as I crossed the main street, now teaming with cars and people. Old ladies in black stooped and carrying heavy bags, two or three in each hand; men, too tired to notice me, unshaven, smoking down the nubs of cigarettes; men, not too tired, twisting their heads to get a better look, whistling low; hot and exhausted young mothers hauling several sticky kids, one in the arms, filthy, gnawing at a mouthful of candy.

The shop had its door opened on to the street to let the heat out, only to cause an eruption at the threshold where the two masses of heat, one from the searing street, the other from the steamer and the sewing machines, met and collided upwards. A sign over the door read Susie's Sportswear, though I had no idea who Susie was. Ma's bosses were Luigi, called Lou and his wife, Josephine, called Josey. Daddy said they were the cheapest sons of bitches he'd ever seen or heard of because they had the most incredible house and went on vacations all the time, but they paid Ma chicken shit and made her work like a slave for it, through lunch sometimes and staying late with no overtime. They were supposed to pick her up early in the morning on their way, but they wouldn't come to the house; they made her walk to a certain place by the side of the highway in all kinds of weather. Infuriated, Daddy told her to quit, just quit, like he would have. Ma said, "Shut up, we need the money." I'd been to Lou and Josey's house. One Christmas, Will, Don Don, Junie and I went up to North Revere to see the spectacular Christmas decorations on the houses there that everyone was talking about, "Oh, you gotta go up to North Revere and see the Christmas town!" So, we drove up, and crawled along in the bumper-to-bumper traffic of sightseers. There, the snow was lighted red and green from the extravaganza of bulbs over the crusted houses and trees. The doors to the houses were open and the people were inviting the strollers in for drinks. I found myself in Lou and Josey's. There they were amidst plastic garlands of evergreens and red berries, two white and gold artificial Christmas trees, more than one chandelier per room, glass elephants and birds and giraffes on shelves, silk flower arrangements in tall vases and a floor covered so thickly with rugs, there were layers of rugs, layers! "Have a glass of Christmas cheer!" they said, recognizing me. "No, thank you."

On this day, I could tell the bosses weren't at the shop even before I walked in, because the shouts of women giggling with absolute abandon cascaded out on to the street along with the loud, wild music from the Italian radio station. Lou wouldn't let them talk while they worked, let alone play the radio.

The girls, as Ma called them, were calling to each other in Italian, loud enough to be heard over the music and the rattling drone of the dusty black sewing machines. One girl would stop her machine, drop her head to bite the thread in two, never missing a rhythmic, babbling word to her friends; the machine started up with a deep-throated whirr. A couple of the bolder women sang out insults and jokes; the others laughed. Ma held a secret smile on her sweet lips, listening to them. The women's arms were bare, in the dim light, their skin dark as Africans; a single light bulb hung over each girl like a halo; their white bra straps slipped, caught on their firm flesh which vibrated as their muscles flexed and relaxed.

Ma's was the first machine when you came in the door, because she was the last, the finisher, she was called, the one who put on the zippers and the buttons and the buttonholes. One time, I think of it every time I think of her there, the needle went right through her fingernail and finger and she had to stop for the day and go home.

A huge pile of clothes with loose threads hovered over her on her right side and a smaller, neater pile, the finished pile hugged her on the left because she was a leftie. One of Lou and Josey's kids usually came in and sat on a tall stool behind Ma to pull the loose threads and wind the cute, colorful tags around a button, but not today. No bosses were in, not even their kids, who, like mute, midget policemen, kept a silent watch over the girls and kept them muted, in turn.

It was Nora herself who jumped up from her machine as I crossed the threshold into the dark room and exclaimed, "Look! Madonn'! It's Rosa herself walking in! Look! Twenty-five years ago! It's Rosa! My God!"

She ran toward me, her arms open for me. Ma beamed proudly at her machine. A dozen or so women leapt from their work to surround me, asking Ma one question after another, too fast for her to answer. Dark, sweaty faces like those in Italian Renaissance paintings beamed and glowed at me. Ma turned and laughed with happiness.

"How old is she, Madonn'?"

"Look at her!"

"The angel! Tsk, the angel, Madonn'!"

"Oh, Rosa! You must have the boys coming around, eh, Rosa?"

"Never mind! She's too young for that! Plenty of time! Plenty of time!"

"You coming to work here, like your mother?"

"Get out! She's going to college!" Ma piped in.

"Oooh! College! God bless her! God bless her!"

"She's going to teach her Uncle Sonny how to read! He's thirty years old and he never learned!"

"Thirty years old! Madonn'!"

"See what happens!"

"He didn't pay attention in school, he didn't pay!"

"Is that what you're gonna be, a teacher?"

I nodded and smiled, weakly. It was easy to let the bad experience submerge itself into these women touching me, kissing me; they stroked away the some of the horror of the slimy touch of Dr. Nathan. I gave myself to their eager, sweating faces, dark and lush in the heat. From over their bare shoulders, I could see the only man in the shop, the presser, standing behind his ironing board, a man dressed only in pants and an athletic T-shirt, his black hair and moustache matted with sweat and lint. He smoked a cigarette, which was forbidden whether the boss was there or not. A NON FUMÉ sign hung just over his shoulder. He regarded me: he sent thick waves of rhythmic steam hissing into the already heavy air by lowering the cover of his presser. It was a power he possessed: his machine was powerful at making people hotter and more uncomfortable.

I could have stood forever being stroked with love by beautiful, lush Italian women, but at the first mention of college, they had begun to disperse and lose interest. I felt a pang of loneliness as they all turned from me and went back to their work.

"You get the papers?" Ma asked me. I handed them to her. She dug out her pocketbook from the employee's toilet and stuffed the precious, official papers down to the deepest part where they wouldn't fall out and get lost.

After Ma finished work, we walked together the five blocks to Grandma's. Grandma met us at the front door sounding its familiar alarm.

She eased her wriggling, whining, so-happy-to-see-us boxer, GiGi, back with one foot in the old nurse's shoes, like nuns and World War I nurses wore with heels and laced up pointed toes. She moaned. "Rosa! And Gloria! Come in! Eh! Come in!"

"What a hot day! Ma, you got the fans going?"

"Oh, yeah! I got them! I got them! Your Uncle is here, Gloria, waiting for you."

Like a mournful song, her voice sang to me. I wanted to kiss her, to throw myself down on her sweet softness and cry and cry, to go back to her and never leave. But, then I would have to tell them. I couldn't bear to pollute them with it.

"Gloria! Gloria!" Uncle Sonny called me from the kitchen. He was running around, eager as a puppy. "Gloria! Gloria's going to teach me, Rosie! I got everything I need! I got pens! I got paper! I'm just like you, Gloria!"

They all laughed and so did I, though I wanted to cry.

"Gloria knows everything about reading!" he said, trying to make us laugh, which he did. His long eyelashes fluttered shyly. His chubby, pockmarked cheeks turned the red of roses caught between the palest flush of pink and deep veins of crimson. He had started life as a sleek, young seal, but had grown to be overweight and awkward. His beautiful eyes remained and his shy earnestness, but these were not enough to attract a woman to appreciate him.

Nona was there. She was ancient and almost dissolved. It was during the time when she was traded from daughter to daughter just before she became transparent forever. Grandma had been feeding her. Around her neck, Nona wore a dishtowel stained with orange mash, carrot or squash, that Grandma had made fresh for her. Her old head nodded forward like an infant's on its insufficient neck. The tiny diamonds winked on her folded up ears.

"I gotta start the food, Rosa. Can you feed her for me?"

"Yeah, sure! Hi, Nona! Nona! Nona!"

Ma took over Grandma's place beside Nona, who didn't know her, but continued to nod into her napkin like she understood everything.

Uncle Sonny had part of the Formica table set up with papers and pens.

"Sit down, Gloria! I wanna learn how to read!"

"You don't need papers and pens to learn how to read, Uncle Sonny."

"You don't?"

"Nope. I brought a book for you. You can keep it two weeks, then I have to return it to the library."

I showed him. The book was on electricity. He laughed.

"I know all about electricity, Gloria," he bragged.

"That's good. Then, you'll know all the words I don't. You should read something you're interested in. That's what reading is all about."

"Really?"

I opened the book and began Chapter One, The Elements of Electricity, first explaining what the word elements meant, then, burying the individual letters with my finger when he didn't know the word, letting him sound it out. It was torture for him, at first, and embarrassing because it was with me. But, after a while, he could see that I was serious, that I meant it, that I wasn't the Gloria who sat next to him, but the real person underneath, and soon, he lost self-consciousness and gained speed and the words fell into place, one after another.

We sat like that for an hour or more. Ma finished feeding Nona and cleaned her up. Grandma took the opportunity to do a few chores, including hanging clothes out the kitchen window.

"You don't have to wear your blanket today, Grandma!" I kidded her. Grandma had a coat she'd made out of an American Airlines blanket, given to her by Uncle Salvi, who cleaned the planes at American. Army green and rough, it read AMERICAN across her back when she hung out clothes.

"Yeah, the planes'll wave to you, Ma!" laughed Uncle Sonny.

"Never mind! It keeps me warm in the winter, it keeps me!" Grandma groaned from out the window where she knelt and leaned on the straining tips of her toes. Grandma wouldn't let anyone help her hang clothes. She had a certain way of hanging them, and no one else could do it right.

Grandma was still making her house clothes out of pieces of old things: old bathrobes, old towels, parts of dresses and even Uncle Sonny's discarded sweaters or pants; a leg here, an arm or bodice there. She was a walking, living quilt. Everyone in the family made fun of her for it, especially her sisters and her sons. Uncle Vickie was the worst. He offered her money to buy new clothes.

"What do I want with new?" Grandma cried, "Get out of here! New clothes! I don't go anywhere, except to church!"

After she finished hanging the laundry, we ate covatellis, a special curled macaroni that Grandma made by pressing her thumb into the dough, salad and bread and wine. Uncle Sonny exuberantly played the part of Grandpa sawing the thick loaf of bread, handing a ragged piece to each of us, our hands reaching to him over the table, over the bowls and the stout glasses filled with wine. Uncle Sonny was less kingly than Grandpa, who had been kindly, but aloof. Uncle Sonny was a foolish and jolly prince, not a king.

"This is from your Great Uncle Dominic's vine," Uncle Sonny told me, in ceremony of a fact I already knew.

"Yeah, but his son makes the wine now," Grandma sneered with a mouthful of food.

"So! It's still better than the store!" Uncle Sonny defended his cousin, who was his own age exactly.

Grandma made a face again.

"He leaves too many stems," Ma agreed with her mother, since she also remembered better than Uncle Sonny, the taste of her great uncle's miraculous wine.

"I think Benny does a good job! Right, Gloria?"

He raised his glass to me.

"Great job!" I agreed, thinking it was probably the last homemade wine I'd ever taste. "I always come here for good wine."

Grandma laughed.

"You shouldn't drink!" Ma snapped. "You're too young!"

"Ah, we always gave to the kids! A little water, a little wine, remember, Gloria?"

"Yup!"

The little glasses of half wine, half water, and, at home, half ginger ale, a "winecooler," Daddy called it, a little "popsicle."

"What's the secret to reading, Gloria? I think I'm gonna like reading. I'm gonna get a lamp for my bed, Ma, one of those kind that swivel, Ma, so I can read in bed."

"There's no secret to reading, Uncle Sonny, just keep reading. Practice, practice, practice, I guess. You'll just get better and better."

"See? She knows! Gloria knows! You gonna be a teacher, Gloria? You're a good teacher already. You should teach in the night school, they got a lousy teacher there now. She's ugly, too!"

"Hey! A teacher doesn't have to be pretty to teach!" Grandma scolded him; he laughed, we all laughed, including Grandma.

"Have a pear, Gloria! They're from the North End. Here!"

He rubbed the pear gently on the pristinely clean dishcloth Grandma kept on the table for just this kind of purpose. The sweet and juicy pear, washed by Grandma, rubbed like Aladdin had rubbed the lamp to a blushing sheen, the delicate skin ready to tear with flavor; he sliced it deftly with the razor sharp knife in one hand, offering it to me, resting light as air against the blade and his outstretched thumb, I could have wept to take the slice, wet and pure and so heavenly sweet to my tongue, I wanted to die there, to dissolve like the pear, like Nona asleep, maybe dying, in her little bed; like the Holy Host at mass, the morsel of pear melted on my tongue, entering a confused and aching soul, giving pain and comfort.

After dinner, Uncle Sonny went outside to pick arugula for Ma to take home. We never left without heavy bags laden with foodstuffs, clothes and bargains from the store. Ma and Grandma wanted to be alone, so they wouldn't let me help with the dishes. They sent me out with Uncle Sonny, who clambered over the garden like a happy puppy, calling, "You gotta have some red peppers too, Gloria! Oh, your mother's eyes will water when she eats these, I'll bet!" In triumph, he held over his head a fat bunch of arugula and a sagging bouquet of top-heavy red peppers.

"This enough? I'll get more!" he answered himself.

The evening cooled as darkness fell over the freshly watered garden. After "giving the plants to drink," Uncle Sonny then took the hose and forced the boxer's shit into the alley.

The garden next door, the old man's garden, the old man who had been Nona's great friend, who had worn the floppy straw hat, was gone. Chicory, ragweed and Queen Anne's lace choked the overgrown, coarse scrub that had once been corn and broccoli, asparagus, lettuce, squash and tomato. The rusted body of a dead refrigerator, hairy with weeds was stuck in the middle.

"What happened to the old man's garden?" I asked.

"He died, Gloria! The garden is gone now," Uncle Sonny replied.

"The new people didn't keep it up?"

"Get out! Are you kidding? They put in a new fence, see? We had a fight, Gloria! They said our tomatoes was growing into their yard! So, we had to cut them down! Eh! Forget about it!"

*Cool as a knife, a memory cut back to me. I was in Grandma's bedroom; it was night. What was I doing there? Marie was with me. It was because the Buddha was in the alley! The night of the Buddha in the alley!*

*I'd been asleep, sticky with sand and suntan lotion, my skin still raw and burned by the sun. I woke to find myself in Grandma's bedroom. Voices, I could hear voices. Marie was asleep, her breathing sweet as candy beside me. I could hear Grandma and Ma, and the voices, muffled, of policemen and their feet heavily scraping the kitchen floor in their monstrous shoes. But, other voices, there were voices singing! Where?*

*I'd crept off the soft bedspread to look in the direction of the music. I'd walked barefoot and sandy on the cool linoleum of night to the backdoor, which was in Grandma's bedroom. I had to bend the blinds, which crackled, to peek out.*

*There was a light across the way, a big light, in someone's house. No, not a house, I'd thought, sleepily, outside! The lights were hanging from the trees outside and a group of people, a party, were seated around a long table and in the illumination, golden and far away, they were singing together, clear and beautiful, a happy song in Italian, laughing, celebrating, while, in our alley, a man's naked bloody body had been carried away. And, it seemed absolutely right. I'd returned to bed, nuzzled beside Marie, and I was smiling.*

We were sleepy now, all of us, and saying good night. Uncle Sonny was going to drive us home, because it was dark. I kissed Nona's soft, melting cheek as she slept, I leaned my slimy lips to touch Grandma's baby cheek, and briefly, to Uncle Sonny's evening stubble. He blushed shyly and said, "All right! Let's go!" And I was horrified that I could even exist in the same, dazzling white kitchen as they, that I could breathe the same air without making them choke.

But, it was all right. Because it had to be.

AUGUST 21, 1968
RADIO FREE PRAGUE

I opened the front door, it made that peculiar squeech sound, and Ma had the TV turned up real loud and my ears were shocked with static and a young voice, terrified that he couldn't speak fast enough, "This is Radio Free Prague!" static as though he'd been stopped, then again "This is Radio Free Prague!" static as though he'd been stopped and "This is Radio Free Prague!" static as though he'd been - and I asked Ma, "What happened?" and she said, staring at the TV, her arms folded in front of her, the cigarette burning in her hand, "They went in with tanks again." "This is Radio Free Prague!" the young man's voice called out "This is Radio Free Prague!" static

EAST BOSTON, 1954

When Mama opened the door and looked into the room, she screamed.

Her life was changed forever.

Daddy and I looked up.

Daddy laughed.

"Cut it out, Rosie! She's okay. It doesn't hurt her!"

Mama cried and ran to pick me up.

Daddy stood and zipped his pants.

Mama screamed and cried. She ran into another room and slammed the door, pow!

I MUST BE ABOUT THE WORK OF MY MOTHER (II)

Ma had trouble with her intestines. They gurgled. She went to the doctor, the big doctor at the hospital, Brigham and Women's or something, and he told her she would have to have seven feet of her large intestine taken out because they were dead and while they had her open, was she finished having children or did she plan to have any more? Oh, she was finished. Well, then, the doctor said, he could fix her so she would be better than she had ever dreamed. That's how it happened that along with her intestinal surgery, Ma had a hysterectomy. I could see by the word that that which had made her hysterical had been removed.

June and I stood on the enclosed balcony of Ma's hospital room, high on a stone precipice, placing us in the very tree tops where a light rain fell overlooking an avalanche of pink and grey boulders that formed the hillside. We stood, it seemed with nothing under our feet at all, and I could think of only one thing: my mother had tubes running from her pretty little nose and mouth, tubes that gurgled every time she breathed. Now she gurgled from everywhere at once. Every tremor seemed full of pain; every vibration, every bubble gurgled painfully through her veins and my own veins.

Grandma was in the room sitting by Ma's side and we could hear her moaning on and on about her own previous operations. She held Ma's hand and moaned, "And with my gall bladder, they told me not to do too much work afterwards, but eh, what are you gonna do, Rosa? I'm telling you, there was plenty to do! I had five children! You know! You helped me take care of them! You know!"

Ma could barely moan a response through her many tubes. Her skin, slack across her cheekbones, had turned pink and grey as the gargantuan boulders falling down the hill, my foundation, my mother, crumbling like Italian marble.

"If she doesn't stop, Gloria, I'm gonna go insane!" June whispered harshly in my ear.

June, I would stop calling her Junie now most of the time, never called me Gloria, that wasn't good. Her sharp tone and my formal name, snapped me out of my stupor.

"What?"

"Your grandmother is describing her operations! It's terrible! Your mother is suffering, Ri! Can't you stop her?"

"I can't. In my family, you have to be older than the person to say anything bad to them."

Stop Grandma? The thought never would have occurred to me. I wondered if Ma felt the same as June. Was it terrible for Mama to listen to her mother? I listened, and her mournful tone was like a wind crying through an ancient, abandoned temple, a Tibetan om echoing through the antiseptic halls of the hospital, "Oh, oh, Rosa, what are you gonna do, my Rosa, my Rose, my God, mmm," the rosary ran through her pink arthritic fingers. Ma nodded in half consciousness, as if agreeing with her, and in doing so, bent the nose tube backward. A terrible gurgle, then calm as Ma adjusted her head and the tube relaxed again.

I shuddered as if the tube had jammed me in the nose, the plastic tubes keeping Ma alive. I put my head on June's shoulder. The window was open slightly and the aroma came to me of pinecones and rain, like a damp summer cottage.

"What is it?" June patted my hair.

"Those tubes."

Daddy came out.

"I'm gonna grab a smoke," he said. "You girls all right?"

We nodded. But, he could see my crazed eyes. He came over and eased me from June and held me close against his scratchy jacket.

"She's all right; she'll be home soon," he said. "It looks worse than it is, she'll get better."

I wanted to be his little girl and burst out crying in his strong arms, but I couldn't let June see me like that - relying on him - and I wasn't his little girl. I'd been his wife and not his wife. The confused emotions struggled in me, the pain gurgling through Ma's body and through my own, Ma's pain, through me and right through Daddy too. I mourned what never had been as though it had died like a parent; I mourned not having been his daughter. The tree tops swam in mist and rain and tears, my chest sank from misery and, at the same time, swelled with the pride coming from June standing by me, and I kept myself from falling down the hillside on to the boulders.


I nursed my mother. I stayed home from school for weeks. I maneuvered her excruciatingly from the bed, in slow, torturous jerks from the cool sheets, painfully, painfully, she lifted her foot into the slipper and slid along the floor, with many stops along the way to the bathroom for her to sob with the pain of sliding against her wounds, against the friction of the sheets, against the movement of her legs, her own muscles traitors to themselves, stabbing her up the anus, deeply, up the vagina, her sobs in my arms, proclaiming each a different part of her body, "Oh, my legs, my God, my behind, my insides, my insides."

I held her up under the arms while she attempted to sit on the toilet and pee and move her bowels. I knelt before her as she screamed into my chest. And screamed at me for hurting her, for holding her too tightly.

"Get me paper!" she wept and I quickly rolled the toilet paper and handed it to her.

"That's too much!" she moaned. "You waste it! You always waste it!" Leaning on one thigh, she sobbed in pain as she wiped herself.

After she was well, and able to stand and walk and use the bathroom without too much pain, I went back to school, but it wasn't for long. I collapsed in English, and I was glad to collapse there. Mr. Dokes called home and Jakey came for me with Annie Likus, who'd left her job at the A&P to come get me. I hardly knew them. I was too weak to be afraid. Ma put me in her bed, in the lovely four-poster, with its massive mahogany headboard blocking half the bay window, down in what had been the old, spare room. She closed the broken yellow blinds as best she could to make the room dark. Daddy slept on the couch as usual, and Ma slept beside me. There was no coughing or sneezing, only fever.

A dusty darkness hung in the room. I was only vaguely aware of night or day, except night was blacker and lonely as death, when I seemed to float bodiless in outer space, the dusty grains of darkness were my stars.

Days passed with no sounds of life, feverish and so blaring hot, I had no sense of humans around me. It was more than a week before I recognized the soothing tap of pans in the kitchen.

In my feverish dreams, I saw the dancers I used to see as a child, a man and a woman, waltzing in and out of the shapes bombarding me with their masses! Too thick! As thick as the legs of Picasso's women! Elephant legs! Massive concrete squares suddenly changing into hair-like thinness! Too thin! Flying in my face, as thin as horror! And the dancers danced on, oblivious!

"Mama!"

My throat ceased up, burning dry. I opened my eyes, glazed over. With a burning hand, I pointed at the dark wall. "There! The man, the lady! Make them stop! The shapes!"

"Mama!" I clutched at her old nightgown.

"Sh!" she commanded, without sympathy. "Sh!"

She bathed my head in cold water. In her own dear little hands, she held my hot hands in the cold washcloth and pressed the fever out of them and into the cloth where she washed it away over and over.

"Mama!" I screamed. "There!"

"You're dreaming!" She lost patience because it was too painful for her, and she was exhausted.

"No! I can still see them!" I pointed to the dark air.

"You're hallucinating from the fever," she told me.

And, suddenly, no longer so terrible, the figures were dancing in a dream world, another world called Hallucination, in front of me, right before my open eyes. I watched them in awe as they swirled and dipped gracefully. My pounding heart quickened as a thick slab whirled and spun in my face, but it spun away just as fast and I smiled to myself in relief and a hair shape startled me with terror from the side! The thin ones! The feel of a single strand of hair is terrifying even now! The dancers stepped in front. It wasn't real, I told myself, and closed my eyes to blackness.

I opened my eyes to an absolute flood of white light. June was standing alone at the foot of my bed. Gently, frightened, she looked at me. I tried to reassure her, because, after all, she was there, that's all I needed, but my eyes closed down again.

Then, just as suddenly as it had come, the fever broke. I was sitting up in bed accepting cards from neighbors and wild bouquets from June of Chinese lanterns, chicory, Queen Anne's lace, silver dollars, and roses from Agnes herself. Joey DiPietro came, looking guilty, with two gallons of ice cream, strawberry and vanilla. June and I, both of us sitting on the bed, attacked these with two spoons. June brought stacks of homework papers stuffed in textbooks for me to work on.

I was still shuffling weakly about in my pajamas and old nylon quilted robe with the long, nylon threads hanging loose, when Joey came to tell me he didn't want to go out with me anymore. He had a new girlfriend he'd met down the beach. They'd been playing pinball together and now he wanted to go out with her.

He took me into his lap, to comfort me. I perched there, without comfort.

"You met her, at the prom," he said. "She went with Mike."

A flash of realization came over me. My prom, the one I'd begged Joey to take me to, but he'd said it cost too much. He'd finally relented, begrudged. The image came to me of this greasy haired girl in her rented, torn lace gown that had once been white. Her clunky black shoes that didn't match her dress at all. (When I'd agonized over every detail of my gown and shoes, hair and coat. I'd worn smooth pink satin I made myself, pink satin shoes died to match, long pink gloves and a white brocade coat Ma and I had splurged to have made by the seamstress who'd left one sleeve inside out and we'd fixed it in a mad dash that very afternoon. My hair was a tumble of Shirley Temple curls caught up in pins and pink satin ribbons, cascading in formal ringlets. Joey had worn his father's tuxedo jacket which hung too broadly at the shoulders and too long at the wrists, covering his hands, making him look like a little kid.) "What was she doing with Mike?" I'd kept asking myself. Mike, this shy, sweet guy whom I'd just met that night. He looked embarrassed every time she leaned over to whisper her smudged lips next to Joey's ear, every time she laughed too loud. I remembered how her taut breasts had teased Joey's arm and Mike had looked away.

Joey didn't know that while he and she were doing the swim on the dance floor, while she was holding her nose and shimmying down Joey's legs, Mike had taken me aside and said, "I'm not really with her. I don't want you to think I'm really with her. Joey made me take her."

All this came to me in a flash as I sat on his lap. He'd found a girl down the beach to do it with him and he'd made his sweet friend, Mike, take her to my prom.

He'd found her in that dark place, down the Hurley's Hurdles, far deep in the glittery Penny Arcade, smashing with metal and glass, clanging with sirens and bells. They'd stood knee deep in Frozen Custard, slid on half-eaten pieces of Bill Ash's pizza, dragged Joe and Nemo's hot dogs around on their shoes. She reeked of Woolworth's perfume rubbed with Joey's Canoe on her neck and breasts, the way I used to smell it, mellow and green, lingering on my hair. He'd climbed on top of her behind Bluebeard's Cove, in The Pit, gyrating with the Tilt a' Whirl, their naked bodies long and lurid in the Funhouse mirrors. *The Funhouse, where they made me go, on a field trip to Canobie Lake Park in the eighth grade (I know I should have told you). I was so scared; I had to go in alone. I was too shy to have any friends. As I stepped into the blackness, sliding down the tilted corridor, I lost the floor; I lost up and down! I put my hands out to steady myself, but the walls were slanted outward! I must have come to a corner, because the wall suddenly bumped my shoulder and sent me in another direction. That's when the silence erupted into boys' shouts and hands grabbing my vagina, grabbing my breasts, twisting, laughing, laughing, someone screamed! It was only me.*

He'd found her there, waiting in the Funhouse for his hands to grab her as she came round the corner. He'd won her at the Shoot & Win; he'd paid some toothless carnie with a scar for a lip all his nickels for her. She smelled also of nickels, metallic, acidic. They'd had their black and white photos taken: she was on his lap like I was now, only she was laughing with her red mouth opened wide, his dark brown eyes, his heavy lips, openly drooping. They were picture perfect for each other, and how close I'd come to being just like her with my Boy Scouts and my Love Parties! Thank God for June! Thank God for books! And painting and writing!

"I don't care," I said to Joey.

He ran his fingers nervously through his long, dark hair, which fell, charmingly, into his liquid eyes that had never been liquid enough to possess me. He sucked air through his teeth, which I'd always found adorable and I did now, but objectively, and that surprised me.

"You're not upset?" he asked, incredulous.

"No," I told him.

He licked his beautiful lips. I would miss those.

"Are you sure?"

"Yup."

I got off his lap.


The second he left, I felt free. I attacked my homework and reading assignments with renewed energy. Ma, no longer limping, cooked and watched Merv Griffin. Arthur Treacher was making jokes and she was laughing.

A thrill of expectation shivered through me as I worked. I loved my work, I realized, more than anything. I wouldn't give it up even for June, and if she left me, I would still have it, more precious than life and family. No, I was wrong, my work was the same as my life and my family - there could be no difference. I resolved to take a sketchpad everywhere, no matter how anyone made fun of me, as I'd often wished I had the guts to do. How many times I'd wished I had one with me! I was thrilled with this new decision!

The homework assignment seemed remarkably exciting. The food we were going to have for dinner, steak cooked rare, baked potatoes, salad with Ma's oil and vinegar dressing seemed divine, fit for the gods! I couldn't wait to chew that thick slab of juicy meat Ma was sizzling right now in the pan, and to dip my bread into the steak juices and the salad dressing right now filling the kitchen and piquing my nostrils with their pungency! I could just about taste that potato whose skin was crisping in the oven as the butter oozed in shimmering rivulets from its frothy white peaks. I wondered if I should write a story about what had just happened with Joey. Yes! June would love it!

I looked at Ma, working so happily. She had no sex organs inside her. What was that like? Would it be better, like the doctor said, to be sexless? Was she sexless?

Look at her! How clearly she was a woman! How soft and round she was! Look at her crusted feet, how they worked! They were like loaves of bread! Her capable hands, working so easily, intuitively, yet, look how daintily they lifted to her mouth when she laughed! What was a woman, then, I mused as I watched Ma move with true purpose around the kitchen, but someone who loved and took care of her loved ones. And, yes, the definition was the same for a man.

Still, I considered it: cutting off my hair and breasts like an Amazon, like I'd thought of doing after the doctor had cupped them in his scaly hands. (It's true, I should have told you, how I had stood in Grandma's bathroom, which smelled so innocently of Ivory Snow and Johnson & Johnson's baby powder, products she loved to use, and, miserably, I had considered taking my uncle's razor to my shining head. How I wanted to shave my face off, continuing down my neck and breasts, until I was free of all that had attracted him to me. I didn't, miserable as I was, for the simple reason I would have had to explain why I'd mutilated myself and was bleeding to death when I came out of the bathroom.) Or, I thought, I could get really thin and my breasts would disappear and my period would stop. I could cut off my hair and renounce sex forever.

No. I decided. I wanted my hair, my crown, my banner. I wanted my breasts, both shield and soft underbelly. And my rounded ass like Ma's: a woman's ass, for myself. For my beauty. For my honor. For my sex.

I was very happy that afternoon.


## PREY

Before I tell you what happened, I want you to know, Marie and Jakey had done what I did hundreds of times before. The only unusual thing was: it was me who walked across the street to the Likus' house to look for Ma.

What was equally unusual: Rick answered the door instead of one of the girls.

I was only slightly taken aback. After all, he lived there and, if Ma wasn't at home, she was probably at Annie's.

"Is my mother here?" I asked him, warily.

"Yeah," and he stepped back to let me in.

I stepped into the dim hallway.

The second I was in the darkened hue of the Likus house, the second I smelled the musky odor of Likuses, the heavy, bodily odor of their chaos and mystery, the second I saw the amused face of Rick's pal, Frankie Campbell peering at me from the end of the hall, I knew in a flash of absolute terror - Ma wasn't there!

I turned to run out, but landed right in Rick's arms.

Down the dark tunnel, he carried me and every step was a jolt I emphasized, almost comically, with a cry of "Rick! Rick! Rick!"

He threw me down on the couch and jumped on top of me.

I scrambled underneath him.

"Don't! Rick! Don't!"

Frankie stood in the corner. He was blonde and narrow, smirking nervously.

"You're fuckin' nuts, man," Frankie told him.

"Come on!" he said, struggling with me. "You can do it too!"

He unsnapped my dungarees. The zipper slid open though I grabbed at frantically.

He unclenched my fingers, threw my hands down and held them over my head.

He laughed. Neither of us could move.

"Gloria!" he smiled down at me, his blue eyes sparkling against his dark skin, against the raw, white flesh of his scar like a twisted, agonized bolt of lightning from his damaged mind.

At that moment, I was terrified of him and I hated him, but I recognized him. He was the Nazi. A small part, a very strong small part of me wanted to throw my arms around him and pull him down on me. I've often wondered, though I hardly need to wonder, what I would have done if Frankie hadn't been there, standing, watching idiotically, altering the chemistry of the room. In my memory, I think of it sometimes as the death embrace of animals, the lioness teething upon the throat of her victim. I know she must love her prey: how much of her hunger and her agony she's put into pursuing it's delicious flesh and blood that will feed her and her babies and keep them alive and I know her mate has teased her throat with his teeth in much the same way when he took her and the love embrace and the death embrace are almost identical. So it was with me and Rick as we looked into each other's eyes in stalemate that dark afternoon. And I was the prey who entered into a special, familiar, and just relationship with its killer. I loved him and hated him as surely as I loved and hated myself.

But, I had too much to live for and I had to go on living. I couldn't let him! When he let go of me to unbuckle his belt, I pulled at his hands hysterically, not letting him. He laughed and laughed. He never once hit me. I didn't even know till years later that women were hit, or worse, during a rape. Then, he grabbed my pants legs around my thighs and yanked hard; traitors, they slid down to my knees.

"Wow! Look at this!" Rick said about my underwear, tiny bikini panties with little pink rosebuds.

"Hey, Likus, isn't that your grandmother coming?" Frankie drawled stupidly from the window.

"Shit!" Rick spat.

Rick picked me up by the shoulders and threw me off the couch toward the direction of the kitchen. I landed awkwardly in my bunched up pants, but before I could fall over, he had picked me up again and pushed me further toward the kitchen and again, I was being flung out the back door where I landed on my shoulder in a heap by the garbage pail, fish and banana peels cooking in the hot sun, buzzing with flies at the foot of his back steps. I could hear him answer his grandmother while his face was still toward me. He latched the backdoor shut.

I struggled to come to my senses. I couldn't be seen like this and in Rick's backyard! I didn't know whether to run first or pull up my pants. I pulled up my pants and zipped the fly.

I knew I couldn't simply walk out the driveway to the front.

Shaking with terror that I might be seen in Rick's yard, possibly I already had and with my pants down, I hid myself in the thick tangle of brush that grew against the tall wooden fence that separated the Likus's yard from the Strummer's. I considered the track side, but the fence there was even taller and since, I had to throw myself over, I didn't know what kind of shopping cart or soaked mattress or broken bottle I'd land on down by the tracks. The Strummer's yard beckoned me with the soft, green memories of its apple tree.

Thorns of scrub rose sliced at my arms and ankles as I tried to gain a foothold on the smooth fence. By sheer will and emergency, I smashed myself into the boards and catapulted my aching body over. I tumbled on to the grass.

I let myself stop for a minute. I panted heavily, hoping for that moment when my breath would come easily. I wanted to cry. I think the tears started to come and I wiped them away and they continued and I wiped them away again, streaking my face with dirt and blood from my hands.

Johnny came out of his house and rushed toward me. I was so glad to see him! He was married and didn't live there any more, but he was home on leave from the Army before going to Vietnam, I remembered all this at once, in my daze. But, there was something wrong about him! His hair was gone! His beautiful, sun-filled hair! And his expression was wrong! He wasn't happy to see me! He looked furious!

"Get the hell out of my yard!" he yelled at me.

His handsome face was twisted. His sunny hair had been shaved along the bumpy round of his skull like a prisoner of war.

"I couldn't help it," I mumbled, stunned and unsure what was happening.

"Get up!"

He also pulled me by the neck, like a small animal, and threw me in the direction he wanted me to go, toward the front walk. I thought, "If Rick's watching, he'll laugh."

"What are you doing, Johnny?" A soft voice called him sweetly from the front door. "Who is that?"

I looked up through my tears to see the vague shape of a woman wavering there behind the blackened screen door. It was Johnny's mother.

"Why it's Gloria! Gloria Wisher! Hello, dear! How is your mother? I never see her anymore!"

"Fine," I sniffed.

I figured she must be drunk. She didn't have the slightest idea what was going on. She had never called my mother or spoken much to her unless she happened to be out on the porch when Ma walked by. But, Celia Strummer never came out of the house these days. I didn't even think she was a nurse anymore. I was surprised, somewhere on top of my misery, that she even knew my name.

The metal gate made a high-pitched squeal like a caught pig as I opened it and Johnny Strummer, my beloved sun-kissed sweetheart, kicked me real hard in the behind and sent me flying forward out the gate so fast I fell hard on the cement scraping my palms, tearing my pants open and raking my knees in long, bloody scratches.

His mother was shocked.

"Johnny!"

"And stay out!" he screamed, crazily. "Get back in the house!" He turned and strode up the porch steps toward his mother.

I could hear her voice, retreating, protesting sweetly, that she "didn't see why -"

I went home, to my room, to mourn and lick my wounds and gather my strength. Maybe Johnny was mad at me because I hadn't gone for a ride with him. Maybe he was mad because he'd had to get married or because he had to go to war. But, really, it didn't matter why. It was an odd circumstance of my life that so many people had behaved so strangely for so long that when, suddenly, someone I'd trusted and believed in, like Johnny or my pediatrician or Daddy, for no reason viciously struck out at me, when it had happened for the thousandth time, I simply went home, washed and salved my wounds, and prepared myself for the next onslaught. Rick had caught me off guard, but I never thought for a moment he'd acted out of character. Somehow, in Revere, that was a virtue. It created a warped kind of trust.

EAST BOSTON, 1954

I was three years old when Mama opened the door and looked into the room. She screamed.

Her life was changed forever.

Daddy and I looked up.

Daddy laughed.

"Cut it out, Rosie! She's okay. It doesn't hurt her!"

Mama cried and ran to pick me up.

Daddy stood and zipped up his pants.

Mama screamed and cried. She ran into another room and slammed the door, pow!

Mama looked around for a way to kill herself and me.

THAILAND

"They're sending your Uncle Sonny to Thailand," Ma informed me.

"Thailand? I thought the war was in Vietnam?"

"How the hell do I know? You go where they send you! They told him he's going to Thailand."

"Wow. That's heavy."

"He wants you to take care of his car."

"What?"

"His green convertible. He said to keep it in the yard and, every once in a while, just start it up for him."

Uncle Sonny came over a couple of weeks later on a Saturday afternoon. The double gates at the bottom of the yard by the old, grassed-over driveway that we never used were suddenly opened. June and I watched as the green Chrysler convertible with the black canvas top eased itself in to its new home.

Then, the most remarkable thing happened.

Uncle Sonny handed me the keys.

"I know you'll take good care of my car, Gloria. You take good care of everything. And if yous get your licenses, yous can drive it anywheres you want, except the ocean, don't drive it into the ocean. Okay?"

June and I stood with our mouths gaping.

"Okay?" he repeated.

"Okay! Okay!" we answered together.

He went inside the house to visit with Ma.

June and I were silent. Staring at the car's majesty, the sharp lines of its torso, we walked slowly around its body from the trunk to the fierce grill like dragon's teeth above the chrome fender, shined by Uncle Sonny's caring hands to a stunning reflection of sunlight and the wavy figures of two awestruck girls. The tires were gleaming clean. The hubcaps were revolving mirrors.

I peered inside its black vinyl depths.

"It has a radio," I said, foolishly.

I saw lots of curious knobs and levers, glistening silver in the dark of the interior. I felt like Alice in Wonderland, only too scared to touch anything.

"Wonder what all this stuff is."

I opened the door.

"What stuff?" June asked, distractedly.

"These knobs and stuff," I said, stroking them.

"Tweet."

"What?"

"We're getting our licenses."

"We are?"

"Yup."

"How?"

"At school."

"At school? You're kidding!"

"There's a program."

"Where did you hear that?"

"They told us. I thought about doing it, but now, we're definitely gonna."

"Gee, they never tell the Accelerated Class anything like that," I said, peering at the dashboard clock, which, unlike any of the clocks we had in the house, actually worked.

So, we learned to drive. One of the teachers I didn't know from the high school taught us. He was very kind and patient, but his huge bulk was monstrous and threatening in the close confines of the instructional sedan.

I sweated buckets out the back of my blue workshirt, so that when I emerged from each lesson, I had an enormous perspiration stain on my back like a laborer. June was cool and collected. She got out of the car calculating her remaining lessons.

I waited for her to return from her lessons outside the chain link fence where the men's industrial leagues played baseball. The small park was next to the driving school. Johnny Strummer used to play there. While I waited, I pretended I was watching him play.

His long hair was gleaming with sun; it flew in curls about his neck where it fell outside his cap. His blue eyes sparkled as he saw me; his hand shot up to wave to me. He winked, "Hey, Bleachie!" He came running over the next chance he got, huffing and puffing, "You come to see me play?"

I nodded happily.

"I'm learning to drive!" I answered, pointing to the school. "My uncle gave me his car!"

"Oh, yeah? Maybe you can take me for a ride sometime?"

"Oh, Johnny! You're married!"

"So? We can still go for a ride!"

"John-ny!" His friends called him and he ran back to his game.

"The streets ain't gonna be safe with you on them, Bleachie!"

Then, as I watched him dash back to his friends who weren't there, older boys I didn't know took their place, yelling and cursing each other on the field and the whole daydream slipped away. The sickening realization of what had happened took its place, and the even more frightening reality that

Johnny wasn't here at all. He could not be playing ball with his friends in the sun. He was far away, in the jungle.


JOHNNY ROZINSKY

One summer Saturday, I stepped out on the porch and saw a tall, tanned young man dressed in white dungarees and a madras shirt across the street; he was leaning lazily on the railing of Connie's porch. He stood languidly as a Southerner against the railing, as limp as a person used to breathing slowly and easily in tropical heat. I peeked at him through the screen. He had a big nose, long and slightly bulbous on the end, but somehow, it worked on his face to make him seem a bit studious and sweetly approachable. When he looked up, I could just make out: his eyes were heavily lidded, giving him a gentle, sleepy expression. He was doing something I'd never seen a fine looking boy do before.

He was reading a book.

"Who's that?" I asked Ma.

"Who?"

"That's what I wanna know."

"DON'T GET SMART!" I think she said that about a hundred times a day, mostly to me.

"Who's that across the street on Connie's porch?"

She left the stove where she was boiling water laced with mustard for the three pounds of hot pastrami she cooked up every Saturday. Like a sorceress, she boiled the huge pot and leaned over it with a long fork, stirring the sweet strands of pink and fatty meat. She came over to the window, stood next to me and rested her chin on my shoulder.

"Oh," she said.

Then she got that mischievous Mona Lisa smile and walked away.

"Ma! Who is he?"

She smiled secretly.

"That's Johnny Roz-Roz-blah, I don't know how to say it, one of those Polish names. He's Connie's husband's cousin. He used to live there in that house. Do you remember him?"

Amazed, I looked out the window.

"No. He used to live here? When?"

"You were about eight or nine. We just moved here when they moved away. He's about six years older than you."

"Is he moving back here?" I asked hopefully regarding his handsome, self-assured form. I liked the way his long fingers stroked the page a long time before he turned it, almost making love to the book, like he loved it. I admitted to myself immediately, I had a real weakness for the name Johnny.

Like the aunt in *A Tree Grows in Brooklyn*, I would have liked to name them all Johnny. "So, is he gonna live with Connie now? Is she moving out?"

"He's going to Vietnam," Ma said with a sigh, and I knew she was thinking about her little brother, about Johnny Strummer and Jakey's brother, my cousin, Peter who'd been there for a while now. "He wanted to see his old home before he left."

I took this information in while Ma went about her work for a few minutes. All the older boys were going. My darling Cousin Peter who had gone and actually signed up again, Uncle Sonny, Johnny Strummer, now this boy. They appeared to my mind as a huge mass of men, going.

"Why don't you go over and talk to him? He remembers you."

"Don't encourage her." Daddy spoke from the table where he was doing a crossword puzzle. I could forget about him and suddenly he'd speak and I'd be shocked. He interjected a bad feeling, making me uncomfortable about whether to speak to this new boy. He was right, of course, I had that about me, that desire, that urge: I liked it. He knew that. It was between him and me; this thing was in me. I got it from him.

"Did he ask about me?" I asked, tentatively.

"Oh, yeah. He wanted to know about all you kids; he asked about Jakey and Marie and you."

I studied him, hoping I'd remember something.

"He lived in California all this time! I'd love to live there and be nice and warm every day and have palm trees. The lemons and oranges grow right in your Aunt Doris' yard in Florida! I'm sick of the winter!"

"Yeah, it's the winter that keeps the cockroaches out of your bed," said Daddy.

I thought about California. At the mention of the word California, it came to me as though I recognized it: a soft blur instead of a boy, but a memory nevertheless, a vague softness, a gentle spirit. Was that Johnny?

"Go ahead! Don't be shy!"

"I am shy."

"So's he. He used to be real shy. Well, you got two weeks to make up your mind, then he's leaving for Vietnam."

That decided it, though it still took all my courage to go outside. I walked like I was going somewhere in particular; my eyes locked on him, so that when he looked up -

"Hi!"

He spoke slowly, drawling out the short word with purpose. I realized he knew I'd come out. He'd been trying to get me to come out.

"Hi, I'm Gloria. Do you remember me?" I asked as I approached him. He also walked toward me, slow and lazy as a cat that takes its time, even to the point of stopping for a bath. Johnny didn't do that, but he gave the impression of not caring, not hurrying.

We met at Connie's gate.

"Little Gloria."

"I'm not little any more."

"I can see that."

I let myself into that trap, I thought.

"What are you reading?" I asked.

"There's really not much to read in here. I got this for the photographs. Come see."

He had an accent, slow as his walk, as his languid, sleepy manner of moving his arms and hands. He pronounced each and every syllable almost perfectly. I'd never heard anyone pronouce r and t before, except on television.

"Where are you from?"

"California."

It was worth asking, just to hear him say the word. His voice conjured up all the warmth and fragrance of an orange grove, all the suntanned, shipwrecked glamour of surfers, even the romantic dash of cowboys as I'd seen them on "Bonanza" or "Big Valley." Johnny was someone who knew about the reality of those things first hand.

He opened the book on the hood of Connie's old car. It was one of those large hardcover photo books, like the kind made for coffee tables by Life magazine that you can get out of the library. Only he'd bought it. The idea of someone buying a hardcover book was so foreign to me, I assumed, he's either rich or he doesn't mind spending all his money on one thing.

"I got it because it had such beautiful pictures of Polish people. I'm Polish," he smiled sleepily.

"I know," I told him. "My mother can't say your name."

"It's Rozinsky," he laughed. "It's not that hard. Look!"

I wonder if you realize how remarkable this was: not only was he reading a book, openly, in public: he also wanted to talk with me about it. I sneaked a glance at him. His skin was the color of coffee and cream against the faded, real madras of his short-sleeved shirt, the kind surfers wore. ("Real" madras was woven; it was the same vivid color on the inside of the shirt as on the outside. The difference between Johnny's madras and mine was something Johnny liked to show me. My shirt was printed junk Ma had bought at Zayre's; it was white on the inside.) Johnny's hair had been shaved by the United States Army. It was very short along the nape of his neck, where the muscles moved, and the sun sparkled off the shaved ends of its delicate fuzz. His sleepy eyes and rounded nose, as he bent his head to look at the book, drew me down to him in a soft and friendly way.

Johnny Rozinsky opened the book to a shiny full-page photo of a very old woman in a kerchief. She was smiling broadly with no teeth.

"Isn't she beautiful?" he asked in a reverent voice I'd only heard inside my own head or whispered in my ear from June's or Ma's appreciative mouths.

"Yes!" I agreed wholeheartedly. "She looks exactly like my Nona!" And she did, with her ancient skin and laughing eyes.

"Is that your grandmother?" he asked.

"My great-grandmother."

"Your great grandmother is still alive? Wow! That's beautiful, man!"

We looked at all the photos and then we looked at them again. He asked me if I'd like to go down Shirley Ave and eat potato pancakes at the deli for supper.

I told him I'd never been to the deli and I'd never had potato pancakes. He was shocked.

"Oh! You gotta have potato pancakes!" And his face lit up with such an appreciation for potato pancakes! I'd never seen anyone outside my family appreciate food like that!

Ma was pleased and very conspiratorial when I came busting in to tell her. I swear, as I got dressed, her body thrilled as much as mine.

"Where's my dungarees?"

"In the dryer."

"What! Don't put my dungs in the dryer! They'll shrink! The seams will twist!" I cried, pulling them out as though saving the life of a small child.

"Excuse *me*!!" she laughed.

I put them on damp.

Ma shook her head.

"They'll dry," I said.

I told him I had a car, but he wanted to walk. He said he'd been walking all around Revere and he loved Revere. He said he loved the Ave and loved the deli. He talked about how he used to hang out at Shirley Drug when they had a soda fountain.

"I never heard it called a 'soda fountain' except on TV," I told him.

"Why? What do you call it?" he drawled.

"We just call it a 'counter.'"

"Yeah, I remember that."

The potato pancakes were greasier then I could have imagined, but Johnny reached over in his gentle way and patted them with a napkin for me. The yellow grease oozed out of the patties into the napkin. He then showed me how to put applesauce and sour cream on them. He told me potato pancakes were Polish food.

"I'm half Italian and half English."

"That's beautiful. The English are so beautiful! And, the Italians! Wow!"

He looked at me with dreamy eyes and I knew he was thinking that I was as beautiful as the English, the Italians and the Polish. I knew what he was saying. His message came to me as an enormous relief from the prejudice and Polish jokes that surrounded me. He was telling me that all people were beautiful, that even Revere was beautiful, and I also knew it was his way of holding on to himself, of holding on to the life he'd known and loved: eating as much as he could of potato pancakes, Revere, the Poles, even me, before he left the United States of America and disappeared into the jungle.

Afterwards, we walked along the dull grey beach by the quiet, residential end, far from the bright and noisy concessions. A slim fog hid the neon lights from the bars in a dull wash, and the lonely beach echoed Johnny's loneliness, which I could see him pushing away with soft smiles and plans for what we should do tomorrow. Streetlights sent a stream of gold across the sand and he ran into the water up to his knees, pulling me in with him. We splashed knee deep in the dirty water and we laughed and laughed. We laughed! And I couldn't remember ever having laughed so much and so freely with a boy.

As we walked home, he knelt and rung out my dungarees with his hands. I told him how I'd rescued them from the dryer. He laughed. He said jeans (a new word) should dry on to make them tight, and then he stood up, and there, at the top of Centennial, he kissed me.

"I love you," he told me.

I didn't know whether to believe him, but I knew this: Johnny washed away his loneliness in love and beauty. He washed away his fear.

He loved to walk in Boston too. He took me to Boston and we walked all day. Johnny loved everything. He bought donuts and coffee at the steaming teapot and we carried them, the cups too hot to hold, the bag still steaming with oven heat coming from the squishy flesh of the donuts, down to the pier to eat and drink while we watched the longshoremen, as Daddy called them, loading up the boats. The early morning sea air entering our mouths made the coffee especially rich and satisfying and the donuts, absolutely wonderful.

"Drink out of my cup," Johnny said, all dreamy eyed.

I drank from it, the sweet coffee and cream tasted like his very skin.

"Now, drink from mine," I said, and he did, linking our eyes with his gaze over the rim.

We looked in shop windows. He admired the sparkling jewels at Shreve's, but said he could never buy one. In real life, on women, he said, they were cold and ugly. But, he had praise for the deep blue velvet that set them off. He said he'd like to see me in a dress made of it.

We looked at leather and books and paintings and statues. We fed the pigeons and squirrels and the ducks in the Public Garden. He admired the people we saw, people of all kinds - babies! A pretty fat woman! A stout working man! A slim policeman on horseback! A homeless man!

I felt myself falling into adoration of Johnny and then he said, as we were crossing the street, "Have you seen 2001 yet?"

Vaguely, I knew it was a movie.

"No."

"Would you like to?"

"Yeah!"

"Okay, let's get a paper."

"Right now?"

He smiled that slow smile.

"Yeah."

I'd never heard of anyone deciding to go to a movie just like that, in the middle of the street! For certain, I adored him!

2001 was a revelation and a shock. We talked enthusiastically about the monolith, the apes, the music, the planets, the spaceships.

"What did it mean?" I asked. "Where was the old man? Was he the astronaut? The baby looked like him too."

Johnny just shrugged and smiled as though he knew, but couldn't tell me because I had to decide for myself.

"Your big eyes and your high forehead make you look like the baby at the end," he said, "Rebirth."

He held my hand as we walked home. He looked at it as though it were something precious. He said my name.

"I love you," he told me, over and over every day. "I love you." And, he repeated this: "Will you marry me?"

"I'm too young to get married."

The diapers I'd seen when Dinghy wanted to marry me had suddenly appeared hanging over my head like little guillotines.

"We could eat toast and read books all day," he said, making me laugh. He loved toast. He buttered it and folded it and ate it in big, hungry bites.

"That's how my mother eats pizza," I'd told him. "She pours hot pepper on a pizza half and folds it over. Then, her eyes tear and she says, 'Oh, that's good!'"

"Your mother's beautiful. You'll have beautiful children, just like she did. We can get married before I leave. I love you."

"No," I said. "You'll fall in love with a native girl in Vietnam."

One night, on the beach, he tried to make love to me. His hands urged me, along the sides of my breasts, down my back, he caressed my arms, my neck, he insisted silently with urgent kisses, but I couldn't let him. I couldn't. And I was beginning to think, if I couldn't go all the way with Johnny, whom I truly loved, was there ever going to be anyone? But, I couldn't let go of my dream to go to college! I could get pregnant there, where the street light fell on the dirty sand, my face next to someone's used tampon while the bums burped and rolled over in their sandy beds nearby.

I took him to the airport. With cold, nervous lips, we kissed goodbye in utter shock. I lost the car in the vast multi-layered parking lot. A boy on a scooter helped me find it. I followed along behind him miserably.

Icy, trembling, I realized, Johnny was gone. I knew I'd been right not to get married; I didn't regret not having sex. But, I missed his sweet sense of what was good and his calm, easy presence by my side.

I didn't know if it would ever happen for me again, but I'd been completely happy for two weeks.

## JOHNNY'S LETTERS

Johnny wrote me twenty letters a day from Vietnam. They arrived in neat red, white and blue bundles of special tissue paper envelopes that unfolded in an extraordinary way to be the letters themselves. Soldiers got postage free and I could tell by the way Johnny wrote the word, big and bold, *FREE*, in the right hand corner where the stamp should be that he meant it literally: he meant his spirit was still free even though his body was in the Army.

After a few weeks, the mailman knocked on our door to meet me.

"I had to see for myself who you were," he said, sheepishly. He was a young man, pleasant looking and trim in his civilian uniform. "My kids ask me every day, 'How many today, Dad?' You must have boxes of them by now."

"Yes," I nodded. "Boxes." I wondered what it was like to be that young, as young as Johnny Strummer and have kids.

"I like the things he writes on the outside of the envelope. Like this - he pointed to one, 'Wear your love like heaven.' That's nice."

"It's from a song. By Donovan."

"Oh, yeah? That's nice."

"He's very poetic."

"That must be nice. I don't know anything about poetry myself. Well, I wish you both luck," he said after a minute of staring at me.

Johnny Rozinsky, as I'd expected, wrote letters about the beautiful people of Vietnam. He wrote about his Mama San, Song, an older woman who did his laundry while he was in base camp. I sent him a large sketch I'd done of a little Vietnamese boy in Time magazine. Johnny placed this on the wall over his bed. His Mama San asked if the boy was his son.

Johnny asked me to draw my house.

I knew he wanted this because it was the precious view he'd seen from his window. I got my sketchpad and pencil and went across the street and stood in front of Connie's house and faced my soul. It was almost unbearable.

The peaked roof pierced my heart. The window, the porch, the bay window, the steps, the little door under the porch all whispered secrets I'd rather have forgotten, pornographic faces of dark, twisted teachings. The face of the house was like dirty underwear turned inside out, like a person naked that you aren't supposed to see naked, like a teacher or a priest - or a father. And peculiarly, it was the face of an old family of railroad workers, some unknown ancestors, who'd sheltered themselves within the very same flesh and blood of the very same wood and warmth.

I began a drawing, but every line, every shadow was a torment to me, one that I couldn't finish, one that I could never send to Johnny: a picture of my nightmares. He begged for photos, but I didn't have a camera, nor did I have the kind of money it took to buy film and get it developed. I told him I couldn't send photos and this unbalanced correspondence, I felt it, thousands and thousands of miles away, marked a disappointment, which, more than the distance, was the real beginning of our drift apart.

Johnny's letters were beautiful. He didn't write about the war. Ma said, "Johnny's letters" with a wistful tone and everyone knew what she meant. He had a trick of writing a funny idea or a new thought on the inside flap of the envelope just as you opened it, so you had to be careful to cut the envelope just right or you'd miss his message. He wrote ordinary words, but in such a way as to make them poetry. "The jungle trees whisper your name." He wrote, "The rain washes the faces of flowers." He wrote about things we'd seen together in Boston, "The balloon man must be an extraordinary man!" and "The only real gold on earth gleams from the State House dome." He asked me to feed the pigeons for him and to salute George Washington. As if to match him, I wrote the nuns went by two by two, like "the black flags of surrender."

Johnny Rozinsky didn't die as you may have thought. He just didn't come home to me. It was classic. His beautiful letters slowly became less and less beautiful, dwindled and disappeared. After his tour of duty was over, he went home to California and became engaged to the girl next door. In a few years, he opened a Sports Equipment store, specializing in running gear, though nobody in New England would know what "running" meant, and, after we discovered what running was, Johnny would seem like the last person who would make a career out of physical activity. After a few weeks, however, I asked Connie for his phone number and June and I gathered as many coins as we could and went up to the payphone at the sub shop on the highway behind my house and called him in California.

My heart banged out of my chest, but I was determined. I pretended I was calling one of those rock n' roll stars in their room, but this time I didn't need the British accent.

His voice was slow and lazy as I remembered it, and, for a second, his voice, a sweet, painful jolt along thousands of miles of phone line, almost made me cry.

"Johnny. It's Gloria. I just wanted to know, are you coming back?"

"No," he said, and I could hear he was laughing a little.

"How come?"

"I dunno. I'm just not."

"You asked me to marry you, Johnny."

"I know," he laughed.

"I hear you're engaged to the girl next door."

"Yeah."

"That's really funny, Johnny."

"Yeah, I guess."

"I want you to know, I'm not mad. I expected something like this. I wouldn't have been too surprised if you'd told me you were gonna marry your Mama San."

He laughed.

"Have a good life. I mean it."

And, I did, too.

"Yeah, thanks - you, too!"

"Oh, I will! Bye."

"Bye."

Connie told me I had guts. I guess I knew instinctively about traveling 180 degrees away from home, that it changes you to your opposite. But, you know, I don't really think it changed Johnny at all.

GUIDANCE RHS

I graduated from Revere High School with a gold and white tassel for Honors. I would have felt pretty smart, except for someone I hadn't known existed before the last few weeks of school - my guidance counselor.

One day in class, we were told we'd be going down to the office to see our guidance counselors that day.

"What the heck's a 'guidance counselor'?" I asked the girl behind me.

She shrugged. She never knew she had one either.

There were three guidance counselors, so we went down alphabetically in threes. My guidance counselor was a woman. She seemed very small and tidy in a brown suit behind her very large wooden desk. All of guidance was in the same room: Guidance. Guidance was divided into three cubicles made of three-quarter cork walls. The other guidance counselors were dumpy men in grimy suits, whom I'd seen roaming the corridors and didn't care enough to give a moment to wonder who they were or what they did. Each had a student fidgeting in the folding chair in front of them. Faded government posters, advertising the four food groups and certain postal rules using leering, badly drawn government-issue cartoon characters decorated the cork partitions and the industrial green walls.

My counselor, Mrs. Murphy, impatiently slid a paper clip back and forth along some papers and told me neatly as she did, that all the scholarships had been taken by the spectacular grades and achievements of my classmates, most of them scientists, who'd received full scholarships to Harvard, BU, MIT and - this hurt - Radcliffe! She said my SAT's weren't anywhere near good enough for a scholarship, nor had I applied early enough.

"Why didn't you tell me what I needed to be doing?" I asked her, "Where were you all these years?"

"Dear, you couldn't have competed with your classmates."

These were the same kids who couldn't get the symbolic color code of Stephen Crane's even when it was explained to them? Who needed to be taken by the hand and led through *The Great Gatsby*? And spoon-fed a silly romp like *The Importance of Being Ernest*?

Mrs. Murphy suggested a state school.

Why not a state prison?

She suggested Salem State or the University of Massachusetts, if I wanted to live away.

"How much is an application to Harvard?" I asked.

"That costs - she searched her list - fifteen dollars."

I didn't have fifteen dollars.

"Forget Harvard, Gloria. You're simply NOT Harvard material. Let's apply to Salem State. It's free!"

Yeah, let's. I guessed she was going with me.

"What will your major be?"

"What's a major?"

She smiled, a real simpy smile, like she was so smart and I was so stupid.

"A 'major' is your field, dear. What is your favorite subject?"

"English."

"English," she repeated, writing it down. "And you'll minor in Education."

"What does that mean?"

"Your minor is unimportant, but if you have an Education minor, you'll get a teaching certificate," she nodded efficiently.

"Wait a minute! I don't want to teach!"

"Oh, don't be silly. What else would you do with English?"

"Write!"

She smiled that simpy smile again. I wanted to wipe it off her face with that huge, thick book of colleges she had on her desk from which she could only find one, the most local.

"But, how would you make a living, Gloria?"

"By writing. And I'd like to minor in Art."

Her eyes fell to the sketchpad on my lap. For a second, I time traveled, ever so peacefully, to the places Johnny had let me sketch him: leaning against the stone fountain in Boston Common; sitting on the front steps of Connie's house reading, eating toast folded like a letter.

"Art is a nice hobby, dear, but what are you going to do when you get out of school?"

"The same thing I'm doing now, write, draw and study. I'm going to be a writer," I added, though I wanted to scream, "I already am a goddamn godforsaken writer, God help me!"

"You should be a teacher," she replied, with decision.

"Let me ask you something," I said, "this minor in Education, does that mean they actually teach you how to teach English?"

"Yes!" she said, brightly, as though I were finally getting it.

What a waste of time, I thought.

"Let me think about this at home," I told her. "I'll let you know."

"Yes, good idea! Consult with your parents and let me know by Monday!" She smiled knowingly, like a used car salesman who knows you'll be back.

I had no intention of consulting with Ma and Daddy. They knew less than I did.

HEAD

It was my fault. What happened with June: we'd been so close, I panicked. She still said things to me, things I knew she had to say. It had been hard enough to hear them in high school. I could not, no, I would not hear them in college! I needed so desperately to go to college, to not be undermined there. So that, when she said she'd go to Salem State too, I asked her not to go there. I asked her to go someplace else. I needed to go to college alone.

I was shocked by my decision, but I went to her anyway, frightened, determined, just like the night when I had run across the highway in my pajama top and dungarees to tell her about my father. This night, I knew she was babysitting at Connie's and I told her we needed to talk. She smirked.

Junie once told me that she'd been an evil sucker in a previous life and she felt there were moments when that evil spirit came through.

"Junie," I began, "for a long time now..."

"Wait a minute – is this rehearsed?" she grinned.

"Yes." My heart felt sick. But, I told myself I was protecting my work. My soul. "For a long time now, you've been saying things to me, hurtful things and I don't want to take all that to college with me. I don't want you to go to Salem State with me. I want you to go somewhere else."

How could I have done this to Junie? I don't know.

It broke her heart and drove her right into Aaron Goldman's arms. Junie decided to go to Northeastern in Boston, where Aaron was already a sophomore. Surprisingly, we still remained friends, still walked to school together, went shopping, did all the same things we used to do, and to tell the truth, I felt relieved. I needed to be free. I didn't realize, I had sent her into a situation where *she* would be the under dog.

Aaron was a legend; he was a sexual legend, the way Rick was a criminal. He'd opened the first head shop down the Ave in Revere, called simply, HEAD. He sold posters, incense, earrings, beads, T-shirts, pottery and baskets. We wondered, you know, if he sold anything else.

He stood at the doorway of his shop and watched us walk by. He looked at Junie with his startling blue eyes from behind the black curtain of his wavy hair.

"Hey!" he called to us, "You want some beads?"

We crossed the street. It was that simple to change your life.

Junie knew Aaron from school. He passed her notes asking her out. She said she was going out with someone and he wrote back, "What can I say?" In order to deal with her frustration, Junie would smack me with that line all day long. "What can I say?" she'd smirk at me at hurtful moments, real cool, like she didn't care about me. Even before I had asked her to go to college somewhere else, it was another smart remark at my expense that I didn't want to hear in college, a smart remark that I knew had come from Aaron, so that, right away, even before I met him, I started to hate Aaron Goldman.

Smiling, exotically suntanned in the grey damp of March, he placed two necklaces of ugly brown beads over our heads.

"These are from Peru," he told us.

"You've been to Peru?" June asked, enraptured, pouring the dreamy blue water of her eyes into the sparkling blue depths of his. I couldn't help thinking how potentially beautiful their progeny would be.

"Yeah! I just got back!" he grinned, invigorated, it seemed from his travels.

"What were you doing there?" I asked, jealously. I didn't want him impressing Junie.

"Oh, exploring, thinking! Climbing the spectacular mountains! You should see them! The colors are beautiful, like nothing you've ever seen! The people use the colors of the land in their weaving. Come inside! I've got some blankets and pottery! The people are so beautiful, you really should go!"

Junie was transported. Like two naive savages, we followed him inside, to view his wares, perhaps to be given smallpox blankets or to sell our virgin land for beads.

Once inside, I saw a young man, as if part of the shadowy wall, one of his friends startled me by standing in the darkness smoking a cigarette just like Frankie Campbell had stood by in the dark Likus hallway, and then I saw, it *was* Frankie Campbell and I froze.

It's okay, I told myself, other people are here; you're safe. Aaron was busy showing Junie some ponchos. I could feel Frankie's smirk on my back. I tried to ignore him, but while Aaron was busy with Junie, Frankie leaned over and whispered in my ear, "You look good with your pants down!"

His breath passed into my ear with a burning sensation and he passed the cigarette he was smoking to Aaron who accepted it.

"You ever smoke a joint?" Aaron held his breath and asked, squinting into the smoke. He offered it to Junie who had watched him suck in deeply and taking the twisted little cigarette from him, did exactly the same, holding her breath. Aaron motioned her to pass it to me, and I took it between my fingers and looked at it, burning and twisting.

"Don't just look at it! Take a toke and pass it," Frankie laughed.

I knew he wanted it in my mouth. He wanted to watch it go into my mouth, so I let him. I turned so he could see me take the first toke of my life. I sucked deeply and let the smoke fill my brain. Frankie's beady little eyes went all gooshy and gratified. "Yeah!" he said. June and Aaron somehow faded behind a wall of haze as the joint got passed around another time.

"Got this in Mexico on my way back," Aaron said.

Some time passed in a cushioned haze of sweet, floating smoke, and then, unbelievably, I turned to take another toke and a policeman was handing the joint to me! He was young and handsome, no one I knew, with laughing eyes glaring at me from under his slick visor; his badge twinkled in the semi-darkness, and he laughed, and his teeth glowed brightly in the dark, "Don't worry, sweetheart! Jeez, your friends are paranoid!"

The cop was holding a fat wad of money, which he folded and put in his pocket. He laughed again, "I'm telling you, Goldman, I'm gonna have to close you down anyway! You gotta have a bathroom, state law!" he sniffed, enthusiastically, "Good shit!"

I heard Aaron say he couldn't afford to put a bathroom in the tiny head shop, which was no bigger than a closet itself. Frankie slinked into a corner.

The cop filled the little shop with his uniform. I think I forgot how to breathe and June was suddenly beside me and we were out in the sunshine while the painted lines on the street wiggled like jump ropes and the cop car went by a minute later and whooped its siren at us just for fun. Getting high would always seem a male intrusion upon my brain. Even with friends, I could hardly wait to be myself again, after the heady cloud had passed, like the passing of the clouds blocking the sun on the purple mountaintops of Peru.

Aaron asked June out that day and the rest is history: the peculiar history of Aaron and June, which was to go on for years.

Like the time Aaron brought her into the Brigham's on the beach where Will Cullen had gotten a job behind the counter. June ordered an ice cream cone and Will made it so big and floppy she couldn't hold it. Aaron just laughed at him, and Will, sullen and serious, turned a livid crimson. Or, the time Aaron walked right up to Will and June while they were walking down Broadway and stole June's attention long enough for a bird to shit on Will's head. Will spent the rest of the walk home behind June and Aaron, rustling the bushes, trying to wipe the mess from his hair with leaves. With every rustle of leaves, Aaron and June burst out laughing.

Aaron liked to grab June while the three of us were walking or talking somewhere and kiss her forever, while I waited and waited. I worried about her because I felt guilty about having told her to go to a different college and because I knew Aaron would overpower her. But, I also understood everyone wanted to be alone with June. Not only me. She was, and still is, lovely to be alone with.

Ma and I hashed it out over my future until that teaching certificate started to look good. I could see it in my hand, officially telling me I could teach, as Ma put it, "just in case." I "decided" to go to Salem State. I didn't choose it as much as it chose me, like so many of the so-called choices people make in life.

June rode the train in to Northeastern with Aaron, except for the first few days of school, when she actually had to go in by herself. Aaron had to go to a funeral. On their way to school, Aaron and his best friend, Neil had found Neil's father shot in the head, slumped over the steering wheel of his own car, parked right in front of his own house.

Ma yelled, "See! See! All the stolen cars we find outside of the house, with their insides stripped out, I told you someday there's gonna be a dead body in one of them!"

I said, "Ma, this isn't a dead body, this is his best friend's father!"

Nevertheless, as a precaution, or an excuse, she got a police radio, "to hear what's going on around here!" Every morning amidst the gentle tinkling sounds of Ma and Daddy sitting down to sip their breakfast coffee silently together I'd hear the violent blast of static from the little black box on the kitchen counter. Ma started talking about "youths" and "vehicles" and "altercations." The cops' raspy voices talked in numbers, "10-4" or "That's a 351" so the people who were listening couldn't understand what was happening. Somehow, Ma got a list of what the number codes meant and she taped it to the side of the box.

I wondered how much of what she was hearing was really happening like the Revere cop in the Head Shop. You could run your finger down the list and see it was a "robbery in progress" or a "domestic disturbance," but you couldn't see and you couldn't hear what was really happening, not really. Listening to the police radio was like reading between the lines in a newspaper: there was a lot going on in those blank spaces between the words, between the blasts of static hitting our ears like gunshots.


TWO THINGS

You could say the murder was caused by this or that but really it was caused by everything. By everything that happened, by the way it all happened, by things that came before, and, crazily enough, by things that came after.

It was all one, somehow.

Two things happened before the murder, and before them, the inevitable, unstoppable, loss of June had begun.

The first thing:

I was eating at the kitchen table, whether it was supper or breakfast, I don't remember. Daddy came in and saw me. He saw that I was alone, and he came over to me. He had a look in his eye that made me look around for

Ma! Ma! Ma! She wasn't around; I was relieved and panicked at the same time.

He reached down and unzipped my dungarees. It happened so fast. They unzipped real easy and my small stomach bulged naked, except for the tiny triangle of bikini underwear and the small tuft of light brown curls popping out.

"There it is!" Daddy grinned, "I miss it!"

He hadn't bothered me in almost two years, not since what I called "Gatsby night" when he'd come into the bedroom while I was studying Gatsby and I'd hollered at him to get out. Gatsby was sacred and I had, almost ridiculously, jumped up to defend literature.

I'd begun to put it all in the past and not expect it anymore.

Can you believe what made me mad - that there was something forbidden about his touching my dungarees! As the stiff, protective canvas fell away I became infuriated that he had no right to touch something so sanctified by my youth, that he had crossed into territory exclusively mine! The dungarees seemed almost as sacred as Gatsby!

I zipped them back up, the zipper biting his hand, which was reaching in.

Protected by my youthful armor, I spit at him, "I'm not your wife!"

He actually growled at me! His upper lip quivered like a growling dog and he skulked away.

I continued eating, though every organ in my body shook. People like me have learned how to eat anyway.


The second thing:

I was sewing downstairs. I was embroidering little multi-colored flowers on the pockets of a skirt I was making for college. I'd been breaking the threads with my teeth, but that was messy for embroidery and dangerous for my gums. I told myself, "Don't be so lazy! Go upstairs and get the scissors!"

I was alone in the house.

I climbed the stairs and as I passed Jakey's room, I heard a rattle and then, scraping and again, a rattle. I peeked in to see Rick Likus at the window jimmying the screen.

When he saw me, he smiled in greeting, as though nothing were out of the ordinary. He stepped into the house with the screen in his hand.

Dumbfounded, I stood facing him. Jakey's bed was between us.

I should have run, I know, but at that moment I wasn't afraid of him.

"I'm going to Vietnam, Gloria," he stated.

"So? What? You thought you'd just sneak in here first?"

"Yeah!" he laughed.

"You're rotten scum, Rick! If you were on the pond, the frogs wouldn't even eat you!"

He laughed and lunged over the bed at me. That's when I ran, screaming, "You're scum! Scum!"

Our feet pounded down the stairs. I was almost half way down when he leaped on me. I'd had dreams in which I was falling down these same stairs, when the sensation of falling jerks in my stomach like a brake and I suddenly float, empowered and strong, down the rest of the way, hovering peacefully as a seagull, sometimes landing quietly on my belly.

We landed in a painful heap against the edges of the steps.

"Damn you, Rick! I hate you! I hate you!" I screamed as I struggled.

"You hate me? You don't hate me, you love me!"

He laughed like it was a big joke to him. His hands grabbed me all over, taking a handful of my behind, squeezing my breasts playfully, meanly. He looked directly into my eyes as he rubbed his hand between my legs. His scarred blue eye, strange, yet as recognizable as my own.

"Stop it! I hate you!"

"You know you love me."

He kissed me, pressing his mouth into mine. I turned my head and spit his saliva out and his mouth traveled down my neck to my breast. He smelled like dirt and the dank dirty sweat of performing a crime. His teeth sunk into the soft cotton of my shirt, into the flesh above my bra.

"No!" I screamed. I wanted to scream, "I'm GLORIA! Get off of me!"

"Shit! That's my ear!" he laughed.

Too bad for me, I was wearing cotton shorts. He took the crotch in his hand and tore it away, panties and all.

"God!" I screamed again and he laughed.

"Mmm, nice," he moaned, cupping me in his hand.

Crazily, I thought, if I drop my legs, maybe he won't be able to see my private parts and if I lifted my legs, maybe I could get my foot into his stomach or his chest and push him off, but I couldn't move when I tried.

"Oh, Rick, please!" I begged, pulling at his hands, which seemed a thousand times stronger then they had been before, why? Had he been only playing with me then? He unzipped himself and took out the second penis I'd ever seen in my life, somewhat bigger than Daddy's and like his, erect and fierce, "Please, Rick! I'm a virgin, Rick!" I choked.

His eyes lit up.

"Oh, yeah?" he laughed, as he entered me, "Not any more!"

I was dry with fear. My vagina resisted him.

"It hurts! God, stop! You're hurting me!"

"Kiss me, it'll feel better!" he urged, gasping.

God help me, he kissed me and I kissed him back and it did start to feel better, but it still hurt, it hurt, it hurt every time he thrust me and pulled back and thrust and thrust again, I hated him for pushing me down on the dirty stairs, for smelling like dirt, I hated him and wished I could just love him instead.

"I wanna see you naked," he said, suddenly stopping.

He was getting up. As he did, he burrowed his head into my belly and lifted me over his shoulders. He started climbing the stairs, but I was struggling so much, we fell against the wall.

"Cut it out!" he laughed. He grunted and heaved forward and made it the rest of the way up the stairs to Jakey's bedroom where he tossed me on the bed.

I jumped up but he was already coming down on top of me.

He landed on my chest, knocking the breath out of me, pinning my arms open; his sweating palms wrapped around my wrists like ropes.

"Someone's going to come!" I gasped. "My mother's gonna come home from work!"

She wasn't. She was going to my grandmother's.

"No, she ain't," he said, matter-of-factly. "She's going to your grandmother's."

I felt the blood go out of my face.

"How did you know that?" I asked him.

He laughed and put his face close to my face.

"Your brother told me," he said.

Jakey?

He let go of my wrists and yanked my shirt over my head, where it stuck, smothering me, blinding me.

And I went cold suddenly realizing what that meant, about my brother, about Jakey.

"I should leave you like that, but I wanna see your face!"

He yanked the shirt off and unhooked my bra and wrenched it off of me. My breasts came tumbling out, round and beautiful and I didn't want him to see them; they were too beautiful for him! I thought, I should have shown them to Johnny! I covered them like a little fool with my arms across my chest while he tore away what was left of my shorts and underwear.

He laughed, almost affectionately, at my foolishness; he opened my arms as he straddled me. Then, he got off me and stood by the bed, his dungarees open, his penis large and red from my blood, sticking out.

"Jeez, you're nice, Gloria! You know that? You got nice! You make my dick hard, man, just fucking walking by me on the street."

He started taking off his shoes and socks. He took off his pants. I thought, if I run out the window, I'll have to go out naked. I hesitated too long.

He was looking around for something. He found my bra and, as in a nightmare, started tying my hands to the bedstead.

"No! Rick! Don't tie me up! Please! I won't run away! I won't fight you, I promise! Please!"

He softened, loosening the bra. With tremendous relief, I heard it hit the floor.

"You like it, don't you, Gloria?"

"Yes! I like it! I like it!"

"I knew you would," he stroked my leg, looking at me.

"I never seen a blonde one before; it's not really blonde, though, huh? Kind of light brown," he said, petting me like a kitten.

I was afraid to speak. I wanted to beg him, to try to convince him to let me go, but I was afraid he'd tie me up if I gave him trouble.

Then, he mounted me again. But, he didn't do what I thought he was going to do. He scooted toward my face, on his fists, like an ape.

"What're you doing?" I gasped.

"If you bite my cock," he looked me in the eye, scaring me; I didn't know what he meant, what was a cock? "Before the cock crows three times," was all I knew, he must mean himself. I wouldn't bite him, I wasn't sure what he was capable of, I suddenly realized, his dark existence, his damaged mind, the true meaning of the jagged scar, was as dark and foreign to me as that jungle they were all going to halfway around the world, "You'll be fuckin' sorry," he spoke deep in his throat, growling with desire like an animal, again I think of the lions, how I never knew if I was in the love embrace or the death, the lust of lions, how they growl-purr deep in their larynx as they eat their prey and take each other's sex, "Now, open your mouth."

I clamped my teeth shut and I also growled, a low moan of helplessness, of pleading and terror, twisting my head from side to side. I didn't understand what he was going to do. Not knowing was frightening, knowing turned out to be worse. You have no idea what this is like until it's done to you.

He took one of his dirty fingers and tried to worm it between my teeth. He couldn't get it in, so he grabbed my jaw with one hand and pressed it like a vise in exactly the right place to make it pop open.

"Relax," he said, jamming his penis into my mouth already gasping with pain. I started to cry then, "Sh, Sh," he said.

"Open wide," he joked.

Back and forth, he eased his penis, tasting of my blood and his urine, back and forth along my crying lips. "It's okay," his voice trembled, "just relax, open your mouth," his stomach alternately smothered me in his disregard and let into my shocked nostrils a welcome rush of tainted air, smelling of him, his dank flesh, perspiring between his legs, smelling of his shit, his pubic hairs brushing my throat like a small, wet animal foraging there, "Sh, sh, stop cryin', it's o-kay," he could barely speak, he squeezed my cheeks painfully to increase his pleasure, his fingers tasted of salt and dirt, "Sh," he seemed to tell himself.

My own sobs were choking me; in order to breathe, I had to stop crying, but the tears still ran down my face. It went on forever, and then, it was over. He yanked out his reddened penis just as it shuddered visibly and throbbed white juices right in my face, salty as a thick white ocean, pouring warm from him and with my tears over my burning cheeks and my lips rubbed raw. I'd never seen semen before and I was terrified.

"Ah! Ah!" he groaned in ecstasy, leaning back, while I sobbed and choked and gasped for my breath, under depths I didn't know.

"You're crazy! Oh, God! I hate you!" I cried and he fell on me. He laughed and took me in his arms.

He licked my face with a broad and eager tongue, like the lion, as unconscionable as the lion.

"Here, I'll eat some too, look!"

He licked me again and I watched as he swallowed tears and semen. He kissed me. Incredibly, he held me tenderly as a lover. He wiped the semen from my face with his dirty hand, gently, streaking my face with dirt and semen. He held my buttocks and pushed me against him.

"Gloria, you're fuckin' nice."

"I hate you!" I sobbed into his sweating chest.

"I wanna take you with me in my fuckin' bag and take you out every fucking night and fuck you in the fuckin' jungle."

He kissed me, mashing my lips with his lips thick and heavy with passion. He opened my mouth with his tongue and fucked my mouth over and over with his salty, foreign and familiar tongue. He got hard again and slid into me from the side, holding me in his arms, lifting my leg over his body, kissing me.

"Hold me!" he urged. "Put your arms around me like you mean it."

And I did.


While he was putting on his clothes, I asked him.

"What did you give Jakey for this?"

He grinned, one foot suspended in a pants leg. "He's waiting at my house. You was supposed to be tied up."

I must have gone completely white, because he looked at my face and laughed, reassuringly, "Don't worry! I'll tell him you wasn't home."

Then, he leaned over my body and kissed me on the belly, an affectionate kiss goodbye, and he said, "Your boyfriend lied about you."

"What do you mean, 'my boyfriend'?"

"Ruzzy, he said he gotcha."

Ruzzy was Johnny Rozinsky.

Just before he went out the window, he turned and said something even more unbelievable than that.

He said, "I'll call you."


Jakey got home about four minutes later. I was in my bedroom. I'd just had time to straighten Jakey's bedspread and get back to my room. I yanked on some clean shorts as he ran up the stairs and burst open the door to my room.

"Hey! You better learn how to knock!" I yelled at him.

He looked so confused, I almost laughed that Nazi laugh for the first time in my life.

"Did Rick come here?" he asked, confusedly.

"What? Rick? Why would Rick come here? What're you talking about?" I yelled as loud and aggressively as I could, all the while backing him out of my room. Maybe it was my face, savage and streaked with a kind of war paint that scared Jakey so much. "What the hell's going on?" I screeched at him, like a madwoman. "What are you doing?"

"Nothin'," his freckled face, which should have been innocent, but had never been, screwed up in distaste and confusion.

"Get out of my room!"

He left and I collapsed on my bed.

My virgin blood and Rick's semen had dried on my face. Blood and semen poured out of my vagina, making my fresh clothing sticky.

I didn't know that most girls take a shower after they're raped, scrubbing themselves raw, sometimes for hours, and they still don't feel clean.

I didn't wash right away. I lay on my bed. I could still feel him on top of me. I shuddered, as his memory smothered me with his flesh. I could smell him. His smell was rising from my skin. Dirt and salt and blood and urine. Like a little dog panting with an open mouth, I lay there and smelled and felt him. I opened my shorts and moving his semen and my own juices around on the erect lips of my vagina, I pretended he was loving me, the way he had at the end, touching me gently, saying sweet things. I heard him and I didn't even believe my imagination: he said, "You're fuckin' nice," and "You're so beautiful," slowly at first, then quicker and rougher and harder till I came in a tender, frightened shudder of love and pain and abject horror at what I'd done.

I cried, the sobs heaving deeply from my bowels, wrenching my stomach till I vomited nothing but bitter saliva on to my pillow. Again, my tears mixed with my blood and his semen that came alive on my face in a sticky, itchy mask and I swallowed the mixture as he had. I wondered why I was so depraved. Why was it like this? Why was there love and fear, and even hate at the same time? Was I going to hell? For loving too much?

GOOD, CLEAN FUN

The very next night, Rick, unbelievably true to his word, called me. I was reading on Ma's bed when the phone rang.

"Gloria," he said, "Wanna go to the show or somethin'?"

His voice, low and dangerous, directed at me, not asking for Jakey, was frightening and sent cold blood down my back.

"Or somethin'?" I gathered all my strength to ask this.

He laughed.

"Yeah. What time shall I pick you up?"

He had a way of speaking, I realized, with his mouth open that sounded like little sucks of breath on the phone, like you'd imagine a snake would talk.

"Never!"

I hung up on him.

The phone rang immediately.

Ma shouted from downstairs, "Who the hell is that?"

I picked up the receiver.

"Come on, Gloria."

"No, Rick."

He sighed.

"I thought you liked me."

"I'm not getting into a car with you."

I may have fantasized about his loving me. I may even have fantasized about his friends. But, I wasn't crazy. When I dreamed, I was in control. I didn't have to remind myself how mean Rick could be, how insane and unpredictable. I could very easily walk into a trap of him and five of his friends. A date with Rick wouldn't be dinner and a movie. It could be a beer and a gang rape.

"Come on, let's go out and have some good, clean fun."

I had to laugh.

He laughed, too.

"Okay?" he asked, hopefully.

"No, Rick!"

I hung up.

The phone rang again, but I didn't answer it.


I know it sounds like I was taking things well. I wasn't. For weeks, I cried at the strangest moments: during supper, I'd have to excuse myself and run upstairs, running the water in the sink to cover my sobs, a trick I'd learned from Eleanor Roosevelt's autobiography because she wasn't allowed to cry when her child died; I woke up crying, choking on tears that had caught in my throat and run into my nostrils; I cried in school, covering my face with a Kleenex, hunkering down behind my history book.

I cried because Rick had been so brutal which for him, had been affectionate. I cried because my brother had sold me like one of those Vietnamese boys who sell their sisters in the alleys of Saigon. I cried because Johnny had been a lie.

For comfort, I took out my old Robin Hood book. At first, I just held it as a beloved relic from another time, one I really couldn't call "more innocent." It's hard covers were strong and sheltering as a father's embrace should be. That also made me cry. Then, I read aloud to myself just to hear the beautiful words, as if the book could speak to me in another's voice, the calming voice of a friend or a parent, a guardian from fear and trouble. I read at random:

*So Robert was tied fast, hand and foot, with bow-strings, and carried to where the dead hart lay. When they had stripped away the hot skin with their keen hunting-knives and laid it flat on the greensward, they rudely threw him upon it and bound it with thongs over his body, leaving naught uncovered but his head. Robert's blood boiled, and he struggled with might and main to loosen the bonds which cut and pained him ever the more as he tried to free himself. Anon two strong fellows came, bearing a stout oak limb on their shoulders, to which the shapeless bundle was tied...Robert was no great burden. Indeed, his body was but a plaything...Much they marveled that he made no outcry... As for Robert, he set his teeth and prayed inwardly...his wits began to reel..."*

Some of his captors felt pity for him and set him loose because he had been one of the best archers they'd ever seen. I began to wish for a longbow and sheaf of arrows. I fell asleep, clutching the book so tightly, my hand and arm were numb and rigid when I woke the next morning. I had dreamed of myself as an archer, standing tall. I shone, dressed in silver and white. I shot an arrow of light straight and true into a marker, a bulky shape, hideously dark and moving swiftly toward me.

## ROBERT OF LOCKSLEY

When June and I drove down the beach in the car, we were two dazzling blondes in a convertible. Boys with tanned hard bodies lined the boulevard and shouted to us, their bulging muscles in arms and chest and thighs, dark with oil and days and days of sun. The girls' flat stomachs and firm buttocks and rounded breasts competed; their coarse hair was sun-streaked, but no competition for the real thing flying by on wings, just out of reach. We drove past Point of Pines' quiet, rambling homes just touching the cove; past Roland's, where on Friday and Saturday nights, the boys liked to gorge themselves on Mount Fujiyama's, ice cream mounds, lighted on fire and dripping with several different sauces; past The Clam Spot, oozing fried yellow air on to the Lynnway, shooting out the causeway to another world, the blue waters and grassy dunes of Nahant where we spent hours and hours there playing in the clear water, reading or drawing on the pale sand, or just watching the clean view, broken only by white gulls crying plaintively.

We went to the beach a lot that summer, but we also went to Boston, which we called, "town," the place we seemed to crave every Saturday afternoon, winter or summer, fall or spring, for its elite, insular charms of soft gaslights, bumpy cobblestones, old bricks, delicate gardens, shining brass railings and painted front doors. We peeked in the paned windows at elegant furnishings, ceiling-high bookshelves, carved picture frames, formal portraits and candelabra glistening over dining tables and hearths dancing with flames. We admired summer flowers tumbling out of window boxes or pressed against the frosted glass of February. On Tremont Street, we visited the Lionel toy trains in a little shop hidden along a row of low, Dickensian storefronts tucked mysteriously behind the street, there we also discovered a little tobacco shop where the proprietor allowed us just to breathe in the scents, look and admire, as though in a museum. One day, Junie bought a pipe there and we made our own tobacco blend, smelling of vanilla and wood smoke. Out on a bench by the fountain, we shared the pipe, got giddy and then a little sick, curing us of smoking, but Junie kept the pipe anyway. We ate town with our eyes and ears and craved it as if it had a certain taste and flavor which needed to be replenished every weekend.

Once, in Louisburg Square, I glimpsed a nun high in a window, bending to water a plant; she carried a long necked watering can, her habit floated above her head in a span of great white wings. In the golden reflection of sunset, she shone warm and at peace.

Elegant old ladies, ladies such as I had never seen except in old black and white movies, passed us in proper woolen suits, properly ornamented with sedate brooches, trim hats and white gloves.

At Christmastime, June and I stood gaping at the store windows of Jordan Marsh and Filene's where a whole miniature village of Christmas celebrants had been assembled, figures poised and animated, cooking Christmas dinner, opening Christmas gifts around the tree, selling pies or toys, going to their Christmas Eve sleep or singing Christmas carols. The colors shone festive gold and crimson, forest green and snowy white. We'd take the escalator upstairs in Jordan's, past the rows and rows of sleek clothing, past the sparkling housewares, past the textured rugs and curtains, far into the secret bowels of the store, past the spring and fall runways for the fashion shows, secreted far inside, past the offices, cold and remote, with phones ringing and the smooth voices of girls answering in singing tones, past the restrooms in vacant white corridors, like long vacuum tunnels, round the corner to The Enchanted Village, a much larger, child-sized, almost village-sized version of what was downstairs in the street windows. The figures curtsied and bowed somewhere around our waists. Like us, the children passed, hot in their winter coats, but beaming as if with the glass eyes and painted cheeks of the Enchanted people.

In Boston, on fine fall days, the deep hued leaves floated to the ground and students sat on the grass or on benches or fountains and talked about art and literature and the meaning of life. June and I caught surprising snippets of their conversation, falling like bright leaves around our heads. Often, a student played his flute or violin for free, not asking for money, sitting cross-legged on a car while his friends ate lunch. Once, we heard a clarinet while going down the long alley behind the townhouses and once, a woman rehearsing operatic scales as she walked home.

Sometimes, I had to beg Ma for the change to go. It cost twenty-five cents each way and we always needed an extra quarter for an ice cream cone at Brighams. Sometimes Ma wouldn't give it to me and I'd cry and June would get it from Agnes. That was humiliating. But, it had to be done. Town was sacred.

On this day, I had saved my money from babysitting to have a large sum to shop for something nice and on the day of the murder I had over sixty dollars!

It had been two days since Rick had broken into our house and raped me and I hadn't told June. I was hiding, I think, from her and from myself. June was very subdued that day herself, because Will was heartbroken over her, still calling and coming to the house. That very morning he'd shown up at her house while she did her chores. He'd simply sat outside, not trying to come in; he sat there outside her bedroom window on the curb and we'd had to pass him on our walk to the train station. June had made her choice and it was a sad one for Will.

Downtown Boston was a hot concrete box. The cars steamed the narrow streets in bumper-to-bumper traffic, honking and screaming, hissing hot smoke like fissures from the earth. We always went to Filene's basement, a gold mine of bargains, the only place we could afford, where the clothes were piled in mad jumbles you had to dig through like an archaeologist through eons of rubble to find anything valuable.

That day our eyes were caught by a pile of shining disco wigs.

"Look at these funny wigs for five dollars!" I had some money in my purse and I think I went a little hysterical trying to have some fun.

June tried on a wig that looked like the silver tinsel for a Christmas tree. I busted out laughing. Even the salesgirl laughed, because June's perfect, natural face peeked out like a kitten caught in a ball of tinsel.

"A red one!" I exclaimed, pulling out a short red gamin wig, shot with gold disco threads.

The salesgirl said, "I can't believe you're gonna get all that beautiful blonde hair under that little wig!"

Deftly, I twisted all my hair into a tight spiral and tucked it under the wig, which I yanked down to sit snugly around my ears.

"She did!" The salesgirl cried in approval. She held up a mirror in her hand, the nails of which curled around the mirror's handle in broken red chips.

"Look at your eyes! They're green like a redhead's!" she cooed, sucking a piece of hard candy balled up in her cheek.

"I always wished I could have short hair, but only sometimes, you know?"

"Yeah!" June nodded in agreement. "You look like a pretty boy."

I shivered a little, because I was enjoying myself, in spite of everything. I paid for the wig, leaving it on, and we went up the escalator to the seventh floor where June liked to try on the "real clothes," just to see what they looked like on her. She tried on a Mary Quant plaid skirt and a black sweater. "You could go out with Mick Jagger," I told her. "Or Paul McCartney, take your pick!" She tried on a suede jacket and jodhpurs. I said, "You could ride to hounds!" She replied, "I would never chase a fox!" I tried on a short black velvet dress with a lace collar. "You look like Twiggy, except a redhead!" We had a good laugh. The idea that I could look like Twiggy!

We were going down the escalator.

"We looked positively regal in your silver hair, if I do say so myself!" I said.

"Regal! I like that!" said June, trying out a new word. She was cheering up, so was I; it was, as I've said, so lovely to be with June.

That's when we passed the Sport's Equipment as we rounded the corner by the escalator. I'd never really noticed Sport's Equipment before, except to see a jumble of rifles, basketballs and tennis rackets. But on this day, I saw, as the moving steps descended, there, shining, polished wood in the tall, angelically arched shape I longed for - a long bow with arrows.

"June, look!" I whispered, breathless as I ran to it.

"What? What?"

She followed me.

"A long bow!"

Carefully, I picked it up. It was magnificent. Light as a feather and rounded so that it fit in my grip. It was tall, at least a foot taller than I was.

"But, is it made from yew," I pondered.

"Yes," someone said.

I turned to see a stout older woman with short, brown hair. She wore no makeup; unlike the salesgirl downstairs whose lashes had been thick with black grease. This was a solid, no nonsense kind of person.

"It's probably too tall for me," I mused.

"That's the smallest we have, six feet."

I pulled the bow string back, as Robin had described, to my cheek, feeling the stiff pull, hearing the slight song of the string as it whispered near my ear.

I had to have it, even just to hold it and look at it.

"How much is it?" I asked the woman.

"The bow is forty, on sale. The arrows are extra, twenty-seven for the sheaf," she replied, eying my disco wig.

"It's a wig." I told her.

"I can see that."

I didn't have enough money. I started to put the bow back, but as I did, my hand rebelled. It wouldn't put the beautiful bow aside. I looked at the arrows, straight and neat in their leather sheaf.

"Does the leather sheaf come with them?" I asked, stalling.

"Oh, yes, we wouldn't just hand them to you, you know."

"Pie?" I said.

I called her Pie when I needed a favor.

"How much?"

"Just a few dollars."

She handed me a twenty.

"That's too much!"

"Take it!"

The bow and arrows were paid for.

"I've never seen a girl buy one of these before," the saleswoman said as she started wrapping them in paper.

"Could I - carry it, just like that?" I asked her.

"Sure, just let me tag it for you and here's your receipt. Wait till you're out of the store before you shoot any arrows," she joked.

I slung the leather sheaf over my chest, cradling the arrows under my arm. I rested the bow on my shoulder.

"I must be out of my mind," I told June.

"What're you gonna do with it?" she asked as we took the escalator down.

"I don't know, maybe practice a few shots in the yard. Probably, it'll wind up on my wall. But, I don't care. I just want to have it."

"Where'd you want to go next? Want to check out Jordan's or cross down to the park? Or go have a coffee? I got fifteen dollars left. How about you - oh, yeah, you're in debt."

I laughed, hugging my insane purchase, "Only temporarily."

"Then, let's go to Jordan's, okay?"

We were going into Jordan's through the beautiful copper and glass doors, the beautiful double doors where crowds pile in and out at the same time. I was chattering gaily. "What do you want to look at first?" I asked her.

There was no answer.

"Hey! Where do you want to go first? Which floor?" I turned, smiling, and saw her.

Her childlike face was the color of ashes.

"What is it? What happened? Are you sick?" My heart pounded hard, yet all my warm blood seemed to desert me. What had happened to her?

We stood stock still while people streamed around us.

"A man just grabbed me by my breasts," June said in a small voice.

My heart leapt, jerking crazily in my cold chest. Several people turned to look at June as she spoke.

"He twisted my breasts and walked away," she said, tears forming in her eyes.

"Who? Where? Is he here? Where'd he go?"

"He went out the doors."

"What'd he look like?"

She shook her head, "I only saw his hands. He was wearing a suit."

"A suit? A suit?" I cried in disbelief. A man wearing a suit should never do something like that! A man wearing a suit should know better! He should *be* better!

I know it was madness, but I ran out after him. I heard June call, "No! Don't!" I didn't care. I had to get him. I had to! That was all I knew in that moment. No one hurt June while I was with her, not while I could protect her! It was easy, so easy to feel rage for someone else, and not for myself. So easy, so easy, the fury rose up in me, from everywhere at once, I was made of it! I think I was going to beat him senseless with my fists, when I nearly tripped over the long bow and realized I had it.

I saw him! That summer day, there were hardly any men wearing suits, and there he was sauntering slowly down the sidewalk like nothing was wrong in the whole wide world.

"Clear the way!" I shouted to the crowd.

I took an arrow out of the sheaf and placed it against the bowstring. I stood in the same position I'd seen archers stand in books and I pulled back the string.

People murmured and fell back. A few laughed nervously. The man stopped when everyone else did. He turned and faced me and I admit, I hesitated. I had entered a place that hadn't existed before: a small space floating in time like a dream and for a split second, it wavered.

Then the man laughed out loud.

"What're you nuts, you crazy cunt? Is it Halloween yet?" he asked the crowd.

"Halt and take thy punishment!"

I didn't even know I'd said it till June told me later.

"Suck my dick!" the man said.

I lost my mind.

"Nay, suck mine!"

From deep inside it came, a cry of such fury, the news would call it a warrior's cry, "Ugggh!" I screeched and the people screeched too and from way down it came; I saw and heard and smelled everything all at once: huge, monstrous orgasmic: the inside my father's underwear, the pungent, rank odor of it, the tickling hairs, the soft leaves, the hard trunk of a tree; the liquid eyes of my cousins, the collapsed head of my doll; the barren streets of East Boston and the graffiti and the screwed up faces of the teenagers yelling on their outstretched toes, "FUCK!" Uncle Sonny's sweet hand holding mine, his sweet smile, the sweet taste of caramel on my tongue; the wondrous palaces of magic we'd gone into for a few short hours; the rats running in the subway; the blood dripping from the headless chickens, the sour smell of them rotting; the red apple hanging in the kitchen, Daddy fingering it thoughtfully; Grandpa handing me a luscious fruit along the knife; Grandma's thin bow mouth, the white cloth she carried, the bowl; the clothes soaking in bleach and water; the bitter taste of the delicate, fresh-plucked arugula; Nona's diamond pierced ancient ear, her silent laugh; the White House, stately on its green lawn; the dead Buddha in the alley, the drop of blood from his temple; the scent of suntan lotion, the grit of sand, the revelers singing in the night; the little airport of small white planes on a grassy field, "Feast your eyes! You won't see this again!" the sparrows splashing in the glowing dust of sunset; my father's tongue inside me, his hands, "Let me see, I made it"; the priest how he turned his head away from me; the perfect leg of my godmother poised to enter the car, saying, "Better than you, better than you!" the lamplight on trees; the doctor's hands relieving my pain with a stinging needle, and under my dress, "I've always loved you, Gloria!" the oil tanks seeping heavy clouds of stinking oil; the graceful horses going round and round the exercise yard; the cop in the Head Shop; Will Cullen waving from the telephone pole; Aaron slipping beads over our heads; his best friend's dad slumped over the steering wheel; the black lace bridge; the dancers who drowned, fairly spinning into the fiery sea; Dorothy's fat stomach erupting from her white cotton panties and the sweet chocolatey fat girl sweat of her; the happy face of Mrs. Church on the inside of the pouring wet window, her husband's screaming not an inch away on the outside, the black hairs escaping from her scarlet panties; the grey vomit of mushy gushy, the leering faces of kids wearing makeup and negligees; Helen Krauss' thin, thin black hairs on her haggard head; Richie Silva holding me gently in my dreams after Daddy left; my sister's palms branded with stars; Agnes eagerly pressing the marijuana leaf onto the tablecloth; Jimmy Priestley's spectral walking; Jack's sparkling blue eyes, his carefree laughter; the priests ushering the boys into the sacristy; the unbearably tenderly blossoming pear tree; June crying in my arms, "Am I ugly, Ri? Am I stupid?" the seagulls, aloft and pure; the planes screaming and scraping the houses with their bellies; the trains rolling over the tracks like far-away thunder; Ma screaming her pain into my chest; the dirty Q-tips at Daddy's elbow; the savior, my savior, Mr. Luke Garante bellowing the life-saving lessons of literature; Rick's big hard penis jamming my mouth; Rick, Rick, Rick! as he carried me unwilling into his house; I heard Grandma then, she opened the front door setting off the buzzer, in her wavering, old voice, she called, "Rosa?" and the arrow shot out from all this, this whirlwind of anguish and horror and love, taking it all along its shaft down the long tunnel of nightmares, hurling through the short space I didn't think I could travel into the dark shape that ran toward me and he staggered a moment in disbelief and I watched him not understanding a thing and he fell and the crowd screamed again and gathered round him. Someone yanked me by the back of my shirt and it was June and we were running as fast as we could and it wasn't till we had gone up Washington Street and State Street, across the park to Beacon that I realized what had happened and we were running into the maze of tiny, drunken streets of Beacon Hill for shelter.

The sirens of police cars screamed from all directions. We stopped many times, heaving dangerously close to losing our breath completely, heaving dryly in alcoves and doorways. Then, June pulled me into a narrow alley, really a space of about twelve inches between two buildings. We ran sideways down this long vise to an opening that turned out to be a small courtyard.

We collapsed, gasping for breath, against a stone fountain. A fat cupid playing a pipe from which water trickled peacefully.

We sat on the brick and just breathed for several minutes, gazing blankly at each other.

Then, June said, still heaving for breath, "You killed him."

"Who?"

Not my father, I loved him! Not my rapist, I loved him!

She stared at me. "That man!"

The man in the suit? Incredible!

"*Killed* him?" I asked.

She looked around the silent courtyard. The intense quiet buzzed in our ears. The delicate ivy, the calm statue, the spiraling brick, the splashing water existed on its own plane of serenity. Far away the sirens flew about the streets.

"I had to do something," I said.

"I know."

She took me in her arms. For only a second, we trembled there together, trying to breathe. Then, from behind us, a voice spoke calmly.

"I think you girls had better come in here."

We turned to see a woman standing in a doorway. An elaborate lion's head crowned the archway over her head. She was older, maybe fifty, her dark hair was streaked with grey; it settled about her serious face like a dark cloud. She wore a red dress, cut in mock sailor style with brass buttons and a white collar. The room behind her was beautiful. I glimpsed: shelves of books, stuffed chairs, a fireplace covered by an antique screen, paintings and flowers and green plants. In the room, a gentle music was playing. I think I was drawn by these as well as by her elegant presence when I got up, and June did too, as if under a spell.

She closed the door behind us.

"Sit down," she said.

I sat on something soft. June landed at my feet.

"I'll take that," the woman said, reaching for the long bow, which had fallen to the floor.

I handed it to her.

"And those."

She meant the arrows. Her hand was held out for them. Without thinking, her presence was so commanding, I gave them to her and watched in shock as she tossed them and the long bow into the fireplace.

"No!" I gasped, but it came out as a whisper.

"I don't think you have a choice, do you?"

The woman leaned to make a fire. June and I watched in awe; it was all so interesting and terrifying.

"How did you know?" June asked her.

"I was on the phone with my editor. We had a Saturday lunch planned. Her office overlooks Washington Street. Her assistant happened to be on an errand when there was a lot of commotion outside one of the stores."

The flames caught the beautiful shining arch of the bow. The leather sheaf like a living thing caught fire; it writhed and twisted before our eyes. The arrows became arrows of fire with points of flickering stars. The harsh odor of chemical finish stung our eyes and nostrils while the fire flared high as if in protest and then, resigned to burn steadily.

The woman held out her hand for our wigs. We took them off and handed them to her without thinking. She tossed them into the flames. The wigs also jumped up and hissed and gave off a sharp protesting smell of chemicals, then settled down to shrivel and burn.

The woman bent over a silver coffee service sparkling in the firelight. She asked if we'd like some - or something stronger? We shook our heads in amazement. She poured herself some coffee and reached to turn on the TV. She switched a few channels.

"Sure enough," she said.

There, on the screen, was a photo of me standing with bow and arrow aimed. The anchorwoman was talking, something about interrupting the regularly scheduled programs, something about a tourist snapping a Polaroid. There I was, arms poised, legs apart, the wig shining - and there was the man, facing me, laughing. It was all fuzzy and blurred, but clear enough.

"People are already calling her Joan of Arc or the Bow and Arrow Killer, but the young woman who shot an arrow into a crowd of downtown shoppers and killed an unidentified man just moments ago has already sparked everyone's interest. Police are not releasing the name of the murder victim, pending notification of his family. According to witnesses, he allegedly grabbed one of the girls forcibly *by her breasts* while she and her friend were going through the street doors at Jordan Marsh Department Store on Washington Street in downtown Boston. The other girl, allegedly wearing a *fashion wig* at the time, pursued the victim and shot him with a *bow and arrow*! A manhunt - or should I say - a womanhunt is currently underway in the downtown area."

"Well, Liz, I guess that just goes to show fact is stranger than fiction!" the co-anchor quipped.

"It certainly is, Jack! You go to lunch and anything can happen! Still, I don't suppose those two girls expected to be molested in broad daylight while shopping in a crowded department store!"

"Certainly not, we have more on this bizarre occurrence in downtown Boston, live on the scene with correspondent, Judy Harrison. Judy? What do you have for us?"

"How long were we running?" I asked June.

"I don't know."

"It seemed like seconds."

"Jack," said a woman standing in front of Jordan Marsh with a microphone, "I'm here at the scene of the alleged murder and I'm talking to Gregory Di Angelo. Gregory? Tell us what you saw."

A young man in a T-shirt spoke excitedly. His eyes beamed with absolute joy. "I couldn't believe my eyes! She just ran out here and told everybody to get out of the way! She was unbelievable!"

"Did she say anything else?"

"Yeah!" the young man said, "I don't remember what she said, exactly, but she was English, I'll tell you that!"

"English?"

"Yeah, the one with the bow and arrow, she talked real funny!"

June and I just looked at each other.

The woman was smiling, like Ma did sometimes, a pretty Mona Lisa smile.

Then, replacing the young man, an elderly woman was on the screen, also beaming excitedly, as though the best thing in the world had happened. "She let out the most ungodly screech," she declared to the reporter, "like a wild Indian!"

"Jack," the reporter, Judy Harrison, spoke into her microphone, "Sylvia Leonard is upstairs right now in Filene's Sport's Department where the young Joan of Arc seems to have purchased her bow and arrow quite possibly only an hour ago!"

The scene suddenly switched to the Sport's Department. There was the gruff saleswoman. My heart sank. Now, she would tell them what she knew about us, June, as well as me!

"Jack, Liz, I'm speaking with Margery Holbright, the clerk who sold the young lady the bow and arrow just moments before she used it to kill a man out on the street! Do you remember what she looked like?" the reporter asked the saleswoman.

"You have a picture of her, don't you?" Margery Holbright responded, stiffly.

My heart fairly jumped out of my chest. June let out a huge puff of air, covering her face with her hands.

"What about her companion? What did she look like?"

"A teenager, skinny, dressed like a hippie."

"Did the girls say or do anything unusual in your opinion?"

"In *my* opinion?" Margery Holbright bristled. "In my opinion, she did what any self-respecting woman would love to do! She killed the - *blip!*"

The reporter, flustered, recovered herself and turned quickly to the camera, saying, "Feelings are running pretty strong down here this afternoon, Jack, as the Bow and Arrow Killer seems to have acted for many women when she took a deadly stand today against a common molester."

"Thank you, Sylvia. I understand we also have a statement from the saleswoman who sold this girl the fashion wig?" His tone was perplexed and mocking.

"Ah, yes, Jack," replied Sylvia, "the saleswoman in Filene's Basement told us just moments ago that the young lady had the wig on when she turned around to help her, so she also didn't get to see the killer's real hair or anything about her, as the transaction was completed very quickly and she was very busy at the time."

Here, I stopped hearing anything because I started to cry. The woman turned off the television. She said nothing while I sobbed. June put her head on my knees. I buried my face in her soft hair and let loose my tears. June's hand wrapped around mine, tightly she gripped me, till finally, I stopped and looked up.

"They're not telling," I said.

"No," the woman replied.

"Why are you helping us?" June asked her.

The woman made a visible effort to calm herself. She lifted her chin and set it firmly before speaking, her expression went inward and distant.

"Six years ago, I was raped on Christmas Eve outside in the courtyard."

"In *that* courtyard?" June asked, incredulous. "On Christmas Eve?"

"Yes," the woman smiled, "Hard to believe anything like that could happen there, isn't it?"

She continued, "I was coming home with presents and goodies; you know, my arms were full, I was distracted by the anticipation of the holiday. I didn't see him hiding behind the trash cans."

"You stayed here!" June said in amazement.

"Yes. This is my house. I was born in this house. It was my mother's house before me." She sighed, "Every time I think I've made peace, it just seems to come back."

"Ma'ry," I murmured, unconsciously.

The woman laughed, "You do talk funny!"

"Sorry, I've been reading too much Robin Hood, I guess."

Unbelievably, they both laughed very well at that. It was a lovely sight to see them laugh: June, all shining with firelight reflected in her tears, this woman, shaking her dark curls, throwing back her head.

For the first time, I relaxed a bit and really looked around the room.

I saw that I was sitting in a plush chair; it was deep crimson and thrown over the back, was a tan shawl that must have been cashmere, because it was softer than anything I'd ever felt before. I saw that June was sitting on a low embroidered stool, whose little wooden feet were carved like claws.

Across the room, I saw a squarely built oak desk and on it, a typewriter with paper in it, stacks of paper to each side, one high, one low, like the stacks of sportswear to the left and right of Ma at her machine, which was her finished work and her work to be done, and I imagined it was the same here. Little pieces of paper were tacked to the wall; a few articles cut from a newspaper and photos of places, making the physical collage of a story. A tall vase of flowers, a small clock, an open greeting card, stood on the desk, which faced out into the room toward the hearth.

Then I recalled her words, "I was on the phone with my editor" and it came to me as though I had been asleep, "You're a writer!" I exclaimed.

"Yes."

"Wow! I don't know any living writers!" I said, looking her up and down.

She laughed, good-naturedly throwing back her head full of peppered curls again.

"I need a drink!" she said, getting up.

My eyes followed her into a compact kitchen with butcher block counters where she kept a neat array of colorful bottles and glasses on shelves and copper pans hanging from a wooden rack above her head. I saw dark green walls and a Renaissance style painting of fruit and flowers.

"I'm going to have a Renaissance kitchen someday," I said to June. She nodded, following my gaze.

Our dark guardian angel returned with two small brandies in those lovely curved bowls called "snifters."

"They are the wine dark seas of little planets," I whispered in awe as I took one from her hands.

The woman nodded, smiling, without surprise.

June said, "She says things."

The woman smiled, "I'll bet she does." Then she raised her glass, like ours. "To Robin Hood!" she said.

Now, my face contorted once more into pain and tears, but I lifted my glass to meet hers, and June's.

"To Robin!" I said.

"Robin!" said June.

We clicked our glasses together, forever linking our souls as outlaws; we drank firelight and brandy.

Hours later, for she'd insisted we stay as long as possible, she held open the heavy wooden door for us to leave.

I didn't want to go. That small room had been one of those places in your life that speaks so clearly to you, speaking your name in another language you don't speak yet, but instinctively understand. You find yourself in a place outside yourself that knows you and when your body tries to leave it, your heart and soul try to stay where they had felt entirely at peace for the first time.

"I want very much to come back here. May I visit you?" I asked.

She smiled so sweetly, I thought, for a minute, her answer would be yes, but with a kind and almost welcoming face, she told me, "I don't think that would be wise."

June and I took the train home like we always did. We had to hurry. June had to be home at four. No one paid any attention to us. When we stepped out on the platform at Revere Beach, a suddenly icy summer breeze from the ocean wrapped around us like the fierce and enveloping spirit we knew so well, obliterating the hot breath of the departing train, obliterating, as always the feeling of town.

The derelicts going to the track turned their racing forms over and over, searching for the one hope to win. They couldn't have cared less who had killed the man with the bow and arrow. We passed through their hunched bodies without being noticed, even for our sex.

We walked in a daze of sun and shock and exhaustion, climbing the vertical Centennial Ave. first, as we did when we were most tired, just to get the hardest part of the journey out of the way.

"I'm glad I didn't know I could kill him, June! I'm glad! I might not have had the guts to go after him! Do you think the police will come to my door?"

"I don't know."

"What would you do if they come and ask you about me?"

"Oh, I'll tell them where you live!"

I looked at her sharply.

She laughed.

"Man!" I shook my head. "I'm not sorry for what I did, but I'm sorry, so very sorry, for what he did! Why do they do things like that? Why?"

"I don't know."

"I don't feel guilty, June. I feel - right! I feel right! My God, I don't know right from wrong!"

"Yes, you do."

"No, no! I'm not even sure of up and down anymore! It's always like that! It's like being in total darkness, you can't tell up and down!"

She reached for me and took me in her arms.

A car went by and a guy yelled, "Lesbos!" but we were used to it, we blocked it out and slid our consciousness elsewhere because we had to hear what each other had to say, like prisoners who endure the confines of their cells by astral projecting themselves wherever they need to go.

"Then, I don't care," she told me, "I don't care what's right or wrong, what's up or down! I don't care! Whatever you say is right is right! Whatever you say is up is up!"

I nodded weakly, the tears came from out of nowhere, streaming down my face; I doubted I could judge for her when I had no judgment anymore.

"I feel vindicated, Ri! Come here."

We stopped walking and sat down on a low stonewall outside someone's house.

"Uncle Bob paid us another visit last night."

Indignation and rage flooded over me and I wanted to rush out again with my bow and arrows to hunt down this other man! Instead, I shook with quiet anger, shivering in the hot sun while June spoke.

"I was sitting in my Dad's recliner. My brothers were in the room, Ri! They were on the floor in front of me, so they couldn't see. He came over to me and I thought he was going to kiss me goodbye, you know, like an uncle, but he started kissing me like a lover. He put his tongue into my mouth and he put his hands all over my breasts. Then, he just walked away and cheerfully said goodnight to everyone at the door. Ri, you tell me what's right and wrong!"

I buried my head in her lap again. Maybe someone was watching us from a window, maybe an old lady, but no one ever walked around that part of Centennial. We were alone.

"June," I spoke into her lap; I couldn't raise my head. "Rick Likus sneaked into my house and raped me two days ago."

"What? You didn't tell me?" Her fingers dug into my shoulders.

"No, I don't know how I feel about it. I only know it wouldn't have happened if I'd been the one in control."

"What do you mean, 'you don't know how you feel about it?'"

"There's some part of me that loves him, like I love my father, like I love and despise - (I wanted to say *everything*, but it came out) - *home*."

She nodded.

"But, maybe you didn't want to be raped."

I looked up then.

"He can't love me," I said.

It was ironic, two murderers had to hurry home for curfew, but we did. Because we'd stopped for a minute, we had to run the rest of the way. Then we walked the last few feet in case her mother or father were looking out the window and saw us hurrying, they'd know we were late. It was as bizarre as murder. We were both four minutes late that day, as I was staying over her house. However, no one was in the kitchen when we came in, so no one noticed.


UNDER THE PEAR TREE

I left her asleep and climbed out the window. I wanted to be alone for a while. I wanted to see if I *could* be alone. I felt no guilt. There was nothing to feel guilty about. Junie had been with me. That's all that mattered.

As soon as I landed on the damp, cool grass outside June's window, I felt the same rush of excitement I usually felt at the solitude of night. I decided to go home and write or read for a while in my room.

The abandoned highway whooshed with only the occasional, almost musical, car. Hichborn Street was silvery with leaves rustling in silence.

Approaching the street, I felt an almost holy uplifting of myself, there in the lamplight illuminating trees, in the soft salty wind that moved the light blue clouds over the face of the moon. The wind seemed to move, not the clouds, pulling earth and me along; it seemed to support me and move me. As I walked straight, with my own energy, the wind agreed and lifted me. My hair lifted from my neck luxuriously; my feet were buoyant with power.

I walked into the yard and saw him there.

I could see his silhouette clearly. He stood by the pear tree as though ready to pounce, his arms bent, his fingers extended as though ready to grab.

And, then, he changed his mind. I could see by his silhouette, which suddenly relaxed and just stood, facing me.

He wanted me to choose. He waited. But, I could see, he would try to run after me if I chose no. He wouldn't make it. I was closer to the door.

We faced each other, as we had once before. But, this time, as equals.

The wind blew my hair out, all around me, in that wild way, straight out and crazy. It felt about to rain, so pregnant was the air, salty and warm.

I chose. I ran into his arms.

He held me too hard, he kissed me too hard and I did the same. I hated him and loved him. He was every smell I ever smelled that sickened me or gave me joy, every bite of food, every sip of drink, every word I ever read, every drawing I did to escape, every hope, every pain, every fear, all the filth, all the cleaning to deny it, all the terror and all the love and I kissed him fully.

What are children to do with what they are given? What can we do? If we reject it, we commit suicide.

Rick pushed me hard into the trunk of the pear tree. I welcomed the rough touch of the bark, I welcomed it! Then, against the rough bark, he gave me a gentle kiss and I realized he was trying to tell me something! Was he sorry? Was he trying to - love me?

I kissed him gently. His lips searched mine, and I answered him. It occurred to me, he meant nothing but pleasure, that I was imagining the tenderness, as girls will imagine the tenderness they cannot live without. But, something more was happening. Something more is always happening. I was empowered and terrorized by murder. He was going off to become a murderer. Murder was a new sacrament joining us together as one. The pear tree was our priest, obscenities were our vows, the highways were our rings wrapped round and round us happy to strangle us as easily as bind us, our ceremony was a futile parade of anguish headed by a mute, hand-painted statue of the Virgin Mary.

The things we did together shocked me, but I did them to sanctify murder.

"Take off your clothes," he whispered, hoarse with passion.

He wanted me naked while he was clothed. I understood this.

Under the heavily laden pear tree, the pears, not pear shaped yet, pulled the branches down like a canopy around us, he sat down and admired me in the streetlight flickering through pears and leaves.

He unzipped himself and took out his penis, already strong and high. He held it tightly in his fist, like a man who admires his erection.

"Come here," he said. "Sit down on it."

I hesitated. How was that possible? Surely, his penis was so big it wouldn't fit!

"Get down here!" he commanded, about to pull me down, then he changed and murmured, his head reeling to the side with passion and intent, "it's okay, come on."

I straddled him. Under the dim canopy, I heard him moan to see me do this. I slid down, gingerly, still holding myself up by my palms against the rough bark of the tree.

Lightning flashed as I found him. I eased myself down.

"That's it!" he gasped.

Thunder boomed, far away and I hesitated again.

"Don't worry, come on," he kissed the hollow of my throat.

I let myself go the rest of the way, to my knees.

His lips were against my breasts, when he gasped, "Ah!" sucking in my flesh.

He moved me, taking me by the hips, he shifted me from side to side, then up and down, obscenely, violently; I was horrified that I was moving like an animal!

Harshly, he whispered, "You do it!" and I did, feeling his skin against mine, inside and out, not sure after a while which was inside which was outside, which was the unctuous scent of pear and which the pungency of skin, every nerve flailed about like loose wires electrocuting flesh and blood and bones.

His fingers pressed into my buttocks were charged. His tongue rolling with my tongue, first in his mouth, then in mine, became as animals, oblivious to themselves having transmuted into pure sensation.

The storm came closer; thunder followed lightning quicker and quicker.

He found the right nerve, he worked it over and over and my eyelids, heavy and drugged, tried to lift themselves in surprise as the sensation I'd always felt on the outside grew and grew against his penis, overwhelming, erasing everything but itself; I shuddered terrifically and passed into oblivion. I felt him pulsating within me as I collapsed against him, breathing his strong scent of dirt through his damp shirt, tasting with my open mouth the fabric that was Rick.

"Jesus Christ, Gloria, was that you? Fuckin' A, that was you!" He kissed me, his lips landed awkwardly on my cheek as he gasped for breath. "I never felt anything like that before!"

He held me tight, and kissed me, breathing heavily. "We came together! Fuck!" Again, he kissed me in amazement. "That's never happened to me before!"

"Me either," I panted.

He laughed and kissed me, turning me off him. Globs of semen poured out as he slid from me. I sat beside him almost chastely. He put his arm around me like a boy on a date.

Lightning illuminated us with its weird blue light. Thunder cracked immediately. A second passed like a vacuum, then fat drops of rain began to fall. He pulled me closer.

"I think we're all right."

He took out his cigarettes with one hand, lighting one an inch in front of my face. He dragged, and the red tip of his cigarette and his teeth became the only things visible until the lightning flashed, when my body shone blue, then disappeared.

He offered me a drag on his cigarette, putting the paper to my lips.

"I'll cough," I refused.

"Take it."

I did, holding the bitter smoke in my mouth.

"Inhale."

The smoke burned my throat and lungs and came out, burning my nostrils and lips. I choked, coughing deeply. He laughed, taking the cigarette from me.

"You shouldn't smoke, it's bad for you."

Then, he said, "You're all right, Gloria, you know that?"

"Yeah, I know."

I was thinking, how should I think about this, how real is any of it, when he suddenly took his cigarette and twisted the burning tip into one of my breasts.

He was just as quick to cover my mouth with his hand as I screamed.

"What'd you do that for? Let me go!" I screamed under his grimy hand.

We squirmed; he fell on me, just hanging on as I scrambled for my clothes. "No! Stay! Stay!" he begged.

"Please!" he said, his face against my belly as he crawled over me.

"Why'd you do that?" Fierce little knives of pain stabbed my breast. I couldn't move from the weight of him.

"I don't want you to forget me," he said.

"I won't forget you, you jerk. How could I? You think I do this every night?"

He laughed.

"Why the hell can't you just love me?" I asked, then I kind of froze, waiting for him to answer; it wasn't the kind of question anyone really asked Rick.

"Come off it! I love ya! That's just my way of showing affection!"

That's it, I thought, this is all you're going to get. Open your senses as always. Take in the crushed grass, the deluge of rain, the scent of wood and green, rain and pears ripening above you; take him, that's what there is, take him.

I reached up and stroked his twisted eyebrow. He couldn't look at me then. His answer was to shock me once again by turning his cock into my mouth, by turning me, easing me into his mouth. This was too much for me! Too shocking! I was buried, his zipper rhythmically cutting into my cheek, his burning tongue forcing me into wanting exactly what he wanted; we came almost together again, in rapid succession, like twins being born.

He crawled over me again, back to my face where his semen was half swallowed, half dripping. He kissed me, over and over, heedless of semen. Then, he crawled up to the porch like a thief and while my father snored, his legs open and his hairy crotch sticking out, Rick stole his blanket and brought it out to us.

We huddled under the rough army blanket from World War II, which seemed to absorb the dampness right from the air. Rick lit another cigarette.

"I'm leaving tomorrow," he said, spitting some tobacco.

"For Vietnam?"

"Nah, they send you to South Carolina first. Fuckin' boot camp."

"Oh, yeah," I said, recalling.

We were silent. The rain stopped suddenly, then pattered again in fat drops, and stopped.

"We should get married, Gloria, then we can come together every night."

"Yeah, right."

I didn't think for a second he meant it, till I heard the flat note of disappointment in his voice.

"Yeah, right," he said.

I was astonished. From out of nowhere, the diapers appeared hanging on clotheslines over my head and I was horrified! Why hadn't I thought of it before! I'd spent so many years trying not to get pregnant! When I was raped, I'd only thought about being raped. As though reading my thoughts, Rick exclaimed, "Hey! What if you got a little Rick in there? Then, we'd have to get married!"

He took a drag, nonchalantly.

"I'd kill myself," I said, and instantly regretted it for the rest of my life. His face fell so low.

"Yeah, I don't blame you," he said.

I couldn't take it back, you couldn't say you were sorry to a guy like Rick and, anyway, it was impossible, I couldn't marry him. We were married already. We always would be, and, in sexual law, Annie Likus would be my mother, unless I found a way out.

He put out his cigarette, this time on the grass. He pulled me against him.

"Think we got enough time to sleep?" he asked, peering around the branches at the sky.

"Some."

"Good."

We slept for a couple of hours. The sparrows woke us. I looked straight into his damaged crystal blue eye and he kissed me once more, I assumed, for the last time.

BURNING THE BRA

When I walked into the house, Ma was just getting up. She thought I was coming home from Junie's.

"What are you doing home so early?" she yawned.

"Couldn't sleep."

As I walked up the stairs, I heard the TV come on.

"Look at that!" Ma cried out to herself in the kitchen in a singsong voice that was amazed and impressed.

I ran back down the stairs to see the blurry Polaroid of myself on television again.

"The Bow n' Arrow Killer! My God!" Ma sang.

"Wow!" I agreed, marveling that my own mother didn't recognize me, even wearing the same cutoffs and poor boy.

Ma tsked at the story of what the man had done, "What a world!" she sang, gaily, "What a world!" Immediately, she went over to the telephone and started dialing.

"Who are you calling?" I asked, as it was only five o'clock.

She spoke into the receiver.

"Yeah, hi, you watchin' television? Whaddaya think?" Ma took a drag on her cigarette as she cradled the receiver in the crook of her neck and started the coffee.

She turned on the police radio, which was local and had nothing on it about the murder. Some cop was describing the diamond earrings he'd bought his girlfriend.

Daddy came into the kitchen from his sleep on the porch, scratching his stomach, his head, whatever needed scratching, "What's all the commotion? What are you doing up?" he asked me.

"Nothing. I'm going to bed."

"What?"

"Nothing."

"Hurry up with that coffee," he complained, half-joking.

He sat down at the table and lit a cigarette.

"I'm making it!" Ma yelled, "He's up! He's up!" she told Annie, also half-joking. "I gotta go!"

The news commentator had finished the story. It hadn't changed much from yesterday's, except, while Daddy and Ma were talking, I heard something about "a furniture salesman killed" and "police on the lookout for two young girls, about high school age, possibly visiting from the British Isles, anyone with any information..." but I didn't want to think about murder.

I wanted to be alone, to think about Rick.

Upstairs, I stood in front of the mirror. I was too keyed up to sleep.

I thought about a story Jakey told me about the raunchy male business teacher who never stopped making sexual remarks. He loved to embarrass the few female members of the class by telling dirty jokes all day. It was a ploy to get girls to stop taking business. Once, the young and lovely Miss DiMicco walked by in the hall and they could hear her high heels approaching. The whole class listened and snickered, except the girls, who waited uneasily and fidgeted in their seats. Sure enough, as she passed the quiet room, you could have heard the proverbial pin drop and Mr. Rauncho hollered down the hall, "Smell your fingers!" The high heels stopped dead in their tracks and then, continued on their way. Every male in the class exploded with laughter.

I couldn't resist. I smelled every part of myself, like an animal, memorizing him and me. I sniffed my fingers - they smelled salty, pungent, musky, my underarms - high pitched and rancid, fruit warm and overripe in a bowl, the bend in my elbow - there the scent of green pulp from the grass - my hair, his cigarette smoke, or was it Ma's? Or Daddy's? I didn't know.

I thought about how Ma had made me sleep in Rick's bed up at the Likus' cabin on the lake in New Hampshire. I was about ten and I'd cried and cried and begged to let Marie sleep in it instead because it was so full of dirt. Ma and Marie were sleeping on cots and I'd begged, "Please, Mama! Please! I can't sleep in here!" But, Ma had laughed at me and said, "Go to sleep! All the beds got sand in them!"

I recalled the story of how Rick's gang had stood and cheered for him when he'd finally graduated high school, as violently and happily as the troops had cheered for Marilyn Monroe, and Rick had bowed for them, diploma in hand.

I thought about how some girls were burning their bras and how Will Cullen's sister had been called down to the assistant principal's office for not wearing one and for having her skirt too short - if you knelt down and the hem didn't touch the floor, it was too short and you were sent home.

Just the thought of taking off my bra aroused me. I unhooked it and slid it off, one arm at a time, pulling it through a sleeve. As the cloth of my poor boy came down over my nipples - the sensation nearly dropped me to my knees. I knew I would never want to wear a bra again. I didn't burn it though; bras were too expensive to just toss. I folded it carefully and tucked it into the back of my underwear drawer in case I needed it. Maybe for a job. Or to teach school. Maybe.

I had to go out. To June's. This was too good to experience alone. I changed clothes quickly, to a T-shirt and dungarees, sandals instead of moccasins, thinking maybe I'd better not walk around in the same outfit as a killer, even in Revere.

My breasts swayed deliciously against the cotton fabric exciting me beyond belief as I skipped down the very steps where Rick had raped me.

I wondered if he'd be proud of me if he knew I'd killed somebody.

## DOWN AT DUNKIN'

"They'll get her!" a truck driver took a huge tear out of his jelly donut, leaving a glob of jelly dangling from his lip. "Look at her! They got her picture!" He emphasized this by sucking up the glob.

Everyone at Dunkin'' was talking about the murder. The Record American had me on the front page. The glaring title read, "BULL'S EYE!"

Junie and I sat with our heads down, sipping our sweet coffee and cream, nibbling silently on our honey dips. Dunkin' Donuts had just come into Bell Circle; it was an affordable, quiet haven open 24 hours that Junie and I could walk to any time we needed.

"You're damn right we'll get her!" a cop boomed, thick and heavy in his uniform, filling the space with the authority and power of his gun belt, his blue and gold patches, his nightstick, his glistening visor.

I suppose it was my training that made it possible for me to sit there and listen to them with an innocent, calm face, eating and drinking and talking quietly with Junie while my heart pounded fast and icy and my palms and every other part of me sweated, as men say, bullets.

"So, who'd she kill?" a longhaired, young guy in a T-shirt and cut offs asked everyone in general.

"Some guy who tweaked her girl friend," the truck driver answered.

"Hey, watch it!" one of the waitresses, a young woman in a messy brown ponytail, hollered over to him. "I don't blame her for killing the bastard! He had it comin'!"

"What do you mean, 'tweaked'?" the young guy asked, sipping his coffee out of a to-go cup.

It was a good thing for men, I thought, that women weren't armed. I recalled my theory of giving women five legal shots at birth. The word "tweaked" would have been enough for me to use up one of my five shots, if I had them. But, men would have to speak a lot more respectfully, if every woman in the room had five legal shots in reserve.

"He grabbed her by the breasts and twisted her nips while she was coming through the doors at - what? Filene's?" said a bearded guy in a greasy car mechanic's uniform emblazoned with Buddy's Garage in red letters on the back.

"Jordan's!" an older waitress corrected him.

"Jeez, what, was she built?" the young guy asked.

"Ha! Hope so, for his sake!" exclaimed the cop.

"You guys better watch your mouths! Jeez, I can't believe they actually got a word for it." the older waitress exclaimed, reaching with her back to them for another cup from a tall stack of thick, ceramic cups.

"Hey, get a load of this!" the younger waitress read, excitedly, "'The murdered man, Harold Hap-pen-blah - sorry - Happenblocker, a furniture salesman with Loritz Furniture of Boston, was divorced with four children. His ex-wife, Marion Finley, commented, through her tears, ("Mmm," the waitress sympathized) when informed of the tragic event yesterday, 'I could have told you he'd end up like this! He had it coming a long time!' ("See! I told you!" the waitress interjected, then continued) 'But, an arrow to the heart,' the waitress read more slowly, 'was too good for him.' Imagine that," the waitress mused.

"I'd like to see that paper," I said to her.

"Here, honey!" The older waitress slid a copy over to us. There were several on the counter.

Hello again. There I was. And I saw something new: there were Junie's sandals, right between my outstretched legs, as though we formed a crazy new four-legged animal. Because I'd been closer to the camera, Junie was hidden from view.

"Wow," was all I could say. I swayed a little on the stool. The cops, the waitresses' light-hearted tone, Junie's feet, my unreal, outstretched form and the waitress's words, "to the heart" were having a mesmerizing effect on me. I could still feel a dull throb in my right breast from the bowstring. Was that why the Amazons used to cut off one of their breasts? Or was I feeling pain from the burn Rick had given me?

"Ah, you can't tell nothin' from this picture!" the older waitress said, stabbing her frosted white fingernail on the page. She had puffed yellow hair to rival any of the donuts.

"They'll blow it up! You know that movie, 'Blow Up'? Then we'll see who she is!" the cop declared.

"I wanna see that movie," I said to Junie, trying to act casual.

"Yeah, me too."

"When you blow up a picture, it gets even fuzzier!" the younger waitress told him. "My boyfriend works at Kodak developing. He could tell you."

"They got ways! They got ways! Maybe they'll get the FBI in on it!" the car mechanic laughed.

"Screw the FBI!" the cop said. "Oh, sorry girls."

"You look like nice girls," the cop then said to us. "Would you kill somebody for molesting your friend?"

He directed his question at Junie. I guessed I was the friend.

We both looked at him. I thought, surely he can read the truth where it was written: plainly, on our faces. A moment of such complete silence passed, I wondered if my heart had stopped beating and I had died of shock.

"I don't have a bow n' arrow," Junie said.

Everybody laughed. On the rush of laughter, I felt the life run back into me.

"Ah, she must be an archer," the cop went on, "They'll check out all the archery classes. She's gotta be an A student; she got him in the heart!"

"You're dreaming! They're not gonna find her! They say she was wearing a wig!"

"Yeah, women! You can change your appearance in a second! It's not fair, I tell you! You're no good!

"Look it!" said the younger waitress, holding up the newspaper, "the wig salesgirl said, 'I sell a lot of wigs! I can't remember everybody!'"

June and I knew the salesgirl in the Basement remembered us. She'd made a big deal about my hair and my eyes. We didn't dare look at each other.

"Good thing you sell coffee every day, Pauline!" the mechanic said, holding out his cup.

"Yeah, good thing for you!" the younger waitress replied, pouring him some more.

"That's what I mean!"

"Hey! Ginny! Pauline! Duty calls! Catch ya later!" the cop sang out, finishing off his cup.

"Go get 'em, Mike!"

"You bet! Revere's finest are on the case!"


JULY 19, 1969
MARY JO

A few days later, I heard Ma call out again from the kitchen with that sing-song voice of incredible glee, "Oh, my God! Woooow!"

"What?" I asked, my heart thumping.

The news was on again, photos of some political guy in a suit I'd seen often enough, but didn't know his name. Then, pictures of a rickety old bridge in Cape Cod, pictures of the Kennedy Compound in Hyannis and the words, "Hyannis, Kennedy Compound, Chappaquiddik, Mary Jo Kopechne, party, car, bridge, water, night, drunk, sank, swam" were repeated till the words took on a life of their own and became an entity called Chappaquiddik and nobody cared about The Bow and Arrow Killer any more.

"What happened?"

"Ted Kennedy went off a bridge with a girl in his car and she drowned!"

"Who's Ted Kennedy?"

"Your Senator!"

"Is he a real Kennedy?" I asked as the photos and the words flashed by me on TV.

"Of course he's a real Kennedy! He's John Kennedy's brother!"

"So, what's he doing with a girl in his car? He's old, isn't he married?"

"He's married to *Joan!*" She said the name "Joan" with tremendous significance and glee.

"How come she drowned?" I think I was asking myself.

"She was in the car! When a car falls into the water you can't get out!"

"How come he got out?"

She shrugged, "Who knows?"

"Is he going to jail?"

"What are you nuts? Are you kidding me? The Kennedys?"

Ma gazed reverently at the photos of the Compound.

"I wanna bring Grandma here and make a compound like the Kennedys have, so we can all be together. That's what I want to do."

Over the days that followed, my own thoughts turned to Mary Jo Kopechne and one thing would become very clear: she'd trusted him implicitly. I could see her laughing as she got into his car.

I could feel her terror submerged in that blackness.


## INSURANCE COMPANIES

To pay for college, which was only $250 a year, June and I got full time summer jobs together in an insurance agency in town. We simply walked into the long sea of blue and white cubicles and told the kindly personnel manager we'd like two clerical jobs together and he gave them to us. We told him we had decided not to go to college.

It was strange being back in town so soon, back in the awful hot grittiness, which we hated and were drawn into, even though murder had been committed there. I wondered how many other murders had been committed, behind which windows in which alleys, on which streets and at what times? How many unsolved murders? How many people were killing and being killed as we walked past to and from work?

The insurance company was on Atlantic Ave down by the wharves, but the ocean couldn't compete with the hot blasts from the cars and the surging masses of bodies that were caught between the steel buildings, rushing back and forth against the high walls.

There was no place to eat. We took bagged lunches and stood in Bailey's where the marble floors and tables would have been an icy relief if they hadn't been mobbed with exhausted workers trying to get their midday meal.

We were fired from this job because we got the place in such good shape they wanted to move us up in the company. We'd totally updated the filing system, replacing all the old worn folders and tags with crisp new ones. We'd accomplished our typing so quickly and neatly every day - I looked at the keys, June never did - they wanted to train us to type summonses, and here is where I got in trouble.

I told them I'd rather not. I'd just read "Bartleby the Scrivener: A Story of Wall Street" and I realized from his example that I could just decline. I didn't want to be responsible for typing something so unpleasant. So, I was fired and June quit.

In a month I had made enough money to pay my tuition. June contributed to hers, which was considerably more, $1,000. But her family could afford to help her, mine couldn't.

I would repeat this pattern the next year without June, getting another bogus job in another insurance agency. I told them I had tried college and didn't like it. They were eager to believe in my inferiority. This time it was 1970: I wore no makeup, an Indian headband and moccasins. The boss, a fat young man in a pale green polyester suit, took me into his office and gave me a lecture on appearances. He told me the comfortable "walking shoes" were fine, but the headband would have to go. He told me he expected me to wear stockings. He philosophized a bit, leaning back in his chair, examining his fat, childish fingers, "Time is money, don't you agree?" I thought of Albert Einstein riding the trolley, coming to the vivid and sudden realization of the true nature of time and space and motion. This was no Einstein.

My desk faced a billboard on a brick wall. On rainy days, a radial tire ad would get soaked and a bank ad would seep through. My boss sauntered over to my desk one day during my lunch break. I was re-reading *Tess of the D'Urbervilles*.

"Oh, yeah," he bragged, puffing out his chest, "I was supposed to read that in school. I never did!"

NOT reading a book had become an accomplishment.

The secretaries flirted with him. They were semi-beautiful girls in their late twenties, encased in nylon stockings and polyester dresses, their hair sprayed, their nails painted, their lips and eyes greased, their necks and wrists heavy with gold plated chains. They told me about the boy who used to sit at my desk before me. Apparently, he'd boiled turnips in their coffee pot and eaten with chopsticks. "He ruined our coffee pot! You would have liked him!" they laughed.

I would have.

I learned quickly that the business world pretended to have evolved further than humans. Nothing human was allowed. In business, a person wasn't supposed to be late, sick, have a hair out of place or a stain or a wrinkle on their clothes. People were not supposed to sweat, fart, stink, (though many did), eat or get hungry, go to the bathroom, have friends or family, pain or emergency. The cleaning lady told me that if one of her kids were sick, she had to say she was sick and take a sick day. Business denied the human body like nothing else.

The differences between business and me reached a climax one unnaturally hot day when I was supposed to deliver some reports to the annex office.

The day was stifling hot, not a breeze to refresh the very real, tortured bodies of human beings, just a hot blast from the buildings and the cars. Heat rose from the sidewalks in visible, rippling waves. Around me, the people forced their bodies along in a drowsy haze. Deflated, their shoulders hunched, they staggered and slipped off the curb, they bumped into each other blindly and stumbled on their way. The despair of people in their jobs was as heavy as the buildings and as thick as the air. I couldn't breathe! The nylons business made me wear were suffocating me! Every inch of my legs wanted a breath! I decided to rip them off right there in the street!

I was pulling the stockings blessedly off of me when the first paper flew out of its folder and onto the wind.

It was beautiful!

It filled with air like a sail! It waved goodbye to me like a seagull's wing!

I threw another! The reports of people's pain and suffering flew into the air, one after the other, till they became a celebration, a liberation, an exhilarating ticker tape parade of sails and wings! They dashed about like white butterflies! They rose high, high, sucked by the vacuum of business caught between the tall buildings! Graceful and cool as white doves, they settled on the hot streets.

From that day on, I had nothing more to do with business. I told June I'd never trade time for money again. She'd gone to work for the telephone company where she'd learned how to make calls for free from any phone booth in America. But, she didn't last there. The supervisors roamed the switchboards like Gestapo. To watch if she were talking to customers, invisibly, like part of the machine, they'd click in. To watch if she were having a coffee or a cookie, they'd peer over her shoulder. June started to drink after work and she stayed up almost all night trying to prolong her free time. She got so sick she had to quit. Then, she went to work apprenticing for the Florentine jeweler we used to know on Winter Street. She was excited about that, about making the beautiful lacey gold, setting any stone she wanted, aquamarine, garnet, turquoise! She promised to make me bracelets and rings, a necklace I'd imagined, of thin beaten gold and a tear-shaped ruby! June was thrilled with this new and promising occupation, until the old jeweler fell in love with her and she had to leave that place too.

EAST BOSTON, 1954

I was three years old when Mama opened the door and looked into the room. She screamed.

Her life was changed forever.

Daddy and I looked up.

Daddy laughed.

"Cut it out, Rosie! She's okay. It doesn't hurt her!"

Mama cried and ran to pick me up.

Daddy stood and zipped up his pants.

Mama screamed and cried. She ran into another room and slammed the door, pow!

Mama looked around for a way to kill herself and me.

But, she didn't kill us. Mama chose life.

AUGUST 11, 1969
WOODSTOCK

On the weekend of August 11 and 12, 1969, Happy Jack White traveled to upstate New York to a free outdoor rock concert called Woodstock that we were not allowed to attend. That Saturday afternoon, after finishing our morning chores, June and I got into the convertible and drove. Our plan was to follow the coast north to see what was there.

We'd just been fired from the first insurance company and the feeling of liberation was intense. The music coming from the radio lifted the car off the road as it flew along Revere Beach Boulevard.

We were two real blondes in a convertible and as usual, the men and boys on the street reacted violently to us by yelling and screaming after us, "Hey! Is it true blondes have more fun?"

We got a least five or six of that particular question every time we went out, because of a commercial for hair color on television.

We waved back, "It's true!"

We drove. Past Joe Nemo's Grinders and Pizza, past Anna's, past the Arcade and Bluebeard's Cove, past the Tom Tom Room, past the Cyclone and the bumper cars and the merry-go-round, past elegant Point of Pines, past the long Lynnway crammed full of car dealerships, which I taught June to "erase," that is, to demolish the Lynnway mess with one imaginative sweep and change everything ugly into the tall, green reeds blowing in the wind the way the Lynnway was supposed to be, the way it used to be - and for the first time, we drove past pretty little sun-bleached Nahant.

Now, we were on the way to somewhere we'd never been. The road curved out at the ocean in a long blue arch round the bend of a town called Swampscott, where the blue water filled the stone bowl formed by the road, and at night, we'd find, the water turned black as onyx, so that as we passed, the onyx tilted and winked at us, twinkling with the reflection of white and red city lights. Crooked trees, stooped by the wind, inclined and with stout, piney fingers seemed to ache for the horizon.

"Trees sculpted by the wind!"

"Yes!"

"Look at that little yacht club, Pie!"

A compact mansion, built of sun-bleached driftwood, perched on the edge of a wharf like a barnacle. Little white boats bobbed on the blue and gold shore. Big white boats stood in line as if waiting their turn, grounded for now, almost blocking the sidewalk. We drove close, dwarfed by them.

"Wow! They're giants! Can you read their names?"

"Weekend Obsession, Melissa, Sunny!"

"Man!"

"Imagine having a boat!"

"Imagine *living* on a boat!"

We sailed past houses white as yachts on lawns of wide green seas.

"Look at that house! It's humungous! I love it! Look at the enclosed porch on the side! And the windows around back must face the ocean! Imagine waking up there! Or writing there!"

We kept on. Counting chimneys and estimating fireplaces, judging the houses by the number of fireplaces, whether fireplaces were in the bedrooms ("Imagine, a fireplace in the bedroom!"), or in the living rooms (sitting by the fire!), we saw balconies (Imagine having coffee on the balcony!), pillars, porches, doors of many paned windows that opened on to lawns, pools, stables, garages that used to be stables, circular driveways, pine trees taller than hills. And the ocean beyond.

The streets got narrower. The neighborhood closer. Now the houses stood boldly on the edge of the curb. They stood straight, flat faced and simple. Their wooden faces, for the most part, were made of that straight, slatted wood found in the poorest neighborhoods, yet it seemed elegant, clean and fine. Poor and elegant. This we had never seen before. Another way of life began to present itself. A possibility. We traveled more slowly. There was more to see, though the simplicity was mind-boggling. Instead of gazing admirably at driveways and pools, we found ourselves remarking on window boxes overflowing with flowers, trailing green and flowery vines. We noticed narrow brick walkways and dainty, lattice worked gables, wrought iron and old-fashioned mailboxes. The houses were tucked neatly into spaces so small, the charm of modesty and simplicity sent shivers through us. The thrill of seeing houses and trees wrapped around one another as if in a fairy tale, gardens tumbling through porches, iron tables and chairs tucked into flowery nooks, stone statues of children or animals peeking from ivy and moss, simple wooden houses bearing wreaths and happy flags, houses painted bright yellow or sky blue or long ago soft greens and browns deep as earth.

"You couldn't leave these wreaths and statues out in Revere, they'd be smashed. What is this place?" I asked June.

"I don't know."

A small rabbit scurried across the road and ran up the steps of a white, steepled church. I hit the brakes out of sheer amazement.

"A rabbit!" we exclaimed together. We became like little children, gawking in wonder.

We came to a street of little shops. People walked by in relaxed clothes, tanned people with sun-bleached hair and clothes faded from years and years of sun. People walked two by two! They were conversing! They held hands! Men held their wives' hands! Teenagers held hands!

"Look, June, those kids are holding hands!"

"Wow! I've never seen people walking and holding hands before!"

"I saw a boy in Revere shoving a girl into a car once. I called the cops, but they never came."

"Some of these houses have historical plaques on them like they have in Boston. Want to stop and read them?"

It was hard to find a parking place. Most of the streets had restrictions because they were so very narrow. After ten minutes, we found one on a street called Pearl. We got out and started walking around with our necks stretched like long cranes, turning and turning.

"There's a plaque!" June pointed to a pearl grey house. Pearl grey on Pearl Street, I thought. The plaque was made of wood, unlike the bronze plaques in Boston, and shaped like a little house. It read "William Goodwin, housewright, 1729." We read aloud in unison, without thinking.

"Man!"

"It was right to build houses. House-wright," I mused.

We walked and walked, passing beautiful gardens and houses as old as time. Houses with faces we loved instantly. Faces we would remember and visit often.

"These houses are loved, June. It's obvious. Look at the care given even the doorknobs and hinges. They shine in the sun."

"Built for Ruth Morse, widow, 1750," June read. "I love the names. Built for Ruth Morse, widow," she repeated, "Did someone build it for her because she was a widow?"

Houses, like ships, flew flags from their doors. Flags! From houses! We'd never seen anything like it! Not only American flags brilliant in the seashore sun, but flags of watermelon slices, tulips, sailboats, snapping into the wind a philosophy of enjoyment and optimism.

We heard nothing but a hush on the air. We stood still and listened to silence - on a street. A seagull cried. Far off and muffled, some people laughed. A foghorn, long and muted. Then, that hush again. Hush, like a whoosh you could feel in your ears. Sh, sh, sh, like the inside of a seashell, but this was the inside of a street, a soul.

"A house without walls," I said, "Whatever it's name, it's a house without walls."

"Yes!" said June.

"Darling Street! Oh, we have to go there!"

Just as we turned the corner of Darling Street, we saw it there, at the base of the charming street of cottages, perched on a rocky hillock - a castle.

"Oh, God! June, it's real! Isn't it? It's really there!"

We ran to it. I placed my hand against the cool stone, pink and grey and veined with white.

"June, touch it! It's real! Put your hand on it! You can touch it!"

"Ri! I wonder who built it!"

The small, square castle stood on a hill, really green grass poured over a pile of marble boulders, part of which stretched out into a park where people walked their dogs or lazed on the green lawn. The ocean, filled with summer yachts filing back and forth in and out of the harbor, appeared blue and white just over the hill's crest. The castle had four scalloped towers from which nautical flags of every pattern and color flung themselves brightly into the wind.

We ran round and round the castle, discovering its narrow garden overgrown, choked with weedy red berries and pink wild roses sparse and starving, wrought iron lawn furniture toppled over and rusted, slits in the stone that were windows with junk crammed against them. Clearly, the place was unoccupied and that was sad, but full of the opportunity for romance and speculation, not to mention the possibility, however remote, that one of us could live there! We imagined this freely.

We saw more beautiful houses. A long yellow farm house, in front of which stood a garden of grasses, aromatic, I plucked the tip of one, white green and pressed it to my nose, and another, purple flower, till I saw amanda and realized it was an herb garden. We saw a trellis of massive, Heavenly Blue morning glories growing out of an old fashioned washing tub.

An old lady, wearing a blue dress and carrying a watering can, came out of her small white house with green shutters. She smiled at us. Two cats ran out mewing after her, they raced across the neat lawn chasing a squirrel that leaped over a low stone wall. Over the edge of the hill, a scrap of blue ocean winked in the sun. A ship's bell clanged in the distance. And, the hush.

"What is this place?" I asked the old lady.

"You don't know where you are?" she smiled at the idea.

"No," we shook our heads.

"Why, you're in Marblehead!" she said with enthusiasm, and, did I imagine, a hint of mischief? "Marblehead," she repeated as though the name was significant.

We nodded. In my mind, I repeated, Marblehead, like a charm.

"Marblehead is enchanted," I said to June, as we walked on.

"Yes, it is," she agreed.

We read the plaque on a white house nestled into the hillside: Built for John Boden, shoreman, 1710, Boden's Lookout. We stepped carefully down a narrow stone stairway, down the hill, past houses clustered prettily there. We emerged on another street and walked on till we came to a small cove.

The ocean splashed over dark rocks at the mouth of the harbor. On the far shore, we could see perched, an iron lighthouse, large homes and I counted, at least three yacht clubs. Seagulls swooped and called out long, piercing songs. Two elderly women stood at easels set up on the rocks.

"Look, Pie! Those women are painting!"

The women were elderly, but their thin limbs were strong and bronzed by the sun. They were dressed in ragged shorts, cut off at the knees, their slender legs open to the breeze. Their shirts were sun-bleached and torn with wear. Their bare feet clung firmly to the rocks. On their heads were old cloth hats, under which their profiles stood out, sure and clear. One of them stopped her work. She turned her lined face in our direction, her blue eyes sparkled and her voice was clear with energy. "Hello!" she sang out to me, looking me directly in the eye, as though laughing that she had me by the eyes and was communicating an idea to me, "Be-au-ti-ful day!" she called. Dimly, I heard June call back, "Hello!" in a voice that also sang, and then the woman turned back to her painting.

Tears sprang into my eyes, I was so moved. I wasn't sure what her message had been, but I knew she had told me something. I followed June quite blindly until we came to a small café.

A painted sign hung by a wrought iron rail, in the old fashioned manner. It read, "King's Rook."

"King's Rook. I think that's from chess. Ri, shall we go in?"

"I don't have much money," I said.

"I think it's okay," she told me.

"Oh, look!" June pointed across a driveway only large enough for a very small car, beyond which a field of about 300 sunflowers fixed their blazing faces to the sun.

I couldn't speak.

We entered the café and were immediately blinded by the darkness. Eventually, the tiny flames of candles bobbed about and we were able to distinguish tables made of thick slabs of old wood, on each a candle held by a small glass. A waiter approached us. He was very young and tanned, dressed in khaki shorts and a faded pink polo shirt.

"Two?"

"Yes," we replied, stunned by it all.

Classical music was playing.

"I wonder what music that is," I said to June.

The waiter answered me, somewhat serious and bored. He couldn't have been more than sixteen.

"It's Mozart's Piano Concerto, number 19."

We looked at him, amazed.

"Thank you," I said.

He gave us menus and went off.

"Pie?"

"Yeah?" She was reading the menu, which was a small dark red leather bound book with pages of crumbly yellow paper.

"He knew what the music was."

"I know!"

"I'm going to learn about music."

"Yes! Me too! Let's!"

We ordered the cheapest thing we could find, two American coffees, but we read the entire menu aloud, pronouncing the exotic names of the rich coffees and desserts, wines, liqueurs and strange aperitifs as though the menu were a book of poetry in a new language or a book of secrets in an old one.

"Cassis," June read, for she loved a new word. "Crème de Menthe, Kahlua, I wonder what they are."

"Liqueurs, it says, I only know Pernod from Hemingway and anisette which is like licorice and from my childhood."

The wood of the table was old, a thick slab that could have been cut from an ancient ship. We ran our fingers over it's pitted and notched surface, dark with the oil from many thousands of fingers.

"June, I think the Revolution may have begun here."

We looked around at the old mirror in its brass frame, at the prints, by Sargeant and Renoir, at the remarkably detailed Victorian silhouettes, of ladies and gentlemen on a windy day in the country, at the local art, landscapes and seascapes of Marblehead.

Again, I repeated the word, like a magic spell, Marblehead. Like the spell cast by the writer's house who'd helped us the day of the murder, whom we'd named Isis, after the Egyptian Goddess of Magic and Life, because we didn't know her name, but this was an entire *place*, not just a room!

"I think those two men are playing chess!" I said, referring to two old gentlemen who smoked their pipes and leaned intently over a board at a nearby table. Like characters out of a novel, I thought, but they're real.

"Yes! And look at those women over there! They're beautiful and they must be forty - or older!"

I saw them, relaxed in their pretty summer dresses, talking eagerly over glasses of wine. I saw their delicately wrinkled faces, their soft hair, one short and fine, the other longer and held back by a soft bow. I saw the gold and pearl bracelet on one slender arm, the hand gesturing finely, demonstratively, the lacey earrings dangling only a little - and I knew what the painter, the elderly woman on the rocks, had told me.

"June, today I've seen women I want to be like! For the first time in my life, except for Isis who was remarkable and only one, I've seen women I could admire! Not just love because they are my family, but admire!"

June was silent, but it was clear, she understood.

Then, she said, "There's hope."

"The woman who was painting, she was telling me, this is what life can be like! Every day! I know it! We can make life beautiful, June! I know it."

Our coffees came and we sipped them slowly. The cups were glass, like they didn't exist at all. The simplicity of the place overcame me. I wanted to say something, but I was sure, if I did, something would click in the universe and my words would be irrevocable. I knew I'd entered a magic place, enchanted and charged, I spoke anyway, and I meant it.

"Pie," I whispered.

She looked at me.

"I'm taking a vow of poverty right here and now."

"What?" She was amazed. "Are you serious?"

"Yes! I'll probably regret it, and I know, this Marblehead probably reeks of money, I mean, sometimes you can see it's money, but sometimes, you can see, it's not money, it's caring. I want to do it without money. I'm stubborn enough to try it and I've got enough endurance to stick it out. I want to make life beautiful and I want to do it in simple ways that don't take money. I hate money, I always have. I hate having to have it. I hate the way things like food and flowers and having a place to live depend on money. I've got to find a way to earn just enough money to live on, some job I like and feel good about and then paint and write the rest of the time. I want to marry someone who feels the same way, if I marry at all, and have one child who understands. I'm not afraid of daily work, I welcome it."

June nodded, thoughtfully.

"You know, when you look around this town, you're right - you can see sometimes it's money, but sometimes, it's more than that," she said.

"Yes!"

"After all, there's plenty of money in Revere and look at it!"

"Yeah, because all that money just goes into somebody's pocket so he can double park his fat Cadillac down at the track. Sometimes my mother talks about hot topping the whole yard, pear tree and all, because they're getting too lazy to take care of it! It scares me, I think she means it."

"But, you can see here, just by planting seeds in an old tub or by spending a day painting by the ocean, beautiful music, a cat -"

"It's more than things, it's knowing what to do."

"Yes, and it's real."

"As real as castles."

"I'm going to do it," I vowed. I knew what it was, what I needed and I had it already. So did June.

"You'd think we'd seen bluebirds flying about with ribbons," I mused.

"We *have* seen bluebirds flying about with ribbons!" June confirmed.

We listened to the music, which had drifted into the most far-reaching tones I'd ever heard. Not a flute, but something deeper and all the while high and the beauty of not knowing was better than knowing for the notes sang to me only of themselves and the purity of music and of moments strung of bliss.

We came to Marblehead often. At night, we walked and imagined what life was like in the lighted houses. Through lace curtains, we saw tables arranged for dinner parties with eight or ten place settings, glowing invitingly with candles, flowers in vases, fireplaces burning, filling the street with the sweet and musky scent of wood smoke.

High in a house, overlooking the ocean, a small window lighted and a head bent over a desk - someone was writing! This writer kept me company for years; as I worked, I often thought of him working.

We climbed the cliffs at Fort Sewall. The ocean roared black and frothy white. We stood on the edge of the precipice and held out our arms to the moon as though we could walk the path of its reflection. We imagined clippers and yachts and a woman clutching her shawl, standing on one of the many widow's walks crowning the roofs around us.

We went to Marblehead to celebrate birthdays and holidays. We went to talk out our loneliness, our anger, our fears. We sat for hours and hours at The King's Rook or on the rocks or the grass and Marblehead never failed to exorcise our terrors, neither did it ever fail to exalt our joys.

Soon, it would be hard to get June away from Aaron even for a few hours, and for years and years, I was happy, ecstatic for whatever I could get. It made June and it made Marblehead all the more gratifying.

Soon, parts of Marblehead would need to be erased: condominiums that blocked the view of a little bay by taking the view all to themselves; wires that crisscrossed in front of the graceful, old buildings almost crossing them out with black lines; too many cars so that the dear, little streets were heaving with loud, impatient traffic and, in summer, hundreds of swarming bodies.

Still, we erased what we had to; it was by far the most beautiful place we knew. We went there to fill ourselves with beauty, with the unique quality Marblehead had of rough beauty next to polished, all the more real and, at the same time, fantastic, because of it: sometimes a shack next to a mansion, an crumbling stone wall in full view of a splendid yacht, dying sunflowers nodding their heads to pretty hats in a window.

Marblehead trees and rocks, historic in shape, seemed to hold ghosts and spirits and thousands of stories within. Houses as well as hillsides, blended like living parts into the marble mountains and rocky coasts, old, from a time when men and women lived in thin houses, only an inch from the storm. A place sometimes as breathtaking as postcard vistas right before your eyes or quaint as ducks on a pond, sometimes decrepit and falling asunder, but always, always, beautiful. We walked and walked, we talked, we sat and listened and absorbed, until we had enough beauty to take home and last us like massive doses of painkillers - a long, long while.

# Book Six

## Renaissance Woman

Revere

1969-1973

MARY ANN

We drove to Salem State that first morning in a black rainstorm. About eight girls were crammed into my new car, just about everybody from Revere was going to Salem State College.

Uncle Sonny had come home finally and taken back his convertible. He went to work at Edison as an electrician, which had been his dream, using skills he'd learned in the Army.

Daddy found me another car. It had to be a convertible. After having had one, I was spoiled for anything else. At Daddy's work, the bookkeeper, Muriel, was selling hers: a sweet little white Mustang with a red interior. We bought it for $200. I got a waitress job at the new Howard Johnson's at Gateway on weekends so I could pay Ma and Dad back for the car and insurance, $10 a week, out of my tips. I felt that waitressing was really the only honorable job I could do. After all, bringing food to hungry people was a good thing.

Driving to Salem State that first day in a blinding rainstorm was even more blinding because the windshield wipers on the new car didn't work. I was driving by judging my distance from the guardrail with my window wide open. The Mustang also didn't have heat, which was not an issue because the window had to be open. Needless to say, all my passengers found other arrangements right away. At first, it was G and I silently projecting down the highway, then the frigid breeze blowing constantly over her body got to her and I was driving alone within days. And glad of it.

On this day, I had G with me, the Pansky twins who kept cooing "twinish!" at everything they said, Donna somebody and a mush of bodies I couldn't distinguish. G was Paula Giardini, who was so smart she hated talking. She just sat and smoked one Marlboro after another. In high school, she could take an essay test on any novel without reading it and get an A. At the time, I loved her for that, but, later, I'd find out she was just good at lying. She and I had poured over the Beatles' records in an attempt to solve the "Paul is dead" riddle. We accomplished what we'd set out to do after days and days of concentrated effort: Paul was, in fact, dead.

G and I became tenuous friends, tenuous because I know she thought I was a little idiot. I didn't mind. Compared to her, I was. I remember her standing up in senior English class and telling the teacher she thought Tess of the D'Urbervilles should have just slept with the guy to get it out of the way so they could have gone on with their relationship. Very sophisticated! G obviously didn't know Rick Likus, but, as usual, I always think I'm the innocent when in the company of sophisticates. One day, June and I realized what a liar she'd been all along. She'd told us she had two boy friends,

Gordon, and his friend, Peter from another town and one day, June and I were crossing the street and suddenly their names came together in a new way and we just looked at each other in the middle of the road and cried, "Peter and Gordon!" The rock duo.

So, it was this way: G thought I was a fool and I let her.

The first day, which was Registration, was so dark and confusing, I left the headlights on and spent hours at the end of the day trying to get someone with jumper cables to help us. I was already drenched with rain from judging the road through an open window. The walk up from the parking lot left us all squishing in our shoes.

Salem State was a cute little campus of square yellow buildings set round a grassy quadrangle. A white cement square took up the center like a Greek forum. But, on this dark day, nothing was visible but sheets of rain.

In the dry fluorescent brilliance of the Registration Room, I set to work like an archeologist would set to digging. I asked some older kids who was the hardest teacher for English Composition and I took him. I asked who was the easiest for Math and Science, and I took him. Then, I told G, "We have to find the newspaper and join it."

G and I hunted down the newspaper office through bright yellow corridors, some of them deserted and silent. Finally, we turned a corner and came up against a small bustle of bodies rushing through a glass door with the legend, in script, The Lantern, the same name as the Revere High School newspaper.

The editor, a surprisingly beautiful young woman, was at her desk. She drew us in with her homey, soft good looks: long strawberry blonde hair, round cheeks and a pert Irish nose. At the same time, her confidence and ability were obvious and somewhat daunting. Behind her, and I'll always associate her with her own soft color and the stark black and white image behind her, was a huge black and white poster which I would have to get used to seeing in the halls, in the women's' bathrooms, in apartments, but this was the first time I was seeing it and it was quite a shock. My mouth fell open, as I stood before myself, practically life-size, in the tourist's blurred Polaroid. The waitress in Dunkin' Donuts had been right. When you blow up a picture, it just gets fuzzier. A tagline had been added at the bottom in violent red letters, I assumed, by feminists: it read, "SUCK MINE!"

It was too incredible.

"What do you think of her?" the young woman behind the desk asked me.

I couldn't answer. No words, only a tangle of emotions, would come.

I heard G say, matter-of-factly, "She's a goddess."

I turned and looked at her in utter shock. If G knew, she'd respect me. Or, she wouldn't believe it, even with proof.

"Amen!" said the editor.

"Hi," she stood and reached over the desk to shake our hands, "I'm Mary Ann Callahan, editor-in-chief of The Lantern. What can I do for you?"

"We'd like to work for the paper," G told her.

"Frosh?"

"What?" G asked, confused.

"Freshmen?" Mary Ann laughed.

"Yeah," G said. I nodded.

"Any experience?"

"High school newspaper, short stories," I managed.

"If you're freshmen, where are your beanies and pillowcases?" she teased.

"Our what?"

"You're supposed to go down to the bookstore and buy a beanie and a pillowcase to carry your books in, so everyone will know you're freshmen."

"We're supposed to *buy* our own humiliation?" I fumed, forgetting the poster.

She laughed.

"Write about it, it'll be your first assignment."

So, G and I collaborated on "For What It's Worth," a short piece about our reluctance to subject ourselves to tradition. We wrote for The Lantern for the first few weeks of school. It was a great, professional rush to hurry into The Lantern office, greet Mary Ann, greet fellow reporters, check the board for assignments, make phone calls, go out on interviews, sit in on political meetings of the many committees at school.

Things were changing constantly and fast, even in a small school like Salem State, which mimicked the demonstrations it saw in other parts of the country, like Berkley and Ohio State. However, Salem State usually had to content itself with making large issues out of small ones, like a certain teacher's tenure or distribution of a free magazine on campus considered too adult to be passed around near an elementary school, which was adjacent to us. G and I were part of it all. Once, a student wore a fairy dress of pink tulle to a committee meeting to show her contempt, and another time, a fire truck was driven on to the quadrangle to hose down the smut of the free magazine. We wrote about a Black Panther style poverty breakfast program that was discontinued for lack of funds and a clock tower put up instead, "Harding's Last Erection," named after the departing college president who'd insisted on building it.

I didn't care about issues so much as I did about writing. I knew, the issues came and went; it was the emotions underneath that interested me.

Fiction was my true love and I knew I'd have to get back to it. Facts were too limiting.

By some rare chance, Mary Ann Callahan's locker was next to mine. There were four tennis courts on campus and she played every day. She sailed by like a fresh breeze in her short, white tennis skirt, her long legs tanned and strong. Always, she gave my quiet, thoughtful spirit an enthusiastic hello: she knew her energy encouraged me. She was happy and athletic; she never stopped. It came naturally to her. She made me feel like a writer. She made me feel like a person - a working, valuable person. It was beautiful to have - an editor and a friend.

Once, she caught me looking at the poster.

"You never told me what you think of her," she said.

After a moment's reflection, I said, "I feel sorry she had to do something like that."

"Do you blame her?"

"No, she had to," I said, sadly.

She regarded me, seriously. I blinked back the tears forming in my eyes.

"She's a hero of mine. I wish there were more like her," she said, getting back to work.

Early one Monday morning, I went in as usual to get my assignment off the board. The office was in chaos. I looked around, but no one I knew was there, not even G. Not Mary Ann. Everyone was strange: strange bodies, everywhere, yelling at once.

An ugly little guy with a straggly, half-formed beard was tearing down the poster behind Mary Ann's desk. He was wearing a dirty plaid shirt and dungarees.

"What are you doing? That's not your property! Where's Mary Ann?" I ran over to her desk and confronted him.

"Who the hell are you?" he squinted over his shoulder through large, horn-rimmed glasses.

That was the closest I've ever come to wanting to tell someone exactly who I was. I felt the same murderous urge I'd felt before.

"I'm a reporter on this paper." I said, instead, "I work here. Who the hell are you?"

"We'll see if you still work here or not. Everyone's under review," he said, rolling up the poster.

"That's Mary Ann's," I insisted, infuriated. "Where is she?"

He adjusted his glasses.

"She's dead," he said, handing me the poster. "You want this?"

A cold tidal wave washed over me and reality spun me under water.

Limply, I took the poster from his outstretched hand.

"What do you mean, dead?" I asked, weakly, hoping he'd change his mind and say otherwise.

"I mean dead. This newspaper is being seized by the SDS. If you want to write for us, leave your name, check back in a week and we'll let you know."

"What the hell is the SDS?"

"Students for a Democratic Society, I can't believe you've never heard of us. It doesn't look good for you writing for us, girlie."

I leaned over the desk and put myself right in his scruffy face. "What's so 'democratic' about a hostile take-over? Sounds a lot like Prague to me." I said as menacingly as I could manage, shaking and fighting back tears.

"You obviously don't know what we're about," he said, stepping back.

"I don't follow little Nazis!" I slammed the poster down so close to him, he jumped.

I struggled down to the campus bowling alley where G worked, palming the kids' money and ringing up 0 on the register. She told me "the scruffy little guy," she laughed at my description, was Fred Wiener and that people called him "the Whiner." The SDS, she said, not Wiener, had actually done some good work down South getting the vote for black people and working in the War on Poverty, but the Republicans, she said, got scared when it looked like blacks were starting to get educated and move into better neighborhoods. *Republican neighborhoods!* The poverty program was working too well, and they put a stop to it. She also told me that Wiener was hooked on uppers and downers. She knew because they had the same dealer. I just nodded, employing my usual method of understanding, which I'd used since childhood: take it all in, meditate, study, and hopefully understand at some point.

It took me days to find out what had happened to Mary Ann. She'd died of mononucleosis over the weekend. I hadn't even known she was sick. I wrote a poem about her, anonymously, and it was published next to her picture, full page, in her yearbook. It was the greatest honor I had ever achieved.

That's how I never became a newspaper reporter. That's how I got a poster of myself committing murder in my room.

G stopped talking to me altogether after a while. She no longer needed a ride to school because she crashed in Salem most nights. She got lost on speed. She spent most days coming down from the night before, laid out on the bowling alley's plastic settee. If I said, "Hey, G," she would ignore me, or simply get up and walk away. People told me, let her go; you can't reach them if they want to go.

I don't think I've ever met anyone who respected me for being good, except Junie, Mrs. French, Mr. Garante and Mary Ann. And I never met anyone who wasn't awed by murder.


## FRANK

I'd been dancing, in a sari, part of a special Indian dance class at the school given by a visiting artist. Ma had given me a length of kelly green cotton that I'd wrapped and wrapped around me. The Indian lady taught us how to wrap our saris just before she taught us how to dance. There's a picture of me in my yearbook, startled by the camera, dancing, the red smudge of a Brahmin she rubbed on to my forehead, she said, "You would be a Brahmin," incongruous with my long yellow hair.

I couldn't take the sari off. I couldn't. I walked around campus to all my classes wrapped in green cloth over my rotted jeans and work boots, serene as an Indian princess.

I was sitting with this Italian girl I knew, I was ranting something about why should everyone have a toaster, a blender, a dog, a house, and she answered, "Don't do drugs, Gloria! Your mind is already too conscious, I don't know what would happen to you, you're already where drugs are supposed to take you!" A guy came over to us and greeted her and after a minute, she introduced me to him, Frank Murphy.

Though the campus was small, I had never seen him before.

He was stocky and squarely handsome in a neat, almost military way. He had a way of jutting his square jaw out while his brown eyes looked down his nose at me as if to say, "I know all about you, before you ever will," and that not only frightened me, it possessed me. Feeling afraid, it felt familiar. Perhaps I recognized him.

"Hey, where's your sari?" Frank called out to me the next time he saw me.

"Back at the palace."

Actually, Ma had made me wrap it back around the bolt.

"You don't belong to a harem, do you?"

I laughed.

"Yeah, I might ever."

He looked at me, like he was thinking about me in a harem. Maybe, his harem.

"Want some coffee?"

We walked across campus to Scarborough Fair, a small café in the basement of the Student Union. Along the way, people stared at us and a lot of people said hello to Frank. They reached out and grabbed him, physically grabbed him, like they needed to touch him; some slapped him on the back or squeezed his shoulder, mostly guys, saying, "How ya doin', man?" And, they looked me up and down.

I was with him.

I was known around campus a little bit myself, for the Indian headband I wore: I was "that blonde with the headband." And I was known, in some circles for the stories I'd written, not only for the paper, but two fiction pieces in particular. One about the astronauts landing on the moon while an invisible society in another dimension observes them with amusement; another about the astronaut who could no longer walk on earth after having walked on the moon, because his body no longer responded to gravity. I know the moonwalk was supposed to be the biggest thing mankind ever did, but I couldn't help seeing it through a poet's eyes: man putting his annoying foot down on the sacred moon.

But, I supposed these people - mostly guys - wouldn't have known me for my stories. They knew me because I was with Frank.

I liked the way he moved. Even standing, his body sat back like he couldn't care less. He was strong. His thighs swelled in his dungarees. His muscles moved under the denim.

He laughed with great enjoyment at something one of the guys had said to him. I had no idea what it meant, though I'd heard it, and I was back, suddenly, in that foreign land of an unknown language - my own. Frank threw back his head and laughed with full abandon, not ungracefully, with a long "Ah!" at the end, and it was clear to me, he thoroughly enjoyed himself because he owned his world, and equally clear - I could join him there, if I wanted.

Inside the Union, a freshman walked by with a Boycott Grapes sticker plastered on his binder.

"A rebel with a cause," I said, unkindly, to impress him.

Frank laughed; he struck the heel of one boot to the toe of the other with delight. I'd made him laugh!

He stroked his moustache. It was a mannerism I'd see often. Later, he would tell me, it felt like a pussy.

"You're not a freshman?" he asked.

"Me? Not really."

Our eyes met. We had a small conspiracy against causes.

As we passed the radio station, the DJ gave Frank the peace sign. I decided to join Frank. He was going to take me in and teach me. It was going to be like Fagin taking in Oliver Twist.

Bob Dylan was playing when we ducked into the darkness of Scarborough Fair. The records were donations and were replayed over and over. Coffee was free, with a donation.

In the candlelight, Frank told me he was twenty-eight years old, a Vietnam veteran there on the GI Bill.

I asked him about Vietnam. Maybe I said, "What was it like?"

He narrowed his eyes offensively, "What do you want to know, Gloria?" He set his jaw.

I couldn't speak. It was obvious: I didn't know anything. He was insinuating I probably wouldn't even survive hearing about it.

He talked about school instead. He laughed about the four tennis courts, calling it The Country Club. He laughed about the easy courses, calling it Salem State High. He asked what my major was. His was Business. He also told me proudly that he had a BSA motorcycle.

English, I told him when he asked my major. And I told him about my editor, how she'd played tennis, how her locker had been next to mine, how she'd died of mono.

"Only the good die young," Frank said.

"She was my editor."

I didn't know what else to say about what she'd meant to me.

"I'm hip," Frank said.

I told him about the poem.

"Published?"

"Full page, right next to her."

"Full page!"

I'd impressed him, and with my writing.

"Then the newspaper was taken over by the SDS."

Frank nearly spewed his coffee.

"You mean that little shit, Whiner?"

"Yeah, Fred Wiener."

"That's him. The Whiner."

"I take it you're not political."

In those days, there was a certain amount of guilt attached to not being involved politically in some way.

"What do you mean? I'm political!" He showed me the holes in his dungarees. I smiled warmly at his flesh, showing smooth and baby soft through the white threads. "Right here, look, these are my politics!"

Slowly, I took off my beat up leather jacket from the thrift store on Canal Street. He watched me, mesmerized.

I pulled off my sweater, Navy issue, over my head. Underneath, an olive green Army T-shirt, the neck cut low with a scissors. My heavy breasts swung freely and stopped. The nipples showed, plainly.

"These are my politics," I said.

I suppose I was ready.

Frank kept trying, of course. He'd inch his hand over my breast till I finally allowed him to have my breasts. Then, of course, he moved for my dungarees, his hands rubbing my ass, rubbing my vagina through the cloth. I wouldn't let him open the zipper.

He kept trying. He was patient. Very unlike himself.

Then, one night, we were kissing on his couch, and I heard him. It was only a murmur against my throat, a muffled whisper, almost a secret, "I love you, Gloria. I love you."

I warmed to him. I didn't let him that night; I waited until it was safe. It was a day or so after my next period, and when he tried, when his penis tip was soft at the edge of my vagina, I turned and let him slip in, and he was astonished. He looked at me.

"It's okay," I told him, "It's okay."

He went about having his own orgasm, and came inside me with a shudder.

On Frank's stereo, the Rolling Stones were singing my favorite song, the Vienna Boys Choir angelically chanting, "You Can't Always Get What You Want."


## CLEANING THE KI

Rita and I were naked, kneeling on the floor, surrounded by a couple of kilos of "some of the finest shit" Frank and his roommate and old Army buddy, Payton had ever scored, and they knew about dope after having smoked "some of the most potent on the planet" in Nam. Frank told me the old ladies squatting on the streets in Nam smoked joints rolled "as big as dicks."

Our job was to break up the kilos, spread the dry weed open and pick out as many seeds as we could. Frank prided himself on his dope not having seeds that not only added artificially to the weight but snapped in your eyes while you were enjoying your smoke.

What happened was, I'd started sorting on the floor in Frank's room after we'd made love and Payton's girlfriend, Rita had come to help. When she saw me naked, she said, "Oh!" and started taking off her clothes too.

Rita was a poor Portuguese girl from Gloucester. She was the oldest in a family of seven children, and had spent most of her life caring for little ones. She worked on the pier in the Mighty Mac factory making winter coats. Rita was part American Indian giving her a broad, flat nose, dark skin and the deepest blackest hair I'd ever seen; it shone blue as a raven's wing; it shimmered flat and smooth in the candlelight by which we worked.

I said, "This is primitive!"

"Yeah!" she giggled, her deep, guttural laugh.

The men were clothed; they passed in and out, bagging the fine dope into little plastic Baggies, weighing them to an even pound. They seemed disinterested in our bodies, though Payton would look over occasionally and his pale eyebrow would go up in mock appreciation. Frank went by and wagged his tongue at Rita, who giggled again, stoned and deep.

Sometimes, it was like they were all ahead of me and even though I wasn't sure if it was a place I wanted to go, I was still trying to keep up. Sometimes, I think they actually caused me to retreat.

Like the time Frank sang "Midnight Rambler" to me. We were driving in the Rambler. A square station wagon with curtains over the windows in back, it reminded me of the recreation rooms people used to "finish" in their basements. The faded striped curtains hung on string, as though they'd been meant to be cheerful, but just came out looking tired. The Rambler was grey; Frank called her "The Grey Ghost."

The Stones' "Midnight Rambler" was on the radio and Frank spit the words at me with that special emphasis of his own, a special, clear pronunciation that was violent and scary in itself.

"Did you hear about the Midnight Rambler? the knife-sharpened tippie-toe...gambler...the one you never seen before...his footsteps down your marble hall..put a fist through your steel-plated door."

I let him sing at me. I knew what the song was about; I'd heard it before. Cringing, I slid lower and lower down in my seat next to him, hoping to slide down far enough so the words wouldn't be hitting me so directly, sliding down in my seat as if to guzzle liquor from a tilted bottle, another thing I did that scared the daylights out of me, but I did it anyway.

Frank screwed up his face in mock pain, "Don't chyou do that, don't chyou do that, don't chyou do that." He started off soft and low, building the tension, getting louder and louder, he screwed up his face to imitate the wail of the slide guitar, "Don't chyou do that, don't chyou do that," like he was so cool, like he knew what it was to be at someone's mercy, he was so tough, he could take it, he told me himself the girls were crying about a broomstick, could he take the broomstick and still keep singing, "Don't chyou do that, don't chyou do that," he ended with his fist against the dashboard, "I'll stick a knife right down your throat an' it HURTS!" It was like the deformed fetuses of the Beardsley drawings, a shock at first, but then, slowly, like the trucks and planes rumbling and screaming over the house, the scream becomes a part of your life, a part of who you are, and the sound is no longer a shock, but a comfort, a bad thing that seems to understand you, a painful thing that has a way of anesthetizing pain, the memory of Frank singing would turn Jagger's voice into my voice, but it would take years of conditioning to transform the Boston Strangler into a song.

I still hadn't gotten used to Rita's T-shirt showing Mickey Mouse with a hard-on. She was seventeen when I first met her, the same age as me, but much tougher and easier about things. When people are tougher than me, I always assume, they've seen worse. It had been her job to take me to the Family Planning Clinic. She was an old hand at it, having had sex with Payton for two years before I'd come along.

If the church represents spiritual confession, then the doctor represents physical confession. I'm amazed that the church ever gave up this power. How much more control they could have had over people if they'd combined the two terrors of both spiritual and physical confession! Nothing, however, does that all by itself as perfectly as the sexual examination.

I had to pick up Rita at North Shore Community College where I found her sitting cross-legged on the grass wearing tired old clothes that looked like she'd been in them a week, a limp navy blue man's T-shirt, limp dungarees. Meanwhile, I'd dressed carefully again, causing me to look ridiculously stylish in a sheer white blouse under a white sweater vest, khaki skirt and lace-up sandals.

When she saw me, she stood up without saying hello, listless and disinterested.

"You look awful!" escaped from me before I could hold it back.

"I feel awful," she moaned. She stood a little hunched over, with her hand holding her stomach.

I'd never seen Rita looking like this, run down and dull. I was used to her laugh, her casual, playful attitude.

"I got a shittin' flu," she complained.

I drove and Rita briefed me, miserably, about how to lie. You had to say you had a husband, otherwise they weren't supposed to give you any contraception. The doctor was a woman and she understood; Rita babysat for her, so it was okay. Just come up with a name for a husband.

Mrs. Frank Murphy was horrifying. Mrs. Rick Likus was out of the question. There was only one choice.

I'd just seen him.


It was unseasonably cool and grey, one of the last days of summer. I was used to seeing him suddenly like that, maybe once or twice a year; he wasn't in my life, no, I wasn't in his life, though I always loved him best. There was a storm somewhere off the Florida coast and it was sending huge waves and heavy winds our way. The ocean was swirling grey and dangerous and all the tough kids had gone down to the beach to surf.

I was driving by and I saw them, so I stopped to watch. They didn't have surfboards, of course; they were using long pieces of cardboard.

The waves were crashing ten or twelve feet high. Richie Silva was there with about twelve other kids flying on top of the iron-grey water. They couldn't stand on the flimsy cardboard: they lay their bodies along the cardboard and let the waves take them furiously, sometimes over the sea wall, sometimes crashing headlong into it. Some of the wilder girls were surfing, screaming like crazy people and flying up over the seawall.

The ocean roared with its own lungs, the waves roared like lions running with kids on their backs, screaming with terror and delight.

Richie didn't yell. His body hit the wall and tumbled over right by me. He was breathless and grinning as the grey ocean emptied out at his feet; he stumbled up.

"Hi," he said, seeing me.

"Hi," I said, full of love and surprise.

His body was black and blue, like sewn patches. His lips shivered blue, his skin went sickly white all over and black and blue.

"Aren't you getting hurt?" I asked, wanting to reach out and touch his shivering skin.

"Nah! Feels great!"

This was the most we'd ever said to each other.

"You should've brought your bathing suit!"

Then, he jumped over the wall and was gone on the next wave.


"How long have you been married, Mrs. Silva?" the receptionist was asking me.

"Four years."

She smiled knowingly.

Rita laughed. She knew everyone. The doctor came out and greeted Rita, not me. She never even looked at me. It was worse than receiving communion with an unconfessed sin on your soul. At least that was private, between you and God, and, unlike the doctor, you knew all along God would understand and love you.

I wore Ma's old wedding band, the one I used at work. At HoJo's, it had had the opposite effect, so I'd had to stop wearing it. Instead of keeping the men away from me as I'd hoped, they were fascinated.

"You're *married?*" they'd panted enthusiastically, looking me over, up and down.

I had to put the band away in Ma's little hope chest, only to take it out again for this foray into Family Planning.

It was nice having a woman doctor, I suppose, but a woman and a doctor are two different things. A woman doctor is still a doctor and she's not being motherly when she asks you to put your feet into the cold metal stirrups and says, "You're gonna feel a lit-tle pres-sure, there!" and the instrument is bigger than you are and colder and harder than ice and it stretches you larger than you ever thought possible, larger than a glacier shifting, and every first vaginal examination is like the shifting of the Poles for every woman as the vast ice comes down and changes the very climate you're used to and like a Nazi the doctor exclaims, "Very interesting!" and you'd swear the instrument should come out bloody and you're fucked all over again without even a kiss.

Rick Likus had had more love in his touch when he raped me.

But, I got what Frank sent me for - the pill.

It was better than having a fake ID. A license to have sex. Little soldiers marching round an oval field. Little killers. The pill was going to organize me in a new masculine, militaristic way.


COMBAT ZONE

I was younger than the others, too young for a long time. There was trouble every time we went somewhere. Either I couldn't get in or I couldn't get a drink. Rita looked older, so no one gave her trouble. She had that deep voice and dark hair, she was tall and big breasted. I was a tiny baby face next to her.

We were in a bar in the Combat Zone. The streets and the bar, there was no difference between them; you could walk in or out and the dank smell, the darkness, the smoke, the bodies were tightly packed and steaming against each other. In the thick smoke, the waitress kind of flung herself against our table from the crush of the bodies behind her, "Whad'll ya have?" Frank ordered beer, so did Payton and Rita, and I said, "Yeah, I'll have a beer, too." and she said, "How old are you, honey?" I said, "Twenty-one" in a real sweet voice and Frank groaned. Payton covered his mouth with his hand and Rita looked around the room. The waitress said, "I'll have to see some ID."

I was silent.

That's when Frank grabbed me and pulled me outside and told me, "Next time the waitress asks you for an ID, Wisher, tell her to go FUCK herself!"

He had me by the shoulder and I looked across the dark street and I saw a prostitute with her hand in some guy's back pocket and I wondered if she was picking his pocket.

I said, "I can't say that to the waitress."

"Yes, you can, Wisher!" He squeezed my shoulder hard, "Just say it - FUCK! Just say it!"

He had his face screwed up again and his square, soldier chin jutted out at me. He was mad. Mad at me.

"Why should I swear at the waitress?"

"FUCK! Say it! Say it!"

The tears swelled in my eyes.

"I can't."

"Ah! Cry! That's all you can do is fuckin' cry! FUCK!"

We went back inside and I just sat with them. Rita and Payton were tripping too, while they drank.

We rode Frank's BSA home, and as we drove along Memorial Drive, curving black and slick, I held on to him but the tears made the lights drip long lines of red and yellow, long lines of green, like Rita and Payton see when they trip. I was low, terribly low, thinking I would never be as smart and cool as the others, thinking how easy it would be to just let go and give up. I'd slide across Memorial Drive and be beaten to death by the onslaught of cars and trucks, for a second, I would know what it had been like to be Rick Likus smashed in the head and then, I wouldn't know anything.

I came so close, when I think of it, I shudder to think how very close I came to complete and utter failure.

When I got home, I saw the prostitute with her hand in the guy's pants on the late news. She had been robbing him and a surveillance team had taken her picture from a parked car. It was an eerie feeling, seeing a reality from my life played out on the TV. Tired and beat, with Frank's semen stuck up my panties, I went to bed.


## GOLDEN DREAMS

I lost track of the years again, probably because June wasn't with me. I sometimes think, if we'd still been together, we would have been stronger. Things would have gone better for us. She moved out of her house. One day, while Agnes wept, June passed trash bag after trash bag of her things out the Princess curtains to Aaron who waited on the lawn. They got a place together in Winthrop. June was eighteen. That's when she quit Northeastern and went to work at the phone company.

I don't know what year it was, only that they'd changed the drinking age to eighteen and I was eighteen. Old enough to drink or carry drinks. Oh, and old enough to be fucked, legally.

"You should get a job," Frank said as we drove down the Lynnway.

He drove relaxed, leaning back in his seat, his barefoot pressed against the dashboard, his knee poking out of his torn dungarees.

"I have a job," I reminded him.

He sneered.

"You call that a job, Gloria? That's piss n' shit money."

"The basics," I shrugged.

Frank hated my casual attitude toward money. But, I wasn't as calm as I sounded. My heart beat fast because we'd had this argument before and I didn't want to have it again.

"That's because you live at home with your moth-er!" he taunted. Then he went on.

"My mother makes more than you do when she returns something to the store..."

Here we go.

"She returned a coat the other day because the lining was ripped and when they wouldn't take it back, she stood in the store and screamed for the manager. She yelled real loud until he gave her the money back. *She'd had the coat for three years - and she didn't even buy it in that store!"*

"That's disgusting," I said.

He always had a story like this about his mother. She was always returning something.

"That's a typical response from you! That's life, Wisher! You could never do that, could you? I'd like to see you do that!"

"I never would."

"Don't have to tell me," he said, flatly.

Hot tears came to my eyes. I made a mental note not to forget this horrible feeling, no matter how good things got, never forget how degraded Frank could make me feel and never, never marry into this family, never have Frank's mother as your mother-in-law, I told myself. With Frank, the diapers were *always* hanging over my head.

I was silent for a while, listening to Janis Joplin scream on the radio. Fantastically, she lulled me to feeling a little better, her wail, her pain, how her mother had said, "Janis, you have such a nice voice, why do you scream?" The idea made me smile, in spite of myself. I knew why she screamed. She screamed for all of us. Then, I recalled how Frank had bragged that he'd seen her and Big Brother and someone in the audience had called out, "I wanna ball you!" And Janis had said, "Okay, but, one at a time!" He wished I would say that to a few hundred guys; I knew it from the way he told me. He'd had that "You'd never do that, Wisher, would you?" smirk on his face.

We were stopped at a red light and Frank looked over at this seamy looking dive called Viceroy's, a long red box in a parking lot.

"There! You can get a job in there! By Friday, Gloria, you can be making a couple a hundred bucks every weekend! Just wiggle your little ass for them, bend over and show a little tit!"

The tears fought with me, but the more I fought, the more tears came and swelled until I sniffed them back and gave myself away.

"Bullshit, Wisher! Bullshit!" he yelled. "You can get a job in there and make some real money!"

I looked over at the sickly red brickface of Viceroy's. A few Cadillacs were scattered around the lot in the middle of the day.

"I don't want to get a job in there," I said, with a small voice.

"Don't give me that wimpy whine of yours! Listen, those guys drop a lot of cash. When they belt back a few, they get real generous!"

If Uncle Vickie caught me in a place like Viceroy's, he'd yank me out of there so fast, like Uncle Sonny did the night I brought Marie into the Tom Tom Room after the Boston Ballet. Uncle Sonny had cried, "What are you doing here?" and he'd thrown us into a cab.

"I promised her a Golden Dream!" I'd said.

Who'd given me my first Golden Dream? That frothy, foamy orange cream in a long-stemmed bowl that tickled my nose like champagne; sweetly as a child's vanilla orange pushup, it bubbled my brain.

It was Peter, Jakey's brother, on leave, in Uncle Vickie's bar, in the Tom Tom Room, with all my uncles in a row at the bar, like they would be at a wedding or a wake, their wide Buonocorso eyes, their bulging Buonocorso noses, high elegant foreheads, all in a line. The music blasted the room, creating a wall of vibration, a shimmering wave of celebration. Peter was celebrating, like he always did, celebrating being happy and being on leave. He'd said, "Oh, you gotta have a Golden Dream!" I was too young to drink, so he bought them for me. He watched me drink the first one, with great anticipation. He watched my lips approach the rim of the champagne glass. He leaned over with absolute delight in his eyes. "Whoop!" I said as the bubbles hit my nose. Peter threw back his head and laughed, "Go on, take a sip! Don't be afraid!" He bought me Golden Dream after Golden Dream.

The night Frank brought me to the Tom Tom, Uncle Vickie got drunk and told the female bartender over and over, "That's my niece! She's as old as you!"

"Yeah, right, she's as old as me?" The bartender wouldn't believe him.

Uncle Vickie thought it was a great joke. He laughed and laughed at the bartender, who just looked at him sadly with her kohl-blackened eyes.

That night, maybe because Frank brought me, we saw Uncle Vickie smoking a joint and they were roasting a whole pig on a spit. The pig dripped fat, hiss! on to the fire, hiss! The smell was odious, filthy greasy and people kept shouting, "Mmm, when's the pig gonna be done, Vic?" The tinny music smashed against you like you were the cymbal, so loud that Frank had to scream everything he said. When we ordered, he wouldn't buy me a Golden Dream. He said I was out of my mind: they were too expensive. However, the gins and tonics we drank kept piling up in front of us; so many people sent drinks over out of respect for Vic's niece. That was the night Frank told me I had to move out of my mother's house. I couldn't imagine leaving a space in which I was actually freer than I would be in an apartment where Frank could spend the night any time he wanted.

I snapped back to the present when I noticed Frank had pulled into the Viceroy's parking lot.

"What're we doing here?" I asked, alarmed.

"You're getting a job."

"I have a job." My heart slammed, almost out of my chest.

"Go on, they're gonna love you!"

"They'll want me to work weekends! I work at Howard Johnson's! What's Gladys gonna do?"

"Tell her you quit!"

"You know, Frank," I began to argue, "being a student is my job." I believed it too, it was hard enough to work weekends, study and go out with Frank. My grades weren't close to what I wanted as it was. I'd dreamed about a perfect average, but I had plenty of B's and at least one D, in Health, because the course was really about disease. We were forced to memorize long lists of horrible exotic diseases, their nasty symptoms, incubation periods and medicinal cures. After a while, they all seemed like one big disease.

"Look, this is bullshit, Wisher! You want to be a writer, go in there and find out about life! I wanted to be a general! You know how much ass you have to kiss to make general? I wouldn't have respected myself if I'd made it to general! If you were a *real writer*, you'd be published and have some *real money!*"

I got out of the car just to shut him up.

Walking across the parking lot, I looked down and saw the sparkling bits of glass and I time traveled to another day: early in the morning, I was walking across the Salem State campus, absolutely alone in a wide vista of dazzling white snow and across it, the hush of history whooshed my ears. As I stopped and looked out over the expanse of pure white softness, snow-filled, sparkling wind blew across my cold cheeks. I disappeared into its beauty. It was more than an hour before the first classes started. Not a soul was around. This freezing white emptiness, I thought, shivering deeply, chilled to the bone from having driven the thirty miles without heat, is what the first Salem winters had been like for the pilgrims. As I walked, the silence lifted me as in a dream. I shivered under the grey seal coat I'd bought for ten dollars at the thrift store on Canal Street and I wished for a dime to get a hot cup of coffee at the school cafeteria.

That second, I looked down and there, glinting in the snow was a dime at my feet. Not a mark, not a footprint except my own and a dime on top of the soft snow. With numb fingers, I picked it up and carried the precious dime to the cafeteria where I bought a steaming cup of coffee, sweetened with cream, cradled it in my hands and read my new French words in heavenly bliss.

When I told my boss Gladys I was quitting to work at the Viceroy, she said, "Oh, no! Not that place! You don't belong there!" She told me to return any time and she'd give me my job back.

I was hired by an undernourished, greyish-yellow bartender who looked like he hadn't seen daylight in years. The Viceroy during the day was dank with the odor of undersmells, grease and spilled drinks. The bartender told me my hours would be five to three. I thought he had that backwards. He shook his head, no. Drinks through dinner, drinks again, then breakfast.

Frank said, "I knew you'd make a bundle!"

Viceroy's at night was a sinister red and black cavern that crashed with a bad band whose singer wore a bad toupee and mimicked Top 40 hits from the AM radio. The place pounded with people drinking and dancing. The bartender lost his yellow tinge and glowed red in the bar lights. But, he wasn't the devil in charge: that was the dishwasher, a dark, wiry young guy with a narrow black moustache who stood inside the dishwasher that wound around him like a snake and screamed and groaned and spit hot water and garbage on to us while we waited for our trays. The dishwasher regarded us silently from under his flimsy paper hat that sat on his thick black brows and made him look somehow more evil.

But, Frank was right, I made at least a hundred or more a weekend, mostly from the drinkers and dancers, as long as I could remember who drank what and kept their glasses coming. The night was a torture of bad music and bad talk until somewhere near two in the morning, long after last call, the band would mercifully stop playing and put down their instruments, sit down for a cup of coffee, light a cigarette. The lights would come up to a normal level. And the most beautiful people I'd ever seen wandered in from their own night's work waiting tables at the posh club in Nahant, Tony G's, owned by a famous baseball player. Handsome men, beautiful women, movie star beautiful; the men dressed in tuxedos, the women, in black gowns and sparkling jewelry. They spoke in soft, exhausted tones, ordering breakfast and coffee. I remember one woman whose white blonde hair drifted over her bare shoulders, the creamy pearls on her ears, her voice, so kind, so considerate. They talked quietly for an hour or more. You could tell they knew what it was like to wait on people; they were so nice to me. Frank always wanted to know how much they left, and it was always a lot. He was pleased.

Every time we passed a box on the highway, Frank would say, "You can get a job there!" I had a job at Kentucky Fried Chicken where the creepy little manager, short and fat and scruffy with his three hairs slicked over his bald head, ashes and crumbs littering his tight jacket, asked me in to his office one afternoon.

He showed me my application. Someone, probably the assistant manager, a young silly guy who was always fooling around, had altered the F I'd put in the SEX square to read, OFTEN. The manager looked me up and down and said, "If someone's putting out in my place, I want to know about it." I said I wasn't, that I didn't know how that had gotten there. He looked me up and down again and let me go back to cleaning out the black gunk from under the refrigerator.

I had a job at Firelli's, where the men came and went out the back way from the kitchen all day and all night with to go orders, usually a calzone, where I was advised by the men who hung around the kitchen, if I wanted to get a teaching job, I needed to campaign for whoever was running for mayor of Revere, then I'd get a teaching job. That's where I met Benzarro, whom I would pay to get me a teaching job. The salad girl asked me to be the godmother of her baby. I turned her down because of what had happened with Ma and Margaret Flannagan. I told her as nicely as I could that she should ask someone in her family. I was fired from Firelli's for talking back to a customer.

I worked at The Driftwood where I was fired for tending the customers too much, customers who wanted to be alone in a dark corner with their mistresses.

At one time, I had three jobs at once and was going to school. Frank still wasn't satisfied because though I had plenty of money, I only saved it or used small amounts to buy books or paints or canvas. He wanted me to be rich. But, I felt poor, very, very poor. Because, you see, not only did I stare all night into the black puddles of parking lots, not only did I scrub the undersides of scummy shelves, not only did I have greasy guys snap their fingers for me, or try to put their hands up the short skirt I had to wear, not only did fellow workers steal my tips or my jacket from the employees room, not only did I not believe in any of the things I served people or any of the ugly, violent places in which I served them, but

I no longer had to wish for God given dimes to appear in the ethereal snow of historical mornings. And that was a sad loss.


SAVING THINGS

You're probably wondering why I was with Frank.

Sometimes, after Frank had made me feel particularly bad I would lie on my bed and stare through the darkness at the beautiful, strong shape of myself standing erect and firm, bowstring pulled back, unafraid, sure, and I would wonder who I was and why couldn't I be more like myself, as I had been that day? Frank would admire me finally if he knew I had committed murder. That's when the tears of self-pity would flow, and then the tears of anger, because *she* would never have cried for herself!

Then, I would miss June's strong, thin arms about me. I'd imagine Richie Silva. I still gained comfort from his imaginary arms, more than I did from Frank's real ones.

I would think of Rick Likus - where was he in the jungle? Did he think of me? I'd never told Frank about him. I never told Frank about Daddy. In fact, I'd begun to "save" things from Frank in order to save their meaning and their value. I saved them to tell June, of course, because she was the only one who could appreciate them.

An example happened on a day Frank and I took a drive up by Essex. Our first afternoon together had been spent in Essex, where Frank had pulled over by a meadow, damp and freezing in the fresh marsh air, still and thick with mud, where rows and rows of yellow school buses were lined up like bright toys upon the black ground. I'd thrown my arms about him and exclaimed, "Oh, don't ever take me away from this place!" catching him completely off guard, warming him to me. I'd never seen real school buses so squat and cute before, like bumble bees in a row, only the long, green evil kind we'd had in Revere.

We were in Essex this day and Frank had refused to take me to the lovely little Essex Clams where lovers could sit outside on the weathered wood porch overlooking the ocean and eat fried clams out of baskets. He said it was a fuckin' tourist trap, and I said, "I know *that*, but it's so nice!" He said he wouldn't waste his money. Instead, he drove to a Seven Eleven where he left me, "Keep an eye on the BSA," in the searing hot parking lot while he went in to "get us some lunch." I could still smell the crisp, oily fried clams across the way, and the salt of the ocean breezing with gulls.

I spent most of the time with my eyes glued to the horizon, blue and glimmering with sun stars on a strip of water. Tall, fresh green grass swayed in the foreground - I wished I had my paints. I hadn't done a lot of painting - or writing - since going out with Frank. He didn't have the patience to wait for me to sketch, let alone paint. As for my stories, he insisted they weren't any good because they weren't published outside of school. He insisted that Salem State would publish anything, and that the A+ I'd gotten in Creative Writing was a joke. Anybody, he said, could get an A+ in Creative Writing, that's why everybody took Creative Writing in the first place, to get an easy grade. He wouldn't believe me that I'd deserved it, he had to ask practically everybody on campus if Creative Writing was hard to get an A in, he'd ask a total stranger walking by before he'd believe me.

I was meditating on the soft, watery grass. You could feel its soft texture just by looking at it dip and sway. I pretended I was sitting on the porch at Essex Clams, which I could see over the water, when all of a sudden, from out of the grass popped a doe, not ten feet from me. Her ears flicked, gently startled, but her liquid gaze was all serenity. She had no other language but this and I tried to fill my eyes with gratitude back to her for letting me look so long into her lovely face.

Then, she was gone.

"I can't wait to tell June!" I thought. That's when I knew for certain that I had been holding things back from Frank.

When Frank returned with an open bag of white bread and a package of baloney he was already gobbling, I couldn't bring myself to tell him. He would've said, "They got fucking ticks, Wisher. I hope you didn't touch her!"

You see, I was with Frank because I knew he could teach me unrelentingly about reality. He was my road trip to reality. Joni Mitchell has a line in one of her songs that describes it perfectly: "He gives me things I can't give up just yet."

Now, I'll tell you about those things.

The night on Plum Island. We intended to sleep the night there on the beach, which was illegal. Frank loved to do stuff that was illegal. We'd already made love in our sleeping bag, raunchy with sand and musky with three years of lovemaking. Then, Frank said he wanted to go for a ride on the shore, he'd always dreamed of riding there, under the stars.

I started to put my clothes on, but he stopped me. He kissed me and led me by the hand to the BSA. Naked, he started her up, lifting the kickstand with a sharp kick of his bare heel.

Fearful and excited, I let him guide me to sit, not only in front of him, facing him, but joined with him.

"Can we do this?" I was breathless.

He kissed me deeply with his tongue.

"I want to try."

I eased myself on, feeling the machine trembling too, feeling myself fill with him. I went limp with desire, sinking into his chest, my face buried in him, his heart pounding against my cheek.

He drove slowly down the beach, the water made long swirls round our ankles. We didn't dare move while the BSA purred gently along and through us till I couldn't tell where the sensations were coming from, the machine or me, from Frank's penis or from his heart, was the wind inside me or outside, was the skin I felt his or mine? The ocean, moon and stars alike melted together into pure vibration.

He finally had to stop the bike. We tumbled over on to the sand, where he fell on top of me, nearly burying me into the earth with his thrusts.

He fell off me just as suddenly, gasping, "That was the most intense sexual experience of my life!"

On the black sand, the only light visible from the overturned bike, I kissed him in agreement, letting him assume it was also mine. But, I never had an orgasm with Frank. He was a selfish lover. Nevertheless, for me it was a celibate-like duration of sustained lust, years of an almost nourishing yearning.


## EPIPHANY

Often, I didn't know where I was, but getting there was an essential part of the sacrament.

The concert was the new mass. Here was another element of Frank I needed for the time being. Frank always knew where the best concerts were.

In a communal confession, a ritual prelude to the epiphany, we'd prepare ourselves by drinking and smoking in the dark space of the Rambler, levitating down the highway on music and lights. The music was wind, the music was pure spiritual absolution: the greatest guitars, the greatest voices, sent by heaven to tell us something, and we listened, it was a new gospel! The rock star sang and his breath filled our lungs! His breath lifted our bodies, our vehicle, sending us flying over time and space like it was nothing, sending us flying into the night on our way to see for ourselves - demi-gods.

The run from the car was a penance. We'd fall out of the Rambler, Frank, Payton, Rita and I, to great gusts of Boston wind that instantly dispersed the clouds of dope that came out with us, great blasts of the coldest, or the hottest, most furious wind caught between the towering office buildings. Shivering or burning uncontrollably, we'd run as fast as we could to get away from it.

Waiting in line was the benediction. Freezing in winter or sweating in summer, the elements continued our penance during the blessing. We wore ceremonial robes: old fur coats, matted and torn; Army jackets, green or camouflaged; dungaree jackets, holy as priests' raiment, sewn with peace signs and fists, embroidered with flowers or suns or stars, stiff with years of worship, stiff as with the blood of soldiers; for tramping through life, the Frye boots, heavy and serious, the sandals, biblical and gentle; the dungarees, the basic uniform, torn, graphitized, decorated as a prison wall with body fluids, pictures of our souls, bits of ribbon, scraps of memory;

headbands, flowers, earrings, beads, the musky, reverential scent of patchouli oil mingled with marijuana that said, "We're one," all come here to celebrate and give birth to a new life form.

We didn't know each other, but we entered the new church and fused into one body. The anticipation quickened our pulses. The sight of the stars on earth shot our hearts to heaven. Their notes played on our hormones, their voices stroked our dreams, their guitars plucked our nerves like strings, sending ecstatic tremors through us. We raised our hands in exaltation and called out to them to see us, hear us, commune with us: justify us! We swayed rhythmically or danced in our seat or in the aisles to the music that caused us to disappear into it, the way an orgasm causes lovers to disappear. The music was a sacramental climax: the dance, a mystery of transmutation. We let the gods in, their voices became our blood, their words became our flesh. The stairway to heaven went both ways. They'd come for our souls; we took theirs away with us. They were ours: we belonged to them.

The experience was heightened because I was stoned and innocent and I didn't know where I was; I would be carried along on a wave and suddenly find myself in front of a stage, in smoking darkness, pressed against bodies, breathing, hearing, smelling, tasting, as with one strange sense alone, a sensation so foreign I often wondered if it was my sense and not coming from another person, the one next to me, or behind me, or in front of me on the stage? It was a new high there together I'd always reached alone in my room without drugs, only the concentration of my own senses. But, now, I was feeling everybody else's. I felt Jim Morrison's voice surging up my own throat. I felt his bark in my stomach. I saw and smelled the blue smoke rising from Tina Turner's straining muscles. It smelled like singed roses. Janis screamed like an airplane going over the house, she was a screaming oracle, blasting through me, coming out my fingertips. You could pray with Crosby, Stills and Nash. You could reach heights on their harmony, or you could pillow into their sweetness. Jimi Hendrix's inner intensified cosmic wail made deep ecstasy, made deep spiritual sex. Carlos Santana could pluck a woman's vulva in places her boyfriend couldn't touch.

After Altamont, I thought I was going to die at the next Rolling Stones' concert held at Boston Garden. After Altamont, the Rolling Stones' concert where a boy was knifed to death right in front of the stage by Hell's Angels security, the love started to fade, the nation got tired, the love children couldn't bear the pain.

The Garden, that huge concrete box, was ninety-eight degrees at four in the afternoon the day of the show, before it was filled with thousands of boiling bodies. Security was rampant. No drugs would be tolerated, no liquor, no weapons. Because I was the smallest and most innocent looking, wearing only a halter and cut-offs with my hiking boots, I was chosen to carry the Army canteen, the dope, the blade. Frank said there was no way he was going in there without a weapon.

The cop stopped me at the door.

"What's in the canteen?" he asked, official and solemn.

Frank answered, "Water, man."

The cop opened the canteen, which was strung around my neck and sniffed. Water. Frank had organized this outing like a military campaign. He said he wasn't going in without water either.

The cop smiled at the water, screwed the cap back on with one deft flick of his finger. Stoned, I thought, he's a vet. I'd seen Frank do that a million times.

He let us pass.

The heat was smothering. We waited two hours. No Stones. Next to us, a nervous little guy with an electric hairdo told us his name and asked if we knew him. His name was a household word, but Frank said, "No, man, I don't know you." The guy offered us speed to help us stay awake. "I can't believe you don't know me, man," he said. It was funny. We took his speed and promised him we'd try to listen to him on the radio. "FM, man," he said. FM was something new, better than what we'd gotten on AM.

Then, the mayor of Boston, handsome Kevin White, was on the stage.

"What's he doing there?" I asked Frank.

"My city is in flames!" the mayor cried, dramatically. No one knew what he was talking about. "And the Rolling Stones are, at this moment, in Philadelphia in jail."

We understood this part. An enormous groan went up from the audience.

"It is now twelve o'clock, midnight," the mayor went on, "Southie is burning..."

"He loves this!" Frank exclaimed.

"and I am working furiously to get the Stones out of jail. (A groan went up from the audience!) Apparently, one of them – I apologize, I don't know which one - hit a photographer at the Philadelphia airport. We've spoken to authorities in Philadelphia and we think we can get a judge to hear the case AS WE SPEAK! Then, I am going to get them on a chartered plane and fly them to Logan. They should be here in an hour, less, if I have my way - I beg your indulgence, you've been a great audience so far, please, don't let me down!"

It was beautiful, this break in time. We wandered the Garden. The time went by so fast; the Stones were in front of us before we knew it. Mick's wormlike body snaked along the stage; remarkably skinny, he filled the space with his movements and with a red scarf that danced like a snake, as long as the stage. He flung and twisted its silky skin; he charmed us with the snake. He was the demon we'd been waiting for, and then, he was gone! We screamed for him, but no one came out.

The empty stage could not be willed to hold him again. We had to go away starving.

It happened again and again, one minute we'd be laughing ecstatically getting out of the car, the next minute, as if by magic, the heavy black door to a club would open and slam behind me and I'd be standing in another world.

I was facing a long aisle going down a ramp. Around me was a deep blue cloud, the color of midnight. Surging with smoke, the darkness surrounded me. My companions fell away. And I saw, at the foot of the ramp, a pale, thin group clutching guitars and microphones, leaning on their instruments for their last breaths of life, their heads nodded downward, the drumsticks hit the drums, bah, bam, bah, bam, slooooowly, slooowly, as in a dream of hitting the drum, as in a dream when you want to speak but can't, as in a dream when you must run, but your limbs are heavy and numb. A woman with ice blonde hair tapped the drum, unheard of, a woman drummer. "Her----" sang the singer, holding the word so I couldn't identify it, "her---", he drifted, forgetting to sing. I waited mesmerized, I waited, while he drew out the word, "her--", he was singing to his lover, his soul, "her---" he breathed, and then, "oo--in." And again, he held and drifted us with him, "Her---oo--in", he sang to his demon and his dream.

Heroin. A beautiful song about heroin.

Where on earth was I?

As in a dream, the scene shifted and I was in a dark cave, really a series of caverns, curling with smoke, dark, so that faces suddenly popped in front of my face, frighteningly real, as in a dream. I held on to Frank's hand for dear life as we approached alcoves and small caves off to the side where there appeared to be people, squatting primitively around candles, orange flames twitched horrifically, throwing gigantic, twisted shadows against the walls. The people were doing something, what?

"What are they doing?" I asked Frank, holding his hand and peering nervously through the thick, sweet smelling smoke. "Smoking?"

"Yeah!" Frank laughed. "Smoking!"

"Come on," I urged, "Were some of those people making love?"

"Fucking!" Frank corrected me.

He actually left me and went to get drinks.

I was surrounded by a group of beautiful, young Arabs.

"Such eyes!" One of them said to his friend, smiling at me. They all had the liquid eyes of Arabs, black as olives, shining temptingly in the flashing lights. I felt myself intrigued. I felt myself going toward them in their silk suits and crisp white collars. Such eyes!

But, I was not to be captured by Arabs. Frank came back, with gins and tonics and I was almost disappointed.

Then, as in a dream, the scene shifted and I was standing close to the stage. Closer than I wanted to be. I didn't know who the band was. The smoke from The Tea Party filled my head. I couldn't hear the band because they were too loud. They banged and crashed, and somewhere, inside, the plaintive cry of the guitar as though trying to get out.

In front was a wild man with wild beard and wild hair. His eyes locked on to the wide eyes of a scared young girl in front of him. He saw me and he was delighted. He knew I was scared. He grinned evilly as a Nazi and picked up his long leather belt with two leather balls on the end and started twirling it in my face round and round like a lasso. He was skeletal, demonically tall. His cheeks sucked in, his eyes bulged out. On the end of the leather straps were bolero balls, he swung these as if to show me, show me, show me, here, little girl, here, here! How many times had I heard it? This wasn't what I wanted, old and evil, here was the real demon, here, with searing eyes, circled in black! They were the circle the devil would come through! Here, little girl! Here! I couldn't move, he had me, and his message was the opposite of the lovely old ladies I'd seen on the shore, opposite the love and peace and spiritual orgasm. Pretty girl, here! His old hair leaping, his leering eyes, his devilish grin, the music, no longer a soothing ocean, screaming and crashing like hellfire! That's what he told me, here's what we came for, here, sex, little girl, come n' get it, little girl, sex, sex!

## FUCKING WHORES

Rick Likus came home from Vietnam, but I didn't see him until one Saturday afternoon when I had the hose out and a pail of soapy water and I was washing my car.

I'd discovered the only way to make my poor things look really good was to keep them clean. So, I knew what he meant, I understood completely, when my darling neighborhood rapist turned around at his door and shouted up the street at me, "WASH THE WORLD!"

He was right. Like Daddy, he knew me well. Daddy said I actually enjoyed doing the cleaning chores. He was right. Cleaning things gave me a feeling of control. It felt good to see things come clean. Daddy also said, once, "If you're lucky Gloria, maybe that little Likus shit will rape you."

Uncle Vickie was over our house. He had one of his flashy girlfriends with him. I wasn't impressed by his girlfriends' cleavage anymore, since I had cleavage of my own. And I was no longer mesmerized by their long plastic earrings or their red talons since I didn't choose to have those at all.

Uncle Vickie was very drunk. I realized Uncle Vickie had probably always been drunk, I just never knew it. He'd asked me about Frank and when I told him Frank had a job as a bellhop down at the Fenway Motor Inn, Uncle Vickie got on a tangent and he wouldn't let up. Frank had simply decided one day that he wanted to be a bellhop; he thought it sounded like a cool job.

"Ah, he's got a girlfriend on the side. You know how it is, all them bellhops got girlfriends, they get every broad that comes in! They get them first! He's got a girl stashed in the hotel! You mark my words, Gloria! He's got a girl!"

I'd never seen Uncle Vickie like this, railing, bitter. He had a new scar under his chin that grinned lasciviously from ear to ear like a second, but more sickening, smile. He told us he had to carry a baseball bat to his car now, because "the niggas are gettin' so bad in town, Rosie! They tore up the convertible, Rosie! My beautiful convertible!" He complained to his older sister, like she would go downtown and scold them about it.

"Ah, he's screwin' all them hookas at the hotel!"

I could see Frank in the elevator with some woman, charming her with his smart remarks, his sharp good looks; my heart sank so low.

Uncle Vickie kept talking, his fat jowly chin red blotched, swinging with emphasis, dug up and scarred with that new deep red scar wiggling across the front of his throat from ear to ear. I no longer felt admiration. He reminded me of the red, drippy pig going round on the spit, everyone shouting, "Hey, Vic! When's that pig gonna be done?" and Frank hissing in my ear that I still lived with my "par-ents," when was I gonna MOVE OUT!

I felt the same sadness and fear I had felt that night on the BSA, the same confusion. My temperature shot up a hundred degrees, the tears pushed at my eyes. I didn't want Uncle Vickie to see me cry.

I jumped up and ran from the kitchen table.

"You're a chump!" Uncle Vickie laughed after me.

I made it up the stairs.

"Gloria!" It was Daddy's voice behind me.

"What?" I sobbed, stopping short. I stood stiffly in the hall, wondering what was coming next.

Daddy came up very close to me and took me in his arms.

"Don't pay any attention to your Uncle, that's the only life he knows," Daddy said.

I tried to hold back my tears, but I could feel some seeping out, wetting Daddy's T-shirt, yellowed with age, reeking of range oil and beer.

We stood next to the very spot where Rick had raped me, where Daddy himself had caught me and sucked my breasts while company sat downstairs. I let myself be held. I let him try to be a father to me. But, I knew, I was my own father.

He kissed my forehead.

"Your Uncle doesn't know everything."

"I know," I said. Then I reached up and kissed him too. "Thank you, Daddy," I said, and I meant it. I believed him more than I would have believed myself about what Frank was doing.

Daddy let me go. He turned and started down the stairs.

"You gonna be okay?"

"Yeah."

I went into my room, face to face with the woman I admired most in the world. I wondered if I would ever have the courage to be her again.

As I looked at my bed, there, with its bedspread made of two kinds of curtains, I saw me and Daddy on it. We were talking and I was asking him why he'd never put it in me and he said, he didn't think it would fit. Then, he bounced me on it a couple of times, soft as a baby's skin and hard at the same time. Sometimes I wished it had gone in, but it hadn't.

I was grateful, as I stood there in front of my heroine, that on this night, I only had to worry about whether Frank was fucking whores at the hotel.


## JAKEY AND DIANE, HENRY AND MARIE

Marie described Diane.

"She has a drug store in her purse."

Ma and I had a good laugh at that.

Marie could open her monkey mouth and like a little animal surprise everyone, not only that she could speak, but that she could be clever too.

Diane was Jakey's girl friend. The first one we ever knew about. We were used to the phone ringing for Jakey, but it'd never been a female of the species.

Diane talked so fast nobody but Jakey could understand her. We'd pick up the phone and hear, "Jakeythe'ah?"

"Excuse me?" I asked.

"Jakeythe'ah?"

"I'm sorry, I think you have the wrong number."

The phone rang as soon as I hung up.

"Jakeythe'ah?"

Okay, maybe, I thought I heard "Jakey" in there somewhere.

"Just a minute."

"Ja-key! It's for you! A gi-rl!"

Jakey snatched the receiver from me and mumbled into it. The Revere Mumble, which means, I'm too tough to pronounce consonants, but apparently, Diane understood every word. Daddy said Diane was going a million miles an hour; Jakey was at idle.

"Ya, wha? Ya, ya, ya, ya. Wha? Nah." You could hear Diane's voice from across the room. It was obvious to me and Ma and Marie that she was telling him what he'd be doing. "Ya, ya wen? Ya right. Ya, ok, ya. Ya."

Jakey didn't live with us any more. He brought Diane to see us one night, or she just happened to be with him when he dropped in to pick up something. She looked so much like a monkey, small and dark, with a tight, aggressive nervousness, that she made the slow monkey faced Marie look evolved to a much higher level of evolution.

She gave us a grudging, general hello, and at the same time, plopped her oversized black leather purse open on to the kitchen table. Not quickly enough, we shoved our coffee and tea cups out of the way, spilling some hot liquid over ourselves, while she dug a small skittish hand in, sending vials of drugs flying up and out. She banged her hand down on each stray bottle and threw it back in violently. The small dark hand remerged with a bent pack of Marlboro's. She stuck one in her mouth and lighted it, squinting. Her lips were a few shades blacker than her skin. She wore no lipstick or makeup of any kind. Her hair was neither short nor long: it clung to her neck and fell in her eyes in thick black clumps.

"So, Gloria, you in college?" she asked me, blowing out smoke.

Marie and I had watched the entire ceremony of her digging out her cigarettes with fascination. Diane had burst into Ma's kitchen and in two seconds, she was dominating Ma's domain and our home. All our personalities at once were dwarfed. Her relationship to Jakey became crystal clear. It was fascinating.

"Uh, yeah."

Diane raised her eyebrows, probably thinking I was as stupid as I looked.

"That's nice. I always wanted to go to college. Never got around to it. You like shoes?"

"Um, yeah. I like shoes."

"I can get you all the shoes you want. What's your size?"

"Um, five and a half, six. But, I don't need shoes."

She stopped smoking and looked me dead in the eye.

"What do you mean you don't need shoes? Everybody needs shoes for Chrissake!"

Okay. I got it. If I didn't need shoes, I was disrespectful. I realized a little more about Jakey and Diane's relationship.

"My Uncle Enio has a shoe store, anything you want! You just tell me. You like these? You like platforms?"

She showed me her shoes, turning one leg to the side, while she lit another cigarette from the one that was only half dead in her hand.

She was wearing black vinyl platforms that curled around a donut hole in the heel. "Cute, huh? My uncle's got tons a these." She looked down at my boots.

"You like boots? He's got boots too. Not like those. Nice ones. Real nice, from Italy."

About this time, Marie met Henry at the Abraham Lincoln School. They bumped into each other in the hall on April 9th, 1970 and it was love.

He was famous in our house for being hunted on the police radio.

Bursts of static.

"Ah, a youth has been reported walking along the railroad tracks with a rifle over his shoulder."

Static, static.

"Ah, 10-4."

We'd all shout, in the direction of the little box, "Run, Henry, run!"

It turned out Henry had whittled the rifle out of wood. He was just practicing for the day he really could go duck hunting.

The fact that Henry truly loved the monkey face just the way she was and didn't think she was fat or stupid or needed makeup or a hairdo was enough to recommend him to us. He was charming. Wiry and clever, his dirty blonde bowl cut lopped continually into his blue eyes but didn't seem to slow him down. He could draw anything in a minute; a ballpoint pen and an inch in the margins of his notebook was all he needed to render a sketch of amazing detail and shading.

"Where'd you learn how to do that?" I asked, impressed.

"Oh, my father could draw," he said. "I just, you know, kept trying."

He was Henry VI, in a line of Henry's from the last century. In spite of his formal name, his family lived in a low house on the flats off the marsh. His father was on disability. His mother was a confused image to me. Tall and fashionably thin, she smoked like Diane and her bag too, opened up to a pile of medicines. Once, I told Henry his mother was pretty. He said, "Yours is beautiful." I knew what he meant. Ma cooked and invited people in. Henry's mother threw him out a lot. He fit right into our lives; soon, he moved into our house permanently.

I began to realize, Henry moved in, and Jakey had been adopted, and when he was on leave Peter ate with us and slept over with his buddies in tow, and Aunt Lettie and Uncle Gus had lived with us for a while, and even Uncle Freddie's pregnant girl friend had moved in till she had her baby (and

Uncle Freddie married her), that our house *was* a kind of foster home. Ma and Daddy always had their arms open for others.

Henry's thin fingers were always scarred and torn up from his long walks in the coarse fields of the marsh. Henry actually immersed himself into those tall green reeds I always dreamed about replacing the entire highway with, he walked and knew every inch of the mud and water, the grass and rocks. He knew which plants and birds and animals lived there. He could draw them and tell about their habits. He also knew the stars and photography. He built rockets and really sent them blasting skyward. He built a rowboat, a smokehouse and a wishing well for Ma in the backyard. Some of his projects, though, like the toolshed and the pizza oven, remained half finished in our yard, in a crumbled, broken heap.

One morning, I was slinking home from Frank's house, Ma and Daddy were in New Hampshire, where they went occasionally with Daddy's club to gamble and also, out of practicality, to buy liquor and cigarettes with no tax, when I opened the front door and was greeted by Ma's terrier, nervously twitching and whining to me.

"What's the matter, Tiny?" This was Ma's fourth or fifth little terrier. As each one died, Ma replaced it, or actually, Uncle Vickie would bring her a new one, wriggling nervously under his coat. They all looked the same, black and white, pink-eared, doe-eyed. They all were named Teeny or Tiny or Tareyton.

Tiny was even more nervous than usual. She licked her little snout. She dug my calves with her claws. Her black eyes teared a bit, worried as could be, and looked pleadingly into mine.

I walked into the house, wondering how much I should make of a neurotic dog's nerves. As I passed Ma's bedroom, which was now downstairs in what used to be the spare room where Rick had tried to have sex with me the night Get Smart was on TV, I saw something wrong out of the corner of my eye. I turned to see Jakey's naked body sprawled in the double bed with Diane's naked body sprawled across his buttocks. Ma's white chenille bedspread was caught, tangled very prettily round her leg.

I stood dumbstruck. The grey stillness of morning hung suspended over the scene, giving it an unreality, a sensation that if I shouted, "Hey!" it would disappear. I tried to take in what I was seeing: my brother's blonde head, his slack, open mouth drooling on to the pillow, Diane's dark form, slender, tight as metal, clenched over his.

In Ma's bed.

I decided not to wake them. After all, I'd just come from Frank's, and I had told Ma I'd been at Melanie's, a strange girl who did not even exist? I was no better. But, in Ma's bed!

I went upstairs to change for work.

As I passed Marie's bedroom, my eyes caught an unfamiliar shape there also.

Henry and Marie were fast asleep, her curly head cradled under his arm, his lips resting on her forehead.

They were fully clothed.

I changed for work and left silently.

I couldn't resist telling Ma about Jakey and Diane. It bothered me for days; I kept seeing her in my mother's bed. Ma was very cool about it. I was surprised. I think she was happy to confront Diane with something juicy.

We all thought it was hilarious when Diane bared her teeth and told us vehemently, "Jakey never touched me! Never!"

She turned to me, "Your mind is in the gutter, Gloria! In the gutter!"

"I always like to be elevated," I replied.

"What? What's that, college talk?"

I shook my head.

Then she got vicious as only a monkey can.

"Yous think you're so smart! What, are yous better than me? Huh? Jakey loves me! He loves me! He don't love yous! He told me! He can't stand yous! You people ain't even his real family! I don' know why he calls you Dad and Ma - he don't have to! You're not his real father and mother!"

This speech fell on Daddy like a bomb.

But, he just hung his head and listened to her tirade. After she and Jakey went out the door, Daddy started the story, "I took him in when my own brother..." but he couldn't finish it. He cried, right there at the kitchen table, with his head down by his dish of cold, half-eaten food; down by his used handkerchief all green and stuck together; by his used Q-tip, all yellow and blackened; by his half bottle of beer gone flat. He sobbed, and my stomach twisted with each scraping heave of his throat, with each long effort to sniff back the tears. It was still a fact of life that when Daddy cried, I felt his pain inside me. It's ironic, isn't it how they call sex "the facts of life"? They are the same, life and sex. They never separate.

Diane crept under our lives till she caused a fissure that Jakey fell through. I suppose that was inevitable.

I think it was maybe the third time Jakey brought her home, only about two weeks after she'd insisted he never had touched her, never, that she told us she was pregnant, that they were married and that Jakey had joined the Marines.

Daddy regarded them both. They stood together in the archway Daddy had made between the kitchen and den: Jakey, smirking like he'd put one over on them. Diane, with her thick monkey lips pursed up righteously.

"Maybe it'll make a man out of you," Daddy said.

"He *is* a man!" she cried. "I'm pregnant, ain't I?"

Daddy just looked past her skinny form in its tight pants at the television, which was right behind them.

The Wizard of Oz was on, a Special Television Event we didn't dare miss, even though it was on every year and we'd seen it several times already.

Jakey and Diane went upstairs to his old room to pack the rest of his stuff in a bag. We didn't care what else they did at this point. They could have been humping up there like two dogs for all we cared.

The actors were singing and skipping down the yellow brick road as the two lovebirds were going out the door. Daddy just stared at the TV. I thought, he can't be interested in this! But there was nothing he could say. His son was going out the door and there was nothing to say.

Just before he disappeared forever, Jakey turned, nodded toward the TV and said directly to me, "Let me know how it turns out!"

We heard from him, though Ma cried, "I don't want to hear from him!" He sent us a photo, like a school photo, of himself in his uniform. Jakey didn't look like a real Marine. He looked like a fraud. The uniform wore him. It was bigger than Jakey. He didn't have the pride or the concentration a real Marine has. He didn't have the belief.

After he was discharged from the Marines, Jakey turned to crime for a career. He grew up to be a con man. Every now and then the police called Ma and asked if she'd seen or heard from him. The cops from Suffolk County called and said he was wanted in Suffolk County. The cops from Essex County called and told her he was wanted in Essex County. And Middlesex. Other states called: Florida, New Jersey, West Virginia. Ma told all the cops she didn't want to hear from him.

Diane had her baby, a boy she named Enio after her father. Little Enio was three when Diane was arrested for armed robbery of a liquor store and the kidnapping of the old man who was behind the counter. Ma opened the Record American one morning and there on the front-page was a photo of Diane and her accomplice, some guy in an torn T-shirt, being hauled off by cops. Diane was baring her teeth in that familiar, vicious way, clutching the crucifix that was around her neck in one hand and brandishing it at the camera. Our name, WISHER, was drilled across the front page under this photo, DIANE WISHER, ARRESTED FOR ARMED ROBBERY AND KIDNAPPING. A crushed automobile was in the background.

Little Enio was taken in by the elder Enio, until he died, and then, Peter, Jakey's saintly brother repeated history and adopted his nephew into his own blossoming family of two pretty little girls.

Jakey was still at large.

CASTLE HILL

Someone once said he knew the revolution was over when he saw a young hippie girl standing on the corner eating a can of dog food with a spoon.

What had begun for me on the curbstone by June's house when I told her about my father and she loved me anyway had reached its boundaries and crossed a line it probably shouldn't have. Even pagans like me have rules of behavior, sometimes involving very strict standards and very severe penalties.

I suppose, if Frank had respected me, as with most women, I would have been lost, I would have done anything, maybe even wound up in jail like Diane, but he reminded me daily that he didn't, so that when he, for instance, put his hand on the back of my head and pushed it down and said, "Suck my dick!" he had it fixed so I'd feel like a whore if I did and like a prude if I didn't.

We were at a wedding. The bride was a friend of Payton's family. Payton's family had streets named after them in Salem, Boston and Arlington. I didn't have really nice things to wear, so I'd improvised a little black slip dress with Frye boots. Rita borrowed a silk shawl shot with silver threads from me, but she ruined the effect by throwing it over a purple velvet gown, linty as an old couch, and saying, "I love playing dress up, don't you?" I was offended. The scarf was important to me; I'd bought it at a thrift shop; it had belonged to someone once. I don't know why, but I was a serious dresser. Everything I wore was religious and political. Frank looked '70s cool in the white cotton suit I'd embroidered with sparkling beads, all down the pants seams and around the cuffs of the shirt. He called it his Elvis suit. Payton was elegant in upper class linen.

The wedding was being held at the Crane mansion on Castle Hill in Ipswich. We stood high as kites tethered to the crest of the Hill on the lawn that was tender and fine as baby's skin, while the sun set in gorgeous layers of pinks and yellows, purples and scarlets. We listened to the quiet ceremony, with overtones of the whine and grate of the last guest arriving, his Porsche whining around every curve of the road spiraling up the hill. Next to me, Frank's body cringed.

"He's gonna murder that engine."

It was Freddie and Melanie in the Porsche. Freddie's family knew the bride too. Freddie was Frank's protégé. When Frank met him he was Fred Doyle, insurance agent, enrolled at Salem State business school nights, driving a '68 station wagon, married a year to a girl who'd gotten pregnant on their third date. Two weeks later, Freddie Doyle was dealing right along side Frank, driving a Harley and a sleek red Porsche, separated from his wife and baby, living in a Washington Square apartment with Melanie, a girl he'd met in a local biker bar. He'd grown a long handlebar moustache, similar to Peter Fonda's in "Easy Rider," a movie he'd seen seventeen times. I know this because Frank used to ask him at parties, "Hey, Freddie! Tell everybody how many times you've seen 'Easy Rider'!" Every party, the number would go up. Freddie also had a ski rack on his Porsche, but he never skied. Frank laughed his ass off.

They finally arrived, the Porsche got louder at every turn till it nearly exploded in the parking area and a tousled Freddie and Melanie rushed up to the edge of the ceremony. Nobody turned. Freddie made some kind of motion to Frank like he'd been fucking and Frank, Payton and Rita stifled a giggle.

People looked at us a lot at the reception, we stood out from the others. The women wore lace collars that rested quietly as lambs on beds of pink flowers. The men were tightly buttoned into navy blue or brown.

We sat around one of those huge round tables covered by yards of pink linen. The vista in front of us through the floor to ceiling windows was of the infinite lawn in twilight. The lights of the party gathered like glistening drops on the glass, the classical white statues, illuminated one by one, stood sentinel at the edges of the wood that surrounded the mansion. The night folded its wings around us.

You'd think I was beyond participating in my own torture by now. The food was delicately cut roast beef, not as succulent as Ma's, the gravy was ordinary, not as divine as I was used to, the bread was an American joke - soggy outside with powdery inside, the mashed potatoes, it didn't matter anyway, just eating wasn't enough for freaks, food had to be special - that's what real hippies called themselves, never hippies, we were freaks – we didn't eat. Around the table facing Frank and I were two young couples we didn't know, Rita next to me, Payton next to her, Freddie opposite in dark glasses he never took off and Melanie. Freddie poked at the food like it was made of rubber. Payton made motion of eating, so did Frank and Rita. I figured they'd done speed before I got there. I ate a little, of course, I always did. I was used to American food from the Whites. Melanie just looked at her dish.

The couples we didn't know made small talk, asking Frank about the business administration course at Salem State, and I could see he didn't want to talk. His answer was to look directly at this young man, clean shaven and neat, and at his pretty, fat faced wife who was "expecting in July" and talk in general terms while his hand crept under my dress.

I had no choice. You may think I had, but if I didn't ease myself down like I did, so that his fingers could make their way into the folds of my vulva, there'd be a nasty fight afterwards. I'd be accused of not being liberated.

Frank asked the young man about the law firm he was joining, where their offices were located, what kind of law did they practice, (Here, Frank guided my hand to his zipper.) whether he and his wife wanted a boy or a girl, the young woman blushed and said, either sex was fine with them as long as the baby was healthy.

They had the sweet cream cheeks of cherubs. They had the curled red lips of babies.

Frank's zipper slid noiselessly down the white cotton. I could feel the beads against my palm as my hand took his erect penis and slowly moved up and down, slowly so as not to be detected, I moved only from the wrist down.

Now, Frank had my juices flowing, so it was easier to do what he wanted. We looked into the faces of innocent people, nice people and they spoke to us, the young man seemed to falter, as Frank came quickly and thrust a napkin, fine and pink, over my hand. He snapped my panties closed like something he was done with. I watched, astonished, as he rubbed his fingers along his lips and sniffed deeply.

The conversation continued for half a minute more when the young man scraped his chair back and stood abruptly. His jaw trembled, his face got flushed as he spoke to Frank.

"May I see you outside?"

"Sure, man," Frank replied amiably.

The young wife's little pink mouth hung open at the sight of her husband suddenly getting up in the middle of a conversation and going out of the room with a stranger.

"What happened?" she asked me with innocent confusion.

I shrugged and looked at Rita, who was playing with her mashed potatoes, building a miniature lake on her plate. Somehow, by the way she was doing this, I knew she knew what had happened. I looked at Payton, who understood and got up with a clearing of his throat and followed the sound of the young man's voice, which squeaked with emotion in the mansion's marble foyer.

"Did something happen to your boy friend?" the young wife asked me with concern.

I shook my head, no.

"I can hear Jonathan," she said, quietly to herself. "He sounds upset."

Freddie, still wearing the dark glasses now low on his nose, was slumped way down in his chair half asleep and waiting for the whole thing to be over. Melanie looked bored.

The shouting outside was muffled, civilized, then the young man returned to the table with his crisp white shirt torn away from its collar and a decorous line of blood dripping from his still trembling lip.

"Jonathan! What happened to you?" his wife cried.

"What's going on here?" came the boom of an older man's voice, "Jonathan?"

People started to crowd around our table.

"Ah, where's Frank?" Freddie sat up suddenly and asked me. "Can we go get something to eat now? I'm starving, man."

"These people -" he began, sniffing back blood, which his wife was trying to blot with a dinner napkin.

"Come on -" Rita said, decisively, getting up and taking us all outside.

"Good! You don't belong here! I don't know who invited them," he mumbled after us.

We found Frank and Payton sharing a joint, sitting with their asses resting on the pedestal of one of the statues. The two of them were unscathed. Slightly wrinkled and aggravated, but comfortably justified and relaxed after a job well done.

Frank offered me the joint and I shook my head, no. He gave me a look, so I tried to take it but he passed it on to Payton who laughed at me, then Rita, then Freddie and Melanie, who gave the joint to me. I didn't smoke. I gave it to Frank.

He sneered into the smoke, holding it in and talking at the same time, "What's the matter with you?"

At first I didn't answer him, then I heard myself say, "He was right."

Payton kind of moaned and rubbed his beard. Rita giggled, that deep, guttural laugh of hers. I wanted to rip my beautiful scarf right off her. She didn't deserve to wear it.

"We should not have done that in there."

"You did it too, Wisher, you're no better."

"No, but I want to be."

"FUCK!" Frank said, "Come down out of your ivory tower and join the human race!"

Payton just got up and left. Rita and Melanie followed. Freddie ran after them, saying, "Here, I got another one."

They had a way, when they laughed at me or turned their backs on me, of making me wonder if I were wrong, but this time, I was too shaken to wonder.

Frank got up, dropped the live roach and rubbed it into the grass, rubbed it till the red glow went out and the body turned black. Then he reached down and picked it up and put the tiny piece of charred remains in his pocket. Frank was very careful about not leaving roaches behind.

He looked back at the mansion. People were dancing in the lighted room. The music drifted out to us, sweetly.

"Nice fuckin' pad," Frank said. "Ah," he threw his arm around me and led me to the car, "I've been thrown out of better places," he laughed.

I hadn't.

Something had shifted for me, when the young woman had turned and with her soft, cherub face had asked with real concern, "Did something happen to your boy friend?" Something had changed.

I kept getting glimpses, only glimpses.


## WHEN YOUR RAPIST REJECTS YOU

I was walking back to my car after having checked out the shoe stores on Shirley Ave. There was a crowd in front of Shirley Drug like there used to be only they were slightly older now. They were Rick's gang, clustered on the cement steps, spilling in and out the glass doors of the drugstore, spilling themselves over the sidewalk and curb.

It was the same old dilemma. If I crossed the street, they'd know I was avoiding passing between them. If I walked through them, I might touch their hard bodies. Power exuded from their tight bodies. They were laughing, that mean laugh that meant they were enjoying themselves at someone else's expense, their lips would lift over their white teeth almost like a dog's snarl.

They were happy because Rick was with them again.

He was there. My heart beat fast. I'd decided without my knowing it, I was going to walk through them.

He was close. I could see out the corner of my eye, his dark cheek, his filthy hand as he brought the cigarette butt to his mouth.

His mouth.

As I passed through them, my legs turned to water. He was talking to someone. He said, "Yeah, tell me about it."

Just as I passed, he turned his back to me.

I walked on to my car, my stomach twisted as though I had swallowed a weird poison of disappointment and loss. Why should I feel that way? Why did I? Shouldn't I be happy that my rapist rejected me?


## TOOL & DIE

Don't ask me when this happened. Sometimes Daddy was there and sometimes he wasn't.

Work was hard to find. So, Daddy found himself temporarily living and working in Providence, Rhode Island at Mason Tool & Die. On July 3, Daddy volunteered to climb the flagpole to untangle the pulley so the American flag could go up for the celebration. The old flagpole cracked and Daddy, who was used to accidents, decided quickly he would ride it down.

But, he was on a metal ladder. Instead of sailing slowly down on the weight of the dead flagpole, it hung itself on a high-tension wire and Daddy became the fireworks. He exploded in midair and fell into the decorative shrubbery where he broke his hip.

Now, he was in the hospital in Providence, Rhode Island.

Ma had already been down, but she couldn't stay. She had to work and take care of Marie.

Frank offered to take me down. I said I didn't want to go. The idea horrified me. Frank said I should. Daddy was alone down there, Frank told me.

Marie gave me her old stuffed bear to take to him, to keep him company, she said. I'd bought him a funny card, of a leering sexy nurse and a small vase of multi-colored flowers.

Providence was grimmer than Chelsea or Dorchester had ever been. It was hard to believe. I put a lot of faith in words and with a word like Providence, I thought it would be a fairly nice place. Perhaps it had been nice at one time. Not any more. As we drove through we saw a desolate collection of black buildings, row after row of abandoned factories and warehouses covered with a kind of black shingle, opaque and final. We drove past gangs of boys with mullet hair wearing chains and black T-shirts with skulls. The Revolution was clearly over. None of us would have worn a skull. Unless we put a daisy chain on its head.

We drove by several darkly dressed young men where they huddled under a bridge, under a thick black iron overpass painted with a huge white peace sign that dripped white drops of paint. The boys had long hair down their backs, like hippies, but in the front their skulls were shorn. Their hair wasn't beautiful or flowing, it looked hopeless, dreary - violent. They weren't laughing. They hung together with shoulders sagging into their pockets; they eyed each passing car with dangerous suspicion.

"We're close," Frank said.

Providence Hospital was a pile of brick buildings. I made it past the front desk, where they asked if we were relatives, up the elevator, which sent my stomach turning. I made it down the long antiseptic corridor with its black edges full of dirt.

But, at the door to Daddy's room, where two grown men lay wrapped in white bedclothes, drifting on the ethereal grey sunlight that filtered through the grimy windows, pale and floating was Daddy, there I lost my legs and Frank had to catch me.

"Hey! You all right?" Frank asked. It was more a command than a question.

Daddy looked over and greeted us, in a hoarse, small, only vaguely familiar voice, "Hi-o!"

All the strength had gone out of him and like a cold river; it went out of me too.

Frank was cheerful, "Hey, Bill!" He strode into the room.

I looked at him, instantly realizing, if I married Frank, he and Daddy would get along great. Frank could take a lot of Daddy off of me.

I leaned on Frank's arm and fell against Daddy's bedside where I bent to kiss his lips, now dry and rigid as a chicken's beak, as thin and non-existent as Grandma's and Ma's had become.

We were very quiet because the old man next to Daddy was asleep. I managed to prop up the worn teddy bear Marie had sent, the vase of flowers which he said were nice and the card I gave him, which he chuckled at, on the dusty windowsill with all his get well cards, arranged like cheery little pink and yellow tombstones.

But, we knew he wasn't going to die. Weakly, happily, even boastingly, he described the accident in detail. He bragged about the steel pin the doctors were going to put in his leg. He'd always walk with a limp, he declared, and he'd be on a walker for a while, then a cane. But he was optimistic, he said, he'd be "good as new in no time."

He and Frank talked hospitals, which Frank knew about because his mother was a nurse administrator. He and Frank talked sports and workman's comp. I asked if any of his nurses were pretty. He laughed and said they were all taking great care of him.

Then, Daddy's listless eyes started to close. Frank nodded to me. I got up from the metal chair I'd been sitting on. I kissed him once more, this time on his pocky, broken cheek, like kissing the craters of the moon.

"Ok, slugger," he whispered hoarsely, "I'll be seein' ya."

I had to let Frank support me as we walked out. I looked back to see Marie's little teddy bear on the windowsill just about brimming with vitality compared to everything else in the room.


"THAT WAS JUST A DREAM SOME OF US HAD"

It's a line from a Joni Mitchell song, "California" from 1970. It describes her feelings about the Revolution being over. Every time I think of that line, I can hear John Lennon saying, just before he died, "Hey, man, the '70s, weren't they awful? How did you survive them, man?" We didn't.

Certainly, not without him. In that decade, he had retired from public life for a while, and, well, we needed someone like him to remind people that it hadn't been just a way to dress or wear you hair.

Frank's tenement in Beverly was owned by a car thief. Looking down from any of the back windows, you could see a dirt parking lot of decrepit old jalopies; these sputtered in and out all day. I suppose, if I'd paid attention, I might have realized they were never the same cars. The landlord's wife, I suppose you could say she was the landlady, took speed and painted abstracts all day, till the day she came rushing upstairs to show us one of her paintings, because she had just seen the face of Jesus in it. We told her, "Oh, yeah, wow!" though we couldn't see a thing. Then, she had to run back downstairs because her cookies were burning. Frank said speed freaks always burned their cookies. She only painted the face of Jesus after that.

Frank called his landlord "an entrepreneur, a property owning entrepreneur." He was proud of knowing criminals, what he called, "ex-offenders." Frank would pronounce the word, "offenders" violently, clutching his lower lip with his upper teeth on the "fs." "Good people," Frank said, "really, really good people." It was really the same thing I was doing with Frank, I would come to realize, this sticking your hand deep down in the mud to find the truth, though, of course, Frank accused me of always looking for it in the clouds.

Payton had taken to playing mournful Joan Baez tunes over and over, "I dreamed I saw Joe Hill last night alive as you or me," her sad voice dragging all through the apartment. They had a new poster, a black background and a quote from Thoreau, "Most men lead lives of quiet desperation." And the classic, "Coke" written in Coca Cola script. It was their way of saying they were freaking out now that it was time to graduate.

Payton was playing pool. They had a pool table. Their pool table had tears and ruts in the felt that you had to play around. I was playing with him and he was pretty edgy every time I got a shot. So, when Frank called me into the living room, "Hey, Stella! Get in here, I want you to see this!" Payton got a little grin on under his beard.

I noticed Frank was careful not to use my name. He usually called me Wisher. That's because a thief was with him. Someone who came there to buy drugs, and Frank was nervous because the guy was a bad character. The fact that he had called me Stella and had called me into the same room with them meant that we were playing a game. The game where the thief was now going to be a normal person, a guest in our home and thief etiquette was now in play. This meant, "Tread carefully." It was a kind of twisted decorum, a tremendous respect you had to give, or all hell could break loose.

I'd seen him come in. I was down by the bedroom door and Frank had turned him down the hall the opposite way, so he wouldn't see me.

We'd never had anyone so big in the place before, usually just students, or friends. But this guy was huge, so broad, even his back lunged out from his shoulders. He wore a denim vest sort of cut apart to let his bulky arms breathe. Underneath, he had only his hairy chest and a lot of tattoos to keep him warm, and it was not summertime. His boots had made a lot of noise clunking against the wood floors; with each step, they'd dragged metal chains that wound around his ankles. His hair was as blonde as mine and wavy. It curled around his dark, hairy shoulders. I couldn't help seeing him in his mother's arms when he'd been born, the way I had seen Daddy. Blonde, curly fluff on his little pink head. I saw his mother turn and name him with promise in her heart.

I figured I was going in to see some kind of weapon.

The thief had a look of respectful anticipation when he saw me and I knew it was going to be okay, but Frank was still nervous. He rubbed his lip.

"Come over here, this is Manuel. Manny, this is my lady, Stella." Frank thought it was funny to call me Stella sometimes. He said it was a good whore's name for me.

Manny nodded, "Nice to meet you, Stella."

As I came closer, I noticed he had a little trouble breathing like a lot of big people. I could hear each breath come raspy and strangled.

Opened on the coffee table was a briefcase that, like Manny, had seen better days. It was beaten on the corners, like someone had thrown it against the wall a few times. The leather had come away in places, revealing a yellow underside. Like a perverse salesman, Manny was showing his wares: twelve neat rows of ladies' rings, all stolen.

The thief eyed me sneakily from under his hair, a kind of sneaky pride in what he did for a living.

The rings were sunk in blue velvet. Most of them were tarnished, large fakes or modest diamonds, blackened by wear, the crevices of their gold filled with the dreams and toil of women.

I assumed I was supposed to say something appreciative.

"Wow! They're really nice!"

The thief beamed.

"Pick one," offered Manny. "My treat."

So, that's why I was called in. Bimbo treat. Frank must have given him a great deal on some hash. No good refusing politely. That wasn't in the cards.

I had to choose one. Most of the bigger diamonds sat in the dirtier slits in the velvet, as though more hands had reached in for them. But, I didn't want one that had been someone's wedding or engagement ring. I didn't want a huge, flashy fake. A small one. That would be polite, too, I thought, since the thief could get more money for a larger one.

Then, I saw it. Its blue velvet slot was almost clean. It was buried so deeply, if I hadn't been looking for the very smallest ring I could find, I never would have - wait, my fingers shook as they closed around its slender band, it couldn't be, that would be too weird, impossible, impossible, I held it's white gold band, it's two heart shaped rubies, its diamond chip winked at me.

I held it in my hand.

"That little thing! I'll give you a nicer one!"

His filthy fingernail poked at a cocktail diamond, probably a fake, surrounded by fat aquamarines.

I was in danger now of insulting him.

"No, thanks, really," I managed. "I like this one." To be polite, I looked directly into his unshaven, blotchy face. "Please," I said.

"Sure," he shrugged his enormous shoulders.

"Let's see," Frank held out his hand for it. Reluctantly, I handed it over to him. He turned it round, making a face.

"Hey!" Frank cried out, as he noticed the split in its band, "It's busted! Ah, no offense, man."

I got so scared they might take it away from me, to give me a better one.

"No! No! I don't care! I want this one! Please!"

I rescued it from Frank.

The thief shrugged again.

"Your lady has good taste," he declared.

To change the awkward subject, Frank said, "Show her your tattoo, man," and to me, "Chicks love it."

He took off the vest, breathing heavily with the effort. There, across his back, was a lovely, curvaceous archer done in the style of Greek mythology. Except for her short red hair and a ribbon banner under her sandaled feet that read, "Suck Mine!" I never would have presumed that it was me.

"His Mama made him get it," Frank laughed. "He was fucked out of his mind!"

Manny looked proud and sheepish at the same time.

"Nah, she's my fuckin' idol, man! She's got fuckin' balls, ya know? I fuckin' dream about ballin' her." Then, he added against all thief/dealer etiquette, sucking in his breath, "She's got great tits like ya lady here!"

For half a second, there was a silence as when a bomb is falling to earth. Then, Frank laughed, uneasily, "Watch it, man," he said.

"Hey, no offense, man." Manny shrugged, pulling his vest back on.

"None taken," Frank replied.

That was the trouble with being an icon. You don't get to choose your fans.

I put my mother's love ring back on my little finger where it belonged.

"Thank you, Manny," I said.

"No problem." And to Frank, "How'd a shit bum like you get such a classy lady?"

Frank laughed good-naturedly, because he laughed with tremendous relief. Manny was leaving peacefully.

Looking down at the ring on my finger, I knew I also had what I'd come for.


## HOLLYHOCKS AND RUGOSA

I was getting into my car to go to school, when I saw a very strange shape laboring up the hill. At first, I thought, what is that? Then, I thought, it's a very small man carrying a huge load, much bigger than himself. He was packed up like a prospector's mule. Every step seemed awkward and painful, as the load swung from side to side, almost knocking the person over - was it a man? It seemed too fragile.

Then, the shape struck a sharp cord in my memory, suddenly as familiar as my own shape.

It was June.

I ran down to her as fast as I could.

I tried to grab stuff and pull it off of her.

"What's going on? Why do you have all this stuff on you?"

"No! Don't! Let's wait till we get to your house, it's all balanced."

She was carrying the portrait of her grandfather in her hands. A fat backpack, over packed and bulging at the seams sat on top of her neck. She looked exhausted. Her light was out. Her luminous skin was flat and pale, her bright eyes dulled.

"Aaron threw me out," she said without emotion, "this is all my stuff."

"He threw you out?"

Right away, I erased Aaron Goldman. He didn't exist for me. I put him away in a box only June could open.

"How come? What happened?"

She didn't cry. She looked absolutely serious, like she was about to tell me what she had done to deserve being thrown out.

"He said he couldn't do the laundry because it was damp out."

"And you had a fight?"

She nodded.

"It's always damp out! It's New England! If we waited till it wasn't damp out, we'd all smell like we did in the Middle Ages!"

She actually laughed. We were standing in the middle of the street, about where Johnny Strummer's old dog used to sleep. She said her load was bearing into her back, so we went on up the hill.

"Did he hit you, June?"

"No."

But, I knew Aaron.

"He hit you with words."

"You still say things," she said, quietly.

"Will you stay at my house?" I asked.

"I don't know. I'd like to take a shower, though. There's a cottage in Gloucester I need to look at." She laughed derisively, at herself, "a shed, really."

"I'll take you!" I offered, forgetting about school for the day.

Carefully, we removed the entire load from her back where it had dug red grooves. She took a shower and came out smelling fresh, of her own peppermint soap, but dressed in the same clothes, a wrinkled turtleneck jersey and limp corduroys.

"Don't you want to change your clothes?" I asked. "Do you want to borrow some?"

"No," she replied, sadly. She was so damned independent, like a cat you wanted to cuddle and kiss, but it just walks away. "But, it still feels good, Ri."

Just hearing her call me Ri again in person was almost worth the pain of not being able to help her.

"June," I ventured, "you traded Agnes for Aaron."

"I know," she agreed, calmly, drying her wet hair with a towel.

We took the long shore route up to Gloucester, stopping at a little café on the ocean in Marblehead called America East. The weak autumn sun paled in a yellow and charcoal sky, the ocean was without horizon, choppy and grey, but it was the winter ocean we knew so well, the one that kept the company of winter soldiers.

The wind blew steadily through the crevices of the old bay window. We sat upon a cold wooden bench, hugging our coffee cups for warmth. A smattering of older people, who seemed to make a second home there sat around a picnic table set under an ancient life preserver and photograph gone sepia of the Constitution, Boston's sacred ship, in Marblehead Harbor for Fourth of July. We sat under a faded nautical map showing shipwrecks around the Marblehead and Salem coasts. One of the men at the picnic table was dressed like a shabby sea captain in an old cap and worn seaman's sweater. A large black dog slept at his feet. The dog wore a red bandana tied around its thick neck and occasionally woke to nudge or lick his master's hand, which rested on his head. Next to him, an old blonde with a raspy voice would say something, and the whole café would turn around and laugh with her. I'd never seen that before, a whole restaurant talking and laughing across tables. Several people walked in while we were there, one at a time, asking the general company, "Janice here?" The cry went up from the picnic table that she was expected any minute. The man with the dog called out, jovially, as he got up, went behind the counter and poured his own coffee into a real mug, "Not yet! Later! She's making soup! Come back in twenty minutes!" After an hour or so, Janice herself came in, a tall, round woman with shocking red hair, beaming, "Hi, hi, hi," to individuals around the room. She carried a huge pan of soup, careful not to slosh its heavy load, held across her middle like a pregnant belly.

June and I leaned back into this affection like refuges.

"June," I said, "I broke up with Frank."

It was amazing, that June could be away so long and not really leave me. Perhaps she was too exhausted to register surprise, but she looked at me, took me in, and said, "You're okay."

I nodded.

"He keeps calling me and he won't let me hang up. Sometimes, I just leave the receiver lying there. I can come back an hour later and he's still on the line. He sent me roses."

She shook her head slowly from side to side.

"Just what you always wanted," she said.

"They're dead now. They look more appropriate all black and dried up. I'm going to keep them that way, for a while, anyway."

She laughed, sadly, "I remember your telling me he said he was going to teach your children to say, 'FUCK' all the time."

"Yeah, one time we were talking about my being an English teacher and Frank told me he was going to teach his kids to tell the teacher to go fuck herself. That was the day I realized, I was letting myself slide into marrying him by accident."

"What do you mean, 'by accident'?"

"Some people just fall into marriage because they think there's nothing better. I think I came close to doing that. His mother told him he lost a good woman. Imagine.

It also gave me a chance to get off the pill," I informed her.

"How does *that* feel?"

"Liberating."

She sighed, "Maybe I should get rid of the shield."

June had been using the new Dalcon shield. It caused her a lot of problems. How often during her periods would I walk behind her, checking her skirt or dungarees for stains, worse, for signs of the deluge she was feeling, following her faithfully as a little dog into strange public toilets where she had to stick two pads and a tampon on herself as her body tried in vain to pass the clawlike piece of plastic.

"I don't think he ever read one of my stories." I continued to change the subject, which I knew June was pondering: the dilemma of whether she could get the thing taken out. "Your body's trying to reject it." I'd told her. "I know." she replied. But, there remained the problem: as long as she was with Aaron, she needed the shield.

"I didn't write very much in the three years we were together," I continued, "Or paint. Since we broke up, he met a woman; he really enjoyed telling me on one of his phone calls that he'd gone out with someone. Not only that, but he loved telling me she was a *published writer*, who had *two books of poetry* out. Payton also fucked her and Frank said she'd shaved off all her pubic hair."

"Wait a minute! Wait a minute! What? She shaved herself? I never heard of that!" Her voice fell to a whisper, "All of it?"

I shrugged, "I guess!"

June didn't even shave her underarms because we'd seen hair under the women's arms in "Women in Love" and she'd liked it so much she let hers grow. Luckily, Aaron also liked it.

"And what about Payton? He slept with Frank's girlfriend? Isn't he with Rita?"

"Maybe it was pretty casual with Frank. Besides, that's Payton's hobby, cheating on Rita. You know, there was something I always hated about Payton. Whenever we saw a young girl, I mean really young, like a pre-teen, Payton would say something crude about where he'd like to put his dick. A few times, I wanted to leave for that reason alone. I mean, this was a guy who was so-called "well-brought up," he'd had every advantage, as they say."

"Ugh," June agreed.

"I wasted a lot of time, June, not being loved. You know, it was incredible, one of the things Frank said to me when I told him I wanted to break up was 'I thought we'd get married.' June, I would have sworn he didn't even *like* me! He never really respected anything about me.

You know how I always see the diapers over my head?"

"Yeah."

"You know, one day I was watching television, crosslegged on the floor, switching channels to find something interesting, when I happened upon this woman standing at a podium outside, the audience was sprawled out on the grass, and she said, 'Oh, honey, if men could get pregnant, abortion would be a sacrament.' I don't know who she was, but I knew what she'd said was true. I wasn't ready to hear it. The whole history of the world rushed out from under me like the ocean does when the waves get sucked back from under your feet. It's funny, that's exactly what happened when President Kennedy was shot. The sidewalk rushed out from under me. Everything changed after that. That woman's remark about abortion, it rewrites history! I understood so much at that moment, about men and women. How they fear us, how they fear the vagina, how they love us, and at the same time, want to overpower us any way they can. June, I don't want an abortion. I want a man with whom I want to have children."

"I've had two abortions already," June confided.

I began to mourn immediately. They had been my children too, June's children, they would have been my children too. My nieces or nephews. I began to understand even more about abortion. I still wouldn't have denied a woman's right, but it hurt. The hurt was very real.

"Aaron doesn't want children yet," she said, quietly.

"He wants all your attention."

I had to put this away: this was too much for now.

"Remember I told you about the thief?"

"Yeah."

I showed her the love ring on my finger.

"It's come home," June said.

The peace of resting in each other's company. It always amazed me how June and I could talk about horrific things, and still rest in each other's company.

We live our lives for moments like these: everyday memories that become blessed: a talk, a café, a cottage, a swim.

*One morning, early, before class, I had gone down alone to America East, to this very café by the sea and ordered coffee there amongst the fishermen. They had smelled strongly of fish, clean and hard as salt. The coffee was good and fresh as the fresh sea air.*

*They had respected me to walk out amongst them, a girl with long, blonde hair and a book bag on her shoulder, a girl in trailing blue jeans and a thin shirt, without a sidelong glance, without a derisive word. They had respected me to walk out the café door and stand with them facing the harbor, as one of them, knowing I was a worker like them with a job to do that day. They respected me.*

*An elder fisherman nodded to me, "'Mornin'." Another, with the slender jaw of youth, blushed and ducked his head.*

*I stood with them and drank in the peace of morning.*

*It was a moment like being with June, so good, so pure, so flooded with contentment.*


The cottage was no bigger than a closet, but it had a kitchen with a window over the sink, a bathroom and a small place for a bed. It stood sentry on a wide lawn with a little path leading from its brightly painted blue door to the main cottage, a small white house of gables clustered round a brick chimney. Beyond this was the wide sea smashing against the rocky shore.

The landlady, Mrs. Harwood, came out to greet us. She was a neat woman, chubby, in a green dress. She clutched a fluffy yellow sweater to herself as she led us cheerfully up the path. The blue eyes of a little girl looked out from her pink and wrinkled face. She offered June the use of her oven, the use of her telephone, her television, her shower, whenever she liked, her door was always open. Of course, there was no heat in the little house, was June sure she wanted it? Well, she could come up to the main cottage anytime and curl up on the sofa to keep warm!

"Is there electricity?" I asked.

"Oh, yes, dear!"

Secretly, I planned to buy June an electric blanket.

June was still so exhausted and shocked about being thrown out; I practically had to hold her up. We stood in front of the little house while the cold wind from the sea whipped around us. The sun had come out, bright and cold. It shone on the pastel remains of hollyhocks that flanked the tiny entryway.

"June, you have hollyhocks," I said.

She nodded, sadly.

We stopped at Crane's Beach. Because it was out of season, we drove right in and parked in the lot. We strolled the cold water's edge without talking. Then, suddenly, June began to take off her clothes.

"June! It's freezing!"

Without listening to me, she kicked off her shoes and yanked off her socks. She tore the clothes from herself, corduroys, sweater, jersey, panties, till she was completely naked.

"You're not!" I was freezing, pulling my sweater around me.

You've never seen a woman so beautiful. Her limbs had always been smooth and fine, her tummy and buttocks rounded only a little, her breasts much larger than they should be on such a slender girl. Her hair, a sheet of white gold. She dove into the water, now bright blue green, sparkling with white crests.

"June! You're out of your mind!"

She laughed at me and did this Junie thing she always liked to do. She floated on her back and laughed, she spit huge spouts of ocean like a whale.

"Come on in, wimp!"

I shook my head, thinking, this was nuts, but I started to strip anyway. I had to go fast before I changed my mind. I leaped into the icy water, screaming.

"June, I hope you know what to do if I have a heart attack!"

"Shut up and float!"

I was the most shivering whale ever, but I floated. The water lapped around our forms, making islands of our pubis and breasts.

"Hey, Ri, don't you just love pubic hair?" She spouted water again.

"Man, this is crazy!" I said through clenched teeth.

We swam and splashed each other like kids. We swam under water. We ran out and picked the last of the pink rugosa roses also shivering in the wind, cutting our fingers on the thorns and stubborn stalks firmly rooted in the sand, we floated them in the water with us.

A uniformed young man in a Range Rover who was patrolling the dunes drove by on the shore. We hid from him under water, but he saw our clothes and called to us. We said we were all right, but he told us if we weren't out of the water and gone by the time he drove back, he'd arrest us. Nude bathing was illegal, he yelled. He lingered for half a minute, watching us, then left.

We came out and dressed in our sandy clothes, our bodies still tingling and icy, the sweaters felt warm from the sun, warm as though we wrapped a living thing around us.


CROSSROADS

Now came a time of such sweet joy, it had to be followed by a time of sorrow.

June lived between our two houses for three weeks until she could take the cottage. Mrs. Harwood was going away and she insisted June wait until she got back. During that time, except for being rigid as cats every time the phone rang or there was a knock at the door, because we were sure Aaron would call or come after her, June and I thoroughly enjoyed being together.

One night, I danced for her and her mother and father.

The four of us were sitting at her kitchen table, illuminated only by the yellow glow of the overhead lamp, and the stove light still on, a quiet night, talking and listening to an old Donovan album of soft and lilting country songs about tinkers, starfish and looking glasses made of sand.

She said I got up, so casually, they thought I might be getting a drink of water, but I began to dance, a slow, graceful gypsy dance to Donovan's

"The Enchanted Gypsy." I raised my arms above my head, I lifted the hem of my long skirt and twirled it prettily in my hand, I moved my hands and feet in a delicate manner and I turned like an Arab girl. She said everyone was mesmerized, they watched, in an amazed contentment as my arms lifted and fell in languid spirals, they watched as my hands formed arches, as I lifted my feet and pointed my toes. I spun, finally, spinning and spinning to the music, with little dips and turns, till finally, I dropped to the floor and bowed my head.

No one could believe what I'd done. They burst into applause. Mrs. White exclaimed, "Well! Gloria!" "Ho, ho, ho!" Mr. White rolled his embarrassed laughter out. (Although it had been the most chaste dance of clothed dips and swirls, later, Ted confided secretly to June, "Gloria's must not be a virgin any more if she can dance like that!) "Ri," June laughed with delight, "that was great!" "Thanks," I said, "I don't know what made me do that!"

But, I did know. The music was so beautiful and I was so happy, the moment had simply lifted me out of my chair.

Another night, June and I stayed up almost all night on the floor in my room, with a large bottle of Kahlua, a large bottle of cream and a metal tray of ice cubes. The glasses were huge, probably made for frappes, but we had what Daddy called, "a popsicle." In hushed voices, hiding behind the bed, we poured and stirred and drank and laughed on the cold linoleum floor.

Then, June went to the bathroom and locked the door, like all the Whites did when they went to the bathroom, but, unfortunately, she passed out. I could see her there, the pattern of her pajamas, through the old keyhole; I couldn't wake her with my knocking or calling her name. There was nothing to do but go to sleep right there while June slept on the floor on the other side of the door.

She went to school with me, carrying her "sustenance" for the day on her back. One of my friends, the very tall Stewart Land, who stuttered painfully, (but it was such a tremendous thrill to wait to hear what he had to say, I would wait patiently), took one look at her opening up the contents of her backpack and placing her package of tea and small container of brown rice and vegetables on the little table at Scarborough Fair, and he said, "Y-y-y-you h-h-ha-have a v-v-ver-ri-veri-ta-verita-ble gro-ce-ry store in th-th-there!"

She and Aaron had changed their diets and together, June and I cooked these new and outrageous things, which were really, ancient and quite natural, in Ma's kitchen and in Agnes'. We made brown rice and vegetables; sea vegetables, long and black or slick and green; we roasted sesame seeds and fried tofu, a pure white bean cake like soft cheese; we sliced carrots into matchsticks and braised them with onions and tamari, soy sauce aged in wood and sea salt. We ground our own flour using a mill that clamped on to the table: June planted her bare foot firmly on Ma's linoleum floor to balance the work of her turning the grinder's handle. To Ma's amazement, the fresh wheat berries were poured into the mouth of the grinder, and the freshly ground flour flowed out! "So, that's how they make flour!" Ma exclaimed. We made our own bread because good bread was almost impossible to find now. Even the bakeries were using fake ingredients. Ma had started to use Crisco in her cooking instead of the homemade lard she used to collect in a jar from the sizzling steaks and juicy pork chops. We tried to tell her not to do that because Crisco was like eating plastic, but she wouldn't listen. Grandma never used Crisco. She would have twisted her face in disgust. But Ma was amazed as June and I toasted the flat, crisp nori sea vegetable sheets over an open flame then wrapped the toasted nori around fried tofu and dipped these in ginger sauce. We made tempura, deep-frying broccoli florets in batter. Ma liked the crispy tempura with its tangy ginger dip sauce, "Oh, that's good!" We made salads of arugula and sesame dressing. From a macrobiotic cookbook with wooden spoons on its cover, we made ancient recipes and found new flavors and new life. We wondered what our kitchens would look like. Recalling the Renaissance kitchen of Isis, June said, yes, we would have a Renaissance kitchen with wooden bowls and freshly ground flour for our bread and lace curtains and hand hewn, hand painted furniture and I would paint my own pictures for the walls and borders of flowers or birds and maybe even a statue of a woman or a cherub to stand in the garden.

We took ballet lessons at the adult education school of The Boston Ballet, arriving around seven in the evening, just as the real dancers were leaving. They gathered in the dirty wooden corridor. Young men and women dressed in crazy layers of rags, cloths swaddled around their fragile limbs as though to hold them together, woolen socks with holes worn through and the feet cut off, pulled over pink satin toe shoes faded and broken as the shoes of beggars in the Bible or Napoleon's soldiers marching to Moscow, leotards thin as skin draped with chiffon skirts and scarf ropes knotted about their ethereal waists.

June and I took off our coats with our dance clothes already on, while the dancers stripped naked in front of us. They smelled strongly of pungent underarms and the musky smell of working feet. We loved them, the sweat pouring down their faces, necks and backs, they wiped at themselves casually with a towel, their muscles swelling and straining, the ordinary clothing of pants and sweaters going on them in a way only dancers would wear pants and sweaters, the tight knot of the women's hair let loose suddenly and falling in two-foot tendrils greasy from sweating so hard. They wrapped woolen scarves in a manner only dancers would, causing them to look like ballet dancers even in their coats. They stopped in the doorways to watch their fellows still dancing. Their profiles were disdainful as they commented harshly on the performances: "She'll never be on stage, never, not with that body!" "She's good, but she'll have to lose two hundred pounds." "Oh, look at that ankle! My God! If I did that, I'd be finished!" "Pitiful."

Our teacher was an old dancer named Thadea, thin and hard, with a tight bun of grey hair a top her head. Thadea worked us nearly to death. We dripped sweat from our hair and eyes, down our fronts and backs, while she tortured our adult bodies into unnatural shapes and positions, holding us there till we groaned and begged. Once, I saw myself on pointe in the mirror and the sight was so beautiful, my hands arched over my head held high, my black leotard in perfect sculpture, my pink tights straight and fine, one knee bent exactly right, so wonderful, I couldn't bear it, I fell over immediately.

After class, we drove down the few blocks to The Seventh Inn natural foods restaurant on Boylston Street, a serene oasis of rice paper and bamboo, on every table fresh flowers that seemed to swell with the playing of flute and harp. We sat delicately as on egg shells in our leotards, our hair up in ballet dancer's knots a top long, graceful necks, listening carefully to the many conversations in the many accents going on around us, eating and relishing the treats of these words as much as we ate and relished our hiziki salads and sipped our glasses of wine. It was amazing, how much we relied on eavesdropping. We learned the most interesting things just by being quiet, rare things unique to the universal crossroads of The Seventh Inn.

"I wanted the building to be integrated into its environment," a man next to us said to his friend. "I used organic materials as much as possible, glass and stone, for instance...there was a very large boulder I wanted to incorporate into the living room."

"He spoke to me about the new system, but I'm afraid, I have to disagree..."

"The stage would have to be stark white, with only a silken swing hanging center stage!"

"I might have a chance to sing! I think there's a part for me!"

"A student asked me today if I thought poetry was alive."

The waitress asked if we were dancers. Flattered, we said no. She said we looked like dancers. We thoroughly enjoyed this illusion that made us feel part of the culture churning there.

The walls were decorated with original art that seemed an odd mixture of Japanese and American influence, falling leaves, an infant just born, vegetables cut and open as a sculptured form, all signed in a Japanese character.

"Who is the artist?" I asked the waitress. "Is he Japanese?"

"Oh, he's American. He comes here all the time. That's him over there! I'm not sure what his name is."

We looked to see an older man whose grey hair was held at the nape of his neck by a cord of black cotton cloth wrapped in the style of a Japanese samurai. He was dressed in a short kimono of dark cotton and black Japanese pants that clung to his legs. He wore a sheath dangling from his broad sash.

"Does he have a sword?" I asked.

"Oh, no! That's a kendo stick! But, it can be just as deadly as a sword. From what I hear, he's able to defend himself quite well with it."

June and I were delighted to be in this atmosphere of artists, good food, wine and music. It was a time of discovery of self outside our selves, a time of embarkation.

Until the night Aaron drove up outside The Center for the Performing Arts after our ballet class, just as we were going to the car and chattering happily about going to The Seventh Inn for dinner.

All he had to do was drive up and she disappeared into his van. They sat in there, talking, I could see their heads, while I sat in my car waiting, for more than an hour.

Then, June came out and told me she was going with him. She was eating a strawberry.

"Where did you get the strawberry?" I asked.

"Aaron's got boxes of them, want some?"

"No, thanks. Where'd he get strawberries?"

She shrugged, "Some hothouse." He was always doing that. He'd walk into a natural foods store and buy their whole display of energy bars, sign and all, and just give them away by the handfuls.

She told me also that she wouldn't be going to ballet class any more, but that I could still go by myself if I wanted to.

Then, she kissed my cheek, hastily, and she was gone.

I was way too lonely to go to The Seventh Inn. I stopped in Kappy's and got myself a jug of Paul Masson and went home by myself.


RICHIE SILVA

Near the middle of June's stay with me, one cloudy Sunday afternoon, we walked over to her house because Happy Jack, who no longer lived at home, was going to be there especially to see her.

When we opened the front door, Ted and all the boys were in the living room together and the roar of men watching a football game punched us in the face. Ted was sitting on the edge of his recliner, the others were standing in the middle of the room, or on the arms of the chairs, pounding the chairs with their fists and screaming at the television, "Get him! Get him! Get him!" as if their lives depended on it. Jack yelled, "Hey, hey, hey!" at the sight of his sister and threw his arms around her, but watched the TV from over her shoulder. He screamed at the TV right into her ear, "That's it! Got it! Go, go, go, go!"

Without realizing it, he dropped her and reached over to punch his brother Joe's shoulder, "I'm gonna win this one, buddy!"

"You're dreamin' - oh, no!" Joey yelled.

"Ha, ha!"

June and I wandered into the kitchen where Agnes was sitting at the table reading the Sunday paper, her bi-focals down on the tip of her freckled turned-up nose. I felt a sudden affection for her, quietly seated under the soft yellow light spilling from the overhead.

"Junie! Gloria! You knew Richie Silva, didn't you?"

"Richie," I fumbled, stunned by the sudden mention of the name I treasured secretly.

"Yes! I thought I saw you talking to him one day right out front!"

More like not talking to him. I remembered that day, I'd passed him on the same side of the street, not a week ago, just as I was going into June's house, so suddenly, he was there in front of me, once again I was so full of emotion for him, my knees went out from under me and all I could say was, "Hi."

"Hi," he said, with affection.

We'd stood and stared at each other a moment, and then, inexplicably, passed on. How many times have I relived that moment? How many times have I stopped him in time, tried unsuccessfully to hold him there, powerless in memory? Why could I never speak to him? What words would I have used?

"What about Richie?" June asked, casually, turning the newspaper around to find the comics.

You won't believe how cheerfully Agnes said this, how rosy her cheeks were, how her eyes danced with electric light.

"He hung himself last night. His mother found him in his closet."

Her words passed into me and ground to a stop, he-hung-him-self-last-night like the words of a nightmare, the nightmare was in me and I couldn't get it out, he-hung-himself-last-night, he-hung-himself-last-night, he-hung-himself-last-night-his-mother-found-him-in-the-closet-his-mother-he-hung-himself-found-him-in-the-closet-last-night-he-hung-himself-last-night…he was afraid, alone, afraid…I didn't know, I should have known, I could have helped, I could have loved him and he didn't know! His pain! His-mother-found-him-hanging-in-the-closet-in the closet! His mother, the same woman who'd chased me away and called me a whore! She loved him too! Why couldn't *she* help him? Why hadn't she?

Agnes was still talking, "Jack told us about it. They'll probably call it an accidental death, but Jack told me, it was probably a sexual experiment gone wrong." She laughed. She laughed!

I vomited all over the kitchen floor, falling into it on knees that finally gave way.

"Gloria!" Agnes yelled, jumping up, grabbing a whole roll of paper towel.

I watched her, numbly, thinking what a waste. Ma would never waste paper towel like that; she'd use a rag and wash it out. Kneeling there on the floor, I hated Agnes for wasting paper towel.

I felt what felt like June's thin arms go around me, and then I saw the feet of all the brothers crowding round my face down on the floor.

I heard their voices far away, still mumbling about the football game, still laughing, who's that on the floor?

But, it wasn't fair to blame them. They loved a good scandal, a good laugh, a good sex experiment! I didn't know if it was a sexual experiment. I wasn't trying to deny sex, I just I couldn't help thinking - it was my fault. That was clear, I could have saved him. I could have loved him. I could have held him in my arms. That was obvious. I knew I could have kept him alive. I could never explain it to them, they were so far away in their happy world, it was my fault, my fault...

I was running, running, away from the Whites, toward a place where I could be alone with him.

A heavy rain was falling right into me, icy, icy as knives, it screamed, "Richie! Richie!" It felt good! It felt right!

I past his house where he had died; I ran to the sea wall where the waves crashed over grey and cold the way they had that day he'd surfed them: crazy, happy, the grey water streaming over his white limbs, the black and blues all over his shivering body. I looked into his eyes, the lashes were wet and dark, his dewy brown eyes, they laughed at me, they laughed and mourned, "You should've brought your bathing suit!"

I couldn't cry deeply enough. My sobs were as deep as the waves that crashed over me, that sucked back into an ocean of sorrow and spilled over without relief, without end. I could cry every tear in the ocean and more would rain from the sky.

June was beside me. Through a wash of tears I saw her profile and a heavy rubber slicker came down over both of us, large and yellow as a strange sea animal; it smelled like an old whale kept beached in an attic. How long had she been there? How long had we huddled inside the whale? She held my wet hand; she kissed my hand, inside the belly of the whale.

Then, she got up and was gone! Why did she have to go? Why couldn't she stay with me forever? That was my fault too! I turned my head to see my car, to see June hurrying back to me; she'd gotten my car and come after me. She had a candle in her hand! From the dashboard, we kept a candle there for talking in the car during late night stops for coffee.

Without speaking, she placed the bit of candle with us under the yellow fin of the whale. Reverently, she lighted it, sticking it to the concrete wall. It flickered bravely and we tried to shelter its flame from the constant spray. For a brief moment, it shone sweet and bright under the yellow skin and together we prayed for him. We prayed that he was at peace, that he was not lonely any more, or afraid, or, we guessed, he was no longer horny – a bit of a shaky chuckle there - then the small flame sputtered and went out. We tried again and again to light it, but couldn't.

But, the physical act of trying to light the candle calmed me down. I leaned against June. Soon, the ocean also became calmer; the tide seemed to be going out. We huddled together under the smelly, old slicker that was no longer a whale.

"Ri, it's not your fault."

"What?"

"You were screaming on the kitchen floor, that it was your fault," she sounded annoyed with me, which was unusual for her.

"Yeah, that's me, the over-reactor."

"It's not your fault."

"Yeah, right."

"Ri, people who are that desperate need more help than you could give them."

"June, I could have loved him."

"You did love him. And he loved you."

Then, I realized: she was right, it was so clear. That was the way I loved Richie and the way he'd loved me. Silently, dearly, from across the street, that had been the way we'd kept each other close.

"I'll always love him," I said.

"I know."


When I awoke the next morning, my eyes opened directly into the face of a picture I'd cut out of a magazine and framed, a painting by Degas, "The Head of a Young Woman." She wore a simple brown dress and her hair was caught up, giving her a boyish look. Something in her serene and gentle gaze had made me frame this picture and put it on my wall. I'd always been puzzled by that, because it was so brown and so very plain.

But, on this morning, my eyes met her large brown eyes and her soft sweet gaze; they rested on her round, full cheeks that only added to her peace, and I knew I looked into the face of Richie Silva.

## FOURS YEARS IN COLLEGE

I had three good teachers at Salem State College.

The first, a tired, handsome Greek, taught me to read poetry. He was reciting T.S. Eliot, when, passing my desk, he reached over and grabbed my arm. He held it up to the light as he recited the next line, with a disgusted, even horrified voice, he cried, *"but in the lamplight, downed with light brown hair!"* Instantly, all poetry became vivid.

The second was a tall Englishman who read us Chaucer aloud in Olde English, that is, pronouncing every letter so that English sounded French and rang with a lilt almost Celtic. He asked us questions we had to decipher before we could search for the answers, which we then wrote in long essays full of logic so involved and convoluted, I couldn't believe I was capable of such thoughts! He took us far beyond ourselves.

The third, a short, disheveled philosophy professor who taught without a text or notes of any kind. He simply entered the classroom, took off his watch, placed it before him on the desk, picked up a piece of broken chalk and proceeded to dazzle us. Once, I passed him in a tender spring drizzle, when he lifted his finger to the sky and declared, "Who will tell the philosopher it is raining?" I was only going to say hello.

I learned from G, who finally only went to school to crash on the plastic sofa in the Union, that not every one likes you and you can't force them to like you.

I learned from the beautiful blonde student who had had a four-year affair with a beautiful blonde professor. We saw them, everyday, playing tennis in the sun or in the fog, glowing like movie stars. One day, near graduation, I saw her alone in the library. I'd heard they'd broken up, that she had quit school in despair. There she was studying, several volumes opened around her. I said hello, how are you and she said, with shocked, glassy eyes, "I'm great! I've never learned so much in all four years of school as I have in these last few weeks."

And from Stewart Land, who stuttered horribly, but always stuttered the truth; I learned the most sublime lesson of all. I entered the classroom early one dark rainy morning; deep inside the weird yellow buildings only the fluorescent lights were on and the historic Salem sky looked black as midnight. Stewart was alone at his desk and he said, "L-L-L-Lis-ten t-t-to th-th-this!" Then, he read a long passage from the book he held in his hand, Proust's *Remembrance of Things Past*. I don't think he stuttered once, while he read a long piece of such closely worked detail, it was like a painting no one could duplicate, and when he came to the final words, Stewart said, in a voice as full of emotion and control as the finest actor, he said, "it was the rain."

I decided then and there, I must not read Proust until I was much older.

Then, Stewart gave me the most valuable truth of my life: "I th-th-think l-l-l-life is sym-b-b-b-bol-ic, i-i-if on-ly we c-c-c-can re-re-read it."

That was the beginning of my understanding, when I began to take out all the things I had put away in my heart.

## USED TO THINK OF IT AS MY SCHOOL, NOT HIGH SCHOOL

Revere High was four years dirtier and in need of repair. The window shades that had been ripped as though a fist had gone through them, now hung in brittle shreds. The windows that had once been grimy were now grimy and broken; the broken windows were boarded up. The halls were choked with garbage from kids' lunches, orange rinds, banana peels, wax paper wrung around salami sandwiches, as well as trash the kids threw down, test or homework papers, candy wrappers, pages of text books that floated up on the gusts made by the traffic of hundreds of feet. The stairwells lurked blacker than ever, except for dope smokers hiding under them, the tiny planets that hung suspended in the darkness, that glowed red and smelled of smoke, the muffled giggles, the reflective eyes of primitive beings huddled around a fire.

I was there to student teach and things were so much worse. Teachers did their work by rote, stunned and dazed. The dress code had been abolished and institutional, packaged food had replaced the cooked meals in the cafeteria and at home. Instead of straight backed, straight laced students, well fed and well rested, I was faced with a room full of slumped, exhausted kids, derelicts too young, in torn jeans and black T-shirts bearing skulls and devils. The boys in the back slept and I let them because they looked so tired, so wasted and hollow, it seemed useless to wake them. They looked up at me through layers of stringy hair, faces that had aged already, pimpled and pocked as Daddy's, puffy and wrinkled around the eyes, chins scarred with red crevices. Their long legs stuck out into the aisles; their sneakers were rotted open and black.

The girls sat on the edge of their seats in tight ass jeans. They brushed their big hair, painted their nails black or purple, snapped clouds of sweet, airy bubble gum.

I let them do all these things, because I understood. I was a little scared of them; they were tough and impenetrable. Some of them looked like they could hang out with Rick Likus. But, worse, because Rick's crowd had at least been natural, sun-bleached and dirty. These were like tight black machines, metallic and hard-edged. I didn't know if I had it in me to do anything for them, or even interest them for five minutes. Then, I set about deserving their attention.

I guess it was lucky Frank had made me work in all those jobs, because I was able to redesign the English lessons to try and solve some the kids' real life problems. Of course, I got in trouble for this with the kids' regular teachers whom I was replacing for six weeks. One woman told me, "Just give them a sheet of yellow paper and tell them to write an essay on democracy or something and give them a sheet of white paper and tell them to copy it over. That takes them the whole period." More than once I had to defend what I was doing, and after a while, I started to think, maybe I'd make a pretty good lawyer. But, I didn't believe in the law. The practice of law, the courts, it was all trickery.

I got stacks of job applications from different companies and together, we talked about how to fill them out, even the importance of handwriting and signatures, what you could tell from a person's application before reading it. We wrote resumes for each and every kid, letters asking for a raise, speeches asking for a raise. We approached the boss, in skits during class, to ask for a raise or to complain about a problem we had in the workplace. We studied how to buy a used car, choosing an insurance company, which led to a little law, civil rights, privileges and responsibilities, including marriage, divorce, and custody.

After a few weeks, no one was sleeping; no one was doing her nails.

I began a unit on witchcraft. I admit, at first, only to entertain them, but after a few days, I realized, they were thinking symbolically. I got in a lot of trouble for teaching this subject. The head of the English Department, a too neat little man in a tight bow tie, interrogated me almost as severely as the justices of the Salem witch trials. I thought I might be banned in Revere for sending home mimeographed papers explaining witches and devils and snakes and other familiars. But, the kids loved it and appreciated learning about something they never would have known existed.


"Stand up and describe your mother to me. Let's see, Reneé."

Reneé made a face. She stood, reluctantly.

"Before you begin, think. Careful. Use real words. No slang. No ums, no you knows. Get it straight, then tell me."

"My mother is about thirty-five years old. She's not tall. She's short."

The kids laughed. It could be a slow process.

"Go on."

"Her hair is black. It's curly. Um, oh, sorry. It's not natural. She gets a perm. I give it to her."

More laughter.

"Thank you. You can sit down. Mike. Stand up and describe your job."

Mike was a huge, grubby boy. His T-shirt always came out of the back of his jeans. He was so wide, his bulk was slung over the edge of the too-small seats the desks had now and he didn't fit into a desk with a table top, he had to use one that had had its top torn off in a classroom fight. Mike worked at McDonald's. Everyone knew that.

"My boss is an asshole," Mike said.

The class burst out laughing.

"No. Try again."

He sighed.

"I work at McDonald's," he said, exasperated.

Laughter.

"Yes?"

"Nuf said."

Laughter.

He started to sit down.

"No."

"It sucks!" he said, getting frustrated and angry.

"No."

"*You* ever work at McDonald's?"

"No."

He mumbled something and sat down.

"Kentucky Fried Chicken."

"YOU!"

"Yes. And The Viceroy, The Driftwood, Howard Johnson's. Right now, I work nights at Firelli's and after school, I tutor."

Murmurs of appreciation.

"Who do you tutor, Miss Wisher?" a girl named Monica asked.

"Mike!" one of the boys remarked to more laughter.

"I tutor a little boy in his reading." This was true. I'd needed a Community Involvement credit, so I called up one of the new families on our street, the Pizzaros and asked if Nickie Pizzaro needed any help with his homework. His mother said sure and I found myself nodding at the Pizzaro kitchen table after school while Nickie droned through a small paperback on baseball heroes. Nevertheless, his grade improved from a D to a B, from the practice alone.

I told them about this and the whole class smiled with affection, whether for Nickie or for my falling asleep, I didn't know.

"Before you sit down Mike, tell us why your boss is an asshole."

"Woo! Way to go, Miss Wish!"

I had to laugh. It was good to laugh in high school. I never had before when I was there.

There were moments, like this one, or when the bell would suddenly ring and they'd all get up and leave without saying goodbye, that I'd feel so suddenly lonely and so in love with them, I wanted to shout to their backs walking out of the empty classroom, "Hey! Wait a minute! Come back!"

Then I knew. I was a teacher as well as a writer and an artist. It came as quite a shock.


## THE THUNDERBOLT

In *A Room With a View*, when George Emerson argues with Mr. Beebe about what brought him to Lucy, he says, "It is Fate that I am here...But you can call it Italy if it makes you less unhappy." Italians themselves call it "the thunderbolt."

When I was struck, it was hard, irrevocable and without warning. I was afraid and I struggled against nature, but it was no good. I was already in the grip of sexual law.

In my college course, things were not as simple for me as things were in the general classes. Things are never really simple, but sometimes, we sneak by. Not this time.

In my college course, I taught three sets of twins: Mickey and Matt, the blonde hockey players; Susan and Sharon, slim, gamin blondes with small, delicate features; Brian and Sean, two Irish saints with black, electric hairdos as fuzzy dark halos surrounding their long noses and prominent chins. The twins weren't the problem. You would think they'd give me trouble, but my college course was so much the sweetest group of human beings put together in one room, I couldn't believe I was still in Revere. You could tell most of them came from caring homes: they radiated a certain confident optimism: they wore pastel colors, their hair and clothes were clean, including their jeans and sneakers, which could dazzle your eyes with their whiteness.

I was calling attendance on the first day, simple enough. It was really fun to see the faces come to life with names, especially twin faces which, if you looked closely, looked, that is, with all your senses, the differences jumped out at you.

"Luciano Merano?" I called.

The class roared with laughter. All together, they seemed to let go of a cumbersome weight and let out something they'd been wanting to express.

"What? What is it?" I looked around the room, confused. "Who is Luciano?"

Off to my left, a boy raised his hand, laxly.

He wasn't the pretty kind of handsome I always like Italians to be. His nose was too wide for that. But he had a distinction, the manner of someone out of his time, set apart from the place he found himself, yet with none of the immigrant's confusion in his manner or in his dress. He seemed older and wiser than the others; he was patient with them, indulgent. His long, brown hair fell about his face with the softness of a girl's, but his limbs were thick and strong as a workingman's. He reminded me immediately of the young men in Zeffirelli's "Romeo and Juliet," young Renaissance boys, ready and not ready to be men.

"Why is everyone laughing?" I asked, generally.

"You're supposed to call him, Luke! Ha, ha! Luke!" Mickey punched Luke on the shoulder.

These twins were so powerful, their athletic arms and legs struck out from the confines of their desks and filled the aisles; they seemed to play hockey with their limbs even while they tried to sit still.

Matt smiled in his quiet way, "You're not supposed to call him Luciano. It makes him mad."

"It doesn't make me mad when she says it, only when you goons say it!"

He didn't have the same street accent the other kids had. His accent was from Italy, soft, refined, delectable as the rumcake we used to have at Easter, the sweet and liquory rumcake I hadn't had since Nona's last birthday on earth.

"Oh, oh! But, *she* can say it!"

"I like the way it sounds when she says it. She says it right!"

"Yeah," Mickey laughed, "Most of the teachers say, 'Lucy-anno'! Ha, ha! Lucy-anno!" The whole class cracked up.

It was true, I pronounced the ci as chi, the way it was supposed to be, the way I'd heard it pronounced all my life, rolling over the smooth tongues of Grandma and Grandpa, Nona and Mama.

"Okay, okay, quiet down. I'll try to remember, but I might slip up now and then. It's written in front of me as Luciano."

"They made me write my full name."

Mickey cracked up.

Luke leaned over to him, "That's pretty funny coming from a guy who calls himself 'Mick-ey, Mick-ey!' Like a little mouse!"

The whole class laughed.

"He's going back to Italy," Mickey explained when he caught his breath, "So, it doesn't matter!"

"His parents made him come here to go to school," Matt said. "We've been best friends since he moved here. He's a lot older than we are! Tell her how old you are, Luke!"

Luke sighed, "Twenty."

Mickey and Matt laughed.

"Tell her about the castles!"

Luke was silent.

"There are three hundred and fifty castles where he comes from!" Susan piped in, "Right by the place he lived!"

"Really?" I asked. "I never knew about this. Where is this place?"

"Tirolo," Luke said. "It's in the Alps, almost."

"Castles in the clouds!" Mickey exclaimed, waving his arms over imaginary mountains. "He's getting married and he's taking his bride back to his castle in the clouds!"

"I don't have a castle," Luke told him. "They're all mostly ruins and museums now, anyway," he explained shyly, only half-looking up at me.

"His parents want him to go to Harvard, but he wants to be a shoemaker and go back to Italy."

"Are your parents here, Luke?"

"No, my father has a restaurant back in Tirolo and a couple more in Rome and Milan."

"But Luke's gonna be a little Geppetto type guy!" Mickey kidded.

"Geppetto was a woodcarver, Mickey," I said.

"He was? I thought he was a shoemaker!"

"See?" Luke said, "You learned something already!"

Luke smiled at me and our eyes met and that's when the thunderbolt hit hard.

The classroom slid into a whirlpool, my blood pulsed rhythmically in my ears as though trying to speak to tell me what I already knew: I was afraid.

This couldn't happen. He was my student, so I erased this, and when it wouldn't erase, I pushed it aside.

"Let's start our grammar," I said.

They groaned.

"Open your books to page, 112, past perfect. I'll finish attendance while you read."

I knew their regular teacher could hear everything from her desk on the other side of the pea green partition where she was monitoring me. She was a stout, elderly lady with a frothy pink flip that looked like perky cotton candy on her head. She was very kind to me, but she was a stickler for grammar, though she'd promised I could teach a novel next.

Occasionally, I found myself looking at Luke, marveling that such a young person (less than a year younger than me) wanted a simpler life. Who was he? I wondered as his head was bent to his work. Imagine, finding someone like him at Revere High.

Then, he looked up and all the other heads were down. The thunderbolt cracked hard. He held my eyes, seriously, even a little sadly. There was something always a little sad about him, which caused my heart to go out to him. But, this time when my heart left my body, another heart entered.

I looked down at the attendance sheet, trying to remember who I was.


## A RIDE TO SCHOOL

I don't know why I was walking to school, probably my old car was down, but one sunny Spring day, awash with fresh sea breezes mingling tantalizingly with the tired exhaust from the road, a bright red sportscar slowed by my side and it was Luke.

"Miss Wisher! Do you want a ride to school?" He gestured toward the road, as if to say, hey, it's just a few feet down the road. The white road that led straight to the little white Immaculate Conception Church and straight to the red brick box where the devil went to school, this day sparkling with sun on its white concrete back.

"Sure!" I said, without hesitation, and I got right in.

I think I couldn't resist the chance to be alone with him. I had gotten used to the idea that Luke was off limits: a) he was my student b) he was engaged to be married. So, I'd decided over the first few days to put my own feelings aside and relax. I think it was really my way of fooling myself and enjoying him every minute I could. And, as if in collusion, the green things were stirring underground, breaking through the dead layers of winter leaves. The gulls were crying to me, flying ahead, showing the way.

"You have too many books," he laughed as I sat down with them stacked primly on my lap. In fact, I dressed rather primly for school, always in long skirts and ribbed sweaters, my hair up in a schoolmarm bun. It was a romantic, '20s and '30s style that was current then, after the influence of the "Bonnie and Clyde" movie as well as "Women in Love"; but it suited my needs at Revere High, the creative severity helped inspire authority. Otherwise, I looked exactly like one of the kids.

"Yeah, story of my life, I guess. Too many books."

"This is a nice car!" I remarked after a moment, looking around with some surprise at the black leather seats and the complicated dashboard glistening with dials and levers that made my car look like a covered wagon. The inside smelled richly of leather and the sweet green scent of a light aftershave.

"Yeah, my girl friend likes it. It's an old Alfa Romeo. Best kept secret in the world that shoe repair makes good money, especially if you're the only place in town," he sighed.

"What's the sigh for?"

He looked at me, "Ha! You caught me. Ah, my girlfriend, Debbi, every time I say that, I can see the little heart she makes over the i and I feel guilty talking about her, but, I'll tell you - he paused to think - she likes the money part all right, but not the shoe repair so much."

"I guess its not really about being a shoe "maker" anymore, is it?" I ventured.

"Naw! Nobody makes the shoes anymore. Except the fine Italian houses like Gucci."

"How did you get into this business and not the restaurant business like your dad?"

"Well, my parents wanted me to go to school in the United States."

He shrugged, like he couldn't see why, but he'd done what they'd asked. "I went to live with my aunt and uncle and I just started working in my uncle's shop after school - on Broadway. I liked it, you know. I like being independent. I make good money." He sighed again, and his hand on the wheel went up in a gesture that meant, this baffles me, "My father thinks I should be a lawyer."

"I wanted to go to Harvard," I smiled, almost nostalgically.

"Really?"

"Yes."

"I thought only men could go to Harvard."

I gave him a look. He smiled and shrugged apologetically.

"Women go to Radcliffe."

"Oh. Why didn't you go to Radcliffe? Is that part of Harvard? I've heard of it."

"It is. I wasn't smart enough or rich enough. I went to The School of Earth and Salt Water instead."

"What's that?"

"Just a little college called Salem State." And to change the subject, I added, "I know that shop of yours."

"Do you go there? I've never seen you," he paused, "I'd remember."

"I take pretty good care of my stuff, I guess I could use some new heels on my Frye boots soon."

"Take them in, I'll do a good job."

"Maybe, when I can afford it." This seemed so illicit that I knew I'd never take the boots to him.

"Don't worry about that," he said, as if reading my mind.

Then, we were at school. I got out of the car quickly and waved goodbye, openly, as though nothing in the world was wrong.

But, I kept talking to him all that day, in my mind. We carried on many conversations. I chattered about everything I did, everything I believed in and loved, no matter how insignificant, because I wanted Luke to know.

Occasionally, I came up against some things I didn't want him to know, and I fell silent.

## ALSO THE SUN ALSO RISES

No bigger than a closet, the novel storeroom at Revere High stank of age and mildew. Faded paperbacks were stacked haphazardly to the ceiling, their ragged pages sticking out like exhausted tongues. The yellow light from the overheard bulb made the paper look ancient and parched.

Finally, I was able to start a literary unit and I was in the storeroom searching for a book for us to read. I needed a novel with enough copies for a class of thirty-five.

I counted twenty-six and a half copies of *Catcher in the Rye*. Yes, there was actually half a book. I picked it up in disbelief and discovered that every single swear word had been rubbed out with an eraser, rubbed so hard, in fact, that little holes dotted the pages.

I laughed out loud.

Someone was walking by and his head turned just as I looked up, laughing. He'd tell me later that the golden light reflected off the old books behind me had been the light of Italy, warm and full of peace, that I had looked like a saint, not a sad and suffering saint, but, as though there were such a thing, a laughing one.

And, all this was in his eyes as he looked at me.

"Luke!"

"Miss Wisher, what are you doing in the closet?"

He stepped into the small room, very close to me, and I felt my body respond to him, without my consent, my legs slackened and my back wanted to arch. I stood up straight. He put his books down with a thud, and I told myself, in order to gather my wits, now, Luke is putting down his books.

"I'm trying to find a novel for us to read in class," I told him. "That will be our next project. You can help me, if you have the time."

"Sure."

"You don't have to get to work?"

He shook his head. He nodded to the book I held in my hand.

"Is that one funny?" he asked.

"Well, yes." I showed him the tiny holes. "All the swear words have been rubbed out for us!"

"You're joking!" His face studied the page in disbelief. Then he grinned and lit up.

"All these holes are swears? So - we can just fill them in!"

"Exactly!"

I put the book back.

"It's only half a book anyway. We need at least thirty-five books. Want to help me count each title and see how close we can come?"

"Still," he said, intrigued by *The Catcher in the Rye*, "I'd like to read that one. I always wanted to."

I gave him one.

"Return it to me when you're done."

"Ok," his soft eyes were already delving into its first pages.

I began counting books. In a minute, he was beside me, also counting. I loved having him near me and if I had to subdue myself in order to have him there, then I would.

"Don't bother with *Pride and Prejudice*," I said. "Let's see, not *The Red Pony* either, too simple, not *The Good Earth* or *The Yearling*."

"You don't like those?"

"Not for your class. Count, *A Farewell to Arms*."

"*Great Gatsby* is not here," I said, "that's a good one."

"How many?" I asked.

"Twenty-six *A Farewell to Arms*. *Moby Dick*?" He asked.

I sighed, "How many?"

He counted quickly, in groups of ten. "Fifty," he announced.

"Figures."

"I'd love to do *The Sun Also Rises*," I said.

I'd been saving it for last, afraid to count.

"Twenty-nine."

"We need five."

"What about the library?" he asked.

"Well, I doubt if we'd get more than one copy there, and you couldn't write in it or damage it in any way. I'd like you guys to have your own copies in paperback, if possible." I spoke while checking the condition of what I had, keeping my head down. "I'm making sure most of the pages are here. We'll have to watch out for that."

He shook his head in amazement at the condition of the books.

"I guess I'll have to buy us some," I said.

"Buy them? Yourself? Let us buy them!"

"I can't do that!"

"Sure! We'll just go to the bookstore. Where is it?"

"There isn't one in Revere."

"Nobody reads here?"

"Don't make me laugh." I bent to pick up the stack of good *Suns* we'd made.

"I like it when you laugh," he said a little too quietly with that soft accent that could melt a stone, and I was no stone.

"I like it when you don't laugh, too," he said after a minute of silence.

I knew if looked up at him, our eyes would lock. I struggled with this. I kept my head down. Then, in an effort to be efficient and do the next thing I needed to do to get out of that room, I reached up and pulled the string to turn off the lightbulb, then quickly bent to pick up the stack and carry it out when he said in the sudden darkness, "Let me help you," and he bent also and our heads collided over the stack.

"Ow!" I jumped back.

"Oh! I'm sorry! Madonn', your head is hard!"

"Did I hurt you?" I reached out my hand for the light pull, which was swinging, and I touched his head instead.

"No," he whispered, affected. Then, I felt his arms go around me, his body pressed against me.

"Oh, Luke, no! This can't happen!" I cried in one breath.

"It has happened," he whispered in my ear.

I pushed him away and backed up against the wall of books. I kept my hands up as though to keep him away and he kept back. I was shaking and the tears started to come. I wiped them away quickly.

"This isn't a joke to me, Luke."

"I know that."

Several people had walked by the open storeroom while we'd been there, but, in those few seconds, everything had changed. We were no longer just teacher and student, and someone was walking by now so I said, in a harsh voice, "That's got the light. Help me with these. We'll take them to the classroom." I walked out ahead of him with a stack and he followed.

It was only a disinterested student who kept his back to us.

As we passed the vacant window frame overlooking the interior well that was formed by the U shape of the school building, I thought I saw out of the corner of my eye, the bright blue and yellow cover of *The Sun Also Rises* down on the trash heap.

"Just a minute, Luke."

"Miss Wisher, I'm sorry," he began, putting his stack down as I had done and walking toward me.

Now, I had to look into his eyes, like a teacher, cold and severe. "I know. It won't happen again. Will it?"

"No," he shook his head. "What are you looking at down there?" he asked, seriously.

I pointed into the well.

"Look! I think there are at least three copies down there! I wonder if they're whole."

"I'll go down and find out." He looked around for a way down.

"No! I can't let you do that! It's a long way down there! How would you get down, how would you get back up? Besides, I'm sure it's illegal for me to let you do that!"

He laughed.

"Don't worry about it. Come on. You'll have your books tomorrow on your desk."

"Luke -"

But, he had picked up the stack of books again and his stocky form was quickly disappearing down the dim corridor.

I felt a pang for him, as his legs moved and his arms embraced the books. Something familiar hurt me, someone I loved walking away from me with short legs, and arms carrying, always carrying.

Was I so hopeless to fall in love with a student while I was still a student myself? Stunned by my depravity, stunned that it should feel so keenly divine, I also picked up my books and followed him.

The three of them, Luke, Mickey and Matt, while I was busy carrying trays, had simply gotten a ladder, gone down the well and retrieved the copies of *The Sun Also Rises*. Later that night, they'd driven into Harvard Square to the Harvard Coop bookstore and purchased the remaining two copies, the last two in the store.

On my desk the next morning, I found three copies that had been wiped with soap and water and were still a little slimy, one with a few pages missing, and two brand new shiny copies all tied together with a new pink ribbon and a note that read, "Also The Sun Also Rises."

The three books that had been down in the well smelled almost overpoweringly of bananas, tuna fish (I hoped it was tuna fish) and bologna. I tried to give at least two of my heroes the new books, but they refused, handing these over to Susan and Sharon instead and taking the smelly ones for themselves.

"You're going to think this book stinks," I joked.

"Naw, we're used to it," bragged Mickey. "You should smell our room!"

We set to work.

I got books on bullfighting and, with the help of a reluctant employee of the Salem State Multi-Media Department, made a slide show of what a bullfight was like. I played old recordings of 1920s music to show how frivolous life had become in the States. I spoke to them plainly and clearly about Jake's injury, looking them straight in the eye and they appreciated my respect for them and it was returned to me a thousand fold.

We talked openly about Jake's pain, about war, frustration; watching your friends screw up what you wish you had, having to live without dignity, without reward. About drinking and partying too much - this was funny to them, and not funny. We talked about the lost generation. We concluded every generation was lost if it wanted to be. We talked about the boundaries between countries. I asked them why the old man had been allowed to pass the border guard without papers. The quietest boy in the class, who often slept because he worked nights, surprised me with the answer.

"Because he was there before the boundaries."

"Yes!"

I was deeply in love.


## THE LAST DAY OF HIGH SCHOOL FOR ME

He'd driven me to school many times, always calling to me in a friendly way as I walked, but this day was different.

He pulled the Romeo over abruptly and waited, motor running, by the curb. Even by the way he drove, I knew something was wrong. When I reached the car, he had the passenger door open and I just got in. He sped away, angrily, it seemed.

"What is it?" I asked, alarmed.

His face was turned away from me, looking at the road or looking thoughtfully out the window by his side. He didn't say anything the whole ride and then we were at school. I started to get out of the car.

He put his hand over mine on the seat.

"No, stay with me, please," he said.

I sat back and waited. He still hadn't looked at me. Kids streamed around us, some of them peering into the car to see if they knew us.

"Do you have a boyfriend?" he asked.

He wasn't calling me Miss Wisher any more. Something had changed.

"No. I did, but I broke up with him."

"Why?"

"We didn't want the same things."

"What did he want?"

I gave a little laugh, "I think he wanted to make money illegally."

"Was he Mafia?"

"No, drugs."

He looked at me then. I could see he hadn't slept; his face was ashen and weak.

"And what is it you want?"

His hand still covered mine. I looked down at our hands. His olive flesh was thick and wide, the fingernails were blackened from his work like Daddy's and I didn't know if this quickening of my heart at the sight of them was fright or recognition or love. My own hand, pale and very small, peeked out under from his with pink fingertips.

"I want a full, creative life. I want to write something good," I said, answering his question. "In my mind, I see a small cottage surrounded by flowers, the sea beyond, sometimes a blonde child is playing in the yard. I'm writing or painting, cooking or hanging clothes on a clothesline. I want to do good work and take care of a family too, I know I can do it."

He listened without saying anything, as though he were picturing this too.

Then, he said, "Yesterday was my birthday."

"You don't want me to say Happy Birthday, do you?"

"No."

He went on, "Debbi told me she'd never wanted to go to Italy with me. She'd always hoped I'd change my mind."

"Luke, I'm so sorry!" My eyes filled with tears for him.

He shrugged, but I could see how hurt he was.

"She works as the receptionist at Firestone Tire, you know the place?"

I nodded, "On the Parkway."

"Yeah. They want to promote her to, just a minute. I want to get it right - sales rep. And she accepted."

"My God! Spend her days in Firestone on the Parkway, or driving to other places like that, instead of Italy!"

"That's what I said, and she said, 'Everybody wants to get out of the old country and come here - everybody but you, you're the only one who wants go back'!"

"What are you going to do? Are you still going?"

I held my breath waiting for the answer.

"Yeah, I'm going. But, not so happily. And, I'm not so set on Tirolo any more. My father is there and I don't know if I could take hearing about Harvard every day of my life, especially now. I'm open. There's a place in the South I'd like to try, Vieste, it's a nice place," he looked at me intently, "a fishing village, nice little houses, good food, lots of flowers and ocean. Not so many shoes," he added with a laugh.

He picked up my hand and looked at it for just a second. I didn't have the heart to take it away, and then he pressed its palm to his lips, very hard and emotionally, causing me to gasp. Without looking at me, he let go of my hand, and in a reflex, I put my hand over my mouth, wetting my own lips from his. Just as suddenly, I pulled my hand away and left it limp and shaking in my lap.

"I should let you go," he said. "You must have some kids waiting for you somewhere."

He smiled, "See you later." But, he didn't come to class that day.

Just before I left the car, with tears gathering in my eyes, I turned to him and said, "Luke, I always thought your girlfriend had to be the luckiest girl in the world."

His expression softened to such sweet surprise, I was afraid to stay in the car a moment longer.


## HOW TO GET A TEACHING JOB IN REVERE

I would have had a teaching job at the new high school they were building, like Lisa Sarno who married the coach's son, if I had married the coach's son. If I'd campaigned for the new mayor, like Karen Minelli and David Santoro, I would have gotten a job, not in my field, but I'd have gotten a job. Several of my classmates were given teaching jobs. None of them had a job in their field. Lisa Sarno would be teaching typing. She'd studied math. Karen got a kindergarten position. She'd studied junior high science. David would be teaching history. He'd also studied science.

My uncle owned a club; that was another way to get a teaching job.

I was tending my plants on the porch. I'd turned Ma's porch into a greenhouse of plants: hanging green tendrils wound around the pillars, filled the windows, hung over the ledges, trailed the floor. Flowers of many kinds, pink and red geraniums, petals colored so deeply, they seemed unreal; petunias, petals of pale, anemic skin; begonias, petals of sugar; fuchsia, hanging bright vessels turned upside down and emptied out; miniature roses, trying so hard to be roses; pansies, with their screwed up, thoughtful faces; sunflowers in pots and outside, around the house, nodding over the fence where the heavenly blue morning glories covered every chain link, inside again, the portulacca, which broke my heart, with their succulent multi-colored cups on one little plant, because they were from Italy.

Ma came out to the porch one day and asked gruffly, "Do you want a job in Somerville?"

"What?" I asked, like a startled bird. My heart pounded hard.

"Your Uncle Vic says he can get you a job in Somerville, you know, where your Cousin Bernadette lives with her husband."

"Yeah, Ma, I know Somerville." And I knew Bernadette had quit college already pregnant to get married and moved into the apartment over her mother's.

I froze. Somerville was one rough place on this planet. Revere compared to Somerville was the difference between an alley during the day and an alley at night.

"No," I said, picking off a dead leaf from the pink geranium.

"*NO?*" She hollered. "You want me to tell your Uncle no? He's all excited!"

"Can he get me a job in Revere? At least I know Revere." The devil I knew.

I checked the water content of the soil. My fingers shook under the earth, poor roots, I thought.

She went to ask him. I could hear her yelling into the phone. Because Uncle Vickie had lost a lot of his hearing from the loud bands at the club, she yelled at the top of her voice, "I don't know why! Don't ask *me*! She's nuts! She's nuts! She wants a job in Revere!"

She came back out to the porch and announced, "He can't get you a teaching job in Revere!"

"Not even at the new high school?"

"No."

She sat down on the narrow bed where Daddy slept in the warm weather. She got busy lighting a cigarette. Tiny jumped up nervously behind her, wiggling because she knew Ma was mad. The dirty old blankets were thick with clusters of white dog hairs.

"I'll get my own teaching job." I said.

"Yeah, good luck!" Ma said, disgusted.


Step 1: My "Guidance" Counselor

Mrs. Murphy, my ex-guidance counselor, was now the principal of the Coffin School, where I'd gone to school in the eighth grade, walking through my own Sherwood Forest, pretending to be Maid Marion meeting her dearest Robin.

I got dressed in my most professional manner and paid her a visit in her office. She was thrilled to see me! So glad to hear that I'd followed her advice and gone to Salem State and studied teaching!

Then, she opened the top drawer of her desk.

"Look what I just took away from a first grader at recess," she said blithely, as though anticipating impressing me.

She held up a perfect life-size hangman's noose.

"One of the boys was chasing the girls with it. He had it around a little girl's neck when I took it away."

I couldn't speak. The whole incident was too Revere.

"Now, what can I do for you, dear?"

"I was hoping you'd be able to help me to get a teaching job."

Her face fell to the floor. Her complexion went grey and two ridiculous dots of red rouge stood out on each cheek.

"There are no jobs," she said, weakly.

Why was she so nervous, I wondered?

"But, you advised me to go into teaching."

"Yes, in 1969 there were jobs. Now, there are none," she held out her empty hands.

"They're building a new high school."

"Those jobs are all taken."

"You're a principal! You must know of a job in one of the schools."

"The only job I know of was taken by Mrs. Hovey."

"Mrs. Hovey who taught Science here?" She'd been a lousy Science teacher.

"Yes! Did you have her, dear?"

"Yes." That's where Benny Mann had felt up my breasts.

"Imagine that, how time flies. Yes, Mrs. Hovey had been waiting twelve years for an opening in English."

"She was really an *English* teacher all that time?" I couldn't believe someone without a soul would go into English.

"You could re-locate to the Mid-West. I hear they need teachers."

She put the noose back in her drawer after having held it on her lap during our conversation. I supposed this meant our chat was over.

"Good idea. The Mid-West. Thank you so much, Mrs. Murphy. I'll look into that."

What was I, a Guernsey?

"Wonderful! Let me know how you do! Good luck!"

"You too."

## Step 2:  Another Reluctant Principal

In 1973, the principal of Revere High School, Mr. Suosso, was the same principal who'd been there when I went to school, but no one had ever seen him. He hadn't come out of his office for over twenty-five years. I made an appointment to go in.

Since the actual principal never moved from his office, the assistant principal, Mr. Dokes, the ex-Marine, had done all the disciplinary patrolling and presided over all the ceremonies. The every day business of papers being filled out and filed, the phone calls being made and maintenance being supervised had been accomplished by the nameless secretaries in the main office who ran the affairs of the students, teachers, administration and the building like those of a small country.

I was led into the sanctuary by Mr. Suosso's personal secretary, a hunched over woman in one of those old blue silk dresses Miss Tower had once worn with so much dignity and grace.

Mr. Suosso's quivering shrunken little body barely peeked over the desktop. A deformed head, yellow and brown spotted, too round on one side with thinning, greasy, black hair, sat a top a scrawny neck in a too large starched collar and bobbed like one of those dogs set on the rear windows of cars. If it weren't for this slight, irregular tremor, I would have wondered if he was alive. I know you're thinking I'm exaggerating just to be smart, but this is exactly what he looked like.

I introduced myself. His expression did not change. He didn't offer to shake hands. Again, I wondered if I should call someone or check for a pulse.

Then, he said, "Sit down," accusingly, in a small, high-pitched voice.

I sat in the regulation wooden chair set out for visitors. The office was dark; the blinds snapped shut. The bookshelves that lined the walls were filled with dark backed books that seemed an irretrievable part of the wall. The green bottle lamp on the desktop gave no light whatsoever.

"Mr. Suosso," I launched into my rehearsed speech, "I was a student here at Revere High and, just recently, I completed my student teaching here. During that time, I was able to help a lot of students and I really feel I could make a difference at Revere High. I feel strongly that my work here is not finished. The students here need someone like me. I'm from Revere, I know Revere. I could -"

"I can't help you," he interrupted.

"I thought, at the new high school -"

"There are no jobs," he interrupted again.

"None?"

He bobbed his head from side to side.

I got foolhardy.

"Coach DeCicco's son's fiancée' got a job teaching typing. Francine Nuncio, whose mother works in the mayor's office, got a job teaching fifth grade at the Liberty. Mr. Donolley is retiring. Mrs. Finley is leaving to have a baby and she told me she's never coming back." Her exact words were a lot stronger.

"There are no jobs," he said, louder and squeakier.

That weird little voice carried a lot of weight.

Step 3: The Payoff

A lot of guys came and went out of the back kitchen at Firelli's where I still waitressed two evenings a week. They came in shiny silk suits and black shoes that glistened. They came in workmen's overalls, or in white aprons splashed with blood. Their meaty hands reached into the pots and pans on the huge double industrial stove and with scoops made from hunks of bread, they dipped, and ladled other people's meals into their mouths. They stuck their fingers delicately into the salad girl's station and munched on lettuce while they nodded and bent their heads to Mr. Firelli's nodding head. They carried out the long white boxes of calzone or the flat boxes, piled one on the other of pizzas. They left boxes behind, stacked in the corners, covered with clear plastic wrap, the lettering on the cardboard blotted out.

One of these guys heard that I wanted a teaching job in Revere.

He came over to me where I stood waiting to pick up my order.

"Hey, I hear ya wanna teaching job. I can getcha a job."

"Oh, yeah?"

I didn't look at him.

"Yeah," he leaned back and checked my legs. He made a face. My legs aren't the kind men like; they're short and stubby like Ma's. This time I was glad. And what Ma calls "burned up" at the same time; that's when your stomach gets fiery hot from indignation. It never has ceased to amaze me, how ugly men think they should get beautiful women. By the disgusted look on his face, I knew he thought I wasn't nearly good enough for him - well, good. This guy was round as a bull. His bald head was hung with clumps of black fuzz that seemed to slide down his face into grubby sideburns. Around his fleshy neck, he'd gathered as many gold chains as he could find. A dirty fake diamond made vain attempts to flash from his oily, fat pinky.

"It'll cost ya, though," he said, rifling a mushroom and steak tip from one of the plates. He shrugged, apologetically. "Hey, whaddaya gonna do? Everythin' costs somethin', right?"

"How much?"

I looked at him. He shrugged again, "Three hundred bucks."

"Three hundred bucks for a teaching job? In Revere? In my subject?"

He shrugged. "Yeah. What's ya subject?"

"English."

I knew he had no idea what that meant.

"No problem."

I said okay, even though I guess I knew better, I had to take the chance. Three hundred dollars sounded kind of cheap. Even so, I had to scrounge for it. Daddy sighed, "I doubt it, but go ahead anyway." Ma said, "Jesus Christ! Jesus Christ! Your Uncle could have gotten you a job in Somerville, but you didn't want it, you didn't want it! Here's your three hundred bucks! We'll never see it again!"

The guy's name was "Goomba" Paul Benzarro. You called him Paulie or you called him Goomba. He'd told me to meet him at the Dunkin' Donuts on the Lynnway at four o'clock the following afternoon. I'd never been to that Dunkin' Donuts, because it was so forbiddingly dark and small; it sat on a long, remote parking lot next to another lot and a Minute Man Insurance Agency and a vacant factory building. The Lynnway rushed past. The men and women who pulled in to this particular Dunkin' Donuts or wandered in from the narrow highway sidewalk were grim with despair; grim with a darkness that had settled on their shoulders like a shroud out of the grimy air. They were stooped and dangerous, or they were wary of danger from all sides and ready for it. As a matter of fact, almost every Dunkin' Donuts in Revere had slid from its original, wholesome, pink and orange sheen to a sleazy, dark grime, from clean, homey places of refreshment to dusty, lost way stations where poor people could find a phone, make a dinner of a donut, get a fix

Or a teaching job.

Goomba Paul was early. His shiny butt lapped over the counter stool as he pivoted to watch me walk in. He munched the end of a sugar cruller, smacking his lips noisily.

"Wanna cup a coffee?" Goomba asked.

He made a blasé nod to the waitress who eyed me suspiciously.

"How'd ya like ya coffee?" Goomba asked me.

"Cream, no sugar," I told the waitress.

She plunked the cup down so that it rattled in the saucer and spilled over.

Goomba laughed. Clearly, in her mind, she and Goomba had a relationship and I was an unwanted interference. She was one of those girls who hid their face under tall hair and thick purple lipstick. Her Dunkin' uniform groaned across ample buttocks. Her black stockings had runs behind the knees, where some girls think runs are invisible.

"Looks like rain, whaddya think, Darlene?" He winked at the waitress, who turned her black head in his direction and smiled provocatively. "We need rain. Into every life a little rain must fall, eh, Darlene? Give me a couple a jelly donuts, sweetie pie. Wan' somethin' ta eat?" he asked me.

"No, thanks."

"So, you're gonna be a teacher? That's nice. Tha world needs teachers. Maybe I'll see you; I'm gonna be starting at the new high school. I'm gonna be in charge of perveyin' for the cafeteria."

Goomba Paul Benzarro would be arrested in 1985 for embezzlement from the Commonwealth of Massachusetts and for parceling meat products out the back door of the new high school to the trunks of his friends' cars. Of course, arrests like this didn't just happen. Goomba Paul had to have made somebody mad, and I couldn't imagine Goomba making anyone mad.

But, sitting in the Dunkin' Donuts that afternoon, trying to weasel a teaching job, the announcement of his new position was just another turn of the screw.

He made more small talk about the weather and about my so-called future. He asked if I had a boyfriend and why I wasn't married.

"A girl like you is ripe! Ya ripe! Ya know? Ya ripe, don' wait too long!"

He said he'd take me out himself if he wasn't married, or, maybe, he snuck a glance at me, he'd take me out anyway. When I didn't reply, he asked if I'd brought it. I handed him an envelope of cash, three crisp one hundred dollar bills Ma had taken out of the Chelsea Savings Bank a few days before, telling me "they" needed to have cash.

Goomba Paul slurped down the rest of his coffee, stuck a twenty into the puddle under his cup and said to me, as if in dismissal, "Ah, it's probably ya face! Ya face is too fuckin' smart fa a girl, ya know that? Ya give me the creeps just lookin' at cha."

"See ya tomorrow, Darlene, my love!" he called as he ambled out the glass doors.

"You wan' anythin' else?" Darlene asked me, ripping a separate check for me off her pad.

"No, thanks, I've had enough."

The people around me turned and looked me up and down. It happened to me a lot in places like this, places where I didn't belong. The people around me started to throw me out with their eyes.

It was in the way Goomba had gone out the glass doors; it was in the way Darlene had looked at me when she handed me the check; it was in the way the people around me had regarded me when I was left alone at the counter: Goomba Paul had absolutely no intention of ever getting me a teaching job. He was probably on his way to the track right now with Ma's three hundred dollars.

Uncle Vickie was right: I was a chump.


## I HAVE A NERVOUS BREAKDOWN AND GO TO HARVARD

I entered a bad time. My student teaching was over. With that had gone a strong sense of worth. Now, I had only a quarter semester left and if I wanted to graduate with my class, I had to double up on my courses.

My hands started sweating again. I wondered if I had done a foolish thing by turning Luke away. I drove past his uncle's shop, lonely for him. I told myself I had to stop thinking about him, but thoughts of him were becoming a haven to me, a soft place to lie down. I let myself sometimes think of his profile that seemed to evoke his sweet patience, his wisdom. I thought of his arms. I could still feel them around me in the dark in that small room of books. I thought of his strong legs and I yearned for them also, and that made me insane with desire for him, and then, I thought, yes, now I am insane.

I saw a play at school with a boy from one of my classes. He ran his hand down my back and whispered in my ear, "You're not wearing a brassiere this evening." I liked him. He knew things about the paintings of Christ that he told me over Chinese food that was much too sweet to eat about the thin Christ and the muscular Christ. But one of the girls in class liked him too, and she made some kind of remark as we were leaving the play and though I hadn't heard the words, I heard the tone of her voice and it hurt me so much to think she had vindictiveness toward me. When I made love to him, his penis rattled around in me like a pencil, I felt nothing and I searched and searched for sensation under my closed eyes. When I put his penis in my mouth, he moaned, "No one's ever done that to me before," and it was so thin, the nightmare of thick and thin overwhelmed me again and I had to stop abruptly. I cried over his penis being so thin, so very unbelievably thin, I was in terror of its thinness, and I mourned it. He sat up and put his cold, thin arms around me. He was cold because the historic Salem apartment was so cold; it ran through with wind. "Don't cry," he comforted me, "I understand, most girls don't like to do that, you don't have to, don't feel like you have to." He ran a cold hand over my breasts, "You're so beautiful." I shriveled with coldness.

I wandered. When I wasn't reading or doing papers or attending class, I couldn't sleep, I was so wired. I couldn't stop thinking, speeding so far ahead of myself; my eyes bugged out of my head like a crazy woman's. I drove at night, visiting all the places June and I had gone, visiting them like a ghost in the darkness where we had walked in the day. I drove to Marblehead and stood at the water's edge, looking out at the Green Light. I could smell roses and mint and the sweet green of freshly cut grass. Just as it had before, the silvery path of the moon reached out to me and the water lapped against the rocks. Then, a woman screamed, once, only once, hideously, piteously, and all was quiet again, the lapping water, the rush of ocean, making me wonder if it had been real. Or had it been my own self?

I tore an application for teaching jobs in Australia from the bulletin board inside the Union building. I'd missed the informational seminar, but I made out the application and sent it off to Sydney.

I envisioned crystal clear beaches, red, red earth and naked Aborigine children. Friends at school told me I was nuts if I thought they would send me to a city like Sydney; I would probably be sent to the Outback. Ma said, "You're out of your mind! You should have gone to Somerville, you should have gone, to Somerville!" She sucked on her cigarette helplessly. All of my classmates were going on to graduate school. "What's graduate school?" I asked. I was afraid. In Australia, I knew in no time at all I would fall for a handsome cowboy and marry him and have children out of sheer lust and find myself buried there in the Australian desert on the other side of the world, unable to make my way back. But why should I want to go back? I could write in Australia like *My Brilliant Career:"You shall have a little writing desk."*

I got a wild crush on the delicate teacher who taught "Dickens & Dostoyevsky," an elective that was overwhelming me with reading. I loved being near her; her long dresses, her necklace like rosary beads, her dangling earrings, her long throat, the silly girlish voice she had that made Dickens' characters even more charming. I brought her tangerines and a bottle of red wine, thinking maybe she would talk to me for a while, about anything, but the door to her office was locked. I left the pile of sweet gifts at her locked door like a demented lover.

There was a career day and when I walked past one of the booths, I heard a familiar voice. A strange, bearded young man was speaking to passers by and handing out leaflets. The voice came from so far within me, I thought, how far away this person must be in my memory, but he wasn't that far away - it was Will Cullen, but he wore the full beard and matted hair of a mountain man.

Nevertheless, I was so excited to see him as though I had stumbled across another human being in the wilderness! "Will! Will! Hi! It's me, it's Gloria!"

But his eyes wouldn't focus on me. He said, "Read this! The coal miners of West Virginia are suffering, they need your help!" He looked at me wildly, but he didn't see me.

"But, Will," I couldn't believe his eyes couldn't see me; I was right in front of him! "Will, don't you know me?" I desperately needed him to see me!

"Yes, I know who you are. The coal miners of West Virginia are starving. They want the basic necessities of life. They need your help!"

He turned away from me and handed leaflets to the other people passing by, who looked at them and threw them on the ground. I put all the money I had in my wallet, nine dollars and change, into his cash box, but he didn't acknowledge me.

When I told June, she said Donald Donnelly had told her one day that Will had become a coal miner in West Virginia because he felt he couldn't serve their cause without suffering their pain along with them. I couldn't tell if he had achieved his destiny or if he had avoided it. Surely, as a miner, he could not help them.

At home, Ma put the Want Ads from the Sunday Herald American on my bed next to the stacks of neatly folded laundry she'd washed. Just the sight of the businesses in their little advertising squares like little office buildings in tall columns of bigger office buildings made me crazy with rage! I tore them, I tore them, and tore them and tore them! I couldn't get the pieces small enough to make them disappear.

One night, one of my old professors called me on the telephone. He said he had been thinking about me, about something I'd said once in class about the collective consciousness, if I had a moment, would I like to discuss it with him for his future reference? Of course, I said, and I got comfortable on Ma's bed, talking into her Princess phone.

"You said the 'universal soul' sounded absolutely real to you?"

"Yes," I agreed, eager for companionship.

"But, t-tell me, I recall a conversation we had once about twilight, what Forster calls 'the hour of unreality.' You said it was your favorite time of day. Could that be because you have trouble with reality?"

"I don't trust reality. I want to make my own reality."

That's when I heard his bath water slosh. I froze. He was calling me from the bathtub? I recalled this professor liked to read Jung in the bathtub.

He went on to praise Jung. I could hear the pages flipping.

"Don't you f-find C-Camp-bell too col-lo-qui-al?"

"I like that kind of searching quality, feeling blindly," I replied, wondering if it was okay to call someone from the bathtub. I supposed it was.

"Oh, oh, y-yes!" he stuttered, but without the eloquence I was used to in stutterers.

He talked on for a few moments, degenerating finally into "Ha-ha-ha" sounds and short breaths of agreement. The water sloshed violently. Shaking, I hung up, but I doubt if he noticed.

Maybe, I thought, I had trouble with reality because I had to spend so much time trying to reconcile with it.

Daddy took that moment to come in. He must have heard me on the phone, on the bed. He struggled in on his cane and sat down heavily on the side of the bed. I watched in horror as he smiled and began to rub my leg.

The shock was too much for me. I screamed at him without thinking Ma could hear me, "Get away from me you dirty old man! Get away! Get away!"

He got off the bed so fast, he fell over on to it again as I ran out of the room.

I called June late that night, where she lived now with Aaron as caretakers to the some rich guy's estate in Arlington. Aaron had found her in the cottage in Gloucester and brought her back, just as we'd feared. I lay with my cheek against the cold kitchen floor in a puddle of tears. June fell asleep while I told her my troubles. I listened to her dear breath. I listened to her ignoring me until I also fell asleep, there on the floor.

The one place I found solace was the Harvard Coop. I liked to go there and stand in the H's and sometimes, just hold a copy of *The Sun Also Rises* in my hand, and sometimes read it. I read it so many times, standing up in the bookstore, I thought, now maybe I've read it as many times as Hemingway re-wrote it. I imagined Luke came there too, that maybe he held the same book in his hands, so that one day, as I walked down the fiction aisle, wearing a long summer dress I'd made of a voile of pink roses and green leaves, I remember the pattern swishing comfortingly about my legs as I walked, when I looked up and saw him there, I was sure it was a dream, part of my tense and tortured haze. I put my head down to the roses and up again and he was still there, holding the very book I usually held. "Luke," I said, dreamily, weakly, as though about to tell him how funny it was that I thought I saw him there. At the sound of my voice, he looked up. He dropped the book in amazement. He reached for me and took me in his arms.

I felt his lips on my cheek, against the soft flesh of my temple I felt them, and his voice rolling down the tunnel of my ear, "Gloria!" he said, the way I'd been waiting to hear it all my life, a recognition, a confirmation, a refuge, a castle.

BOWER

We walked to the Café Algiers, but not before Luke purchased the book we'd both held in our hands.

Downstairs in the dark café, he moved his chair very close to mine, saying, "I don't want a table between us." We ordered Arab coffees, but we hardly drank them.

"That classroom was dead without you. She went on a spelling war, telling us our spelling needed a lot of work."

"You guys did need work on your spelling."

"Not me!"

"No, not you."

Luke always got an easy A; I never understood what he was doing there.

"All anyone ever talked about was you. It was torture."

"No one knew about us," I said.

"I did."

"Yes, you did."

I rested in his eyes looking on me with love. I'd rested with June, but never with a man before. The sensation was so full, here and now, past and future, swelling my body with desire and peace and affection for him.

"Gloria, do you ever think about me? About going to Italy with me?" he asked, softly, unsure of himself.

"I dream about it."

"So do I." He tapped his demitasse with a nervous finger. "Does that mean," he looked at me, a little frightened, "Will you marry me?"

I didn't hesitate. I even saw the diapers hanging over my head in a very poor room, where the ancient stucco was cracked and the light golden with warmth. For the first time, I wasn't afraid. The diapers didn't scare me any more. They looked interesting, challenging; I wanted to know more about them - of course, really about the baby who wore them. My vision followed the clothesline outside. Suddenly, they were no longer inside, but blowing in the fresh air on a clothesline where I had hung them myself. I saw that the small house was surrounded by flowers and sunlight; the child was playing in the yard, and the ocean stretched beyond.

"Yes," I said.

He kissed me then, our first kiss, in the dark café smelling sweetly of coffee and musk, trilling with Arabian flute. I knew he was kissing Gloria, this person he knew from his heart, but there was another Gloria I had to show him.

"Luke," I said, knowing I could be throwing away the best thing I'd ever found, "there's something you have to see first."

At first, we couldn't open the porch door. A mattress frame had fallen from its usual place balanced against the wall, blocking the door. By wheedling the storm door inch by inch, we managed to get it open. Luke supported the frame, leaning dangerously in midair and pushed it back into place.

Things had gotten worse in the last few years.

The smell hit us right away. An open, empty bottle of salad dressing greeted us, standing on the windowsill. The second I'd opened the porch door, we were hit by the sharp odor of salad dressing, beer and whiskey, old nicotine that reeked pungently of sulphur, along with years of human perspiration from under the arms and feet that had somehow worked its way into the old fabric of the furniture, years of pastrami and tomatoes, garlic and oregano that were no longer edible, but poisonous even to the nose.

His baffled gaze followed the mess as we walked by, much of which I'd tried to clean up or throw away, but no one would let me. The smelly old furniture was stacked with dusty cardboard boxes of discarded clothes and shoes that poked their damaged arms and legs and broken toes over the edges. On top of these, part of a toy telephone with Mickey Mouse's dirty face leering at us; a filthy plastic duck with a hole punched through its head; the decrepit runners of a sled; the bent handlebars of a two wheeler bike; a rusted hospital potty; an ancient dictionary with its center cut out for hiding things inside; damp, old telephone books; Marie's Easter bonnet from several years ago, now torn and flaking apart like dandruff. Disabled chairs were piled haphazardly in a corner. One dirty skate, a banana peel and a stained American flag were stuffed into the dusty mailbox. Junk mail, some of it quite old, was piled on the windowsill. Newspapers stacked, rotten and yellow. Stacks of moldy paperbacks; a toppled pile of bald bicycle tires; a small plastic wastebasket overflowing with ashes and papers and cigarette butts, a skirt of ashes around its base; the stub of a broom; stinking, empty beer bottles in a paper shopping bag; bottle caps; used Q-tips; a broken pair of child's plastic sunglasses permanently lodged in the aluminum window sill. Among these were my plants.

"These are your flowers," Luke said. "They look like you."

The way into the house used to be tenuous. I'd had a method of talking to a boyfriend just as we entered, to make him turn his head toward me and away from the couch where Daddy could be lying, but this time, we walked right in and the couch was empty.

We passed the living room where Daddy had pulled down a wall and was putting up a half wall to look out into the kitchen.

"Watch out for the nails," I warned, as we passed through a field of large penny nails rolling around the floor.

The living room was a sand dune of plaster and sawdust tracked in a long trail. Tools were left every which way, including a power saw plugged in with a long red snake of a wire coiled on the floor. Plywood and dry wall, their paper half pulled down, the markings still clear from the lumber company, leaned against the living room's paneling, making long, horizontal gashes in the wooden wall Ma had once been so proud of making Daddy build. Dirty socks lay tangled up in the dust.

Newspapers and coupons were thrown down on the kitchen table, along with a few coffee cups. Two cigarettes smoked in an ashtray already choked with butts next to Daddy's balled up handkerchief, some dirty spoons stuck with coffee to the table, and a half eaten hardboiled egg sitting in a saucer of beer. One of Henry's rockets stood three feet tall on the newspapers as though ready for lift off.

Ma came in the back door, her muddy terrier dashing in front of her, yapping furiously at us. Ma bent to pick up the squirmy little dog.

"Look out! She's got shit on her! Stay still, you little shit!" Her cigarette gripped tenaciously between her teeth. She plunged the terrier into the sink, rattling dishes aside. "Jesus Christ!"

"Ma, this is Luke. Luke, this is my mother. We're going upstairs, Ma," I said. "We'll see you later."

She half-turned to give me a look, like I was going up there to have wild, insane sex with him. Little did she know, we'd been having sex all afternoon, and we were making love right now before her very eyes.

"Your mother -" he began, but couldn't finish.

"I know."

Now, we were walking up the dark stairway. At the turn, Luke was ahead of me.

"I was raped on these stairs by the boy across the street. I was a virgin."

Luke stopped in his tracks.

"Why are you doing this?" he asked after a moment of rigid silence.

"I have to."

He waited for me at the top of the stairs.

"You have to know."

His face had twisted with bewilderment and pain.

"Please, Luke, I can't just go away with you without letting you see all this. Here's my room," I told him. I had the room all to myself now; Marie had taken over Jakey's.

I let him walk in first.

"My God, it's unbelievable! What a difference!" he exclaimed. But, I heard that sadness that was always with him.

"It's beautiful," he said, turning to me. "Like the flowers, it also looks like you."

He meant the meditative flow of the sheer, white curtains. He meant the clean, polished wood surfaces that radiated peace. He meant my paintings on the walls; the flowers and green leaves of living plants like musical notes; he meant the books, solid and calm, and the typewriter that showed I was working. On the windowsill, in silhouette against the sky, the serenity of the bisque statue of a lady kneeling and arranging her hair. The exotic bedspread of Indian purple and gold, the slippers side by side on the soft blue rug.

His gaze stopped at the poster.

"I've heard of her," he began to say, then suddenly, "Gloria!" he whispered in awe, "My God, it's you!"

I couldn't speak. I hadn't expected this. It wasn't the poster I'd brought him to see.

He looked at me in amazement.

"You're the only one who's ever recognized me."

"Your mother never did?"

"No. No one."

"Not your friends?"

"My friend was there. He hurt her."

I would have been afraid, except for the expression of rapt admiration on his face.

"I saw this on the news. I remember reading about it."

"I wanted to destroy him," I said.

His back was turned to me. "Yes," he said, studying the poster.

"But, I never thought I could. I was as surprised as anyone."

"No one has ever come to your door about this? Not the police?"

I shook my head.

"What happened to your hair? It looks strange."

"It's a disco wig."

"A disco wig!" he laughed. "Now I remember all the girls were buying them, trying to look like her. To look like you," he corrected himself.

"Are you going to turn me in?" I asked, without thinking.

He grimaced, "Don't insult me."

"Where did you learn how to shoot a bow and arrow?"

"Robin Hood," I smiled.

He turned and looked at me a minute.

"I read that book," he nodded.

"I want to see the view from your window," he said.

He walked over to my window, and there he was, clearly, the man I loved, standing on my side of the glass, in the exact spot I'd stood and dreamed of him, who would he be, what form would he take, standing framed by the miraculous pear blossoms and the slight breeze lifting the curtains. All my memories had shaped him.

"Show me his house," Luke said.

Then, I stood beside him at my childhood window.

"That one, with the lilacs growing over the door."

"Do you want me to do anything? Kill him?"

My heart nearly broke through my chest.

"No!"

"No? I'm not afraid," he regarded the house, as though measuring that he could kill its occupants. I was terrified Rick might come out. His Triumph was parked outside.

"No. Luke - that wasn't the only time."

He looked at me.

"You were in love with him?"

"Yes. The second time was my idea."

"Ah!"

We didn't kiss. We didn't make love. We didn't even talk much. He told me about Italy, we thought about what we'd like to do.

When we went downstairs, it was dark. The lights were on in the kitchen. Ma had supper ready. The house smelled of crispy steak and potatoes, the tang of oil and vinegar dressing on the salad. I was too frightened and exhausted and in love to be hungry, and with all that, I felt the hunger pang burn me at the aromas of Ma's cooking. I could see Daddy's half-eaten food already on the counter, the steak fat congealed around the rim of the dish. I hadn't even heard him come home. Ma asked Luke to stay to supper. He refused, politely, saying he was glad to have met her.

On the way out, Daddy was on the couch. The light was on, the television was blaring a screaming car chase through hillbilly country. By now, we had a television in every room, each turned to a different channel. We could hear Ma's TV in the kitchen hollering out a mayonnaise ad. Daddy's legs were wide open, one foot on the floor, the other on the back of the couch. His hands were tucked down the front of his boxer shorts. The hole in front was gaping, black with pubic hair. Daddy's head was thrown back, pumping snores.

We wonder sometimes what hell is like. Catholics have been warned every day of their lives; descriptions have been written by those self-satisfied old men sitting round that large mahogany table, descriptions of horror that keep the public under control, that keep even kings cowering under their power. We've been told there's no relief from the pain, not even to take a breath and brace for the next pain. We're told we are tortured next to murderers and thieves by fire, ice, knives, demons eating our insides while we're alive, like my re-occurring nightmare of a monster Daddy eating me from the vagina while I lay sleeping. But if I go to hell, I will not be stabbed with knives or burned with fire or frozen or eaten by demons.

I will relive over and over again that moment when the serene and beautiful Renaissance face of Luciano Merano whirled round distorted, gripped with disgust and horror.

"This is your father!"

"Yes." I met his eyes.

"He has no respect for you!"

Again, I met his eyes.

He stared at me, questioningly. I held his eyes, as he so often loved to hold mine. I looked straight at him and with my eyes alone I told him everything.

His head dipped to one side, questioning, disbelieving, then, abruptly, he took his arm and wrapped it around my neck and pulled me outside on to the porch. He slammed the door shut behind us.

I closed my eyes and prayed I hadn't hurt him too much. I didn't dare hope I hadn't lost him.

He held me close like that and then I felt his lips pressing into my head. I felt his lips pressing so hard that I was sure I felt my own hair on my own lips. I could feel his lips trembling, and his other arm wrapped around me and pulled me close, so close, I thought, now he's trying to pull me into him.

"My brother is a wanted criminal. His wife is in jail for armed robbery and kidnapping."

"Gloria - stop!" he said, and I thought, now, now he will go away and be clean.

"How much of this do you think I can take?" he asked, looking at me sternly.

I shook my head, "I don't know."

"A lot! Do you hear me? A lot! Do you think you can tell me enough bad to erase all the good I see, all the good I feel, in you? You can't! You can't erase my love for you - you only make me love you more!"

Then, he kissed me, wrapping me in him, and though I'd dreamed of a bower and not a filthy porch, his heart beat warmly in my chest and took me to that soft place I was seeking.

## AND FINALLY, YIELD

The day of my last final, the phone started ringing off the wall at 7:30 in the morning. I got ready for school, while Ma ran up and down the stairs, answering the telephone, sometimes in her bedroom, sometimes in the kitchen, with tremendous glee and breathless excitement.

She ran outside and stood looking up the hill, expectantly, tapping her little foot, smacking her face with the cigarette; she ran back into the house, the phone burst, she answered it, ecstatically.

Uncle Vickie's Cadillac swooped down in front of the house. Ma ran out, puffing smoke like an excited chimney. Stealthily, she opened the Cadillac door and slid in.

The two of them sat in there for an hour, the motor running, spewing exhaust up the street like emissions of the aggravation and enthusiasm from their secret discussion within.

I knew what they were talking about. Grandma had fallen in love with a man she'd met at the meat store. I thought the pun was lovely – she met him at the meat store. All the sons were in an uproar because she wanted to get re-married. Ma kept herself neutral, agreeing with each of her brothers in turn.

Uncle Vickie was incensed that his mother wanted to disgrace the sacred memory of his father. Uncle Salvi, who now had nine children, wasn't crazy about the idea, but he didn't want to stand in her way, if that's what she wanted. Uncle Freddie thought she was nuts, getting married at sixty-four, who was this guy, who'd he think he was, anyway? Only Uncle Sonny smiled and said, "That's nice."

The phone rang again. Ma was still outside hunkered down in the Cadillac. I hesitated, then, answered it.

"Hello?"

"Who's this?" a man demanded.

"It's Gloria, Uncle Freddie."

"Where's your mother?" he barked.

"Outside in Uncle Vickie's -"

"Get her!"

Ma came running in on radar alone, grabbing the phone from my hand, her eyes on fire.

"Yeah? Yeah, Freddie, yeah, Vickie's here, yeah, Okay, yeah!"

She ran outside again.

I suppose it was the sudden rush of silence, but I had the sensation of being alone with Grandma. I had one sock pulled on, the other in my hand, standing in the kitchen, when I picked up the phone and dialed her number.

"Hello?" said her mournful, worried voice.

"Grandma! It's Gloria!"

"Oh, Gloria, what's the matter? Aren't you supposed to be in school? Is your mother all right?"

"She's fine, Grandma. I'm going to take my last final in a few minutes."

"What's a final?"

"That's a big test to see how much I've learned. I'm graduating cum laude."

"That's Latin! What's that mean?"

"I don't know. They gave me a little pin to wear. I think it means I got all A's and B's."

"Oh, you're a smart girl, Gloria."

She moaned. I knew why.

"Ma's outside with Uncle Vickie."

"Oh," she moaned, "they're mad at me."

"No, they're not! They're loving every minute! They're just in shock. They'll get used to the idea. Don't worry. You do what you want. Gee whiz, Grandma, how old are you anyway? You look like a young peach!"

She laughed out loud.

"Ha, ha! Oh, Gloria! You always make me laugh! A peach! I'm sixty-four! A peach!"

"Your cheeks are like a peach. I wish I had cheeks like that."

"You do! You do! Oh, I wish I was twenty-one again."

"Grandma, I think it's great that you can be in love again at sixty-four!"

"Oh," she moaned again, "I don't know, Gloria. You know, Leo is a good man; he seems like a nice man. We met at the meat store, you know, at the meat store. (I smiled again to myself at this pun.) Umm, I don' know. I'm afraid. My first marriage was not happy, not happy. Your Grandfather Vic was hard, hard! Nobody knew how hard he was! What am I gonna do? I get afraid sometimes to marry again, what if Leo is like that after we get married?"

"I remember, Grandma, how sad you always looked."

"Umm, but Leo is a nice man, we get along. It's good to have someone in your old age."

"Grandma, I have my passport, you know. I'm also getting married."

"Gloria! You're going away from us! Aren't you gonna be at my wedding?"

I laughed. So, she was planning to get married, regardless of her sons' opinions.

"Oh, yes, Grandma, I'll be at your wedding. Grandma, what's Italy like?"

"Oh, terrible!" she cried, then, in a softer voice, "but beautiful." And I heard that singing sound of Italy I didn't hear so often any more.

"I think once I eat the food in Italy, I won't be able to leave."

"Yeah, that's true, the food is good in Italy! Yeah."

"It's getting hard to find real food here now. Everything is becoming artificial."

"I have real food, I have!" Grandma bragged. Uncle Sonny traveled into Boston to bring her the best from the North End market. I was also making a weekly journey into Boston, to Erewhon to get natural foods.

"I know, Grandma. You always have good food."

There was a silence while we each had our own thoughts.

"Well, I should go to school," I said.

"Good luck on your test, Gloria," Grandma said.

"Thank you. I'll do well now that you've blessed me."

"Oh!" she laughed. "Only God and the Blessed Virgin bless us, not me, not me!"

You're wrong, Grandma.

"You stand up for yourself, Grandma. Don't let them tell you what to do! And don't let them make you feel bad!"

"Okay. Goodbye."

I could hear Ma and Uncle Vickie downstairs, and I heard Uncle Salvi arrive to the terrier's sharp yaps. I heard the tinkling of coffee cups and the metal click of spoons dumped angrily on the table.

Uncle Vickie boomed, "Some guy she met!"

Uncle Salvi urged, quietly, "Calm down, Vic, she's a grown woman. I don't like it either, but we gotta get used to it."

"Get used to it? My ass!"

Uncle Freddie arrived, screaming as loud as the dog, "I had to come all the way from Rockland in my truck! Where's Sonny?"

"He ain't here yet."

"Jesus Christ! Do you know how much work I'm missing?"

"Naw, just sugar, Rosie, black an' sweet, like my women."

"Jeez, Vic," Uncle Salvi mumbled.

I was brushing my hair when Marie came out of the bathroom, getting ready for school. I saw her reflection in my mirror, her robe clutched around her, her dark hair tumbling down her back, she was barefoot; she looked, in the misty steam from the shower, like a painting. I was struck again by the beauty of women, by each little daily task they did, carrying, washing, walking, reaching to light or extinguish the lamp, each simple movement was the soul of life, the true worship of God, without thinking, without self-consciousness; I thought how beautiful she was, just walking, she was becoming a woman.

The phone rang again.

Looking at her, I wasn't afraid, not of life or its simplicity, not of the tender tasks that seem to rob us of life but are life itself. Looking at women, I could make peace with the washing of clothes, diapers, cleaning the house, cooking the food, dressing and the brushing of hair, the piles of books and papers that meant I was working, all of it made me eager to begin work again. The voices of my uncles complaining were like birds chattering to each other about the weather to which they were absolute slaves, while the women went on about the real tasks of life, getting dressed, making coffee, preparing themselves and everyone else for the day.

Then, Ma broke into my thoughts when she hung up the phone and screamed, frightened and bewildered, up the stairs to me and Marie, "RICK LIKUS IS DEAD!"

I stopped what I was doing and stared into the mirror without seeing myself.

"What happened?" Marie yelled back, leaning over the hall railing.

"He crashed his car into a tree last night! Annette just called; Linda won't be going to school today, Marie! You have to go alone!"

"What is it, Rosie? Who's that?" Uncle Vickie wanted to know.

I could hear the murmur of Ma explaining.

I started to shake. I took hold of the bureau, but I was shaking. Tears came, but I was shaking and trying to control myself from shaking. I didn't cry.

I felt him go from me. I felt his penis go from my mouth and from inside me, I felt his semen wash from my face, I felt his dirty fingers come off my tongue. I felt him go out of me, out of my life, out of his house, out of my house. He lifted off my shoulders, where I hadn't realized he'd been, from out of my soul, out from my nostrils and fingertips; he left my mind, my skin, my blood, where I would have carried him for years.

I wasn't sorry. I was glad. I rejoiced, the way people should rejoice when someone dies and a spirit is freed. My spirit. He had been imprisoned and had taken his prison with him, but I was free.

"There was a bottle on the floor. His little sister, Chelsea was on the extension and she - can you believe it? Out of the mouths of babes," Ma went on.

I used to ask, why couldn't he just love me? I didn't care anymore.

I was not going to miss Rick Likus, but I was glad that he had lived. And glad he'd died the way he'd lived, crashing hard into a tree. I was grateful for him, in a rush of incredible love and gratitude to God, and to Rick, I was grateful to have had him. Over me came a flood of gratitude to God for everything, for sex and squalor and pain and murder, for Daddy.

In my heart, I began to pray, not in words, but in a complicated rush of visions of pain and joy.

Lamb of God, who takes away the sins of the world, thank you for the corruption of old men and the dirty hands of young men, that I may know injustice.

Lamb of God, who takes away the sins of the world, thank you for the dank smell of urine and the salty taste of it in my mouth, that I may smell it and taste it and spit it out.

Lamb of God, who takes away the sins of the world, thank you for the scream of the airplane screaming through my heart, and the truck barreling through my brain.

Lamb of God, who takes away the sins of the world, thank you for the golden sparrows playing in the golden dust.

Lamb of God, who takes away the sins of the world, thank you for the brown weeds, their delicate lace silhouetted against the snow, that I may know I am alive in winter. Thank you for the Nazi.

Lamb of God, who takes away the sins of the world, thank you for the horses treading lightly round the crushed glass.

Lamb of God, who takes away the sins of the world, thank you for the green islands hungering, biting the backs of highways for their lives.

Lamb of God, who takes away the sins of the world, thank you for the scent of the sea, of diesel and of roses, lilies, grass, rot, shit, blood, basil, amanda, wet wooden trunks of trees, all these smoking into the summer heat.

Lamb of God, who takes away the sins of the world, thank you for the seagull, who will forever fly ahead to show me the way, that I may be free, and grateful.

Lamb of God, who takes away the sins of the world, thank you for the soft, brown eyes of Richie Silva, who held me in his arms in my imagination that I might be comforted.

Lamb of God, who takes away the sins of the world, thank you for the sad, soft eyes of Luciano Merano, that I may be loved by them.

Lamb of God, who takes away the sins of the world, thank you for June who saw my light dying and shared with me her own.

Lamb of God, who takes away the sins of the world, thank you for the hands and the ways of women, that they are wise and resourceful, that they are my hands and my ways.

Lamb of God, who takes away the sins of the world, thank you for my sins.

Yes, thank you.

Ah, Daddy, you've given me more than any other father could give: you've made me my own father.

You've given me wounds and the salt to heal them. I thank you.

With your black-rimmed fingernails that you put up inside me, you injected me with terror and the fearlessness to face it. I thank you. With the fiery, black hairs of your belly, you smothered me. Now, I can breathe. With your tongue, smooth and horrifying, you gave me the balm to carry and carry and carry and finally, yield.

I thank you.

I love you and I don't care why. I'm depraved enough to be glad, to be often proud of having had sex with you.

I'm twisted and proud and aching with eagerness.

I thank you.

I was finished getting ready. Carefully, I put my hairbrush down on the bureau, placing it in a ceremonial, final act. Rick was dead. I had my passport.

I went to school.

Other Books by Patricia Goodwin

Fiction:
*When Two Women Die*
*Dreamwater*

Poetry:
*Atlantis*
*Java Love*
*Marblehead Moon*

Anthology:
*Under Her Skin: How Girls Experience Race in America*

# About the Author

Patricia Goodwin grew up in an Italian-American neighborhood north of Boston. She was the first in her family to finish high school and go to college. She graduated cum laude from Salem State College, Salem, MA where she earned a BA in English Literature. In the early days of the natural foods movement, she created and taught macrobiotic educational programs for the East West Foundation, now the Kushi Institute. A portion of "A Child's Christmas in Revere," a chapter from her novel, *Holy Days* was previously published in the anthology, *Under Her Skin: How Girls Experience Race in America* (Seal Press, 2004). Her poetry has been published in *Marblehead Magazine, IndeArts, Runes, nthposition.com, Pemmican Press, Radius: Poetry from the Center to the Edge* and *The Potomac*, among others. She has three books of poetry: *Marblehead Moon* (1993), *Java Love* (1997) and *Atlantis* (2006). *Dreamwater* (2013) is the sequel to her historical novella, *When Two Women Die* (2012). With the exception of her essay in the *Under Her Skin* anthology, all of her books have been published under the imprint of Plum Press. As a practicing macrobiotic of over 40 years, Patricia has written many articles about organic food, health, and the dangers of GMOs. Patricia lives with her husband and daughter in a historic seacoast town in Massachusetts. When she isn't writing books, Patricia Goodwin loves to paint.

For more information about the author, including blog, new work, events, and videos, please visit patriciagoodwin.com.